Alistai[...] [...]nister, was
brough[...] [...]n 1941, at
the age of eighteen, he joined the [...] Navy; two
and a half years spent aboard a cruiser were later to
give him the background for *HMS Ulysses*, his first
novel, the outstanding documentary novel on the
war at sea. After the war, he gained an English
Honours degree at Glasgow University, and became
a schoolmaster. In 1983 he was awarded a D.Litt
from the same university.

Alistair MacLean is now recognized to be the
outstanding writer of our time in his genre. He
wrote twenty-nine world bestsellers, many of
which have been turned into films – *The Guns of
Navarone, Force 10 from Navarone, Where Eagles
Dare* and *Bear Island* are among the most famous.
Alistair MacLean died in 1987.

ALISTAIR MACLEAN

Navarone Omnibus

THE GUNS OF NAVARONE &
FORCE 10 FROM NAVARONE

HarperCollins*Publishers*

HarperCollins*Publishers*
77–85 Fulham Palace Road,
Hammersmith, London W6 8JB

This one-volume edition 1996
3 5 7 9 8 6 4 2

First published in Great Britain in two volumes:

The Guns of Navarone published by Collins 1957
Previously published in paperback by Fontana 1959
Reprinted fifty-six times
And by HarperCollins*Publishers* 1993
Copyright © Devoran Trustees Ltd 1957

Force 10 from Navarone published by Collins 1968
Previously published in paperback by Fontana 1970
Reprinted twenty-six times
And by HarperCollins*Publishers* 1994
Copyright © Devoran Trustees Ltd 1968

This one-volume edition copyright © Devoran Trustees Ltd 1996

ISBN 0 00 649910 4

Set in Trump Mediaeval

Printed in Great Britain by
Caledonian International Book Manufacturing Ltd, Glasgow

THE GUNS OF NAVARONE

CONTENTS

CHAPTER 1

Prelude: Sunday

0100–0900

The match scratched noisily across the rusted metal of the corrugated iron shed, fizzled, then burst into a sputtering pool of light, the harsh sound and sudden brilliance alike strangely alien in the stillness of the desert night. Mechanically, Mallory's eyes followed the cupped sweep of the flaring match to the cigarette jutting out beneath the Group-Captain's clipped moustache, saw the light stop inches away from the face, saw too the sudden stillness of that face, the unfocused vacancy of the eyes of a man lost in listening. Then the match was gone, ground into the sand of the airfield perimeter.

'I can hear them,' the Group-Captain said softly. 'I can hear them coming in. Five minutes, no more. No wind tonight – they'll be coming in on Number Two. Come on, let's meet them in the interrogation room.' He paused, looked quizzically at Mallory and seemed to smile. But the darkness deceived, for there was no humour in his voice. 'Just curb your impatience, young man – just for a little longer. Things haven't gone too well tonight. You're going to have all your answers, I'm afraid, and have them all too soon.' He turned abruptly, strode off towards the squat buildings that loomed vaguely against the pale darkness that topped the level horizon.

Mallory shrugged, then followed on more slowly, step for step with the third member of the group, a broad, stocky figure with a very pronounced roll in his gait. Mallory wondered sourly just how much practice Jensen had required to achieve that sailorly effect. Thirty years at sea, of course – and Jensen had done exactly that – were sufficient warrant for a man to dance a hornpipe as he walked; but that wasn't the point. As the brilliantly successful Chief of Operations of the Subversive Operation Executive in Cairo, intrigue, deception, imitation and disguise were the breath of life to Captain James Jensen, D.S.O., R.N. As a Levantine stevedore agitator, he had won the awed respect of the dock-labourers from Alexandretta to Alexandria: as a camel-driver, he had blasphemously out-camel-driven all available Bedouin competition: and no more pathetic beggar had ever exhibited such realistic sores in the bazaars and market-places of the East. Tonight, however, he was just the bluff and simple sailor. He was dressed in white from cap-cover to canvas shoes, the starlight glinted softly on the golden braid on epaulettes and cap peak.

Their footsteps crunched in companionable unison over the hard-packed sand, rang sharply as they moved on to the concrete of the runway. The hurrying figure of the Group-Captain was already almost lost to sight. Mallory took a deep breath and turned suddenly towards Jensen.

'Look, sir, just what *is* all this? What's all the flap, all the secrecy about? And why am *I* involved in it? Good lord, sir, it was only yesterday that I was pulled out of Crete, relieved at eight hours' notice. A month's leave, I was told. And what happens?'

'Well,' Jensen murmured, 'what did happen?'

'No leave,' Mallory said bitterly. 'Not even a night's sleep. Just hours and hours in the S.O.E. Headquarters. answering a lot of silly, damnfool questions about climbing in the Southern Alps. Then hauled out of bed at midnight, told I was to meet you, and then driven for hours across the blasted desert by a mad Scotsman who sang drunken songs and asked hundreds of even more silly, damnfool questions!'

'One of my more effective disguises, I've always thought,' Jensen said smugly. 'Personally, I found the journey most entertaining!'

'One of your — ' Mallory broke off, appalled at the

8

memory of things he had said to the elderly bewhiskered Scots captain who had driven the command vehicle. 'I – I'm terribly sorry, sir. I never realised – '

'Of course you didn't!' Jensen cut in briskily. 'You weren't supposed to. Just wanted to find out if you were the man for the job. I'm sure you are – I was pretty sure you were before I pulled you out of Crete. But where you got the idea about leave I don't know. The sanity of the S.O.E. has often been questioned, but even *we* aren't given to sending a flying-boat for the sole purpose of enabling junior officers to spend a month wasting their substance among the flesh-pots of Cairo,' he finished dryly.

'I still don't know – '

'Patience, laddie, patience – as our worthy Group-Captain has just advocated. Time is endless. To wait, and to keep on waiting – that is to be of the East.'

'To total four hours' sleep in three days is not,' Mallory said feelingly. 'And that's all I've had.... Here they come!'

Both men screwed up their eyes in automatic reflex as the fierce glare of the landing lights struck at them, the flare path arrowing off into the outer darkness. In less than a minute the first bomber was down, heavily, awkwardly, taxiing to a standstill just beside them. The grey camouflage paint of the after fuselage and tail-planes was riddled with bullet and cannon shells, an aileron was shredded and the port outer engine out of commission, saturated in oil. The cabin Perspex was shattered and starred in a dozen places.

For a long time Jensen stared at the holes and scars of the damaged machine, then shook his head and looked away.

'Four hours' sleep, Captain Mallory,' he said quietly. 'Four hours. I'm beginning to think that you can count yourself damn lucky to have had even that much.'

The interrogation room, harshly lit by two powerful, unshaded lights, was uncomfortable and airless. The furniture consisted of some battered wall-maps and charts, a score or so of equally scuffed chairs and an unvarnished deal table. The Group-Captain, flanked by Jensen and Mallory, was sitting behind this when the door opened abruptly and the first of the flying crews entered, blinking rapidly in the fierceness of the unaccustomed light. They were led by a dark-haired, thick-set pilot, trailing helmet and flying-suit in his left hand. He had an Anzac bush helmet crushed on the back of his head, and the word 'Australia' emblazoned in white across each khaki shoulder. Scowling, wordlessly and without permission, he sat down in front of them, produced a pack of cigarettes and rasped a match across the surface of the table. Mallory looked furtively at the Group-Captain. The Group-Captain just looked resigned. He even sounded resigned.

'Gentlemen, this is Squadron Leader Torrance. Squadron Leader Torrance,' he added unnecessarily, 'is an Australian.' Mallory had the impression that the Group-Captain rather hoped this would explain some things, Squadron Leader Torrance among them. 'He led tonight's attack on Navarone. Bill, these gentlemen here – Captain Jensen of the Royal Navy, Captain Mallory of the Long Range Desert Group – have a very special interest in Navarone. How did things go tonight?'

Navarone! So that's why I'm here tonight, Mallory thought. Navarone. He knew it well, rather, knew of it. So did everyone who had served any time at all in the Eastern Mediterranean: a grim, impregnable iron fortress off the coast of Turkey, heavily defended by – it was thought – a mixed garrison of Germans and Italians, one of the few Aegean islands on which the Allies had been unable to establish a mission, far less recapture, at some period of the war.... He realised that Torrance was speaking, the slow drawl heavy with controlled anger.

'Bloody awful, sir. A fair cow, it was, a real suicide do.' He broke off abruptly, stared moodily with compressed lips through his own drifting tobacco smoke. 'But we'd like to go back again,' he went on. 'Me and the boys here. Just once. We were talking about it on the way home.' Mallory caught the deep murmur of voices in the background, a growl of agreement. 'We'd like to take with us the joker who thought this one up and shove him out at ten thousand over Navarone, without benefit of a parachute.'

'As bad as that, Bill?'

'As bad as that, sir. We hadn't a chance. Straight up, we really hadn't. First off, the weather was against us – the jokers in the Met. office were about as right as they usually are.'

'They gave you clear weather?'

'Yeah. Clear weather. It was ten-tenths over the target,' Torrance said bitterly. 'We had to go down to fifteen hundred. Not that it made any difference. We would have to have gone down lower than that anyway – about three thousand feet below sea-level then fly up the way: that cliff overhang shuts the target clean off. Might as well have dropped a shower of leaflets asking them to spike their own bloody guns.... Then they've got every second A.A. gun in the south of Europe concentrated along this narrow 50-degree vector – the only way you can approach the target, or anywhere near the target. Russ and Conroy were belted good and proper on the way in. Didn't even get half-way towards the harbour.... They never had a chance.'

'I know, I know.' The Group-Captain nodded heavily. 'We heard. W/T reception was good.... And McIlveen ditched just north of Alex?'

'Yeah. But he'll be all right. The old crate was still awash when we passed over, the big dinghy was out and it was as smooth as a millpond. He'll be all right,' Torrance repeated.

The Group-Captain nodded again, and Jensen touched his sleeve.

11

'May I have a word with the Squadron Leader?'

'Of course, Captain. You don't have to ask.'

'Thanks.' Jensen looked across at the burly Australian and smiled faintly.

'Just one little question, Squadron Leader. You don't fancy going back there again?'

'Too bloody right, I don't!' Torrance growled.

'Because?'

'Because I don't believe in suicide. Because I don't believe in sacrificing good blokes for nothing. Because I'm not God and I can't do the impossible.' There was a flat finality in Torrance's voice that carried conviction, that brooked no argument.

'It is impossible, you say?' Jensen persisted. 'This is terribly important.'

'So's my life. So are the lives of all these jokers.' Torrance jerked a big thumb over his shoulder. 'It's impossible, sir. At least, it's impossible for us.' He drew a weary hand down his face. 'Maybe a Dornier flying-boat with one of these new-fangled radio-controlled glider-bombs might do it and get off with it. I don't know. But I do know that nothing we've got has a snowball's chance in hell. Not,' he added bitterly, 'unless you cram a Mosquito full of T.N.T. and order one of us to crash-dive it at four hundred into the mouth of the gun cave. That way there's always a chance.'

'Thank you, Squadron Leader – and all of you.' Jensen was on his feet. 'I know you've done your very best, no one could have done more. And I'm sorry....Group-Captain?'

'Right with you, gentlemen.' He nodded to the bespectacled Intelligence officer who had been sitting behind them to take his place, led the way out through a side door and into his own quarters.

'Well, that is that, I suppose.' He broke the seal of a bottle of Talisker, brought out some glasses. 'You'll have to accept it as final, Jensen. Bill Torrance's is the senior, most experienced squadron left in Africa today. Used to pound the Ploesti oil well and think it a helluva skylark. If anyone could have done tonight's job it was Bill Torrance, and if he says, it's impossible, believe me, Captain Jensen, it can't be done.'

'Yes.' Jensen looked down sombrely at the golden amber of the glass in his hand. 'Yes, I know now. I *almost* knew before, but I couldn't be sure, and I couldn't take the chance of being wrong.... A terrible pity that it took the lives of a dozen men to prove me right.... There's just the one way left, now.'

'There's just the one,' the Group-Captain echoed. He lifted his glass, shook his head. 'Here's luck to Kheros!'

'Here's luck to Kheros!' Jensen echoed in turn. His face was grim.

'Look!' Mallory begged. 'I'm completely lost. Would somebody please tell me – '

'Kheros,' Jensen interrupted. 'That was your cue call, young man. All the world's a stage, laddie, etc., and this is where you tread the boards in this particular little comedy.' Jensen's smile was quite mirthless. 'Sorry you've missed the first two acts, but don't lose any sleep over that. This is no bit part: you're going to be the star, whether you like it or not. This is it. Kheros, Act 3, Scene 1. Enter Captain Keith Mallory.'

Neither of them had spoken in the last ten minutes. Jensen drove the big Humber command car with the same sureness, the same relaxed efficiency that hall-marked everything he did: Mallory still sat hunched over the map on his knees, a large-scale Admiralty chart of the Southern Aegean illuminated by the hooded dashboard light, studying an area of the Sporades and Northern Dodecanese heavily squared off in red pencil. Finally he straightened up and shivered. Even in Egypt these late November nights could be far too cold for comfort. He looked across at Jensen.

'I think I've got it now, sir.'

'Good!' Jensen gazed straight ahead along the winding grey ribbon of dusty road, along the white glare of the headlights that cleaved through the darkness of the desert. The beams lifted and dipped, constantly, hypnotically, to the cushioning of the springs on the rutted road. 'Good!' he repeated. 'Now, have another look at it and imagine yourself standing in the town of Navarone — that's on that almost circular bay on the north of the island. Tell me, what would you see from there?'

Mallory smiled.

'I don't have to look again, sir. Four miles or so away to the east I'd see the Turkish coast curving up north and west to a point almost due north of Navarone — a very sharp promontory, that, for the coastline above curves back almost due east. Then, about sixteen miles away, due north beyond this promontory — Cape Demirci, isn't it? — and practically in a line with it I'd see the island of Kheros. Finally, six miles to the west is the island of Maidos, the first of the Lerades group. They stretch away in a north-westerly direction, maybe fifty miles.'

'Sixty.' Jensen nodded. 'You have the eye, my boy. You've got the guts and the experience — a man doesn't survive eighteen months in Crete without both. You've got one or two special qualifications I'll mention by and by.' He paused for a moment, shook his head slowly. 'I only hope you have the luck — all the luck. God alone knows you're going to need it.'

Mallory waited expectantly, but Jensen had sunk into some private reverie. Three minutes passed, perhaps five, and there was only the swish of the tyres, the subdued hum of the powerful engine. Presently Jensen stirred and spoke again, quietly, still without taking his eyes off the road.

'This is Saturday — rather, it's Sunday morning now. There are one thousand two hundred men on the island of Kheros — one thousand two hundred British soldiers —

14

who will be dead, wounded or prisoner by next Saturday. Mostly they'll be dead.' For the first time he looked at Mallory and smiled, a brief smile, a crooked smile, and then it was gone. 'How does it feel to hold a thousand lives in your hands, Captain Mallory?'

For long seconds Mallory looked at the impassive face beside him, then looked away again. He stared down at the chart. Twelve hundred men on Kheros, twelve hundred men waiting to die. Kheros and Navarone, Kheros and Navarone. What was that poem again, that little jingle that he'd learnt all these long years ago in that little upland village in the sheeplands outside Queenstown? Chimborazo – that was it. 'Chimborazo and Cotopaxi, you have stolen my heart away.' Kheros and Navarone – they had the same ring, the same indefinable glamour, the same wonder of romance that took hold of a man and stayed with him. Kheros and – angrily, almost he shook his head, tried to concentrate. The pieces of the jigsaw were beginning to click into place, but slowly.

Jensen broke the silence.

'Eighteen months ago, you remember, after the fall of Greece, the Germans had taken over nearly all the islands of the Sporades: the Italians, of course, already held most of the Dodecanese. Then, gradually, we began to establish missions on these islands, usually spear-headed by your people, the Long Range Desert Group or the Special Boat Service. By last September we had retaken nearly all the larger islands except Navarone – it was too damned hard a nut, so we just by-passed it – and brought some of the garrisons up to, and beyond, battalion strength.' He grinned at Mallory. 'You were lurking in your cave somewhere in the White Mountains at the time, but you'll remember how the Germans reacted?'

'Violently?'

Jensen nodded.

'Exactly. Very violently indeed. The political importance of Turkey in this part of the world is impossible to over-estimate – and she's always been a potential partner for either Axis or Allies. Most of these islands are only a few miles off the Turkish coast. The question of prestige, of restoring confidence in Germany, was urgent.'

'So?'

'So they flung in everything – paratroopers, airborne troops, crack mountain brigades, hordes of Stukas – I'm told they stripped the Italian front of dive-bombers for these operations. Anyway, they flung everything in – the lot. In a few weeks we'd lost over ten thousand troops and every island we'd ever recaptured – except Kheros.'

'And now it's the turn of Kheros?'

'Yes.' Jensen shook out a pair of cigarettes, sat silently until Mallory had lit them and sent the match spinning through the window towards the pale gleam of the Mediterranean lying north below the coast road. 'Yes, Kheros is for the hammer. Nothing that we can do can save it. The Germans have absolute air superiority in the Aegean...'

'But – but how can you be so sure that it's this week?' Jensen sighed.

'Laddie, Greece is fairly hotching with Allied agents. We have over two hundred in the Athens-Piraeus area alone and – '

'Two hundred!' Mallory interrupted incredulously. 'Did you say – '

'I did.' Jensen grinned. 'A mere bagatelle, I assure you, compared to the vast hordes of spies that circulate freely among our noble hosts in Cairo and Alexandria.' He was suddenly serious again. 'Anyway, our information is accurate. An armada of caiques will sail from the Piraeus on Thursday at dawn and island-hop across the Cyclades, holing up in the islands at night.' He smiled. 'An intriguing situation, don't you think? We daren't move in the Aegean in the daytime or we'd be bombed out of the water. The Germans don't dare move at night. Droves of our destroyers and M.T.B.s and gun-boats move into the

Aegean at dusk: the destroyers retire to the south before dawn, the small boats usually lie up in isolated island creeks. But we can't stop them from getting across. They'll be there Saturday or Sunday — and synchronise their landings with the first of the airborne troops: they've scores of Junkers 52s waiting just outside Athens. Kheros won't last a couple of days.' No one could have listened to Jensen's carefully casual voice, his abnormal matter-of-factness and not have believed him.

Mallory believed him. For almost a minute he stared down at the sheen of the sea, at the faerie tracery of the stars shimmering across its darkly placid surface. Suddenly he swung round on Jensen.

'But the Navy, sir! Evacuation! Surely the Navy—'

'The Navy,' Jensen interrupted heavily, 'is not keen. The Navy is sick and tired of the Eastern Med. and the Aegean, sick and tired of sticking out its long-suffering neck and having it regularly chopped off — and all for sweet damn all. We've had two battleships wrecked, eight cruisers out of commission — four of them sunk — and over a dozen destroyers gone... I couldn't even start to count the number of smaller vessels we've lost. And for what? I've told you — for sweet damn all! Just so's our High Command can play round-and-round-the-rugged-rocks and who's-the-king-of-the-castle with their opposite numbers in Berlin. Great fun for all concerned — except, of course, for the thousand or so sailors who've been drowned in the course of the game, the ten thousand or so Tommies and Anzacs and Indians who suffered and died on these same islands — and died without knowing why.'

Jensen's hands were white-knuckled on the wheel, his mouth tight-drawn and bitter. Mallory was surprised, shocked almost, by the vehemence, the depth of feeling; it was so completely out of character.... Or perhaps it was in character, perhaps Jensen knew a very great deal indeed about what went on on the inside....

'Twelve hundred men, you said, sir?' Mallory asked

17

quietly. 'You said there were twelve hundred men on Kheros?'

Jensen flickered a glance at him, looked away again.

'Yes. Twelve hundred men.' Jensen sighed. 'You're right, laddie, of course you're right. I'm just talking off the top of my head. Of course we can't leave them there. The Navy will do its damnedest. What's two or three more destroyers – sorry, boy, sorry, there I go again.... Now listen, and listen carefully.'

'Taking 'em off will have to be a night operation. There isn't a ghost of a chance in the daytime – not with two-three hundred Stukas just begging for a glimpse of a Royal Naval destroyer. It'll have to be destroyers – transports and tenders are too slow by half. And they can't possibly go north about the northern tip of the Lerades – they'd never get back to safety before daylight. It's too long a trip by hours.'

'But the Lerades is a pretty long string of islands,' Mallory ventured. 'Couldn't the destroyers go through – '

'Between a couple of them? Impossible.' Jensen shook his head. 'Mined to hell and back again. Every single channel. You couldn't take a dinghy through.'

'And the Maidos-Navarone channel. Stiff with mines also, I suppose?'

'No, that's a clear channel. Deep water – you can't moor mines in deep water.'

'So that's the route you've got to take, isn't it, sir? I mean, they're Turkish territorial waters on the other side and we – '

'We'd go through Turkish territorial waters tomorrow, and in broad daylight, if it would do any good,' Jensen said flatly. 'The Turks know it and so do the Germans. But all other things being equal, the Western channel is the one we're taking. It's a clearer channel, a shorter route – and it doesn't involve any unnecessary international complications.'

'All other things being equal?'

18

'The guns of Navarone.' Jensen paused for a long time, then repeated the words, slowly, expressionlessly, as one would repeat the name of some feared and ancient enemy. 'The guns of Navarone. They make everything equal. They cover the Northern entrances to both channels. We could take the twelve hundred men off Kheros tonight – if we could silence the guns of Navarone.'

Mallory sat silent, said nothing. He's coming to it now, he thought.

'These guns are no ordinary guns,' Jensen went on quietly. 'Our naval experts say they're about nine-inch rifle barrels. I think myself they're more likely a version of the 210 mm. 'crunch' guns that the Germans are using in Italy – our soldiers up there hate and fear those guns more than anything on earth. A dreadful weapon – shell extremely slow in flight and damnably accurate. Anyway,' he went on grimly, 'whatever they were they were good enough to dispose of the *Sybaris* in five minutes flat.'

Mallory nodded slowly.

'The *Sybaris*! I think I heard – '

'An eight-inch cruiser we sent up there about four months ago to try conclusions with the Hun. Just a formality, a routine exercise, we thought. The *Sybaris* was blasted out of the water. There were seventeen survivors.'

'Good God!' Mallory was shocked. 'I didn't know – '

'Two months ago we mounted a large-scale amphibious attack on Navarone.' Jensen hadn't even heard the interruption. 'Commandos, Royal Marine Commandos and Jellicoe's Special Boat Service. Less than an even chance, we knew – Navarone's practically solid cliff all the way round. But then these were very special men, probably the finest assault troops in the world today.' Jensen paused for almost a minute, then went on very quietly. 'They were cut to ribbons. They were massacred almost to a man.

'Finally, twice in the past ten days – we've seen this

attack on Kheros coming for a long time now – we sent in parachute saboteurs: Special Boat Service men.' He shrugged his shoulders helplessly. 'They just vanished.'

'Just like that?'

'Just like that. And then tonight – the last desperate fling of the gambler and what have you.' Jensen laughed, briefly and without humour. 'That interrogation hut – I kept pretty quiet in there tonight, I tell you. I was the "joker" that Torrance and his boys wanted to heave out over Navarone. I don't blame them. But I had to do it, I just had to do it. I knew it was hopeless – but it had to be done.'

The big Humber was beginning to slow down now, running silently between the tumble-down shacks and hovels that line the Western approach to Alexandria. The sky ahead was already beginning to streak in the first tenuous greys of the false dawn.

'I don't think I'd be much good with a parachute,' Mallory said doubtfully. 'In fact, quite frankly, I've never even *seen* a parachute.'

'Don't worry,' Jensen said briefly. 'You won't have to use one. You're going into Navarone the hard way.'

Mallory waited for more, but Jensen had fallen silent, intent on avoiding the large potholes that were beginning to pock the roadway. After a time Mallory asked:

'Why me, Captain Jensen?'

Jensen's smile was barely visible in the greying darkness. He swerved violently to avoid a gaping hole and straightened up again.

'Scared?'

'Certainly I'm scared. No offence intended, sir, but the way you talk you'd scare anyone.... But that wasn't what I meant.'

'I know it wasn't. Just my twisted humour.... Why you? Special qualifications, laddie, just like I told you. You speak Greek like a Greek. You speak German like a German. Skilled saboteur, first-class organiser and

20

eighteen unscathed months in the White Mountains of Crete – a convincing demonstration of your ability to survive in enemy-held territory.' Jensen chuckled. 'You'd be surprised to know just how complete a dossier I have on you!'

'No, I wouldn't.' Mallory spoke with some feeling. 'And,' he added, 'I know of at least three other officers with the same qualifications.'

'There are others,' Jensen agreed. 'But there are no other Keith Mallorys. Keith Mallory,' Jensen repeated rhetorically. 'Who hadn't heard of Keith Mallory in the palmy, balmy days before the war? The finest mountaineer, the greatest rock climber New Zealand has ever produced – and by that, of course, New Zealanders mean the world. The human fly, the climber of the unclimbable, the scaler of vertical cliffs and impossible precipices. The entire south coast of Navarone,' said Jensen cheerfully, 'consists of one vast, impossible precipice. Nary a hand- or foot-hold in sight.'

'I see,' Mallory murmured. 'I see indeed. "Into Navarone the hard way." That was what you said.'

'That was,' Jensen acknowledged. 'You and your gang – just four others. Mallory's Merry Mountaineers. Handpicked. Every man a specialist. You'll meet them all tomorrow – this afternoon, rather.'

They travelled in silence for the next ten minutes, turned up right from the dock area, jounced their uncomfortable way over the massive cobbles of the Rue Soeurs, slewed round into Mohammed Ali square, passed in front of the Bourse and turned right down the Sherif Pasha.

Mallory looked at the man behind the wheel. He could see his face quite clearly now in the gathering light.

'Where to, sir?'

'To see the only man in the Middle East who can give you any help now. Monsieur Eugene Vlachos of Navarone.'

★   ★   ★

21

'You are a brave man, Captain Mallory.' Nervously Eugene Vlachos twisted the long, pointed ends of his black moustache. 'A brave man and a foolish one, I would say – but I suppose we cannot call a man a fool when he only obeys his orders.' His eyes left the large drawing lying before him on the table and sought Jensen's impassive face.

'Is there no other way, Captain?' he pleaded.

Jensen shook his head slowly:

'There are. We've tried them all, sir. They all failed. This is the last.'

'He must go, then?'

'There are over a thousand men on Kheros, sir.'

Vlachos bowed his head in silent acceptance, then smiled faintly at Mallory.

'He calls me "sir". Me, a poor Greek hotel-keeper and Captain Jensen of the Royal Navy calls me "sir". It makes an old man feel good.' He stopped, gazed off vacantly into space, the faded eyes and tired, lined face soft with memory. 'An old man, Captain Mallory, an old man now, a poor man and a sad one. But I wasn't always, not always. Once I was just middle-aged, and rich and well content. Once I owned a lovely land, a hundred square miles of the most beautiful country God ever sent to delight the eyes of His creatures here below, and how well I loved that land!'

He laughed self-consciously and ran a hand through his thick, greying hair. 'Ah, well, as you people say, I suppose it's all in the eye of the beholder. "A lovely land," I say. "That blasted rock," as Captain Jensen has been heard to describe it out of my hearing.' He smiled at Jensen's sudden discomfiture. 'But we both give it the same name – Navarone.'

Startled, Mallory looked at Jensen. Jensen nodded.

'The Vlachos family has owned Navarone for generations. We had to remove Monsieur Vlachos in a great hurry eighteen months ago. The Germans didn't care

22

overmuch for his kind of collaboration.'

'It was – how do you say – touch and go.' Vlachos nodded. 'They had reserved three very special places for my two sons and myself in the dungeons in Navarone.... But enough of the Vlachos family. I just wanted you to know, young man, that I spent forty years on Navarone and almost four days' – he gestured to the table – 'on that map. My information and that map you can trust absolutely. Many things will have changed, of course, but some things never change. The mountains, the bays, the passes, the caves, the roads, the houses and, above all, the fortress itself – these have remained unchanged for centuries, Captain Mallory.'

'I understand, sir.' Mallory folded the map carefully, stowed it away in his tunic. 'With this, there's always a chance. Thank you very much.'

'It is little enough, God knows.' Vlachos's fingers drummed on the table for a moment, then he looked up at Mallory. 'Captain Jensen informs me that most of you speak Greek fluently, that you will be dressed as Greek peasants and will carry forged papers. That is well. You will be – what is the word? – self-contained, will operate on your own.' He paused, then went on very earnestly.

'Please do not try to enlist the help of the people of Navarone. At all costs you must avoid that. The Germans are ruthless. I know. If a man helps you and is found out, they will destroy not only that man but his entire village – men, women and children. It has happened before. It will happen again.'

'It happened in Crete,' Mallory agreed quietly. 'I've seen it for myself.'

'Exactly.' Vlachos nodded. 'And the people of Navarone have neither the skill nor the experience for successful guerrilla operations. They have not had the chance – German surveillance has been especially severe in our island.'

'I promise you, sir – ' Mallory began.

Vlachos held up his hand.

'Just a moment. If your need is desperate, really desperate, there are two men to whom you may turn. Under the first plane tree in the village square of Margaritha – at the mouth of the valley about three miles south of the fortress – you will find a man called Louki. He has been the steward of our family for many years. Louki has been of help to the British before – Captain Jensen will confirm that – and you can trust him with your life. He has a friend, Panayis: he, too, has been useful in the past.'

'Thank you, sir. I'll remember. Louki and Panayis and Margaritha – the first plane tree in the square.'

'And you will refuse all other aid, Captain?' Vlachos asked anxiously. 'Louki and Panayis – only these two,' he pleaded.

'You have my word, sir. Besides, the fewer the safer for us as well as your people.' Mallory was surprised at the old man's intensity.

'I hope so, I hope so.' Vlachos sighed heavily.

Mallory stood up, stretched out his hand to take his leave.

'You're worrying about nothing, sir. They'll never see us,' he promised confidently. 'Nobody will see us – and we'll see nobody. We're after only one thing – the guns.'

'Ay, the guns – those terrible guns.' Vlachos shook his head. 'But just suppose – '

'Please. It will be all right,' Mallory insisted quietly. 'We will bring harm to none – and least of all to your islanders.'

'God go with you tonight,' the old man whispered. 'God go with you tonight. I only wish that I could go too.'

CHAPTER 2

Sunday Night

1900–0200

'Coffee, sir?'

Mallory stirred and groaned and fought his way up from the depths of exhausted sleep. Painfully he eased himself back on the metal-framed bucket-seat, wondering peevishly when the Air Force was going to get round to upholstering these fiendish contraptions. Then he was fully awake, tired, heavy eyes automatically focusing on the luminous dial of his wrist-watch. Seven o'clock. Just seven o'clock – he'd been asleep barely a couple of hours. Why hadn't they let him sleep on?

'Coffee, sir?' The young air-gunner was still standing patiently by his side, the inverted lid of an ammunition box serving as a tray for the cups he was carrying.

'Sorry, boy, sorry.' Mallory struggled upright in his seat, reached up for a cup of the steaming liquid, sniffed it appreciatively. 'Thank you. You know, this smells just like real coffee.'

'It is, sir.' The young gunner smiled proudly. 'We have a percolator in the galley.'

'He has a percolator in the galley.' Mallory shook his head in disbelief. 'Ye gods, the rigours of war in the Royal Air Force!' He leaned back, sipped the coffee luxuriously and sighed in contentment. Next moment he was on his feet, the hot coffee splashing unheeded on his bare knees as he stared out the window beside him. He looked at the gunner, gestured in disbelief at the mountainous landscape unrolling darkly beneath them.

'What the hell goes on here? We're not due till two hours after dark – and it's barely gone sunset! Has the pilot – ?'

25

'That's Cyprus, sir.' The gunner grinned. 'You can just see Mount Olympus on the horizon. Nearly always, going to Castelrosso, we fly a big dog-leg over Cyprus. It's to escape observation, sir; and it takes us well clear of Rhodes.'

'To escape observation, he says!' The heavy transatlantic drawl came from the bucket-seat diagonally across the passage: the speaker was lying collapsed – there was no other word for it – in his seat, the bony knees topping the level of the chin by several inches. 'My Gawd! To escape observation!' he repeated in awed wonder. 'Dog-legs over Cyprus. Twenty miles out from Alex by launch so that nobody ashore can see us takin' off by plane. And then what?' He raised himself painfully in his seat, eased an eyebrow over the bottom of the window, then fell back again, visibly exhausted by the effort. 'And then what? Then they pack us into an old crate that's painted the whitest white you ever saw guaranteed visible to a blind man at a hundred miles – 'specially now that it's gettin' dark.'

'It keeps the heat out,' the young gunner said defensively.

'The heat doesn't worry me, son.' The drawl was tireder, more lugubrious than ever. 'I like the heat. What I don't like are them nasty cannon shells and bullets that can ventilate a man in all the wrong places.' He slid his spine another impossible inch down the seat, closed his eyes wearily and seemed asleep in a moment.

The young gunner shook his head admiringly and smiled at Mallory.

'Worried to hell, isn't he, sir?'

Mallory laughed and watched the boy disappear for'ard into the control cabin. He sipped his coffee slowly, looked again at the sleeping figure across the passage. The blissful unconcern was magnificent: Corporal Dusty Miller of the United States, and more recently of the Long Range Desert Force, would be a good man to have around.

26

He looked round at the others and nodded to himself in satisfaction. They would all be good men to have around. Eighteen months in Crete had developed in him an unerring sense for assessing a man's capacity for survival in the peculiar kind of irregular warfare in which he himself had been so long engaged. Off-hand he'd have taken long odds on the capacity of these four to survive. In the matter of picking an outstanding team Captain Jensen, he reckoned, had done him proud. He didn't know them all yet – not personally. But he was intimately acquainted with the exhaustive dossier that Jensen held on each one of them. These were reassuring, to say the least.

Or was there perhaps a slight question mark against Stevens? Mallory wondered, looking across the passage at the fair-haired, boyish figure gazing out eagerly beneath the gleaming white wing of the Sunderland. Lieutenant Andy Stevens, R.N.V.R., had been chosen for this assignment for three reasons. He would navigate the craft that was to take them to Navarone: he was a first-class Alpinist, with several outstanding climbs to his record: and, the product of the classical side of a red-brick university, he was an almost fanatical philhellene, fluent in both Ancient and Modern Greek, and had spent his last two long vacations before the war as a tourist courier in Athens. But he was young, absurdly young, Mallory thought as he looked at him, and youth could be dangerous. Too often, in that island guerrilla warfare, it had been fatal. The enthusiasm, the fire, the zeal of youth was not enough: rather, it was too much, a positive handicap. This was not a war of bugle calls and roaring engines and magnificent defiance in the clamour of battle: this was a war of patience and endurance and stability, of cunning and craft and stealth, and these were not commonly the attributes of youth.... But he looked as if he might learn fast.

Mallory stole another glance at Miller. Dusty Miller, he decided, had learnt it all a long, long time ago. Dusty

Miller on a white charger, the bugle to his lips – no, his mind just refused to encompass the incongruity of it. He just didn't look like Sir Lancelot. He just looked as if he had been around for a long, long time and had no illusions left.

Corporal Miller had, in fact, been around for exactly forty years. By birth a Californian, by descent three parts Irish and one part Central European, he had lived and fought and adventured more in the previous quarter of a century than most men would in a dozen lifetimes. Silver-miner in Nevada, tunneller in Canada and oil-fire shooter all over the globe, he had been in Saudi Arabia when Hitler attacked Poland. One of his more remote maternal ancestors, some time around the turn of the century, had lived in Warsaw, but that had been affront enough for Miller's Irish blood. He had taken the first available plane to Britain and lied his way into the Air Force, where, to his immense disgust, and because of his age, he was relegated to the rear turret of a Wellington.

His first operational flight had been his last. Within ten minutes of taking off from the Menidi airfield outside Athens on a January night in 1941, engine failure had brought them to an ignominious though well-cushioned end in a paddy field some miles north-west of the city. The rest of the winter he had spent seething with rage in a cookhouse back in Menidi. At the beginning of April he resigned from the Air Force without telling anyone and was making his way north towards the fighting and the Albanian frontier when he met the Germans coming south. As Miller afterwards told it, he reached Nauplion two blocks ahead of the nearest panzer division, was evacuated by the transport *Slamat*, sunk, picked up by the destroyer *Wryneck*, sunk, and finally arrived in Alexandria in an ancient Greek caique, with nothing left him in the world but a fixed determination never again to venture in the air or on the sea. Some months later he was operating with a long-range striking force behind the enemy lines in Libya.

He was, Mallory mused, the complete antithesis to Lieutenant Stevens. Stevens, young, fresh, enthusiastic, correct and immaculately dressed, and Miller, dried-up, lean, stringy, immensely tough and with an almost pathological aversion to spit and polish. How well the nickname 'Dusty' suited him: there could hardly have been a greater contrast. Again, unlike Stevens, Miller had never climbed a mountain in his life and the only Greek words he knew were invariably omitted from the dictionaries. And both these facts were of no importance at all. Miller had been picked for one reason only. A genius with explosives, resourceful and cool, precise and deadly in action, he was regarded by Middle East Intelligence in Cairo as the finest saboteur in southern Europe.

Behind Miller sat Casey Brown. Short, dark and compact, Petty Officer Telegraphist Brown was a Clydesider, in peace-time an installation and testing engineer in a famous yacht-builder's yard on the Gareloch. The fact that he was a born and ready-made engine-room artificer had been so blindingly obvious that the Navy had missed it altogether and stuck him in the Communications Branch. Brown's ill luck was Mallory's good fortune. Brown would act as the engineer of the boat taking them to Navarone and would maintain radio contact with base. He had also the further recommendation of being a first-class guerrilla fighter: a veteran of the Special Boat Service, he held the D.C.M. and D.S.M. for his exploits in the Aegean and off the coast of Libya.

The fifth and last member of the party sat directly behind Mallory. Mallory did not have to turn round to look at him. He already knew him, knew him better than he knew anyone else in the world, better even than he knew his own mother. Andrea, who had been his lieutenant for all these eighteen interminable months in Crete.

Andrea of the vast bulk, the continual rumbling laughter and tragic past, with whom he had eaten, lived and slept in caves, rock-shelters and abandoned shepherd's huts while constantly harried by German patrols and aircraft — that Andrea had become his *alter ego*, his *doppel: gänger* remind himself what he was like.... There was no question as to why Andrea had come along. He wasn't there primarily because he was a Greek himself, with an intimate knowledge of the islanders' language, thought and customs, nor even because of his pefect understanding with Mallory, although all these things helped. He was, instead, there exclusively for the protection and safety he afforded. Endlessly patient, quiet and deadly, tremendously fast in spite of his bulk, and with a feline stealth that exploded into berserker action, Andrea was the complete fighting machine. Andrea was their insurance policy against failure.

Mallory turned back to look out the window again, then nodded to himself in imperceptible satisfaction. Jensen probably couldn't have picked a better team if he'd scoured the whole Mediterranean theatre. It suddenly occurred to Mallory that Jensen probably had done just that. Miller and Brown had been recalled to Alexandria almost a month ago. It was almost as long since Stevens's relief had arrived aboard his cruiser in Malta. And if their battery-charging engine hadn't slipped down that ravine in the White Mountains, and if the sorely harassed runner from the nearest listening post hadn't taken a week to cover fifty miles of snowbound, enemy-patrolled mountains and another five days to find them, he and Andrea would have been in Alexandria almost a fortnight earlier. Mallory's opinion of Jensen, already high, rose another notch. A far-seeing man who planned accordingly, Jensen must have had all his preparations for this made even before the first of the two abortive parachute landings on Navarone.

★　　★　　★

30

It was eight o'clock and almost totally dark inside the plane when Mallory rose and made his way for'ard to the control cabin. The captain, face wreathed in tobacco smoke, was drinking coffee: the co-pilot waved a languid hand at his approach and resumed a bored scanning of the scene ahead.

'Good evening.' Mallory smiled. 'Mind if I come in?'

'Welcome in my office any time,' the pilot assured him. 'No need to ask.'

'I only thought you might be busy...' Mallory stopped and looked again at the scene of masterly inactivity. 'Just who is flying this plane?' he asked.

'George. The automatic pilot.' He waved a coffee-cup in the direction of a black, squat box, its blurred outlines just visible in the near darkness. 'An industrious character, and makes a damn sight fewer mistakes than that idle hound who's supposed to be on watch... Anything on your mind, Captain?'

'Yes. What were your instructions for tonight?'

'Just to set you blokes down in Castelrosso when it was good and dark.' The pilot paused, then said frankly, 'I don't get it. A ship this size for only five men and a couple of hundred odd pounds of equipment. Especially to Castelrosso. Especially after dark. Last plane that came down here after dark just kept on going down. Underwater obstruction – dunno what it was. Two survivors.'

'I know. I heard. I'm sorry, but I'm under orders too. As for the rest, forget it – and I mean forget. Impress on your crew that they mustn't talk. They've never seen us.'

The pilot nodded glumly. 'We've all been threatened with court-martial already. You'd think there was a ruddy war on.'

'There is.... We'll be leaving a couple of cases behind. We're going ashore in different clothes. Somebody will be waiting for our old stuff when you get back.'

'Roger. And the best of luck, Captain. Official secrets, or no official secrets, I've got a hunch you're going to need it.'

31

'If we are, you can give us a good send-off.' Mallory grinned. 'Just set us down in one piece will you?'

'Reassure yourself, brother,' the pilot said firmly. 'Just set your mind at ease. Don't forget – I'm in this ruddy plane too.'

The clamour of the Sunderland's great engines was still echoing in their ears when the stubby little motor-boat chugged softly out of the darkness and nosed alongside the gleaming hull of the flying-boat. There was no time lost: there were no words spoken; within a minute the five men and all their gear had been embarked; within another the little boat was rubbing to a stop against the rough stone Navy jetty of Castelrosso. Two ropes were spinning up into the darkness, were caught and quickly secured by practised hands. Amidships, the rust-scaled iron ladder, recessed deep into the stone, stretched up into the star-dusted darkness above: as Mallory reached the top a figure stepped forward out of the gloom.

'Captain Mallory?'

'Yes.'

'Captain Briggs, Army. Have your men wait here, will you? The colonel would like to see you.' The nasal voice, peremptory in its clipped affectation, was far from cordial. Mallory stirred in slow anger, but said nothing. Briggs sounded like a man who might like his bed or his gin, and maybe their late visitation was keeping him from either or both. War was hell.

They were back in ten minutes, a third figure following behind them. Mallory peered at the three men standing on the edge of the jetty, identified them, then peered around again.

'Where's Miller got to?' he asked.

'Here, boss, here.' Miller groaned, eased his back off a big, wooden bollard, climbed wearily to his feet. 'Just restin', boss. Recuperatin', as you might say, from the nerve-rackin' rigours of the trip.'

'When you're all *quite* ready,' Briggs said acidly, 'Matthews here will take you to your quarters. You are to remain on call for the Captain, Matthews. Colonel's orders.' Briggs's tone left no doubt that he thought the colonel's orders a piece of arrant nonsense. 'And don't forget, Captain – two hours, the Colonel said.'

'I know, I know,' Mallory said wearily. 'I was there when he said it. It was to me he was talking. Remember? All right, boys, if you're ready.'

'Our gear, sir?' Stevens ventured.

'Just leave it there. Right, Matthews, lead the way, will you?'

Matthews led the way along the jetty and up interminable flights of steep, worn steps, the others followed in Indian file, rubber soles noiseless on the stone. He turned sharply right at the top, went down a narrow, winding alley, into a passage, climbed a flight of creaking, wooden stairs, opened the first door in the corridor above.

'Here you are, sir. I'll just wait in the corridor outside.'

'Better wait downstairs,' Mallory advised. 'No offence. Matthews, but the less you know of this the better.'

He followed the others into the room, closing the door behind him. It was a small, bleak room, heavily curtained. A table and half a dozen chairs took up most of the space. Over in the far corner the springs of the single bed creaked as Corporal Miller stretched himself out luxuriously, hands clasped behind his head.

'Gee!' he murmured admiringly. 'A hotel room. Just like home. Kinda bare, though.' A thought occurred to him. 'Where are all you other guys gonna sleep?'

'We aren't,' Mallory said briefly. 'Neither are you. We're pulling out in less than two hours.' Miller groaned. 'Come on, soldier,' Mallory went on relentlessly. 'On your feet.'

Miller groaned again, swung his legs over the edge of the bed and looked curiously at Andrea. The big Greek was quartering the room methodically, pulling out lockers, turning pictures, peering behind curtains and under the bed.

33

'What's he doin'?' Miller asked. 'Lookin' for dust?'

'Testing for listening devices,' Mallory said curtly. 'One of the reasons why Andrea and I have lasted so long.' He dug into the inside pocket of his tunic, a dark naval battledress with neither badge nor insignia, pulled out a chart and the map Vlachos had given him, unfolded and spread them out. 'Round the table, all of you. I know you've been bursting with curiosity for the past couple of weeks, asking yourselves a hundred questions. Well, here are all the answers. I hope you like them... Let me introduce you to the island of Navarone.'

Mallory's watch showed exactly eleven o'clock when he finally sat back, folded away the map and chart. He looked quizzically at the four thoughtful faces round the table.

'Well, gentlemen, there you have it. A lovely set-up, isn't it?' He smiled wryly. 'If this was a film, my next line should be, "Any questions, men?" But we'll dispense with that because I just wouldn't have any of the answers. You all know as much as I do.'

'A quarter of a mile of sheer cliff, four hundred feet high, and he calls it the only break in the defences.' Miller, his head bent moodily over his tobacco tin, rolled a long, thin cigarette with one expert hand. 'This is just crazy, boss. Me, I can't even climb a bloody ladder without falling off.' He puffed strong, acrid clouds of smoke into the air. 'Suicidal. That's the word I was lookin' for. Suicidal. One buck gets a thousand we never get within five miles of them gawddamned guns!'

'One in a thousand, eh?' Mallory looked at him for a long time without speaking. 'Tell me, Miller, what odds are you offering on the boys on Kheros?'

'Yeah.' Miller nodded heavily. 'Yeah, the boys on Kheros. I'd forgotten about them. I just keep thinkin' about me and that damned cliff.' He looked hopefully across the table at the vast bulk of Andrea. 'Or maybe Andrea there

34

would carry me up. He's big enough, anyway.'

Andrea made no reply. His eyes were half-closed, his thoughts could have been a thousand miles away.

'We'll tie you hand and foot and haul you up on the end of a rope,' Stevens said unkindly. 'We'll try to pick a fairly sound rope,' he added carelessly. The words, the tone, were jocular enough, but the worry on his face belied them. Mallory apart, only Stevens appreciated the almost insuperable technical difficulties of climbing a sheer, unknown cliff in the darkness. He looked at Mallory questioningly. 'Going up alone, sir, or – '

'Excuse me, please.' Andrea suddenly sat forward, his deep rumble of a voice rapid in the clear, idiomatic English he had learnt during his long association with Mallory. He was scribbling quickly on a piece of paper. 'I have a plan for climbing this cliff. Here is a diagram. Does the Captain think this is possible?'

He passed the paper across to Mallory. Mallory looked at it, checked, recovered, all in one instant. There was no diagram on it. There were only two large, printed words: 'Keep talking.'

'I see,' Mallory said thoughtfully. 'Very good indeed, Andrea. This has distinct possibilities.' He reversed the paper, held it up before him so that they could all see the words. Andrea had already risen to his feet, was padding cat-footed towards the door. 'Ingenious, isn't it, Corporal Miller,' he went on conversationally. 'Might solve quite a lot of our difficulties.'

'Yeah.' The expression on Miller's face hadn't altered a fraction, the eyes were still half-closed against the smoke drifting up from the cigarette dangling between his lips. 'Reckon that might solve the problem, Andrea – and get me up in one piece, too.' He laughed easily, concentrated on screwing a curiously-shaped cylinder on the barrel of an automatic that had magically appeared in his left hand. 'But I don't quite get that funny line and the dot at – '

It was all over in two seconds — literally. With a deceptive ease and nonchalance Andrea opened the door with one hand, reached out with the other, plucked a wildly-struggling figure through the gap, set him on the ground again and closed the door, all in one concerted movement. It had been as soundless as it had been swift. For a second the eavesdropper, a hatchet-faced, swarthy Levantine in badly-fitting white shirt and blue trousers, stood there in shocked immobility, blinking rapidly in the unaccustomed light. Then his hand dived in under his shirt.

'Look out!' Miller's voice was sharp, the automatic lining up as Mallory's hand closed over his.

'Watch!' Mallory said softly.

The men at the table caught only a flicker of blued steel as the knife arm jerked convulsively back and plunged down with vicious speed. And then, incredibly, hand and knife were stopped dead in mid-air, the gleaming point only two inches from Andrea's chest. There was a sudden scream of agony, the ominous cracking of wrist bones as the giant Greek tightened his grip, and then Andrea had the blade between finger and thumb, had removed the knife with the tender, reproving care of a parent saving a well-loved but irresponsible child from himself. Then the knife was reversed, the point was at the Levantine's throat and Andrea was smiling down pleasantly into the dark and terror-stricken eyes.

Miller let out a long breath, half-sigh, half-whistle.

'Well, now,' he murmured, 'I guess mebbe Andrea has done that sort of thing before?'

'I guess maybe he has,' Mallory mimicked. 'Let's have a closer look at exhibit A, Andrea.'

Andrea brought his prisoner close up to the table, well within the circle of light. He stood there sullenly before them, a thin, ferret-faced man, black eyes dulled in pain and fear, left hand cradling his crushed wrist.

'How long do you reckon this fellow's been outside, Andrea?' Mallory asked.

Andrea ran a massive hand through his thick, dark, curling hair, heavily streaked with grey above the temples.

'I cannot be sure, Captain. I imagined I heard a noise – a kind of shuffle – about ten minutes ago, but I thought my ears were playing tricks. Then I heard the same sound a minute ago. So I am afraid – '

'Ten minutes, eh?' Mallory nodded thoughtfully, then looked at the prisoner. 'What's your name?' he asked sharply. 'What are you doing here?'

There was no reply. There were only the sullen eyes, the sullen silence – a silence that gave way to a sudden yelp of pain as Andrea cuffed the side of his head.

'The Captain is asking you a question,' Andrea said reproachfully. He cuffed him again, harder this time. 'Answer the Captain.'

The stranger broke into rapid, excitable speech, gesticulating wildly with both hands. The words were quite unintelligible. Andrea sighed, shut off the torrent by the simple expedient of almost encircling the scrawny throat with his left hand.

Mallory looked questioningly at Andrea. The giant shook his head.

'Kurdistan or Armenian, Captain, I think. But I don't understand it.'

'I certainly don't,' Mallory admitted. 'Do you speak English?' he asked suddenly.

Black, hate-filled eyes glared back at him in silence. Andrea cuffed him again.

'Do you speak English?' Mallory repeated relentlessly.

'Eenglish? Eenglish?' Shoulders and upturned palms lifted in the age-old gesture of incomprehension. 'Ka Eenglish!'

'He says he don't speak English,' Miller drawled.

'Maybe he doesn't and maybe he does,' Mallory said evenly. 'All we know is that he *has* been listening and that we can't take any chances. There are far too many

37

lives at stake.' His voice suddenly hardened, the eyes were grim and pitiless. 'Andrea!'

'Captain?'

'You have the knife. Make it clean and quick. Between the shoulder blades!'

Stevens cried out in horror, sent his chair crashing back as he leapt to his feet.

'Good God, sir, you can't – '

He broke off and stared in amazement at the sight of the prisoner catapulting himself bodily across the room to crash into a distant corner, one arm up-curved in rigid defence, stark, unreasoning panic lined in every feature of his face. Slowly Stevens looked away, saw the triumphant grin on Andrea's face, the dawning comprehension in Brown's and Miller's. Suddenly he felt a complete fool. Characteristically, Miller was the first to speak.

'Waal, waal, whaddya know! Mebbe he *does* speaka da Eenglish after all.'

'Maybe he does,' Mallory admitted. 'A man doesn't spend ten minutes with his ear glued to a keyhole if he doesn't understand a word that's being said.... Give Matthews a call, will you, Brown?'

The sentry appeared in the doorway a few seconds later.

'Get Captain Briggs here, will you, Matthews?' he asked. 'At once please.'

The soldier hesitated.

'Captain Briggs has gone to bed, sir. He left strict orders that he wasn't to be disturbed.'

'My heart bleeds for Captain Briggs and his broken slumbers,' Mallory said acidly. 'He's had more sleep in a day than I've had in the past week.' He glanced at his watch and the heavy brows came down in a straight line over the tired, brown eyes. 'We've no time to waste. Get him here at once. Understand? At once!'

Matthews saluted and hurried away. Miller cleared his throat and clucked his tongue sadly.

'These hotels are all the same. The goin's-on – you'd

never believe your eyes. Remember once I was at a convention in Cincinnati – '

Mallory shook his head wearily.

'You have a fixation about hotels, Corporal. This is a military establishment and these are army officers' billets.'

Miller made to speak but changed his mind. The American was a shrewd judge of people. There were those who could be ribbed and those who could not be ribbed. An almost hopeless mission, Miller was quietly aware, and as vital as it was, in his opinion, suicidal; but he was beginning to understand why they'd picked this tough, sunburnt New Zealander to lead it.

They sat in silence for the next five minutes, then looked up as the door opened. Captain Briggs was hatless and wore a white silk muffler round his throat in place of the usual collar and tie. The white contrasted oddly with the puffed red of the heavy neck and face above. These had been red enough when Mallory had first seen them in the colonel's office – high blood pressure and even higher living, Mallory had supposed. the extra deep shades of red and purple now present probably sprang from a misplaced sense of righteous indignation. A glance at the choleric eyes, gleaming light-blue prawns afloat in a sea of vermilion, was quite enough to confirm the obvious.

'I think this is a bit much, Captain Mallory!' The voice was high pitched in anger, more nasal than ever. 'I'm not the duty errand-boy, you know. I've had a damned hard day and—'

'Save it for your biography,' Mallory said curtly, 'and take a gander at this character in the corner.'

Briggs's face turned an even deeper hue. He stepped into the room, fists balled in anger, then stopped in his tracks as his eye lit on the crumpled, dishevelled figure still crouched in the corner of the room.

'Good God!' he ejaculated. 'Nicolai!'

'You know him.' It was a statement, not a question.

'Of course I know him!' Briggs snorted. 'Everybody knows him. Nicolai. Our laundry-boy.'

'Your laundry-boy! Do his duties entail snooping around the corridors at night, listening at keyholes?'

'What do you mean?'

'What I say.' Mallory was very patient. 'We caught him listening outside the door.'

'Nicolai? I don't believe it!'

'Watch it, mister,' Miller growled. 'Careful who you call a liar. We all saw him.'

Briggs stared in fascination at the black muzzle of the automatic waving negligently in his direction, gulped, looked hastily away.

'Well, what if you did?' He forced a smile. 'Nicolai can't speak a word of English.'

'Maybe not,' Mallory agreed dryly. 'But he understands it well enough.' He raised his hand. 'I've no desire to argue all night and I certainly haven't the time. Will you please have this man placed under arrest, kept in solitary confinement and incommunicado for the next week at least. It's vital. Whether he's a spy or just too damned nosy, he knows far too much. After that, do what you like. My advice is to kick him out of Castelrosso.'

'*Your advice*, indeed!' Briggs's colour returned, and with it his courage. 'Who the hell are you to give me advice or to give me orders, Captain Mallory?' There was a heavy emphasis on the word 'captain'.

'Then I'm asking it as a favour,' Mallory pleaded wearily. 'I can't explain, but it's terribly important. There are hundreds of lives – '

'Hundreds of lives!' Briggs sneered. 'Melodramatic stuff and nonsense!' He smiled unpleasantly. 'I suggest you keep that for *your* cloak-and-dagger biography, Captain Mallory.'

Mallory rose, walked round the table, stopped a foot away from Briggs. The brown eyes were still and very cold.

'I could go and see your colonel, I suppose. But I'm tired of arguing. You'll do exactly as I say or I'll go straight to Naval H.Q. and get on the radio-telephone to Cairo. And if I do,' Mallory went on, 'I swear to you that you'll be on the next ship home to England – and on the troop-deck, at that.'

His last words seemed to echo in the little room for an interminable time: the stillness was intense. And then, as suddenly as it had arisen, the tension was gone and Briggs's face, a now curiously mottled white and red, was slack and sullen in defeat.

'All right, all right,' he said. 'No need for all these damned stupid threats – not if it means all that much to you.' The attempt to bluster, to patch up the shredded rags of his dignity, was pathetic in its transparency. 'Matthews – call out the guard.'

The torpedo-boat, great aero engines throttled back half speed, pitched and lifted, pitched and lifted with monotonous regularity as it thrust its way into the long, gentle swell from the W.N.W. For the hundredth time that night Mallory looked at his watch.

'Running behind time, sir?' Stevens suggested.

Mallory nodded.

'We should have stepped straight into this thing from the Sunderland – there was a hold-up.'

Brown grunted. 'Engine trouble, for a fiver.' The Clydeside accent was very heavy.

'Yes, that's right.' Mallory looked up, surprised. 'How did you know?'

'Always the same with these blasted M.T.B. engines,' Brown growled. 'Temperamental as a film star.'

There was silence for a time in the tiny blacked-out cabin, a silence broken only by the occasional clink of a glass. The Navy was living up to its traditional hospitality.

'If we're late,' Miller observed at last, 'why doesn't the

skipper open her up? They tell me these crates can do forty to fifty knots.'

'You look green enough already,' Stevens said tactlessly. 'Obviously, you've never been in an M.T.B. full out in a heavy sea.'

Miller fell silent a moment. Clearly, he was trying to take his mind off his internal troubles. 'Captain?'

'Yes, what is it?' Mallory answered sleepily. He was stretched full length on a narrow settee, an almost empty glass in his fingers.

'None of my business, I know, boss, but – would you have carried out that threat you made to Captain Briggs?'

Mallory laughed.

'It *is* none of your business, but – well, no, Corporal, I wouldn't. I wouldn't because I couldn't. I haven't all that much authority invested in me – and I didn't even know whether there was a radio-telephone in Castelrosso.'

'Yeah. Yeah, do you know, I kinda suspected that.' Corporal Miller rubbed a stubbled chin. 'If he'd called your bluff, what would you have done, boss?'

'I'd have shot Nicolai,' Mallory said quietly. 'If the colonel had failed me. I'd have had no choice left.'

'I knew that too. I really believe you would. For the first time I'm beginning to believe we've got a chance... But I kinda wish you *had* shot him – *and* little Lord Fauntleroy. I didn't like the expression on old Briggs's face when you went out that door. Mean wasn't the word. He coulda killed you then. You trampled right over his pride, boss – and to a phony like that nothin' else in the world matters.'

Mallory made no reply. He was already sound asleep, his empty glass fallen from his hand. Not even the banshee clamour of the great engines opening full out as they entered the sheltered calm of the Rhodes channel could plumb his bottomless abyss of sleep.

CHAPTER 3

Monday

0700–1700

'My dear fellow, you make me feel dreadfully embarrassed.' Moodily the officer switched his ivory-handled fly-
swat against an immaculately trousered leg, pointed a
contemptuous but gleaming toe-cap at the ancient caique,
broad-beamed and two-masted, moored stern on to the
even older and more dilapidated wooden pier on which
they were standing. 'I am positively ashamed. The clients
of Rutledge and Company, I assure you, are accustomed
only to the best.'

Mallory smothered a smile. Major Rutledge of the Buffs,
Eton and Sandhurst as to intonation, millimetrically
tooth-brushed as to moustache, Savile Row as to the quite
dazzling sartorial perfection of his khaki drill, was so
magnificently out of place in the wild beauty of the rocky,
tree-lined bluffs of that winding creek that his presence
there seemed inevitable. Such was the major's casual
assurance, so dominating his majestic unconcern, that it
was the creek, if anything, that seemed slightly out of
place.

'It *does* look as if it has seen better days,' Mallory
admitted. 'Nevertheless, sir, it's exactly what we want.'

'Can't understand it, I really can't understand it.' With
an irritable but well-timed swipe the major brought down
a harmless passing fly. 'I've been providing chaps with
everything during the past eight or nine months – caiques,
launches, yachts, fishing boats, everything – but no one
has ever yet specified the oldest, most dilapidated derelict
I could lay hands on. Quite a job laying hands on it, too, I
tell you.' A pained expression crossed his face. 'The chaps
know I don't usually deal in this line of stuff.'

43

'What chaps?' Mallory asked curiously.

'Oh, up the islands, you know.' Rutledge gestured vaguely to the north and west.

'But – but those are enemy held – '

'So's this one. Chap's got to have his H.Q. somewhere,' Rutledge explained patiently. Suddenly his expression brightened. 'I say, old boy, I know just the thing for you. A boat to escape observation and investigation – that was what Cairo insisted I get. How about a German E-boat, absolutely perfect condition, one careful owner. Could get ten thou. for her at home. Thirty-six hours. Pal of mine over in Bodrum – '

'Bodrum?' Mallory questioned. 'Bodrum? But – but that's in Turkey, isn't it?'

'Turkey? Well, yes, actually, I believe it is,' Rutledge admitted. 'Chap has to get his supplies from somewhere, you know,' he added defensively.

'Thanks all the same' – Mallory smiled – 'but this is exactly what we want. We can't wait, anyway.'

'On your own heads be it!' Rutledge threw up his hands in admission of defeat. 'I'll have a couple of my men shove your stuff aboard.'

'I'd rather we did it ourselves, sir. It's – well, it's a very special cargo.'

'Right you are,' the major acknowledged. 'No questions Rutledge, they call me. Leaving soon?'

Mallory looked at his watch.

'Half an hour, sir.'

'Bacon, eggs and coffee in ten minutes?'

'Thanks very much.' Mallory grinned. 'That's one offer we'll be very glad to accept.'

He turned away, walked slowly down to the end of the pier. He breathed deeply, savouring the heady, herb-scented air of an Aegean dawn. The salt tang of the sea, the drowsily sweet perfume of honeysuckle, the more delicate, sharper fragrance of mint all subtly merged into an intoxicating whole, indefinable, unforgettable. On either

44

side, the steep slopes, still brilliantly green with pine and walnut and holly, stretched far up to the moorland pastures above, and from these, faintly borne on the perfumed breeze, came the distant melodic tinkling of goats' bells, a haunting, a nostalgic music, true symbol of the leisured peace the Aegean no longer knew.

Unconsciously almost, Mallory shook his head and walked more quickly to the end of the pier. The others were still sitting where the torpedo boat had landed them just before dawn. Miller, inevitably, was stretched his full length, hat tilted against the golden, level rays of the rising sun.

'Sorry to disturb you and all that, but we're leaving in half an hour; breakfast in ten minutes. Let's get the stuff aboard.' He turned to Brown. 'Maybe you'd like to have a look at the engine?' he suggested.

Brown heaved himself to his feet, looked down unenthusiastically at the weather-beaten, paint-peeled caique.

'Right you are, sir. But if the engine is on a par with this bloody wreck...' He shook his head in prophetic gloom and swung nimbly over the side of the pier.

Mallory and Andrea followed him, reaching up for the equipment as the other two passed it down. First they stowed away a sackful of old clothes, then the food, pressure stove and fuel, the heavy boots, spikes, mallets, rock axes and coils of wire-centred rope to be used for climbing, then, more carefully, the combined radio receiver and transmitter and the firing generator fitted with the old-fashioned plunge handle. Next came the guns – two Schmeissers, two Brens, a Mauser and a Colt – then a case containing a weird but carefully selected hodge-podge of torches, mirrors, two sets of identity papers and, incredibly, bottles of Hock, Moselle, ouzo and retsina.

Finally, and with exaggerated care, they stowed away for'ard in the forepeak two wooden boxes, one green in colour, medium sized and bound in brass, the other small

45

and black. The green box held high explosive – T.N.T., amatol and a few standard sticks of dynamite, together with grenades, gun-cotton primers and canvas hosing; in one corner of the box was a bag of emery dust, another of ground glass, and a sealed jar of potassium, these last three items having been included against the possibility of Dusty Miller's finding an opportunity to exercise his unique talents as a saboteur. The black box held only detonators, percussion and electrical, detonators with fulminates so unstable that their exposed powder could be triggered off by the impact of a falling feather.

The last box had been stowed away when Casey Brown's head appeared above the engine hatch. Slowly he examined the mainmast reaching up above his head, as slowly turned for'ard to look at the foremast. His face carefully expressionless, he looked at Mallory.

'Have we got sails for these things, sir?'

'I suppose so. Why?'

'Because God only knows we're going to need them!' Brown said bitterly. 'Have a look at the engine-room, you said. This isn't an engine-room. It's a bloody scrap-yard. And the biggest, most rusted bit of scrap down there is attached to the propeller shaft. And what do you think it is? An old Kelvin two-cylinder job built more or less on my own doorstep – about thirty years ago.' Brown shook his head in despair, his face as stricken as only a Clydeside engineer's can be at the abuse of a beloved machine. 'And it's been falling to bits for years, sir. Place is littered with discarded bits and spares. I've seen junk heaps off the Gallowgate that were palaces compared to this.'

'Major Rutledge said it was running only yesterday,' Mallory said mildly. 'Anyway, come on ashore. Breakfast. Remind me we're to pick up a few heavy stones on the way back, will you?'

'Stones!' Miller looked at him in horror. 'Aboard that thing?'

Mallory nodded, smiling.

'But that gawddamned ship is sinkin' already!' Miller protested. 'What do you want stones for?'

'Wait and see.'

Three hours later Miller saw. The caique was chugging steadily north over a glassy, windless sea, less than a mile off the coast of Turkey, when he mournfully finished lashing his blue battledress into a tight ball and heaved it regretfully over the side. Weighted by the heavy stone he had carried aboard, it was gone from sight in a second.

Morosely he surveyed himself in the mirror propped up against the for'ard end of the wheelhouse. Apart from a deep violet sash wrapped round his lean middle and a fancifully embroidered waistcoat with its former glory mercifully faded, he was dressed entirely in black. Black lacing jackboots, black baggy trousers, black shirt and black jacket: even his sandy hair had been dyed to the same colour.

He shuddered and turned away.

'Thank Gawd the boys back home can't see me now!' he said feelingly. He looked critically at the others, dressed, with some minor variations, like himself. 'Waal, mebbe I ain't quite so bad after all.... Just what is all this quick-change business for, boss?'

'They tell me you've been behind the German lines twice, once as a peasant, once as a mechanic.' Mallory heaved his own ballasted uniform over the side. 'Well, now you see what the well-dressed Navaronian wears.'

'The double change, I meant. Once in the plane, and now.'

'Oh, I see. Army khaki and naval whites in Alex, blue battledress in Castelrosso and now Greek clothes? Could have been – almost certainly were – snoopers in Alex or Castelrosso or Major Rutledge's island. And we've changed from launch to plane to M.T.B. to caique. Covering our tracks, Corporal. We just can't take any chances.'

Miller nodded, looked down at the clothes sack at his

47

feet, wrinkled his brows in puzzlement, stooped and dragged out the white clothing that had caught his eye. He held up the long, voluminous clothes for inspection.

'To be used when passing through the local cemeteries, I suppose.' He was heavily ironic. 'Disguised as ghosts.'

'Camouflage,' Mallory explained succinctly. 'Snow-smocks.'

'What!'

'Snow. That white stuff. There are some pretty high mountains in Navarone, and we may have to take them. So – snow-smocks.'

Miller looked stunned. Wordlessly he stretched his length on the deck, pillowed his head and closed his eyes. Mallory grinned at Andrea.

'Picture of a man getting his full quota of sunshine before battling with the Arctic wastes... Not a bad idea. Maybe you should get some sleep, too. I'll keep watch for a couple of hours.'

For five hours the caique continued on its course parallel to the Turkish coast, slightly west of north and rarely more than two miles off-shore. Relaxed and warm in the still kindly November sun, Mallory sat wedged between the bulwarks of the blunt bows, his eyes ceaselessly quartering sky and horizon. Amidships, Andrea and Miller lay asleep. Casey Brown still defied all attempts to remove him from the engine-room. Occasionally – very occasionally – he came up for a breath of fresh air, but the intervals between his appearances steadily lengthened as he concentrated more and more on the aged Kelvin engine, regulating the erratic drip-fed lubrication, constantly adjusting the air intake: an engineer to his fingertips, he was unhappy about that engine: he was drowsy, too, and headachy – the narrow hatchway gave hardly any ventilation at all.

Alone in the wheelhouse – an unusual feature in so tiny a caique – Lieutenant Andy Stevens watched the Turkish coast slide slowly by. Like Mallory's, his eyes moved ceaselessly, but not with the same controlled wandering. They shifted from the coast to the chart: from the chart to the islands up ahead off the port bow, islands whose position and relation to each other changed continually and deceptively, islands gradually lifting from the sea and hardening in definition through the haze of blue refraction: from the islands to the old alcohol compass swinging almost imperceptibly on corroded gimbals, and from the compass back to the coast again. Occasionally, he peered up into the sky, or swung a quick glance through a 180-degree sweep of the horizon. But one thing his eyes avoided all the time. The chipped, fly-blown mirror had been hung up in the wheelhouse again, but it was as if his eyes and the mirror were of opposite magnetic poles: he could not bring himself to look at it.

His forearms ached. He had been spelled at the wheel twice, but still they ached, abominably: his lean, tanned hands were ivory-knuckled on the cracked wheel. Repeatedly, consciously, he tried to relax, to ease the tension that was bunching up the muscles of his arms; but always, as if possessed of independent volition, his hands tightened their grip again. There was a funny taste in his mouth, too, a sour and salty taste in a dry, parched mouth, and no matter how often he swallowed, or drank from the sun-warmed pitcher at his side, the taste and the dryness remained. He could no more exorcise them than he could that twisting, cramping ball that was knotting up his insides, just above the solar plexus, or the queer, uncontrollable tremor that gripped his right leg from time to time.

Lieutenant Andy Stevens was afraid. He had never been in action before, but it wasn't that. This wasn't the first time he had been afraid. He had been afraid all his life, ever since he could remember: and he could remember a long way back, even to his early prep-school days when his famous father, Sir Cedric Stevens, the most celebrated

49

explorer and mountaineer of his time, had thrown him bodily into the swimming pool at home, telling him that this was the only way he could learn to swim. He could remember still how he had fought and spluttered his way to the side of the pool, panic-stricken and desperate, his nose and mouth blocked with water, the pit of his stomach knotted and constricted in that nameless, terrifying ache he was to come to know so well: how his father and two elder brothers, big and jovial and nerveless like Sir Cedric himself, had wiped the tears of mirth from their eyes and pushed him in again....

His father and brothers.... It had been like that all through his schooldays. Together, the three of them had made his life thoroughly miserable. Tough, hearty, open-air types who worshipped at the shrine of athleticism and physical fitness, they could not understand how anyone could fail to revel in diving from a five-metre springboard or setting a hunter at a five-barred gate or climbing the crags of the Peak district or sailing a boat in a storm. All these things they had made him do and often he had failed in the doing, and neither his father nor his brothers could ever have understood how he had come to dread those violent sports in which they excelled, for they were not cruel men, nor even unkind, but simply stupid. And so to the simple physical fear he sometimes and naturally felt was added the fear of failure, the fear that he was bound to fail in whatever he had to do next, the fear of the inevitable mockery and ridicule: and because he had been a sensitive boy and feared the ridicule above all else, he had come to fear these things that provoked the ridicule. Finally, he had come to fear fear itself, and it was in a desperate attempt to overcome this double fear that he had devoted himself – this in his late teens – to crag and mountain climbing: in this he had ultimately become so proficient, developed such a reputation, that father and brothers had come to treat him with respect and as an equal, and the ridicule had ceased. But the fear had not ceased; rather it had grown by what it fed on, and often, on a particularly difficult climb, he had all but fallen to his death, powerless in the grip of sheer, unreasoning terror. But this terror he had always sought, successfully so far, to conceal. As now. He was trying to overcome, to conceal that fear now. He was afraid of failing – in what he wasn't quite sure – of not measuring up to expectation: he was afraid of being afraid: and he was desperately afraid, above all things, of being seen, of being known to be afraid....

The startling, incredible blue of the Aegean; the soft, hazy silhouette of the Anatolian mountains against the washed-out cerulean of the sky; the heart-catching, magical blending of the blues and violets and purples and indigoes of the sun-soaked islands drifting lazily by, almost on the beam now; the iridescent rippling of the water tanned by the gentle, scent-laden breeze newly sprung from the south-east; the peaceful scene on deck, the reassuring, interminable thump-thump thump-thump of the old Kelvin engine.... All was peace and quiet and contentment and warmth and languor, and it seemed impossible that anyone could be afraid. The world and the war were very far away that afternoon.

Or perhaps, after all, the war wasn't so far away. There were occasional pin-pricks – and constant reminders. Twice a German Arado seaplane had circled curiously overhead, and a Savoia and Fiat, flying in company, had altered course, dipped to have a look at them and flown off, apparently satisfied: Italian planes, these, and probably based on Rhodes, they were almost certainly piloted by Germans who had rounded up their erstwhile Rhodian allies and put them in prison camps after the surrender of the Italian Government. In the morning they had passed within half a mile of a big German caique – it flew a German flag and bristled with mounted machine-guns and a two-pounder far up in the bows; and in the early afternoon a high-speed German launch had roared by so closely that their caique had rolled wickedly in the wash of its passing: Mallory and Andrea had shaken their fists and cursed loudly and fluently at the grinning sailors on deck. But there had been no attempts to molest or detain them: neither British nor German hesitated at any time to violate the neutrality of Turkish territorial waters, but by the strange quixotry of a tacit gentlemen's agreement hostilities between passing vessels and planes were almost unknown. Like the envoys of warring countries in a neutral capital, their behaviour ranged from the impeccably and frigidly polite to a very pointed unawareness of one another's existence.

These, then, were the pin-pricks – the visitation and by-goings, harmless though they were, of the ships and planes of the enemy. The other reminders that this was no peace but an illusion, an ephemeral and a frangible thing, were more permanent. Slowly the minute hands of their watches circled, and every tick took them nearer to that great wall of cliff, barely eight hours away, that had to be climbed somehow: and almost dead ahead now, and less than fifty miles distant, they could see the grim, jagged peaks of Navarone topping the shimmering horizon and reaching up darkly against the sapphired sky, desolate and remote and strangely threatening.

At half-past two in the afternoon the engine stopped. There had been no warning coughs or splutters or missed strokes. One moment the regular, reassuring thump-thump: the next, sudden, completely unexpected silence, oppressive and foreboding in its absoluteness.

Mallory was the first to reach the engine hatch.

'What's up, Brown?' His voice was sharp with anxiety. 'Engine broken down?'

'Not quite, sir.' Brown was still bent over the engine, his voice muffled. 'I shut it off just now.' He straightened his back, hoisted himself wearily through the hatchway, sat on deck with his feet dangling, sucking in great draughts of fresh air. Beneath the heavy tan his face was very pale.

Mallory looked at him closely.

'You look as if you had the fright of your life.'

'Not that.' Brown shook his head. 'For the past two-three hours I've been slowly poisoned down that ruddy hole. Only now I realise it.' He passed a hand across his brow and groaned. 'Top of my blinkin' head just about lifting off, sir. Carbon monoxide ain't a very healthy thing.'

'Exhaust leak?'

'Aye. But it's more than a leak now.' He pointed down at the engine. 'See that stand-pipe supporting that big iron ball above the engine – the water-cooler? That pipe's as thin as paper, must have been leaking above the bottom flange for hours. Blew out a bloody great hole a minute ago. Sparks, smoke and flames six inches long. Had to shut the damned thing off at once, sir.'

Mallory nodded in slow understanding.

'And now what? Can you repair it, Brown?'

'Not a chance, sir.' The shake of the head was very definite. 'Would have to be brazed or welded. But there's a spare down there among the scrap. Rusted to hell and about as shaky as the one that's on.... I'll have a go, sir.'

'I'll give him a hand,' Miller volunteered.

'Thanks, Corporal. How long, Brown, do you think?'

'Lord only knows, sir. Two hours, maybe four. Most of the nuts and bolts are locked solid with rust: have to shear or saw 'em – and then hunt for others.'

Mallory said nothing. He turned away heavily, brought up beside Stevens who had abandoned the wheelhouse and was now bent over the sail locker. He looked up questioningly as Mallory approached.

Mallory nodded. 'Just get them out and up. Maybe four hours, Brown says. Andrea and I will do our landlubbery best to help.'

Two hours later, with the engine still out of commission, they were well outside territorial waters, closing on a big island some eight miles away to the W.N.W. The wind, warm and oppressive now, had backed to a darkening and thundery east, and with only a lug and a jib – all the sails they had found – bent to the foremast, they could make no way at all into it. Mallory had decided to make for the island – the chances of being observed there were far less than in the open sea. Anxiously he looked at his watch then stared back moodily at the receding safety of the Turkish shore. Then he stiffened, peered closely at the dark line of sea, land and sky that lay to the east.

'Andrea! Do you see – '

'I see it, Captain.' Andrea was at his shoulder. 'Caique. Three miles. Coming straight towards us,' he added softly.

'Coming straight towards us,' Mallory acquiesced. 'Tell Miller and Brown. Have them come here.'

Mallory wasted no time when they were all assembled. 'We're going to be stopped and investigated,' he said quickly. 'Unless I'm much mistaken, it's that big caique that passed us this morning. Heaven only knows how, but they've been tipped off and they're going to be as suspicious as hell. This'll be no kid-glove, hands-in-the-pockets inspection. They'll be armed to the teeth and hunting trouble. There's going to be no half-measures. Let's be quite clear about that. Either they go under or we do: we can't possibly survive an inspection – not with all the gear *we've* got aboard. And,' he added softly, 'we're not going to dump that gear.' Rapidly he explained his plans. Stevens, leaning out from the wheelhouse window, felt the old sick ache in his stomach, felt the blood leaving his face. He was glad of the protection of the wheelhouse that hid the lower part of his body: that old familiar tremor in his leg was back again. Even his voice was unsteady.

'But, sir – sir – '

54

'Yes, yes, what is it, Stevens?' Even in his hurry Mallory paused at the sight of the pale, set face, the bloodless nails clenched over the sill of the window.

'You — you can't do *that*, sir!' The voice burred harshly under the sharp edge of strain. For a moment his mouth worked soundlessly, then he rushed on. 'It's massacre, sir, it's — it's just murder!'

'Shut up, kid!' Miller growled.

'That'll do, Corporal!' Mallory said sharply. He looked at the American for a long moment then turned to Stevens, his eyes cold. 'Lieutenant, the whole concept of directing a successful war is aimed at placing your enemy at a disadvantage, at *not* giving him an even chance. We kill them or they kill us. They go under or we do — and a thousand men on Kheros. It's just as simple as that, Lieutenant. It's not even a question of conscience.'

For several seconds Stevens stared at Mallory in complete silence. He was vaguely aware that everyone was looking at him. In that instant he hated Mallory, could have killed him. He hated him because — suddenly he was aware that he hated him only for the remorseless logic of what he said. He stared down at his clenched hands. Mallory, the idol of every young mountaineer and cragsman in pre-war England, whose fantastic climbing exploits had made world headlines, in '38 and '39: Mallory, who had twice been baulked by the most atrocious ill-fortune from surprising Rommel in his desert headquarters: Mallory, who had three times refused promotion in order to stay with his beloved Cretans who worshipped him the other side of idolatry. Confusedly these thoughts tumbled through his mind and he looked up slowly, looked at the lean, sunburnt face, the sensitive, chiselled mouth, the heavy, dark eyebrows bar-straight over the lined brown eyes that could be so cold or so compassionate, and suddenly he felt ashamed, knew that Captain Mallory lay beyond both his understanding and his judgment.

55

'I am very sorry, sir.' He smiled faintly. 'As Corporal Miller would say, I was talking out of turn.' He looked aft at the caique arrowing up from the south-east. Again he felt the sick fear, but his voice was steady enough as he spoke. 'I won't let you down, sir.'

'Good enough. I never thought you would.' Mallory smiled in turn, looked at Miller and Brown. 'Get the stuff ready and lay it out, will you? Casual, easy and keep it hidden. They'll have the glasses on you.'

He turned away, walked for'ard. Andrea followed him.

'You were very hard on the young man.' It was neither criticism nor reproach – merely statement of fact.

'I know.' Mallory shrugged. 'I didn't like it either.... I had to do it.'

'I think you had,' Andrea said slowly. 'Yes, I think you had. But it was hard.... Do you think they'll use the big guns in the bows to stop us?'

'Might – they haven't turned back after us unless they're pretty sure we're up to something fishy. But the warning shot across the bows – they don't go in for that Captain Teach stuff normally.'

Andrea wrinkled his brows.

'Captain Teach?'

'Never mind.' Mallory smiled. 'Time we were taking up position now. Remember, wait for me. You won't have any trouble in hearing my signal,' he finished dryly.

The creaming bow-wave died away to a gentle ripple, the throb of the heavy diesel muted to a distant murmur as the German boat slid alongside, barely six feet away. From where he sat on a fish-box on the port of the fo'c'sle, industriously sewing a button on to the old coat lying on the deck between his legs, Mallory could see six men, all dressed in the uniform of the regular Germany Navy – one crouched behind a belted Spandau mounted on its tripod just aft of the two-pounder, three others bunched amidships each armed with an automatic machine carbine – Schmeissers, he thought – the captain, a hard,

56

cold-faced young lieutenant with the Iron Cross on his tunic, looking out the open door of the wheelhouse and, finally, a curious head peering over the edge of the engine-room hatch. From where he sat, Mallory couldn't see the poop-deck – the intermittent ballooning of the lug-sail in the uncertain wind blocked his vision; but from the restricted fore-and-aft lateral sweep of the Spandau, hungrily traversing only the for'ard half of their one caique, he was reasonably sure that there was another machine-gunner similarly engaged on the German's poop.

The hard-faced young lieutenant – a real product of the Hitler Jugend that one, Mallory thought – leaned out of the wheelhouse, cupped his hand to his mouth.

'Lower your sails!' he shouted.

Mallory stiffened, froze to immobility. The needle had jammed hard into the palm of his hand, but he didn't even notice it. The lieutenant had spoken in English! Stevens was so young, so inexperienced. He'd fall for it, Mallory thought with a sudden sick certainty, he's bound to fall for it.

But Stevens didn't fall for it. He opened the door, leaned out, cupped his hand to his ear and gazed vacantly up to the sky, his mouth wide open. It was so perfect an imitation of dull-witted failure to catch or comprehend a shouted message that it was almost a caricature. Mallory could have hugged him. Not in his actions alone, but in his dark, shabby clothes and hair as blackly counterfeit as Miller's, Stevens was the slow, suspicious island fisherman to the life.

'Eh?' he bawled.

'Lower your sails! We are coming aboard!' English again, Mallory noted; a persistent fellow this.

Stevens stared at him blankly, looked round helplessly at Andrea and Mallory: their faces registered a lack of comprehension as convincing as his own. He shrugged his shoulders in despair.

'I am sorry, I do not understand German,' he shouted.

57

'Can you not speak my language?' Stevens's Greek was perfect, fluent and idiomatic. It was also, the Greek of Attica, not of the islands; but Mallory felt sure that the lieutenant wouldn't know the difference.

He didn't. He shook his head in exasperation, called in slow, halting Greek: 'Stop your boat at once. We are coming aboard.'

'Stop my boat!' The indignation was so genuine, the accompanying flood of furious oaths so authentic, that even the lieutenant was momentarily taken aback. 'And why should I stop my boat for you, you – you – '

'You have ten seconds,' the lieutenant interrupted. He was on balance again, cold, precise. 'Then we will shoot.'

Stevens gestured in admission of defeat and turned to Andrea and Mallory.

'Our conquerors have spoken,' he said bitterly. 'Lower the sails.'

Quickly they loosened the sheets from the cleats at the foot of the mast. Mallory pulled the jib down, gathered the sail in his arms and squatted sullenly on the deck – he knew a dozen hostile eyes were watching him – close by the fish-box. The sail covering his knees and the old coat, his forearms on his thighs, he sat with head bowed and hands dangling between his knees, the picture of heart-struck dejection. The lug-sail, weighted by the boom at the top, came down with a rush. Andrea stepped over it, walked a couple of uncertain paces aft, then stopped, huge hands hanging emptily by his sides.

A sudden deepening of the muted throbbing of the diesel, a spin of the wheel and the big German caique was rubbing alongside. Quickly, but carefully enough to keep out of the line of fire of the mounted Spandaus – there was a second clearly visible now on the poop – the three men armed with the Schmeissers leapt aboarad. Immediately one ran forward, whirled round level with the foremast, his automatic carbine circling gently to cover all of the crew. All except Mallory – and he was leaving Mallory in the safe hands of the Spandau gunner in the bows. Detachedly, Mallory admired the precision, the timing, the clockwork inevitability of an old routine.

He raised his head, looked around him with a slow, peasant indifference. Casey Brown was squatting on the deck abreast the engine-room, working on the big ball-silencer on top of the hatch-cover. Dusty Miller, two paces farther for'ard and with his brows furrowed in concentration, was laboriously cutting a section of metal from a little tin box, presumably to help in the engine repairs. He was holding the wire-cutting pliers in his left hand – and Miller, Mallory knew, was right-handed. Neither Stevens nor Andrea had moved. The man beside the foremast still stood there, eyes unwinking. The other two were walking slowly aft, had just passed Andrea, their carriage relaxed and easy, the bearing of men who know they have everything so completely under control that even the idea of trouble is ridiculous.

Carefully, coldly and precisely, at point-blank range and through the folds of both coat and sail, Mallory shot the Spandau machine-gunner through the heart, swung the still chattering Bren round and saw the guard by the mast crumple and die, half his chest torn away by the tearing slugs of the machine-gun. But the dead man was still on his feet, still had not hit the deck, when four things happened simultaneously. Casey Brown had had his hand on Miller's silenced automatic, lying concealed beneath the ball-silencer, for over a minute. Now he squeezed the trigger four times, for he wanted to mak' siccar; the after machine-gunner leaned forward tiredly over his tripod, lifeless fingers locked on the firing-guard. Miller crimped the three-second chemical fuse with the pliers, lobbed the tin box into the enemy engine-room, Stevens spun the armed stick-grenade into the opposite wheelhouse and Andrea, his great arms reaching out with all the speed and precision of striking cobras, swept the Schmeisser gunners' heads together with sickening force. And then all five men had hurled themselves to the deck and the German caique was erupting in a roar of flame and smoke and flying débris: gradually the echoes faded away over the sea and there was left only the whining stammer of the Spandau, emptying itself uselessly skyward; and then the belt jammed and the Aegean was as silent as ever, more silent than it had ever been.

Slowly, painfully, dazed by the sheer physical shock and the ear-shattering proximity of the twin explosions, Mallory pushed himself off the wooden deck and stood shakily on his feet. His first conscious reaction was that of surprise, incredulity almost: the concussive blast of a grenade and a couple of lashed blocks of T.N.T., even at such close range, was far beyond anything he had expected.

The German boat was sinking, sinking fast. Miller's home-made bomb must have torn the bottom out of the engine-room. She was heavily on fire amidships, and for one dismayed instant Mallory had an apprehensive vision of towering black columns of smoke and enemy reconnaissance planes. But only for an instant: timbers and planking, tinder-dry and resinous, were burning furiously with hardly a trace of smoke, and the flaming, crumpling deck was already canted over sharply to port: she would be gone in seconds. His eyes wandered to the shattered skeleton of the wheelhouse, and he caught his breath suddenly when he saw the lieutenant impaled on the splintered wreck of the wheel, a ghastly, mangled caricature of what had once been a human being, decapitated and wholly horrible: vaguely, some part of Mallory's mind registered the harsh sound of retching, violent and convulsive, coming from the wheelhouse, and he knew Stevens must have seen it too. From deep within the sinking caique came the muffled roar of rupturing fuel tanks: a flame-veined gout of oily black smoke erupted from the engine-room and the caique miraculously struggled back on even keel, her gunwales almost awash, and then the hissing waters had overflowed and overcome the decks and the twisting flames, and the caique was gone, her slender masts sliding vertically down and vanishing in a turbulent welter of creaming foam and oil-filmed bubbles. And now the Aegean was calm and peaceful again, as placid as if the caique had never been, and almost as empty: a few charred planks and an inverted helmet drifted lazily on the surface of the shimmering sea.

With a conscious effort of will, Mallory turned slowly to look to his own ship and his own men. Brown and Miller were on their feet, staring down in fascination at where the caique had been. Stevens was standing at the wheelhouse door. He, too, was unhurt, but his face was ashen: during the brief action he had been a man above himself, but the aftermath, the brief glimpse he'd had of the dead lieutenant had hit him badly. Andrea, bleeding from a gash on the cheek, was looking down at the two Schmeisser gunners lying at his feet. His face was expressionless. For a long moment Mallory looked at him, looked in slow understanding.

'Dead?' he asked quietly.

Andrea inclined his head.

'Yes.' His voice was heavy. 'I hit them too hard.'

Mallory turned away. Of all the men he had ever known, Andrea, he thought, had the most call to hate and to kill his enemies. And kill them he did, with a ruthless efficiency appalling in its single-mindedness and thoroughness of execution. But he rarely killed without regret, without the most bitter self-condemnation, for he did not believe that the lives of his fellow-men were his to take. A destroyer of his fellow-man, he loved his fellow-man above all things. A simple man, a good man, a killer with a kindly heart, he was for ever troubled by his conscience, ill at ease with his inner self. But over and above the wonderings and the reproaches, he was informed by an honesty of thought, by a clear-sighted wisdom which sprang from and transcended his innate simplicity.

61

Andrea killed neither for revenge, nor from hate, nor nationalism, nor for the sake of any of the other 'isms' which self-seekers and fools and knaves employ as beguilement to the battlefield and justification for the slaughter of millions too young and too unknowing to comprehend the dreadful futility of it all. Andrea killed simply that better men might live.

'Anybody else hurt?' Mallory's voice was deliberately brisk, cheerful. 'Nobody? Good! Right, let's get under way as fast as possible. The farther and the faster we leave this place behind, the better for all of us.' He looked at his watch. 'Almost four o'clock – time for our routine check with Cairo. Just leave that scrap-yard of yours for a couple of minutes, Chief. See if you can pick them up.' He looked at the sky to the east, a sky now purply livid and threatening, and shook his head. 'Could be that the weather forecast might be worth hearing.'

It was. Reception was very poor – Brown blamed the violent static on the dark, convoluted thunderheads steadily creeping up astern, now overspreading almost half the sky – but adequate. Adequate enough to hear information they had never expected to hear, information that left them silenced, eyes stilled in troubled speculation. The tiny loud-speaker boomed and faded, boomed and faded, against the scratchy background of static.

'Rhubarb calling Pimpernel! Rhubarb calling Pimpernel!' These were the respective code names for Cairo and Mallory. 'Are you receiving me?'

Brown tapped an acknowledgment. The speaker boomed again.

'Rhubarb calling Pimpernel. Now X minus one. Repeat, X minus one.' Mallory drew in his breath sharply. X – dawn on Saturday – had been the assumed date for the German attack on Kheros. It must have been advanced by one day – and Jensen was not the man to speak without certain knowledge. Friday, dawn – just over three days.

'Send "X minus one understood",' Mallory said quietly.

'Forecast, East Anglia,' the impersonal voice went on: the Northern Sporades, Mallory knew. 'Severe electrical storms probable this evening, with heavy rainfall. Visibility poor. Temperature falling, continuing to fall next twenty-four hours. Winds east to south-east, force six, locally eight, moderating early tomorrow.'

Mallory turned away, ducked under the billowing lug-sail, walked slowly aft. What a set-up, he thought, what a bloody mess. Three days to go, engine u.s. and a first-class storm building up. He thought briefly, hopefully, of Squadron Leader Torrance's low opinion of the backroom boys of the Met. Office, but the hope was never really born. It couldn't be, not unless he was blind. The steep-piled buttresses of the thunderheads towered up darkly terrifying, now almost directly above.

'Looks pretty bad, huh?' The slow nasal drawl came from immediately behind him. There was something oddly reassuring about that measured voice, about the steadiness of the washed-out blue of the eyes enmeshed in a spider's web of fine wrinkles.

'It's not so good,' Mallory admitted.

'What's all this force eight business, boss?'

'A wind scale,' Mallory explained. 'If you're in a boat this size and you're good and tired of life, you can't beat a force eight wind.'

Miller nodded dolefully.

'I knew it. I might have known. And me swearing they'd never get me on a gawddamned boat again.' He brooded a while, sighed, slid his legs over the engine-room hatchway, jerked his thumb in the direction of the nearest island, now less than three miles away. 'That doesn't look so hot, either.'

'Not from here,' Mallory agreed. 'But the chart shows a creek with a right-angle bend. It'll break the sea and the wind.'

'Inhabited?'

'Probably.'

'Germans?'

'Probably.'

Miller shook his head in despair and descended to help Brown. Forty minutes later, in the semi-darkness of the overcast evening and in torrential rain, lance-straight and strangely chill, the anchor of the caique rattled down between the green walls of the forest, a dank and dripping forest, hostile in its silent indifference.

CHAPTER 4

Monday Evening

1700 – 2330

'Brilliant!' said Mallory bitterly. 'Ruddy well brilliant! "Come into my parlour said the spider to the fly."' He swore in chagrin and exasperated disgust, eased aside the edge of the tarpaulin that covered the for'ard hatchway, peered out through the slackening curtain of rain and took a second and longer look at the rocky bluff that elbowed out into the bend of the creek, shutting them off from the sea. There was no difficulty in seeing now, none at all: the drenching cloudburst had yielded to a gentle drizzle, and grey and white cloud streamers, shredding in the lifting wind, had already pursued the blackly towering cumulonimbus over the far horizon. In a clear band of sky far to the west, the sinking, flame-red sun was balanced on the rim of the sea. From the shadowed waters of the creek it was invisible, but its presence unmistakable from the gold-shot gauze of the falling rain, high above their heads.

The same golden rays highlighted the crumbling old watch-tower on the very point of the cliff, a hundred feet above the river. They burnished its fine-grained white Parian marble, mellowed it to a delicate rose: they gleamed on the glittering steel, the evil mouths of the Spandau machine-guns reaching out from the slotted embrasures in the massive walls, illumined the hooked cross of the swastika on the flag that streamed out stiffly from the staff above the parapet. Solid even in its decay, impregnable in its position, commanding in its lofty outlook, the tower completely dominated both waterborne approaches, from the sea and, upriver, down the narrow, winding channel that lay between the moored caique and the foot of the cliff.

Slowly, reluctantly almost, Mallory turned away and gently lowered the tarpaulin. His face was grim as he turned round to Andrea and Stevens, ill-defined shadows in the twilit gloom of the cabin.

'Brilliant!' he repeated. 'Sheer genius. Mastermind Mallory. Probably the only bloody creek within a hundred miles – and in a hundred islands – with a German guard post on it. And of course I had to go and pick it. Let's have another look at that chart, will you, Stevens?'

Stevens passed it across, watched Mallory study it in the pale light filtering in under the tarpaulin, leaned back against the bulkhead and drew heavily on his cigarette. It tasted foul, stale and acrid, but the tobacco was fresh enough, he knew. The old, sick fear was back again, as strongly as ever. He looked at the great bulk of Andrea across from him, felt an illogical resentment towards him for having spotted the emplacement a few minutes ago. They'll have cannon up there, he thought dully, they're bound to have cannon – couldn't control the creek otherwise. He gripped his thigh fiercely, just above the knee, but the tremor lay too deep to be controlled: he blessed the merciful darkness of the tiny cabin. But his voice was casual enough as he spoke.

'You're wasting your time, sir, looking at that chart and blaming yourself. This is the only possible anchorage within hours of sailing time from here. With that wind there was nowhere else we could have gone.'

'Exactly. That's just it.' Mallory folded the chart, handed it back. 'There was nowhere else we could have gone. There was nowhere else anyone could have gone. Must be a very popular port in a storm, this – a fact which must have become apparent to the Germans a long, long time ago. That's why I should have known they were almost bound to have a post here. However, spilt milk, as you say.' He raised his voice. 'Chief?'

'Hallo!' Brown's muffled voice carried faintly from the depths of the engine-room.

'How's it going?'

'Not too bad, sir. Assembling it now.'

Mallory nodded in relief.

'How long?' he called. 'An hour?'

'Aye, easy, sir.'

'An hour.' Again Mallory glanced through the tarpaulin, looked back at Andrea and Stevens. 'Just about right. We'll leave in an hour. Dark enough to give us some protection from our friends up top, but enough light left to navigate our way out of this damned corkscrew of a channel.'

'Do you think they'll try to stop us, sir?' Stevens's voice was just too casual, too matter of fact. He was pretty sure Mallory would notice.

'It's unlikely they'll line the banks and give us three hearty cheers,' Mallory said dryly. 'How many men do you reckon they'll have up there, Andrea?'

'I've seen two moving around,' Andrea said thoughtfully. 'Maybe three or four altogether, Captain. A small post. The Germans don't waste men on these.'

'I think you're about right,' Mallory agreed. 'Most of them'll be in the garrison in the village – about seven miles from here, according to the chart, and due west. It's not likely – '

He broke off sharply, stiffened in rigid attention. Again the call came, louder this time, imperative in its tone. Cursing himself for his negligence in not posting a guard – such carelessness would have cost him his life in Crete – Mallory pulled the tarpaulin aside, clambered slowly on to the deck. He carried no arms, but a half-empty bottle of Moselle dangled from his left hand; as part of a plan prepared before they had left Alexandria, he'd snatched it from a locker at the foot of the tiny companionway.

He lurched convincingly across the deck, grabbed at a stay in time to save himself from falling overboard. Insolently he stared down at the figure on the bank, less than ten yards away – it hadn't mattered about a guard, Mallory realised, for the soldier carried his automatic carbine slung over his shoulder – insolently he tilted the wine to his mouth and swallowed deeply before condescending to talk to him.

He could see the mounting anger in the lean, tanned face of the young German below him. Mallory ignored it. Slowly, an inherent contempt in the gesture, he dragged the frayed sleeve of his black jacket across his lips, looked the soldier even more slowly up and down in a minutely provocative inspection as disdainful as it was prolonged.

'Well?' he asked truculently in the slow speech of the islands. 'What the hell do you want?'

Even in the deepening dusk he could see the knuckles whitening on the stock of the carbine, and for an instant Mallory thought hē had gone too far. He knew he was in no danger – all noise in the engine-room had ceased, and Dusty Miller's hand was never far from his silenced automatic – but he didn't want trouble. Not just yet. Not while there were a couple of manned Spandaus in that watch-tower.

With an almost visible effort the young soldier regained his control. It needed little help from the imagination to see the draining anger, the first tentative stirrings of hesitation and bewilderment. It was the reaction Mallory had hoped for. Greeks – even half-drunk Greeks – didn't talk to their over-lords like that – not unless they had an overpoweringly good reason.

'What vessel is this?' The Greek was slow and halting but passable. 'Where are you bound for?'

Mallory tilted the bottle again, smacked his lips in noisy satisfaction. He held the bottle at arm's length, regarded it with a loving respect.

'One thing about you Germans,' he confided loudly. 'You do know how to make a fine wine. I'll wager *you* can't lay your hands on this stuff, eh? And the swill they're making up above' – the island term for the main-

68

land – 'is so full of resin that it's only good for lighting fires.' He thought for a moment. 'Of course, if you know the right people in the islands, they *might* let you have some ouzo. But some of us can get ouzo *and* the best Hocks *and* the best Moselles.'

The soldier wrinkled his face in disgust. Like almost every fighting man he despised Quislings, even when they were on his side: in Greece they were very few indeed.

'I asked you a question,' he said coldly. 'What vessel, and where bound?'

'The caique *Aigion*,' Mallory replied loftily. 'In ballast, for Samos. Under orders,' he said significantly.

'Whose orders?' the soldier demanded. Shrewdly Mallory judged the confidence as superficial only. The guard was impressed in spite of himself.

'Herr Commandant in Vathy. General Graebel,' Mallory said softly. 'You will have heard of the Herr General before, yes?' He was on safe ground here, Mallory knew. The reputation of Graebel, both as a paratroop commander and an iron disciplinarian, had spread far beyond these islands.

Even in the half-light Mallory could have sworn that the guard's complexion turned paler. But he was dogged enough.

'You have papers? Letters of authority?'

Mallory sighed wearily, looked over his shoulder.

'Andrea!' he bawled.

'What do you want?' Andrea's great bulk loomed through the hatchway. He had heard every word that passed, had taken his cue from Mallory: a newly-opened wine bottle was almost engulfed in one vast hand and he was scowling hugely. 'Can't you see I'm busy?' he asked surlily. He stopped short at the sight of the German and scowled again, irritably. 'And what does this halfling want?'

'Our passes and letters of authority from Herr General. They're down below.'

Andrea disappeared, grumbling deep in his throat. A rope was thrown ashore, the stern pulled in against the sluggish current and the papers passed over. The papers — a set different from those to be used if emergency arose in Navarone — proved to be satisfactory, eminently so. Mallory would have been surprised had they been anything else. The preparation of these, even down to the photostatic facsimile of General Graebel's signature, was all in the day's work for Jensen's bureau in Cairo.

The soldier folded the papers, handed them back with a muttered word of thanks. He was only a kid, Mallory could see now — if he was more than nineteen his looks belied him. A pleasant, open-faced kid — of a different stamp altogether from the young fanatics of the S.S. Panzer Division — and far too thin. Mallory's chief reaction was one of relief: he would have hated to have to kill a boy like this. But he had to find out all he could. He signalled to Stevens to hand him up the almost empty crate of Moselle. Jensen, he mused, had been very thorough indeed: the man had literally thought of everything... Mallory gestured in the direction of the watch-tower.

'How many of you are up there?' he asked.

The boy was instantly suspicious. His face had tightened up, stilled in hostile surmise.

'Why do you want to know?' he asked stiffly.

Mallory groaned, lifted his hands in despair, turned sadly to Andrea.

'You see what it is to be one of them?' he asked in mournful complaint. 'Trust nobody. Think everyone is as twisted as...' He broke off hurriedly, turned to the soldier again. 'It's just that we don't want to have the same trouble every time we come in here,' he explained. 'We'll be back in Samos in a couple of days, and we've still another case of Moselle to work through. General Graebel keeps his — ah — special envoys well supplied.... It must be thirsty work up there in the sun. Come on, now, a bottle each. How many bottles?'

The reassuring mention that they would be back again, the equally reassuring mention of Graebel's name, plus, probably, the attraction of the offer and his comrades' reaction if he told them he had refused it, tipped the balance, overcame scruples and suspicions.

'There are only three of us,' he said grudgingly.

'Three it is,' Mallory said cheerfully. 'We'll bring you some Hock next time we return.' He tilted his own bottle. '*Prosit!*' he said, an islander proud of airing his German, and then, more proudly still, '*Auf Wiedersehen!*'

The boy murmured something in return. He stood hesitating for a moment, slightly shame-faced, then wheeled abruptly, walked off slowly along the river bank, clutching his bottles of Moselle.

'So!' Mallory said thoughtfully. 'There are only three of them. That should make things easier—'

'Well done, sir!' It was Stevens who interrupted, his voice warm, his face alive with admiration. 'Jolly good show!'

'Jolly good show!' Miller mimicked. He heaved his lanky length over the coaming of the engine hatchway, '"Good" be damned! I couldn't understand a gawddamned word, but for my money that rates an Oscar. That was terrific, boss!'

'Thank you, one and all,' Mallory murmured. 'But I'm afraid the congratulations are a bit premature.' The sudden chill in his voice struck at them, so that their eyes aligned along his pointing finger even before he went on. 'Take a look,' he said quietly.

The young soldier had halted suddenly about two hundred yards along the bank, looked into the forest on his left in startled surprise, then dived in among the trees. For a moment the watchers on the boat could see another soldier, talking excitedly to the boy and gesticulating in the direction of their boat, and then both were gone, lost in the gloom of the forest.

'That's torn it!' Mallory said softly. He turned away.

71

'Right, that's enough. Back to where you were. It would look fishy if we ignored that incident altogether, but it would look a damned sight fishier if we paid too much attention to it. Don't let's appear to be holding a conference.'

Miller slipped down into the engine-room with Brown, and Stevens went back to the little for'ard cabin. Mallory and Andrea remained on deck, bottles in their hands. The rain had stopped now, completely, but the wind was still rising, climbing the scale with imperceptible steadiness, beginning to bend the tops of the tallest of the pines. Temporarily the bluff was affording them almost complete protection. Mallory deliberately shut his mind to what it must be like outside. They had to put out to sea – Spandaus permitting – and that was that.

'What do you think has happened, sir?' Stevens's voice carried up from the gloom of the cabin.

'Pretty obvious, isn't it?' Mallory asked. He spoke loudly enough for all to hear. 'They've been tipped off. Don't ask me how. This is the second time – and their suspicions are going to be considerably reinforced by the absence of a report from the caique that was sent to investigate us. She was carrying a wireless aerial, remember?'

'But why should they get so damned suspicious all of a sudden?' Miller asked. 'It doesn't make sense to me, boss.'

'Must be in radio contact with their H.Q. Or a telephone – probably a telephone. They've just been given the old tic-tac. Consternation on all sides.'

'So mebbe they'll be sending a small army over from their H.Q. to deal with us,' Miller said lugubriously.

Mallory shook his head definitely. His mind was working quickly and well, and he felt oddly certain, confident of himself.

'No, not a chance. Seven miles as the crow flies. Ten, maybe twelve miles over rough hill and forest tracks – and in pitch darkness. They wouldn't think of it.' He waved his bottle in the direction of the watch-tower. 'Tonight's their big night.'

'So we can expect the Spandaus to open up any minute?' Again the abnormal matter-of-factness of Stevens's voice.

Mallory shook his head a second time.

'They won't. I'm positive of that. No matter how suspicious they may be, how certain they are that we're the big bad wolf, they are going to be shaken to the core when that kid tells them we're carrying papers and letters of authority signed by General Graebel himself. For all they know, curtains for us may be the firing squad for them. Unlikely, but you get the general idea. So they're going to contact H.Q., and the commandant on a small island like this isn't going to take a chance on rubbing out a bunch of characters who may be the special envoys of the Herr General himself. So what? So he codes a message and radios it to Vathy in Samos and bites his nails off to the elbow till a message comes back saying Graebel has never heard of us and why the hell haven't we all been shot dead?' Mallory looked at the luminous dial of his watch. 'I'd say we have at least half an hour.'

'And meantime we all sit around with our little bits of paper and pencil and write out our last wills and testaments.' Miller scowled. 'No percentage in that, boss. We gotta *do* somethin'.'

Mallory grinned.

'Don't worry, Corporal, we are going to do something. We're going to hold a nice little bottle party, right here on the poop.'

The last words of their song — a shockingly corrupted Grecian version of 'Lilli Marlene', and their third song in the past few minutes — died away in the evening air. Mallory doubted whether more than faint snatches of the singing would be carried to the watch-tower against the wind, but the rhythmical stamping of feet and waving of bottles were in themselves sufficient evidence of drunken musical hilarity to all but the totally blind and deaf. Mallory grinned to himself as he thought of the complete confusion and uncertainty the Germans in the tower must have been feeling then. This was not the behaviour of enemy spies, especially enemy spies who know that suspicions had been aroused and that their time was running out.

Mallory tilted the bottle to his mouth, held it there for several seconds, then set it down again, the wine untasted. He looked round slowly at the three men squatting there with him on the poop, Miller, Stevens and Brown. Andrea was not there, but he didn't have to turn his head to look for him. Andrea, he knew, was crouched in the shelter of the wheelhouse, a waterproof bag with grenades and a revolver strapped to his back.

'Right!' Mallory said crisply. 'Now's your big chance for *your* Oscar. Let's make this as convincing as we can.' He bent forward, jabbed his finger into Miller's chest and shouted angrily at him.

Miller shouted back. For a few moments they sat there, gesticulating angrily and, to all appearances, quarrelling furiously with each other. Then Miller was on his feet, swaying in drunken imbalance as he leaned threateningly over Mallory, clenched fists ready to strike. He stood back as Mallory struggled to his feet, and in a moment they were fighting fiercely, raining apparently heavy blows on each other. Then a haymaker from the American sent Mallory reeling back to crash convincingly against the wheelhouse.

'Right, Andrea.' He spoke quietly, without looking round. 'This is it. Five seconds. Good luck.' He scrambled to his feet, picked up a bottle by the neck and rushed at Miller, upraised arm and bludgeon swinging fiercely down. Miller dodged, swung a vicious foot, and Mallory roared in pain as his shins caught on the edge of the bulwarks. Silhouetted against the pale gleam of the creek, he stood poised for a second, arms flailing wildly, then plunged heavily, with a loud splash, into the waters of the creek.

For the next half-minute — it would take about that time for Andrea to swim underwater round the next upstream corner of the creek — everything was a confusion and a bedlam of noise. Mallory trod water as he tried to pull himself aboard: Miller had seized a boathook and was trying to smash it down on his head: and the others, on their feet now, had flung their arms round Miller, trying to restrain him: finally they managed to knock him off his feet, pin him to the deck and help the dripping Mallory aboard. A minute later, after the immemorial fashion of drunken men, the two combatants had shaken hands with one another and were sitting on the engine-room hatch, arms round each other's shoulders and drinking in perfect amity from the same freshly-opened bottle of wine.

'Very nicely done,' Mallory said approvingly. 'Very nicely indeed. An Oscar, definitely, for Corporal Miller.'

Dusty Miller said nothing. Taciturn and depressed, he looked moodily at the bottle in his hand. At last he stirred.

'I don't like it, boss,' he muttered unhappily. 'I don't like the set-up one little bit. You shoulda let me go with Andrea. It's three to one up there, and they're waiting and ready.' He looked accusingly at Mallory. 'Dammit to hell, boss, you're always telling us how desperately important this mission is!'

'I know,' Mallory said quietly. 'That's why I didn't send you with him. That's why none of us has gone with him. We'd only be a liability to him, get in his way.' Mallory shook his head. 'You don't know Andrea, Dusty.' It was the first time Mallory had called him that: Miller was warmed by the unexpected familiarity, secretly pleased. 'None of you know him. But I know him.' He gestured towards the watch-tower, its square-cut lines in sharp silhouette against the darkening sky. 'Just a big, fat, good-natured chap, always laughing and joking.' Mallory paused, shook his head again, went on slowly. 'He's up there now, padding through that forest like a cat, the biggest and most dangerous cat you'll ever see. Unless they offer no resistance – Andrea never kills unnecessarily – when I send him up there after these three poor bastards I'm executing them just as surely as if they were in the electric chair and I was pulling the switch.'

In spite of himself Miller was impressed, profoundly so. 'Known him a long time, boss, huh?' It was half question, half statement.

'A long time. Andrea was in the Albanian war – he was in the regular army. They tell me the Italians went in terror of him – his long-range patrols against the Iulia division, the Wolves of Tuscany, did more to wreck the Italian morale in Albania than any other single factor. I've heard a good many stories about them – not from Andrea – and they're all incredible. And they're all true. But it was afterwards I met him, when we were trying to hold the Servia Pass. I was a very junior liaison lieutenant in the Anzac brigade at the time. Andrea' – he paused deliberately for effect – 'Andrea was a lieutenant-colonel in the 19th Greek Motorised Division.'

'A *what*?' Miller demanded in astonishment. Stevens and Brown were equally incredulous.

'You heard me. Lieutenant-colonel. Outranks me by a fairish bit, you might say.' He smiled at them quizzically. 'Puts Andrea in rather a different light, doesn't it?'

They nodded silently but said nothing. The genial, hail-fellow Andrea – a good-natured, almost simple-minded buffoon – a senior army officer. The idea had come too suddenly, was too incongruous for easy assimilation and immediate comprehension. But, gradually, it began to make sense to them. It explained many things about Andrea to them – his repose, his confidence, the unerring sureness of his lightning reactions, and, above all, the implicit faith Mallory had in him, the respect he showed for Andrea's opinions whenever he consulted him, which was frequently. Without surprise now, Miller slowly recalled that he'd never yet heard Mallory give Andrea a direct order. And Mallory never hesitated to pull his rank when necessary.

'After Servia,' Mallory went on, 'everything was pretty confused. Andrea had heard that Trikkala – a small country town where his wife and three daughters lived – had been flattened by the Stukas and Heinkels. He reached there all right, but there was nothing he could do. A land-mine had landed in the front garden and there wasn't even rubble left.'

Mallory paused, lit a cigarette. He stared through the drifting smoke at the fading outlines of the tower.

'The only person he found there was his brother-in-law, George. George was with us in Crete – he's still there. From George he heard for the first time of the Bulgarian atrocities in Thrace and Macedonia – and his parents lived there. So they dressed in German uniforms – you can imagine how Andrea got those – commandeered a German army truck and drove to Protosami.' The cigarette in Mallory's hand snapped suddenly, was sent spinning over the side. Miller was vaguely surprised: emotion, or rather, emotional displays, were so completely foreign to that very tough New Zealander. But Mallory went on quietly enough.

'They arrived in the evening of the infamous Protosami massacre. George has told me how Andrea stood there, clad in his German uniform and laughing as he watched a party of nine or ten Bulgarian soldiers lash couples together and throw them into the river. The first couple in were his father and stepmother, both dead.'

'My Gawd above!' Even Miller was shocked out of his usual equanimity. 'It's just not possible—'

'You know nothing,' Mallory interrupted impatiently. 'Hundreds of Greeks in Macedonia died the same way – but usually alive when they were thrown in. Until you know how the Greeks hate the Bulgarians, you don't even begin to know what hate is.... Andrea shared a couple of bottles of wine with the soldiers, found out that they had killed his parents earlier in the afternoon – they had been foolish enough to resist. After dusk he followed them up to an old corrugated-iron shed where they were billeted for the night. All he had was a knife. They left a guard outside. Andrea broke his neck, went inside, locked the door and smashed the oil lamp. George doesn't know what happened except that Andrea went berserk. He was back outside in two minutes, completely sodden, his uniform soaked in blood from head to foot. There wasn't a sound, not even a groan to be heard from the hut when they left, George says.'

He paused again, but this time there was no interruption, nothing said. Stevens shivered, drew his shabby jacket closer round his shoulders: the air seemed to have become suddenly chill. Mallory lit another cigarette, smiled faintly at Miller, nodded towards the watch-tower.

'See what I mean by saying we'd only be a liability to Andrea up there?'

'Yeah. Yeah, I guess I do,' Miller admitted. 'I had no idea, I had no idea.... Not *all* of them, boss! He couldn't have killed—'

'He did,' Mallory interrupted flatly. 'After that he formed his own band, made life hell for the Bulgarian outposts in Thrace. At one time there was almost an entire division chasing him through the Rhodope mountains. Finally he was betrayed and captured, and he, George and four others were shipped to Stavros – they were to go on to Salonika for trial. They overpowered their guards – Andrea got loose among them on deck at night – and sailed the boat to Turkey. The Turks tried to intern him – they might as well have tried to intern an earthquake. Finally he arrived in Palestine, tried to join the Greek Commando Battalion that was being formed in the Middle East – mainly veterans of the Albanian campaign, like himself.' Mallory laughed mirthlessly. 'He was

78

arrested as a deserter. He was released eventually, but there was no place for him in the new Greek Army. But Jensen's bureau heard about him, knew he was a natural for Subversive Operations... And so we went to Crete together.'

Five minutes passed, perhaps ten, but nobody broke the silence. Occasionally, for the benefit of any watchers, they went through the motions of drinking; but even the half-light was fading now and Mallory knew they could only be half-seen blurs, shadowy and indistinct, from the heights of the watch-tower. The caique was beginning to rock in the surge from the open sea round the bluff. The tall, reaching pines, black now as midnight cypress and looming impossibly high against the star-dusted cloud wrack that scudded palely overhead, were closing in on them from either side, sombre, watchful and vaguely threatening, the wind moaning in lost and mournful requiem through their swaying topmost branches. A bad night, an eerie and an ominous night, pregnant with that indefinable foreboding that reaches down and touches the well-springs of the nameless fears, the dim and haunting memories of a million years ago, the ancient racial superstitions of mankind: a night that sloughed off the tissue veneer of civilisation and the shivering man complains that someone is walking over his grave.

Suddenly, incongruously, the spell was shattered and Andrea's cheerful hail from the bank had them all on their feet in a moment. They heard his booming laugh and even the forests seemed to shrink back in defeat. Without waiting for the stern to be pulled in, he plunged into the creek, reached the caique in half a dozen powerful strokes and hoisted himself easily aboard. Grinning down from his great height, he shook himself like some shaggy mastiff and reached out a hand for a convenient wine bottle.

'No need to ask how things went, eh?' Mallory asked, smiling.

'None at all. It was just too easy. They were only boys and they never even saw me.' Andrea took another long swig from the bottle and grinned in sheer delight. 'And I didn't lay a finger on them,' he went on triumphantly. 'Well, maybe a couple of little taps. They were all looking down here, staring out over the parapet when I arrived. Held them up, took their guns off them and locked them in a cellar. And then I bent their Spandaus – just a little bit.'

This is it, Mallory thought dully, this is the end. This is the finish of everything, the strivings, the hopes, the fears, the loves and laughter of each one of us. This is what it all comes to. This is the end, the end for us, the end for a thousand boys on Kheros. In unconscious futility his hand came up, slowly wiped lips salt from the spray bulleting off the wind-flattened wave-tops, then lifted farther to shade bloodshot eyes that peered out hopelessly into the storm-filled darkness ahead. For a moment the dullness lifted, and an almost intolerable bitterness welled through his mind. All gone, everything – everything except the guns of Navarone. The guns of Navarone. They would live on, they were indestructible. Damn them, damn them, damn them! Dear God, the blind waste, the terrible uselessness of it all!

The caique was dying, coming apart at the seams. She was literally being pounded to death, being shaken apart by the constant battering shocks of wind and sea. Time and time again the poop-deck dipped beneath the foam-streaked cauldron at the stern, the fo'c'sle rearing crazily into the air, dripping forefoot showing clear: then the plummeting drop, the shotgun, shuddering impact as broad-beamed bows crashed vertically down into the cliff-walled trough beyond, an explosive collision that threw so unendurable a strain on the ancient timbers and planks and gradually tore them apart.

It had been bad enough when they'd cleared the creek just as darkness fell, and plunged and wallowed their way through a quartering sea on a northward course for Navarone. Steering the unwieldy old caique had become difficult in the extreme: with the seas fine on the starboard quarter she had yawed wildly and unpredictably through a fifty degree arc, but at least her seams had been tight then, the rolling waves overtaking her in regular formation and the wind settled and steady somewhere east of south. But now all that was gone. With half a dozen planks sprung from the stem-post and working loose from the apron, and leaking heavily through the stuffing-gland of the propeller shaft, she was making water far faster than the ancient, vertical hand-pump could cope with: the wind-truncated seas were heavier, but broken and confused, sweeping down on them now from this quarter, now from that: and the wind itself, redoubled in its shrieking violence, veered and backed insanely from south-west to south-east. Just then it was steady from the south, driving the unmanageable craft blindly on to the closing iron cliffs of Navarone, cliffs that loomed invisibly ahead, somewhere in that all-encompassing darkness.

Momentarily Mallory straightened, tried to ease the agony of the pincers that were clawing into the muscles of the small of his back. For over two hours now he had been bending and straightening, bending and straightening, lifting a thousand buckets that Dusty Miller filled interminably from the well of the hold. God only knew how Miller felt. If anything, he had the harder job of the two and he had been violently and almost continuously seasick for hours on end. He looked ghastly, and he must have been feeling like death itself: the sustained effort, the sheer iron will-power to drive himself on in that condition reached beyond the limits of understanding. Mallory shook his head wonderingly. 'My God, but he's tough, that Yank.' Unbidden, the words framed themselves in his mind, and he shook his head in anger, vaguely conscious of the complete inadequacy of the words.

Fighting for his breath, he looked aft to see how the others were faring. Casey Brown, of course, he couldn't see. Bent double in the cramped confines of the engine-room, he, too, was constantly sick and suffering a blinding headache from the oil fumes and exhaust gases still filtering from the replacement stand-pipe, neither of which could find any escape in the unventilated engine-room: but, crouched over the engine, he had not once left his post since they had cleared the mouth of the creek, had nursed the straining, ancient Kelvin along with the loving care, the exquisite skill of a man born into a long and proud tradition of engineering. That engine had only to falter once, to break down for the time in which a man might draw a deep breath, and the end would be as immediate as it was violent. Their steerage way, their lives, depended entirely on the continuous thrust of that screw, the laboured thudding of that rusted old two-cylinder. It was the heart of the boat, and when that heart stopped beating the boat died too, slewed broadside on and foundering in the waiting chasms between the waves.

For'ard of the engine-room, straddle-legged and braced against the corner pillar of the splintered skeleton that was all that remained of the wheelhouse, Andrea laboured unceasingly at the pump, never once lifting his head, oblivious of the crazy lurching of the deck of the caique, oblivious, too, of the biting wind and stinging, sleet-cold spray that numbed bare arms and moulded the sodden shirt to the hunched and massive shoulders. Ceaselessly, tirelessly, his arm thrust up and down, up and down, with the metronomic regularity of a piston. He had been there for close on three hours now, and he looked as if he could go on for ever. Mallory, who had yielded him the pump in complete exhaustion after less than twenty minutes' cruel labour, wondered if there was any limit to the man's endurance.

He wondered, too, about Stevens. For four endless hours now Andy Stevens had fought and overcome a wheel that

82

leapt and struggled in his hands as if possessed of a convulsive life and will of its own – the will to wrench itself out of exhausted hands and turn them into the troughs: he had done a superb job, Mallory thought, had handled the clumsy craft magnificently. He peered at him closely, but the spray lashed viciously across his eyes and blinded him with tears. All he could gather was a vague impression of a tightly-set mouth, sleepless, sunken eyes and little patches of skin unnaturally pale against the mask of blood that covered almost the entire face from hairline to throat. The twisting, towering comber that had stove in the planks of the wheelhouse and driven in the windows with such savage force had been completely unexpected: Stevens hadn't had a chance. The cut above the right temple was particularly bad, ugly and deep: the blood still pulsed over the ragged edge of the wound, dripped monotonously into the water that sloshed and gurgled about the floor of the wheelhouse.

Sick to his heart, Mallory turned away, reached down for another bucket of water. What a crew, he thought to hmself, what a really terrific bunch of – of... He sought for words to describe them, even to himself, but he knew his mind was far too tired. It didn't matter anyway, for there were no words for men like that, nothing that could do them justice.

He could almost taste the bitterness in his mouth, the bitterness that washed in waves through his exhausted mind. God, how wrong it was, how terribly unfair! Why did such men have to die, he wondered savagely, why did they have to die so uselessly. Or maybe it wasn't necessary to justify dying, even dying ingloriously empty of achievement. Could one not die for intangibles, for the abstract and the ideal? What had the martyrs at the stake achieved? Or what was the old tag – *dulce et decorum est pro patria mori*. If one lives well, what matter how one dies. Unconsciously his lips tightened in quick revulsion and he thought of Jensen's remarks about the High

Command playing who's-the-king-of-the-castle. Well, they were right bang in the middle of their playground now, just a few more pawns sliding into the limbo. Not that it mattered – they had thousands more left to play with.

For the first time Mallory thought of himself. Not with bitterness or self-pity or regret that it was all over. He thought of himself only as the leader of this party, his responsibility for the present situation. It's my fault, he told himself over and over again, it's all my fault. I brought them here. I made them come. Even while one part of his mind was telling him that he'd had no option, that his hand had been forced, that if they had remained in the creek they would have been wiped out long before the dawn, irrationally he still blamed himself the more. Shackleton, of all the men that ever lived, maybe Ernest Shackleton could have helped them now. But not Keith Mallory. There was nothing he could do, no more than the others were doing, and they were just waiting for the end. But he was the leader, he thought dully, he should be planning something, he should be doing something.... But there was nothing he could do. There was nothing anyone on God's earth could do. The sense of guilt, of utter inadequacy, settled and deepened with every shudder of the ancient timbers.

He dropped his bucket, grabbed for the security of the mast as a heavy wave swept over the deck, the breaking foam quicksilver in its seething phosphorescence. The waters swirled hungrily round his legs and feet, but he ignored them, stared out into the darkness. The darkness – that was the devil of it. The old caique rolled and pitched and staggered and plunged, but as if disembodied, in a vacuum. They could see nothing – not where the last wave had gone, nor where the next was coming from. A sea invisible and strangely remote, doubly frightening in its palpable immediacy.

Mallory stared down into the hold, was vaguely conscious of the white blur of Miller's face: he had swallowed some sea-water and was retching painfully, salt water laced with blood. But Mallory ignored it, involuntarily: all his mind was concentrated elsewhere, trying to reduce some fleeting impression, as vague as it had been evanescent, to a coherent realisation. It seemed desperately urgent that he should do so. Then another and still heavier wave broke over the side and all at once he had it.

The wind! The wind had dropped away, was lessening with every second that passed. Even as he stood there, arms locked round the mast as the second wave fought to carry him away, he remembered how often in the high hills at home he had stood at the foot of a precipice as an onrushing wind, seeking the path of least resistance, had curved and lifted up the sheer face, leaving him standing in a pocket of relative immunity. It was a common enough mountaineering phenomenon. And these two freak waves – the surging backwash! The significance struck at him like a blow. The cliffs! They were on the cliffs of Navarone!

With a hoarse, wordless cry of warning, reckless of his own safety, he flung himself aft, dived full length through the swirling waters for the engine-room hatchway.

'Full astern!' he shouted. The startled white smudge that was Casey Brown's face twisted up to his. 'For God's sake, man, full astern! We're heading for the cliffs!'

He scrambled to his feet, reached the wheelhouse in two strides, hand pawing frantically for the flare pocket.

'The cliffs, Stevens! We're almost on them! Andrea – Miller's still down below!'

He flicked a glance at Stevens, caught the slow nod of the set, blood-masked face, followed the line of sight of the expressionless eyes, saw the whitely phosphorescent line ahead, irregular but almost continuous, blooming and fading, blooming and fading, as the pounding seas smashed against and fell back from cliffs still invisible in the darkness. Desperately his hands fumbled with the flare.

And then, abruptly, it was gone, hissing and spluttering

along the near-horizontal trajectory of its flight. For a moment, Mallory thought it had gone out, and he clenched his fists in impotent bitterness. Then it smashed against the rock face, fell back on to a ledge about a dozen feet above the water, and lay there smoking and intermittently burning in the driving rain, in the heavy spray that cascaded from the booming breakers.

The light was feeble, but it was enough. The cliffs were barely fifty yards away, black and wetly shining in the fitful radiance of the flare – a flare that illuminated a vertical circle of less than five yards in radius, and left the cliff below the ledge shrouded in the treacherous dark. And straight ahead, twenty, maybe fifteen yards from the shore, stretched the evil length of a reef, gap-toothed and needle-pointed, vanishing at either end into the outer darkness.

'Can you take her through?' he yelled at Stevens.

'God knows! I'll try!' He shouted something else about 'steerage way', but Mallory was already half-way to the for'ard cabin. As always in an emergency, his mind was racing ahead with that abnormal sureness and clarity of thought for which he could never afterwards account.

Grasping spikes, mallet and a wire-cored rope, he was back on deck in seconds. He stood stock still, rooted in an almost intolerable tension as he saw the towering, jagged rock bearing down upon them, fine on the starboard bow, a rock that reached half-way to the wheelhouse. It struck the boat with a crash that sent him to his knees, rasped and grated along half the length of the buckled, splintered gunwales: and then the caique had rolled over to port and she was through. Stevens frantically spinning the wheel and shouting for full astern.

Mallory's breath escaped in a long, heavy sigh of relief – he had been quite unaware that he had stopped breathing – and he hurriedly looped the coil of rope round his neck and under his left shoulder and stuck spikes and hammer in his belt. The caique was slewing heavily round now, port side to, plunging and corkscrewing violently as she began to fall broadside into the troughs of the waves, waves shorter and steeper than ever under the double thrust of the wind and the waves and the backwash recoiling from the cliffs: but she was still in the grip of the sea and her own momentum, and the distance was closing with frightening speed. It's a chance I have to take, Mallory repeated to himself over and over again; it's a chance I have to take. But that little ledge remote and just inaccessible, was fate's last refinement of cruelty, the salt in the wound of extinction, and he knew in his heart of hearts that it wasn't a chance at all, but just a suicidal gesture. And then Andrea had heaved the last of the fenders – worn truck tyres – outboard, and was towering above him, grinning down hugely into his face: and suddenly Mallory wasn't so sure any more.

'The ledge?' Andrea's vast, reassuring hand was on his shoulder.

Mallory nodded, knees bent in readiness, feet braced on the plunging, slippery deck.

'Jump for it,' Andrea boomed. 'Then keep your legs stiff.'

There was no time for any more. The caique was swinging in broadside to, teetering on the crest of a wave, as high up the cliff as she would ever be, and Mallory knew it was now or never. His hands swung back behind his body, his knees bent farther, and then, in one convulsive leap he had flung himself upwards, fingers scrabbling on the wet rock of the cliff, then hooking over the rim of the ledge. For an instant he hung there at the length of his arms, unable to move, wincing as he heard the foremast crash against the ledge and snap in two, then his fingers left the ledge without their own volition, and he was almost half-way over, propelled by one gigantic heave from below.

He was not up yet. He was held only by the buckle of his belt, caught on the edge of the rock, a buckle now dragged up to his breastbone by the weight of his body. But he did not paw frantically for a handhold, or wriggle his body or flail his legs in the air – and any of these actions would have sent him crashing down again. At last, and once again, he was a man utterly at home in his own element. The greatest rock climber of his time, men called him, and this was what he had been born for.

Slowly, methodically, he felt the surface of the ledge, and almost at once he discovered a crack running back from the face. It would have been better had it been parallel to the face – and more than the width of a match-stick. But it was enough for Mallory. With infinite care he eased the hammer and a couple of spikes from his belt, worked a spike into the crack to obtain a minimal purchase, slid the other in some inches nearer, hooked his left wrist round the first, held the second spike with the fingers of the same hand and brought up the hammer in his free hand. Fifteen seconds later he was standing on the ledge.

Working quickly and surely, catlike in his balance on the slippery, shelving rock, he hammered a spike into the face of the cliff, securely and at a downward angle, about three feet above the ledge, dropped a clove hitch over the top and kicked the rest of the coil over the ledge. Then, and only then, he turned round and looked below him.

Less than a minute had passed since the caique had struck, but already she was a broken-masted, splintered shambles, sides caving in and visibly disintegrating as he watched. Every seven or eight seconds a giant comber would pick her up and fling her bodily against the cliff, the heavy truck tyres taking up only a fraction of the impact that followed, the sickening, rending crash that reduced the gunwales to matchwood, holed and split the sides and cracked the oaken timbers: and then she would roll clear, port side showing, the hungry sea pouring in through the torn and ruptured planking.

Three men were standing by what was left of the

wheelhouse. *Three* men — suddenly, he realised that Casey Brown was missing, realised, too, that the engine was still running, its clamour rising and falling then rising again, at irregular intervals. Brown was edging the caique backwards and forwards along the cliff, keeping her as nearly as humanly possible in the same position, for he knew their lives depended on Mallory — and on himself. 'The fool!' Mallory swore. 'The crazy fool!'

The caique surged back in a receding trough, steadied, then swept in against the cliff again, heeling over so wildly that the roof of the wheelhouse smashed and telescoped against the wall of the cliff. The impact was so fierce, the shock so sudden, that Stevens lost both hand-grip and footing and was catapulted into the rock face, upflung arms raised for protection. For a moment he hung there, as if pinned against the wall, then fell back into the sea, limbs and head relaxed, lifeless in his limp acquiescence. He should have died then, drowned under the hammer-blows of the sea or crushed by the next battering-ram collision of caique and cliff. He should have died and he would have died but for the great arm that hooked down and plucked him out of the water like a limp and sodden rag doll and heaved him inboard a bare second before the next bludgeoning impact of the boat against the rock would have crushed the life out of him.

'Come on, for God's sake!' Mallory shouted desperately. 'She'll be gone in a minute! The rope — use the rope!' He saw Andrea and Miller exchange a few quick words, saw them shake and pummel Stevens and stand him on his feet, dazed and retching sea-water, but conscious. Andrea was speaking in his ear, emphasising something and guiding the rope into his hands, and then the caique was swinging in again, Stevens automatically shortening his grip on the rope. A tremendous boost from below by Andrea, Mallory's long arm reaching out and Stevens was on the ledge, sitting with his back to the cliff and hanging on to the spike, dazed still and shaking a muzzy head, but safe.

'You're next, Miller!' Mallory called. 'Hurry up, man — jump for it!'

Miller looked at him and Mallory could have sworn that he was grinning. Instead of taking the rope from Andrea, he ran for'ard to the cabin.

'Just a minute, boss!' he bawled. 'I've forgotten my toothbrush.'

He reappeared in a few seconds, but without the toothbrush. He was carrying the big, green box of explosives, and before Mallory had appreciated what was happening the box, all fifty pounds of it, was curving up into the air, upthrust by the Greek's tireless arms. Automatically Mallory's hands reached for and caught it. He overbalanced, stumbled and toppled forward, still clutching the box, then was brought up with a jerk. Stevens, still clutching the spike, was on his feet now, free hand hooked in Mallory's belt: he was shivering violently, with cold and exhaustion and an oddly fear-laced excitement. But, like Mallory, he was a hillman at home again.

Mallory was just straightening up when the waterproofed radio set came soaring up. He caught it, placed it down, looked over the side.

'Leave that bloody stuff alone!' he shouted furiously. 'Get up here yourselves — now!'

Two coils of rope landed on the ledge beside him, then the first of the rucksacks with the food and clothing. He was vaguely aware that Stevens was trying to stack the equipment in some sort of order.

'Do you hear me?' Mallory roared. 'Get up here at once! That's an order. The boat's sinking, you bloody idiots!'

The caique *was* sinking. She was filling up quickly and Casey Brown had abandoned the flooded Kelvin. But she was a far steadier platform now, rolling through a much shorter arc, less violent in her soggy, yielding collisions with the cliff wall. For a moment Mallory thought the sea was dropping away, then he realised that the tons of water in the caique's hold had drastically lowered her centre of gravity, were acting as a counter-balancing weight.

Miller cupped a hand to his ear. Even in the near darkness of the sinking flare his face had an oddly greenish pallor.

'Can't hear a word you say, boss. Besides, she ain't sinkin' yet.' Once again he disappeared into the for'ard cabin.

Within thirty seconds, with all five men working furiously, the remainder of the equipment was on the ledge. The caique was down by the stern, the poop-deck covered and water pouring down the engine-room hatchway as Brown struggled up the rope, the fo'c'sle awash as Miller grabbed the rope and started after him, and as Andrea reached up and swung in against the cliff his legs dangled over an empty sea. The caique had foundered, completely gone from sight: no drifting flotsam, not even an air bubble marked where she had so lately been.

The ledge was narrow, not three feet wide at its broadest, tapering off into the gloom on either side. Worse still, apart from the few square feet where Stevens had piled the gear, it shelved sharply outwards, the rock underfoot treacherous and slippery. Backs to the wall, Andrea and Miller had to stand on their heels, hands outspread and palms inward against the cliff, pressing in to it as closely as possible to maintain their balance. But in less than a minute Mallory had another two spikes hammered in about twenty inches above the ledge, ten feet apart and joined with a rope, a secure lifeline for all of them.

Wearily Miller slid down to a sitting position, leaned his chest in heartfelt thankfulness against the safe barrier of the rope. He fumbled in his breast pocket, produced a pack of cigarettes and handed them round, oblivious to the rain that soaked them in an instant. He was soaking wet from the waist downwards and both his knees had been badly bruised against the cliff wall: he was bitterly cold, drenched by heavy rain and the sheets of spray that

91

broke continually over the ledge: the sharp edge of the rock bit cruelly into the calves of his legs, the tight rope constricted his breathing and he was still ashen-faced and exhausted from long hours of labour and seasickness: but when he spoke, it was with a voice of utter sincerity.

'My Gawd!' he said reverently. 'Ain't this wonderful!'

CHAPTER 5

Monday Night

Ninety minutes later Mallory wedged himself into a natural rock chimney on the cliff face, drove in a spike beneath his feet and tried to rest his aching, exhausted body. Two minutes' rest he told himself, only two minutes while Andrea comes up: the rope was quivering and he could just hear, above the shrieking of the wind that fought to pluck him off the cliff face, the metallic scraping as Andrea's boots struggled for a foothold on that wicked overhang immediately beneath him, the overhang that had all but defeated him, the obstacle that he had impossibly overcome only at the expense of torn hands and body completely spent, of shoulder muscles afire with agony and breath that rasped in great gulping inhalations into his starving lungs. Deliberately he forced his mind away from the pains that racked his body, from its insistent demands for rest, and listened again to the ringing of steel against rock, louder this time, carrying clearly even in the gale.... He would have to tell Andrea to be more careful on the remaining twenty feet or so that separated them from the top.

At least, Mallory thought wryly, no one would have to tell him to be quiet. He couldn't have made any noise with his feet if he'd tried – not with only a pair of torn socks as cover for his bruised and bleeding feet. He'd hardly covered his first twenty feet of the climb when he'd discovered that his climbing boots were quite useless, had robbed his feet of all sensitivity, the ability to locate and engage the tiny toe-holds which afforded the only sources of purchase. He had removed them with great difficulty, tied them to his belt by the laces – and lost them, had them torn off, when forcing his way under a projecting spur of rock.

The climb itself had been a nightmare, a brutal, gasping agony in the wind and the rain and the darkness, an agony that had eventually dulled the danger and masked the suicidal risks in climbing that sheer unknown face, in interminable agony of hanging on by fingertips and toes, of driving in a hundred spikes, of securing ropes then inching on again up into the darkness. It was a climb such as he had not ever made before, such as he knew he would not ever make again, for this was insanity. It was a climb that had extended him to the utmost of his great skill, his courage and his strength, and then far beyond that again, and he had not known that such reserves, such limitless resources, lay within him or any man. Nor did he know the well-spring, the source of that power that had driven him to where he was, within easy climbing reach of the top. The challenge to a mountaineer, personal danger, pride in the fact that he was probably the only man in southern Europe who could have made the climb, even the sure knowledge that time was running out for the men on Kheros – it was none of these things, he knew that: in the last twenty minutes it had taken him to negotiate that overhang beneath his feet his mind had been drained of all thought and all emotion, and he had climbed only as a machine.

Hand over hand up the rope, easily, powerfully, Andrea hauled himself over the smoothly swelling convexity of the overhang, legs dangling in mid-air. He was festooned with heavy coils of rope, girdled with spikes that protruded from his belt at every angle and lent him the incongruous appearance of a comic-opera Corsican bandit. Quickly he hauled himself up beside Mallory, wedged himself in the chimney and mopped his sweating forehead. As always, he was grinning hugely.

Mallory looked at him, smiled back. Andrea, he reflected, had no right to be there. It was Stevens's place, but Stevens had still been suffering from shock, had lost much blood: besides, it required a first-class climber to bring up the rear, to coil up the ropes as he came and to remove the spikes – there must be no trace left of the ascent: or so Mallory had told him, and Stevens had reluctantly agreed, although the hurt in his face had been easy to see. More than ever now Mallory was glad he had resisted the quiet plea in Stevens's face: Stevens was undoubtedly a fine climber, but what Mallory had required that night was not another mountaineer but a human ladder. Time and time again during the ascent he had stood on Andrea's back, his shoulders, his upturned palm and once – for at least ten seconds and while he was still wearing his steel-shod boots – on his head. And not once had Andrea protested or stumbled or yielded an inch. The man was indestructible, as tough and enduring as the rock on which he stood. Since dusk had fallen that evening, Andrea had laboured unceasingly, done enough work to kill two ordinary men, and, looking at him then, Mallory realised, almost with despair, that even now he didn't look particularly tired.

Mallory gestured at the rock chimney, then upwards at its shadowy mouth limned in blurred rectangular outline against the pale glimmer of the sky. He leant forward, mouth close to Andrea's ear.

'Twenty feet, Andrea,' he said softly. His breath was still coming in painful gasps. 'It'll be no bother – it's fissured on my side and the chances are that it goes up to the top.'

Andrea looked up the chimney speculatively, nodded in silence.

'Better with your boots off,' Mallory went on. 'And any spikes we use we'll work in by hand.'

'Even on a night like this – high winds and rain, cold and black as a pig's inside – and on a cliff like this?' There was neither doubt nor question in Andrea's voice: rather it was acquiescence, unspoken confirmation of an unspoken thought. They had been so long together, had reached such a depth of understanding that words between them were largely superfluous.

Mallory nodded, waited while Andrea worked home a spike, looped his ropes over it and secured what was left of the long ball of twine that stretched four hundred feet below to the ledge where the others waited. Andrea then removed boots and spikes, fastening them to the ropes, eased the slender, double-edged throwing-knife in its leather shoulder scabbard, looked across at Mallory and nodded in turn.

The first ten feet were easy. Palms and back against one side of the chimney and stocking-soled feet against the other, Mallory jack-knifed his way upwards until the widening sheer of the walls defeated him. Legs braced against the far wall, he worked in a spike as far up as he could reach, grasped it with both hands, dropped his legs across and found a toe-hold in the crevice. Two minutes later his hands hooked over the crumbling edge of the precipice.

Noiselessly and with an infinite caution he fingered aside earth and grass and tiny pebbles until his hands were locked on the solid rock itself, bent his knee to seek lodgment for the final toe-hold, then eased a wary head above the cliff-top, a movement imperceptible in its slow-motion, millimetric stealth. He stopped moving altogether as soon as his eyes had cleared the level of the cliff, stared out into the unfamiliar darkness, his whole being, the entire field of consciousness, concentrated into his eyes and his ears. Illogically, and for the first time in all that terrifying ascent, he became acutely aware of his own danger and helplessness, and he cursed himself for his folly in not borrowing Miller's silenced automatic.

The darkness below the high horizon of the lifting hills beyond was just one degree less than absolute: shapes and angles, heights and depressions were resolving themselves in nebulous silhouette, contours and shadowy profiles emerging reluctantly from the darkness, a darkness suddenly no longer vague and unfamiliar but disturbingly reminiscent in what it revealed, clamouring for recognition. And then abruptly, almost with a sense of shock, Mallory had it. The cliff-top before his eyes was exactly as Monsieur Vlachos had drawn and described it – the narrow, bare strip of ground running parallel to the cliff, the jumble of huge boulders behind them and then, beyond these, the steep scree-strewn lower slopes of the mountains. The first break they'd had yet, Mallory thought exultantly – but what a break! The sketchiest navigation but the most incredible luck, right bang on the nose of the targe – the highest point of the highest, most precipitous cliffs in Navarone: the one place where the Germans never mounted a guard, because the climb was impossible! Mallory felt the relief, the high elation wash through him in waves. Jubilantly he straightened his leg, hoisted himself half-way over the edge, arms straight, palms down on the top of the cliff. And then he froze into immobility, petrified as the solid rock beneath his hands, his heart thudding painfully in his throat.

One of the boulders had moved. Seven, maybe eight yards away, a shadow had gradually straightened, detached itself stealthily from the surrounding rock, was advancing slowly towards the edge of the cliff. And then the shadow was no longer 'it'. There could be no mistake now – the long jack-boots, the long greatcoat beneath the waterproof cape, the close-fitting helmet were all too familiar. Damn Vlachos! Damn Jensen! Damn all the know-alls who sat at home, the pundits of Intelligence who gave a man wrong information and sent him out to die. And in the same instant Mallory damned himself for his own carelessness, for he had been expecting this all along.

For the first two or three seconds Mallory had lain rigid and unmoving, temporarily paralysed in mind and body: already the guard had advanced four or five steps, carbine held in readiness before him, head turned sideways as he listened into the high, thin whine of the wind and the deep and distant booming of the surf below, trying to isolate the sound that had aroused his suspicions. But now the first shock was over and Mallory's mind was working again. To go up on to the top of the cliff would be suicidal: ten to one the guard would hear him scrambling over the edge and shoot him out of hand: and if he did get up he had neither the weapons nor, after the exhausting climb, the strength to tackle an armed, fresh man. He would have to go back down. But he would have to slide down slowly, an inch at a time. At night, Mallory knew, side vision is even more acute than direct, and the guard might catch a sudden movement out of the corner of his eye. And then he would only have to turn his head and that would be the end: even in that darkness, Mallory realised, there could be no mistaking the bulk of his silhouette against the sharp line of the edge of the cliff.

Gradually, every movement as smooth and controlled as possible, every soft and soundless breath a silent prayer, Mallory slipped gradually back over the edge of the cliff. Still the guard advanced, making for a point about five yards to Mallory's left, but still he looked away, his ear turned into the wind. And then Mallory was down, only his finger-tips over the top, and Andrea's great bulk was beside him, his mouth to his ear.

'What is it? Somebody there?'

'A sentry,' Mallory whispered back. His arms were beginning to ache from the strain. 'He's heard something and he's looking for us.'

Suddenly he shrank away from Andrea, pressed himself as closely as possible to the face of the cliff, was vaguely aware of Andrea doing the same thing. A beam of light, hurtful and dazzling to eyes so long accustomed to the dark, had suddenly stabbed out at an angle over the edge of the cliff, was moving slowly along towards them. The German had his torch out, was methodically examining the rim of the cliff. From the angle of the beam, Mallory judged that he was walking along about a couple of feet from the edge. On that wild and gusty night he was taking no chances on the crumbly, treacherous top-soil of the cliff: even more likely, he was taking no chances on a pair of sudden hands reaching out for his ankles and jerking him to a mangled death on the rocks and reefs four hundred feet below.

Slowly, inexorably, the beam approached. Even at that slant, it was bound to catch them. With a sudden sick certainty Mallory realised that the German wasn't just suspicious: he *knew* there was someone there, and he wouldn't stop looking until he found them. And there was nothing they could do, just nothing at all... Then Andrea's head was close to his again.

'A stone,' Andrea whispered. 'Over there, behind him.'

Cautiously at first, then frantically, Mallory pawed the cliff-top with his right hand. Earth, only earth, grass roots and tiny pebbles – there was nothing even half the size of a marble. And then Andrea was thrusting something against him and his hand closed over the metallic smoothness of a spike: even in that moment of desperate urgency, with the slender, searching beam only feet away, Mallory was conscious of a sudden brief anger with himself – he had still a couple of spikes stuck in his belt and had forgotten all about them.

His arm swung back, jerked convulsively forward, sent the spike spinning away into the darkness. One second passed, then another, he knew he had missed, the beam was only inches from Andrea's shoulders, and then the metallic clatter of the spike striking a boulder fell upon his ear like a benison. The beam wavered for a second, stabbed out aimlessly into the darkness and then whipped round, probing into the boulders to the left. And then the sentry was running towards them, slipping and stumbling in his haste, the barrel of the carbine gleaming in the light of the torch held clamped to it. He'd gone less than ten yards when Andrea was over the top of the cliff like a great, black cat, was padding noiselessly across the ground to the shelter of the nearest boulder. Wraith-like, he flitted in behind it and was gone, a shadow long among shadows.

The sentry was about twenty yards away now, the beam of his torch darting fearfully from boulder to boulder when Andrea struck the haft of his knife against a rock, twice. The sentry whirled round, torch shining along the line of the boulders, then started to run clumsily back again, the skirts of the greatcoat fluttering grotesquely in the wind. The torch was swinging wildly now, and Mallory caught a glimpse of a white, straining face, wide-eyed and fearful, incongruously at variance with the gladiatorial strength of the steel helmet above. God only knew, Mallory thought, what wild and panic-stricken thoughts were passing through his confused mind: noises from the cliff-top, metallic sound from either side among the boulders, the long, eerie vigil, afraid and companionless, on a deserted cliff edge on a dark and tempest-filled night in a hostile land – suddenly Mallory felt a deep stab of compassion for this man, a man like himself, someone's well-loved husband or brother or son who was only doing a dirty and dangerous job as best he could and because he was told to, compassion for his loneliness and his anxieties and his fears, for the sure knowledge that before he had drawn breath another three times he would be dead.... Slowly, gauging his time and distance, Mallory raised his head.

'Help!' he shouted. 'Help me! I'm falling!'

The soldier checked in mid-stride and spun round, less than five feet from the rock that hid Andrea. For a second the beam of his torch waved wildly around, then settled on Mallory's head. For another moment he stood stock still then the carbine in his right hand swung up, the left hand reached down for the barrel. Then he grunted once, a violent and convulsive exhalation of breath, and the thud of the hilt of Andrea's knife striking home against the ribs carried clearly to Mallory's ears, even against the wind....

Mallory stared down at the dead man, at Andrea's impassive face as he wiped the blade of his knife on the greatcoat, rose slowly to his feet, sighed and slid the knife back in its scabbard.

'So, my Keith!' Andrea reserved the punctilious 'Captain' for company only. 'This is why our young lieutenant eats his heart out down below.'

'That is why,' Mallory acknowledged. 'I knew it – or I almost knew it. So did you. Too many coincidences – the German caique investigating, the trouble at the watchtower – and now this.' Mallory swore, softly and bitterly. 'This is the end for our friend Captain Briggs of Castelrosso. He'll be cashiered within the month. Jensen will make certain of that.'

Andrea nodded.

'He let Nicolai go?'

'Who else could have known that we were to have landed here, tipped off everyone along the line?' Mallory paused, dismissed the thought, caught Andrea by the arm. 'The Germans are thorough. Even although they must know it's almost an impossibility to land on a night like this, they'll have a dozen sentries scattered along the cliffs.' Unconsciously Mallory had lowered his voice. 'But they wouldn't depend on one man to cope with five. So – '

'Signals,' Andrea finished for him. 'They must have some way of letting the others know. Perhaps flares – '

'No, not that,' Mallory disagreed. 'Give their position away. Telephone. It has to be that. Remember how they were in Crete – miles of field telephone wire all over the shop?'

Andrea nodded, picked up the dead man's torch, hooded it in his huge hand and started searching. He returned in less than a minute.

'Telephone it is,' he announced softly. 'Over there, under the rocks.'

'Nothing we can do about it,' Mallory said. 'If it does ring, I'll have to answer or they'll come hot-footing along. I only hope to heaven they haven't got a bloody password. It would be just like them.'

He turned away, stopped suddenly.

'But someone's got to come sometime – a relief, sergeant of the guard, something like that. Probably he's supposed to make an hourly report. Someone's bound to come – and come soon. My God, Andrea, we'll have to make it fast!'

'And this poor devil?' Andrea gestured to the huddled shadow at his feet.

'Over the side with him.' Mallory grimaced in distaste. 'Won't make any difference to the poor bastard now, and we can't leave any traces. The odds are they'll think he's gone over the edge – this top soil's as crumbly and treacherous as hell... You might see if he's any papers on him – never know how useful they might be.'

'Not half as useful as these boots on his feet.' Andrea waved a large hand towards the scree-strewn slopes. 'You are not going to walk very far there in your stocking soles.'

Five minutes later Mallory tugged three times on the string that stretched down into the darkness below. Three answering tugs came from the ledge, and then the cord vanished rapidly down over the edge of the overhang, drawing with it the long, steel-cored rope that Mallory paid out from the coil on the top of the cliff.

The box of explosives was the first of the gear to come up. The weighted rope plummeted straight down from the point of the overhang, and padded though the box was on every side with lashed rucksacks and sleeping-bags it still crashed terrifyingly against the cliff on the inner arc of every wind-driven swing of the pendulum. But there was no time for finesse, to wait for the diminishing swing of the pendulum after each tug. Securely anchored to a rope that stretched around the base of a great boulder, Andrea leaned far out over the edge of the precipice and reeled in the seventy-pound deadweight as another man would a trout. In less than three minutes the ammunition box lay beside him on the cliff-top; five minutes later the firing generator, guns and pistols, wrapped in a couple of other sleeping-bags and their lightweight, reversible tent – white on one side, brown and green camouflage on the other – lay beside the explosives.

A third time the rope went down into the rain and the darkness, a third time the tireless Andrea hauled it in, hand over hand. Mallory was behind him, coiling in the slack of the rope, when he heard Andrea's sudden exclamation: two quick strides and he was at the edge of the cliff, his hand on the big Greek's arm.

'What's up, Andrea? Why have you stopped – ?'

He broke off, peered through the gloom at the rope in Andrea's hand, saw that it was being held between only finger and thumb. Twice Andrea jerked the rope up a foot or two, let it fall again: the weightless rope swayed wildly in the wind.

'Gone?' Mallory asked quietly.

Andrea nodded without speaking.

'Broken?' Mallory was incredulous. 'A wire-cored rope?'

'I don't think so.' Quickly Andrea reeled in the remaining forty feet. The twine was still attached to the same place, about a fathom from the end. The rope was intact.

'Somebody tied a knot.' Just for a moment the giant's voice sounded tired. 'They didn't tie it too well.'

Mallory made to speak, then flung up an instinctive arm as a great, forked tongue of flame streaked between the cliff-top and unseen clouds above. Their cringing eyes were still screwed tight shut, their nostrils full of the acrid, sulphurous smell of burning, when the first volley of thunder crashed in Titan fury almost directly overhead, a deafening artillery to mock the pitiful efforts of embattled man, doubly terrifying in the total darkness that followed that searing flash. Gradually the echoes pealed and faded inland in diminishing reverberations, were lost among the valleys of the hills.

'My God!' Mallory murmured. 'That was close. We'd better make it fast, Andrea – this cliff is liable to be lit up like a fairground any minute... What was in that last load you were bringing up?' He didn't really have to ask – he himself had arranged for the breaking up of the equipment into three separate loads before he'd left the ledge. It wasn't even that he suspected his tired mind of playing tricks on him; but it was tired enough, too tired, to probe the hidden compulsion, the nameless hope that prompted him to grasp at nameless straws that didn't even exist.

'The food,' Andrea said gently. 'All the food, the stove, the fuel – and the compasses.'

For five, perhaps ten seconds, Mallory stood motionless. One half of his mind, conscious of the urgency, the desperate need for haste, was jabbing him mercilessly: the other half held him momentarily in a vast irresolution, an irresolution of coldness and numbness that came not from the lashing wind and sleety rain but from his own mind, from the bleak and comfortless imaginings of lost wanderings on that harsh and hostile island, with neither food nor fire.... And then Andrea's great hand was on his shoulder, and he was laughing softly.

'Just so much less to carry, my Keith. Think how grateful our tired friend Corporal Miller is going to be... This is only a little thing.'

'Yes,' Mallory said. 'Yes, of course. A little thing.' He turned abruptly, tugged the cord, watched the rope disappear over the edge.

Fifteen minutes later, in drenching, torrential rain, a great, sheeting downpour almost constantly illuminated by the jagged, branching stilettos of the forked lightning, Casey Brown's bedraggled head came into view over the edge of the cliff. The thunder, too, emptily cavernous in that flat and explosive intensity of sound that lies at the heart of a thunderstorm, was almost continuous: but in the brief intervals, Casey's voice, rich in his native Clydeside accent, carried clearly. He was expressing himself fluently in basic Anglo-Saxon, and with cause. He had had the assistance of two ropes on the way up – the one stretched from spike to spike and the one used for raising supplies, which Andrea had kept pulling in as he made the ascent. Casey Brown had secured the end of this round his waist with a bowline, but the bowline had proved to be nothing of the sort but a slip-knot, and Andrea's enthusiastic help had almost cut him in half. He was still sitting on the cliff-top, exhausted head between his knees, the radio still strapped to his back, when two tugs on Andrea's rope announced that Dusty Miller was on his way up.

Another quarter of an hour elapsed, an interminable fifteen minutes when, in the lulls between the thunderclaps, every slightest sound was an approaching enemy patrol, before Miller materialised slowly out of the darkness, halfway down the rock chimney. He was climbing steadily and methodically, then checked abruptly at the cliff-top, groping hands pawing uncertainly on the top-soil of the cliff. Puzzled, Mallory bent down, peered into the lean face: both the eyes were clamped tightly shut.

'Relax, Corporal,' Mallory advised kindly. 'You have arrived.'

Dusty Miller slowly opened his eyes, peered round at the edge of the cliff, shuddered and crawled quickly on hands and knees to the shelter of the nearest boulders. Mallory followed and looked down at him curiously.

'What was the idea of closing your eyes coming over the top?'

'I did not,' Miller protested.

Mallory said nothing.

'I closed them at the bottom,' Miller explained wearily. 'I opened them at the top.'

Mallory looked at him incredulously.

'What! All the way?'

'It's like I told you, boss,' Miller complained. 'Back in Castelrosso. When I cross a street and step up on to the sidewalk I gotta hang on to the nearest lamp-post. More or less.' He broke off, looked at Andrea leaning far out over the side of the cliff, and shivered again. 'Brother! Oh, brother! Was I scared!'

Fear. Terror. Panic. Do the thing you fear and the death of fear is certain. Do the thing you fear and the death of fear is certain. Once, twice, a hundred times, Andy Stevens repeated the words to himself, over and over again, like a litany. A psychiatrist had told him that once and he'd read it a dozen times since. Do the thing you fear and the death of fear is certain. The mind is a limited thing, they had said. It can only hold one thought at a time, one impulse to action. Say to yourself, I am brave, I am overcoming this fear, this stupid, unreasoning panic which has no origin except in my own mind, and because the mind *can* only hold one thought at a time, and because thinking and feeling are one, then you *will* be brave, you *will* overcome and the fear will vanish like a shadow in the night. And so Andy Stevens said these things to himself, and the shadows only lengthened and deepened, lengthened and deepened, and the icy claws of fear dug ever more savagely into his dull exhausted mind, into his twisted, knotted stomach.

His stomach. That knotted ball of jangled, writhing nerve-ends beneath the solar plexus. No one could ever know how it was, how it felt, except those whose shredded minds were going, collapsing into complete and final breakdown. The waves of panic and nausea and faintness that flooded up through a suffocating throat to a mind dark and spent and sinewless, a mind fighting with woollen fingers to cling on to the edge of the abyss, a tired and lacerated mind, only momentarily in control, wildly rejecting the clamorous demands of a nervous system, which had already taken far too much, that he should let

106

go, open the torn fingers that were clenched so tightly round the rope. It was just that easy. 'Rest after toil, port after stormy seas.' What was that famous stanza of Spenser's? Sobbing aloud, Stevens wrenched out another spike, sent it spinning into the waiting sea three hundred long feet below, pressed himself closely into the face and inched his way despairingly upwards.

Fear. Fear had been at his elbow all his life, his constant companion, his *alter ego*, at his elbow, or in close prospect or immediate recall. He had become accustomed to that fear, at times almost reconciled, but the sick agony of this night lay far beyond either tolerance or familiarity. He had never known anything like this before, and even in his terror and confusion he was dimly aware that the fear did not spring from the climb itself. True, the cliff was sheer and almost vertical, and the lightning, the ice-cold rain, the darkness and the bellowing thunder were a waking nightmare. But the climb, technically, was simple: the rope stretched all the way to the top and all he had to do was to follow it and dispose of the spikes as he went. He was sick and bruised and terribly tired, his head ached abominably and he had lost a great deal of blood: but then, more often than not, it is in the darkness of agony and exhaustion that the spirit of man burns most brightly.

Andy Stevens was afraid because his self-respect was gone. Always before, that had been his sheet anchor, had tipped the balance against his ancient enemy – the respect in which other men had held him, the respect he had had for himself. But now these were gone, for his two greatest fears had been realised – he was known to be afraid, he had failed his fellow-man. Both in the fight with the German caique and when anchored above the watch-tower in the creek, he had known that Mallory and Andrea knew. He had never met such men before, and he had known all along that he could never hide his secrets from such men. He should have gone up that cliff with Mallory, but Mallory had made excuses and taken Andrea instead – Mallory *knew* he was afraid. And twice before, in Castelrosso and when the German boat had closed in on them, he had almost failed his friends – and tonight he had failed them terribly. He had not been thought fit to lead the way with Mallory – and it was he, the sailor of the party, who had made such a botch of tying that last knot, had lost all the food and the fuel that had plummeted into the sea a bare ten feet from where he had stood on the ledge... and a thousand men on Kheros were depending on a failure so abject as himself. Sick and spent, spent in mind and body and spirit, moaning aloud in his anguish of fear and self-loathing, and not knowing where one finished and the other began, Andy Stevens climbed blindly on.

The sharp, high-pitched call-up buzz of the telephone cut abruptly through the darkness on the cliff-top. Mallory stiffened and half-turned, hands clenching involuntarily. Again it buzzed, the jarring stridency carrying clearly above the bass rumble of the thunder, fell silent again. And then it buzzed again and kept on buzzing, peremptory in its harsh insistence.

Mallory was half-way towards it when he checked in mid-step, turned slowly round and walked back towards Andrea. The big Greek looked at him curiously.

'You have changed your mind?'

Mallory nodded but said nothing.

'They will keep on ringing until they get an answer,' Andrea murmured. 'And when they get no answer, they will come. They will come quickly and soon.'

'I know, I know.' Mallory shrugged. 'We have to take that chance – certainty rather. The question is – how long will it be before anyone turns up.' Instinctively he looked both ways along the windswept cliff-top: Miller and Brown were posted one on either side about fifty yards away, lost in the darkness. 'It's not worth the risk. The more I think of it, the poorer I think my chances would be

108

of getting away with it. In matters of routine the old Hun tends to be an inflexible sort of character. There's probably a set way of answering the phone, or the sentry has to identify himself by name, or there's a password – or maybe my voice would give me away. On the other hand the sentry's gone without trace, all our gear is up and so's everyone except Stevens. In other words, we've practically made it. We've landed – and nobody knows we're here.'

'Yes.' Andrea nodded slowly. 'Yes, you are right – and Stevens should be up in two or three minutes. It would be foolish to throw away everything we've gained.' He paused, then went on quietly: 'But they are going to come running.' The phone stopped ringing as suddenly as it had started. 'They are going to come now.'

'I know. I hope to hell Stevens...' Mallory broke off, spun on his heel, said over his shoulder, 'Keep your eye open for him, will you? I'll warn the others we're expecting company.'

Mallory moved quickly along the cliff-top, keeping well away from the edge. He hobbled rather than walked – the sentry's boots were too small for him and chafed his toes cruelly. Deliberately he closed his mind to the thought of how his feet would be after a few hours' walking over rough territory in these boots: time enough for the reality, he thought grimly, without the added burden of anticipation... He stopped abruptly as something hard and metallic pushed into the small of his back.

'Surrender or die!' The drawling, nasal voice was positively cheerful: after what he had been through on the caique and the cliff face, just to set feet on solid ground again was heaven enough for Dusty Miller.

'Very funny,' Mallory growled. 'Very funny indeed.' He looked curiously at Miller. The American had removed his oilskin cape – the rain had ceased as abruptly as it had come – to reveal a jacket and braided waistcoat even more sodden and saturated than his trousers. It didn't make sense. But there was no time for questions.

'Did you hear the phone ringing just now?' he asked.

'Was that what it was? Yeah, I heard it.'

'The sentry's phone. His hourly report, or whatever it was, must have been overdue. We didn't answer it. They'll be hot-footing along any minute now, suspicious as hell and looking for trouble. Maybe your side, maybe Brown's. Can't approach any other way unless they break their necks climbing over these boulders.' Mallory gestured at the shapeless jumble of rocks behind them. 'So keep your eyes skinned.'

'I'll do that, boss. No shootin', huh?'

'No shooting. Just get back as quickly and quietly as you can and let us know. Come back in five minutes anyway.'

Mallory hurried away, retracing his steps. Andrea was stretched full length on the cliff-top, peering over the edge. He twisted his head round as Mallory approached.

'I can hear him. He's just at the overhang.'

'Good.' Mallory moved on without breaking step. 'Tell him to hurry, please.'

Ten yards farther on Mallory checked, peered into the gloom ahead. Somebody was coming along the cliff-top at a dead run, stumbling and slipping on the loose gravelly soil.

'Brown?' Mallory called softly.

'Yes, sir. It's me.' Brown was up to him now, breathing heavily, pointing back in the direction he had just come. 'Somebody's coming, and coming fast! Torches waving and jumping all over the place – must be running.'

'How many?' Mallory asked quickly.

'Four or five at least.' Brown was still gasping for breath. 'Maybe more – four or five torches, anyway. You can see them for yourself.' Again he pointed backwards, then blinked in puzzlement. 'That's bloody funny! They're all gone.' He turned back swiftly to Mallory. 'But I can swear – '

'Don't worry,' Mallory said grimly. 'You saw them all

110

right. I've been expecting visitors. They're getting close now and taking no chances... How far away?'

'Hundred yards – not more than a hundred and fifty.'

'Go and get Miller. Tell him to get back here fast.'

Mallory ran back along the cliff edge and knelt beside the huge length of Andrea.

'They're coming, Andrea,' he said quickly. 'From the left. At least five, probably more. Two minutes at the most. Where's Stevens? Can you see him?'

'I can see him.' Andrea was magnificently unperturbed. 'He is just past the overhang...' The rest of his words were lost, drowned in a sudden, violent thunderclap, but there was no need for more. Mallory could see Stevens now, climbing up the rope, strangely old and enfeebled in action, hand over hand in paralysing slowness, half-way now between the overhang and the foot of the chimney.

'Good God!' Mallory swore. 'What's the matter with him? He's going to take all day...' He checked himself, cupped his hands to his mouth. 'Stevens! Stevens!' But there was no sign that Stevens had heard. He still kept climbing with the same unnatural over-deliberation, a robot in slow motion.

'He is very near the end,' Andrea said quietly. 'You see he does not even lift his head. When a climber does not lift his head, he is finished.' He stirred. 'I will go down for him.'

'No.' Mallory's hand was on his shoulder. 'Stay here. I can't risk you both... Yes, what is it?' He was aware that Brown was back, bending over him, his breath coming in great heaving gasps.

'Hurry, sir, hurry, for God's sake!' A few brief words but he had to suck in two huge gulps of air to get them out. 'They're on top of us!'

'Get back to the rocks with Miller,' Mallory said urgently. 'Cover us... Stevens! Stevens!' But again the wind swept up the face of the cliff, carried his words away.

'Stevens! For God's sake, man! Stevens!' His voice was

low-pitched, desperate, but this time some quality in it must have reached through Stevens's fog of exhaustion and touched his consciousness, for he stopped climbing and lifted his head, hand cupped to his ear.

'Some Germans coming!' Mallory called through funnelled hands, as loudly as he dared. 'Get to the foot of the chimney and stay there. Don't make a sound. Understand?'

Stevens lifted his hand, gestured in tired acknowledgment, lowered his head, started to climb up again. He was going even more slowly now, his movements fumbling and clumsy.

'Do you think he understands?' Andrea was troubled.

'I think so. I don't know.' Mallory stiffened and caught Andrea's arm. It was beginning to rain again, not heavily yet, and through the drizzle he'd caught sight of a hooded torch beam probing among the rocks thirty yards away to his left. 'Over the edge with the rope,' he whispered. 'The spike at the bottom of the chimney will hold it. Come on – let's get out of here!'

Gradually, meticulous in their care not to dislodge the smallest pebble, Mallory and Andrea inched back from the edge, squirmed round and headed back for the rocks, pulling themselves along on their elbows and knees. The few yards were interminable and without even a gun in his hand Mallory felt defenceless, completely exposed. An illogical feeling, he knew, for the first beam of light to fall on them meant the end not for them but for the man who held the torch. Mallory had complete faith in Brown and Miller... That wasn't important. What mattered was the complete escape from detection. Twice during the last endless few feet a wandering beam reached out towards them, the second a bare arm's length away: both times they pressed their faces into the sodden earth, lest the pale blur of their faces betray them, and lay very still. And then, all at once it seemed, they were among the rocks and safe.

112

In a moment Miller was beside them, a half-seen shadow against the darker dusk of the rocks around them.

'Plenty of time, plenty of time,' he whispered sarcastically. 'Why didn't you wait another half-hour?' He gestured to the left, where the flickering of torches, the now clearly audible murmur of guttural voices, were scarcely twenty yards away. 'We'd better move farther back. They're looking for him among the rocks.'

'For him or for his telephone,' Mallory murmured in agreement. 'You're right anyway. Watch your guns on these rocks. Take the gear with you... And if they look over and find Stevens we'll have to take the lot. No time for fancy work and to hell with the noise. Use the automatic carbines.'

Andy Stevens had heard, but he had not understood. It was not that he panicked, was too terrified to understand, for he was no longer afraid. Fear is of the mind, but his mind had ceased to function, drugged by the last stages of exhaustion, crushed by the utter, damnable tiredness that held his limbs, his whole body, in leaden thrall. He did not know it, but fifty feet below he had struck his head against a spur of rock, a sharp, wicked projection that had torn his gaping temple wound open to the bone. His strength drained out with the pulsing blood.

He had heard Mallory, had heard something about the chimney he had now reached, but his mind had failed to register the meaning of the words. All that Stevens knew was that he was climbing, and that one always kept on climbing until one reached the top. That was what his father had always impressed upon him, his brothers too. You must reach the top.

He was half-way up the chimney now, resting on the spike that Mallory had driven into the fissure. He hooked his fingers in the crack, bent back his head and stared up towards the mouth of the chimney. Ten feet away, no more. He was conscious of neither surprise nor elation. It was just there: he had to reach it. He could hear voices, carrying clearly from the top. He was vaguely surprised that his friends were making no attempt to help him, that they had thrown away the rope that would have made those last few feet so easy, but he felt no bitterness, no emotion at all: perhaps they were trying to test him. What did it matter anyway – he had to reach the top.

He reached the top. Carefully, as Mallory had done before him, he pushed aside the earth and tiny pebbles, hooked his fingers over the edge, found the same toe-hold as Mallory had and levered himself upwards. He saw the flickering torches, heard the excited voices, and then for an instant the curtain of fog in his mind lifted and a last tidal wave of fear washed over him and he knew that the voices were the voices of the enemy and that they had destroyed his friends. He knew now that he was alone, that he had failed, that this was the end, one way or another, and that it had all been for nothing. And then the fog closed over him again, and there was nothing but the emptiness of it all, the emptiness and the futility, the overwhelming lassitude and despair and his body slowly sinking down the face of the cliff. And then the hooked fingers – they, too, were slipping away, opening gradually, reluctantly as the fingers of a drowning man releasing their final hold on a spar of wood. There was no fear now, only a vast and heedless indifference as his hands slipped away and he fell like a stone, twenty vertical feet into the cradling bottle-neck at the foot of the chimney.

He himself made no sound, none at all: the soundless scream of agony never passed his lips, for the blackness came with the pain: but the straining ears of the men crouching in the rocks above caught clearly the dull, sickening crack as his right leg fractured cleanly in two, snapping like a rotten bough.

CHAPTER 6

Monday Night

0200–0600

The German patrol was everything that Mallory had feared – efficient, thorough and very, very painstaking. It even had imagination, in the person of its young and competent sergeant, and that was more dangerous still.

There were only four of them, in high boots, helmets and green, grey and brown mottled capes. First of all they located the telephone and reported to base. Then the young sergeant sent two men to search another hundred yards or so along the cliff, while he and the fourth soldier probed among the rocks that paralleled the cliff. The search was slow and careful, but the two men did not penetrate very far into the rocks. To Mallory, the sergeant's reasoning was obvious and logical. If the sentry had gone to sleep or taken ill, it was unlikely that he would have gone far in among that confused jumble of boulders. Mallory and the others were safely back beyond their reach.

And then came what Mallory had feared – an organised, methodical inspection of the cliff-top itself: worse still, it began with a search along the very edge. Securely held by his three men with interlinked arms – the last with a hand hooked round his belt – the sergeant walked slowly along the rim, probing every inch with the spot-lit beam of a powerful torch. Suddenly he stopped short, exclaimed suddenly and stooped, torch and face only inches from the ground. There was no question as to what he had found – the deep gouge made in the soft, crumbling soil by the climbing rope that had been belayed round the boulder and gone over the edge of the cliff... Softly, silently, Mallory and his three companions straightened to their knees or to their feet, gun barrels lining along the tops of boulders or peering out between cracks in the rocks. There was no doubt in any of their minds that Stevens was lying there helplessly in the crutch of the chimney, seriously injured or dead. It needed only one German carbine to point down that cliff face, however carelessly, and these four men would die. They would have to die.

The sergeant was stretched out his length now, two men holding his legs. His head and shoulders were over the edge of the cliff, the beam from his torch stabbing down the chimney. For ten, perhaps fifteen seconds, there was no sound on the cliff-top, no sound at all, only the high, keening moan of the wind and the swish of the rain in the stunted grass. And then the sergeant had wriggled back and risen to his feet, slowly shaking his head. Mallory gestured to the others to sink down behind the boulders again, but even so the sergeant's soft Bavarian voice carried clearly in the wind.

'It's Ehrich all right, poor fellow.' Compassion and anger blended curiously in the voice. 'I warned him often enough about his carelessness, about going too near the edge of that cliff. It is very treacherous.' Instinctively the sergeant stepped back a couple of feet and looked again at the gouge in the soft earth. 'That's where his heel slipped – or maybe the butt of his carbine. Not that it matters now.'

'Is he dead, do you think, Sergeant?' The speaker was only a boy, nervous and unhappy.

'It's hard to say... Look for yourself.'

Gingerly the youth lay down on the cliff-top, peering cautiously over the lip of the rock. The other soldiers were talking among themselves, in short staccato sentences when Mallory turned to Miller, cupped his hands to his mouth and the American's ear. He could contain his puzzlement no longer.

'Was Stevens wearing his dark suit when you left him?' he whispered.

116

'Yeah,' Miller whispered back. 'Yeah, I think he was.' A pause. 'No dammit, I'm wrong. We both put on our rubber camouflage capes about the same time.'

Mallory nodded. The waterproofs of the Germans were almost identical with their own: and the sentry's hair, Mallory remembered had been jet black – the same colour as Stevens's dyed hair. Probably all that was visible from above was a crumpled, cape-shrouded figure and a dark head. The sergeant's mistake in identity was more than understandable: it was inevitable.

The young soldier eased himself back from the edge of the cliff and hoisted himself carefully to his feet.

'You're right, Sergeant. It *is* Ehrich.' The boy's voice was unsteady. 'He's alive, I think. I saw his cape move, just a little. It wasn't the wind, I'm sure of that.'

Mallory felt Andrea's massive hand squeezing his arm, felt the quick surge of relief, then elation, wash through him. So Stevens *was* alive! Thank God for that! They'd save the boy yet. He heard Andrea whispering the news to the others, then grinned wryly to himself, ironic at his own gladness. Jensen definitely would not have approved of this jubilation. Stevens had already done his part, navigated the boat to Navarone, and climbed the cliff: and now he was only a crippled liability, would be a drag on the whole party, reduce what pitiful chances of success remained to them. For a High Command who pushed the counters around crippled pawns slowed up the whole game, made the board so damnably untidy. It was most inconsiderate of Stevens not to have killed himself so that they could have disposed of him neatly and without trace in the deep and hungry waters that boomed around the foot of the cliff... Mallory clenched his hands in the darkness and swore to himself that the boy would live, come home again, and to hell with total war and all its inhuman demands... Just a kid, that was all, a scared and broken kid and the bravest of them all.

The young sergeant was issuing a string of orders to his

men, his voice quick, crisp and confident. A doctor, splints, rescue stretcher, anchored sheer-legs, ropes, spikes – the trained, well-ordered mind missed nothing. Mallory waited tensely, wondering how many men, if any, would be left on guard, for the guards would have to go and that would inevitably betray them. The question of their quick and silent disposal never entered his mind – a whisper in Andrea's ear and the guards would have no more chance than penned lambs against a marauding wolf. Less chance even than that – the lambs could always run and cry out before the darkness closed over them.

The sergeant solved the problem for them. The assured competence, the tough, unsentimental ruthlessness that made the German N.C.O. the best in the world gave Mallory the chance he never expected to have. He had just finished giving his orders when the young soldier touched him on the arm, then pointed over the edge.

'How about poor Ehrich, Sergeant?' he asked uncertainly. 'Shouldn't – don't you think one of us ought to stay with him?'

'And what could you do if you did stay – hold his hand?' the sergeant asked acidly. 'If he stirs and falls, then he falls, that's all, and it doesn't matter then if a hundred of us are standing up here watching him. Off you go, and don't forget the mallets and pegs to stay the sheer-legs.'

The three men turned and went off quickly to the east without another word. The sergeant walked over to the phone, reported briefly to someone, then set off in the opposite direction – to check the next guard post, Mallory guessed. He was still in sight, a dwindling blur in the darkness, when Mallory whispered to Brown and Miller to post themselves on guard again: and they could still hear the measured crunch of his firm footfalls on a patch of distant gravel as their belayed rope went snaking over the edge of the cliff, Andrea and Mallory sliding swiftly down even before it had stopped quivering.

Stevens, a huddled, twisted heap with a gashed and

bleeding cheek lying cruelly along a razor-sharp spur of rock, was still unconscious, breathing stertorously through his open mouth. Below the knee his right leg twisted upwards and outwards against the rock at an impossible angle. As gently as he could, braced against either side of the chimney and supported by Andrea, Mallory lifted and straightened the twisted limb. Twice, from the depths of the dark stupor of his unconsciousness, Stevens moaned in agony, but Mallory had no option but to carry on, his teeth clenched tight until his jaws ached. Then slowly, with infinite care, he rolled up the trouser leg, winced and screwed his eyes shut in momentary horror and nausea as he saw the dim whiteness of the shattered tibia sticking out through the torn and purply swollen flesh.

'Compound fracture, Andrea.' Gently his exploring fingers slid down the mangled leg, beneath the lip of the jackboot, stopped suddenly as something gave way beneath his feather touch. 'Oh, my God!' he murmured. 'Another break, just above the ankle. This boy is in a bad way. Andrea.'

'He is indeed,' Andrea said gravely. 'We can do nothing for him here?'

'Nothing. Just nothing. We'll have to get him up first.' Mallory straightened, gazed up bleakly at the perpendicular face of the chimney. 'Although how in the name of heaven – '

'I will take him up.' There was no suggestion in Andrea's voice either of desperate resolve or consciousness of the almost incredible effort involved. It was simply a statement of intention, the voice of a man who never questioned his ability to do what he said he would. 'If you will help me to raise him, to tie him to my back...'

'With his broken leg loose, dangling from a piece of skin and torn muscle?' Mallory protested. 'Stevens can't take much more. He'll die if we do this.'

'He'll die if we don't,' Andrea murmured.

119

Mallory stared down at Stevens for a long moment, then nodded heavily in the darkness.

'He'll die if we don't,' he echoed tiredly. 'Yes, we have to do this.' He pushed outwards from the rock, slid half a dozen feet down the rope and jammed a foot in the crutch of the chimney just below Stevens's body. He took a couple of turns of rope round his waist and looked up.

'Ready, Andrea?' he called softly.

'Ready.' Andrea stooped, hooked his great hands under Stevens's armpits and lifted slowly, powerfully, as Mallory pushed from below. Twice, three times before they had him up, the boy moaned deep down in his tortured throat, the long, quivering 'Aahs' of agony setting Mallory's teeth on edge: and then his dangling, twisted leg had passed from Mallory's reach and he was held close and cradled in Andrea's encircling arm, the rain-lashed, bleeding mask of a face lolling grotesquely backwards, forlorn and lifeless with the dead pathos of a broken doll. Seconds later Mallory was up beside them, expertly lashing Stevens's wrists together. He was swearing softly, as his numbed hands looped and tightened the rope, softly, bitterly, continuously, but he was quite unaware of this: he was aware only of the broken head that lolled stupidly against his shoulder, of the welling, rain-thinned blood that filmed the upturned face, of the hair above the gashed temple emerging darkly fair as the dye washed slowly out. Inferior bloody boot-blacking. Mallory thought savagely: Jensen shall know of this – it could cost a man's life. And then he became aware of his own thoughts and swore again, still more savagely and at himself this time, for the utter triviality of what he was thinking.

With both hands free – Stevens's bound arms were looped round his neck, his body lashed to his own – Andrea took less than thirty seconds to reach the top; if the dragging, one hundred and sixty pounds deadweight on his back made any difference to Andrea's climbing speed and power, Mallory couldn't detect it. The man's endurance was fantastic. Once, just once, as Andrea scrambled over the edge of the cliff, the broken leg caught on the rock, and the crucifying torture of it seared through the merciful shell of insensibility, forced a brief shriek of pain from his lips, a hoarse, bubbling whisper of sound all the more horrible for its muted agony. And then Andrea was standing upright and Mallory was behind him, cutting swiftly at the ropes that bound the two together.

'Straight into the rocks with him, Andrea, will you?' Mallory whispered. 'Wait for us at the first open space you come to.' Andrea nodded slowly and without raising his head, his hooded eyes bent over the boy in his arms, like a man sunk in thought. Sunk in thought or listening, and all unawares Mallory, too, found himself looking and listening into the thin, lost moaning of the wind, and there was nothing there, only the lifting, dying threnody and the chill of the rain hardening to an ice-cold sleet. He shivered, without knowing why, and listened again; then he shook himself angrily, turned abruptly towards the cliff face and started reeling in the rope. He had it all up, lying round his feet in a limp and rain-sodden tangle when he remembered about the spike still secured to the foot of the chimney, the hundreds of feet of rope suspended from it.

He was too tired and cold and depressed even to feel exasperated with himself. The sight of Stevens and the knowledge of how it was with the boy had affected him more than he knew. Moodily, almost, he kicked the rope over the side again, slid down the chimney, untied the second rope and sent the spike spinning out into the darkness. Less than ten minutes later, the wetly-coiled ropes over his shoulder, he led Miller and Brown into the dark confusion of the rocks.

They found Stevens lying under the lee of a huge boulder, less than a hundred yards inland, in a tiny, cleared space barely the size of a billiard table. An oilskin was spread beneath him on the sodden, gravelly earth, a camouflage cape covered most of his body: it was bitterly cold now, but the rock broke the force of the wind, sheltered the boy from the driving sleet. Andrea looked up as the three men dropped into the hollow and lowered their gear to the ground; already, Mallory could see, Andrea had rolled the trouser up beyond the knee and cut the heavy jackboot away from the mangled leg.

'Sufferin' Christ!' The words, half-oath, half-prayer, were torn involuntarily from Miller: even in the deep gloom the shattered leg looked ghastly. Now he dropped on one knee and stooped low over it. 'What a mess!' he murmured slowly. He looked up over his shoulder. 'We've gotta do something about that leg, boss, and we've no damned time to lose. This kid's a good candidate for the mortuary.'

'I know. We've got to save him, Dusty, we've just *got* to.' All at once this had become terribly important to Mallory. He dropped down on his knees. 'Let's have a look at him.'

Impatiently Miller waved him away.

'Leave this to me, boss.' There was a sureness, a sudden authority in his voice that held Mallory silent. 'The medicine pack, quick – and undo that tent.'

'You sure you can handle this?' God knew, Mallory thought, he didn't really doubt him – he was conscious only of gratitude, of a profound relief, but he felt he had to say something. 'How are you going – '

'Look, boss,' Miller said quietly. 'All my life I've worked with just three things – mines, tunnels and explosives. They're kinda tricky things, boss. I've seen hundreds of busted arms and legs – and fixed most of them myself.' He grinned wryly in the darkness. 'I was boss myself, then – just one of my privileges, I reckon.'

'Good enough!' Mallory clapped him on the shoulder. 'He's all yours, Dusty. But the tent!' Involuntarily he looked over his shoulder in the direction of the cliff. 'I mean – '

'You got me wrong, boss.' Miller's hands, steady and precise with the delicate certainty of a man who has spent a lifetime with high explosive, were busy with a swab and disinfectant. 'I wasn't fixin' on settin' up a base hospital. But we need tent-poles – splints for his legs.'

'Of course, of course. The poles. Never occurred to me for splints – and I've been thinking of nothing else for – '

'They're not too important, boss.' Miller had the medicine pack open now, rapidly selecting the items he wanted with the aid of a hooded torch. 'Morphine – that's the first thing, or this kid's goin' to die of shock. And then shelter, warmth, dry clothin' – '

'Warmth! Dry clothing!' Mallory interrupted incredulously. He looked down at the unconscious boy, remembering how Stevens had lost them the stove and all the fuel, and his mouth twisted in bitterness. His own executioner... 'Where in God's name are we going to find them?'

'I don't know, boss,' Miller said simply. 'But we gotta find them. And not just to lessen shock. With a leg like this and soaked to the skin, he's bound to get pneumonia. And then as much sulfa as that bloody great hole in his leg will take – one touch of sepsis in the state this kid's in...' His voice trailed away into silence.

Mallory rose to his feet.

'I reckon you're the boss.' It was a very creditable imitation of the American's drawl, and Miller looked up quickly, surprise melting into a tired smile, then looked away again. Mallory could hear the chatter of his teeth as he bent over Stevens, and sensed rather than saw that he was shivering violently, continuously, but oblivious to it all in his complete concentration on the job in hand. Miller's clothes, Mallory remembered again, were completely saturated: not for the first time, Mallory wondered how he had managed to get himself into such a state with a waterproof covering him.

'You fix him up. I'll find a place.' Mallory wasn't as confident as he felt: still, on the scree-strewn, volcanic slopes of these hills behind, there ought to be a fair chance of finding a rock shelter, if not a cave. Or there would have been in day-light: as it was they would just have to trust to luck to stumble on one.... He saw that Casey Brown, grey-faced with exhaustion and illness — the after-effects of carbon monoxide poisoning are slow to disappear — had risen unsteadily to his feet and was making for a gap between the rocks.

'Where are you going, Chief?'

'Back for the rest of the stuff, sir.'

'Are you sure you can manage?' Mallory peered at him closely. 'You don't look any too fit to me.'

'I don't feel it either,' Brown said frankly. He looked at Mallory. 'But with all respects, sir, I don't think you've seen yourself recently.'

'You have a point,' Mallory acknowledged. 'All right then, come on. I'll go with you.'

For the next ten minutes there was silence in the tiny clearing, a silence broken only by the murmurs of Miller and Andrea working over the shattered leg, and the moans of the injured man as he twisted and struggled feebly in his dark abyss of pain: then gradually the morphine took effect and the struggling lessened and died away altogether, and Miller was able to work rapidly, without fear of interruption. Andrea had an oilskin outstretched above them. It served a double purpose — it curtained off the sleet that swept round them from time to time and blanketed the pinpoint light of the rubber torch he held in his free hand. And then the leg was set and bandaged and as heavily splinted as possible and Miller was on his feet, straightening his aching back.

'Thank Gawd that's done,' he said wearily. He gestured at Stevens. 'I feel just the way that kid looks.' Suddenly he stiffened, stretched out a warning arm. 'I can hear something, Andrea,' he whispered.

124

Andrea laughed. 'It's only Brown coming back, my friend. He's been coming this way for over a minute now.'

'How do you know it's Brown?' Miller challenged. He felt vaguely annoyed with himself and unobtrusively shoved his ready automatic back into his pocket.

'Brown is a good man among rocks,' Andrea said gently; 'but he is tired. But Captain Mallory...' He shrugged. 'People call me "the big cat" I know, but among the mountains and rocks the captain is more than a cat. He is a ghost, and that was how men called him in Crete. You will know he is here when he touches you on the shoulder.'

Miller shivered in a sudden icy gust of sleet.

'I wish you people wouldn't creep around so much,' he complained. He looked up as Brown came round the corner of a boulder, slow with the shambling, stumbling gait of an exhausted man. 'Hi, there, Casey. How are things goin'?'

'Not too bad.' Brown murmured his thanks as Andrea took the box of explosives off his shoulder and lowered it easily to the ground. 'This is the last of the gear. Captain sent me back with it. We heard voices some way along the cliff. He's staying behind to see what they say when they find Stevens gone.' Wearily he sat down on top of the box. 'Maybe he'll get some idea of what they're going to do next, if anything.'

'Seems to me he could have left you there and carried that damned box back himself,' Miller growled. Disappointment in Mallory made him more outspoken than he'd meant to be. 'He's much better off than you are right now, and I think it's a bit bloody much...' He broke off and gasped in pain as Andrea's fingers caught his arm like giant steel pincers.

'It is not fair to talk like that, my friend,' Andrea said reproachfully. 'You forget, perhaps, that Brown here cannot talk or understand a word of German?'

Miller rubbed his bruised arm tenderly, shaking his head in slow self-anger and condemnation.

125

'Me and my big mouth,' he said ruefully. 'Always talkin' outa turn Miller, they call me. Your pardon, one and all... And what is next on the agenda, gentlemen?'

'Captain says we're to go straight on into the rocks and up the right shoulder of this hill here.' Brown jerked a thumb in the direction of the vague mass, dark and strangely foreboding, that towered above and beyond them. 'He'll catch us up within fifteen minutes or so.' He grinned tiredly at Miller. 'And we're to leave this box and a rucksack for him to carry.'

'Spare me,' Miller pleaded. 'I feel only six inches tall as it is.' He looked down at Stevens, lying quietly under the darkly gleaming wetness of the oilskins, then up at Andrea. 'I'm afraid, Andrea – '

'Of course, of course!' Andrea stooped quickly, wrapped the oilskins round the unconscious boy and rose to his feet, as effortlessly as if the oilskins had been empty.

'I'll lead the way,' Miller volunteered. 'Mebbe I can pick an easy path for you and young Stevens.' He swung generator and rucksacks on to his shoulder, staggering under the sudden weight; he hadn't realised he was so weak. 'At first, that is,' he amended. 'Later on, you'll have to carry us both.'

Mallory had badly miscalculated the time it would require to overtake the others; over an hour had elapsed since Brown had left him, and still there were no signs of the others. And with seventy pounds on his back, he wasn't making such good time himself.

It wasn't all his fault. The returning German patrol, after the first shock of discovery, had searched the cliff-top again, methodically and with exasperating slowness. Mallory had waited tensely for someone to suggest descending and examining the chimney – the gouge-marks of the spikes on the rock would have been a dead giveaway – but nobody even mentioned it. With the guard obviously fallen to his death, it would have been a pointless thing to do anyway. After an unrewarding search, they had debated for an unconscionable time as to what they should do next. Finally they had done nothing. A replacement guard was left, and the rest made off along the cliff, carrying their rescue equipment with them.

The three men ahead had made surprisingly good time, although the conditions, admittedly, were now much easier. The heavy fall of boulders at the foot of the slope had petered out after another fifty yards, giving way to broken scree and rain-washed rubble. Possibly he had passed them, but it seemed unlikely: in the intervals between these driving sleet showers – it was more like hail now – he was able to scan the bare shoulder of the hill, and nothing moved. Besides, he knew that Andrea wouldn't stop until he reached what promised at least a bare minimum of shelter, and as yet these exposed windswept slopes had offered nothing that even remotely approached that.

In the end, Mallory almost literally stumbled upon both men and shelter. He was negotiating a narrow, longitudinal spine of rock, had just crossed its razor-back, when he heard the murmur of voices beneath him and saw a tiny glimmer of light behind the canvas stretching down from the overhang of the far wall of the tiny ravine at his feet.

Miller started violently and swung round as he felt the hand on his shoulder; the automatic was half-way out of his pocket before he saw who it was and sank back heavily on the rock behind him.

'Come, come, now! Trigger-happy.' Thankfully Mallory slid his burden from his aching shoulders and looked across at the softly laughing Andrea. 'What's so funny?'

'Our friend here.' Andrea grinned again. 'I told him that the first thing he would know of your arrival would be when you touched him on the shoulder. I don't think he believed me.'

'You might have coughed or somethin',' Miller said defensively. 'It's my nerves, boss,' he added plaintively. 'They're not what they were forty-eight hours ago.'

127

Mallory looked at him disbelievingly, made to speak, then stopped short as he caught sight of the pale blur of a face propped up against a rucksack. Beneath the white swathe of a bandaged forehead the eyes were open, looking steadily at him. Mallory took a step forward, sank down on one knee.

'So you've come round at last!' He smiled into the sunken parchment face and Stevens smiled back, the bloodless lips whiter than the face itself. He looked ghastly. 'How do you feel, Andy?'

'Not too bad, sir. Really I'm not.' The bloodshot eyes were dark and filled with pain. His gaze fell and he looked down vacantly at his bandaged leg, looked up again, smiled uncertainly at Mallory. 'I'm terribly sorry about all this, sir. What a bloody stupid thing to do.'

'It wasn't a stupid thing.' Mallory spoke with slow, heavy emphasis. 'It was criminal folly.' He knew everyone was watching them, but knew, also, that Stevens had eyes for him alone. 'Criminal, unforgivable folly,' he went on quietly, ' – and I'm the man in the dock. I'd suspected you'd lost a lot of blood on the boat, but I didn't know you had these big gashes on your forehead. I should have made it my business to find out.' He smiled wryly. 'You should have heard what these two insubordinate characters had to say to me about it when they got to the top.... And they were right. You should never had been asked to bring up the rear in the state you were in. It was madness.' He grinned again. 'You should have been hauled up like a sack of coals like the intrepid mountaineering team of Miller and Brown... God knows how you ever made it – I'm sure you'll never know.' He leaned forward, touched Stevens's sound knee. 'Forgive me, Andy. I honestly didn't realise how far through you were.'

Stevens stirred uncomfortably, but the dead pallor of the high-boned cheeks was stained with embarrassed pleasure.

'Please, sir,' he pleaded. 'Don't talk like that. It was just one of these things.' He paused, eyes screwed shut and indrawn breath hissing sharply through his teeth as a wave of pain washed up from his shattered leg. Then he looked at Mallory again. 'And there's no credit due to me for the climb,' he went on quietly. 'I hardly remember a thing about it.'

Mallory looked at him without speaking, eyebrows arched in mild interrogation.

'I was scared to death every step of the way up,' Stevens said simply. He was conscious of no surprise, no wonder that he was saying the thing he would have died rather than say. 'I've never been so scared in all my life.'

Mallory shook his head slowly from side to side, stubbled chin rasping in his cupped palm. He seemed genuinely puzzled. Then he looked down at Stevens and smiled quizzically.

'Now I know you *are* new to this game, Andy.' He smiled again. 'Maybe you think I was laughing and singing all the way up that cliff? Maybe you think *I* wasn't scared?' He lit a cigarette and gazed at Stevens through a cloud of drifting smoke. 'Well, I wasn't. "Scared" isn't the word – I was bloody well terrified. So was Andrea here. We knew too much not to be scared.'

'Andrea!' Stevens laughed, then cried out as the movement triggered off a crepitant agony in his bone-shattered leg. For a moment Mallory thought he had lost consciousness, but almost at once he spoke again, his voice husky with pain. 'Andrea!' he whispered. 'Scared! I don't believe it.'

'Andrea *was* afraid.' The big Greek's voice was very gentle. 'Andrea *is* afraid. Andrea is always afraid. That is why I have lived so long.' He stared down at his great hands. 'And why so many have died. They were not so afraid as I. They were not afraid of everything a man could be afraid of, there was always something they forgot to fear, to guard against. But Andrea was afraid of everything – and he forgot nothing. It is as simple as that.'

129

He looked across at Stevens and smiled.

'There are no brave men and cowardly men in the world, my son. There are only brave men. To be born, to live, to die — that takes courage enough in itself, and more than enough. We are all brave men and we are all afraid, and what the world calls a brave man, he, too, is brave and afraid like all the rest of us. Only he is brave for five minutes longer. Or sometimes ten minutes, or twenty minutes — or the time it takes a man sick and bleeding and afraid to climb a cliff.'

Stevens said nothing. His head was sunk on his chest, and his face was hidden. He had seldom felt so happy, seldom so at peace with himself. He had known that he could not hide things from men like Andrea and Mallory, but he had not known that it would not matter. He felt he should say something, but he could not think what and he was deathly tired. He knew, deep down, that Andrea was speaking the truth, but not the whole truth; but he was too tired to care, to try to work things out.

Miller cleared his throat noisily.

'No more talkin', Lieutenant,' he said firmly. 'You gotta lie down, get yourself some sleep.'

Stevens looked at him, then at Mallory in puzzled inquiry.

'Better do what you're told, Andy.' Mallory smiled. 'Your surgeon and medical adviser talking. He fixed your leg.'

'Oh! I didn't know. Thanks, Dusty. Was it very — difficult?'

Miller waved a deprecatory hand.

'Not for a man of my experience. Just a simple break,' he lied easily. 'Almost let one of the others do it... Give him a hand to lie down, will you, Andrea?' He jerked his head towards Mallory. 'Boss?'

The two men moved outside, turning their backs to the icy wind.

'We gotta get a fire, dry clothing, for that kid,' Miller

said urgently. 'His pulse is about 140, temperature 103. He's runnin' a fever, and he's losin' ground all the time.'

'I know, I know,' Mallory said worriedly. 'And there's not a hope of getting any fuel on this damned mountain. Let's go in and see how much dried clothing we can muster between us.'

He lifted the edge of the canvas and stepped inside. Stevens was still awake, Brown and Andrea on either side of him. Miller was on his heels.

'We're going to stay here for the night,' Mallory announced, 'so let's make things as snug as possible. Mind you,' he admitted, 'we're a bit too near the cliff for comfort, but old Jerry hasn't a clue we're on the island, and we're out of sight of the coast. Might as well make ourselves comfortable.'

'Boss . . .' Miller made to speak, then fell silent again. Mallory looked at him in surprise, saw that he, Brown and Stevens were looking at one another, uncertainty, then doubt and a dawning, sick comprehension in their eyes. A sudden anxiety, the sure knowledge that something was far wrong, struck at Mallory like a blow.

'What's up?' he demanded, sharply. 'What is it?'

'We have bad news for you, boss,' Miller said carefully. 'We should have told you right away. Guess we all thought that one of the others would have told you. . . Remember that sentry you and Andrea shoved over the side?'

Mallory nodded, sombrely. He knew what was coming.

'He fell on top of that reef twenty-thirty feet or so from the cliff,' Miller went on. 'Wasn't much of him left, I guess, but what was was jammed between two rocks. He was really stuck good and fast.'

'I see,' Mallory murmured. 'I've been wondering all night how you managed to get so wet under your rubber cape.'

'I tried four times, boss,' Miller said quietly. 'The others had a rope round me.' He shrugged his shoulders. 'Not a

131

chance. Them gawddamned waves just flung me back against the cliff every time.'

'It will be light in three or four hours,' Mallory murmured. 'In four hours they will know we are on the island. They will see him as soon as it's dawn and send a boat to investigate.'

'Does it really matter, sir,' Stevens suggested. 'He could still have fallen.'

Mallory eased the canvas aside and looked out into the night. It was bitterly cold and the snow was beginning to fall all around them. He dropped the canvas again.

'Five minutes,' he said absently. 'We will leave in five minutes.' He looked at Stevens and smiled faintly. 'We are forgetful too. We should have told you. Andrea stabbed the sentry through the heart.'

The hours that followed were hours plucked from the darkest nightmare, endless, numbing hours of stumbling and tripping and falling and getting up again, of racked bodies and aching, tortured muscles, of dropped loads and frantic pawing around in the deepening snow, of hunger and thirst and all-encompassing exhaustion.

They had retraced their steps now, were heading W.N.W. back across the shoulder of the mountain – almost certainly the Germans would think they had gone due north, heading for the centre of the island. Without compass, stars or moon to guide, Mallory had nothing to orientate them but the feel of the slope of the mountain and the memory of the map Vlachos had shown them in Alexandria. But by and by he was reasonably certain that they had rounded the mountain and were pushing up some narrow gorge into the interior.

The snow was the deadly enemy. Heavy, wet and feathery, it swirled all around them in a blanketing curtain of grey, sifted down their necks and jackboots, worked its insidious way under their clothes and up their sleeves, blocked their eyes and ears and mouths, pierced and then anaesthetised exposed faces, and turned gloveless hands into leaden lumps of ice, benumbed and all but powerless. All suffered, and suffered badly, but Stevens most of all. He had lost consciousness again within minutes of leaving the cave and clad in clinging, sodden clothes as he was, he now lacked even the saving warmth generated by physical activity. Twice Andrea had stopped and felt for the beating of the heart, for he thought that the boy had died: but he could feel nothing for there was no feeling left in his hands, and he could only wonder and stumble on again.

About five in the morning, as they were climbing up the steep valley head above the gorge, a treacherous, slippery slope with only a few stunted carob trees for anchor in the sliding scree, Mallory decided that they must rope up for safety's sake. In single file they scrambled and struggled up the ever-steepening slope for the next twenty minutes: Mallory, in the lead, did not even dare to think how Andrea was getting on behind him. Suddenly the slope eased, flattened out completely, and almost before they realised what was happening they had crossed the high divide, still roped together and in driving, blinding snow with zero visibility, and were sliding down the valley on the other side.

They came to the cave at dawn, just as the first grey stirrings of a bleak and cheerless day struggled palely through the lowering, snow-filled sky to the east. Monsieur Vlachos had told them that the south of Navarone was honey-combed with caves, but this was the first they had seen, and even then it was no cave but a dark, narrow tunnel in a great heap of piled volcanic slabs, huge, twisted layers of rock precariously poised in a gully that threaded down the slope towards some broad and unknown valley a thousand, two thousand feet, beneath them, a valley still shrouded in the gloom of night.

It was no cave, but it was enough. For frozen, exhausted, sleep-haunted men, it was more than enough, it was more than they had ever hoped for. There was room for them all, the few cracks were quickly blocked against the drifting snow, the entrance curtained off by the boulder-weighted tent. Somehow, impossibly almost in the cramped darkness, they stripped Stevens of his sea- and rain-soaked clothes, eased him into a providentially zipped sleeping-bag, forced some brandy down his throat and cushioned the bloodstained head on some dry clothing. And then the four men, even the tireless Andrea, slumped down to the sodden, snow-chilled floor of the cave and slept like men already dead, oblivious alike of the rocks on the floor, the cold, their hunger and their clammy, saturated clothing, oblivious even to the agony of returning circulation in their frozen hands and faces.

CHAPTER 7

Tuesday

1500–1900

The sun, rime-ringed and palely luminous behind the drifting cloud-wrack, was far beyond its zenith and dipping swiftly westwards to the snow-limned shoulder of the mountain when Andrea lifted the edge of the tent, pushed it gently aside and peered out warily down the smooth sweep of the mountainside. For a few moments he remained almost motionless behind the canvas, automatically easing cramped and aching leg muscles, narrowed, roving eyes gradually accustoming themselves to the white glare of the glistening, crystalline snow. And then he had flitted noiselessly out of the mouth of the tunnel and reached far up the bank of the gully in half a dozen steps; stretched full length against the snow, he eased himself smoothly up the slope, lifted a cautious eye over the top.

Far below him stretched the great, curved sweep of an almost perfectly symmetrical valley – a valley born abruptly in the cradling embrace of steep-walled mountains and falling away gently to the north. That towering, buttressed giant on his right that brooded darkly over the head of the valley, its peak hidden in the snow clouds – there could be no doubt about that, Andrea thought. Mt Kostos, the highest mountain in Navarone: they had crossed its western flank during the darkness of the night. Due east and facing his own at perhaps five miles' distance, the third mountain was barely less high: but its northern flank fell away more quickly, debouching on to the plains that lay to the north-east of Navarone. And about four miles away to the north-north-east, far beneath the snowline and the isolated shepherds' huts, a tiny, flat-roofed township lay in a fold in the hills, along the bank of the little stream that wound its way through the valley. That could only be the village of Margaritha.

Even as he absorbed the topography of the valley, his eyes probing every dip and cranny in the hills for a possible source of danger, Andrea's mind was racing back over the last two minutes of time, trying to isolate, to remember the nature of the alien sound that had cut through the cocoon of sleep and brought him instantly to his feet, alert and completely awake, even before his conscious mind had time to register the memory of the sound. And then he heard it again, three times in as many seconds, the high-pitched, lonely wheep of a whistle, shrill peremptory blasts that echoed briefly and died along the lower slopes of Mt Kostos: the final echo still hung faintly on the air as Andrea pushed himself backwards and slid down to the floor of the gully.

He was back on the bank within thirty seconds, cheek muscles contracting involuntarily as the ice-chill eyepieces of Mallory's Zeiss-Ikon binoculars screwed into his face. There was no mistaking them now, he thought grimly, his first, fleeting impression had been all too accurate. Twenty-five, perhaps thirty soldiers in all, strung out in a long, irregular line, they were advancing slowly across the flank of Kostos, combing every gully, each jumbled confusion of boulders that lay in their path. Every man was clad in a snow-suit, but even at a distance of two miles they were easy to locate: the arrow-heads of their strapped skis angled up above shoulders and hooded heads: startlingly black against the sheer whiteness of the snow, the skis bobbed and weaved in disembodied drunkenness as the men slipped and stumbled along the scree-strewn slopes of the mountain. From time to time a man near the centre of the line pointed and gestured with an alpenstock, as if co-ordinating the efforts of the search party. The man with the whistle, Andrea guessed.

'Andrea!' The call from the cave mouth was very soft. 'Anything wrong?'

Finger to his lips, Andrea twisted round in the snow. Mallory was standing by the canvas screen. Dark-jowled and crumple-clothed, he held up one hand against the glare of the snow while the other rubbed the sleep from his blood-shot eyes. And then he was limping forward in obedience to the crooking of Andrea's finger, wincing in pain at every step he took. His toes were swollen and skinned, gummed together with congealed blood. He had not had his boots off since he had taken them from the feet of the dead German sentry: and now he was almost afraid to remove them, afraid of what he would find.... He clambered slowly up the bank of the gully and sank down in the snow beside Andrea.

'Company?'

'The very worst of company,' Andrea murmured. 'Take a look, my Keith.' He handed over the binoculars, pointed down to the lower slopes of Mt Kostos. 'Your friend Jensen never told us that they were here.'

Slowly, Mallory quartered the slopes with the binoculars. Suddenly the line of searchers moved into his field of vision. He raised his head, adjusted the focus impatiently, looked briefly once more, then lowered the binoculars with a restrained deliberation of gesture that held a wealth of bitter comment.

'The W.G.B.,' he said softly.

'A Jaeger battalion,' Andrea conceded. 'Alpine Corps – their finest mountain troops. This is most inconvenient, my Keith.'

Mallory nodded, rubbed his stubbled chin.

'If anyone can find us, they can. And they'll find us.' He lifted the glasses to look again at the line of advancing men. The painstaking thoroughness of the search was disturbing enough: but even more threatening, more frightening, was the snail-like relentlessness, the inevitability of the approach of these tiny figures. 'God knows what the Alpenkorps is doing here,' Mallory went on. 'It's enough that they are here. They must know that we've landed and spent the morning searching the eastern saddle of Kostos – that was the obvious route for us to break into the interior. They've drawn a blank there, so now they're working their way over to the other saddle. They must be pretty nearly certain that we're carrying a wounded man with us and that we can't have got very far. It's only going to be a matter of time, Andrea.'

'A matter of time,' Andrea echoed. He glanced up at the sun, a sun all but invisible in the darkening sky. 'An hour, an hour and a half at the most. They'll be here before the sun goes down. And we'll still be here.' He glanced quizzically at Mallory. 'We cannot leave the boy. And we cannot get away if we take the boy – and then he would die anyway.'

'We will not be here,' Mallory said flatly. 'If we stay we all die. Or finish up in one of those nice little dungeons that Monsieur Vlachos told us about.'

'The greatest good of the greatest number,' Andrea nodded slowly. 'That's how it has to be, has it not, my Keith? The greatest number. That is what Captain Jensen would say.' Mallory stirred uncomfortably, but his voice was steady enough when he spoke.

'That's how I see it, too, Andrea. Simple proportion – twelve hundred to one. You know it has to be this way.' Mallory sounded tired.

'Yes, I know. But you are worrying about nothing.' Andrea smiled. 'Come, my friend. Let us tell the others the good news.'

Miller looked up as the two men came in, letting the canvas screen fall shut behind them. He had unzipped the side of Stevens's sleeping-bag and was working on the mangled leg. A pencil flashlight was propped on a rucksack beside him.

'When are we goin' to do somethin' about this kid,

138

boss?' The voice was abrupt, angry, like his gesture towards the sleep-drugged boy beside him. 'This damned waterproof sleeping-bag is soaked right through. So's the kid – and he's about frozen stiff: his leg feels like a side of chilled beef. He's gotta have heat, boss, a warm room and hot drinks – or he's finished. Twenty-four hours.' Miller shivered and looked slowly round the broken walls of the rock-shelter. 'I reckon he'd have less than an even chance in a first-class general hospital... He's just wastin' his time keepin' on breathin' in this gawddamned ice-box.'.

Miller hardly exaggerated. Water from the melting snow above trickled continuously down the clammy, green-lichened walls of the cave or dripped directly on to the half-frozen gravelly slush on the floor of the cave. With no through ventilation and no escape for the water accumulating at the sides of the shelter, the whole place was dank and airless and terribly chill.

'Maybe he'll be hospitalised sooner than you think,' Mallory said dryly. 'How's his leg?'

'Worse.' Miller was blunt. 'A helluva sight worse. I've just chucked in another handful of sulpha and tied things up again. That's all I can do, boss, and it's just a waste of time anyway... What was that crack about a hospital?' he added suspiciously.

'That was no crack,' Mallory said soberly, 'but one of the more unpleasant facts of life. There's a German search party heading this way. They mean business. They'll find us, all right.'

Miller swore. 'That's handy, that's just wonderful,' he said bitterly. 'How far away, boss?'

'An hour, maybe a little more.'

'And what are we goin' to do with Junior, here? Leave him? It's his only chance, I reckon.'

'Stevens comes with us.' There was a flat finality in Mallory's voice. Miller looked at him for a long time in silence: his face was very cold.

'Stevens comes with us,' Miller repeated. 'We drag him

along with us until he's dead – that won't take long – and then we leave him in the snow. Just like that, huh?'

'Just like that, Dusty.' Absently Mallory brushed some snow off his clothes, and looked up again at Miller. 'Stevens knows too much. The Germans will have guessed why we're on the island, but they don't know how we propose to get inside the fortress – and they don't know when the Navy's coming through. But Stevens does. They'll make him talk. Scopolamine will make anyone talk.'

'Scopolamine! On a dying man?' Miller was openly incredulous.

'Why not? I'd do the same myself. If you were the German commandant and you knew that your big guns and half the men in your fortress were liable to be blown to hell any moment, you'd do the same.'

Miller looked at him, grinned wryly, shook his head.

'Me and my – '

'I know. You and your big mouth.' Mallory smiled and clapped him on the shoulder. 'I don't like it one little bit more than you do, Dusty.' He turned away and crossed to the other side of the cave. 'How are you feeling, Chief?'

'Not too bad, sir.' Casey Brown was only just awake, numbed and shivering in sodden clothes. 'Anything wrong?'

'Plenty,' Mallory assured him. 'Search party moving this way. We'll have to pull out inside half an hour.' He looked at his watch. 'Just on four o'clock. Do you think you could raise Cairo on the set?'

'Lord only knows,' Brown said frankly. He rose stiffly to his feet. 'The radio didn't get just the best of treatment yesterday. I'll have a go.'

'Thanks, Chief. See that your aerial doesn't stick up above the sides of the gully.' Mallory turned to leave the cave, but halted abruptly at the sight of Andrea squatting on a boulder just beside the entrance. His head bent in concentration, the big Greek had just finished screwing telescopic sights on to the barrel of his 7.92 mm. Mauser and was now deftly wrapping a sleeping-bag lining round its barrel and butt until the entire rifle was wrapped in a white cocoon.

Mallory watched him in silence. Andrea glanced up at him, smiled, rose to his feet and reached out for his rucksack. Within thirty seconds he was clad from head to toe in his mountain camouflage suit, was drawing tight the purse-strings of his snow-hood and easing his feet into the rucked elastic anklets of his canvas boots. Then he picked up the Mauser and smiled slightly.

'I thought I might be taking a little walk, Captain,' he said apologetically. 'With your permission, of course.'

Mallory nodded his head several times in slow recollection.

'You said I was worrying about nothing,' he murmured. 'I should have known. You might have told me, Andrea.' But the protest was automatic, without significance. Mallory felt neither anger nor even annoyance at this tacit arrogation of his authority. The habit of command died hard in Andrea: on such occasions as he ostensibly sought approval for or consulted about a proposed course of action it was generally as a matter of courtesy and to give information as to his intentions. Instead of resentment, Mallory could feel only an overwhelming relief and gratitude to the smiling giant who towered above him: he had talked casually to Miller about driving Stevens till he died and then abandoning him, talked with an indifference that masked a mind sombre with bitterness at what he must do, but even so he had not known how depressed, how sick at heart this decision had left him until he knew it was no longer necessary.

'I am sorry.' Andrea was half-contrite, half-smiling. 'I should have told you. I thought you understood... It is the best thing to do, yes?'

'It is the only thing to do,' Mallory said frankly. 'You're going to draw them off up the saddle?'

141

'There is no other way. With their skis they would overtake me in minutes if I went down into the valley. I cannot come back, of course, until it is dark. You will be here?'

'Some of us will,' Mallory glanced across the shelter where a waking Stevens was trying to sit up, heels of his palms screwing into his exhaustsed eyes. 'We must have food and fuel, Andrea,' he said softly. 'I am going down into the valley tonight.'

'Of course, of course. We must do what we can.' Andrea's face was grave, his voice only a murmur. 'As long as we can. He is only a boy, a child almost... Perhaps it will not be long.' He pulled back the curtain, looked out at the evening sky. 'I will be back by seven o'clock.'

'Seven o'clock,' Mallory repeated. The sky, he could see, was darkening already, darkening with the gloom of coming snow, and the lifting wind was beginning to puff little clouds of air-spun, flossy white into the little gully. Mallory shivered and caught hold of the massive arm. 'For God's sake, Andrea,' he urged quietly, 'look after yourself!'

'Myself?' Andrea smiled gently, no mirth in his eyes, and as gently he disengaged his arm. 'Do not think about me.' The voice was very quiet, with an utter lack of arrogance. 'If you must speak to God, speak to Him about these poor devils who are looking for us.' The canvas dropped behind him and he was gone.

For some moments Mallory stood irresolutely at the mouth of the cave, gazing out sightlessly through the gap in the curtain. Then he wheeled abruptly, crossed the floor of the shelter and knelt in front of Stevens. The boy was propped up against Miller's anxious arm, the eyes lack-lustre and expressionless, bloodless cheeks deep-sunken in a grey and parchment face. Mallory smiled at him: he hoped the shock didn't show in his face.

'Well, well, well. The sleeper awakes at last. Better late than never.' He opened his waterproof cigarette case, proffered it to Stevens. 'How are you feeling now, Andy?'

'Frozen, sir.' Stevens shook his head at the case and tried to grin back at Mallory, a feeble travesty of a smile that made Mallory wince.

'And the leg?'

'I think it must be frozen, too.' Stevens looked down incuriously at the sheathed whiteness of his shattered leg. 'Anyway, I can't feel a thing.'

'Frozen!' Miller's sniff was a masterpiece of injured pride. 'Frozen, he says! Gawddamned ingratitude. It's the first-class medical care, if I do say so myself!'

Stevens smiled, a fleeting, absent smile that flickered over his face and was gone. For long moments he kept staring down at his leg, then suddenly lifted his head and looked directly at Mallory.

'Look sir, there's no good kidding ourselves.' The voice was soft, quite toneless. 'I don't want to seem ungrateful and I hate even the idea of cheap heroics, but – well, I'm just a damned great millstone round your necks and – '

'Leave you, eh?' Mallory interrupted. 'Leave you to die of the cold or be captured by the Germans. Forget it, laddie. We can look after you – and these ruddy guns – at the same time.'

'But, sir – '

'You insult us, Lootenant.' Miller sniffed again. 'Our feelings are hurt. Besides, as a professional man I gotta see my case through to convalescence, and if you think I'm goin' to do that in any gawddamned dripping German dungeon, you can – '

'Enough!' Mallory held up his hand. 'The subject is closed!' He saw the stain high up on the thin cheeks, the glad light that touched the dulled eyes, and felt the self-loathing and the shame well up inside him, shame for the gratitude of a sick man who did not know that their concern stemmed not from solicitude but from fear that he might betray them... Mallory bent forward and began to unlace his high jackboots. He spoke without looking up.

143

'Dusty.'

'Yeah?'

'When you're finishing boasting about your medical prowess, maybe you'd care to use some of it. Come and have a look at these feet of mine, will you? I'm afraid the sentry's boots haven't done them a great deal of good.'

Fifteen painful minutes later Miller snipped off the rough edges of the adhesive bandage that bound Mallory's right foot, straightened up stiffly and contemplated his handiwork with pride.

'Beautiful, Miller, beautiful,' he murmured complacently. 'Not even in Johns Hopkins in the city of Baltimore...' He broke off suddenly, frowned down at the thickly bandaged feet and coughed apologetically. 'A small point has just occurred to me, boss.'

'I thought it might eventually,' Mallory said grimly. 'Just how do you propose to get my feet into these damned boots again?' He shivered involuntarily as he pulled on a pair of thick woollen socks, matted and sodden with melted snow, picked up the German sentry's boots, held them at arm's length and examined them in disgust. 'Sevens, at the most – and a darned small sevens at that!'

'Nines,' Stevens said laconically. He handed over his own jackboots, one of them slit neatly down the sides where Andrea had cut it open. 'You can fix that tear easily enough, and they're no damned good to me now. No arguments, sir, please.' He began to laugh softly, broke off in a sharply indrawn hiss of pain as the movement jarred the broken bones, took a couple of deep, quivering breaths, then smiled whitely. 'My first – and probably my last – contribution to the expedition. What sort of medal do you reckon they'll give me for that, sir?'

Mallory took the boots, looked at Stevens a long moment in silence, then turned as the tarpaulin was pushed aside. Brown stumbled in, lowered the transmitter and telescopic aerial to the floor of the cave and pulled out a tin of cigarettes. They slipped from his frozen fingers, fell into the icy mud at his feet, became brown and sodden on the instant. He swore briefly, and without enthusiasm, beat his numbed hands across his chest, gave it up and sat down heavily on a convenient boulder. He looked tired and cold and thoroughly miserable.

Mallory lit a cigarette and passed it across to him.

'How did it go, Casey? Manage to raise them at all?'

'They managed to raise me – more or less. Reception was lousy.' Brown drew the grateful tobacco smoke deep down into his lungs. 'And I couldn't get through at all. Must be that damned great hill to the south there.'

'Probably,' Mallory nodded. 'And what news from our friends in Cairo? Exhorting us to greater efforts? Telling us to get on with the job?'

'No news at all. Too damn worried about the silence at this end. Said that from now on they were going to come through every four hours, acknowledgment or no. Repeated that about ten times, then signed off.'

'That'll be a great help,' Miller said acidly. 'Nice to know they're on our side. Nothin' like moral support.' He jerked his thumb towards the mouth of the cave. 'Reckon them bloodhounds would be scared to death if they knew ... Did you take a gander at them before you came in?'

'I didn't have to,' Brown said morosely. 'I could hear them – sounded like the officer in charge shouting directions.' Mechanically, almost, he picked up his automatic rifle, eased the clip in the magazine. 'Must be less than a mile away now.'

The search party, more closely bunched by this time, was less than a mile, was barely half a mile distant from the cave when the Oberleutnant in charge saw that the right wing of his line, on the steeper slopes to the south, was lagging behind once more. Impatiently he lifted his whistle to his mouth for the three sharp peremptory blasts that would bring his weary men stumbling into line again. Twice the whistle shrilled out its imperative urgency, the

145

piercing notes echoing flatly along the snowbound slopes and dying away in the valley below: but the third *wheep* died at birth, caught up again and tailed off in a wailing, eldritch diminuendo that merged with dreadful harmony into a long, bubbling scream of agony. For two or three seconds the Oberleutnant stood motionless in his tracks, his face shocked and contorted: then he jack-knifed violently forward and pitched down into the crusted snow. The burly sergeant beside him stared down at the fallen officer, looked up in sudden horrified understanding, opened his mouth to shout, sighed and toppled wearily over the body at his feet, the evil, whip-lash crack of the Mauser in his ears as he died.

High up on the western slopes of Mount Kostos, wedged in the V between two great boulders, Andrea gazed down the darkening mountainside over the depressed telescopic sights of his rifle and pumped another three rounds into the wavering, disorganised line of searchers. His face was quite still, as immobile as the eyelids that never flickered to the regular crashing of his Mauser, and drained of all feeling. Even his eyes reflected the face, eyes neither hard nor pitiless, but simply empty and almost frighteningly remote, a remoteness that mirrored his mind, a mind armoured for the moment against all thought and sensation, for Andrea knew that he must not think about this thing. To kill, to take the life of his fellows, that was the supreme evil, for life was a gift that it was not his to take away. Not even in fair fight. And this was murder.

Slowly Andrea lowered the Mauser, peered through the drifting gun-smoke that hung heavily in the frosty evening air. The enemy had vanished, completely, rolled behind scattered boulders or burrowed frantically into the blanketing anonymity of the snow. But they were still there, still potentially as dangerous as ever. Andrea knew that they would recover fast from the death of their officer – there were no finer, no more tenacious fighters in Europe than the ski-troops of the Jaeger mountain battalion – and would come after him, catch him and kill him if humanly possible. That was why Andrea's first case had been to kill their officer – he might not have come after him, might have stopped to puzzle out the reason for this unprovoked flank attack.

Andrea ducked low in reflex instinct as a sudden burst of automatic fire whined in murderous ricochet off the boulders before him. He had expected this. It was the old classic infantry attack pattern – advance under covering fire, drop, cover your mate and come again. Swiftly Andrea rammed home another charge into the magazine of his Mauser, dropped flat on his face and inched his way along behind the low line of broken rock that extended fifteen or twenty yards to his right – he had chosen his ambush point with care – and then petered out. At the far end he pulled his snow hood down to the level of his brows and edged a wary eye round the corner of the rock.

Another heavy burst of automatic fire smashed into the boulders he had just left, and half a dozen men – three from either end of the line – broke cover, scurried along the slope in a stumbling, crouching run, then pitched forward into the snow again. *Along* the slope – the two parties had run in opposite directions. Andrea lowered his head and rubbed the back of a massive hand across the stubbled grizzle of his chin. Awkward, damned awkward. No frontal attack for the foxes of the W.G.B. They were extending their lines on either side, the points hooking around in a great, encircling half-moon. Bad enough for himself, but he could have coped with that – a carefully reconnoitred escape gully wound up the slope behind him. But he hadn't foreseen what was obviously going to happen: the curving crescent of line to the west was going to sweep across the rock-shelter where the others lay hidden.

Andrea twisted over on his back and looked up at the evening sky. It was darkening by the moment, darkening with the gloom of coming snow, and daylight was beginning to fail. He twisted again and looked across the great

147

swelling shoulder of Mount Kostos, looked at the few scattered rocks and shallow depressions that barely dimpled the smooth convexity of the slope. He took a second quick look round the rock as the rifles of the W.G.B. opened up once more, saw the same encircling manoeuvre being executed again, and waited no longer. Firing blindly downhill, he half-rose to his feet and flung himself out into the open, finger squeezing on the trigger, feet driving desperately into the frozen snow as he launched himself towards the nearest rock-cover, forty yards away if an inch. Thirty-five yards to go, thirty, twenty and still not a shot fired, a slip, a stumble on the sliding scree, a catlike recovery, ten yards, still miraculously immune, and then he had dived into shelter to land on chest and stomach with a sickening impact that struck cruelly into his ribs and emptied his lungs with an explosive gasp.

Fighting for breath, he struck the magazine cover, rammed home another charge, risked a quick peep over the top of the rock and catapulted himself to his feet again, all inside ten seconds. The Mauser held across his body opened up again, firing downhill at vicious random, for Andrea had eyes only for the smoothly-treacherous ground at his feet, for the scree-lined depression so impossibly far ahead. And then the Mauser was empty, useless in his hand, and every gun far below had opened up, the shells whistling above his head or blinding him with spurting gouts of snow as they ricocheted off the sold rock. But twilight was touching the hills, Andrea was only a blur, a swiftly-flitting blur against a ghostly background, and uphill accuracy was notoriously difficult at any time. Even so, the massed fire from below was steadying and converging, and Andrea waited no longer. Unseen hands plucking wickedly at the flying tails of his snow-smock, he flung himself almost horizontally forward and slid the last ten feet face down into the waiting depression.

Stretched full length on his back in the hollow, Andrea

fished out a steel mirror from his breast pocket and held it gingerly above his head. At first he could see nothing, for the darkness was deeper below and the mirror misted from the warmth of his body. And then the film vanished in the chill mountain air and he could see two, three and then half a dozen men breaking cover, heading at a clumsy run straight up the face of the hill – and two of them had come from the extreme right of the line. Andrea lowered the mirror and relaxed with a long sigh of relief, eyes crinkling in a smile. He looked up at the sky, blinked as the first feathery flakes of falling snow melted on his eyelids and smiled again. Almost lazily he brought out another charger for the Mauser, fed more shells into the magazine.

'Boss?' Miller's voice was plaintive.

'Yes? What is it?' Mallory brushed some snow off his face and the collar of his smock and peered into the white darkness ahead.

'Boss, when you were in school did you ever read any stories about folks gettin' lost in a snowstorm and wanderin' round and round in circles for days?'

'We had exactly the same book in Queenstown,' Mallory conceded.

'Wanderin' round and round until they died?' Miller persisted.

'Oh, for heaven's sake!' Mallory said impatiently. His feet, even in Stevens's roomy boots, hurt abominably. 'How can we be wandering in circles if we're going downhill all the time? What do you think we're on – a bloody spiral staircase?'

Miller walked on in hurt silence, Mallory beside him, both men ankle-deep in the wet, clinging snow that had been falling so silently, so persistently, for the past three hours since Andrea had drawn off the Jaeger search party. Even in mid-winter in the White Mountains in Crete Mallory could recall no snowfall so heavy and continuous. So much for the Isles of Greece and the eternal sunshine that gilds them yet, he thought bitterly. He hadn't reckoned on this when he'd planned on going down to Margaritha for food and fuel, but even so it wouldn't have made any difference to his decision. Although in less pain now, Stevens was becoming steadily weaker, and the need was desperate.

With moon and stars blanketed by the heavy snow-clouds — visibility, indeed, was hardly more than ten feet in any direction — the loss of their compasses had assumed a crippling importance. He didn't doubt his ability to find the village — it was simply a matter of walking downhill till they came to the stream that ran through the valley, then following that north till they came to Margaritha — but if the snow didn't let up their chances of locating that tiny cave again in the vast sweep of the hillsides...

Mallory smothered an exclamation as Miller's hand closed round his upper arm, dragged him down to his knees in the snow. Even in that moment of unknown danger he could feel a slow stirring of anger against himself, for his attention had been wandering along with his thoughts... He lifted his hand as vizor against the snow, peered out narrowly through the wet, velvety curtain of white that swirled and eddied out of the darkness before him. Suddenly he had it — a dark, squat shape only feet away. They had all but walked straight into it.

'It's the hut,' he said softly in Miller's ear. He had seen it early in the afternoon, half-way between their cave and Margaritha, and almost in line with both. He was conscious of relief, an increase in confidence: they would be in the village in less than half an hour. 'Elementary navigation, my dear Corporal,' he murmured. 'Lost and wandering in circles, my foot! Just put your faith..'

He broke off as Miller's fingers dug viciously into his

arm, as Miller's head came close to his own.

'I heard voices, boss.' The words were a mere breath of sound.

'Are you sure?' Miller's silenced gun, Mallory noticed, was still in his pocket.

Miller hesitated.

'Dammit to hell, boss, I'm sure of nothin',' he whispered irritably. 'I've been imaginin' every damn thing possible in the past hour!' He pulled the snow hood off his head, the better to listen, bent forward for a few seconds then sank back again. 'Anyway, I'm sure I *thought* I heard somethin'.'

'Come on. Let's take a look-see.' Mallory was on his feet again. 'I think you're mistaken. Can't be the Jaeger boys – they were half-way back across Mount Kostos when we saw them last. And the shepherds only use these places in the summer months.' He slipped the safety catch of his Colt .455, walked slowly, at a half-crouch, towards the nearest wall of the hut, Miller at his shoulder.

They reached the hut, put their ears against the frail, tar-paper walls. Ten seconds passed, twenty, half a minute, then Mallory relaxed.

'Nobody at home. Or if they are, they're keeping mighty quiet. But no chances, Dusty. You go that way, I'll go this. Meet at the door – that'll be on the opposite side, facing into the valley... Walk wide at the corners – never fails to baffle the unwary.'

A minute later both men were inside the hut, the door shut behind them. The hooded beam of Mallory's torch probed into every corner of the ramshackle cabin. It was quite empty – and earthen floor, a rough wooden bunk, a dilapidated stove with a rusty lantern standing on it, and that was all. No table, no chair, no chimney, not even a window.

Mallory walked over to the stove, picked up the lamp and sniffed it.

'Hasn't been used for weeks. Still full of kerosene,

though. Very useful in that damn dungeon up there – if we can ever find the place...'

He froze into a sudden listening immobility, eyes unfocused and head cocked slightly to one side. Gently, ever so gently, he set the lamp down, walked leisurely across to Miller.

'Remind me to apologise at some future date,' he murmured. 'We have company. Give me your gun and keep talking.'

'Castelrosso again,' Miller complained loudly. He hadn't even raised an eyebrow. 'This is downright monotonous. A Chinaman – I'll bet it's a Chinaman this time.' But he was already talking to himself.

The silenced automatic balanced at his waist, Mallory walked noiselessly round the hut, four feet out from the walls. He had passed two corners, was just rounding the third when, out of the corner of his eye, he saw a vague figure behind him rising up swiftly from the ground and lunging out with upraised arm. Mallory stepped back quickly under the blow, spun round, swung his balled fist viciously and backwards into the stomach of his attacker. There was a sudden explosive gasp of agony as the man doubled up, moaned and crumpled silently to the ground. Barely in time Mallory arrested the downward, clubbing swipe of his reversed automatic.

Gun reversed again, the butt settled securely in his palm, Mallory stared down unblinkingly at the huddled figure, at the primitive wooden baton still clutched in the gloved right hand, at the unmilitary looking knapsack strapped to his back. He kept his gun lined up on the fallen body, waiting: this had been just too easy, too suspicious. Thirty seconds passed and still the figure on the ground hadn't stirred. Mallory took a short step forward and carefully, deliberately and none too gently kicked the man on the outside of the right knee. It was an old trick, and he'd never known it to fail – the pain was brief, but agonising. But there was no movement, no sound at all.

Quickly Mallory stooped, hooked his free hand round the knapsack shoulder straps, straightened and made for the door, half-carrying, half-dragging his captive. The man was no weight at all. With a proportionately much heavier garrison than ever in Crete, there would be that much less food for the islanders, Mallory mused compassionately. There would be very little indeed. He wished he hadn't hit him so hard.

Miller met him at the open door, stooped wordlessly, caught the unconscious man by the ankles and helped Mallory dump him unceremoniously on the bunk in the far corner of the hut.

'Nice goin', boss,' he complimented. 'Never heard a thing. Who's the heavyweight champ?'

'No idea.' Mallory shook his head in the darkness. 'Just skin and bones, that's all, just skin and bones. Shut the door, Dusty, and let's have a look at what we've got.'

CHAPTER 8

Tuesday

1900–0015

A minute passed, two, then the little man stirred, moaned and pushed himself to a sitting position. Mallory held his arm to steady him, while he shook his bent head, eyes screwed tightly shut as he concentrated on clearing the muzziness away. Finally he looked up slowly, glanced from Mallory to Miller and back at Mallory again in the feeble light of the newly-lit shuttered lantern. Even as the men watched, they could see the colour returning to the swarthy cheeks, the indignant bristling of the heavy, dark moustache, the darkening anger in the eyes. Suddenly the man reached up, tore Mallory's hand away from his arm.

'Who are you?' He spoke in English, clear, precise, with hardly a trace of accent.

'Sorry, but the less you know the better.' Mallory smiled, deliberately to rob the words of offence. 'I mean that for your own sake. How are you feeling now?'

Tenderly the little man massaged his midriff, flexed his leg with a grimace of pain.

'You hit me very hard.'

'I had to.' Mallory reached behind him and picked up the cudgel the man had been carrying. 'You tried to hit me with this. What did you expect me to do – take my hat off so you could have a better swipe at me?'

'You are very amusing.' Again he bent his leg, experimentally, looking up at Mallory in hostile suspicion. 'My knee hurts me,' he said accusingly.

'First things first. Why the club?'

'I meant to knock you down and have a look at you,' he explained impatiently. 'It was the only safe way. You might have been one of the W.G.B... Why is my knee – ?'

'You had an awkward fall,' Mallory said shamelessly. 'What are you doing here?'

'Who are you?' the little man countered.

Miller coughed, looked ostentatiously at his watch.

'This is all very entertainin', boss — '

'True for you, Dusty. We haven't all night.' Quickly Mallory reached behind him, picked up the man's rucksack, tossed it across to Miller. 'See what's in there, will you?' Strangely, the little man made no move to protest.

'Food!' Miller said reverently. 'Wonderful, wonderful food. Cooked meat, bread, cheese — and wine.' Reluctantly Miller closed the bag and looked curiously at their prisoner. 'Helluva funny time for a picnic.'

'So! An American, a Yankee.' The little man smiled to himself. 'Better and better!'

'What do you mean?' Miller asked suspiciously.

'See for yourself,' the man said pleasantly. He nodded casually to the far corner of the room. 'Look there.'

Mallory spun round, realised in a moment that he had been tricked, jerked back again. Carefully he leaned forward and touched Miller's arm.

'Don't look round too quickly, Dusty. And don't touch your gun. It seems our friend was not alone.' Mallory tightened his lips, mentally cursed himself for his obtuseness. Voices — Dusty had said there had been voices. Must be even more tired than he had thought...

A tall, lean man blocked the entrance to the doorway. His face was shadowed under an enveloping snow-hood, but there was no mistaking the gun in his hand. A short Lee Enfield rifle, Mallory noted dispassionately.

'Do not shoot!' The little man spoke rapidly in Greek. 'I am almost sure that they are those whom we seek, Panayis.'

Panayis! Mallory felt the wave of relief wash over him. That was one of the names Eugene Vlachos had given him, back in Alexandria.

'The tables turned, are they not?' The little man smiled

at Mallory, the tired eyes crinkling, the heavy black moustache lifting engagingly at one corner. 'I ask you again, who are you?'

'S.O.E.,' Mallory answered unhesitatingly.

The man nodded in satisfaction. 'Captain Jensen sent you?'

Mallory sank back on the bunk and sighed in long relief. 'We are among friends, Dusty.' He looked at the little man before him. 'You must be Louki – the first plane tree in the square in Margaritha?'

The little man beamed. He bowed, stretched out his hand.

'Louki. At your service, sir.'

'And this of course, is Panayis?'

The tall man in the doorway, dark, saturnine, unsmiling, inclined his head briefly but said nothing.

'You have us right!' The little man was beaming with delight. 'Louki and Panayis. They know about us in Alexandria and Cairo, then?' he asked proudly.

'Of course!' Mallory smothered a smile. 'They spoke highly of you. You have been of great help to the Allies before.'

'And we will again,' Louki said briskly. 'Come, we are wasting time. The Germans are on the hills. What help can we give you?'

'Food, Louki. We need food – we need it badly.'

'We have it!' Proudly, Louki gestured at the rucksacks. 'We were on our way up with it.'

'You were on your way...' Mallory was astonished. 'How did you know where we were – or even that we were on the island?'

Louki waved a deprecating hand.

'It was easy. Since first light German troops have been moving south through Margaritha up into the hills. All morning they combed the east col of Kostos. We knew someone must have landed, and that the Germans were looking for them. We heard, too, that the Germans had

156

blocked the cliff path on the south coast, at both ends. So you must have come over the west col. They would not expect that – you fooled them. So we came to find you.'

'But you would never have found us – '

'We would have found you.' There was complete certainty in the voice. 'Panayis and I – we know every stone, every blade of grass in Navarone.' Louki shivered suddenly, stared out bleakly through the swirling snow. 'You couldn't have picked worse weather.'

'We couldn't have picked better,' Mallory said grimly.

'Last night, yes,' Louki agreed. 'No one would expect you in that wind and rain. No one would hear the aircraft or even dream that you would try to jump – '

'We came by sea,' Millter interrupted. He waved a negligent hand. 'We climbed the south cliff.'

'What? The south cliff!' Louki was frankly disbelieving. 'No one could climb the south cliff. It is impossible!'

'That's the way we felt when we were about half-way up,' Mallory said candidly. 'But Dusty, here, is right. That's how it was.'

Louki had taken a step back: his face was expressionless.

'I say it is impossible,' he repeated flatly.

'He is telling the truth, Louki,' Miller cut in quietly. 'Do you never read newspapers?'

'Of course I read newspapers!' Louki bristled with indignation. 'Do you think I am – how you say – illiterate?'

'Then think back to just before the war,' Miller advised. 'Think of mountaineerin' – and the Himalayas. You must have seen his picture in the papers – once, twice, a hundred times.' He looked at Mallory consideringly. 'Only he was a little prettier in those days. You must remember. This is Mallory, Keith Mallory of New Zealand.'

Mallory said nothing. He was watching Louki, the puzzlement, the comical screwing up of the eyes, head cocked to one side: then, all at once, something clicked in the little man's memory and his face lit up in a great, crinkling smile that swamped every last trace of suspicion. He stepped forward, hand outstretched in welcome.

'By heaven, you are right! Mallory! Of course I know Mallory!' He grabbed Mallory's hand, pumped it up and down with great enthusiasm. 'It is indeed as the American says. You need a shave... And you look older.'

'I feel older,' Mallory said gloomily. He nodded at Miller. 'This is Corporal Miller, an American citizen.'

'Another famous climber?' Louki asked eagerly. 'Another tiger of the hills, yes?'

'He climbed the south cliff as it has never been climbed before,' Mallory answered truthfully. He glanced at his watch, then looked directly at Louki. 'There are others up in the hills. We need help, Louki. We need it badly and we need it at once. You know the danger if you are caught helping us?'

'Danger?' Louki waved a contemptuous hand. 'Danger to Louki and Panayis, the foxes of Navarone? Impossible! We are the ghosts of the night.' He hitched his pack higher up on his shoulders. 'Come. Let us take this food to your friends.'

'Just a minute.' Mallory's restraining hand was on his arm. 'There are two other things. We need heat – a stove and fuel, and we need – '

'Heat! A stove!' Louki was incredulous. 'Your friends in the hills – what are they? A band of old women?'

'And we also need bandages and medicine,' Mallory went on patiently. 'One of our friends has been terribly injured. We are not sure, but we do not think that he will live.'

'Panayis!' Louki barked. 'Back to the village.' Louki was speaking in Greek now. Rapidly he issued his orders, had Mallory describe where the rock-shelter was, made sure that Panayis understood, then stood a moment in indecision, pulling at an end of his moustache. At length he looked up at Mallory.

'Could you find this cave again by yourself?'

'Lord only knows,' Mallory said frankly. 'I honestly don't think so.'

'Then I must come with you. I had hoped – you see, it will be a heavy load for Panayis – I have told him to bring bedding as well – and I don't think – '

'I'll go along with him,' Miller volunteered. He thought of his back-breaking labours on the caique, the climb up the cliff, their forced march through the mountains. 'The exercise will do me good.'

Louki translated his offer to Panayis – taciturn, apparently, only because of his complete lack of English – and was met by what appeared to be a torrent of protest. Miller looked at him in astonishment.

'What's the matter with old sunshine here?' he asked Mallory. 'Doesn't seem any too happy to me.'

'Says he can manage O.K. and wants to go by himself,' Mallory interpreted. 'Thinks you'll slow him up on the hills.' He shook his head in mock wonder. 'As if any man could slow Dusty Miller up!'

'Exactly!' Louki was bristling with anger. Again he turned to Panayis, fingers stabbing the empty air to emphasise his words. Miller turned, looked apprehensively at Mallory.

'What's he tellin' him now, boss?'

'Only the truth,' Mallory said solemnly. 'Saying he ought to be honoured at being given the opportunity of marching with Monsieur Miller, the world-famous American climber.' Mallory grinned. 'Panayis will be on his mettle tonight – determined to prove that a Navaronian can climb as well and as fast as any man.'

'Oh, my Gawd!' Miller moaned.

'And on the way back, don't forget to give Panayis a hand up the steeper bits.'

Miller's reply was luckily lost in a sudden flurry of snow-laden wind.

★ ★ ★

That wind was rising steadily now, a bitter wind that whipped the heavy snow into their bent faces and stung the tears from their blinking eyes. A heavy, wet snow that melted as it touched, and trickled down through every gap and chink in their clothing until they were wet and chilled and thoroughly miserable. A clammy, sticky snow that built up layer after energy-sapping layer under their leaden-footed boots, until they stumbled along inches above the ground, leg muscles aching from the sheer accumulated weight of snow. There was no visibility worthy of the name, not even of a matter of feet, they were blanketed, swallowed up by an impenetrable cocoon of swirling grey and white, unchanging, featureless: Louki strode on diagonally upwards across the slope with the untroubled certainty of a man walking up his own garden path.

Louki seemed as agile as a mountain goat, and as tireless. Nor was his tongue less nimble, less unwearied than his legs. He talked incessantly, a man overjoyed to be in action again, no matter what action so long as it was against the enemy. He told Mallory of the last three attacks on the island and how they had so bloodily failed — the Germans had been somehow forewarned of the seaborne assault, had been waiting for the Special Boat Service and the Commandos with everything they had and had cut them to pieces, while the two airborne groups had had the most evil luck, been delivered up to the enemy by misjudgment, by a series of unforeseeable coincidences; or how Panayis and himself had on both occasions narrowly escaped with their lives — Panayis had actually been captured the last time, had killed both his guards and escaped unrecognised; of the disposition of the German troops and check-points throughout the island, the location of the road blocks on the only two roads; and finally, of what little he himself knew of the layout of the fortress of Navarone itself. Panayis, the dark one, could tell him more of that, Louki said: twice Panayis had been inside the fortress, once for an entire night: the guns, the

160

control rooms, the barracks, the officers' quarters, the magazine, the turbo rooms, the sentry points – he knew where each one lay, to the inch.

Mallory whistled softly to himself. This was more than he had ever dared hope for. They had still to escape the net of searchers, still to reach the fortress, still to get inside it. But once inside – and Panayis must know how to get inside... Unconsciously Mallory lengthened his stride, bent his back to the slope.

'Your friend Panayis must be quite something,' he said slowly. 'Tell me more about him, Louki.'

'What can I tell you?' Louki shook his head in a little flurry of snowflakes. 'What do I know of Panayis? What does anyone know of Panayis? That he has the luck of the devil, the courage of a madman and that sooner the lion will lie down with the lamb, the starving wolf spare the flock, than Panayis breathe the same air as the Germans? We all know that, and we know nothing of Panayis. All I know is that I thank God I am no German, with Panayis on the island. He strikes by stealth, by night, by knife and in the back.' Louki crossed himself. 'His hands are full of blood.'

Mallory shivered involuntarily. The dark, sombre figure of Panayis, the memory of the expressionless face, the hooded eyes, were beginning to fascinate him.

'There's more to him than that, surely,' Mallory argued 'After all, you are both Navaronians – '

'Yes yes, that is so.'

'This is a small island, you've lived together all your lives – '

'Ah, but that is where the Major is wrong!' Mallory's promotion in rank was entirely Louki's own idea: despite Mallory's protests and explanations he seemed determined to stick to it. 'I, Louki, was for many years in foreign lands, helping Monsieur Vlachos. Monsieur Vlachos,' Louki said with pride, 'is a very important Government official.'

'I know,' Mallory nodded. 'A consul. I've met him. He is a very fine man.'

'You have met him! Monsieur Vlachos?' There was no mistaking the gladness, the delight in Louki's voice. 'That is good! That is wonderful! Later you must tell me more. He is a great man. Did I ever tell you – '

'We were speaking about Panayis,' Mallory reminded him gently.

'Ah, yes, Panayis. As I was saying, I was away for a long time. When I came back, Panayis was gone. His father had died, his mother had married again and Panayis had gone to live with his stepfather and two little stepsisters in Crete. His stepfather, half-fisherman, half-farmer, was killed in fighting the Germans near Candia – this was in the beginning. Panayis took over the boat of his father, helped many of the Allies to escape until he was caught by the Germans, strung up by his wrists in the village square – where his family lived – not far from Casteli. He was flogged till the white of his ribs, of his backbone, was there for all to see, and left for dead. Then they burnt the village and Panayis's family – disappeared. You understand, Major?'

'I understand,' Mallory said grimly. 'But Panayis – '

'He should have died. But he is tough, that one, tougher than a knot in an old carob tree. Friends cut him down during the night, took him away into the hills till he was well again. And then he arrived back in Navarone, God knows how. I think he came from island to island in a small rowing-boat. He never says why he came back – I think it gives him greater pleasure to kill on his own native island. I do not know, Major. All I know is that food and sleep, the sunshine, women and wine – all these are nothing and less than nothing to the dark one.' Again Louki crossed himself. 'He obeys me, for I am the steward of the Vlachos family, but even I am afraid of him. To kill, to keep on killing, then kill again – that is the very breath of his being.' Louki stopped momentarily, sniffed the air like a hound seeking some fugitive scent, then kicked the snow off his boots and struck off up the hill at a tangent. The little man's unhesitating sureness of direction was uncanny.

'How far to go now, Louki?'

'Two hundred yards, Major. No more.' Louki blew some snow off his heavy, dark moustache and swore. 'I shall not be sorry to arrive.'

'Nor I.' Mallory thought of the miserable, draughty shelter in the dripping rocks almost with affection. It was becoming steadily colder as they climbed out of the valley, and the wind was rising, climbing up the register with a steady, moaning whine: they had to lean into it now, push hard against it, to make any progress. Suddenly both men stopped, listened, looked at each other, heads bent against the driving snow. Around them there was only the white emptiness and the silence: there was no sign of what had caused the sudden sound.

'You heard something, too?' Mallory murmured.

'It is only I.' Mallory spun round as the deep voice boomed out behind him and the bulky, white-smocked figure loomed out of the snow. 'A milk wagon on a cobbled street is as nothing compared to yourself and your friend here. But the snow muffled your voices and I could not be sure.'

Mallory looked at him curiously. 'How come you're here, Andrea?'

'Wood,' Andrea explained. 'I was looking for firewood. I was high up on Kostos at sunset when the snow lifted for a moment. I could have sworn I saw an old hut in a gully not far from here – it was dark and square against the snow. So I left – '

'You are right,' Louki interrupted. 'The hut of old Leri, the mad one. Leri was a goatherd. We all warned him, but Leri would listen and speak to no man, only to his goats. He died in his hut, in a landslide.'

'It is an ill wind...' Andrea murmured. 'Old Leri will

163

keep us warm tonight.' He checked abruptly as the gully opened up at his feet, then dropped quickly to the bottom, sure-footed as a mountain sheep. He whistled twice, a double high-pitched note, listening intently into the snow for the answering whistle, walked swiftly up the gully. Casey Brown, gun lowered, met them at the entrance to the cave and held back the canvas screen to let them pass inside.

The smoking tallow candle, guttering heavily to one side in the icy draught, filled every corner of the cave with dark and flickering shadows from its erratic flame. The candle itself was almost gone, the dripping wick bending over tiredly till it touched the rock, and Louki, snow-suit cast aside, was lighting another stump of candle from the dying flame. For a moment, both candles flared up together, and Mallory saw Louki clearly for the first time – a small, compact figure in a dark-blue jacket black-braided at the seams and flamboyantly frogged at the breast, the jacket tightly bound to his body by the crimson *tsanta* or cummerbund, and, above, the swarthy, smiling face, the magnificent moustache that he flaunted like a banner. A Laughing Cavalier of a man, a miniature d'Artagnan splendidly behung with weapons. And then Mallory's gaze travelled up to the lined, liquid eyes, eyes dark and sad and permanently tired, and his shock, a slow, uncomprehending shock, had barely time to register before the stub of the candle had flared up and died and Louki had sunk back into the shadows.

Stevens was stretched in a sleeping-bag, his breathing harsh and shallow and quick. He had been awake when they had arrived but had refused all food and drink, and turned away and drifted off into an uneasy jerky sleep. He seemed to be suffering no pain at all now: a bad sign, Mallory thought bleakly, the worst possible. He wished Miller would return...

Casey Brown washed down the last few crumbs of bread

with a mouthful of wine, rose stiffly to his feet, pulled the screen aside and peered out mournfully at the falling snow. He shuddered, let the canvas fall, lifted up his transmitter and shrugged into the shoulder straps, gathered up a coil of rope, a torch and a groundsheet. Mallory looked at his watch: it was fifteen minutes to midnight. The routine call from Cairo was almost due.

'Going to have another go, Casey? I wouldn't send a dog out on a night like this.'

'Neither would I,' Brown said morosely. 'But I think I'd better, sir. Reception is far better at night and I'm going to climb uphill a bit to get a clearance from that damned mountain there: I'd be spotted right away if I tried to do that in daylight.'

'Right you are, Casey. You know best.' Mallory looked at him curiously. 'What's all the extra gear for?'

'Putting the set under the groundsheet then getting below it myself with the torch,' Brown explained. 'And I'm pegging the rope here, going to pay it out on my way up. I'd like to be able to get back some time.'

'Good enough,' Mallory approved. 'Just watch it a bit higher up. This gully narrows and deepens into a regular ravine.'

'Don't you worry about me, sir,' Brown said firmly. 'Nothing's going to happen to Casey Brown.' A snow-laden gust of wind, the flap of the canvas and Brown was gone.

'Well, if Brown can do it...' Mallory was on his feet now, pulling his snow-smock over his head. 'Fuel, gentlemen – old Leri's hut. Who's for a midnight stroll?'

Andrea and Louki were on their feet together, but Mallory shook his head.

'One's enough. I think someone should stay to look after Stevens.'

'He's sound asleep,' Andrea murmured. 'He can come to no harm in the short time we are away.'

'I wasn't thinking of that. It's just that we can't take the chance of him falling into German hands. They'd make him talk, one way or another. It would be no fault of his – but they'd make him talk. It's too much of a risk.'

'Pouf!' Louki snapped his fingers. 'You worry about nothing, Major. There isn't a German within miles of here. You have my word.'

Mallory hesitated, then grinned. 'You're right. I'm getting the jumps.' He bent over Stevens, shook him gently. The boy stirred and moaned, opened his eyes slowly.

'We're going out for some firewood,' Mallory said. 'Back in a few minutes. You be O.K.?'

'Of course, sir. What can happen? Just leave a gun by my side – and blow out the candle.' He smiled. 'Be sure to call out before you come in!'

Mallory stooped, blew out the candle. For an instant the flame flared then died and every feature, every person in the cave was swallowed up in the thick darkness of a winter midnight. Abruptly Mallory turned on his heel and pushed out through the canvas into the drifting, wind-blown snow already filling up the floor of the gully, Andrea and Louki close behind.

It took them ten minutes to find the ruined hut of the old goatherd, another five for Andrea to wrench the door off its shattered hinges and smash it up to manageable lengths, along with the wood from the bunk and table, another ten to carry back with them to the rock-shelter as much wood as they could conveniently rope together and carry. The wind, blowing straight north off Kostos, was in their faces now – faces numbed with the chill, wet lash of the driving snow, and blowing almost at gale force: they were not sorry to reach the gully again, drop down gratefully between the sheltering walls.

Mallory called softly at the mouth of the cave. There was no reply, no movement from inside. He called again, listened intently as the silent seconds went by, turned his head and looked briefly at Andrea and Louki. Carefully, he laid his bundle of wood in the snow, pulled out his Colt

166

and torch, eased aside the curtain, lamp switch and Colt safety-catch clicking as one.

The spotlight beam lit up the floor at the mouth of the cave, passed on, settled, wavered, probed into the farthest corner of the shelter, returned again to the middle of the cave and steadied there as if the torch were clamped in a vice. On the floor there was only a crumpled, empty sleeping-bag. Andy Stevens was gone.

CHAPTER 9

Tuesday Night

0015–0200

'So I was wrong,' Andrea murmured. 'He wasn't asleep.'

'He certainly wasn't,' Mallory agreed grimly. 'He fooled me too – *and* he heard what I said.' His mouth twisted. 'He knows now why we're so anxious to look after him. He knows now that he was right when he spoke about a mill-stone. I should hate to feel the way he must be feeling right now.'

Andrea nodded. 'It is not difficult to guess why he has gone.'

Mallory looked quickly at his watch, pushed his way out of the cave.

'Twenty minutes – he can't have been gone more than twenty minutes. Probably a bit less to make sure we were well clear. He can only drag himself – fifty yards at the most. We'll find him in four minutes. Use your torches and take the hoods off – nobody will see us in this damn blizzard. Fan out uphill – I'll take the gully in the middle.'

'Uphill?' Louki's hand was on his arm, his voice puzzled. 'But his leg – '

'Uphill, I said,' Mallory broke in impatiently. 'Stevens has brains – and a damn sight more guts than he thinks we credit him with. He'll figure we'll think he's taken the easy way.' Mallory paused a moment then went on sombrely: 'Any dying man who drags himself out in this lot is going to do nothing the easy way. Come on!'

They found him in exactly three minutes. He must have suspected that Mallory wouldn't fall for the obvious, or he had heard them stumbling up the slope, for he had managed to burrow his way in behind the overhanging snowdrift that sealed off the space beneath a projecting ledge just above the rim of the gully. An almost perfect place of concealment, but his leg betrayed him: in the probing light of his torch Andrea's sharp eyes caught the tiny trickle of blood seeping darkly through the surface of the snow. He was already unconscious when they uncovered him, from cold or exhaustion or the agony of his shattered leg: probably from all three.

Back in the cave again, Mallory tried to pour some ouzo – the fiery, breath-catching local spirit – down Stevens's throat. He had a vague suspicion that this might be dangerous – or perhaps it was only dangerous in cases of shock, his memory was confused on that point – but it seemed better than nothing. Stevens gagged, spluttered and coughed most of it back up again, but some at least stayed down. With Andrea's help Mallory tightened the loosened splints on the leg, staunched the oozing blood, and spread below and above the boy every dry covering he could find in the cave. Then he sat back tiredly and fished out a cigarette from his waterproof case. There was nothing more he could do until Dusty Miller returned with Panayis from the village. He was pretty sure there was nothing that Dusty could do for Stevens either. There was nothing anybody could do for him.

Already Louki had a fire burning near the mouth of the cave, the old, tinder-dry wood blazing up in a fierce, crackling blaze with hardly a wisp of smoke. Almost at once its warmth began to spread throughout the cave, and the three men edged gratefully nearer. From half a dozen points in the roof thin, steadily-increasing streams of water from the melting snows above began to splash down on the gravelly floor beneath: with these and with the heat of the blaze, the ground was soon a quagmire. But, especially to Mallory and Andrea, these discomforts were a small price to pay for the privilege of being warm for the first time in over thirty hours. Mallory felt the glow seep through him like a benison, felt his entire body relax, his eyelids grow heavy and drowsy.

Back propped against the wall, he was just drifting off to sleep, still smoking that first cigarette, when there was a gust of wind, a sudden chilling flurry of snow and Brown was inside the cave, wearily slipping the transmitter straps from his shoulders. Lugubrious as ever, his tired eyes lit up momentarily at the sight of the fire. Blue-faced and shuddering with cold – no joke, Mallory thought grimly, squatting motionless for half an hour on that bleak and frozen hillside – he hunched down silently by the fire, dragged out the inevitable cigarette and gazed moodily into the flames, oblivious alike of the clouds of steam that almost immediately enveloped him, of the acrid smell of his singeing clothes. He looked utterly despondent. Mallory reached for a bottle, poured out some of the heated *retsina* – mainland wine heavily reinforced with resin – and passed it across to Brown.

'Chuck it straight down the hatch,' Mallory advised. 'That way you won't taste it.' He prodded the transmitter with his foot and looked up at Brown again. 'No dice this time either?'

'Raised them no bother, sir.' Brown grimaced at the sticky sweetness of the wine. 'Reception was first class – both here and in Cairo.'

'You got through!' Mallory sat up, leaned forward eagerly. 'And were they pleased to hear from their wandering boys tonight?'

'They didn't say. The first thing they told me was to shut up and stay that way.' Brown poked moodily at the fire with a steaming boot. 'Don't ask me how, sir, but they've been tipped off that enough equipment for two or three small monitoring stations has been sent here in the past fortnight.'

Mallory swore.

'Monitoring stations! That's damned handy, that is!' He thought briefly of the fugitive, nomad existence these

170

same monitoring stations had compelled Andrea and himself to lead in the White Mountains of Crete. 'Dammit, Casey, on an island like this, the size of a soup plate, they can pin-point us with their eyes shut!'

'Aye, they can that, sir,' Brown nodded heavily.

'Have you heard anything of these stations, Louki?' Mallory asked.

'Nothing, Major; nothing.' Louki shrugged. 'I am afraid I do not even know what you are talking about.'

'I don't suppose so. Not that it matters — it's too late now. Let's have the rest of the good news, Casey.'

'That's about it, sir. No sending for me — by order. Restricted to code abbreviations — affirmative, negative, repetitive, wilco and such-like. Continuous sending only in emergency or when concealment's impossible anyway.'

'Like from the condemned cell in those ducky little dungeons in Navarone,' Mallory murmured. '"I died with my boots on, ma."'

'With all respects, sir, that's not funny,' Brown said morosely. 'Their invasion fleet — mainly caiques and E-boats — sailed this morning from the Piraeus,' he went on. 'About four o'clock this morning. Cairo expects they'll be holing up in the Cyclades somewhere tonight.'

'That's very clever of Cairo. Where the hell else could they hole up?' Mallory lit a fresh cigarette and looked bleakly into the fire. 'Anyway, it's nice to know they're on the way. That the lot, Casey?'

Brown nodded silently.

'Good enough, then. Thanks a lot for going out. Better turn in, catch up with some sleep while you can…. Louki reckons we should be down in Margaritha before dawn, hole up there for the day — he's got some sort of abandoned well all lined up for us — and push on to the town of Navarone tomorrow night.'

'My God!' Brown moaned. 'Tonight a leaking cave. Tomorrow night an abandoned well — half-full of water probably. Where are we staying in Navarone, sir. The crypt in the local cemetery.'

'A singularly apt lodging, the way things are going,' Mallory said dryly. 'We'll hope for the best. We're leaving before five.' He watched Brown lie down beside Stevens and transferred his attention to Louki. The little man was seated on a box on the opposite side of the fire, occasionally turning a heavy stone to be wrapped in cloth and put to Stevens's numbed feet, and blissfully hugging the flames. By and by he became aware of Mallory's close scrutiny and looked up.

'You look worried, Major.' Louki seemed vexed. 'You look – what is the word? – concerned. You do not like my plan, no? I thought we had agreed – '

'I'm not worried about your plan,' Mallory said frankly. 'I'm not even worried about you. It's that box you're sitting on. Enough H.E. in it to blow up a battleship – and you're only three feet from that fire. It's not just too healthy, Louki.'

Louki shifted uneasily on his seat, tugged at one end of his moustache.

'I have heard that you can throw this T.N.T. into a fire and that it just burns up nicely, like a pine full of sap.'

'True enough,' Mallory acquiesced. 'You can also bend it, break it, file it, saw it, jump on it and hit it with a sledge-hammer, and all you'll get is the benefit of the exercise. But if it starts to sweat in a hot, humid atmosphere – and then the exudation crystallises. Oh, brother! And it's getting far too hot and sticky in this hole.

'Outside with it!' Louki was on his feet, backing farther into the cave. 'Outside with it!' He hesitated. 'Unless the snow, the moisture – '

'You can also leave it immersed in salt water for ten years without doing it any harm,' Mallory interrupted didactically. 'But there are some primers there that might come to grief – not to mention that box of detonators beside Andrea. We'll just stick the lot outside, under a cape.'

'Pouf! Louki has a far better idea!' The little man was already slipping into his cloak. 'Old Leri's hut! The very place. Exactly! We can pick it up there whenever we want – and if you have to leave in a hurry you do not have to worry about it.' Before Mallory could protest, Louki had bent over the box lifted it with an effort, half-walked, half-staggered round the fire, making for the screen. He had hardly taken three steps when Andrea was by his side, had relieved him firmly of the box and tucked it under one arm.

'If you will permit me – '

'No, no!' Louki was affronted. 'I can manage easily. It is nothing.'

'I know, I know,' Andrea said pacifically. 'But these explosives – they must be carried a certain way. I have been trained,' he explained.

'So? I did not realise. Of course it must be as you say! I, then, will bring the detonators.' Honour satisfied, Louki thankfully gave up the argument, lifted the little box and scuttled out of the cave close on Andrea's heels.

Mallory looked at his watch. One o'clock exactly. Miller and Panayis should be back soon, he thought. The wind had passed its peak and the snow was almost gone: the going would be all that easier, but there would be tracks in the snow. Awkward, these tracks, but not fatal – they themselves would be gone before light, cutting straight downhill for the foot of the valley. The snow wouldn't lie there – and even if there were patches they could take to the stream that wound through the valley, leaving no trace behind.

The fire was sinking and the cold creeping in on them again. Mallory shivered in his still wet clothes, threw some more wood on the fire, watched it blaze up, and flood the cave with light. Brown, huddled on a ground-sheet, was already asleep. Stevens, his back to him, was lying motionless, his breathing short and quick. God only

173

knew how long the boy would stay alive: he was dying, Miller said, but 'dying' was a very indefinite term: when a man, a terribly injured, dying man, made up his mind not to die he became the toughest, most enduring creature on earth. Mallory had seen it happen before. But maybe Stevens didn't want to live. To live, to overcome these desperate injuries – that would be to prove himself to himself, and to others, and he was young enough, and sensitive enough and had been hurt and had suffered so much in the past that that could easily be the most important thing in the world to him: on the other hand, he knew what an appalling handicap he had become – he had heard Mallory say so; he knew, too, that Mallory's primary concern was not for his welfare but the fear that he would be captured, crack under pressure and tell everything – he had heard Mallory say so; and he knew that he had failed his friends. It was all very difficult, impossible to say how the balance of contending forces would work out eventually. Mallory shook his head, sighed, lit a fresh cigarette and moved closer to the fire.

Andrea and Louki returned less than five minutes later, and Miller and Panayis were almost at their heels. They could hear Miller coming some distance away, slipping, falling and swearing almost continuously as he struggled up the gully under a large and awkward load. He practically fell across the threshold of the cave and collapsed wearily by the fire. He gave the impression of a man who had been through a very great deal indeed. Mallory grinned sympathetically at him.

'Well, Dusty, how did it go? Hope Panayis here didn't slow you up too much.'

Miller didn't seem to hear him. He was gazing incredulously at the fire, lantern jaw drooping open as its significance slowly dawned on him.

'Hell's teeth! Would you look at that!' He swore bitterly. 'Here I spend half the gawddamned night climbing up a gawddamned mountain with a stove and enough kerosene to bath a bloody elephant. And what do I find?' He took a deep breath to tell them what he found, then subsided into a strangled, seething silence.

'A man your age should watch his blood pressure,' Mallory advised him. 'How did the rest of it go?'

'Okay, I guess.' Miller had a mug of ouzo in his hand and was beginning to brighten up again. 'We got the beddin', the medicine kit – '

'If you'll give me the bedding I will get our young friend into it now,' Andrea interrupted.

'And food?' Mallory asked.

'Yeah. We got the grub, boss. Stacks of it. This guy Panayis is a wonder. Bread, wine, goat-cheese, garlic sausages, rice – everything.'

'Rice?' It was Mallory's turn to be incredulous. 'But you can't get the stuff in the islands nowadays, Dusty.'

'Panayis can.' Miller was enjoying himself hugely now. 'He got it from the German commandant's kitchen. Guy by the name of Skoda.'

'The German commandant's – you're joking!'

'So help me, boss, that's Gospel truth.' Miller drained half the ouzo at a gulp and expelled his breath in a long, gusty sigh of satisfaction. 'Little ol' Miller hangs around the back door, knees knockin' like Carmen Miranda's castanets, ready for a smart take off in any direction while Junior here goes in and cracks the joint. Back home in the States he'd make a fortune as a cat-burglar. Comes back in about ten minutes, luggin' that damned suitcase there.' Miller indicated it with a casual wave of his hand. 'Not only cleans out the commandant's pantry, but also borrows his satchel to carry the stuff in. I tell you, boss, associatin' with this character gives me heart attacks.'

'But – but how about guards, about sentries?'

'Taken the night off, I guess, boss. Old Panayis is like a clam – never says a word, and even then I can't understand him. My guess is that everybody's out lookin' for us.'

'There and back and you didn't meet a soul.' Mallory filled him with a mug of wine. 'Nice going, Dusty.'

'Panayis's doin', not mine. I just tagged along. Besides, we did run into a couple of Panayis's pals – he hunted them up rather. Musta given him the tip-off about somethin'. He was hoppin' with excitement just afterwards, tried to tell me all about it.' Miller shrugged his shoulders sadly. 'We weren't operatin' on the same wave-length, boss.'

Mallory nodded across the cave. Louki and Panayis were close together, Louki doing all the listening, while Panayis talked rapidly in a low voice, gesticulating with both hands.

'He's still pretty worked up about something,' Mallory said thoughtfully. He raised his voice. 'What's the matter, Louki?'

'Matter enough, Major.' Louki tugged ferociously at the end of his moustache. 'We will have to be leaving soon – Panayis wants to go right away. He has heard that the German garrison is going to make a house-to-house check in our village during the night – about four o'clock, Panayis was told.'

'Not a routine check, I take it?' Mallory asked.

'This has not happened for many months. They must think that you have slipped their patrols and are hiding in the village.' Louki chuckled. 'If you ask me, I don't think they know *what* to think. It is nothing to you, of course. You will not be there – and even if you were they would not find you: and it will make it all the safer for you to come to Margaritha afterwards. But Panayis and I – we must not be found out of our beds. Things would go hard with us.'

'Of course, of course. We must take no risks. But there is plenty of time. You will go down in an hour. But first, the fortress.' He dug into his breast pocket, brought out the map Eugene Vlachos had drawn for him, turned to Panayis and slipped easily into the island Greek. 'Come,

Panayis. I hear you know the fortress as Louki here knows his own vegetable patch. I already know much, but I want you to tell me everything about it – the layout, guns, magazines, power rooms, barracks, sentries, guard routine, exits, alarm systems, even where the shadows are deep and the others less deep – just everything. No matter how tiny and insignificant the details may seem to you, nevertheless you must tell me. If a door opens outwards instead of inwards, you must tell me: that could save a thousand lives.'

'And how does the Major mean to get inside?' Louki asked.

'I don't know yet. I cannot decide until I have seen the fortress.' Mallory was aware of Andrea looking sharply at him, then looking away. They had made their plans on the M.T.B. for entering the fortress. But it was the keystone upon which everything depended, and Mallory felt that this knowledge should be confined to the fewest number possible.

For almost half an hour Mallory and the three Greeks huddled over the chart in the light of the flames, Mallory checking on what he had been told, meticulously pencilling in all the fresh information that Panayis had to give him – and Panayis had a very great deal to tell. It seemed almost impossible that a man could have assimilated so much in two brief visits to the fortress – and clandestine visits in the darkness, at that. He had an incredible eye and capacity for detail; and it was a burning hatred of the Germans, Mallory felt certain, that had imprinted these details on an all but photographic memory. Mallory could feel his hopes rising with every second that passed.

Casey Brown was awake again. Tired though he was, the babble of voices had cut through an uneasy sleep. He crossed over to where Andy Stevens, half-awake now, lay propped against the wall, talking rationally at times, incoherently at others. There was nothing for him to do there, Brown saw: Miller, cleaning, dusting and

177

rebandaging the wounds had had all the help he needed – and very efficient help at that – from Andrea. He moved over to the mouth of the cave, listened blankly to the four men talking in Greek, moved out past the screen for a breath of the cold, clean night air. With seven people inside the cave and the fire burning continuously, the lack of almost all ventilation had made it uncomfortably warm.

He was back in the cave in thirty seconds, drawing the screen tightly shut behind him.

'Quiet, everybody!' he whispered softly. He gestured behind him. 'There's something moving out there, down the slope a bit. I heard it twice, sir.'

Panayis swore softly, twisted to his feet like a wild cat. A foot-long, two-edged throwing knife gleamed evilly in his hand and he had vanished through the canvas screen before anyone could speak. Andrea made to follow him, but Mallory stretched out his hand.

'Stay where you are, Andrea. Our friend Panayis is just that little bit too precipitate,' he said softly. 'There may be nothing – or it might be some diversionary move.... Oh, damn!' Stevens had just started babbling to himself in a loud voice. 'He would start talking now. Can't you do something...'

But Andrea was already bent over the sick boy, holding his hand in his own, smoothing the hot forehead and hair with his free hand and talking to him soothingly, softly, continuously. At first he paid no attention, kept on talking in a rambling, inconsequential fashion about nothing in particular; gradually, however, the hypnotic effect of the stroking hand, the gentle caressing murmur took effect, and the babbling died away to a barely audible muttering, ceased altogether. Suddenly his eyes opened and he was awake and quite rational.

'What is it, Andrea? Why are you – ?'

'Shh!' Mallory held up his hand. 'I can hear someone – '

'It's Panayis, sir.' Brown had his eye at a crack in the curtain. 'Just moving up the gully.'

Seconds later, Panayis was inside the cave, squatting down by the fire. He looked thoroughly disgusted.

'There is no one there,' he reported. 'Some goats I saw, down the hill, but that was all.' Mallory translated to the others.

'Didn't sound like goats to me,' Brown said doggedly. 'Different kind of sound altogether.'

'I will take a look,' Andrea volunteered. 'Just to make sure. But I do not think the dark one would make a mistake.' Before Mallory could say anything he was gone, as quickly and silently as Panayis. He was back in three minutes, shaking his head. 'Panayis is right. There is no one. I did not even see the goats.'

'And that's what it must have been, Casey,' Mallory said. 'Still, I don't like it. Snow almost stopped, wind dropping and the valley probably swarming with German patrols – I think it's time you two were away. For God's sake, be careful. If anyone tries to stop you, shoot to kill. They'll blame it on us anyway.'

'Shoot to kill!' Louki laughed dryly. 'Unnecessary advice, Major, when the dark one is with us. He never shoots any other way.'

'Right, away you go. Damned sorry you've got yourselves mixed up in all this – but now that you are, a thousand thanks for all you've done. See you at half-past six.'

'Half-past six,' Louki echoed. 'The olive grove on the bank of the stream, south of the village. We will be waiting there.'

Two minutes later they were lost to sight and sound and all was still inside the cave again, except for the faint crackling of the embers of the dying fire. Brown had moved out on guard, and Stevens had already fallen into a restless, pain-filled sleep. Miller bent over him for a moment or two, then moved softly across the cave to Mallory. His right hand held a crumpled heap of blood-stained bandages. He held them out towards Mallory.

'Take a sniff at that, boss,' he asked quietly. 'Easy does it.'

Mallory bent forward, drew away sharply, his nose wrinkled in immediate disgust.

'Good lord, Dusty! That's vile!' He paused, paused in sure, sick certainty. He knew the answer before he spoke. 'What on earth is it?'

'Gangrene.' Miller sat down heavily by his side, threw the bandages into the fire. All at once he sounded tired, defeated. 'Gas gangrene. Spreadin' like a forest fire – and he would have died anyway. I'm just wastin' my time.'

CHAPTER 10

Tuesday Night

0400—0600

The Germans took them just after four o'clock in the morning, while they were still asleep. Bone-tired and deep-drugged with this sleep as they were, they had no chance, not the slightest hope of offering any resistance. The conception, timing and execution of the coup were immaculate. Surprise was complete.

Andrea was the first awake. Some alien whisper of sound had reached deep down to that part of him that never slept, and he twisted round and elbowed himself off the ground with the same noiseless speed as his hand reached out for his ready-cocked and loaded Mauser. But the white beam of the powerful torch lancing through the blackness of the cave had blinded him, frozen his stretching hand even before the clipped bite of command from the man who held the torch.

'Still! All of you!' Faultless English, with barely a trace of accent, and the voice glacial in its menace. 'You move, and you die!' Another torch switched on, a third, and the cave was flooded with light. Wide awake, now, and motionless Mallory squinted painfully into the dazzling beams: in the back-wash of reflected light, he could just discern the vague, formless shapes crouched in the mouth of the cave, bent over the dulled barrels of automatic rifles.

'Hands clasped above the heads and backs to the wall!' A certainty, an assured competence in the voice that made for instant obedience. 'Take a good look at them, Sergeant.' Almost conversational now, the tone, but neither torch nor gun barrel had wavered a fraction. 'No shadow of expression in their faces, not even a flicker of the eyes. Dangerous men, Sergeant. The English choose their killers well!'

Mallory felt the grey bitterness of defeat wash through him in an almost tangible wave, he could taste the sourness of it in the back of his mouth. For a brief, heart-sickening second he allowed himself to think of what must now inevitably happen and as soon as the thought had come he thrust it savagely away. Everything, every action, every thought, every breath must be on the present. Hope was gone, but not irrecoverably gone: not so long as Andrea lived. He wondered if Casey Brown had seen or heard them coming, and what had happened to him: he made to ask, checked himself just in time. Maybe he was still at large.

'How did you manage to find us?' Mallory asked quietly.

'Only fools burn juniper wood,' the officer said contemptuously. 'We have been on Kostos all day and most of the night. A dead man could have smelt it.'

'On Kostos?' Miller shook his head. 'How could – ?'

'Enough!' The officer turned to someone behind him. 'Tear down that screen,' he ordered in German, 'and keep us covered on either side.' He looked back into the cave, gestured almost imperceptibly with his torch. 'All right, you three. Outside – and you had better be careful. Please believe me that my men are praying for an excuse to shoot you down, you murdering swine!' The venomous hatred in his voice carried utter conviction.

Slowly, hands still clasped above their heads, the three men stumbled to their feet. Mallory had taken only one step when the whip-lash of the German's voice brought him up short.

'Stop!' He stabbed the beam of his torch down at the unconscious Stevens, gestured abruptly at Andrea. 'One side, you! Who is this?'

'You need not fear from him,' Mallory said quietly. 'He is one of us but he is terribly injured. He is dying.'

'We will see,' the officer said tightly. 'Move to the back of the cave!' He waited until the three men had stepped over Stevens, changed his automatic rifle for a pistol, dropped to his knees and advanced slowly, torch in one hand, gun in the other, well below the line of fire of the two soldiers who advanced unbidden at his heels. There was an inevitability, a cold professionalism about it all that made Mallory's heart sink.

Abruptly the officer reached out his gun-hand, tore the covers off the boy. A shuddering tremor shook the whole body, his head rolled from side to side as he moaned in unconscious agony. The officer bent quickly over him, the hard, clean lines of the face, the fair hair beneath the hood high-lit in the beam of his own torch. A quick look at Stevens's pain-twisted, emaciated features, a glance at the shattered leg, a brief, distasteful wrinkling of the nose as he caught the foul stench of the gangrene, and he had hunched back on his heels, gently replacing the covers over the sick boy.

'You speak the truth,' he said softly. 'We are not barbarians. I have no quarrel with a dying man. Leave him there.' He rose to his feet, walked slowly backwards. 'The rest of you outside.'

The snow had stopped altogether, Mallory saw, and stars were beginning to twinkle in the clearing sky. The wind, too, had fallen away and was perceptibly warmer. Most of the snow would be gone by midday, Mallory guessed.

Carelessly, incuriously, he looked around him. There was no sign of Casey Brown. Inevitably Mallory's hopes began to rise. Petty Officer Brown's recommendation for this operation had come from the very top. Two rows of ribbons to which he was entitled but never wore bespoke his gallantry, he had a formidable reputation as a guerrilla fighter – and he had had an automatic rifle in his hand. If he were somewhere out there... Almost as if he had divined his hopes, the German smashed them at a word.

183

'You wonder where your sentry is, perhaps?' he asked mockingly. 'Never fear, Englishman, he is not far from here, asleep at his post. Very sound asleep, I'm afraid.'

'You've killed him?' Mallory's hands clenched until his palms ached.

The other shrugged his shoulder in vast indifference.

'I really couldn't say. It was all too easy. One of my men lay in the gully and moaned. A masterly performance – really pitiable – he almost had me convinced. Like a fool your man came to investigate. I had another man waiting above, the barrel of his rifle in his hand. A very effective club, I assure you....'

Slowly Mallory unclenched his fists and stared bleakly down the gully. Of course Casey would fall for that, he was bound to after what had happened earlier in the night. He wasn't going to make a fool of himself again, cry 'wolf' twice in succession: inevitably, he had gone to check first. Suddenly the thought occurred to Mallory that maybe Casey Brown *had* heard something earlier on, but the thought vanished as soon as it had come. Panayis did not look like the man to make a mistake: and Andrea never made a mistake; Mallory turned back to the officer again.

'Well, where do we go from here?'

'Margaritha, and very shortly. But one thing first.' The German, his own height to an inch, stood squarely in front of him, levelled revolver at waist height, switched-off torch dangling loosely from his right hand. 'Just a little thing, Englishman. Where are the explosives?' He almost spat the words out.

'Explosives?' Mallory furrowed his brows in perplexity. 'What explosives?' he asked blankly, then staggered and fell to the ground as the heavy torch swept round in a vicious half-circle, caught him flush on the side of the face. Dizzily he shook his head and climbed slowly to his feet again.

'The explosives.' The torch was balanced in the hand again, the voice silky and gentle 'I asked you where they were.'

184

'I don't know what you are talking about.' Mallory spat out a broken tooth, wiped some blood off his smashed lips. 'Is this the way the Germans treat their prisoners?' he asked contemptuously.

'Shut up!'

Again the torch lashed out. Mallory was waiting for it, rode the blow as best he could: even so the torch caught him heavily high up on the cheek-bone, just below the temple, stunning him with its jarring impact. Seconds passed, then he pushed himself slowly off the snow, the whole side of his face afire with agony, his vision blurred and unfocused.

'We fight a clean war!' The officer was breathing heavily, in barely controlled fury. 'We fight by the Geneva Conventions. But these are for soldiers, not for murdering spies '

'We are no spies!' Mallory interrupted. He felt as if his head was coming apart.

'Then where are your uniforms?' the officer demanded. 'Spies, I say – murdering spies who stab in the back and cut men's throats!' The voice was trembling with anger. Mallory was at a loss – nothing spurious about this indignation.

'Cut men's throats?' He shook his head in bewilderment. 'What the hell are you talking about?'

'My own batman. A harmless messenger, a boy only – and he wasn't even armed. We found him only an hour ago. Ach, I waste my time!' He broke off as he turned to watch two men coming up the gully. Mallory stood motionless for a moment, cursing the ill luck that had led the dead man across the path of Panayis – it could have been no one else – then turned to see what had caught the officer's attention. He focused his aching eyes with difficulty, looked at the bent figure struggling up the slope, urged on by the ungentle prodding of a bayoneted rifle. Mallory let go a long, silent breath of relief. The left side of Brown's face was caked with blood from a gash above

185

the temple, but he was otherwise unharmed.

'Right! Sit down in the snow, all of you!' He gestured to several of his men. 'Bind their hands!'

'You are going to shoot us now, perhaps?' Mallory asked quietly. It was suddenly, desperately urgent that he should know: there was nothing they could do but die, but at least they could die on their feet, fighting; but if they weren't to die just yet, almost any later opportunity for resistance would be less suicidal than this.

'Not yet, unfortunately. My section commander in Margaritha, Hauptmann Skoda, wishes to see you first — maybe it would be better for you if I *did* shoot you now. Then the Herr Commandant in Navarone — Officer Commanding of the whole island.' The German smiled thinly. 'But only a postponement, Englishman. You will be kicking your heels before the sun sets. We have a short way with spies in Navarone.'

'But, sir! Captain!' Hands raised in appeal, Andrea took a step forward, brought up short as two rifle muzzles ground into his chest.

'Not Captain — Lieutenant,' the officer corrected him. 'Oberleutnant Turzig, at your service. What is it you want, fat one?' he asked contemptuously.

'Spies! You said spies! I am no spy!' The words rushed and tumbled over one another, as if he could not get them out fast enough. 'Before God, I am no spy! I am not one of them.' The eyes were wide and staring, the mouth working soundlessly between the gasped-out sentences. 'I am only a Greek, a poor Greek. They forced me to come along as an interpreter. I swear it, Lieutenant Turzig, I swear it!'

'You yellow bastard!' Miller ground out viciously, then grunted in agony as a rifle butt drove into the small of his back, just above the kidney. He stumbled, fell forward on his hands and knees, realised even as he fell that Andrea was only playing a part, that Mallory had only to speak half a dozen words in Greek to expose Andrea's lie. Miller twisted on his side in the snow, shook his fist weakly and hoped that the contorted pain on his face might be mistaken for fury. 'You two-faced, double-crossing dago! You gawddamned swine, I'll get you....' There was a hollow, sickening thud and Miller collapsed in the snow: the heavy ski-boot had caught him just behind the ear.

Mallory said nothing. He did not even glance at Miller. Fists balled helplessly at his sides and mouth compressed, he glared steadily at Andrea through narrowed slits of eyes. He knew the lieutenant was watching him, felt he must back Andrea up all the way. What Andrea intended he could not even begin to guess – but he would back him to the end of the world.

'So!' Turzig murmured thoughtfully. 'Thieves fall out, eh?' Mallory thought he detected the faintest overtones of doubt, of hesitancy, in his voice, but the lieutenant was taking no chances. 'No matter, fat one. You have cast your lot with these assassins. What is it the English say? "You have made your bed, you must lie on it."' He looked at Andrea's vast bulk dispassionately. 'We may need to strengthen a special gallows for you.'

'No, no, no!' Andrea's voice rose sharply, fearfully, on the last word. 'It is true what I tell you! I am not one of them, Lieutenant Turzig, before God I am not one of them!' He wrung his hands in distress, his great moonface contorted in anguish. 'Why must I die for no fault of my own? I didn't want to come. I am no fighting man, Lieutenant Turzig!'

'I can see that,' Turzig said dryly. 'A monstrous deal of skin to cover a quivering jelly-bag your size – and every inch of it precious to you.' He looked at Mallory, and at Miller, still lying face down in the snow. 'I cannot congratulate your friends on their choice of companion.'

'I can tell you everything, Lieutenant, I can tell you everything!' Andrea pressed forward excitedly, eager to consolidate his advantage, to reinforce the beginnings of doubt. 'I am no friend of the Allies – I will prove it to you – and then perhaps – '

'You damned Judas!' Mallory made to fling himself forward, but two burly soldiers caught him and pinioned his arms from behind. He struggled briefly, then relaxed, looked balefully at Andrea. 'If you dare to open your mouth, I promise you you'll never live to – '

'Be quiet!' Turzig's voice was very cold. 'I have had enough of recriminations, of cheap melodrama. Another word and you join your friend in the snow there.' He looked at him a moment in silence, then swung back to Andrea. 'I promise nothing. I will hear what you have to say.' He made no attempt to disguise the repugnance in his voice.

'You must judge for yourself.' A nice mixture of relief, earnestness and the dawn of hope, of returning confidence. Andrea paused a minute and gestured dramatically at Mallory, Miller and Brown. 'These are no ordinary soldiers – they are Jellicoe's men, of the Special Boat Service!'

'Tell me something I couldn't have guessed myself,' Turzig growled. 'The English Earl has been a thorn in our flesh these many months past. If that is all you have to tell me, fat one – '

'Wait!' Andrea held up his hand. 'They are still no ordinary men but a specially picked force – an assault unit, they call themselves – flown last Sunday night from Alexandria to Castelrosso. They left that same night from Castelrosso in a motor-boat.'

'A torpedo boat,' Turzig nodded. 'So much we know already. Go on.'

'You know already! But how – ?'

'Never mind how. Hurry up!'

'Of course, Lieutenant, of course.' Not a twitch in his face betrayed Andrea's relief. This had been the only dangerous point in his story. Nicolai, of course, had warned the Germans, but never thought it worth while mentioning the presence of a giant Greek in the party. No reason, of course, why he should have selected him for special mention – but if he had done, it would have been the end.

'The torpedo boat landed them somewhere in the islands, north of Rhodes. I do not know where. There they stole a caique, sailed it up through Turkish waters, met a big German patrol boat – and sunk it.' Andrea paused for effect. 'I was less than half a mile away at the time in my fishing boat.'

Turzig leaned forward. 'How did they manage to sink so big a boat?' Strangely, he didn't doubt that it had been sunk.

'They pretended to be harmless fishermen like myself. I had just been stopped, investigated and cleared,' Andrea said virtuously. 'Anyway, your patrol boat came alongside this old caique. Close alongside. Suddenly there were guns firing on both sides, two boxes went flying through the air – into the engine-room of your boat, I think. Pouf!' Andrea threw up his hands dramatically. 'That was the end of that!'

'We wondered...' Turzig said softly. 'Well, go on.'

'You wondered what, Lieutenant?' Turzig's eyes narrowed and Andrea hurried on.

'Their interpreter had been killed in the fight. They tricked me into speaking English – I spent many years in Cyprus – kidnapped me, let my sons sail the boat – '

'Why should they want an interpreter?' Turzig demanded suspiciously. 'There are many British officers who speak Greek.'

'I am coming to that,' Andrea said impatiently. 'How in God's name do you expect me to finish my story if you keep interrupting all the time? Where was I? Ah, yes. They forced me to come along, and their engine broke down. I don't know what happened – I was kept below. I think we were in a creek somewhere, repairing the engine, and then there was a wild bout of drinking – you will not believe this, Lieutenant Turzig, that men on so desperate a mission should get drunk – and then we sailed again.'

189

'On the contrary, I do believe you.' Turzig was nodding his head slowly, as if in secret understanding. 'I believe you indeed.'

'You do?' Andrea contrived to look disappointed. 'Well, we ran into a fearful storm, wrecked the boat on the south cliff of this island and climbed – '

'Stop!' Turzig had drawn back sharply, suspicion flaring in his eyes. 'Almost I believed you! I believed you because we know more than you think, and so far you have told the truth. But not now. You are clever, fat one, but not so clever as you think. One thing you have forgotten – or maybe you do not know. We are of the *Württembergische Gebirgsbataillon* – we *know* mountains, my friend, better than any troops in the world. I myself am a Prussian, but I have climbed everything worth climbing in the Alps and Transylvania – and I tell you that the south cliff cannot be climbed. It is impossible!'

'Impossible perhaps for you.' Andrea shook his head sadly. 'These cursed Allies will beat you yet. They are clever, Lieutenant Turzig, damnably clever!'

'Explain yourself,' Turzig ordered curtly.

'Just this. They knew men thought the south cliff could not be climbed. So they determined to climb it. You would never dream that this could be done, that an expedition could land on Navarone that way. But the Allies took a gamble, found a man to lead the expedition. He could not speak Greek, but that did not matter, for what they wanted was a man who could climb – and so they picked the greatest rock-climber in the world today.' Andrea paused for effect, flung out his arm dramatically. 'And this is the man they picked, Lieutenant Turzig! You are a mountaineer yourself and you are bound to know him. His name is Mallory – Keith Mallory of New Zealand!'

There was a sharp exclamation, the click of a switch, and Turzig had taken a couple of steps forward, thrust the torch almost into Mallory's eyes. For almost ten seconds he stared into the New Zealander's averted, screwed-up face, then slowly lowered his arm, the harsh spotlight limning a dazzling white circle in the snow at his feet. Once, twice, half a dozen times Turzig nodded his head in slow understanding.

'Of course!' he murmured. 'Mallory — Keith Mallory! Of course I know him. There's not a man in my *Abteilung* but has heard of Keith Mallory.' He shook his head. 'I should have known him, I should have known him at once.' He stood for some time with his head bent, aimlessly screwing the toe of his right boot into the soft snow, then looked up abruptly. 'Before the war, even during it, I would have been proud to have known you, glad to have met you. But not here, not now. Not any more. I wish to God they had sent someone else.' He hesitated, made to carry on, then changed his mind, turned wearily to Andrea. 'My apologies, fat one. Indeed you speak the truth. Go on.'

'Certainly!' Andrea's round moon face was one vast smirk of satisfaction. 'We climbed the cliff as I said — although the boy in the cave there was badly hurt — and silenced the guard. Mallory killed him,' Andrea added unblushingly. 'It was a fair fight. We spent most of the night crossing the divide and found this cave before dawn. We were almost dead with hunger and cold. We have been here since.'

'And nothing has happened since?'

'On the contrary.' Andrea seemed to be enjoying himself hugely, revelling in being the focus of attention. 'Two people came up to see us. Who they were I do not know — they kept their faces hidden all the time — nor do I know where they came from.'

'It is as well that you admitted that,' Turzig said grimly. 'I knew someone had been here. I recognised the stove — it belongs to Hauptmann Skoda!'

'Indeed?' Andrea raised his eyebrows in polite surprise. 'I did not know. Well, they talked for some time and — '

'Did you manage to overhear anything they were

191

talking about?' Turzig interrupted. The question came so naturally, so spontaneously, that Mallory held his breath. It was beautifully done. Andrea would walk into it – he couldn't help it. But Andrea was a man inspired that night.

'Overhear them!' Andrea clamped his lips shut in sorely-tried forbearance, gazed heavenwards in exasperated appeal. 'Lieutenant Turzig, how often must I tell you that I am the interpreter? They *could* only talk through me. Of course I know what they were talking about. They are going to blow up the big guns in the harbour.'

'I didn't think they had come here for their health!' Turzig said acidly.

'Ah, but you don't know that they have plans of the fortress. You don't know that Kheros is to be invaded on Saturday morning. You don't know that they are in radio contact with Cairo all the time. You don't know that destroyers of the British Navy are coming through the Maidos Straits on Friday night as soon as the big guns have been silenced. You don't know – '

'Enough!' Turzig clapped his hands together, his face alight with excitement. 'The Royal Navy, eh? Wonderful, wonderful! *That* is what we want to hear. But enough! Keep it for Hauptmann Skoda and the Kommandant in the fortress. We must be off. But first – one more thing. The explosives – where are they?'

'Alas, Lieutenant Turzig, I do not know. They took them out and hid them – some talk about the cave being too hot.' He waved a hand towards the western col, in the diametrically opposite direction to Leri's hut. 'That way, I think. But I cannot be sure, for they would not tell me.' He looked bitterly at Mallory. 'These Britishers are all the same. They trust nobody.'

'Heaven only knows that I don't blame them for that!' Turzig said feelingly. He looked at Andrea in disgust. 'More than ever I would like to see you dangling from the highest scaffold in Navarone. But Herr Kommandant in

192

the town is a kindly man and rewards informers. You may yet live to betray some more comrades.'

'Thank you, thank you, thank you! I knew you were fair and just. I promise you, Lieutenant Turzig – '

'Shut up!' Turzig said contemptuously. He switched into German. 'Sergeant, have these men bound. And don't forget the fat one! Later we can untie him, and he can carry the sick man back to the post. Leave a man on guard. The rest of you come with me – we must find those explosives.'

'Could we not make one of them tell us, sir?' the sergeant ventured.

'The only man who would tell us, can't. He's already told us all he knows. As for the rest – well, I was mistaken about them, Sergeant.' He turned to Mallory, inclined his head briefly, spoke in English. 'An error of judgment, Herr Mallory. We are all very tired. I am almost sorry I struck you.' He wheeled abruptly, climbed swiftly up the bank. Two minutes later only a solitary soldier was left on guard.

For the tenth time Mallory shifted his position uncomfortably, strained at the cord that bound his hands together behind his back, for the tenth time recognised the futility of both these actions. No matter how he twisted and turned, the wet snow soaked icily through his clothes until he was chilled to the bone and shaking continually with the cold; and the man who had tied these knots had known his job all too well. Mallory wondered irritably if Turzig and his men meant to spend all night searching for the explosives: they had been gone for more than half an hour already.

He relaxed, lay back on his side in the cushioning snow of the gully bank, and looked thoughtfully at Andrea who was sitting upright just in front of him. He had watched Andrea, with bowed head and hunched and lifting shoulders, making one single, titanic effort to free himself seconds after the guard had gestured to them to sit down,

193

had seen the cords bite and gouge until they had almost disappeared in his flesh, the fractional slump of his shoulders as he gave up. Since then the giant Greek had sat quite still and contented himself with scowling at the sentry in the injured fashion of one who has been grievously wronged. That solitary test of the strength of his bonds had been enough. Oberleutnant Turzig had keen eyes, and swollen, chafed and bleeding wrists would have accorded ill with the character Andrea had created for himself.

A masterly creation, Mallory mused, all the more remarkable for its spontaneity, its improvisation. Andrea had told so much of the truth, so much that was verifiable or could be verified, that belief in the rest of his story followed almost automatically. And at the same time he had told Turzig nothing of importance, nothing the Germans could not have found out for themselves – except the proposed evacuation of Kheros by the Navy. Wryly Mallory remembered his dismay, his shocked unbelief when he heard Andrea telling of it – but Andrea had been far ahead of him. There was a fair chance that the Germans might have guessed anyway – they would reason, perhaps, that an assault by the British on the guns of Navarone at the same time as the German assault on Kheros would be just that little bit too coincidental: again, escape for them all quite clearly depended upon how thoroughly Andrea managed to convince his captors that he was all he claimed, and the relative freedom of action that he could thereby gain – and there was no doubt at all that it was the news of the proposed evacuation that had tipped the scales with Turzig: and the fact that Andrea had given Saturday as the invasion date would only carry all the more weight, as that had been Jensen's original date – obviously false information fed to his agents by German counter-Intelligence, who had known it impossible to conceal the invasion preparations themselves; and finally, if Andrea hadn't told Turzig of the destroyers, he might have failed to carry conviction, they might all yet finish on the waiting gallows in the fortress, the guns would remain intact and destroy the naval ships anyway.

It was all very complicated, too complicated for the state his head was in. Mallory sighed and looked away from Andrea towards the other two. Brown and a now conscious Miller were both sitting upright, hands bound behind their backs, staring down into the snow, occasionally shaking muzzy heads from side to side. Mallory could appreciate all too easily how they felt — the whole right-hand side of his face ached cruelly, continuously. Nothing but aching, broken heads everywhere, Mallory thought bitterly. He wondered how Andy Stevens was feeling, glanced idly past the sentry towards the dark mouth of the cave, stiffened in sudden, almost uncomprehending shock.

Slowly, with an infinitely careful carelessness, he let his eyes wander away from the cave, let them light indifferently on the sentry who sat on Brown's transmitter, hunched watchfully over the Schmeisser cradled on his knees, finger crooked on the trigger. Pray God he doesn't turn round, Mallory said to himself over and over again, pray God he doesn't turn round. Let him sit like that just for a little while longer, only a little while longer.... In spite of himself, Mallory felt his gaze shifting, being dragged back again towards that cave-mouth.

Andy Stevens was coming out of the cave. Even in the dim starlight every movement was terribly plain as he inched forward agonisingly on chest and belly, dragging his shattered leg behind him. He was placing his hands beneath his shoulders, levering himself upwards and forwards while his head dropped below his shoulders with pain and the exhaustion of the effort, lowering himself slowly on the soft and sodden snow, then repeating the same heart-sapping process over and over again. Exhausted and pain-filled as the boy might be, Mallory thought, his mind was still working: he had a white sheet

195

over his shoulders and back as camouflage against the snow, and he carried a climbing spike in his right hand. He must have heard at least some of Turzig's conversation: there were two or three guns in the cave, he could easily have shot the guard without coming out at all – but he must have known that the sound of a shot would have brought the Germans running, had them back at the cave long before he could have crawled across the gully, far less cut loose any of his friends.

Five yards Stevens had to go, Mallory estimated, five yards at the most. Deep down in the gully where they were, the south wind passed them by, was no more than a muted whisper in the night; that apart, there was no sound at all, nothing but their own breathing, the occasional stirring as someone stretched a cramped or frozen leg. He's bound to hear him if he comes any closer, Mallory thought desperately, even in that soft snow he's bound to hear him.

Mallory bent his head, began to cough loudly, almost continuously. The sentry looked at him, in surprise first, then in irritation as the coughing continued.

'Be quiet!' the sentry ordered in German. 'Stop that coughing at once!'

'*Hüsten? Hüsten?* Coughing, is it? I can't help it,' Mallory protested in English. He coughed again, louder, more persistently than before. 'It is your Oberleutnant's fault,' he gasped. 'He has knocked out some of my teeth.' Mallory broke into a fresh paroxysm of coughing, recovering himself with an effort. 'Is it my fault that I'm choking on my own blood?' he demanded.

Stevens was less than ten feet away now, but his tiny reserves of strength were almost gone. He could no longer raise himself to the full stretch of his arms, was advancing only a few pitiful inches at a time. At length he stopped altogether, lay still for half a minute. Mallory thought he had lost consciousness, but by and by he raised himself up again, to the full stretch this time, had just begun to pivot himself forward when he collapsed, fell heavily in the snow. Mallory began to cough again, but he was too late. The sentry leapt off his box and whirled round all in one movement, the evil mouth of the Schmeisser lined up on the body almost at his feet. Then he relaxed as he realised who it was, lowered the barrel of his gun.

'So!' he said softly. 'The fledgling has left its nest. Poor little fledgling!' Mallory winced as he saw the back-swing of the gun ready to smash down on Stevens's defenceless head, but the sentry was a kindly enough man, his reaction had been purely automatic. He arrested the swinging butt inches above the tortured face, bent down and almost gently removed the spike from the feebly threatening hand, sent it spinning over the edge of the gully. Then he lifted Stevens carefully by the shoulders, slid in the bunched-up sheet as pillow for the unconscious head against the bitter cold of the snow, shook his head wonderingly, sadly, went back to his seat on the ammunition box.

Hauptmann Skoda was a small, thin man in his late thirties, neat, dapper, debonair and wholly evil. There was something innately evil about the long, corded neck that stretched up scrawnily above his padded shoulders, something repellent about the incongruously small bullet head perched above. When the thin, bloodless lips parted in a smile, which was often, they revealed a perfect set of teeth: far from lighting his face, the smile only emphasised the sallow skin stretched abnormally taut across the sharp nose and high cheek-bones, puckered up the sabre scar that bisected the left cheek from eyebrow to chin: and whether he smiled or not, the pupils of the deep-set eyes remained always the same, still and black and empty. Even at that early hour – it was not yet six o'clock – he was immaculately dressed, freshly shaven, the wetly-gleaming hair – thin, dark, heavily indented above the temples – brushed straight back across his head. Seated behind a flat-topped table, the sole article of furniture in the bench-lined guardroom, only the upper half of his body was visible: even so, one instinctively knew that the crease of the trousers, the polish of the jack-boots, would be beyond reproach.

He smiled often, and he was smiling now as Oberleutnant Turzig finished his report. Leaning far back in his chair, elbows on the arm-rests, Skoda steepled his lean fingers under his chin, smiled benignly round the guardroom. The lazy, empty eyes missed nothing – the guard at the door, the two guards behind the bound prisoner, Andrea sitting on the bench where he had just laid Stevens – one lazy sweep of those eyes encompassed them all.

'Excellently done, Oberleutnant Turzig!' he purred. 'Most efficient, really most efficient!' He looked speculatively at the three men standing before him, at their bruised and blood-caked faces, switched his glance to Stevens, lying barely conscious on the bench, smiled again and permitted himself a fractional lift of his eyebrows. 'A little trouble perhaps, Turzig? The prisoners were not too – ah – co-operative?'

'They offered no resistance, sir, no resistance at all,' Turzig said stiffly. The tone, the manner, were punctilious, correct, but the distaste, the latent hostility were mirrored in his eyes. 'My men were maybe a little enthusiastic. We wanted to make no mistake.'

'Quite right, Lieutenant, quite right,' Skoda murmured approvingly. 'These are dangerous men and one cannot take chances with dangerous men.' He pushed back his chair, rose easily to his feet, strolled round the table and stopped in front of Andrea. 'Except maybe this one, Lieutenant?'

'He is dangerous only to his friends,' Turzig said shortly. 'It is as I told you, sir. He would betray his mother to save his own skin.'

'And claiming friendship with us, eh?' Skoda asked

musingly. 'One of our gallant allies, Lieutenant.' Skoda reached out a gentle hand, brought it viciously down and across Andrea's cheek, the heavy signet ring on his middle finger tearing skin and flesh. Andrea cried out in pain, capped one hand to his bleeding face and cowered away, his right arm raised above his head in blind defence.

'A notable addition to the armed forces of the Third Reich,' Skoda murmured. 'You were not mistaken, Lieutenant. A poltroon – the instinctive reaction of a hurt man is an infallible guide. It is curious,' he mused, 'how often very big men are thus. Part of nature's compensatory process, I suppose.... What is your name, my brave friend?'

'Papagos,' Andrea muttered sullenly. 'Peter Papagos.' He took his hand away from his cheek, looked at it with eyes slowly widening with horror, began to rub it across his trouser leg with jerky, hurried movements, the repugnance on his face plain for every man to see. Skoda watched him with amusement.

'You do not like to see blood, Papagos, eh?' he suggested. 'Especially your own blood?'

A few seconds passed in silence, then Andrea lifted his head suddenly, his fat face screwed up in misery. He looked as if he were going to cry.

'I am only a poor fisherman, your Honour!' he burst out. 'You laugh at me and say I do not like blood, and it is true. Nor do I like suffering and war. I want no part of any of these things!' His great fists were clenched in futile appeal, his face puckered in woe, his voice risen an octave. It was a masterly exhibition of despair and even Mallory found himself almost believing in it. 'Why wasn't I left alone?' he went on pathetically. 'God only knows I am no fighting man – '

'A highly inaccurate statement,' Skoda interrupted dryly. 'That fact must be patently obvious to every person in the room by this time.' He tapped his teeth with a jade cigarette-holder, his eyes speculative. 'A fisherman you call yourself – '

'He's a damned traitor!' Mallory interrupted. The commandant was becoming just that little bit too interested in Andrea. At once Skoda wheeled round, stood in front of Mallory with his hands clasped behind his back, teetering on heels and toes, and looked him up and down in mocking inspection.

'So!' he said thoughtfully. 'The great Keith Mallory! A rather different proposition from our fat and fearful friend on the bench there, eh, Lieutenant?' He did not wait for an answer. 'What rank are you, Mallory?'

'Captain,' Mallory answered briefly.

'Captain Mallory, eh? Captain Keith Mallory, the greatest mountaineer of our time, the idol of pre-war Europe, the conqueror of the world's most impossible climbs.' Skoda shook his head sadly. 'And to think that it should all end like this... I doubt whether posterity will rank your last climb as among your greatest: there are only ten steps leading to the gallows in the fortress of Navarone.' Skoda smiled. 'Hardly a cheerful thought, is it, Captain Mallory?'

'I wasn't even thinking about it,' the New Zealander answered pleasantly. 'What worries me is your face.' He frowned. 'Somewhere or other I'm sure I've seen it or something like it before.' His voice trailed off into silence.

'Indeed?' Skoda was interested. 'In the Bernese Alps, perhaps? Often before the war – '

'I have it now!' Mallory's face cleared. He knew the risk he was taking, but anything that concentrated attention on himself to the exclusion of Andrea was justified. He beamed at Skoda. 'Three months ago, it was, in the zoo in Cairo. A plains buzzard that had been captured in the Sudan. A rather old and mangy buzzard, I'm afraid,' Mallory went on apologetically, 'but exactly the same scrawny neck, the same beaky face and bald head – '

Mallory broke off abruptly, swayed back out of reach as Skoda, his face livid and gleaming teeth bared in rage, swung at him with his fist. The blow carried with it all

Skoda's wiry strength, but anger blurred his timing and the fist swung harmlessly by: he stumbled, recovered, then fell to the floor with a shout of pain as Mallory's heavy boot caught him flush on the thigh, just above the knee. He had barely touched the floor when he was up like a cat, took a pace forward and collapsed heavily again as his injured leg gave under him.

There was a moment's shocked stillness throughout the room, then Skoda rose painfully, supporting himself on the edge of the heavy table. He was breathing quickly, the thin mouth a hard, white line, the great sabre scar flaming redly in the sallow face drained now of all colour. He looked neither at Mallory nor anyone else, but slowly, deliberately, in an almost frightening silence, began to work his way round to the back of the table, the scuffling of his sliding palms on the leather top rasping edgily across over-tautened nerves.

Mallory stood quite still, watching him with expressionless face, cursing himself for his folly. He had overplayed his hand. There was no doubt in his mind – there could be no doubt in the mind of anyone in that room – that Skoda meant to kill him; and he, Mallory, would not die. Only Skoda and Andrea would die: Skoda from Andrea's throwing knife – Andrea was rubbing blood from his face with the inside of his sleeve, fingertips only inches from the sheath – and Andrea from the guns of the guards, for the knife was all he had. You fool, you fool, you bloody stupid fool, Mallory repeated to himself over and over again. He turned his head slightly and glanced out of the corner of his eye at the sentry nearest him. Nearest him – but still six or seven feet away. The sentry would get him, Mallory knew, the blast of the slugs from the Schmeisser would tear him in half before he could cover the distance. But he would try. He must try. It was the least he owed to Andrea.

Skoda reached the back of the table, opened a drawer and lifted out a gun. An automatic, Mallory noted with

201

detachment – a little, blue-metal, snub-nosed toy – but a murderous toy, the kind of gun he would have expected Skoda to have. Unhurriedly Skoda pressed the release button, checked the magazine, snapped it home with the palm of his hand, flicked off the safety catch and looked up at Mallory. The eyes hadn't altered in the slightest – they were cold, dark and empty as ever. Mallory flicked a glance at Andrea and tensed himself for one convulsive fling backwards. Here it comes, he thought savagely, this is how bloody fools like Keith Mallory die – and then all of a sudden, and unknowingly, he relaxed, for his eyes were still on Andrea and he had seen Andrea doing the same, the huge hand slipping down unconcernedly from the neck, empty of any sign of knife.

There was a scuffle at the table and Mallory was just in time to see Turzig pin Skoda's gun-hand to the table-top.

'Not that, sir!' Turzig begged. 'For God's sake, not that way!'

'Take your hands away,' Skoda whispered. The staring, empty eyes never left Mallory's face. 'Take your hands away, I say – unless you want to go the same way as Captain Mallory.'

'You can't kill him, sir!' Turzig persisted doggedly. 'You just can't. Herr Kommandant's orders were very clear, Hauptmann Skoda. The leader must be brought to him alive.'

'He was shot while trying to escape,' Skoda said thickly.

'It's no good.' Turzig shook his head. 'We can't kill them all – and the other prisoners would talk.' He released his grip on Skoda's hands. 'Alive, Herr Kommandant said, but he didn't say how much alive.' He lowered his voice confidentially. 'Perhaps we may have some difficulty in making Captain Mallory talk,' he suggested.

'What! What did you say?' Abruptly the death's head smile flashed once more, and Skoda was completely on balance again. 'You are over-zealous, Lieutenant. Remind me to speak to you about it some time. You under-estimate me: that was exactly what I was trying to do – frighten Mallory into talking. And now you've spoilt it all.' The smile was still on his face, the voice light, almost bantering, but Mallory was under no illusions. He owed his life to the young W.G.B. lieutenant – how easily one could respect, form a friendship with a man like Turzig if it weren't for this damned, crazy war....Skoda was standing in front of him again: he had left his gun on the table.

'But enough of this fooling, eh, Captain Mallory?' The German's teeth fairly gleamed in the bright light from the naked lamps overhead. 'We haven't all night, have we?'

Mallory looked at him, then turned away in silence. It was warm enough, stuffy almost, in that little guardroom, but he was conscious of a sudden, nameless chill; he knew all at once, without knowing why, but with complete certainty, that this little man before him was utterly evil.

'Well, well, well, we are not quite so talkative now, are we, my friend?' He hummed a little to himself, looked up abruptly, the smile broader than ever. 'Where are the explosives, Captain Mallory?'

'Explosives?' Mallory lifted an interrogatory eyebrow. 'I don't know what you are talking about.'

'You don't remember, eh?'

'I don't know what you are talking about.'

'So.' Skoda hummed to himself again and walked over in front of Miller. 'And what about you, my friend?'

'Sure I remember,' Miller said easily. 'The captain's got it all wrong.'

'A sensible man!' Skoda purred – but Mallory could have sworn to an undertone of disappointment in the voice. 'Proceed, my friend.'

'Captain Mallory has no eye for detail,' Miller drawled. 'I was with him that day. He is malignin' a noble bird. It was a vulture, not a buzzard.'

Just for a second Skoda's smile slipped, then it was back again, as rigidly fixed and lifeless as if it had been painted on.

'Very, very witty men, don't you think, Turzig? What the British would call music-hall comedians. Let them laugh while they may, until the hangman's noose begins to tighten...' He looked at Casey Brown. 'Perhaps you – '

'Why don't you go and take a running jump to yourself?' Brown growled.

'A running jump? The idiom escapes me, but I fear it is hardly complimentary.' Skoda selected a cigarette from a thin case, tapped it thoughtfully on a thumb nail. 'Hmm. Not just what one might call too co-operative, Lieutenant Turzig.'

'You won't get these men to talk, sir.' There was a quiet finality in Turzig's voice.

'Possibly not, possibly not.' Skoda was quite unruffled. 'Nevertheless, I shall have the information I want, and within five minutes.' He walked unhurriedly across to his desk, pressed a button, screwed his cigarette into its jade holder, and leaned against the table, an arrogance, a careless contempt in every action, even to the leisurely crossing of the gleaming jackboots.

Suddenly a side door was flung open and two men stumbled into the room, prodded by a rifle barrel. Mallory caught his breath, felt his nails dig savagely into the palms of his hands. Louki and Panayis! Louki and Panayis, bound and bleeding, Louki from a cut above the eye, Panayis from a scalp wound. So they'd got them too, and in spite of his warnings. Both men were shirt-sleeved; Louki, minus his magnificently frogged jacket, scarlet *stanta* and the small arsenal of weapons that he carried stuck beneath it, looked strangely pathetic and woebegone – strangely, for he was red-faced with anger, the moustache bristling more ferociously than ever. Mallory looked at him with eyes empty of all recognition, his face expressionless.

204

'Come now, Captain Mallory,' Skoda said reproachfully. 'Have you no word of greeting for two old friends? No? Or perhaps you are just overwhelmed?' he suggested smoothly. 'You had not expected to see them so soon again, eh, Captain Mallory?'

'What cheap trick is this?' Mallory asked contemptuously. 'I've never seen these men before in my life.' His eyes caught those of Panayis, held there involuntarily: the black hate that stared out of those eyes, the feral malevolence – there was something appalling about it.

'Of course not,' Skoda sighed wearily. 'Oh, of course not. Human memory is so short, is it not, Captain Mallory.' The sigh was pure theatre – Skoda was enjoying himself immensely, the cat playing with the mouse. 'However, we will try again.' He swung round, crossed over to the bench where Stevens lay, pulled off the blanket and, before anyone could guess his intentions, chopped the outside of his right hand against Stevens's smashed leg, just below the knee.... Stevens's entire body leapt in a convulsive spasm, but without even a whisper of a moan: he was still fully conscious, smiling at Skoda, blood trickling down his chin from where his teeth had gashed his lower lip.

'You shouldn't have done that, Hauptmann Skoda,' Mallory said. His voice was barely a whisper, but unnaturally loud in the frozen silence of the room. 'You are going to die for that, Hauptmann Skoda.'

'So? I am going to die, am I?' Again he chopped his hand against the fractured leg, again without reaction. 'Then I may as well die twice over – eh, Captain Mallory? This young man is very, very tough – but the British have soft hearts, have they not, my dear Captain?' Gently his hand slid down Stevens's leg, closed round the stockinged ankle. 'You have exactly five seconds to tell me the truth, Captain Mallory, and then I fear I will be compelled to rearrange these splints – *Gott in Himmel*! What's the matter with that great oaf?'

Andrea had taken a couple of steps forward, was standing only a yard away, swaying on his feet.

'Outside! Let me outside!' His breath came in short, fast gasps. He bowed his head, one hand to his throat, one over his stomach. 'I cannot stand it! Air! Air! I must have air!'

'Ah, no, my dear Papagos, you shall remain here and enjoy – Corporal! Quickly!' He had seen Andrea's eyes roll upwards until only the whites showed. 'The fool is going to faint! Take him away before he falls on top of us!'

Mallory had one fleeting glimpse of the two guards hurrying forwards, of the incredulous contempt on Louki's face, then he flicked a glance at Miller and Brown, caught the lazy droop of the American's eyelid in return, the millimetric inclination of Brown's head. Even as the two guards came up behind Andrea and lifted the flaccid arms across their shoulders, Mallory glanced half-left, saw the nearest sentry less than four feet away now, absorbed in the spectacle of the toppling giant. Easy, dead easy – the gun dangling by his side: he could hit him between wind and water before he knew what was happening...

Fascinated, Mallory watched Andrea's forearms slipping nervelessly down the shoulders of the supporting guards till his wrists rested loosely beside their necks, palms facing inwards. And then there was the sudden leap of the great shoulder muscles and Mallory had hurled himself convulsively sidewards and back, his shoulder socketing with vicious force into the guard's stomach, inches below the breastbone: an explosive *ouf*! of agony, the crash against the wooden walls of the room and Mallory knew the guard would be out of action for some time to come.

Even as he dived, Mallory had heard the sickening thud of heads being swept together. Now, as he twisted round on his side, he had a fleeting glimpse of another guard thrashing feebly on the floor under the combined weights of Miller and Brown, and then of Andrea tearing an automatic rifle from the guard who had been standing at his right shoulder: the Schmeisser was cradled in his great hands, lined up on Skoda's chest even before the unconscious man had hit the floor.

For one second, maybe two, all movement in the room ceased, every sound sheared off by a knife edge: the silence was abrupt, absolute — and infinitely more clamorous than the clamour that had gone before. No one moved, no one spoke, no one even breathed: the shock, the utter unexpectedness of what had happened held them all in thrall.

And then the silence erupted in a staccato crashing of sound, deafening in that confined space. Once, twice, three times, wordlessly, and with great care, Andrea shot Hauptmann Skoda through the heart. The blast of the shells lifted the little man off his feet, smashed him against the wall of the hut, pinned him there for one incredible second, arms outflung as though nailed against the rough planks in spread-eagle crucifixion; and then he collapsed, fell limply to the ground a grotesque and broken doll that struck its heedless head against the edge of the bench before coming to rest on its back on the floor. The eyes were still wide open, as cold, as dark, as empty in death as they had been in life.

His Schmeisser waving in a gentle arc that covered Turzig and the sergeant, Andrea picked up Skoda's sheath knife, sliced through the ropes that bound Mallory's wrists.

'Can you hold this gun, my Captain?'

Mallory flexed his stiffened hands once or twice, nodded, took the gun in silence. In three steps Andrea was behind the blind side of the door leading to the ante-room, pressed to the wall, waiting, gesturing to Mallory to move as far back as possible out of the line of sight.

Suddenly the door was flung open. Andrea could just see the tip of the rifle barrel projecting beyond it.

'Oberleutnant Turzig! *Was ist los? Wer schoss...*' The voice broke off in a coughing grunt of agony as Andrea smashed the sole of his foot against the door. He was round the outside of the door in a moment, caught the man as he fell, pulled him clear of the doorway and peered into the adjacent hut. A brief inspection, then he closed the door, bolted it from the inside.

'Nobody else there, my Captain,' Andrea reported. 'Just the one gaoler, it seems.'

'Fine! Cut the others loose, will you, Andrea?' He wheeled round towards Louki, smiled at the comical expression on the little man's face, the tentative, spreading, finally ear-to-ear grin that cut through the baffled incredulity.

'Where do the men sleep, Louki – the soldiers, I mean?'

'In a hut in the middle of the compound, Major. This is the officers' quarters.'

'Compound? You mean – ?'

'Barbed wire,' Louki said succinctly. 'Ten feet high – and all the way round.'

'Exits?'

'One and one only. Two guards.'

'Good! Andrea – everybody into the side room. No, not you, Lieutenant. You sit down here.' He gestured to the chair behind the big desk. 'Somebody's bound to come. Tell him you killed one of us – trying to escape. Then send for the guards at the gate.'

For a moment Turzig didn't answer. He watched unseeingly as Andrea walked past him, dragging two unconscious soldiers by their collars. Then he smiled. It was a wry sort of smile.

'I am sorry to disappoint you, Captain Mallory. Too much has been lost already through my blind stupidity. I won't do it.'

'Andrea!' Mallory called softly.

'Yes?' Andrea stood in the ante-room doorway.

'I think I hear someone coming. Is there a way out of that side room?'

Andrea nodded silently.

'Outside! The front door. Take your knife. If the Lieutenant...' But he was talking to himself, Andrea was already gone, slipping out through the back door, soundless as a ghost.

'You will do exactly as I say,' Mallory said softly. He took position himself in the doorway to the side room, where he could see the front entrance between door and jamb: his automatic rifle was trained on Turzig. 'If you don't, Andrea will kill the man at the door. Then we will kill you and the guards inside. Then we will knife the sentries at the gate. Nine dead men — and all for nothing, for we will escape anyway... Here he is now.' Mallory's voice was barely a whisper, eyes pitiless in a pitiless face. 'Nine dead men, Lieutenant — and just because your pride is hurt.' Deliberately, the last sentence was in German, fluent, colloquial, and Mallory's mouth twisted as he saw the almost imperceptible sag of Turzig's shoulders. He knew he had won, that Turzig had been going to take a last gamble on his ignorance of German, that this last hope was gone.

The door burst open and a soldier stood on the threshold, breathing heavily. He was armed, but clad only in a singlet and trousers, oblivious of the cold.

'Lieutenant! Lieutenant!' He spoke in German. 'We heard the shots — '

'It is nothing, Sergeant.' Turzig bent his head over an open drawer, pretended to be searching for something to account for his solitary presence in the room. 'One of our prisoners tried to escape... We stopped him.'

'Perhaps the medical orderly — '

'I'm afraid we stopped him rather permanently.' Turzig smiled tiredly. 'You can organise a burial detail in the morning. Meantime, you might tell the guards at the gate to come here for a minute. Then get to bed yourself — you'll catch your death of cold!'

'Shall I detail a relief guard — '

'Of course not!' Turzig said impatiently. 'It's just for a

minute. Besides, the only people to guard against are already in here.' His lips tightened for a second as he realised what he had said, the unconscious irony of the words. 'Hurry up, man! We haven't got all night!' He waited till the sound of the running footsteps died away, then looked steadily at Mallory. 'Satisfied?'

'Perfectly. And my very sincere apologies,' Mallory said quietly. 'I hate to do a thing like this to a man like you.' He looked round the door as Andrea came into the room. 'Andrea, ask Louki and Panayis if there's a telephone switchboard in this block of huts. Tell them to smash it up and any receivers they can find.' He grinned. 'Then hurry back for our visitors from the gate. I'd be lost without you on the reception committee.'

Turzig's gaze followed the broad, retreating back.

'Captain Skoda was right. I still have much to learn.' There was neither bitterness nor rancour in his voice. 'He fooled me completely, that big one.'

'You're not the first,' Mallory reassured him. 'He's fooled more people than I'll ever know... You're not the first,' he repeated. 'But I think you must be just about the luckiest.'

'Because I'm still alive?'

'Because you're still alive,' Mallory echoed.

Less than ten minutes later the two guards at the gates had joined their comrades in the back room, captured, disarmed, bound and gagged with a speed and noiseless efficiency that excited Turzig's professional admiration, chagrined though he was. Securely tied hand and foot, he lay in a corner of the room, not yet gagged.

'I think I understand now why your High Command chose you for this task, Captain Mallory. If anyone could succeed, you would – but you must fail. The impossible must always remain so. Nevertheless, you have a great team.'

'We get by,' Mallory said modestly. He took a last look round the room, then grinned down at Stevens.

'Ready to take off on your travels again, young man, or do you find this becoming rather monotonous?'

'Ready when you are, sir.' Lying on a stretcher which Louki had miraculously procured, he sighed in bliss. 'First-class travel, this time, as befits an officer. Sheer luxury. I don't mind how far we go!'

'Speak for yourself,' Miller growled morosely. He had been allocated first stint at the front or heavy end of the stretcher. But the quirk of his eyebrows robbed the words of all offence.

'Right, then, we're off. One last thing. Where is the camp radio, Lieutenant Turzig?'

'So you can smash it up, I suppose?'

'Precisely.'

'I have no idea.'

'What if I threaten to blow your head off?'

'You won't.' Turzig smiled, though the smile was a trifle lopsided. 'Given certain circumstances, you would kill me as you would a fly. But you wouldn't kill a man for refusing such information.'

'You haven't as much to learn as your late and unlamented captain thought,' Mallory admitted. 'It's not all that important... I regret we have to do all this. I trust we do not meet again – not at least, until the war is over. Who knows, some day we might even go climbing together.' He signed to Louki to fix Turzig's gag and walked quickly out of the room. Two minutes later they had cleared the barracks and were safely lost in the darkness and the olive groves that stretched to the south of Margaritha.

When they cleared the groves, a long time later, it was almost dawn. Already the black silhouette of Kostos was softening in the first feathery greyness of the coming day. The wind was from the south, and warm, and the snow was beginning to melt on the hills.

CHAPTER 11

Wednesday

1400–1600

All day long they lay hidden in the carob grove, a thick clump of stunted, gnarled trees that clung grimly to the treacherous, scree-strewn slope abutting what Louki called the 'Devil's Playground'. A poor shelter and an uncomfortable one, but in every other way all they could wish for: it offered concealment, a first-class defensive position immediately behind, a gentle breeze drawn up from the sea by the sun-baked rocks to the south, shade from the sun that rode from dawn to dusk in a cloudless sky – and an incomparable view of a sun-drenched, shimmering Aegean.

Away to their left, fading through diminishing shades of blue and indigo and violet into faraway nothingness, stretched the islands of the Lerades, the nearest of them, Maidos, so close that they could see isolated fisher cottages sparkling whitely in the sun: through that narrow, intervening gap of water would pass the ships of the Royal Navy in just over a day's time. To the right, and even farther away, remote, featureless, back-dropped by the towering Anatolian mountains, the coast of Turkey hooked north and west in a great curving scimitar: to the north itself, the thrusting spear of Cape Demirci, rock-rimmed but dimpled with sandy coves of white, reached far out into the placid blue of the Aegean: and north again beyond the Cape, haze-blurred in the purple distance, the island of Kheros lay dreaming on the surface of the sea.

It was a breath-taking panorama, a heart-catching beauty sweeping majestically through a great semi-circle over the sunlit sea. But Mallory had no eyes for it, had spared it only a passing glance when he had come on guard less

than half an hour previously, just after two o'clock. He
had dismissed it with one quick glance, settled by the bole
of a tree, gazed for endless minutes, gazed until his eyes
ached with strain at what he had so long waited to see.
Had waited to see and come to destroy – the guns of the
fortress of Navarone.

The town of Navarone – a town of from four to five
thousand people, Mallory judged – lay sprawled round the
deep, volcanic crescent of the harbour, a crescent so deep,
so embracing, that it was almost a complete circle with
only a narrow bottleneck of an entrance to the north-
west, a gateway dominated by searchlights and mortar
and machine-gun batteries on either side. Less than three
miles distant to the north-east from the carob grove, every
detail, every street, every building, every caique and
launch in the harbour were clearly visible to Mallory and
he studied them over and over again until he knew them
by heart: the way the land to the west of the harbour
sloped up gently to the olive groves, the dusty streets
running down to the water's edge: the way the ground
rose more sharply to the south, the streets now running
parallel to the water down to the old town: the way the
cliffs to the east – cliffs pock-marked by the bombs of
Torrance's Liberator Squadron – stretched a hundred and
fifty sheer feet above the water, then curved dizzily out
over and above the harbour, and the great mound of
volcanic rock towering above that again, a mound
barricaded off from the town below by the high wall that
ended flush with the cliff itself: and, finally, the way the
twin rows of A.A. guns, the great radar scanners and the
barracks of the fortress, squat, narrow-embrasured, built
of big blocks of masonry, dominated everything in sight –
including that great, black gash in the rock, below the
fantastic overhang of the cliff.

Unconsciously, almost, Mallory nodded to himself in
slow understanding. This was the fortress that had defied
the Allies for eighteen long months, that had dominated

the entire naval strategy in the Sporades since the Germans had reached out from the mainland into the isles, that had blocked all naval activity in that 2,000 square mile triangle between the Lerades and the Turkish coast. And now, when he saw it, it all made sense. Impregnable to land attack – the commanding fortress saw to that: impregnable to air attack – Mallory realised just how suicidal it had been to send out Torrance's squadron against the great guns protected by that jutting cliff, against those bristling rows of anti-aircraft guns: and impregnable to sea attack – the waiting squadrons of the Luftwaffe on Samos saw to that. Jensen had been right – only a guerrilla sabotage mission stood any chance at all: a remote chance, an all but suicidal chance, but still a chance, and Mallory knew he couldn't ask for more.

Thoughtfully he lowered the binoculars and rubbed the back of his hand across aching eyes. At last he felt he knew exactly what he was up against, was grateful for the knowledge, for the opportunity he'd been given of this long-range reconnaissance, this familiarising of himself with the terrain, the geography of the town. This was probably the one vantage point in the whole island that offered such an opportunity together with concealment and near immunity. No credit to himself, the leader of the mission, he reflected wryly, that they had found such a place: it had been Louki's idea entirely.

And he owed a great deal more than that to the sad-eyed little Greek. It had been Louki's idea that they first move up-valley from Margaritha, to give Andrea time to recover the explosives from old Leri's hut, and to make certain there was no immediate hue and cry and pursuit – they could have fought a rearguard action up through the olive groves, until they had lost themselves in the foothills of Kostos: it was he who had guided them back past Margaritha when they had doubled on their tracks, had halted them opposite the village while he and Panayis had slipped wraith-like through the lifting twilight, picked up outdoor clothes for themselves, and, on the return journey, slipped into the *Abteilung* garage, torn away the coil ignitions of the German command car and truck – the only transport in Margaritha – and smashed their distributors for good measure; it was Louki who had led them by a sunken ditch right up to the road-block guard post at the mouth of the valley – it had been almost ludicrously simple to disarm the sentries, only one of whom had been awake – and, finally, it was Louki who had insisted that they walk down the muddy centre of the valley track till they came to the metalled road, less than two miles from the town itself. A hundred yards down this they had branched off to the left across a long, sloping field of lava that left no trace behind, arrived in the carob copse just on sunrise.

And it had worked. All these carefully engineered pointers, pointers that not even the most sceptical could have ignored and denied, had worked magnificently. Miller and Andrea, who had shared the forenoon watch, had seen the Navarone garrison spending long hours making the most intensive house-to-house search of the town. That should make it doubly, trebly safe for them the following day, Mallory reckoned: it was unlikely that the search would be repeated, still more unlikely that, if it were, it would be carried out with a fraction of the same enthusiasm. Louki had done his work well.

Mallory turned his head to look at him. The little man was still asleep – wedged on the slope behind a couple of tree-trunks, he hadn't stirred for five hours. Still dead tired himself, his legs aching and eyes smarting with sleeplessness, Mallory could not find it in him to grudge Louki a moment of his rest. He'd earned it all – and he'd been awake all through the previous night. So had Panayis, but Panayis was already awakening, Mallory saw, pushing the long, black hair out of his eyes: awake, rather, for his transition from sleep to full awareness was immediate, as fleeting and as complete as a cat's. A

215

N

To Vyoos

Fortress wall

Ordnance depot

A.A. guns

Officers' quarters

Barracks

Batteries and searchlights

Batteries and searchlights

Cliff overhang

The guns immediately below overhangs

Jetties

To Margaritha

To Devil's Playground

1. Main gate
2. Power house
3. Water storage tank
4. Fire control tower
5. Entrance to magazine
6. House in Chapters 15 and 16
7. Tavern in Chapter 15
8. House in Chapter 13

Battery and searchlight

Cave with guns

Fortress building behind cliff top

West side of square

Fortress wall

Cliff overhang

Jetties

View from west of east side of harbour

dangerous man, Mallory knew, a desperate man, almost, and a bitter enemy, but he knew nothing of Panayis, nothing at all. He doubted if he ever would.

Farther up on the slope, almost in the centre of the grove, Andrea had built a high platform of broken branches and twigs against a couple of carob poles maybe five feet apart, gradually filling up the space between slope and trees until he had a platform four feet in width, as nearly level as he could make it. Andy Stevens lay on this, still on his stretcher, still conscious. As far as Mallory could tell, Stevens hadn't closed his eyes since they had been marched away by Turzig from their cave in the mountains. He seemed to have passed beyond the need for sleep, or had crushed all desire for it. The stench from the gangrenous leg was nauseating, appalling, poisoned all the air around. Mallory and Miller had had a look at the leg shortly after their arrival in the copse, uncovered it, examined it, smiled at one another, tied it up again and assured Stevens that the wound was closing. Below the knee, the leg had turned almost completely black.

Mallory lifted his binoculars to have another look at the town, but lowered them almost at once as someone came sliding down the slope, touched him on the arm. It was Panayis, upset, anxious, almost angry looking. He gesticulated towards the westering sun.

'The time, Captain Mallory?' He spoke in Greek, his voice low, sibilant, urgent – an inevitable voice, Mallory thought, for the lean, dark mysteriousness of the man. 'What is the time?' he repeated.

'Half-past two, or thereabouts.' Mallory lifted an interrogatory eyebrow. 'You are concerned, Panayis. Why?'

'You should have wakened me. You should have wakened me hours ago!' He *was* angry, Mallory decided. 'It is my turn to keep watch.'

'But you had no sleep last night,' Mallory pointed out reasonably. 'It just didn't seem fair – '

'It is my turn to keep watch, I tell you!' Panayis insisted stubbornly.

'Very well, then. If you insist.' Mallory knew the high, fierce pride of the islanders too well to attempt to argue. 'Heaven only knows what we would have done without Louki and yourself... I'll stay and keep you company for a while.'

'Ah, so that is why you let me sleep on!' There was no disguising the hurt in the eyes, the voice. 'You do not trust Panayis – '

'Oh, for heaven's sake!' Mallory began in exasperation, checked himself and smiled. 'Of course we trust you. Maybe I should go and get some more sleep anyway; you are kind to give me the chance. You will shake me in two hours' time?'

'Certainly, certainly!' Panayis was almost beaming. 'I shall not fail.'

Mallory scrambled up to the centre of the grove and stretched out lazily along the ledge he had levelled out for himself. For a few idle moments he watched Panayis pacing restlessly to and fro just inside the perimeter of the grove, lost interest when he saw him climbing swiftly up among the branches of a tree, seeking a high lookout vantage point and decided he might as well follow his advice and get some sleep while he could.

'Captain Mallory! Captain Mallory!' An urgent, heavy hand was shaking his shoulder. 'Wake up! Wake up!'

Mallory stirred, rolled over on his back, sat up quickly, opening his eyes as he did so. Panayis was stooped over him, the dark, saturnine face alive with anxiety. Mallory shook his head to clear away the mists of sleep and was on his feet in one swift, easy movement.

'What's the matter, Panayis?'

'Planes!' he said quickly. 'There is a squadron of planes coming our way!'

'Planes? What planes? Whose planes?'

'I do not know, Captain. They are yet far away. But — '

'What direction?' Mallory snapped.

'They come from the north.'

Together they ran down to the edge of the grove. Panayis gestured to the north, and Mallory caught sight of them at once, the afternoon sun glinting off the sharp dihedral of the wings. Stukas, all right, he thought grimly. Seven — no, eight of them — less than three miles away, flying in two echelons of fours, two thousand, certainly not more than twenty-five hundred feet... He became aware that Panayis was tugging urgently at his arm.

'Come, Captain Mallory!' he said excitedly. 'We have no time to lose!' He pulled Mallory round, pointed with outstretched arm at the gaunt, shattered cliffs that rose steeply behind them, cliffs crazily riven by rock-jumbled ravines that wound their aimless way back into the interior — or stopped as abruptly as they had begun. 'The Devil's Playground! We must get in there at once! At once, Captain Mallory!'

'Why on earth should we?' Mallory looked at him in astonishment. 'There's no reason to suppose that they're after us. How can they be? No one know's we're here.'

'I do not care!' Panayis was stubborn in his conviction. 'I know. Do not ask me how I know, for I do not know that myself. Louki will tell you — Panayis knows these things. I know, Captain Mallory, I *know*!'

Just for a second Mallory stared at him, uncomprehending. There was no questioning the earnestness, the utter sincerity — but it was the machine-gun staccato of the words that tipped the balance of instinct against reason. Almost without realising it, certainly without realising why, Mallory found himself running uphill, slipping and stumbling in the scree. He found the others already on their feet, tense, expectant, shrugging on their packs, the guns already in their hands.

'Get to the edge of the trees up there!' Mallory shouted. 'Quickly! Stay there and stay under cover — we're going to

219

have to break for that gap in the rocks.' He gestured through the trees at a jagged fissure in the cliff-side, barely forty yards from where he stood, blessed Louki for his foresight in choosing a hideout with so convenient a bolt-hole. 'Wait till I give the word. Andrea!' He turned round, then broke off, the words unneeded. Andrea had already scooped up the dying boy in his arms, just as he lay in stretcher and blankets and was weaving his way uphill in and out among the trees.

'What's up, boss?' Miller was by Mallory's side as he plunged up the slope. 'I don't see nothin'.'

'You can hear something if you'd just stop talking for a moment,' Mallory said grimly. 'Or just take a look up there.'

Miller, flat on his stomach now, and less than a dozen feet from the edge of the grove, twisted round and craned his neck upwards. He picked up the planes immediately.

'Stukas!' he said incredulously. 'A squadron of gawd-damned Stukas! It can't be, boss!'

'It can and it is,' Mallory said grimly. 'Jensen told me that Jerry has stripped the Italian front of them – over two hundred pulled out in the last few weeks.' Mallory squinted up at the squadron, less than half a mile away now. 'And he's brought the whole damn issue down to the Aegean.'

'But they're not lookin' for us,' Miller protested.

'I'm afraid they are,' Mallory said grimly. The two bomber echelons had just dove-tailed into line-ahead formation. 'I'm afraid Panayis was right.'

'But – but they're passin' us by – '

'They aren't,' Mallory said flatly. 'They're here to stay. Just keep your eyes on that leading plane.'

Even as he spoke, the flight-commander tilted his gull-winged Junkers 87 sharply over to port, half-turned, fell straight out of the sky in a screaming power-dive, plummeting straight for the carob grove.

'Leave him alone!' Mallory shouted. 'Don't fire!' The

Stukas, airbrakes at maximum depression, had steadied on the centre of the grove. Nothing could stop him now – but a chance shot might bring him down directly on top of them: the chances were poor enough as it was... 'Keep your hands over your heads – and your heads down!'

He ignored his own advice, his gaze following the bomber every foot of the way down. Five hundred, four hundred, three, the rising crescendo of the heavy engine was beginning to hurt his ears, and the Stuka was pulling sharply out of its plunging fall, its bomb gone.

Bomb! Mallory sat up sharply, screwing up his eyes against the blue of the sky. Not one bomb but dozens of them, clustered so thickly that they appeared to be jostling each other as they arrowed into the centre of the grove, striking the gnarled and stunted trees, breaking off branches and burying themselves to their fins in the soft and shingled slope. Incendiaries! Mallory had barely time to realise that they had been spared the horror of a 500-kilo H.E. bomb when the incendiaries erupted into hissing, guttering life, into an incandescent magnesium whiteness that reached out and completely destroyed the shadowed gloom of the carob grove. Within a matter of seconds the dazzling coruscation had given way to thick, evil-smelling clouds of acrid black smoke, smoke laced with flickering tongues of red, small at first then licking and twisting resinously upwards until entire trees were enveloped in a cocoon of flame. The Stuka was still pulling upwards out of its dive, had not yet levelled off when the heart of the grove, old and dry and tindery, was fiercely ablaze.

Miller twisted up and round, nudging Mallory to catch his attention through the crackling roar of the flames.

'Incendiaries, boss,' he announced.

'What did you think they were using?' Mallory asked shortly. 'Matches? They're trying to smoke us out, to burn us out, get us in the open. High explosive's not so good among trees. Ninety-nine times out of a hundred this would have worked.' He coughed as the acrid smoke bit into his lungs, peered up with watering eyes through the tree-tops. 'But not this time. Not if we're lucky. Not if they hold off another half-minute or so. Just look at that smoke!'

. Miller looked. Thick, convoluted, shot through with fiery sparks, the rolling cloud was already a third of the way across the gap between grove and cliff, borne uphill by the wandering catspaws from the sea. It was the complete, the perfect smoke-screen. Miller nodded.

'Gonna make a break for it, huh, boss?'

'There's no choice – we either go, or we stay and get fried or blown into very little bits. Probably both.' He raised his voice. 'Anybody see what's happening up top?'

'Queuing up for another go at us, sir,' Brown said lugubriously. 'The first bloke's still circling around.'

'Waiting to see how we break cover. They won't wait long. This is where we take off.' He peered uphill through the rolling smoke, but it was too thick, laced his watering eyes until everything was blurred through a misted sheen of tears. There was no saying how far uphill the smoke-bank had reached, and they couldn't afford to wait until they were sure. Stuka pilots had never been renowned for their patience.

'Right, everybody!' he shouted. 'Fifteen yards along the tree-line to that wash, then straight up into the gorge. Don't stop till you're at least a hundred yards inside. Andrea, you lead the way. Off you go!' He peered through the blinding smoke. 'Where's Panayis?'

There was no reply.

'Panayis!' Mallory called. 'Panayis!'

'Perhaps he went back for somethin'.' Miller had stopped, half-turned. 'Shall I go – '

'Get on your way!' Mallory said savagely. 'And if anything happens to young Stevens I'll hold you...' But Miller, wisely, was already gone, Andrea stumbling and coughing by his side.

For a couple of seconds Mallory stood irresolute, then plunged back downhill towards the centre of the grove. Maybe Panayis had gone back for something – and he couldn't understand English. Mallory had hardly gone five yards when he was forced to halt and fling his arm up before his face: the heat was searing. Panayis couldn't be down there; no one could have been down there, could have lived for seconds in that furnace. Gasping for air, hair singeing and clothes smouldering with fire, Mallory clawed his way back up the slope, colliding with trees, slipping, falling, then stumbling desperately to his feet again.

He ran along to the east end of the wood. No one there. Back to the other end again, towards the wash, almost completely blind now, the super-heated air searing viciously through throat and lungs till he was suffocating, till his breath was coming in great, whooping, agonised breaths. No sense in waiting longer, nothing he could do, nothing anyone could do except save himself. There was a noise in his ears, the roaring of the flames, the roaring of his own blood – and the screaming, heart-stopping roar of a Stuka in a power-dive. Desperately he flung himself forward over the sliding scree, stumbled and pitched headlong down to the floor of the wash.

Hurt or not, he did not know and he did not care. Sobbing aloud for breath, he rose to his feet, forced his aching legs to drive him somehow up the hill. The air was full of the thunder of engines, he knew the entire squadron was coming in to the attack, and then he had flung himself uncaringly to the ground as the first of the high explosive bombs erupted in its concussive blast of smoke and flame – erupted not forty yards away, to his left and ahead of him. *Ahead* of him! Even as he struggled upright again, lurched forward and upward once more, Mallory cursed himself again and again and again. You madman, he thought bitterly, confusedly, you damned crazy madman. Sending the others out to be killed. He should have

223

thought of it – oh, God, he should have thought of it, a five-year-old could have thought of it. Of course Jerry wasn't going to bomb the grove: they had seen the obvious, the inevitable, as quickly as he had, were dive-bombing the pall of smoke between the grove and the cliff! A five-year-old – the earth exploded beneath his feet, a giant hand plucked him up and smashed him to the ground and the darkness closed over him.

CHAPTER 12

Wednesday

1600–1800

Once, twice, half a dozen times, Mallory struggled up from the depths of a black, trance-like stupor and momentarily touched the surface of consciousness only to slide back into the darkness again. Desperately, each time, he tried to hang on to these fleeting moments of awareness, but his mind was like the void, dark and sinewless, and even as he knew that his mind was slipping backwards again, loosing its grip on reality, the knowledge was gone, and there was only the void once more. Nightmare, he thought vaguely during one of the longer glimmerings of comprehension, I'm having a nightmare, like when you know you are having a nightmare and that if you could open your eyes it would be gone, but you can't open your eyes. He tried it now, tried to open his eyes, but it was no good, it was still as dark as ever and he was still sunk in this evil dream, for the sun had been shining brightly in the sky. He shook his head in slow despair.

'Aha! Observe! Signs of life at last!' There was no mistaking the slow, nasal drawl. 'Ol' Medicine Man Miller triumphs again!' There was a moment's silence, a moment in which Mallory was increasingly aware of the diminishing thunder of aero engines, the acrid, resinous smoke that stung his nostrils and eyes, and then an arm had passed under his shoulders and Miller's persuasive voice was in his ear. 'Just try a little of this, boss. Ye olde vintage brandy. Nothin' like it anywhere.'

Mallory felt the cold neck of the bottle, tilted his head back, took a long pull. Almost immediately he had jerked himself upright and forward to a sitting position, gagging, spluttering and fighting for breath as the raw, fiery ouzo

225

bit into the mucous membrane of cheeks and throat. He tried to speak but could do no more than croak, gasp for fresh air and stare indignantly at the shadowy figure that knelt by his side. Miller, for his part, looked at him with unconcealed admiration.

'See, boss? Just like I said – nothin' like it.' He shook his head admiringly. 'Wide awake in an instant, as the literary boys would say. Never saw a shock and concussion victim recover so fast!'

'What the hell are you trying to do?' Mallory demanded. The fire had died down in his throat, and he could breathe again. 'Poison me?' Angrily he shook his head, fighting off the pounding ache, the fog that still swirled round the fringes of his mind. 'Bloody fine physician you are! Shock, you say, yet the first thing you do is administer a dose of spirits – '

'Take your pick,' Miller interrupted grimly. 'Either that or a damned sight bigger shock in about fifteen minutes or so when brother Jerry gets here.'

'But they've gone away. I can't hear the Stukas any more.'

'This lot's comin' up from the town,' Miller said morosely. 'Louki's just reported them. Half a dozen armoured cars and a couple of trucks with field guns the length of a telegraph pole.'

'I see.' Mallory twisted round, saw a gleam of light at a bend in the wall. A cave – a tunnel, almost. Little Cyprus, Louki had said some of the older people had called it – the Devil's Playground was riddled with a honeycomb of caves. He grinned wryly at the memory of his momentary panic when he thought his eyes had gone and turned again to Miller. 'Trouble again, Dusty, nothing but trouble. Thanks for bringing me round.'

'Had to,' Miller said briefly. 'I guess we couldn't have carried you very far, boss.'

Mallory nodded. 'Not just the flattest of country here-abouts.'

226

'There's that, too,' Miller agreed. 'What I really meant is that there's hardly anyone left to carry you. Casey Brown and Panayis have both been hurt, boss.'

'What! Both of them?' Mallory screwed his eyes shut, shook his head in slow anger. 'My God, Dusty, I'd forgotten all about the bomb – the bombs.' He reached out his hand, caught Miller by the arm. 'How–how bad are they?' There was so little time left, so much to do.

'How bad?' Miller shook out a pack of cigarettes and offered one to Mallory. 'Not bad at all – if we could get them into hospital. But hellish painful and cripplin' if they gotta start hikin' up and down those gawddamned ravines hereabouts. First time I've seen canyon floors more nearly vertical than the walls themselves.'

'You still haven't told me – '

'Sorry, boss, sorry. Shrapnel wounds, both of them, in exactly the same place – left thigh, just above the knee. No bones gone, no tendons cut. I've just finished tying up Casey's leg – it's a pretty wicked-lookin' gash. He's gonna know all about it when he starts walkin'.'

'And Panayis?'

'Fixed his own leg,' Miller said briefly. 'A queer character. Wouldn't even let me look at it, far less bandage it. I reckon he'd have knifed me if I'd tried.'

'Better to leave him alone anyway,' Mallory advised. 'Some of these islanders have strange taboos and superstitions. Just as long as he's alive. Though I still don't see how the hell he managed to get here.'

'He was the first to leave,' Miller explained. 'Along with Casey. You must have missed him in the smoke. They were climbin' together when they got hit.'

'And how did I get here?'

'No prizes for the first correct answer.' Miller jerked a thumb over his shoulder at the huge form that blocked half the width of the cave. 'Junior here did his St Bernard act once again. I wanted to go with him, but he wasn't

227

keen. Said he reckoned it would be difficult to carry both of us up the hill. My feelin's were hurt considerable.' Miller sighed. 'I guess I just wasn't born to be a hero, that's all.'

Mallory smiled. 'Thanks again, Andrea.'

'Thanks!' Miller was indignant. 'A guy saves your life and all you can say is "thanks"!'

'After the first dozen times or so you run out of suitable speeches,' Mallory said dryly. 'How's Stevens?'

'Breathin'.'

Mallory nodded forward towards the source of light, wrinkled his nose. 'Just round the corner, isn't he?'

'Yeah, it's pretty grim,' Miller admitted. 'The gangrene's spread up beyond the knee.'

Mallory rose groggily to his feet, picked up his gun. 'How is he really, Dusty?'

'He's dead, but he just won't die. He'll be gone by sundown. Gawd only knows what's kept him goin' so far.'

'It may sound presumptuous,' Mallory murmured; 'but I think I know too.'

'The first-class medical attention?' Miller said hopefully.

'Looks that way, doesn't it?' Mallory smiled down at the still kneeling Miller. 'But that wasn't what I meant at all. Come, gentlemen, we have some business to attend to.'

'Me, all I'm good for is blowin' up bridges and droppin' a handful of sand in engine bearin's,' Miller announced. 'Strategy and tactics are far beyond my simple mind. But I still think those characters down there are pickin' a very stupid way of committin' suicide. It would be a damned sight easier for all concerned if they just shot themselves.'

'I'm inclined to agree with you.' Mallory settled himself more firmly behind the jumbled rocks in the mouth of the ravine that opened on the charred and smoking remains of the carob grove directly below and took another look at the Alpenkorps troops advancing in extended order up the steep, shelterless slope. 'They're no children at this game. I bet they don't like it one little bit, either.'

'Then why the hell are they doin' it, boss?'

'No option, probably. First off, this place can only be attacked frontally.' Mallory smiled down at the little Greek lying between himself and Andrea. 'Louki here chose the place well. It would require a long detour to attack from the rear – and it would take them a week to advance through that devil's scrap-heap behind us. Secondly, it'll be sunset in a couple of hours, and they know they haven't a hope of getting us after it's dark. And finally – and I think this is more important than the other two reasons put together – it's a hundred to one that the commandant in the town is being pretty severely prodded by his High Command. There's too much at stake, even in the one in a thousand chance of us getting at the guns. They can't afford to have Kheros evacuated under their noses, to lose – '

'Why not?' Miller interrupted. He gestured largely with his hands. 'Just a lot of useless rocks – '

'They can't afford to lose face with the Turks,' Mallory went on patiently. 'The strategic importance of these islands in the Sporades is negligible, but their political importance is tremendous. Adolph badly needs another ally in these parts. So he flies in Alpenkorps troops by the thousand and the Stukas by the hundred, the best he has – and he needs them desperately on the Italian front. But you've got to convince your potential ally that you're a pretty safe bet before you can persuade him to give up his nice, safe seat on the fence and jump down on your side.'

'Very interestin',' Miller observed. 'So?'

'So the Germans are going to have no compunction about thirty or forty of their best troops being cut into little pieces. It's no trouble at all when you're sitting behind a desk a thousand miles away... Let 'em come another hundred yards or so closer. Louki and I will start from the middle and work out: you and Andrea start from the outside.'

'I don't like it, boss,' Miller complained.

'Don't think that I do either,' Mallory said quietly. 'Slaughtering men forced to do a suicidal job like this is not my idea of fun – or even of war. But if we don't get them, they get us.' He broke off and pointed across the burnished sea to where Kheros lay peacefully on the hazed horizon, striking golden glints off the western sun. 'What do you think they would have us do, Dusty?'

'I know, I know, boss.' Miller stirred uncomfortably. 'Don't rub it in.' He pulled his woollen cap low over his forehead and stared bleakly down the slope. 'How soon do the mass executions begin?'

'Another hundred yards, I said.' Mallory looked down the slope again towards the coast road and grinned suddenly, glad to change the topic. 'Never saw telegraph poles shrink so suddenly before, Dusty.'

Miller studied the guns drawn up on the roads behind the two trucks and cleared his throat.

'I was only sayin' what Louki told me,' he said defensively.

'What Louki told you!' The little Greek was indignant. 'Before God, Major, the Americano is full of lies!'

'Ah, well, mebbe I was mistaken,' Miller said magnanimously. He squinted again at the guns, forehead lined in puzzlement. 'That first one's a mortar, I reckon. But what in the universe that other weird-looking contraption can be – '

'Also a mortar,' Mallory explained. 'A five-barrelled job, and very nasty. The *Nebelwerfer* or Moanin' Minnie. Howls like all the lost souls in hell. Guaranteed to turn the knees to jelly, especially after nightfall – but it's still the other one you have to watch. A six-inch mortar, almost certainly using fragmentation bombs – you use a

230

brush and shovel for clearing up afterwards.'

'That's right,' Miller growled. 'Cheer us all up.' But he was grateful to the New Zealander for trying to take their minds off what they had to do. 'Why don't they use them?'

'They will,' Mallory assured him. 'Just as soon as we fire and they find out where we are.'

'Gawd help us,' Miller muttered. 'Fragmentation bombs, you said!' He lapsed into gloomy silence.

'Any second now,' Mallory said softly. 'I only hope that our friend Turzig isn't among this lot.' He reached out for his field-glasses but stopped in surprise as Andrea leaned across Louki and caught him by the wrist before he could line the binoculars. 'What's the matter, Andrea?'

'I would not be using these, my Captain. They have betrayed us once already. I have been thinking, and it can be nothing else. The sunlight reflecting from the lenses...'

Mallory stared at him, slowly released his grip on the glasses, nodded several times in succession.

'Of course, of course! I had been wondering... Someone has been careless. There was no other way, there *could* have been no other way. It would only require a single flash to tip them off.' He paused, remembering, then grinned wryly. 'It could have been myself. All this started just after I had been on watch – and Panayis didn't have the glasses.' He shook his head in mortification. 'It *must* have been me, Andrea.'

'I do not believe it,' Andrea said flatly. 'You couldn't make a mistake like that, my Captain.'

'Not only could, but did, I'm afraid. But we'll worry about that afterwards.' The middle of the ragged line of advancing soldiers, slipping and stumbling on the treacherous scree, had almost reached the lower limits of the blackened, stunted remains of the copse. 'They've come far enough. I'll take the white helmet in the middle, Louki.' Even as he spoke he could hear the soft scrape as the three others slid their automatic barrels across and between the protective rocks in front of them, could feel the wave of revulsion that washed through his mind. But his voice was steady enough as he spoke, relaxed and almost casual. 'Right. Let them have it now!'

His last words were caught up and drowned in the tearing, rapid-fire crash of the automatic carbines. With four machine-guns in their hands – two Brens and two 9 mm. Schmeissers – it was no war, as he had said, but sheer, pitiful massacre, with the defenceless figures on the slope below, figures still stunned and uncomprehending, jerking, spinning round and collapsing like marionettes in the hands of a mad puppeteer, some to lie where they fell, others to roll down the steep slope, legs and arms flailing in the grotesque disjointedness of death. Only a couple stood still where they had been hit, vacant surprise mirrored in their lifeless faces, then slipped down tiredly to the stony ground at their feet. Almost three seconds had passed before the handful of those who still lived – about a quarter of the way in from either end of the line where the converging streams of fire had not yet met – realised what was happening and flung themselves desperately to the ground in search of the cover that didn't exist.

The phrenetic stammering of the machine-guns stopped abruptly and in unison, the sound sheared off as by a guillotine. The sudden silence was curiously oppressive, louder, more obtrusive than the clamour that had gone before. The gravelly earth beneath his elbows grated harshly as Mallory shifted his weight slightly, looked at the two men to his right, Andrea with his impassive face empty of all expression, Louki with the sheen of tears in his eyes. Then he became aware of the low murmuring to his left, shifted round again. Bitter-mouthed, savage, the American was swearing softly and continuously, oblivious to the pain as he pounded his fist time and again into the sharp-edged gravel before him.

'Just one more, Gawd.' The quiet voice was almost a prayer. 'That's all I ask. Just one more.'

Mallory touched his arm. 'What is it, Dusty?'

Miller looked round at him, eyes cold and still and empty of all recognition, then he blinked several times and grinned, a cut and bruised hand automatically reaching for his cigarettes.

'Jus' daydreamin', boss,' he said easily. 'Jus' daydreamin'.' He shook out his pack of cigarettes. 'Have one?'

'That inhuman bastard that sent those poor devils up this hill,' Mallory said quietly. 'Make a wonderful picture seen over the sights of your rifle, wouldn't he?'

Abruptly Miller's smile vanished and he nodded.

'It would be all of that.' He risked a quick peep round one of the boulders, eased himself back again. 'Eight, mehbe ten of them still down there, boss,' he reported. 'The poor bastards are like ostriches – trying to take cover behind stones the size of an orange... We leave them be?'

'We leave them be!' Mallory echoed emphatically. The thought of any more slaughter made him feel almost physically sick. 'They won't try again.' He broke off suddenly, flattened himself in reflex instinct as a burst of machine-gun bullets struck the steep-walled rock above their heads and whined up the gorge in vicious ricochet.

'Won't try again, huh?' Miller was already sliding his gun around the rock in front of him when Mallory caught his arm and pulled him back.

'Not them? Listen!' Another burst of fire, then another, and now they could hear the savage chatter of the machine-gun, a chatter rhythmically interrupted by a weird, half-human sighing as its belt passed through the breech. Mallory could feel the prickling of the hairs on the nape of his neck.

'A Spandau. Once you've heard a Spandau you can never forget it. Leave it alone – it's probably fixed on the back of one of the trucks and can't do us any harm... I'm more worried about those damned mortars down there.'

'I'm not,' Miller said promptly. 'They're not firing at us.'

'That's why I'm worried... What do you think, Andrea.'

'The same as you, my Captain. They are waiting. This Devil's Playground, as Louki calls it, is a madman's maze, and they can only fire as blind men – '

'They won't be waiting much longer,' Mallory interrupted grimly. He pointed to the north. 'Here come their eyes.'

At first only specks above the promontory of Cape Demirci, the planes were soon recognisable for what they were, droning in slowly over the Aegean at about fifteen hundred feet. Mallory looked at them in astonishment, then turned to Andrea.

'Am I seeing things, Andrea?' He gestured at the first of the two planes, a high-winged little monoplane fighter. 'That can't be a PZL?'

'It can be and it is,' Andrea murmured. 'An old Polish plane we had before the war,' he explained to Miller. 'And the other is an old Belgian plane – Breguets, we called them.' Andrea shaded his eyes to look again at the two planes, now almost directly overhead. 'I thought they had all been lost during the invasion.'

'Me, too,' Mallory said. 'Must have patched up some bits and pieces. Ah, they've seen us – beginning to circle. But why on earth they use those obsolete death traps – '

'I don't know and I don't care,' Miller said rapidly. He had just taken a quick look round the boulder in front of him. 'Those damned guns down there are just linin' up on us, and muzzle-on they look a considerable sight bigger than telegraph poles. Fragmentation bombs, you said! Come on, boss, let's get the hell outa here!'

Thus the pattern was set for the remainder of that brief November afternoon, for the grim game of tip-and-run, hide-and-seek among the ravines and shattered rocks of the Devil's Playground. The planes held the key to the game, cruised high overhead observing every move of the hunted group below, relaying the information to the guns on the coast road and the company of Alpenkorps that had moved up through the ravine above the carob grove soon after the planes reported that the positions there had been abandoned. The two ancient planes were soon replaced by a couple of modern Henschels – Andrea said that the PZL couldn't remain airborne for more than an hour anyway.

Mallory was between the devil and the deep sea. Inaccurate though the mortars were, some of the deadly fragmentation bombs found their way into the deep ravines where they took temporary shelter, the blast of metal lethal in the confined space between the sheering walls. Occasionally they came so close that Mallory was forced to take refuge in some of the deep caves that honeycombed the walls of the canyons. In these they were safe enough, but the safety was an illusion that could lead only to ultimate defeat and capture; in the lulls, the Alpenkorps, whom they had fought off in a series of brief, skirmishing rearguard actions during the afternoon, could approach closely enough to trap them inside. Time and time again Mallory and his men were forced to move on to widen the gap between themselves and their pursuers, following the indomitable Louki wherever he chose to lead them, and taking their chance, often a very slender and desperate chance, with the mortar bombs. One bomb arced into a ravine that led into the interior, burying itself in the gravelly ground not twenty yards ahead of them, by far the nearest anything had come during the afternoon. By one chance in a thousand, it didn't explode. They gave it as wide a berth as possible, almost holding their breaths until they were safely beyond.

About half an hour before sunset they struggled up the last few boulder-strewn yards of a steeply-shelving ravine floor, halted just beyond the shelter of the projecting wall where the ravine dipped again and turned sharply to the right and the north. There had been no more mortar bombs since the one that had failed to explode. The six-inch and the weirdly-howling *Nebelwerfer* had only a limited range, Mallory knew, and though the planes still cruised overhead, they cruised uselessly: the sun was dipping towards the horizon and the floors of the ravines were already deeply-sunk in shadowed gloom, invisible from above. But the Alpenkorps, tough, dogged, skilful soldiers, soldiers living only for the revenge of their massacred comrades, were very close behind. And they were highly-trained mountain troops, fresh, resilient, the reservoir of their energies barely tapped: whereas his own tiny band, worn out from continuous days and sleepless nights of labour and action...

Mallory sank to the ground near the angled turn of the ravine where he could keep lookout, glanced at the others with a deceptive casualness that marked his cheerless assessment of what he saw. As a fighting unit they were in a pretty bad way. Both Panayis and Brown were badly crippled, the latter's face grey with pain. For the first time since leaving Alexandria, Casey Brown was apathetic, listless and quite indifferent to everything: this Mallory took as a very bad sign. Nor was Brown helped by the heavy transmitter still strapped to his back – with point-blank truculence he had ignored Mallory's categorical order to abandon it. Louki was tired, and looked it: his physique, Mallory realised now, was no match for his spirit, for the infectious smile that never left his face, for the panache of that magnificently upswept moustache that contrasted so oddly with the sad, tired eyes above. Miller, like himself, was tired, but, like himself, could keep on being tired for a long time yet. And Stevens was still conscious, but even in the twilit gloom of the canyon floor his face looked curiously transparent, while the nails, lips and eyelids were drained of blood. And Andrea, who had carried him up and down all these killing canyon tracks – where there had been tracks – for almost two interminable hours, looked as he always did: immutable, indestructible.

Mallory shook his head, fished out a cigarette, made to strike a light, remembered the planes still cruising overhead and threw the match away. Idly his gaze travelled north along the canyon and he slowly stiffened, the unlit cigarette crumpling and shredding between his fingers. This ravine bore no resemblance to any of the others through which they had so far passed – it was broader, dead straight, at least three times as long – and, as far as he could see in the twilight, the far end was blocked off by an almost vertical wall.

'Louki!' Mallory was on his feet now, all weariness forgotten. 'Do you know where you are? Do you know this place?'

'But certainly, Major!' Louki was hurt. 'Have I not told you that Panayis and I, in the days of our youth – '

'But this is a cul-de-sac, a dead-end!' Mallory protested. 'We're boxed in, man, we're trapped!'

Louki grinned impudently and twirled a corner of his moustache. The little man was enjoying himself.

'So? The Major does not trust Louki, is that it?' He grinned again, relented, patted the wall by his side. 'Panayis and I, we have been working this way all afternoon. Along this wall there are many caves. One of them leads through to another valley that leads down to the coast road.'

'I see, I see.' Relief washing through his mind, Mallory sank down on the ground again. 'And where does this other valley come out?'

'Just across the strait from Maidos.'

'How far from the town?'

'About five miles, Major, maybe six. Not more.'

'Fine, fine! And you're sure you can find this cave?'

'A hundred years from now and my head in a goat-skin bag!' Louki boasted.

237

'Fair enough!' Even as he spoke, Mallory catapulted himself violently to one side, twisted in mid-air to avoid falling across Stevens and crashed heavily into the wall between Andrea and Miller. In a moment of unthinking carelessness he had exposed himself to view from the ravine they had just climbed: the burst of machine-gun fire from its lower end – a hundred and fifty yards away at the most – had almost blown his head off. Even as it was, the left shoulder of his jacket had been torn away, the shell just grazing his shoulder. Miller was already kneeling by his side, fingering the gash, running a gently exploratory hand across his back.

'Careless, damn careless,' Mallory murmured. 'But I didn't think they were so close.' He didn't feel as calm as he sounded. If the mouth of that Schmeisser had been another sixteenth of an inch to the right, he'd have had no head left now.

'Are you all right, boss?' Miller was puzzled. 'Did they – '

'Terrible shots,' Mallory assured him cheerfully. 'Couldn't hit a barn.' He twisted round to look at his shoulder. 'I hate to sound heroic, but this really is just a scratch...' He rose easily to his feet, and picked up his guns. 'Sorry and all that, gentlemen, but it's time we were on our way again. How far along is this cave, Louki?'

Louki rubbed his bristly chin, the smile suddenly gone. He looked quickly at Mallory, then away again.

'Louki!'

'Yes, yes, Major. The cave.' Louki rubbed his chin again. 'Well, it is a good way along. In fact, it is at the end,' he finished uncomfortably.

'The *very* end?' asked Mallory quietly.

Louki nodded miserably, stared down at the ground at his feet. Even the ends of his moustache seemed to droop.

'That's handy,' Mallory said heavily. 'Oh, that's very handy!' He sank down to the ground again. 'Helps us no end, that does.'

He bowed his head in thought and didn't even lift it as Andrea poked a Bren round the angle of the rock, and fired a short downhill burst more in token of discouragement than in any hope of hitting anything. Another ten seconds passed, then Louki spoke again, his voice barely audible.

'I am very, very sorry. This is a terrible thing. Before God, Major, I would not have done it but that I thought they were still far behind.'

'It's not your fault, Louki.' Mallory was touched by the little man's obvious distress. He touched his ripped shoulder jacket. 'I thought the same thing.'

'Please!' Stevens put his hand on Mallory's arm. 'What's wrong? I don't understand.'

'Everybody else does, I'm afraid, Andy. It's very, very simple. We have half a mile to go along this valley here – and not a shred of cover. The Alpenkorps have less than two hundred yards to come up that ravine we've just left.' He paused while Andrea fired another retaliatory short burst, then continued. 'They'll do what they're doing now – keep probing to see if we're still here. The minute they judge we're gone, they'll be up here in a flash. They'll nail us before we're half-way, quarter-way to the cave – you know we can't travel fast. And they're carrying a couple of Spandaus – they'll cut us to ribbons.'

'I see,' Stevens murmured. 'You put it all so nicely, sir.'

'Sorry, Andy, but that's how it is.'

'But could you not leave two men as a rear-guard, while the rest – '

'And what happens to the rear-guard?' Mallory interrupted dryly.

'I see what you mean,' he said in a low voice. 'I hadn't thought of that.'

'No, but the rear-guard would. Quite a problem, isn't it?'

'There is no problem at all,' Louki announced. 'The Major is kind, but this is all my fault. I will – '

'You'll do damn all of the kind!' Miller said savagely.

239

He tore Louki's Bren from his hand and laid it on the ground. 'You heard what the boss said – it wasn't your fault.' For a moment Louki stared át him in anger, then turned dejectedly away. He looked as if he were going to cry. Mallory, too, stared at the American, astonished at the sudden vehemence, so completely out of character. Now that he came to think of it, Dusty had been strangely taciturn and thoughtful during the past hour or so – Mallory couldn't recall his saying a word during all that time. But time enough to worry about that later on...

Casey Brown eased his injured leg, looking hopefully at Mallory. 'Couldn't we stay here till it's dark – real dark – then make our way – '

'No good. The moon's almost full tonight – and not a cloud in the sky. They'd get us. Even more important, we have to get into the town between sunset and curfew tonight. Our last chance. Sorry, Casey, but it's no go.'

Fifteen seconds, half a minute passed, and passed in silence, then they all started abruptly as Andy Stevens spoke.

'Louki *was* right, you know,' he said pleasantly. The voice was weak, but filled with a calm certainty that jerked every eye towards him. He was propped up on one elbow, Louki's Bren cradled in his hands. It was a measure of their concentration on the problem on hand that no one had heard or seen him reach out for the machine-gun. 'It's all very simple,' Stevens went on quietly. 'Just let's use our heads, that's all... The gangrene's right up past the knee, isn't it, sir?'

Mallory said nothing: he didn't know what to say, the complete unexpectedness had knocked him off balance. He was vaguely aware that Miller was looking at him, his eyes begging him to say 'No.'

'Is it or isn't it?' There was a patience, a curious understanding in the voice, and all of a sudden Mallory knew what to say.

'Yes,' he nodded. 'It is.' Miller was looking at him in horror.

'Thank you, sir.' Stevens was smiling in satisfaction. 'Thank you very much indeed. There's no need to point out all the advantages of my staying here.' There was an assurance in his voice no one had ever heard before, the unthinking authority of a man completely in charge of a situation. 'Time I did something for my living anyway. No fond farewells, please. Just leave me a couple of boxes of ammo, two or three thirty-six grenades and away you go.'

'I'll be damed if we will!' Miller was up on his feet making for the boy, then brought up abruptly as the Bren centred on his chest.

'One step nearer and I'll shoot you,' Stevens said calmly. Miller looked at him in long silence, sank slowly back to the ground.

'I would, you know,' Stevens assured him. 'Well good-bye, gentlemen. Thank you for all you've done for me.'

Twenty seconds, thirty, a whole minute passed in a queer, trance-like silence, then Miller heaved himself to his feet again, a tall, rangy figure with tattered clothes and a face curiously haggard in the gathering gloom.

'So long, kid. I guess waal, mebbe I'm not so smart after all.' He took Stevens's hand, looked down at the wasted face for a long moment, made to say something else, then changed his mind. 'Be seein' you,' he said abruptly, turned and walked off heavily down the valley. One by one the others followed him, wordlessly, except for Andrea, who stopped and whispered in the boy's ear, a whisper that brought a smile and a nod of complete understanding, and then there was only Mallory left. Stevens grinned up at him.

'Thank you, sir. Thanks for not letting me down. You and Andrea – you understand. You always did understand.'

'You'll – you'll be all right, Andy?' God, Mallory thought, what a stupid, what an insane thing, to say.

'Honest, sir, I'm O.K.' Stevens smiled contentedly. 'No pain left – I can't feel a thing. It's wonderful!'

'Andy, I don't – '

'It's time you were gone, sir. The others will be waiting. Now if you'll just light me a gasper and fire a few random shots down that ravine...'

Within five minutes Mallory had overtaken the others, and inside fifteen they had all reached the cave that led to the coast. For a moment they stood in the entrance, listening to the intermittent firing from the other end of the valley, then turned wordlessly and plunged into the cave. Back where they had left him, Andy Stevens was lying on his stomach, peering down into the now almost dark ravine. There was no pain left in his body, none at all. He drew deeply on a cupped cigarette, smiled as he pushed another clip home into the magazine of the Bren. For the first time in his life Andy Stevens was happy and content beyond his understanding, a man at last at peace with himself. He was no longer afraid.

CHAPTER 13

Wednesday Evening

1800–1915

Exactly forty minutes later they were safely in the heart of the town of Navarone, within fifty yards of the great gates of the fortress itself.

Mallory, gazing out at the gates and the still more massive arch of stone that encased them, shook his head for the tenth time and tried to fight off the feeling of disbelief and wonder that they should have reached their goal at last – or as nearly as made no difference. They had been due a break some time, he thought, the law of averages had been overwhelmingly against the continuation of the evil fortune that had dogged them so incessantly since they had arrived on the island. It was only right, he kept telling himself, it was only just that this should be so: but even so, the transition from that dark valley where they had left Andy Stevens to die to this tumbledown old house on the east side of the town square of Navarone had been so quick, so easy, that it still lay beyond immediate understanding or unthinking acceptance.

Not that it had been too easy in the first fifteen minutes or so, he remembered. Panayis's wounded leg had given out on him immediately after they had entered the cave, and he had collapsed; he must have been in agony, Mallory had thought, with his torn, roughly-bandaged leg, but the failing light and the dark, bitter impassive face had masked the pain. He had begged Mallory to be allowed to remain where he was, to hold off the Alpenkorps when they had overcome Stevens and reached the end of the valley, but Mallory had roughly refused him permission. Brutally he had told Panayis that he was far too valuable to be left there – and that the chances of the Alpenkorps picking that cave out of a score of others were pretty remote. Mallory had hated having to talk to him like that, but there had been no time for gentle blandishments, and Panayis must have seen his point for he had made neither protest nor struggle when Miller and Andrea picked him up and helpd him to limp through the cave. The limp, Mallory had noticed, had been much less noticeable then, perhaps because of the assistance, perhaps because now that he had been baulked of the chance of killing a few more Germans it had been pointless to exaggerate his hurt.

They had barely cleared the mouth of the cave on the other side and were making their way down the tree-tufted sloping valley side towards the sea, the dark sheen of the Aegean clearly visible in the gloom, when Louki, hearing something, had gestured them all to silence. Almost immediately Mallory, too, heard it, a soft guttural voice occasionally lost in the crunch of approaching feet on gravel. Mallory had seen that they were providentially screened by some stunted trees, given the order to stop and sworn in quick anger as he had heard the soft thud and barely muffled cry behind them. He had gone back to investigate and found Panayis stretched on the ground unconscious. Miller, who had been helping him along, had explained that Mallory had halted them so suddenly that he'd bumped into Panayis, that the Greek's bad leg had given beneath him, throwing him heavily, his head striking a stone as he had fallen. Mallory had stooped down in instantly renewed suspicion – Panayis was a throw-back, a natural-born killer, and he was quite capable of faking an accident if he thought he could turn it to his advantage, line a few more of the enemy up on the sights of his rifle... but there had been no fake about that: the bruised and bloodied gash above the temple was all too real.

The German patrol, having had no inkling of their presence, moved noisily up the valley till they had finally gone out of earshot. Louki had thought that the commandant in Navarone was becoming desperate, trying to seal off every available exit from the Devil's Playground. Mallory had thought it unlikely, but had not stayed to argue the point. Five minutes later they had cleared the mouth of the valley, and in another five had not only reached the coast road but silenced and bound two sentries – the drivers, probably – who had been guarding a truck and command car parked by the roadside, stripped them of denims and helmets and bundled them out of sight behind some bushes.

The trip into Navarone had been ridiculously simple, but the entire lack of opposition was easily understand-able, because of the complete unexpectedness of it all. Seated beside Mallory on the front seat, clad, like Mallory, in captured clothes, Louki had driven the big car, and driven it magnificently, an accomplishment so unusual to find in a remote Aegean island that Mallory had been completely mystified until Louki had reminded him that he had been Eugene Vlachos's Consulate chauffeur for many years. The drive into town had taken less than twelve minutes – not only did the little man handle the car superbly, but he knew the road so well that he got the utmost possible out of the big machine, most of the time without benefit of any lights at all.

Not only a simple journey, but quite uneventful. They had passed several parked trucks at intervals along the road, and less than two miles from the town itself had met a group of about twenty soldiers marching in the opposite direction in column of twos. Louki had slowed down – it would have been highly suspicious had he accelerated, endangering the lives of the marching men – but had switched on the powerful headlights, blinding them, and blown raucously on the horn, while Mallory had leaned out of the right-hand window, sworn at them in perfect German and told them to get out of his damned way. This they had done, while the junior officer in charge had come smartly to attention, throwing up his hand in punctilious salute.

Immediately afterwards they had run through an area of high-walled, terraced market gardens, passed between a decaying Byzantine church and a whitewashed orthodox monastery that faced each other incongruously across the same dusty road, then almost at once were running through the lower part of the old town. Mallory had had a vague impression of narrow, winding, dim-lit streets only inches wider than the car itself, hugely cobbled and with almost knee-high pavements, then Louki was making his way up an arched lane, the car climbing steeply all the time. He had stopped abruptly and Mallory had followed his quick survey of the darkened lane; completely deserted though over an hour yet to curfew. Beside them had been a flight of white stone steps innocent of any handrail, running up parallel to the wall of a house, with a highly ornamented lattice-work grille protecting the outside landing at the top. A still groggy Panayis had led them up these stairs, through to a house – he had known exactly where he was – across a shallow roof, down some more steps, through a dark courtyard and into this ancient house where they were now. Louki had driven the car away even before they had reached the top of the stairs; it was only now that Mallory remembered that Louki hadn't thought it worth while to say what he intended to do with the car.

Still gazing out of the windowless hole in the wall at the fortress gate, Mallory found himself hoping intensely that nothing would happen to the sad-eyed little Greek, and not only because in his infinite resource and local knowledge he had been invaluable to them and was likely to prove so again; all these considerations apart, Mallory had formed the deepest affection for him, for his unvarying cheerfulness, his enthusiasm, his eagerness to help and to please, above all for his complete disregard of self. A thoroughly lovable little man, and Mallory's heart warmed to him. More than he could say for Panayis, he thought sourly, and then immediately regretted the thought; it was no fault of Panayis's that he was what he was, and in his own dark and bitter way he had done as much for them as Louki. But the fact remained that he was sadly lacking in Louki's warm humanity.

He lacked also Louki's quick intelligence, the calculated opportunism that amounted almost to genius. It had been a brilliant idea on Louki's part, Mallory mused, that they should take over this abandoned house: not that there had been any difficulty in finding an empty house – since the Germans had taken over the old castle the inhabitants of the town had left in their scores for Margaritha and other outlying villages, none more quickly than those who had lived in the town square itself; the nearness of the fortress wall that formed the north side of the square had been more than many of them could stomach, with the constant coming and going of their conquerors through the fortress gates, the sentries marching to and fro, the never-ceasing reminders that their freedom was a vanished thing. So many gone that more than half the houses on the west side of the square – those nearest the fortress – were now occupied by German officers. But this same enforced close observation of the fortress's activities had been exactly what Mallory had wanted. When the time came to strike they had only yards to go. And although any competent garrison commander would always be prepared against the unexpected, Mallory considered it unlikely indeed that any reasonable man could conceive of a sabotage group so suicidally minded as to spend an entire day within a literal stone's throw of the fortress wall.

Not that the house as such had much to recommend it. As a home, a dwelling place, it was just about as uncomfortable as possible, as dilapidated as it could be without actually falling down. The west side of the square – the side perched precariously on the cliff-top – and the south side were made up of fairly modern buildings of white-washed stone and Parian granite, huddled together in the invariable fashion of houses in these island towns, flat-roofed to catch as much as possible of the winter rains. But the east side of the square, where they were, was made up of antiquated timber and turf houses, of the kind much more often found in remote mountain villages.

The beaten earth floor beneath his feet was hummocky, uneven, and the previous occupants had used one corner of it – obviously – for a variety of purposes, not least as a refuse dump. The ceiling was of rough-hewn, blackened beams, more or less covered with planks, these in turn being covered with a thick layer of trodden earth: from previous experience of such houses in the White Mountains, Mallory knew that the roof would leak like a sieve whenever the rain came on. Across one end of the room was a solid ledge some thirty inches high, a ledge that served, after the fashion of similar structures in Eskimo igloos, as bed, tables or settee as the occasion demanded. The room was completely bare of furniture.

Mallory started as someone touched him on the shoulder and turned round. Miller was behind him mun-ching away steadily, the remains of a bottle of wine in his hand.

'Better get some chow, boss,' he advised. 'I'll take a gander through this hole from time to time.'

'Right you are, Dusty. Thanks.' Mallory moved gingerly towards the back of the room – it was almost pitch dark inside and they dared not risk a light – and felt his way till he brought up against the ledge. The tireless Andrea had gone through their provisions and prepared a meal of sorts – dried figs, honey, cheese, garlic sausages and pounded roast chestnuts. A horrible mixture, Mallory thought, but the best Andrea could do: besides he was too hungry, ravenously so, to worry about such niceties as the pleas-ing of his palate. And by the time he had washed it down with some of the local wine that Louki and Panayis had provided the previous day, the sweetly-resinous rawness of the drink had obliterated every other taste.

Carefully, shielding the match with his hand, Mallory lit a cigarette and began to explain for the first time his plan for entering the fortress. He did not have to bother lowering his voice – a couple of looms in the next house, one of the few occupied ones left on that side of the square, clacked incessantly throughout the evening. Mallory had a shrewd suspicion that this was more of Louki's doing although it was difficult to see how he could have got word through to any of his friends. But Mallory was content to accept the situation as it was, to concentrate on making sure that the others understood his instructions.

Apparently they did, for there were no questions. For a few minutes the talk became general, the usually taciturn Casey Brown having the most to say, complaining bitterly about the food, the drink, his injured leg and the hardness of the bench where he wouldn't be able to sleep a wink all night long. Mallory grinned to himself but said nothing; Casey Brown was definitely on the mend.

'I reckon we've talked enough, gentlemen.' Mallory slid off the bench and stretched himself. God, he was tired! 'Our first and last chance to get a decent night's sleep. Two hour watches – I'll take the first.'

'By yourself?' It was Miller calling softly from the other end of the room. 'Don't you think we should share watches, boss? One for the front, one for the back. Besides, you know we're all pretty well done up. One man by himself might fall asleep.' He sounded so anxious that Mallory laughed.

'Not a chance, Dusty. Each man will keep watch by the window there and if he falls asleep he'll damn soon wake up when he hits the floor. And it's because we're so darned bushed that we can't afford to have anyone lose sleep unnecessarily. Myself first, then you, then Panayis, then Casey, then Andrea.'

249

'Yeah, I suppose that'll be O.K.,' Miller conceded grudgingly.

He put something hard and cold into his hand. Mallory recognised it at once – it was Miller's most cherished possession, his silenced automatic.

'Just so's you can fill any nosy customers full of little holes without wakin' the whole town.' He ambled off to the back of the room, lit a cigarette, smoked it quietly for a few moments, then swung his legs up on the bench. Within five minutes everyone except the silently watchful man at the window was sound asleep.

Two or three minutes later Mallory jerked to unmoving attention as he heard a stealthy sound outside – from the back of the house, he thought. The clacking of the looms next door had stopped, and the house was very still. Again there came the noise, unmistakable this time, a gentle tapping at the door at the end of the passage that led from the back of the room.

'Remain there, my Captain.' It was Andrea's soft murmur, and Mallory marvelled for the hundredth time at Andrea's ability to rouse himself from the deepest of sleeps at the slightest alien sound: the violence of a thunderstorm would have left him undisturbed. 'I will see to it. It must be Louki.'

It was Louki. The little man was panting, near exhaustion, but extraordinarily pleased with himself. Gratefully he drank the cup of wine that Andrea poured for him.

'Damned glad to see you back again!' Mallory said sincerely. 'How did it go? Someone after you?'

Mallory could almost see him drawing himself up to his full height in the darkness.

'As if any of those clumsy fools could see Louki, even on a moonlit night, far less catch him,' he said indignantly. He paused to draw some deep breath. 'No, no, Major, I knew you would be worried about me so I ran back all the way. Well, nearly all the way,' he amended. 'I am not so young as I was, Major Mallory.'

250

'All the way from where?' Mallory asked. He was glad of the darkness that hid his smile.

'From Vygos. It is an old castle that the Franks built there many generations ago, about two miles from here along the coast road to the east.' He paused to drink another mouthful of wine. 'More than two miles, I would say – and I only walked twice, a minute at a time, on the way back.' Mallory had the impression that Louki already regretted his momentary weakness in admitting that he was no longer a young man.

'And what did you do there?' Mallory asked.

'I was thinking, after I left you,' Louki answered indirectly. 'Me, I am always thinking,' he explained. 'It is a habit of mine. I was thinking that when the soldiers who are looking for us out in the Devil's Playground find out that the car is gone, they will know that we are no longer in that accursed place.'

'Yes,' Mallory agreed carefully. 'Yes, they will know that.'

'Then they will say to themselves, "Ha, those *verdammt Englanders* have little time left." They will know that we will know that they have little hope of catching us in the island – Panayis and I, we know every rock and tree and path and cave. So all they can do is to make sure that we do not get into the town – they will block every road leading in, and tonight is our last chance to get in. You follow me?' he asked anxiously.

'I am trying very hard.'

'But first' – Louki spread his hands dramatically – 'but first they will make sure we are not in the town. They would be fools to block the roads if we were already in the town. They *must* make sure we are not in the town. And so – the search. The very great search. With – how do you say? – the teeth-comb!'

Mallory nodded his head in slow understanding.

'I'm afraid he's right, Andrea.'

'I, too, fear so,' Andrea said unhappily. 'We should have

thought of this. But perhaps we could hide – the roof-tops
or – '

'With a teeth-comb, I said!' Louki interrupted impatiently. 'But all is well. I, Louki, have thought it all out. I can smell rain. There will be clouds over the moon before long, and it will be safe to move... You do not want to know what I have done with the car, Major Mallory?' Louki was enjoying himself immensely.

'Forgotten all about it,' Mallory confessed. 'What *did* you do with the car?'

'I left it in the courtyard of Vygos castle. Then I emptied all the petrol from the tank and poured it over the car. Then I struck a match.'

'You did *what*?' Mallory was incredulous.

'I struck a match. I think I was standing too near the car, for I do not seem to have any eyebrows left.' Louki sighed. 'A pity – it was such a splendid machine.' Then he brightened. 'But before God, Major, it burned magnificently.'

Mallory stared at him.

'Why on earth – ?'

'It is simple,' Louki explained patiently. 'By this time the men out in the Devil's Playground must know that their car has been stolen. They see the fire. They hurry back to – how do you say?'

'Investigate?'

'So. Investigate. They wait till the fire dies down. They investigate again. No bodies, no bones in the car, so they search the castle. And what do they find?'

There was silence in the room.

'Nothing!' Louki said impatiently. 'They find nothing. And then they search the countryside for half a mile around. And what do they find? Again nothing. So then they know that they have been fooled, and that we are in the town, and will come to search the town.'

'With the teeth-comb,' Mallory murmured.

'With the teeth-comb. And what do they find?' Louki

paused, then hurried on before anyone could steal his thunder. 'Once again, they will find nothing,' he said triumphantly. 'And why? For by then the rain will have come, the moon will have vanished, the explosives will be hidden – and we will be gone!'

'Gone where?' Mallory felt dazed.

'Where but to Vygos castle, Major Mallory. Never while night follows day will they think to look for us there!'

Mallory looked at him in silence for long seconds without speaking, then turned to Andrea.

'Captain Jensen's only made one mistake so far,' he murmured. 'He picked the wrong man to lead this expedition. Not that it matters anyway. With Louki here on our side, how can we lose?'

Mallory lowered his rucksack gently to the earthen roof, straightened and peered up into the darkness, both hands shielding his eyes from the first drizzle of rain. Even from where they stood – on the crumbling roof of the house nearest the fortress on the east side of the square – the walls stretched fifteen, perhaps twenty feet above their heads; the wickedly out- and down-curving spikes that topped the wall were all but lost in the darkness.

'There she is, Dusty,' Mallory murmured. 'Nothing to it.'

'Nothin' to it!' Miller was horrified. 'I've – I've gotta get over *that*?'

'You'd have a ruddy hard time going through it,' Mallory answered briefly. He grinned, clapped Miller on the back and prodded the rucksack at his feet. 'We chuck this rope up, the hook catches, you shin smartly up – '

'And bleed to death on those six strands of barbed wire,' Miller interrupted. 'Louki says they're the biggest barbs he's ever seen.'

'We'll use the tent for padding,' Mallory said soothingly.

'I have a very delicate skin, boss,' Miller complained. 'Nothin' short of a spring mattress – '

'Well, you've only an hour to find one,' Mallory said indifferently. Louki had estimated that it would be at least an hour before the search party would clear the northern part of the town, give himself and Andrea a chance to begin a diversion. 'Come on, let's cache this stuff and get out of here. We'll shove the rucksacks in this corner and cover 'em with earth. Take the rope out first, though; we'll have no time to start undoing the packs when we get here.'

Miller dropped to his knees, hands fumbling with straps, then exclaimed in sudden annoyance.

'This can't be the pack,' he muttered in disgust. Abruptly his voice changed. 'Here, wait a minute, though.'

'What's up, Dusty?'

Miller didn't answer immediately. For a few seconds his hands explored the contents of the pack, then he straightened.

'The slow-burnin' fuse, boss.' His voice was blurred with anger, with a vicious anger that astonished Mallory. 'It's gone!'

'What!' Mallory stooped, began to search through the pack. 'It can't be, Dusty, it just *can't*! Dammit to hell, man, you packed the stuff yourself!'

'Sure I did, boss,' Miller grated. 'And then some crawlin' bastard comes along behind my back and unpacks it again.'

'Impossible!' Mallory protested. 'It's just downright impossible, Dusty. *You* closed that rucksack – I saw you do it in the grove this morning – and Louki has had it all the time. And I'd trust Louki with my life.'

'So would I, boss.'

'Maybe we're both wrong,' Mallory went on quietly. 'Maybe you did miss it out. We're both helluva tired, Dusty.'

Miller looked at him queerly, said nothing for a

254

moment, then began to swear again. 'It's my own fault, boss, my own damned fault.'

'What do you mean, your own fault? Heavens above, man, I was there when...' Mallory broke off, rose quickly to his feet and stared through the darkness at the south side of the square. A single shot had rung out there, the whiplash crack of a carbine followed the thin, high whine of a ricochet, and then silence.

Mallory stood quite still, hands clenched by his sides. Over ten minutes had passed since he and Miller had left Panayis to guide Andrea and Brown to the Castle Vygos – and they should have been well away from the square by this time. And almost certainly Louki wouldn't be down there, Mallory's instructions to him had been explicit – to hide the remainder of the T.N.T. blocks in the roof and then wait there to lead himself and Miller to the keep. But something could have gone wrong, something could always go wrong. Or a trap, maybe a ruse. But what kind of trap?

The sudden off-beat stammering of a heavy machine-gun stilled his thoughts, and for a moment or two he was all eyes and straining ears. And then another, and lighter machine-gun, cut in, just for a few seconds: as abruptly as they had started, both guns died away, together. Mallory waited no longer.

'Get the stuff together again,' he whispered urgently. 'We're taking it with us. Something's gone wrong.' Within thirty seconds they had ropes and explosives back in their knapsacks, had strapped them on their backs and were on their way.

Bent almost double, careful to make no noise whatsoever they ran across the roof-tops towards the old house where they had hidden earlier in the evening, where they were now to rendezvous with Louki. Still running, they were only feet away from the house when they saw his shadowy figure rise up, only it wasn't Louki. Mallory realised at once, for it was too tall for Louki and without

255

breaking step he catapulted the horizontal driving weight of his 180 pounds at the unknown figure in a homicidal tackle, his shoulder catching the man just below the breast-bone, emptying every last particle of air from the man's lungs with an explosive agonised *whoosh*. A second later both of Miller's sinewy hands were clamped round the man's neck, slowly choking him to death.

And he would have choked to death, neither of the two men were in any mind for half-measures, had not Mallory, prompted by some fugitive intuition, stooped low over the contorted face, the staring, protruding eyes, choked back a cry of sudden horror.

'Dusty!' he whispered hoarsely. 'For God's sake, stop! Let him go! It's Panayis!'

Miller didn't hear him. In the gloom his face was like stone, his head sunk farther and farther between hunching shoulders as he tightened his grip, strangling the Greek in a weird savage silence.

'It's Panayis, you bloody fool, Panayis!' Mallory's mouth was at the American's ear, his hands clamped round the other's wrists as he tried to drag him off Panayis's throat. He could hear the muffled drumming of Panayis's heels on the turf of the roof, tore at Miller's wrists with all his strength: twice before he had heard that sound as a man had died under Andrea's great hands, and he knew with sudden certainty that Panayis would go the same way, and soon, if he didn't make Miller understand. But all at once Miller understood, relaxed heavily, straightened up, still kneeling, hands hanging limply by his sides. Breathing deeply he stared down in silence at the man at his feet.

'What the hell's the matter with you?' Mallory demanded softly. 'Deaf or blind or both?'

'Just one of those things, I guess.' Miller rubbed the back of a hand across his forehead, his face empty of expression. 'Sorry, boss, sorry.'

'Why the hell apologise to me?' Mallory looked away

from him, looked down at Panayis: the Greek was sitting up now, hands massaging his bruised throat, sucking in long draughts of air in great, whooping gasps. 'But maybe Panayis here might appreciate—'

'Apologies can wait,' Miller interrupted brusquely. 'Ask him what's happened to Louki.'

Mallory looked at him for a moment, made to reply, changed his mind, translated the question. He listened to Panayis's halting answer – it obviously hurt him even to try to speak – and his mouth tightened in a hard, bitter line. Miller watched the fractional slump of the New Zealander's shoulders, felt he could wait no longer.

'Well, what is it, boss? Somethin's happened to Louki, is that it?'

'Yes,' Mallory said tonelessly. 'They'd only got as far as the lane at the back when they found a small German patrol blocking their way. Louki tried to draw them off and the machine-gunner got him through the chest. Andrea got the machine-gunner and took Louki away. Panayis says he'll die for sure.'

CHAPTER 14

Wednesday Night

1915–2000

The three men cleared the town without any difficulty, striking out directly across country for the castle Vygos and avoiding the main road. It was beginning to rain now, heavily, persistently, and the ground was mired and sodden, the few ploughed fields they crossed almost impassable. They had just struggled their way through one of these and could just see the dim outline of the keep – less than a cross-country mile from the town instead of Louki's exaggerated estimate – when they passed by an abandoned earthen house and Miller spoke for the first time since they had left the town square of Navarone.

'I'm bushed, boss.' His head was sunk on his chest, and his breathing was laboured. 'Ol' man Miller's on the downward path, I reckon, and the legs are gone. Couldn't we squat inside here for a couple of minutes, boss, and have a smoke?'

Mallory looked at him in surprise, thought how desperately weary his own legs felt and nodded in reluctant agreement. Miller wasn't the man to complain unless he was near exhaustion.

'Okay, Dusty, I don't suppose a minute or two will harm.' He translated quickly into Greek and led the way inside, Miller at his heels complaining at length about his advancing age. Once inside, Mallory felt his way across to the inevitable wooden bunk, sat down gratefully, lit a cigarette then looked up in puzzlement. Miller was still on his feet, walking slowly round the hut, tapping the walls as he went.

'Why don't you sit down?' Mallory asked irritably. 'That was why you came in here in the first place, wasn't it?'

'No, boss, not really.' The drawl was very pronounced. 'Just a low-down trick to get us inside. Two-three very special things I want to show you.'

'Very special? What the devil are you trying to tell me?'

'Bear with me, Captain Mallory,' Miller requested formally. 'Bear with me just a few minutes, I'm not wastin' your time. You have my word, Captain Mallory.'

'Very well.' Mallory was mystified, but his confidence in Miller remained unshaken. 'As you wish. Only don't be too long about it.'

'Thanks, boss.' The strain of formality was too much for Miller. 'It won't take long. There'll be a lamp or candles in here — you said the islanders never leave an abandoned house without 'em?'

'And a very useful superstition it's been to us, too.' Mallory reached under the bunk with his torch, straightened his back. 'Two or three candles here.'

'I want a light, boss. No windows — I checked. O.K.?'

'Light one and I'll go outside to see if there's anything showing.' Mallory was completely in the dark about the American's intentions. He felt Miller didn't want him to say anything, and there was a calm surety about him that precluded questioning. Mallory was back in less than a minute. 'Not a chink to be seen from the outside,' he reported.

'Fair enough. Thanks, boss.' Miller lit a second candle, then slipped the rucksack straps from his shoulders, laid the pack on the bunk and stood in silence for a moment.

Mallory looked at his watch, looked back at Miller.

'You were going to show me something,' he prompted.

'Yeah, that's right. Three things, I said.' He dug into the pack, brought out a little black box hardly bigger than a match-box. 'Exhibit A, boss.'

Mallory looked at it curiously. 'What's that?'

'Clockwork fuse.' Miller began to unscrew the back panel. 'Hate the damned things. Always make me feel like one of those Bolshevik characters with a dark cloak, a moustache like Louki's and carryin' one of those black cannon-ball things with a sputterin' fuse stickin' outa it. But it works.' He had the back off the box now, examining the mechanism in the light of his torch. 'But this one doesn't, not any more,' he added softly. 'Clock's O.K., but the contact arm's been bent right back. This thing could tick till Kingdom Come and it couldn't even set off a firework.'

'But how on earth – ?'

'Exhibit B.' Miller didn't seem to hear him. He opened the detonator box, gingerly lifted a fuse from its felt and cotton-wool bed and examined it closely under his torch. Then he looked at Mallory again. 'Fulminate of mercury, boss. Only seventy-seven grains, but enough to blow your fingers off. Unstable as hell, too – the littlest tap will set it off.' He let it fall to the ground, and Mallory winced and drew back involuntarily as the American smashed a heavy heel down on top of it. But there was no explosion, nothing at all.

'Ain't workin' so good either, is it, boss? A hundred to one the rest are all empty, too.' He fished out a pack of cigarettes, lit one, and watched the smoke eddy and whirl about the heat of the candles. He slid the cigarettes into his pocket.

'There was a third thing you were going to show me,' Mallory said quietly.

'Yeah, I was goin' to show you somethin' else.' The voice was very gentle and Mallory felt suddenly cold. 'I was goin' to show you a spy, a traitor, the most vicious, twistin', murderin', double-crossin' bastard I've ever known.' The American had his hand out of his pocket now, the silenced automatic sitting snugly against his palm, the muzzle trained over Panayis's heart. He went on, more gently than ever. 'Judas Iscariot had nothin' on the boy-friend here, boss… Take your coat off, Panayis.'

'What the devil are you doing? Are you crazy?' Mallory started forward, half-angry, half-amazed, but brought up sharply against Miller's extended arm, rigid as a bar of iron. 'What bloody nonsense is this? He doesn't understand English!'

'Don't he, though? Then why was he out of the cave like a flash when Casey reported hearin' sounds outside... and why was he the first to leave the carob grove this afternoon if he didn't understand your order? Take your coat off, Judas, or I'll shoot you through the arm. I'll give you two seconds.'

Mallory made to throw his arms round Miller and bring him to the ground, but halted in mid-step as he caught the look on Panayis's face – teeth bared, murder glaring out from the coal-black eyes. Never before had Mallory seen such malignity in a human face, a malignity that yielded abruptly to shocked pain and disbelief as the .32 bullet smashed into his upper arm, just below the shoulder.

'Two seconds and then the other arm,' Miller said woodenly. But Panayis was already tearing off his jacket, the dark, bestial eyes never leaving Miller's face. Mallory looked at him, shivered involuntarily, looked at Miller. Indifference, he thought, that was the only word to describe the look on the American's face. Indifference. Unaccountably, Mallory felt colder than ever.

'Turn round!' The automatic never wavered.

Slowly Panayis turned round. Miller stepped forward, caught the black shirt by the collar, ripped it off his back with one convulsive jerk.

'Waal, waal, now, whoever woulda thought it?' Miller drawled. 'Surprise, surprise, surprise! Remember, boss, this was the character that was publicly flogged by the Germans in Crete, flogged until the white of his ribs showed through. His back's in a helluva state, isn't it?'

Mallory looked but said nothing. Completely off balance, his mind was in a kaleidoscopic whirl, his thoughts struggling to adjust themselves to a new set of circumstances, a complete reversal of all his previous thinking. Not a scar, not a single blemish, marked the dark smoothness of that skin.

'Just a natural quick healer,' Miller murmured. 'Only a nasty, twisted mind like mine would think that he had been a German agent in Crete, became known to the Allies as a fifth columnist, lost his usefulness to the Germans and was shipped back to Navarone by fast motor-launch under cover of night. Floggin'! Island-hoppin' his way back here in a row-boat! Just a lot of bloody eyewash!' Miller paused, and his mouth twisted. 'I wonder how many pieces of silver he made in Crete before they got wise to him?'

'But heavens above, man, you're not going to condemn someone just for shooting a line!' Mallory protested. Strangely he didn't feel nearly as vehement as he sounded. 'How many survivors would there be among the Allies if – ?'

'Not convinced yet, huh?' Miller waved his automatic negligently at Panayis. 'Roll up the left trouser leg, Iscariot. Two seconds again.'

Panayis did as he was told. The black venomous eyes never looked away from Miller's. He rolled the dark cloth up to the knee.

'Farther yet? That's my little boy,' Miller encouraged him. 'And now take that bandage off – right off.' A few seconds passed, then Miller shook his head sadly. 'A ghastly wound, boss, a ghastly wound!'

'I'm beginning to see your point,' Mallory said thoughtfully. The dark sinewy leg wasn't even scratched. 'But why on earth – ?'

'Simple. Four reasons at least Junior here is a treacherous, slimy bastard – no self-respectin' rattlesnake would come within a mile of him – but he's a clever bastard. He faked his leg so he could stay in the cave in the Devil's Playground when the four of us went back to stop the Alpenkorps from comin' up the slope below the carob grove.'

'Why? Frightened he'd stop something?'

Miller shook his head impatiently.

'Junior here's scared o' nothin'. He stayed behind to write a note. Later on he used his leg to drop behind us some place, and leave the note where it could be seen. Early on, this must have been. Note probably said that we would come out at such and such a place, and would they kindly send a welcomin' committee to meet us there. They sent it, remember: it was their car we swiped to get to town... That was the first time I got real suspicious of the boyfriend: after he'd dropped behind he made up on us again quick – too damn quick for a man with a game leg. But it wasn't till I opened that rucksack in the square this evenin' that I really knew.'

'You only mentioned two reasons,' Mallory prompted.

'Comin' to the others. Number three – he could fall behind when the welcomin' committee opened up in front – Iscariot here wasn't goin to get himself knocked off before he collected his salary. And number four – remember that real touchin' scene when he begged you to let him stay at the far end of the cave that led into the valley we came out? Goin' to do his Horatio-on-the-bridge act?'

'Going to show them the right cave to pick, you mean.'

'Check. After that he was gettin' pretty desperate. I still wasn't sure, but I was awful suspicious, boss. Didn't know what he might try next. So I clouted him good and hard when that last patrol came up the valley.'

'I see,' Mallory said quietly. 'I see indeed.' He looked sharply at Miller. 'You should have told me. You had no right – '

'I was goin' to, boss. But I hadn't a chance – Junior here was around all the time. I was just startin' to tell you half an hour back, when the guns started up.'

Mallory nodded in understanding. 'How did you happen on all this in the first place, Dusty?'

'Juniper,' Miller said succinctly. 'Remember that's how Turzig said he came to find us? He smelt the juniper.'

263

'That's right. We *were* burning juniper.'

'Sure we were. But he said he smelt it on Kostos – and the wind was blowin' off Kostos all day long.'

'My God,' Mallory whispered. 'Of course, of course! And I missed it completely.'

'But Jerry knew we were there. How? Waal, he ain't got second sight no more than I have. So he was tipped off – he was tipped of by the boy-friend here. Remember I said he'd talked to some of his pals in Margaritha when we went down there for the supplies?' Miller spat in disgust. 'Fooled me all along the line. Pals? I didn't know how right I was. Sure they were his pals – his German pals! And that food he said he got from the commandant's kitchen – he got it from the kitchen all right. Almost certainly he goes in and asks for it – and old Skoda hands him his own suitcase to stow it in.'

'But the German he killed on the way back to the village? Surely to God – '

'Panayis killed him.' There was a tired certainty in Miller's voice. 'What's another corpse to Sunshine here. Probably stumbled on the poor bastard in the dark and had to kill him. Local colour. Louki was there, remember, and he couldn't have Louki gettin' suspicious. He would have blamed it on Louki anyway. The guy ain't human.... And remember when he was flung into Skoda's room in Margaritha along with Louki, blood pourin' from a wound in his head?'

Mallory nodded.

'High-grade ketchup. Probably also from the commandant's kitchen,' Miller said bitterly. 'If Skoda had failed by every other means, there would still have been the boyfriend here as a stool-pigeon. Why he never asked Louki where the explosives were I don't know.'

'Obviously he didn't know Louki knew.'

'Mebbe. But one thing the bastard did know – how to use a mirror. Musta heliographed the garrison from the carob grove and given our position. No other way, boss. Then sometime this morning he must have got hold of my rucksack, whipped out all the slow fuse and fixed the clock fuse and detonators. He should have had his hands blown off tamperin' with them fulminates. Lord only knows where he learnt to handle the damn things.'

'Crete.' Mallory said positively. 'The Germans would see to that. A spy who can't also double as a saboteur is no good to them.'

'And he was very good to them,' Miller said softly. 'Very, very good. They're gonna miss their little pal. Iscariot here was a very smart baby indeed.'

'He was. Except tonight. He should have been smart enough to know that at least one of us would be suspicious – '

'He probably was,' Miller interrupted. 'But he was misinformed. I think Louki's unhurt. I think Junior here talked Louki into letting him stay in his place – Louki was always a bit scared of him – then he strolled across to his pals at the gate, told 'em to send a strong-arm squad out to Vygos to pick up the others, asked them to fire a few shots – he was very strong on local colour, was our loyal little pal – then strolls back across the square, hoists himself up on the roof and waits to tip off his pals as soon as we came in the back door. But Louki forgot to tell him just one thing – that we were goin' to rendezvous on the roof of the house, not inside. So the boy-friend here lurks away for all he's worth up top, waiting to signal his friends. Ten to one that he's got a torch in his pocket.'

Mallory picked up Panayis's coat and examined it briefly. 'He has.'

'That's it, then.' Miller lit another cigarette, watched the match burn down slowly to his fingers, then looked up at Panayis. 'How does it feel to know that you're goin' to die, Panayis, to feel like all them poor bastards who've felt just as you're feeling now, just before they died – all the men in Crete, all the guys in the sea-borne and air

265

landings on Navarone who died because they thought you were on their side? How does it feel, Panayis?'

Panayis said nothing. His left hand clutching his torn right arm, trying to stem the blood, he stood there motionless, the dark, evil face masked in hate, the lips still drawn back in that less than human snarl. There was no fear in him, none at all, and Mallory tensed himself for the last, despairing attempt for life that Panayis must surely make, and then he had looked at Miller and knew there would be no attempt, because there was a strange sureness and inevitability about the American, an utter immobility of hand and eye that somehow precluded even the thought, far less the possibility, of escape.

'The prisoner has nothin' to say.' Miller sounded very tired. 'I suppose I should say somethin'. I suppose I should give out with a long spiel about me bein' the judge, the jury and the executioner, but I don't think I'll bother myself. Dead men make poor witnesses... Mebbe it's not your fault, Panayis, mebbe there's an awful good reason why you came to be what you are. Gawd only knows. I don't, and I don't much care. There are too many dead men. I'm goin' to kill you, Panayis, and I'm goin' to kill you now.' Miller dropped his cigarette, ground it into the floor of the hut. 'Nothin' at all to say?'

And he had nothing at all to say, the hate, the malignity of the black eyes said it all for him and Miller nodded, just once, as if in secret understanding. Carefully, accurately, he shot Panayis through the heart, twice, blew out the candles, turned his back and was half-way towards the door before the dead man had crashed to the ground.

'I am afraid I cannot do it, Andrea.' Louki sat back wearily, shook his head in despair. 'I am very sorry, Andrea. The knots are too tight.'

'No matter.' Andrea rolled over from his side to a sitting position, tried to ease his tightly-bound legs and wrists. 'They are cunning, these Germans, and wet cords can

266

only be cut.' Characteristically, he made no mention of the fact that only a couple of minutes previously he had twisted round to reach the cords on Louki's wrist and undone them with half a dozen tugs of his steel-trap fingers. 'We will think of something else.'

He looked away from Louki, glanced across the room in the faint light of the smoking oil-lamp that stood by the grille door, a light so yellow, so dim that Casey Brown, trussed like a barnyard fowl and loosely secured, like himself, by a length of rope to the iron hooks suspended from the roof, was no more than a shapeless blur in the opposite corner of the stone-flagged room. Andrea smiled to himself, without mirth. Taken prisoner again, and for the second time that day – and with the same ease and surprise that gave no chance at all of resistance: completely unsuspecting, they had been captured in an upper room, seconds after Casey had finished talking to Cairo. The patrol had known exactly where to find them – and with their leader's assurance that it was all over, with his gloating explanation of the part Panayis had played, the unexpectedness, the success of the coup was all too easy to understand. And it was difficult not to believe his assurance that neither Mallory nor Miller had a chance. But the thought of ultimate defeat never occurred to Andrea.

His gaze left Casey Brown, wandered round the room, took in what he could see of the stone walls and floor, the hooks, the ventilation ducts, the heavy grille door. A dungeon, a torture dungeon, one would have thought, but Andrea had seen such places before. A castle, they called this place, but it was really only an old keep, no more than a manor house built round the crenellated towers. And the long-dead Frankish nobles who had built these keeps had lived well. No dungeon this, Andrea knew, but simply the larder where they had hung their meat and game, and done without windows and light for the sake of...

The light! Andrea twisted round, looking at the smoking oil-lamp, his eyes narrowing.

'Louki!' he called softly. The little Greek turned round to look at him.

'Can you reach the lamp?'

'I think so... Yes, I can.'

'Take the glass off,' Andrea whispered. 'Use a cloth – it will be hot. Then wrap it in the cloth, hit it on the floor – gently. The glass is thick – you can cut me loose in a minute or two.'

Louki stared at him for an uncomprehending moment, then nodded in understanding. He shuffled across the floor – his legs were still bound – reached out, then halted his hand abruptly, only inches from the glass. The peremptory, metallic clang had been only feet away, and he raised his head slowly to see what had caused it.

He could have stretched out his hand, touched the barrel of the Mauser that protruded threateningly through the bars of the grille door. Again the guard rattled the rifle angrily between the bars, shouted something he didn't understand.

'Leave it alone, Louki,' Andrea said quietly. His voice was tranquil, unshadowed by disappointment. 'Come back here. Our friend outside is not too pleased.' Obediently Louki moved back, heard the guttural voice again, rapid and alarmed this time, the rattle as the guard withdrew his rifle quickly from the bars of the door, the urgent pounding of his feet on the flagstones outside as he raced up the passage.

'What's the matter with our little friend?' Casey Brown was as lugubrious, as weary as ever. 'He seems upset.'

'He is upset.' Andrea smiled. 'He's just realised that Louki's hands are untied.'

'Well, why doesn't he tie them up again?'

'Slow in the head he may be, but he is no fool,' Andrea explained. 'This could be a trap and he's gone for his friends.'

Almost at once they heard a thud, like the closing of a distant door, the sound of more than one pair of feet running down the passage, the tinny rattling of keys on a ring, the rasp of a key against the lock, a sharp click, the squeal of rusty hinges and then two soldiers were in the room, dark and menacing with their jackboots and ready guns. Two or three seconds elapsed while they looked around them, accustoming their eyes to the gloom, then the man nearest the door spoke.

'A terrible thing, boss, nothin' short of deplorable! Leave 'em alone for a couple of minutes and see what happens? The whole damn bunch tied up like Houdini on an off night!'

There was a brief, incredulous silence, then all three were sitting upright, staring at them. Brown recovered first.

'High time, too,' he complained. 'Thought you were never going to get here.'

'What he means is that he thought we were never going to see you again,' Andrea said quietly. 'Neither did I. But here you are, safe and sound.'

'Yes,' Mallory nodded. 'Thanks to Dusty and his nasty suspicious mind that cottoned on to Panayis while all the rest of us were asleep.'

'Where is he?' Louki asked.

'Panayis?' Miller waved a negligent hand. 'We left him behind – he met with a sorta accident.' He was across at the other side of the room now, carefully cutting the cords that pinioned Brown's injured leg, whistling tunelessly as he sawed away with his sheath knife. Mallory, too, was busy, slicing through Andrea's bonds, explaining rapidly what had happened, listening to the big Greek's equally concise account of what had befallen the other in the keep. And then Andrea was on his feet, massaging his numbed hands, looking across at Miller.

'That whistling, my Captain. It sounds terrible and, what is worse, it is very loud. The guards – '

269

'No worry there,' Mallory said grimly. 'They never expected to see Dusty and myself again... They kept a poor watch.' He turned round to look at Brown, now hobbling across the floor.

'How's the leg, Casey?'

'Fine, sir.' Brown brushed it aside as of no importance. 'I got through to Cairo, tonight, sir. The report – '

'It'll have to wait, Casey. We must get out as fast as we can. You all right, Louki?'

'I am heart-broken, Major Mallory. That a countryman of mine – a trusted friend – '

'That too, will have to wait. Come on!'

'You are in a great hurry,' Andrea protested mildly. They were already out in the passage, stepping over the cell guard lying in a crumpled heap on the floor. 'Surely if they're all like our friend here – '

'No danger from this quarter,' Mallory interrupted impatiently. 'The soldiers in the town – they're bound to know by now that we've either missed Panayis or disposed of him. In either case they'll know that we're certain to come hot-footing out here. Work it out for yourself. They're probably half-way here already, and if they do come...' He broke off, stared at the smashed generator and the ruins of Casey Brown's transmitter set lying in one corner of the entrance hall. 'Done a pretty good job on those, haven't they?' he said bitterly.

'Thank the Lord,' Miller said piously. 'All the less to tote around, is what I say. If you could only see the state of my back with that damned generator – '

'Sir!' Brown had caught Mallory's arm, an action so foreign to the usually punctilious petty officer that Mallory halted in surprise. 'Sir, it's terribly important – the report, I mean. You *must* listen, sir!'

The action, the deadly earnestness, caught and held Mallory's full attention. He turned to face Brown with a smile.

'O.K., Casey, let's have it,' he said quietly. 'Things can't possibly be any worse than they are now.'

'They can, sir.' There was something tired, defeated about Casey Brown, and the great, stone hall seemed strangely chill. 'I'm afraid they can, sir. I got through tonight. First-class reception. Captain Jensen himself, and he was hopping mad. Been waiting all day for us to come on the air. Asked how things were, and I told him that you were outside the fortress just then, and hoped to be inside the magazine in an hour or so.'

'Go on.'

'He said that was the best news he'd ever had. He said his information had been wrong, he'd been fooled, that the invasion fleet didn't hole up overnight in the Cyclades, that they had come straight through under the heaviest air and E-boat escort ever seen in the Med., and are due to hit the beaches on Kheros some time before dawn tomorrow. He said our destroyers had been waiting to the south all day, moved up at dusk and were waiting word from him to see whether they would attempt the passage of the Maidos Straits. I told him maybe something could go wrong, but he said not with Captain Mallory and Miller inside and besides he wasn't – he couldn't risk the lives of twelve hundred men on Kheros just on the off chance that he might be wrong.' Brown broke off suddenly and looked down miserably at his feet. No one else in the hall moved or made any sound at all.

'Go on,' Mallory repeated in a whisper. His face was very pale.

'That's all, sir. That's all there is. The destroyers are coming through the Straits at midnight.' Brown looked down at his luminous watch. 'Midnight. Four hours to go.'

'Oh, God! Midnight!' Mallory was stricken, his eyes for the moment unseeing, ivory-knuckled hands clenched in futility and despair. 'They're coming through at midnight! God help them! God help them all now!'

271

CHAPTER 15

Wednesday Night

2000–2115

Eight-thirty, his watch said. Eight-thirty. Exactly half an hour to curfew. Mallory flattened himself on the roof, pressed himself as closely as possible against the low retaining wall that almost touched the great, sheering sides of the fortress, swore softly to himself. It only required one man with a torch in his hand to look over the top of the fortress wall – a cat-walk ran the whole length of the inside of the wall, four feet from the top – and it would be the end of them all. The wandering beam of a torch and they were bound to be seen, it was impossible not to be seen: he and Dusty Miller – the American was stretched out behind him and clutching the big truck battery in his arms – were wide open to the view of anyone who happened to glance down that way. Perhaps they should have stayed with the others a couple of roofs away, with Casey and Louki, the one busy tying spaced knots in a rope, the other busy splicing a bent wire hook on to a long bamboo they had torn from a bamboo hedge just outside the town, where they had hurriedly taken shelter as a convoy of three trucks had roared past them heading for the castle Vygos.

Eight thirty-two. What the devil was Andrea doing down there, Mallory wondered irritably and at once regretted his irritation. Andrea wouldn't waste an unnecessary second. Speed was vital, haste fatal. It seemed unlikely that there would be any officers inside – from what they had seen, practically half the garrison were combing either the town or the countryside out in the direction of Vygos – but if there were and even one gave a cry it would be the end.

272

Mallory stared down at the burn on the back of his hand, thought of the truck they had set on fire and grinned wryly to himself. Setting the truck on fire had been his only contribution to the night's performance so far. All the other credit went to either Andrea or Miller. It was Andrea who had seen in this house on the west side of the square – one of several adjoining houses used as officers' billets – the only possible answer to their problem. It was Miller, now lacking all time-fuses, clockwork, generator and every other source of electric power who had suddenly stated that he must have a battery, and again it was Andrea, hearing the distant approach of a truck, who had blocked the entrance to the long driveway to the keep with heavy stones from the flanking pillars, forcing the soldiers to abandon their truck at the gates and run up the drive towards their house. To overcome the driver and his mate and bundle them senseless into a ditch had taken seconds only, scarcely more time than it had taken Miller to unscrew the terminals of the heavy battery, find the inevitable jerry-can below the tailboard and pour the contents over engine, cab and body. The truck had gone up in a roar and *whoosh* of flames: as Louki had said earlier in the night, setting petrol-soaked vehicles on fire was not without its dangers – the charred patch on his hand stung painfully – but, again as Louki had said it had burned magnificently. A pity, in a way – it had attracted attention to their escape sooner than was necessary – but it had been vital to destroy the evidence, the fact that a battery was missing. Mallory had too much experience of and respect for the Germans ever to underrate them: they could put two and two together better than most.

He felt Miller tug at his ankle, started, twisted round quickly. The American was pointing beyond him, and he turned again and saw Andrea signalling to him from the raised trap in the far corner: he had been so engrossed in his thinking, the giant Greek so catlike in his silence, that he had completely failed to notice his arrival. Mallory shook his head, momentarily angered at his own abstraction, took the battery from Miller, whispered to him to get the others, then edged slowly across the roof, as noiselessly as possible. The sheer deadweight of the battery was astonishing, it felt as if it weighed a ton, but Andrea plucked it from his hands, lifted it over the trap coaming, tucked it under one arm and nimbly descended the stairs to the tiny hall-way as if it weighed nothing at all.

Andrea moved out through the open doorway to the covered balcony that overlooked the darkened harbour, almost a hundred vertical feet beneath. Mallory, following close behind, touched him on the shoulder as he lowered the battery gently to the ground.

'Any trouble?' he asked softly.

'None at all, my Keith.' Andrea straightened. 'The house is empty. I was so surprised that I went over it all, twice, just to make sure.'

'Fine! Wonderful! I suppose the whole bunch of them are out scouring the country for us – interesting to know what they would say if they were told we were sitting in their front parlour?'

'They would never believe it,' Andrea said without hesitation. 'This is the last place they would ever think to look for us.'

'I've never hoped so much that you're right!' Mallory murmured fervently. He moved across to the latticed railing that enclosed the balcony, gazed down into the blackness beneath his feet and shivered. A long, long drop and it was very cold; that sluicing, vertical rain chilled one to the bone... He stepped back, shook the railing.

'This thing strong enough, do you think?' he whispered.

'I don't know, my Keith. I don't know at all.' Andrea shrugged. 'I hope so.'

'I hope so,' Mallory echoed. 'It doesn't really matter. This is how it has to be.' Again he leaned far out over the railing, twisted his head to the right and upwards. In the rain-filled gloom of the night he could just faintly make out the still darker gloom of the mouth of the cave housing the two great guns, perhaps forty feet away from where he stood, at least thirty feet higher – and all vertical cliff-face between. As far as accessibility went, the cave mouth could have been on the moon.

He drew back, turned round as he heard Brown limping on to the balcony.

'Go to the front of the house and stay there, Casey, will you? Stay by the window. Leave the front door unlocked. If we have any visitors let them in.'

'Club 'em, knife 'em, no guns,' Brown murmured. 'Is that it, sir?'

'That's it, Casey.'

'Just leave this little thing to me,' Brown said grimly. He hobbled away through the doorway.

Mallory turned to Andrea. 'I make it twenty-three minutes.'

'I, too. Twenty-three minutes to nine.'

'Good luck,' Mallory murmured. He grinned at Miller. 'Come on, Dusty. Opening time.'

Five minutes later, Mallory and Miller were seated in a *taverna* just off the south side of the town square. Despite the garish blue paint with which the *tavernaris* had covered everything in sight – walls, tables, chairs, shelves all in the same execrably vivid colour (blue and red for the wine shops, green for the sweetmeat shops was the almost invariable rule throughout the islands) – it was a gloomy, ill-lit place, as gloomy almost as the stern, righteous, magnificently-moustached heroes of the Wars of Independence whose dark, burning eyes glared down at them from a dozen faded prints scattered at eye-level along the walls. Between each pair of portraits was a brightly-coloured wall advertisement for Fix's beer: the effect of the décor, taken as a whole, was indescribable, and Mallory shuddered to think what it would have been like

275

had the *tavernaris* had at his disposal any illumination more powerful than the two smoking oil-lamps placed on the counter before him.

As it was, the gloom suited him well. Their dark clothes, braided jackets, *tsantas* and jackboots looked genuine enough, Mallory knew, and the black-fringed turbans Louki had mysteriously obtained for them looked as they ought to look in a tavern where every islander there – about eight of them – wore nothing else on their heads. Their clothes had been good enough to pass muster with the *tavernaris* – but then even the keeper of a wine shop could hardly be expected to know every man in a town of five thousand, and a patriotic Greek, as Louki had declared this man to be, wasn't going to lift even a faintly suspicious eyebrow as long as there were German soldiers present. And there were Germans present – four of them, sitting round a table near the counter. Which was why Mallory had been glad of the semi-darkness. Not, he was certain, that he and Dusty Miller had any reason to be physically afraid of these men. Louki had dismissed them contemptuously as a bunch of old women – headquarters clerks, Mallory guessed – who came to this tavern every night of the week. But there was no point in sticking out their necks unnecessarily.

Miller lit one of the pungent, evil-smelling local cigarettes, wrinkling his nose in distaste.

'Damn funny smell in this joint, boss.'

Put your cigarette out,' Mallory suggested.

'You wouldn't believe it, but the smell I'm smelling is a damn sight worse than that.'

'Hashish,' Mallory said briefly. 'The curse of these island ports.' He nodded over towards a dark corner. 'The lads of the village over there will be at it every night in life. It's all they live for.'

'Do they have to make that gawddamned awful racket when they're at it?' Miller asked peevishly. 'Toscanini should see this lot!'

276

Mallory looked at the small group in the corner, clustered round the young man playing a *bouzouko* – a long-necked mandolin – and singing the haunting, nostalgic *rembetika* songs of the hashish smokers of the Piraeus. He supposed the music did have a certain melancholy, lotus-land attraction, but right then it jarred on him. One had to be in a certain twilit, untroubled mood to appreciate that sort of thing; and he had never felt less untroubled in his life.

'I suppose it *is* a bit grim,' he admitted. 'But at least it lets us talk together, which we couldn't do if they all packed up and went home.'

'I wish to hell they would,' Miller said morosely. 'I'd gladly keep my mouth shut.' He picked distastefully at the *meze* – a mixture of chopped olives, liver, cheese and apples – on the plate before him: as a good American and a bourbon drinker of long standing he disapproved strongly of the invariable Greek custom of eating when drinking. Suddenly he looked up and crushed his cigarette against the table top. 'For Gawd's sake, boss, how much longer?'

Mallory looked at him, then looked away. He knew exactly how Dusty Miller felt, for he felt that way himself – tense, keyed-up, every nerve strung to the tautest pitch of efficiency. So much depended on the next few minutes; whether all their labour and their suffering had been necessary, whether the men on Kheros would live or die, whether Andy Stevens had lived and died in vain. Mallory looked at Miller again, saw the nervous hands, the deepened wrinkles round the eyes, the tightly compressed mouth, white at the outer corners, saw all these signs of strain, noted them and discounted them. Excepting Andrea alone, of all the men he had ever known he would have picked the lean, morose American to be his companion that night. Or maybe even including Andrea. 'The finest saboteur in southern Europe' Captain Jensen had called him back in Alexandria. Miller had come a long way from Alexandria, and he had come for this alone. Tonight was Miller's night.

Mallory looked at his watch.

'Curfew in fifteen minutes,' he said quietly. 'The balloon goes up in twelve minutes. For us, another four minutes to go.'

Miller nodded, but said nothing. He filled his glass again from the beaker in the middle of the table, lit a cigarette. Mallory could see a nerve twitching high up in his temple and wondered dryly how many twitching nerves Miller could see in his own face. He wondered, too, how the crippled Casey Brown was getting on in the house they had just left. In many ways he had the most responsible job of all – and at the critical moment he would have to leave the door unguarded, move back to the balcony. One slip up there... He saw Miller look strangely at him and grinned crookedly. This had to come off, it just had to: he thought of what must surely happen if he failed, then shied away from the thought. It wasn't good to think of these things, not now, not at this time.

He wondered if the other two were at their posts, unmolested; they should be, the search party had long passed through the upper part of the town; but you never knew what could go wrong, there was so much that could go wrong, and so easily. Mallory looked at his watch again: he had never seen a second hand move so slowly. He lit a last cigarette, poured a final glass of wine, listened without really hearing to the weird, keening threnody of the *rembetika* song in the corner. And then the song of the hashish singers died plaintively away, the glasses were empty and Mallory was on his feet.

'Time bringeth all things,' he murmured. 'Here we go again.'

He sauntered easily towards the door, calling good night to the *tavernaris*. Just at the doorway he paused, began to search impatiently through his pockets as if he had lost something: it was a windless night, and it was raining, he saw, raining heavily, the lances of rain bouncing inches off the cobbled street – and the street itself was deserted as far as he could see in either direction. Satisfied, Mallory swung round with a curse, forehead furrowed in exasperation, started to walk back towards the table he had just left, right hand now delving into the capacious inner pocket of his jacket. He saw without seeming to that Dusty Miller was pushing his chair back, rising to his feet. And then Mallory had halted, his face clearing and his hands no longer searching. He was exactly three feet from the table where the four Germans were sitting.

'Keep quite still!' He spoke in German, his voice low but as steady, as menacing, as the Navy Colt .455 balanced in his right hand. 'We are desperate men. If you move we will kill you.'

For a full three seconds the soldiers sat immobile, expressionless except for the shocked widening of their eyes. And then there was a quick flicker of the eyelids from the man sitting nearest the counter, a twitching of the shoulder and then a grunt of agony as the .32 bullet smashed into his upper arm. The soft thud of Miller's silenced automatic couldn't have been heard beyond the doorway.

'Sorry, boss,' Miller apologised. 'Mebbe he's only sufferin' from St. Vitus' dance.' He looked with interest at the pain-twisted face, the blood welling darkly between the fingers clasped tightly over the wound. 'But he looks kinda cured to me.'

'He is cured,' Mallory said grimly. He turned to the innkeeper, a tall, melancholy man with a thin face and mandarin moustache that drooped forlornly over either corner of his mouth, spoke to him in the quick, colloquial speech of the islands. 'Do these men speak Greek?'

The *tavernaris* shook his head. Completely unruffled and unimpressed, he seemed to regard armed hold-ups in his tavern as the rule rather than the exception.

'Not them!' he said contemptuously. 'English a little,

think – I am sure. But not our language. That I do know.'

'Good. I am a British Intelligence officer. Have you a place where I can hide these men?'

'You shouldn't have done this,' the *tavernaris* protested mildly. 'I will surely die for this.'

'Oh, no, you won't.' Mallory had slid across the counter, his pistol boring into the man's midriff. No one could doubt that the man was being threatened – and violently threatened – no one, that is, who couldn't see the broad wink that Mallory had given the inn-keeper. 'I'm going to tie you up with them. All right?'

'All right. There is a trap-door at the end of the counter here. Steps lead down to the cellar.'

'Good enough. I'll find it by accident.' Mallory gave him a vicious and all too convincing shove that sent the man staggering, vaulted back across the counter, walked over to the *rembetika* singers at the far corner of the room.

'Go home,' he said quickly. 'It is almost curfew time anyway. Go out the back way, and remember – you have seen nothing, no one. You understand?'

'We understand.' It was the young *bouzouko* player who spoke. He jerked his thumb at his companions and grinned. 'Bad men – but good Greeks. Can we help you?'

'No!' Mallory was emphatic. 'Think of your families – these soldiers have recognised you. They must know you well – you and they are here most nights, is that not so?'

The young man nodded.

'Off you go, then. Thank you all the same.'

A minute later, in the dim, candle-lit cellar, Miller prodded the soldier nearest him – the one most like himself in height and build. 'Take your clothes off!' he ordered.

'English pig!' the German snarled.

'Not *English*,' Miller protested. 'I'll give you thirty seconds to get your coat and pants off.'

The man swore at him, viciously, but made no move to

280

obey. Miller sighed. The German had guts, but time was running out. He took a careful bead on the soldier's hand and pulled the trigger. Again the soft *plop* and the man .was staring down stupidly at the hole torn in the heel of his left hand.

'Mustn't spoil the nice uniforms, must we?' Miller asked conversationally. He lifted the automatic until the soldier was staring down the barrel of the gun. 'The next goes between the eyes.' The casual drawl carried complete conviction. 'It won't take me long to undress you, I guess.' But the man had already started to tear his uniform off, sobbing with anger and the pain of his wounded hand.

Less than another five minutes had passed when Mallory, clad like Miller in German uniform, unlocked the front door of the tavern and peered cautiously out. The rain, if anything, was heavier than ever – and there wasn't a soul in sight. Mallory beckoned Miller to follow and locked the door behind him. Together the two men walked up the middle of the street, making no attempt to seek either shelter or shadows. Fifty yards took them into the town square, where they turned right along the south side of the square, then left along the east side, not breaking step as they passed the old house where they had hidden earlier in the evening, not even as Louki's hand appeared mysteriously behind the partly opened door, a hand weighted down with two German Army rucksacks – rucksacks packed with rope, fuses, wire and high explosive. A few yards farther on they stopped suddenly, crouched down behind a couple of huge wine barrels outside a barber's shop, gazed at the two armed guards in the arched gateway, less than a hundred feet away, as they shrugged into their packs and waited for their cue.

They had only moments to wait – the timing had been split-second throughout. Mallory was just tightening the waist-belt of his rucksack when a series of explosions shook the centre of the town, not three hundred yards away, explosions followed by the vicious rattle of a

281

machine-gun, then by further explosions. Andrea was doing his stuff magnificently with his grenades and home-made bombs.

Both men suddenly shrank back as a broad, white beam of light stabbed out from a platform high above the gateway, a beam that paralleled the top of the wall to the east, showed up every hooked spike and strand of barbed wire as clearly as sunlight. Mallory and Miller looked at each other for a fleeting moment, their faces grim. Panayis hadn't missed a thing: they would have been pinned on these strands like flies on fly-paper and cut to ribbons by machine-guns.

Mallory waited another half-minute, touched Miller's arm, rose to his feet and started running madly across the square, the long hooked bamboo pressed close to his side, the American pounding behind him. In a few seconds they had reached the gates of the fortress, the startled guards running the last few feet to meet them.

'Every man to the Street of Steps!' Mallory shouted. 'Those damned English saboteurs are trapped in a house down there! We've got to have some mortars. Hurry, man, hurry, in the name of God!'

'But the gate!' one of the two guards protested. 'We cannot leave the gate!' The man had no suspicions, none at all: in the circumstances – the near darkness, the pouring rain, the German-clad soldier speaking perfect German, the obvious truth that there was a gun-battle being fought near-at-hand – it would have been remarkable had he shown any signs of doubt.

'Idiot!' Mallory screamed at him. '*Dummkopf*! What is there to guard against here? The English swine are in the Street of Steps. They must be destroyed! For God's sake, hurry!' he shouted desperately. 'If they escape again it'll be the Russian Front for all of us!'

Mallory had his hand on the man's shoulder now, ready to push him on his way, but his hand fell to his side unneeded. The two men were already gone, running

282

pell-mell across the square, had vanished into the rain and the darkness already. Seconds later Mallory and Miller were deep inside the fortress of Navarone.

Everywhere there was complete confusion – a bustling, purposeful confusion as one would expect with the seasoned troops of the Alpenkorps, but confusion nevertheless, with much shouting of orders, blowing of whistles, starting of truck engines, sergeants running to and fro chivvying their men into marching order or into the waiting transports. Mallory and Miller ran too, once or twice through groups of men milling round the tailboard of a truck. Not that they were in any desperate hurry for themselves, but nothing could have been more conspicuous – and suspicious – than the sight of a couple of men walking calmly along in the middle of all that urgent activity. And so they ran, heads down or averted whenever they passed through a pool of light, Miller cursing feelingly and often at the unaccustomed exercise.

They skirted two barrack blocks on their right, then the power-house on their left, then an ordnance depot on their right and then the *Abteilung* garage on their left. They were climbing, now, almost in darkness, but Mallory knew where he was to the inch: he had so thoroughly memorised the closely tallying descriptions given him by Vlachos and Panayis that he would have been confident of finding his way with complete accuracy, even if the darkness had been absolute.

'What's that, boss?' Miller had caught Mallory by the arm, was pointing to a large, uncompromisingly rectangular building that loomed gauntly against the horizon. 'The local hoosegow?'

'Water storage tank,' Mallory said briefly. 'Panayis estimates there's half a million gallons in there – magazine flooding in an emergency. The magazines are directly below.' He pointed to a squat, box-like, concrete structure a little farther on. 'The only entrance to the magazine. Locked and guarded.'

They were approaching the senior officers' quarters now – the commandant had his own flat on the second storey, directly overlooking the massive, reinforced ferro-concrete control tower that controlled the two great guns below. Mallory suddenly stopped, picked up a handful of dirt, rubbed it on his face and told Miller to do the same.

'Disguise,' he explained. 'The experts would consider it a bit on the elementary side, but it'll have to do. The lighting's apt to be a bit brighter inside this place.'

He went up the steps to the officers' quarters at a dead run, crashed through the swing doors with a force that almost took them off their hinges. The sentry at the keyboard looked at him in astonishment, the barrel of his sub-machine-gun lining up on the New Zealander's chest.

'Put that thing down, you damned idiot!' Mallory snapped furiously. 'Where's the commandant? Quickly, you oaf! It's life or death!'

'Herr – Herr Kommandant?' the sentry stuttered. 'He's left – they are all gone, just a minute ago.'

'What? All gone?' Mallory was staring at him with narrowed, dangerous eyes. 'Did you say "all gone"?' he asked softly.

'Yes. I – I'm sure they're...' He broke off abruptly as Mallory's eyes shifted to a point behind his shoulder.

'Then who the hell is that?' Mallory demanded savagely.

The sentry would have been less than human not to fall for it. Even as he was swinging round to look, the vicious judo cut took him just below the left ear. Mallory had smashed open the glass of the keyboard before the unfortunate guard had hit the floor, swept all the keys – about a dozen in all – off their rings and into his pocket. It took them another twenty seconds to tape the man's mouth and hands and lock him in a convenient cupboard; then they were on their way again, still running.

One more obstacle to overcome, Mallory thought as they pounded along in the darkness, the last of the triple defences. He did not know how many men would be guarding the locked door to the magazine, and in that moment of fierce exaltation he didn't particularly care. Neither, he felt sure, did Miller. There were no worries now, no taut-nerved tensions or nameless anxieties. Mallory would have been the last man in the world to admit it, or even believe it, but this was what men like Miller and himself had been born for.

They had their hand-torches out now, the powerful beams swinging in wild arcs as they plunged along, skirting the massed batteries of A.A. guns. To anyone observing their approach from the front, there could have been nothing more calculated to disarm suspicion than the sight and sound of the two men running towards them without any attempt at concealment, one of them shouting to the other in German, both with lit torches whose beams lifted and fell, lifted and fell as the men's arms windmilled by their sides. But these same torches were deeply hooded, and only a very alert observer indeed would have noticed that the downward arc of the light never passed backwards beyond the runners' feet.

Suddenly Mallory saw two shadows detaching themselves from the darker shadow of the magazine entrance, steadied his torch for a brief second to check. He slackened speed.

'Right!' he said softly. 'Here they come – only two of them. One each – get as close as possible first. Quick and quiet – a shout, a shot, and we're finished. And for God's sake don't start clubbing 'em with your torch. There'll be no lights on in that magazine and I'm not going to start crawling around there with a box of bloody matches in my hand!' He transferred his torch to his left hand, pulled out his Navy Colt, reversed it, caught it by the barrel, brought up sharply only inches away from the guards now running to meet them.

'Are you all right?' Mallory gasped. 'Anyone been here? Quickly, man, *quickly*!'

'Yes, yes, we're all right.' The man was off guard, apprehensive. 'What in the name of God is all that noise — '

'Those damned English saboteurs!' Mallory swore viciously. 'They've killed the guards and they're inside! Are you sure no one's been here? Come, let me see.'

He pushed his way past the guard, probed his torch at the massive padlock, then straightened his back.

'Thank heaven for that anyway!' He turned round, let the dazzling beam of his torch catch the man square in the eyes, muttered an apology and switched off the light, the sound of the sharp click lost in the hollow, soggy thud of the heel of his Colt catching the man behind the ear, just below the helmet. The sentry was still on his feet, just beginning to crumple, when Mallory staggered as the second guard reeled into him, staggered, recovered, clouted him with the colt for good measure, then stiffened in sudden dismay as he heard the vicious hissing *plop* of Miller's automatic, twice in rapid succession.

'What the hell — '

'Wily birds, boss,' Miller murmured. 'Very wily indeed. There was a third character in the shadows at the side. Only way to stop him.' Automatic cocked in his ready hand, he stooped over the man for a moment, then straightened. 'Afraid he's been stopped kinda permanent, boss.' There was no expression in his voice.

'Tie up the others.' Mallory had only half heard him, he was already busy at the magazine door, trying a succession of keys in the lock. The third key fitted, the lock opened and the heavy steel door gave easily to his touch. He took a last swift look round, but there was no one in sight, no sound but the revving engine of the last of the trucks clearing the fortress gates, the distant rattle of machine-gun fire. Andrea was doing a magnificent job – if only he didn't overdo it, leave his withdrawal till it was too late... Mallory turned quickly, switched on his torch, stepped inside the door. Miller would follow when he was ready.

A vertical steel ladder fixed to the rock led down to the floor of the cave. On either side of the ladder were hollow lift-shafts, unprotected even by a cage, oiled wire ropes glistening in the middle, a polished metal runner at each side of the square to guide and steady the spring-loaded sidewheels of the lift itself. Spartan in their simplicity but wholly adequate, there was no mistaking these for anything but what they were – the shell hoist shafts going down to the magazine.

Mallory reached the solid floor of the cave and swept his torch round through a 180-degree arc. This was the very end of that great cave that opened out beneath the towering overhang of rock that dominated the entire harbour. Not the natural end, he saw after a moment's inspection, but a man-made addition: the volcanic rock around him had been drilled and blasted out. There was nothing here but the two shafts descending into the pitchy darkness and another steel ladder, also leading to the magazine. But the magazine could wait: to check that there were no more guards down here and to ensure an emergency escape route – these were the two vital needs of the moment.

Quickly Mallory ran along the tunnel, flipping his torch on and off. The Germans were past-masters of booby traps – explosive booby traps – for the protection of important installations, but the chances were that they had none in that tunnel – not with several hundred tons of high explosive stored only feet away.

The tunnel itself, dripping-damp and duck-board floored, was about seven feet high and even wider, but the central passage was very narrow – most of the space was taken up by the roller conveyors, one on either side, for the great cartridges and shells. Suddenly the conveyors curved away sharply to the left and right, the sharply-sheering tunnel roof climbed steeply up into the near-darkness of the vaulted dome above, and, almost at his feet, their burnished steel caught in the beam from his torch, twin sets of parallel rails, embedded in the solid stone and twenty feet apart, stretched forward into the lightened gloom ahead, the great, gaping mouth of the cave. And just before he switched off the torch – searchers returning from the Devil's Playground might easily catch the pin-point of light in the darkness – Mallory had a brief glimpse of the turn-tables that crowned the far end of these shining rails and, crouched massively above, like some nightmare monsters from an ancient and other world, the evil, the sinister silhouettes of the two great guns of Navarone.

Torch and revolver dangling loosely in his hands, only dimly aware of the curious tingling in the tips of his fingers, Mallory walked slowly forward. Slowly, but not with the stealthy slowness, the razor-drawn expectancy of a man momentarily anticipating trouble – there was no guard in the cave, Mallory was quite sure of that now – but with that strange, dream-like slowness, the half-belief of a man who has accomplished something he had known all along he could never accomplish, with the slowness of a man at last face to face with a feared but long-sought enemy. I'm here at last, Mallory said to himself over and over again. I'm here at last, I've made it, and these are the guns of Navarone: these are the guns I came to destroy, the guns of Navarone, and I have come at last. But somehow he couldn't quite believe it...

Slowly still Mallory approached the guns, walked half-way round the perimeter of the turn-table of the gun on the left, examined it as well as he could in the gloom. He was staggered by the sheer size of it, the tremendous girth and reach of the barrel that stretched far out into the night. He told himself that the experts thought it was only a nine-inch crunch gun, that the crowding confines of the caves were bound to exaggerate its size. He told himself these things, discounted them: twelve-inch bore if an inch, that gun was the biggest thing he had ever seen. Big? Heavens above, it was gigantic! The fools, the blind crazy fools who had sent the *Sybaris* out against these...

The train of thought was lost, abruptly. Mallory stood quite still, one hand resting against the massive gun carriage and tried to recall the sound that had jerked him back to the present. Immobile, he listened for it again, eyes closed the better to hear, but the sound did not come again, and suddenly he knew that it was no sound at all but the absence of sound that had cut through his thoughts, triggered off some unconscious warning bell. The night was suddenly very silent, very still: down in the heart of the town the guns had stopped firing.

Mallory swore softly to himself. He had already spent far too much time day-dreaming, and time was running short. It *must* be running short – Andrea had withdrawn, it was only a matter of time until the Germans discovered that they had been duped. And then they would come running – and there was no doubt where they would come. Swiftly Mallory shrugged out of his rucksack, pulled out the hundred-foot wire-cored rope coiled inside. Their emergency escape route – whatever else he did he must make sure of that.

The rope looped round his arm, he moved forward cautiously, seeking a belay, but had only taken three steps when his right knee-cap struck something hard and unyielding. He checked the exclamation of pain, investigated the obstacle with his free hand, realised immediately what it was – an iron railing stretched waist-high across the mouth of the cave. Of course! There had been bound to be something like that, some barrier to prevent people from falling over the edge, especially in the darkness of the night. He hadn't been able to pick it up with the binoculars from the carob grove that afternoon – close though it was to the entrance, it had been concealed in the gloom of the cave. But he should have thought of it.

Quickly Mallory felt his way along to the left, to the very end of the railing, crossed it, tied the rope securely to the base of the vertical stanchion next to the wall, paid out the rope as he moved gingerly to the lip of the cave mouth. And then, almost at once, he was there and there was nothing below his probing foot but a hundred and twenty feet of sheer drop to the land-locked harbour of Navarone.

Away to his right was a dark, formless blur lying on the water, a blur that might have been Cape Demirci: straight ahead, across the darkly velvet sheen of the Maidos Straits, he could see the twinkle of far-away lights – it was a measure of the enemy's confidence that they permitted these lights at all, or, more likely, these fisher cottages were useful as a bearing marker for the guns at night: and to the left, surprisingly near, barely thirty feet away in a horizontal plane, but far below the level where he was standing, he could see the jutting end of the outside wall of the fortress where it abutted on the cliff, the roofs of the houses on the west side of the square beyond that, and, beyond that again, the town itself curving sharply down-wards and outwards, to the south first, then to the west, close-girdling and matching the curve of the crescent harbour. Above – but there was nothing to be seen above, that fantastic overhang above blotted out more than half the sky; and below the darkness was equally impenetrable, the surface of the harbour inky and black as night. There were vessels down there, he knew, Grecian caiques and German launches, but they might have been a thousand miles away for any sign he could see of them.

The brief, all encompassing glance had taken barely ten seconds, but Mallory waited no longer. Swiftly he bent down, tied a double bowline in the end of the rope and left it lying on the edge. In an emergency they could kick it out into the darkness. It would be thirty feet short of the water, he estimated – enough to clear any launch or masted caique that might be moving about the harbour.

They could drop the rest of the way, maybe a bone-breaking fall on to the deck of a ship, but they would have to risk it. Mallory took one last look down into the Stygian blackness and shivered: he hoped to God that he and Miller wouldn't have to take that way out.

Dusty Miller was kneeling on the duck-boards by the top of the ladder leading down to the magazine as Mallory came running back up the tunnel, his hands busy with wires, fuses, detonators and explosives. He straightened up as Mallory approached.

'I reckon this stuff should keep 'em happy, boss.' He set the hands of the clockwork fuse, listened appreciatively to the barely audible hum, then eased himself down the ladder. 'In here among the top two rows of cartridges, I thought.'

'Wherever you say,' Mallory acquiesced. 'Only don't make it too obvious – or too difficult to find. Sure there's no chance of them suspecting that we knew the clock and fuses were dud?'

'None in the world,' Miller said confidently. 'When they find this here contraption they'll knock holes in each other's back congratulatin' themselves – and they'll never look any further.'

'Fair enough.' Mallory was satisfied. 'Lock the door up top?'

'Certainly I locked the door!' Miller looked at him reproachfully. 'Boss, sometimes I think...'

But Mallory never heard what he thought. A metallic, reverberating clangour echoed cavernously through the cave and magazine, blotting out Miller's words, then died away over the harbour. Again the sound came, while the two men stared bleakly at one another, then again and again, then escaped for a moment of time.

'Company,' Mallory murmured. 'Complete with sledge-hammers. Dear God, I only hope that door holds.' He was already running along the passage towards the guns, Miller close behind him.

'Company!' Miller was shaking his head as he ran. 'How in the hell did they get here so soon?'

'Our late lamented little pal,' Mallory said savagely. He vaulted over the railing, edged back to the mouth of the cave. 'And we were suckers enough to believe he told the whole truth. But he never told us that opening that door up top triggered off an alarm bell in the guard-room.'

CHAPTER 16

Wednesday Night

2115–2345

Smoothly, skilfully, Miller paid out the wire-cored rope – double-turned round the top rail – as Mallory sank out of sight into the darkness. Fifty feet had gone, he estimated, fifty-five, sixty, then there came the awaited sharp double tug on the signal cord looped round his wrist and he at once checked the rope, stooped and tied it securely to the foot of the stanchion.

And then he had straightened again, belayed himself to the rail with the rope's end, leaned far out over the edge, caught hold of the rope with both hands as far down as he could reach and began slowly, almost imperceptibly at first, then with gradually increasing momentum, to swing man and rope from side to side, pendulum-wise. As the swings of the pendulum grew wider, the rope started to twist and jump in his hands, and Miller knew that Mallory must be striking outcrops of rock, spinning uncontrollably as he bounced off them. But Miller knew that he couldn't stop now, the clanging of the sledges behind him was almost continuous: he only stooped the lower over the rope, flung all the strength of his sinewy arms and shoulders into the effort of bringing Mallory nearer and still nearer to the rope that Brown would by now have thrown down from the balcony of the house where they had left him.

Far below, half-way between the cave mouth and the invisible waters of the harbour, Mallory swung in a great arc through the rain-filled darkness of the sky, forty rushing, bone-bruising feet between the extremities of the swings. Earlier he had struck his head heavily on an outcrop of rock, all but losing consciousness and his grip on the rope. But he knew where to expect that projection now and pushed himself clear each time as he approached it, even although this made him spin in a complete circle every time. It was as well, he thought, that it was dark, that he was independent of sight anyway: the blow had reopened an old wound Turzig had given him, his whole upper face was masked with blood, both eyes completely gummed.

But he wasn't worried about the wound, about the blood in his eyes. The rope – that was all that mattered. Was the rope there? Had anything happened to Casey Brown? Had he been jumped before he could get the rope over the side? If he had, then all hope was gone and there was nothing they could do, no other way they could span the forty sheer feet between house and cave. It just *had* to be there. But if it were there, why couldn't he find it? Three times now, at the right extremity of a swing, he had reached out with his bamboo pole, heard the hook scrape emptily, frustratingly, against the bare rock.

And then, the fourth time, stretched out to the straining limit of both arms, he felt the hook catch on! Immediately he jerked the pole in, caught the rope before he dropped back on the downward swing, jerked the signal cord urgently, checked himself gradually as he fell back. Two minutes later, near exhaustion from the sixty-foot climb up the wet, slippery rope, he crawled blindly over the lip of the cave and flung himself to the ground, sobbing for breath.

Swiftly, without speaking, Miller bent down, slipped the twin loops of the double bowline from Mallory's legs, undid the knot, tied it to Brown's rope, gave the latter a tug and watched the joined ropes disappear into the darkness. Within two minutes the heavy battery was across, underslung from the two ropes, lowered so far by Casey Brown then hauled up by Mallory and Miller. Within another two minutes, but with infinitely more caution, this time, the canvas bag with the nitro, primers and detonators, had been pulled across, lay on the stone floor beside the battery.

All noise had ceased, the hammering of the sledges against the steel door had stopped completely. There was something threatening, foreboding about the stillness, the silence was more menacing than all the clamour that had gone before. Was the door down, the lock smashed, the Germans waiting for them in the gloom of the tunnel, waiting with cradled machine-carbines that would tear the life out of them? But there was no time to wonder, no time to wait, no time now to stop to weigh the chances. The time for caution was past, and whether they lived or died was of no account any more.

The heavy Colt .455 balanced at his waist, Mallory climbed over the safety barrier, padded silently past the great guns and through the passage, his torch clicking on half-way down its length. The place was deserted, the door above still intact. He climbed swiftly up the ladder, listened at the top. A subdued murmur of voices, he thought he heard, and a faint hissing sound on the other side of the heavy steel door, but he couldn't be sure. He leaned forward to hear better, the palm of his hand against the door, drew back with a muffled exclamation of pain. Just above the lock, the door was almost red-hot. Mallory dropped down to the floor of the tunnel just as Miller came staggering up with the battery.

'That door's as hot as blazes. They must be burning – '

'Did you hear anything?' Miller interrupted.

'There was a kind of hissing – '

'Oxy-acetylene torch,' Miller said briefly. 'They'll be burnin' out the lock. It'll take time – that door's made of armoured steel.'

'Why don't they blow it in – gelignite or whatever you use for that job?'

'Perish the thought,' Miller said hastily. 'Don't even *talk* about it, boss. Sympathetic detonation's a funny thing – there's an even chance that the whole damned lot would go up. Give me a hand with this thing, boss, will you?'

Within seconds Dusty Miller was again a man absorbed in his own element, the danger outside, the return trip he had yet to make across the face of the cliff, completely forgotten for a moment. The task took him four minutes from beginning to end. While Mallory was sliding the battery below the floored well of the lift, Miller squeezed in between the shining steel runners of the lift shaft itself, stooped to examine the rear one with his torch and establish, by the abrupt transition from polished to dull metal, exactly where the spring-loaded wheel of the shell-hoist came to rest. Satisfied, he pulled out a roll of sticky black tape, wound it a dozen times round the shaft, stepped back to look at it: it was quite invisible.

Quickly he taped the ends of two rubber-covered wires on the insulated strip, one at either side, taped these down also until nothing was visible but the bared steel cores at the tips, joined these to two four-inch strips of bared wire, taped these also, top and bottom, to the insulated shaft, vertically and less than half an inch apart. From the canvas bag he removed the T.N.T., the primer and the detonator − a bridge mercury detonator lugged and screwed to his own specification − fitted them together and connected one of the wires from the steel shaft to a lug on the detonator, screwing it firmly home. The other wire from the shaft he led to the positive terminal on the battery, and a third wire from the negative terminal to the detonator. It only required the ammunition hoist to sink down into the magazine − as it would do as soon as they began firing − and the spring-loaded wheel would short out the bare wires, completing the circuit and triggering off the detonator. A last check on the position of the bared vertical wires and he sat back satisfied. Mallory had just descended the ladder from the tunnel. Miller tapped him on the leg to draw his attention, negligently waving the steel blade of his knife within an inch of the exposed wires.

'Are you aware, boss,' he said conversationally, 'that if I touched this here blade across those terminals, the whole gawddamned place would go up in smithereens.' He shook his head musingly. 'Just one little slip of the hand, just one teeny little touch and Mallory and Miller are among the angels.'

'For God's sake put that thing away!' Mallory snapped nervously. 'And let's get the hell out of here. They've got a complete half-circle cut through that door already!'

Five minutes later Miller was safe – it had been a simple matter of sliding down a 45-degree tautened rope to where Brown waited. Mallory took a last look back into the cave, and his mouth twisted. He wondered how many soldiers manned the guns and magazine during action stations. One thing, he thought, they'll never know anything about it, the poor bastards. And then he thought, for the hundredth time, of all the men on Kheros and the destroyers, and his lips tightened and he looked away. Without another backward glance he slipped over the edge, dropped down into the night. He was half-way there, at the very lowest point of the curve and about to start climbing again, when he heard the vicious, staccato rattle of machine-gun fire directly overhead.

It was Miller who helped him over the balcony rail, an apprehensive-looking Miller who glanced often over his shoulder in the direction of the gun-fire – and the heaviest concentration of fire, Mallory realised with sudden dismay, was coming from their own, the west side of the square, only three or four houses away. Their escape route was cut off.

'Come on, boss!' Miller said urgently. 'Let's get away from this joint. Gettin' downright unhealthy round these parts.'

Mallory jerked his head in the direction of the fire. 'Who's down there?' he asked quickly.

'A German patrol.'

'Then how in the hell can we get away?' Mallory demanded. 'And where's Andrea?'

'Across the other side of the square, boss. That's who those birds along there are firing at.'

'The other side of the square!' He glanced at his watch. 'Heavens above, man, what's he doing there?' He was moving through the house now, speaking over his shoulder. 'Why did you let him go?'

'I didn't let him go, boss,' Miller said carefully. 'He was gone when I came. Seems that Brown here saw a big patrol start a house to house search of the square. Started on the other side and were doin' two or three houses at a time. Andrea – he'd come back by this time – thought it a sure bet that they'd work right round the square and get here in two or three minutes, so he took off like a bat across the roofs.'

'Going to draw them off?' Mallory was at Louki's side staring out of the window. 'The crazy fool! He'll get himself killed this time – get himself killed for sure! There are soldiers everywhere. Besides, they won't fall for it again. He tricked them once up in the hills, and the Germans – '

'I'm not so sure, sir,' Brown interrupted excitedly. 'Andrea's just shot out the searchlight on his side. They'll think for certain that we're going to break out over the wall and – look, sir, look! There they go!' Brown was almost dancing with excitement, the pain of his injured leg forgotten. 'He's done it, sir, he's done it!'

Sure enough, Mallory saw, the patrol had broken away from their shelter in the house to their right and were running across the square in extended formation, their heavy boots clattering on the cobbles, stumbling, falling, recovering again as they lost footing on the slippery wetness of the uneven stones. At the same time Mallory could see torches flickering on the roofs of the houses opposite, the vague forms of men crouching low to escape observation and making swiftly for the spot where Andrea had been when he had shot out the great Cyclops eye of the searchlight.

'They'll be on him from every side.' Mallory spoke quietly enough, but his fists clenched until the nails cut into the palms of his hands. He stood stock-still for some seconds, stooped quickly and gathered a Schmeisser up from the floor. 'He hasn't a chance. I'm going after him.' He turned abruptly, brought up with equal suddenness: Miller was blocking his way to the door.

'Andrea left word that we were to leave him be, that he'd find his own way out.' Miller was very calm, very respectful. 'Said that no one was to help him, not on any account.'

'Don't try to stop me, Dusty.' Mallory spoke evenly, mechanically almost. He was hardly aware that Dusty Miller was there. He only knew that he must get out at once, get to Andrea's side, give him what help he could. They had been together too long, he owed too much to the smiling giant to let him go so easily. He couldn't remember how often Andrea had come after *him*, more than once when he had thought hope was gone... He put his hand against Miller's chest.

'You'll only be in his way, boss,' Miller said urgently. 'That's what you said...'

Mallory pushed him aside, strode for the door, brought up his fist to strike as hands closed round his upper arm. He stopped just in time, looked down into Louki's worried face.

'The American is right,' Louki said insistently. 'You must not go. Andrea said you were to take us down to the harbour.'

'Go down yourselves,' Mallory said brusquely. 'You know the way, you know the plans.'

'You would let us all go, let us all — '

'I'd let the whole damn world go if I could help him.' There was an utter sincerity in the New Zealander's voice. 'Andrea would never let me down.'

'But you would let him down,' Louki said quietly. 'Is that it, Major Mallory?'

'What the devil do you mean?'

'By not doing as he wishes. He may be hurt, killed even, and if you go after him and are killed too, that makes it all useless. He would die for nothing. Is it thus you would repay your friend?'

'All right, all right, you win,' Mallory said irritably.

'That is how Andrea would want it,' Louki murmured. 'Any other way you would be – '

'Stop preaching at me! Right, gentlemen, let's be on our way.' He was back on balance again, easy, relaxed, the primeval urge to go out and kill well under control. 'We'll take the high road – over the roofs. Dig into that kitchen stove there, rub the ashes all over your hands and faces. See that there's nothing white on you anywhere. And no talking!'

The five-minute journey down to the harbour wall – a journey made in soft-footed silence with Mallory hushing even the beginnings of a whisper – was quite uneventful. Not only did they see no soldiers, they saw no one at all. The inhabitants of Navarone were wisely obeying the curfew, and the streets were completely deserted. Andrea had drawn off pursuit with a vengeance. Mallory began to fear that the Germans had taken him, but just as they reached the water's edge he heard the gunfire again, a good deal farther away this time, in the very north-east corner of the town, round the back of the fortress.

Mallory stood on the low wall above the harbour, looked at his companions, gazed out over the dark oiliness of the water. Through the heavy rain he could just distinguish, to his right and left the vague blurs of caiques moored stern on to the wall. Beyond that he could see nothing.

'Well, I don't suppose we can get much wetter than we are right now,' he observed. He turned to Louki, checked something the little man was trying to say about Andrea.

'You sure you can find it all right in the darkness?' 'It' was the commandant's personal launch, a thirty-six-foot ten-tonner always kept moored to a buoy a hundred feet offshore. The engineer, who doubled as guard, slept aboard, Louki had said.

'I am already there,' Louki boasted. 'Blindfold me as you will and I —'.

'All right, all right,' Mallory said hastily. 'I'll take your word for it. Lend me your hat, will you, Casey?' He jammed the automatic into the crown of the hat, pulled it firmly on to his head, slid gently into the water and struck out by Louki's side.

'The engineer,' Louki said softly. 'I think he will be awake, Major.'

'I think so, too,' Mallory said grimly. Again there came the chatter of machine-carbines, the deeper whiplash of a Mauser. 'So will everyone else in Navarone, unless they're deaf or dead. Drop behind as soon as we see the boat. Come when I call.'

Ten seconds, fifteen passed, then Louki touched Mallory on the arm.

'I see it,' Mallory whispered. The blurred silhouette was less than fifteen yards away. He approached silently, neither legs nor arms breaking water, until he saw the vague shape of a man standing on the poop, just aft of the engine-room hatchway. He was immobile, staring out in the direction of the fortress and the upper town: Mallory slowly circled round the stern of the boat and came up behind him, on the other side. Carefully he removed his hat, took out the gun, caught the low gunwale with his left hand. At the range of seven feet he knew he couldn't possibly miss, but he couldn't shoot the man, not then. The guard-rails were token affairs only, eighteen inches high at the most, and the splash of the man falling into the water would almost certainly alert the guards at the harbour mouth emplacements.

'If you move I will kill you!' Mallory said softly in

German. The man stiffened. He had a carbine in his hand, Mallory saw.

'Put the gun down. Don't turn round.' Again the man obeyed, and Mallory was out of the water and on to the deck, in seconds, neither eye nor automatic straying from the man's back. He stepped softly forward, reversed the automatic, struck, caught the man before he could fall overboard and lowered him quietly to the deck. Three minutes later all the others were safely aboard.

Mallory followed the limping Brown down to the engine room, watched him as he switched on his hooded torch, looked around with a professional eye, looked at the big, gleaming, six-cylinder in-line Diesel engine.

'This,' said Brown reverently, 'is an engine. What a beauty! Operates on any number of cylinders you like. I know the type, sir.'

'I never doubted but you would. Can you start her up, Casey?'

'Just a minute till I have a look round, sir.' Brown had all the unhurried patience of the born engineer. Slowly, methodically, he played the spotlight round the immaculate interior of the engine-room, switched on the fuel and turned to Mallory. 'A dual control job, sir. We can take her from up top.'

He carried out the same painstaking inspection in the wheelhouse, while Mallory waited impatiently. The rain was easing off now, not much, but sufficiently to let him see the vague outlines of the harbour entrance. He wondered for the tenth time if the guards there had been alerted against the possibility of an attempted escape by boat. It seemed unlikely – from the racket Andrea was making, the Germans would think that escape was the last thing in their minds...He leaned forward, touched Brown on the shoulder.

'Twenty past eleven, Casey,' he murmured. 'If these destroyers come through early we're apt to have a thousand tons of rock falling on our heads.'

'Ready now, sir,' Brown announced. He gestured at the crowded dashboard beneath the screen. 'Nothing to it really.'

'I'm glad you think so,' Mallory murmured fervently. 'Start her moving, will you? Just keep it slow and easy.'

Brown coughed apologetically. 'We're still moored to the buoy. And it might be a good thing, sir, if we checked on the fixed guns, searchlights, signalling lamps, life-jackets and buoys. It's useful to know where these things are,' he finished deprecatingly.

Mallory laughed softly, clapped him on the shoulder.

'You'd make a great diplomat, Chief. We'll do that.' A landsman first and last, Mallory was none the less aware of the gulf that stretched between him and a man like Brown, made no bones about acknowledging it to himself. 'Will you take her out, Casey?'

'Right, sir. Would you ask Louki to come here – I think it's steep to both sides, but there may be snags or reefs. You never know.'

Three minutes later the launch was half-way to the harbour mouth, purring along softly on two cylinders, Mallory and Miller, still clad in German uniform, standing on the deck for'ard of the wheelhouse, Louki crouched low inside the wheelhouse itself. Suddenly, about sixty yards away, a signal lamp began to flash at them, its urgent clacking quite audible in the stillness of the night.

'Dan'l Boone Miller will now show how it's done,' Miller muttered. He edged closer to the machine-gun on the starboard bow. 'With my little gun I shall...'

He broke off sharply, his voice lost in the sudden clacking from the wheelhouse behind him, the staccato off-beat chattering of a signal shutter triggered by professional fingers. Brown had handed the wheel over to Louki, was morsing back to the harbour entrance, the cold rain lancing palely through the flickering beams of the lamp. The enemy lamp had stopped but now began again.

'My, they got a lot to say to each other,' Miller said

admiringly. 'How long do the exchange of courtesies last, boss?'

'I should say they are just about finished.' Mallory moved back quickly to the wheelhouse. They were less than a hundred feet from the harbour entrance. Brown had confused the enemy, gained precious seconds, more time than Mallory had ever thought they could gain. But it couldn't last. He touched Brown on the arm.

'Give her everything you've got when the balloon goes up.' Two seconds later he was back in position in the bows, Schmeisser ready in his hands. 'Your big chance, Dan'l Boone. Don't give the searchlights a chance to line up – they'll blind you.'

Even as he spoke, the light from the signal lamp at the harbour mouth cut off abruptly and two dazzling white beams, one from either side of the harbour entrance, stabbed blindingly through the darkness, bathing the whole harbour in their savage glare – a glare that lasted for only a fleeting second of time, yielded to a contrastingly Stygian darkness as two brief bursts of machine-gun fire smashed them into uselessness. From such short range it had been almost impossible to miss.

'Get down, everyone!' Mallory shouted. 'Flat on the deck!'

The echoes of the gunfire were dying away, the reverberations fading along the great sea wall of the fortress when Casey Brown cut in all six cylinders of the engine and opened the throttle wide, the surging roar of the big Diesel blotting out all other sounds in the night. Five seconds, ten seconds, they were passing through the entrance, fifteen, twenty, still not a shot fired, half a minute and they were well clear, bows lifting high out of the water, the deep-dipped stern trailing its long, seething ribbon of phosphorescent white as the engine crescendoed to its clamorous maximum power and Brown pulled the heeling craft sharply round to starboard, seeking the protection of the steep-walled cliffs.

'A desperate battle, boss, but the better men won.' Miller was on his feet now, clinging to a mounted gun for support as the deck canted away beneath his feet. 'My grandchildren shall hear of this.'

'Guards probably all up searching the town. Or maybe there *were* some poor blokes behind those searchlights. Or maybe we just took 'em all by surprise.' Mallory shook his head. 'Anyway you take it, we're just plain damn lucky.'

He moved aft, into the wheelhouse. Brown was at the wheel, Louki almost crowing with delight.

'That was magnificent, Casey,' Mallory said sincerely. 'A first-class job of work. Cut the engine when we come to the end of the cliffs. Our job's done. I'm going ashore.'

'You don't have to, Major.'

Mallory turned. 'What's that?'

'You don't have to. I tried to tell you on the way down, but you kept telling me to be quiet.' Louki sounded injured, turned to Casey. 'Slow down, please. The last thing Andrea told me, Major, was that we were to come this way. Why do you think he let himself be trapped against the cliffs to the north instead of going out into the country, where he could have hidden easily!'

'Is this true, Casey?' Mallory asked.

'Don't ask me, sir. Those two – they always talk in Greek.'

'Of course, of course.' Mallory looked at the low cliffs close off the starboard beam, barely moving now with the engine shut right down, looked back at Louki. 'Are you quite sure..'

He stopped in mid-sentence, jumped out through the wheelhouse door. The splash – there had been no mistaking the noise – had come from almost directly ahead. Mallory, Miller by his side, peered into the darkness, saw a dark head surfacing above the water less than twenty feet away, leaned far over with outstretched arm as the launch slid slowly by. Five seconds later Andrea stood on

305

the deck, dripping mightily and beaming all over his great moon face. Mallory led him straight into the wheelhouse, switched on the soft light of the shaded chart-lamp.

'By all that's wonderful, Andrea, I never thought to see you again. How did it go?'

'I will soon tell you,' Andrea laughed. 'Just after – '

'You've been wounded!' Miller interrupted. 'Your shoulder's kinda perforated.' He pointed to the red stain spreading down the sea-soaked jacket.

'Well, now, I believe I have.' Andrea affected vast surprise. 'Just a scratch, my friend.'

'Oh, sure, sure, just a scratch! It would be the same if your arm had been blown off. Come on down to the cabin – this is just a kindergarten exercise for a man of my medical skill.'

'But the captain – '

'Will have to wait. And your story. Ol' Medicine Man Miller permits no interference with his patients. Come on!'

'Very well, very well,' Andrea said docilely. He shook his head in mock resignation, followed Miller out of the cabin.

Brown opened up to full throttle again, took the launch north almost to Cape Demirci to avoid any hundred to one chance the harbour batteries might make, turned due east for a few miles then headed south into the Maidos Straits. Mallory stood by his side in the wheelhouse, gazing out over the dark, still waters. Suddenly he caught a gleam of white in the distance, touched Brown's arm and pointed for'ard.

'Breakers ahead, Casey, I think. Reefs perhaps?'

Casey looked in long silence, finally shook his head.

'Bow-wave,' he said unemotionally. 'It's the destroyers coming through.'

CHAPTER 17

Wednesday Night

Midnight

Commander Vincent Ryan, R.N., Captain (Destroyers) and Commanding Officer of His Majesty's latest S-class destroyer *Sirdar*, looked round the cramped chart-room and tugged thoughtfully at his magnificent Captain Kettle beard. A scruffier, a more villainous, a more cut and battered-looking bunch of hard cases he had never seen, he reflected, with the possible exception of a Bias Bay pirate crew he had helped round up when a very junior officer on the China Station. He looked at them more closely, tugged his beard again, thought there was more to it than mere scruffiness. He wouldn't care to be given the task of rounding this lot up. Dangerous, highly dangerous, he mused, but impossible to say why, there was only this quietness, this relaxed watchfulness that made him feel vaguely uncomfortable. His 'hatchet-men', Jensen had called them: Captain Jensen picked his killers well.

'Any of you gentlemen care to go below,' he suggested. 'Plenty of hot water, dry clothes — and warm bunks. We won't be using them tonight.'

'Thank you very much, sir.' Mallory hesitated. 'But we'd like to see this through.'

'Right then, the bridge it is,' Ryan said cheerfully. The *Sirdar* was beginning to pick up speed again, the deck throbbing beneath their feet. 'It is at your own risk, of course.'

'We lead charmed lives,' Miller drawled. 'Nothin' ever happens to us.'

The rain had stopped and they could see the cold twinkling of stars through broadening rifts in the clouds. Mallory looked around him, could see Maidos broad off the port bow and the great bulk of Navarone slipping by to starboard. Aft, about a cable length away, he could just distinguish two other ships, high-curving bow-waves piled whitely against tenebrious silhouettes. Mallory turned to the captain.

'No transports, sir?'

'No transports.' Ryan felt a vague mixture of pleasure and embarrassment that this man should call him 'sir'. 'Destroyers only. This is going to be a smash-and-grab job. No time for dawdlers tonight – and we're behind schedule already.'

'How long to clear the beaches?'

'Half an hour.'

'What! Twelve hundred men?' Mallory was incredulous.

'More.' Ryan sighed. 'Half the ruddy inhabitants want to come with us, too. We could still do it in half an hour, but we'll probably take a bit longer. We'll embark all the mobile equipment we can.'

Mallory nodded, let his eye travel along the slender outlines of the *Sirdar*. 'Where are you going to put 'em all, sir.'

'A fair question,' Ryan admitted. 'Five p.m. on the London Underground will be nothing compared to this little lot. But we'll pack them in somehow.'

Mallory nodded again and looked across the dark waters at Navarone. Two minutes, now, three at the most, and the fortress would open behind that headland. He felt a hand touch his arm, half-turned and smiled down at the sad-eyed little Greek by his side.

'Not long now, Louki,' he said quietly.

'The people, Major,' he murmured. 'The people in the town. Will they be all right?'

'They'll be all right. Dusty says the roof of the cave will go straight up. Most of the stuff will fall into the harbour.'

'Yes, but the boats – ?'

'Will you stop worrying! There's nobody aboard

them – you know they have to leave at curfew time.' He looked round as someone touched his arm.

'Captain Mallory, this is Lieutenant Beeston, my gunnery officer.' There was a slight coolness in Ryan's voice that made Mallory think that he wasn't overfond of his gunnery officer. 'Lieutenant Beeston is worried.'

'I *am* worried!' The tone was cold, aloof, with an indefinable hint of condescension. 'I understand that you have advised the captain not to offer any resistance?'

'You sound like a BBC communiqué,' Mallory said shortly. 'But you're right, I did say that. You couldn't locate the guns except by searchlight and that would be fatal. Similarly with gunfire.'

'I'm afraid I don't understand.' One could almost see the lift of the eyebrows in the darkness.

'You'd give away your position,' Mallory said patiently. 'They'd nail you first time. Give 'em two minutes and they'd nail you anyway. I have good reason to believe that the accuracy of their gunners is quite fantastic.'

'So has the Navy,' Ryan interjected quietly. 'Their third shell got the *Sybaris*'s B magazine.'

'Have you got any idea why this should be, Captain Mallory?' Beeston was quite unconvinced.

'Radar-controlled guns,' Mallory said briefly. 'They have two huge scanners atop the fortress.'

'The *Sirdar* had radar installed last month,' Beeston said stiffly. 'I imagine we could register some hits ourselves if – '

'You could hardly miss.' Miller drawled out the words, the tone dry and provocative. 'It's a helluva big island, Mac.'

'Who – who are you?' Beeston was rattled. 'What the devil do you mean?'

'Corporal Miller.' The American was unperturbed. 'Must be a very selective instrument, Lootenant, that can pick out a cave in a hundred square miles of rock.'

There was a moment's silence, then Beeston muttered something and turned away.

'You've hurt Guns's feelings, Corporal,' Ryan murmured. 'He's very keen to have a go — but we'll hold our fire.... How long till we clear that point, Captain?'

'I'm not sure.' He turned. 'What do you say, Casey?'

'A minute, sir. No more.'

Ryan nodded, said nothing. There was a silence on the bridge, a silence only intensified by the sibilant rushing of the waters, the weird, lonesome pinging of the Asdic. Above, the sky was steadily clearing, and the moon, palely luminous, was struggling to appear through a patch of thinning cloud. Nobody spoke, nobody moved. Mallory was conscious of the great bulk of Andrea beside him, of Miller, Brown and Louki behind. Born in the heart of the country, brought up on the foothills of the Southern Alps, Mallory knew himself as a landsman first and last, an alien to the sea and ships: but he had never felt so much at home in his life, never really known till now what it was to belong. He was more than happy, Mallory thought vaguely to himself, he was content. Andrea and his new friends and the impossible well done — how could a man be but content? They weren't all going home, Andy Stevens wasn't coming with them, but strangely he could feel no sorrow, only a gentle melancholy... Almost as if he had divined what Mallory was thinking, Andrea leaned towards him, towering over him in the darkness.

'He should be here,' he murmured. 'Andy Stevens should be here. That is what you are thinking, is it not?'

Mallory nodded and smiled, and said nothing.

'It doesn't really matter, does it, my Keith?' No anxiety, no questioning, just a statement of fact. 'It doesn't really matter.'

'It doesn't matter at all.'

Even as he spoke, he looked up quickly. A light, a bright orange flame had lanced out from the shearing wall of the fortress; they had rounded the headland and he hadn't even noticed it. There was a whistling roar — Mallory thought incongruously of an express train emerging from

310

a tunnel – directly overhead, and the great shell had crashed into the sea just beyond them. Mallory compressed his lips, unconsciously tightened his clenched fists. It was easy now to see how the *Sybaris* had died.

He could hear the gunnery officer saying something to the captain, but the words failed to register. They were looking at him and he at them and he did not see them. His mind was strangely detached. Another shell, would that be next? Or would the roar of the gunfire of that first shell come echoing across the sea? Or perhaps... Once again, he was back in that dark magazine entombed in the rocks, only now he could see men down there, doomed, unknowing men, could see the overhead pulleys swinging the great shells and cartridges towards the well of the lift, could see the shell hoist ascending slowly, the bared, waiting wires less than half an inch apart, the shining, spring-loaded wheel running smoothly down the gleaming rail, the gentle bump as the hoist...

A white pillar of flame streaked up hundreds of feet into the night sky as the tremendous detonation tore the heart out of the great fortress of Navarone. No after-fire of any kind, no dark, billowing clouds of smoke, only that one blinding white column that lit up the entire town for a single instant of time, reached up incredibly till it touched the clouds, vanished as if it had never been. And then, by and by, came the shock waves, the solitary thunderclap of the explosion, staggering even at that distance, and finally the deep-throated rumbling as thousands of tons of rock toppled majestically into the harbour – thousands of tons of rock and the two great guns of Navarone.

The rumbling was still in their ears, the echoes fading away far out across the Aegean, when the clouds parted and the moon broke through, a full moon silvering the darkly-rippling waters to starboard, shining iridescently through the spun phosphorescence of the *Sirdar*'s boiling wake. And dead ahead, bathed in the white moonlight,

311

mysterious, remote, the island of Kheros lay sleeping on the surface of the sea.

FORCE 10 FROM NAVARONE

FORCES FROM BRAZIL

To Lewis and Caroline

Schematic diagram of the River Neretva and the Zenica Cage

11th German Army Corps

The Zenika Gap

Neretva Dam

Units of 11th Army corps

The Western Gap

Major Stephen

dam wall

Colonel Janzy

RIGHT BANK

LEFT BANK

ladder
swing bridge
ford
engine abandoned

The Zenica Cage~ General Vukalovic and his trapped division

Colonel Lazlo

Neretva Gorge

tarmacadam road

Neretva River

bridge

General Zimmerman his two armoured divisions

single track narrow gauge railway

N

CHAPTER ONE

Prelude: Thursday 0000–0600

Commander Vincent Ryan, RN, Captain (Destroyers) and commanding officer of His Majesty's latest S-class destroyer *Sirdar*, leaned his elbows comfortably on the coaming of his bridge, brought up his night-glasses and gazed out thoughtfully over the calm and silvered waters of the moonlit Aegean.

He looked first of all due north, straight out over the huge and smoothly sculpted and whitely phosphorescent bow-wave thrown up by the knife-edged forefoot of his racing destroyer: four miles away, no more, framed in its backdrop of indigo sky and diamantine stars, lay the brooding mass of a darkly cliff-girt island: the island of Kheros, for months the remote and beleaguered outpost of two thousand British troops who had expected to die that night, and who would now not die.

Ryan swung his glasses through 180° and nodded approvingly. This was what he liked to see. The four destroyers to the south were in such perfect line astern that the hull of the leading vessel, a gleaming bone in its teeth, completely obscured the hulls of the three ships behind. Ryan turned his binoculars to the east.

It was odd, he thought inconsequentially, how unimpressive, even how disappointing, the aftermath of either natural or man-made disaster could be. Were it not for that dull red glow and wisping smoke that emanated from the upper part of the cliff and lent

319

the scene a vaguely Dantean aura of primeval menace and foreboding, the precipitous far wall of the harbour looked as it might have done in the times of Homer. That great ledge of rock that looked from that distance so smooth and regular and somehow inevitable could have been carved out by the wind and weather of a hundred million years: it could equally well have been cut away fifty centuries ago by the masons of Ancient Greece seeking marble for the building of their Ionian temples: what was almost inconceivable, what almost passed rational comprehension, was the fact that ten minutes ago that ledge had not been there at all, that there had been in its place tens of thousands of tons of rock, the most impregnable German fortress in the Aegean and, above all, the two great guns of Navarone, now all buried for ever three hundred feet under the sea. With a slow shake of his head Commander Ryan lowered his binoculars and turned to look at the men responsible for achieving more in five minutes than nature could have done in five million years.

Captain Mallory and Corporal Miller. That was all he knew of them, that and the fact that they had been sent on this mission by an old friend of his, a naval captain by the name of Jensen who, he had learnt only twenty-four hours previously – and that to his total astonishment – was the Head of Allied Intelligence in the Mediterranean. But that was all he knew of them and maybe he didn't even know that. Maybe their names weren't Mallory and Miller. Maybe they weren't even a captain and a corporal. They didn't look like any captain or corporal he'd ever seen. Come to that, they didn't look like any soldiers he'd ever seen. Clad in salt-water- and blood-stained German uniforms, filthy, unshaven, quiet and watchful and remote, they belonged to no category of men he'd ever encountered:

all he could be certain of as he gazed at the blurred and blood-shot sunken eyes, the gaunt and trenched and stubbled-grey faces of two men no longer young, was that he had never before seen human beings so ·far gone in total exhaustion.

'Well, that seems to be about it,' Ryan said. 'The troops on Kheros waiting to be taken off, our flotilla going north to take them off and the guns of Navarone no longer in any position to do anything about our flotilla. Satisfied, Captain Mallory?'

'That was the object of the exercise,' Mallory agreed.

Ryan lifted his glasses again. This time, almost at the range of night vision, he focused on a rubber dinghy closing in on the rocky shoreline to the west of Navarone harbour. The two figures seated in the dinghy were just discernible, no more: Ryan lowered his glasses and said thoughtfully:

'Your big friend – and the lady with him – doesn't believe in hanging about. You didn't – ah – introduce me to them, Captain Mallory.'

'I didn't get the chance to. Maria and Andrea. Andrea's a colonel in the Greek army: 19th Motorized Division.'

'Andrea *was* a colonel in the Greek army,' Miller said. 'I think he's just retired.'

'I rather think he has. They were in a hurry, Commander, because they're both patriotic Greeks, they're both islanders and there is much for both to do in Navarone. Besides, I understand they have some urgent and very personal matters to attend to.'

'I see.' Ryan didn't press the matter, instead he looked out again over the smoking remains of the shattered fortress. 'Well, that seems to be that. Finished for the evening, gentlemen?'

Mallory smiled faintly. 'I think so.'

'Then I would suggest some sleep.'

'What a wonderful word that is.' Miller pushed himself wearily off the side of the bridge and stood there swaying as he drew an exhausted forearm over blood-shot, aching eyes. 'Wake me up in Alexandria.'

'Alexandria?' Ryan looked at him in amusement. 'We won't be there for thirty hours yet.'

'That's what I meant,' Miller said.

Miller didn't get his thirty hours. He had, in fact, been asleep for just over thirty minutes when he was wakened by the slow realization that something was hurting his eyes: after he had moaned and feebly protested for some time he managed to get one eye open and saw that that something was a bright overhead light let into the deckhead of the cabin that had been provided for Mallory and himself. Miller propped himself up on a groggy elbow, managed to get his second eye into commission and looked without enthusiasm at the other two occupants of the cabin: Mallory was seated by a table, apparently transcribing some kind of message, while Commander Ryan stood in the open doorway.

'This is outrageous,' Miller said bitterly. 'I haven't closed an eye all night.'

'You've been asleep for thirty-five minutes,' Ryan said. 'Sorry. But Cairo said this message for Captain Mallory was of the greatest urgency.'

'It is, is it?' Miller said suspiciously. He brightened. 'It's probably about promotions and medals and leave and so forth.' He looked hopefully at Mallory who had just straightened after decoding the message. 'Is it?'

'Well, no. It starts off promisingly enough, mind you, warmest congratulations and what-have-you, but after that the tone of the message deteriorates a bit.'

Mallory reread the message: SIGNAL RECEIVED WARM-
EST CONGRATULATIONS MAGNIFICENT ACHIEVEMENT.
YOU BLOODY FOOLS WHY YOU LET ANDREA GET AWAY?
ESSENTIAL CONTACT HIM IMMEDIATELY. WILL EVACUATE
BEFORE DAWN UNDER DIVERSIONARY AIR ATTACK AIR
STRIP ONE MILE SOUTH-EAST MANDRAKOS. SEND CE VIA
SIRDAR. URGENT 3 REPEAT URGENT 3. BEST LUCK. JENSEN.

Miller took the message from Mallory's outstretched
hand, moved the paper to and fro until he had brought
his bleary eyes into focus, read the message in horrified
silence, handed it back to Mallory and stretched out
his full length on his bunk. He said, 'Oh, my God!' and
relapsed into what appeared to be a state of shock.

'That about sums it up,' Mallory agreed. He shook
his head wearily and turned to Ryan. 'I'm sorry, sir, but
we must trouble you for three things. A rubber dinghy,
a portable radio transmitter and an immediate return to
Navarone. Please arrange to have the radio lined up on
a pre-set frequency to be constantly monitored by your
WT room. When you receive a CE signal, transmit it
to Cairo.'

'CE?' Ryan asked.

'Uh-huh. Just that.'

'And that's all?'

'We could do with a bottle of brandy,' Miller said.
'Something – anything – to see us through the rigours
of the long night that lies ahead.'

Ryan lifted an eyebrow. 'A bottle of five-star, no
doubt, Corporal?'

'Would you,' Miller asked morosely, 'give a bottle
of three-star to a man going to his death?'

As it happened, Miller's gloomy expectations of an
early demise turned out to be baseless – for that night,
at least. Even the expected fearful rigours of the long

night ahead proved to be no more than minor physical inconveniences.

By the time the *Sirdar* had brought them back to Navarone and as close in to the rocky shores as was prudent, the sky had become darkly overcast, rain was falling and a swell was beginning to blow up from the south-west so that it was little wonder to either Mallory or Miller that by the time they had paddled their dinghy within striking distance of the shore, they were in a very damp and miserable condition indeed: and it was even less wonder that by the time they had reached the boulder-strewn beach itself, they were soaked to the skin, for a breaking wave flung their dinghy against a sloping shelf of rock, overturning their rubber craft and precipitating them both into the sea. But this was of little enough account in itself: their Schmeisser machine-pistols, their radio, their torches were securely wrapped in waterproof bags and all of those were safely salvaged. All in all, Mallory reflected, an almost perfect three-point landing compared to the last time they had come to Navarone by boat, when their Greek caique, caught in the teeth of a giant storm, had been battered to pieces against the jaggedly vertical – and supposedly unclimbable – South Cliff of Navarone.

Slipping, stumbling and with suitably sulphuric comments, they made their way over the wet shingle and massively rounded boulders until their way was barred by a steeply-angled slope that soared up into the near-darkness above. Mallory unwrapped a pencil torch and began to quarter the face of the slope with its narrow, concentrated beam. Miller touched him on the arm.

'Taking a bit of a chance, aren't we? With that thing, I mean?'

'No chance,' Mallory said. 'There won't be a soldier left on guard on the coasts tonight. They'll all be fighting the fires in the town. Besides, who is left for them to guard against? We are the birds and the birds, duty done, have flown. Only a madman would come back to the island again.'

'I know what we are,' Miller said with feeling. 'You don't have to tell me.'

Mallory smiled to himself in the darkness and continued his search. Within a minute he had located what he had been hoping to find – an angled gully in the slope. He and Miller scrambled up the shale- and rock-strewn bed of the gully as fast as the treacherous footing and their encumbrances would permit: within fifteen minutes they had reached the plateau above and paused to take their breath. Miller reached inside the depths of his tunic, a discreet movement that was at once followed by a discreet gurgling.

'What are you doing?' Mallory enquired.

'I thought I heard my teeth chattering. What's all this "urgent 3 repeat urgent 3" business in the message, then?'

'I've never seen it before. But I know what it means. Some people, somewhere, are about to die.'

'I'll tell you two for a start. And what if Andrea won't come? He's not a member of our armed forces. He doesn't have to come. *And* he said he was getting married right away.'

Mallory said with certainty: 'He'll come.'

'What makes you so sure?'

'Because Andrea is the one completely responsible man I've ever met. He has two great responsibilities – one to others, one to himself. That's why he came back to Navarone – because he knew the people needed him. And that's why he'll leave Navarone when he sees this "urgent 3" signal, because he'll know that someone, in some other place, needs him even more.'

Miller retrieved the brandy bottle from Mallory and thrust it securely inside his tunic again. 'Well, I can tell you this. The future Mrs Andrea Stavros isn't going to be very happy about it.'

'Neither is Andrea Stavros and I'm not looking forward to telling him,' Mallory said candidly. He peered at his luminous watch and swung to his feet. 'Mandrakos in half an hour.'

In precisely thirty minutes, their Schmeissers removed from their waterproof bags and now shoulder-slung at hip level, Mallory and Miller moved swiftly but very quietly from shadow to shadow through the plantations of carob trees on the outskirts of the village of Mandrakos. Suddenly, from directly ahead, they heard the unmistakable clink of glasses and bottlenecks.

For the two men a potentially dangerous situation such as this was so routine as not even to warrant a glance at each other. They dropped silently to their hands and knees and crawled forward, Miller sniffing the air appreciatively as they advanced: the Greek resinous spirit *ouzo* has an extraordinary ability to permeate the atmosphere for a considerable distance around it. Mallory and Miller reached the edge of a clump of bushes, sank prone and looked ahead.

From their richly-befrogged waistcoats, cummerbunds and fancy headgear, the two characters propped against the bole of a plane tree in the clearing ahead were obviously men of the island: from the rifles across their knees, their role appeared to be that of guards of some kind: from the almost vertical angle at which they had to tip the *ouzo* bottle to get at what little was left of its contents, it was equally apparent that they weren't taking their duties too seriously, nor had been for some considerable time past.

Mallory and Miller withdrew somewhat less stealthily than they had advanced, rose and glanced at each other. Suitable comment seemed lacking. Mallory shrugged and moved on, circling around to his right. Twice more, as they moved swiftly into the centre of Mandrakos, flitting from the shadow of carob grove to carob grove, from the shadow of plane tree to plane tree, from the shadow of house to house, they came upon but easily avoided other ostensible sentries, all busy interpreting their duties in a very liberal fashion. Miller pulled Mallory into a doorway.

'Our friends back there,' he said. 'What were they celebrating?'

'Wouldn't you? Celebrate, I mean. Navarone is useless to the Germans now. A week from now and they'll all be gone.'

'All right. So why are they keeping a watch?' Miller nodded to a small, whitewashed Greek Orthodox church standing in the centre of the village square. From inside came a far from subdued murmur of voices. Also from inside came a great deal of light escaping through very imperfectly blacked-out windows. 'Could it be anything to do with that?'

Mallory said: 'Well, there's one sure way to find out.'

They moved quietly on, taking advantage of all available cover and shadow until they came to a still deeper shadow caused by two flying buttresses supporting the wall of the ancient church. Between the buttresses was one of the few more successfully blacked-out windows with only a tiny chink of light showing along the bottom edge. Both men stooped and peered through the narrow aperture.

The church appeared even more ancient inside than

on the outside. The high unpainted wooden benches, adze-cut oak from centuries long gone, had been blackened and smoothed by untold generations of churchgoers, the wood itself cracked and splintered by the ravages of time: the whitewashed walls looked as if they required buttresses within as well as without, crumbling to an extinction that could not now be long delayed: the roof appeared to be in imminent danger of falling in at any moment.

The now even louder hum of sound came from islanders of almost every age and sex, many in ceremonial dress, who occupied nearly every available seat in the church: the light came from literally hundreds of guttering candles, many of them ancient and twisted and ornamented and evidently called out for this special occasion, that lined the walls, the central aisle and the altar: by the altar itself, a priest, a bearded patriarch in Greek Orthodox robes, waited impassively.

Mallory and Miller looked interrogatively at each other and were on the point of standing upright when a very deep and very quiet voice spoke behind them.

'Hands behind the necks,' it said pleasantly. 'And straighten very slowly. I have a Schmeisser machine-pistol in my hands.'

Slowly and carefully, just as the voice asked, Mallory and Miller did as they were told.

'Turn round. Carefully, now.'

So they turned round, carefully. Miller looked at the massive dark figure who indeed had, as he'd claimed, a machine-pistol in his hands, and said irritably: 'Do you mind? Point that damned thing somewhere else.'

The dark figure gave a startled exclamation, lowered the gun to his side and bent forward, the dark, craggy, lined face expressing no more than a passing flicker of surprise. Andrea Stavros didn't go in very much for registering unnecessary emotional displays and the recovery of his habitual composure was instantaneous.

'The German uniforms,' he explained apologetically. 'They had me fooled.'

'You could have fooled me, too,' Miller said. He looked incredulously at Andrea's clothes, at the unbelievably baggy black trousers, the black jackboots, the intricately ornamented black waistcoat and violently purple cummerbund, shuddered and closed his eyes in pain. 'Been visiting the Mandrakos pawn shop?'

'The ceremonial dress of my ancestors,' Andrea said mildly. 'You two fall overboard?'

'Not intentionally,' Mallory said. 'We came back to see you.'

'You could have chosen a more convenient time.' He hesitated, glanced at a small lighted building across the street and took their arms. 'We can talk in here.'

He ushered them in and closed the door behind him. The room was obviously, from its benches and Spartan furnishings, some sort of communal meeting-place, a village hall: illumination came from three rather smoky oil lamps, the light from which was most hospitably reflected by the scores of bottles of spirit and wine and beer and glasses that took up almost every available inch of two long trestle tables. The haphazardly unaesthetic layout of the refreshments bespoke a very impromptu and hastily improvised preparation for a celebration: the serried rows of bottles heralded the intention of compensating for lack of quality by an excess of quantity.

Andrea crossed to the nearest table, picked up three glasses and a bottle of *ouzo*, and began to pour drinks. Miller fished out his brandy and offered it, but Andrea was too preoccupied to notice. He handed them the *ouzo* glasses.

'Health.' Andrea drained his glass and went on thoughtfully: 'You did not return without a good reason, my Keith.'

Silently, Mallory removed the Cairo radio message from its waterproof oilskin wallet and handed it to Andrea, who took it half-unwillingly, then read it, scowling blackly.

He said: 'Urgent 3 means what I think it means?'

Again Mallory remained silent, merely nodding as he watched Andrea unwinkingly.

'This is most inconvenient for me.' The scowl deepened. '*Most* inconvenient. There are many things for me to do in Navarone. The people will miss me.'

'It's also inconvenient for me,' Miller said. 'There are many things *I* could profitably be doing in the West End of London. They miss me, too. Ask any barmaid. But that's hardly the point.'

Andrea regarded him for an impassive moment, then looked at Mallory. '*You* are saying nothing.'

'I've nothing to say.'

The scowl slowly left Andrea's face, though the brooding frown remained. He hesitated, then reached again for the bottle of *ouzo*. Miller shuddered delicately.

'Please.' He indicated the bottle of brandy.

Andrea smiled, briefly and for the first time, poured some of Miller's five-star into their glasses, reread the message and handed it back to Mallory. 'I must think it over. I have some business to attend to first.'

Mallory looked at him thoughtfully. 'Business?'

'I have to attend a wedding.'

'A wedding?' Miller said politely.

'Must you two repeat everything I say? A wedding.'

'But who do *you* know?' Miller asked. 'And at this hour of night.'

330

'For some people in Navarone,' Andrea said drily, 'the night is the only safe time.' He turned abruptly, walked away, opened the door and hesitated.

Mallory asked curiously: 'Who's getting married?'

Andrea made no reply. Instead he walked back to the nearest table, poured and drained a half-tumbler of the brandy, ran a hand through his thick dark hair, straightened his cummerbund, squared his shoulders and walked purposefully towards the door. Mallory and Miller stared after him, then at the door that closed behind him; then they stared at each other.

Some fifteen minutes later they were still staring at each other, this time with expressions which alternated between the merely bemused and slightly stunned.

They were seated in the back seat of the Greek Orthodox church – the only part of any pew in the entire church not now occupied by islanders. From where they sat, the altar was at least sixty feet away but as they were both tall men and sitting by the central aisle, they had a pretty fair view of what was going on up there.

There was, to be accurate, nothing going on up there any more. The ceremony was over. Gravely, the Orthodox priest bestowed his blessing and Andrea and Maria, the girl who had shown them the way into the fortress of Navarone, turned with the slow dignity becoming the occasion, and walked down the aisle. Andrea bent over, tenderness and solicitousness both in expression and manner, and whispered something in her ear, but his words, it would have seemed, bore little relation to the way in which they were expressed, for halfway down the aisle a furious altercation broke out between them. Between, perhaps, is not the right

331

word: it was less an altercation than a very one-sided monologue. Maria, her face flushed and dark eyes flashing, gesticulating and clearly mad through, was addressing Andrea in far from low tones of not even barely-controlled fury: Andrea, for his part, was deprecatory, placatory, trying to hush her up with about the same amount of success as Canute had in holding back the tide, and looking apprehensively around. The reaction of the seated guests varied from disbelief through open-mouthed astonishment and bafflement to downright horror: clearly all regarded the spectacle as a highly unusual aftermath to a wedding ceremony.

As the couple approached the end of the aisle opposite the pew where Mallory and Miller were seated, the argument, if such it could be called, raged more furiously than ever. As they passed by the end pew, Andrea, hand over his mouth, leaned over towards Mallory.

'This,' he said, *sotto voce*, 'is our first married quarrel.'

He was given time to say no more. An imperative hand seized his arm and almost literally dragged him through the church doorway. Even after they had disappeared from sight, Maria's voice, loud and clear, could still be heard by everyone within the church. Miller turned from surveying the empty doorway and looked thoughtfully at Mallory.

'Very high-spirited girl, that. I wish I understood Greek. What was she saying there?'

Mallory kept his face carefully expressionless. 'What about my honeymoon?'

'Ah!' Miller's face was equally dead-pan. 'Don't you think we'd better follow them?'

'Why?'

'Andrea can take care of most people.' It was the usual masterly Miller understatement. 'But he's stepped out of his class this time.'

Mallory smiled, rose and went to the door, followed by Miller, who was in turn followed by an eager press of guests understandably anxious to see the second act of this unscheduled entertainment: but the village square was empty of life.

Mallory did not hesitate. With the instinct born from the experience of long association with Andrea, he headed across the square to the communal hall where Andrea had made the earlier of his two dramatic statements. His instincts hadn't betrayed him. Andrea, with a large glass of brandy in his hand and moodily fingering a spreading patch of red on his cheek, looked up as Mallory and Miller entered.

He said moodily: 'She's gone home to her mother.'

Miller glanced at his watch. 'One minute and twenty-five seconds,' he said admiringly. 'A world record.'

Andrea glowered at him and Mallory moved in hastily.

'You're coming, then.'

'Of course I'm coming,' Andrea said irritably. He surveyed without enthusiasm the guests now swarming into the hall and brushing unceremoniously by as they headed, like the camel for the oasis, towards the bottle-laden tables. 'Somebody's got to look after you two.'

Mallory looked at his watch. 'Three and a half hours yet before that plane is due. We're dead on our feet, Andrea. Where can we sleep — a safe place to sleep. Your perimeter guards are drunk.'

'They've been that way ever since the fortress blew up,' Andrea said. 'Come, I'll show you.'

333

Miller looked around the islanders, who, amid a loud babel of cheerful voices, were already quite exceptionally busy with bottles and glasses. 'How about your guests?'

'How about them, then?' Andrea surveyed his compatriots morosely. 'Just look at that lot. Ever known a wedding reception yet where anybody paid any attention to the bride and groom? Come.'

They made their way southwards through the outskirts of Mandrakos to the open countryside beyond. Twice they were challenged by guards, twice a scowl and growl from Andrea sent them back hurriedly to their *ouzo* bottles. It was still raining heavily, but Mallory's and Miller's clothes were already so saturated that a little more rain could hardly make any appreciable difference to the way they felt, while Andrea, if anything, seemed even more oblivious of it. Andrea had the air of a man who had other things on his mind.

After fifteen minutes' walk, Andrea stopped before the swing doors of a small, dilapidated and obviously deserted roadside barn.

'There's hay inside,' he said. 'We'll be safe here.'

Mallory said: 'Fine. A radio message to the *Sirdar* to send her CE message to Cairo and – '

'CE?' Andrea asked. 'What's that?'

'To let Cairo know we've contacted you and are ready for pick-up ... And after that, three lovely hours' sleep.'

Andrea nodded. 'Three hours it is.'

'Three *long* hours,' Mallory said meditatively.

A smile slowly broke on Andrea's craggy face as he clapped Mallory on the shoulder.

'In three long hours,' he said, 'a man like myself can accomplish a great deal.'

He turned and hurried off through the rain-filled night. Mallory and Miller looked after him with expressionless faces, looked at each other, still with the same expressionless faces, then pushed open the swing doors of the barn.

The Mandrakos airfield would not have received a licence from any Civil Air Board anywhere in the world. It was just over half a mile long, with hills rising steeply at both ends of the alleged runway, not more than forty yards wide and liberally besprinkled with a variety of bumps and potholes virtually guaranteed to wreck any undercarriage in the aviation business. But the RAF had used it before so it was not impossible that they might be able to use it at least once again.

To the south, the airstrip was lined with groves of carob trees. Under the pitiful shelter afforded by one of those, Mallory, Miller and Andrea sat waiting. At least Mallory and Miller did, hunched, miserable and shivering violently in their still sodden clothes. Andrea, however, was stretched out luxuriously with his hands behind his head, oblivious of the heavy drips of rain that fell on his upturned face. There was about him an air of satisfaction, of complacency almost, as he gazed at the first greyish tinges appearing in the sky to the east over the black-walled massif of the Turkish coast.

Andrea said: 'They're coming now.'

Mallory and Miller listened for a few moments, then they too heard it – the distant, muted roar of heavy aircraft approaching. All three rose and moved out to the perimeter of the airstrip. Within a minute, descending rapidly after their climb over the mountains to the south and at a height of less than a thousand feet, a squadron of eighteen Wellingtons, as much heard

335

as seen in the light of early dawn, passed directly over the airstrip, heading for the town of Navarone. Two minutes later, the three watchers both heard the detonations and saw the brilliant orange mushrooming of light as the Wellingtons unloaded their bombs over the shattered fortress to the north. Sporadic lines of upward-flying tracers, obviously exclusively small-arm, attested to the ineffectuality, the weakness of the ground defences. When the fortress had blown up, so had all the anti-aircraft batteries in the town. The attack was short and sharp: less than two minutes after the bombardment had started it ceased as abruptly as it had begun and then there was only the fading dying sound of desynchronized engines as the Wellingtons pulled away, first to the north and then the west, across the still-dark waters of the Aegean.

For perhaps a minute the three watchers stood silent on the perimeter of the Mandrakos airstrip, then Miller said wonderingly: 'What makes us so important?'

'I don't know,' Mallory said. 'But I don't think you're going to enjoy finding out.'

'And that won't be long now.' Andrea turned round and looked towards the mountains to the south. 'Hear it?'

Neither of the others heard it, but they did not doubt that, in fact, there was something to hear. Andrea's hearing was on a par with his phenomenal eyesight. Then, suddenly, they could hear it, too. A solitary bomber – also a Wellington – came sinking in from the south, circled the perimeter area once as Mallory blinked his torch upwards in rapidly successive flashes, lined up its approach, landed heavily at the far end of the airstrip and came taxiing towards them, bumping heavily across the atrocious surface of the airfield. It halted less than a hundred yards from where they stood: then a light started winking from the flight deck.

Andrea said: 'Now, don't forget. I've promised to be back in a week.'

'Never make promises,' Miller said severely. 'What if we aren't back in a week? What if they're sending us to the Pacific?'

'Then when we get back I'll send you in first to explain.'

Miller shook his head. 'I don't really think I'd like that.'

'We'll talk about your cowardice later on,' Mallory said. 'Come on. Hurry up.'

The three men broke into a run towards the waiting Wellington.

The Wellington was half an hour on the way to its destination, wherever its destination was, and Andrea and Miller, coffee mugs in hand, were trying, unsuccessfully, to attain a degree of comfort on the lumpy palliasses on the fuselage floor when Mallory returned from the flightdeck. Miller looked up at him in weary resignation, his expression characterized by an entire lack of enthusiasm and the spirit of adventure.

'Well, what did you find out?' His tone of voice made it abundantly clear that what he had expected Mallory to find out was nothing short of the very worst. 'Where to, now? Rhodes? Beirut? The flesh-pots of Cairo?'

'Termoli, the man says.'

'Termoli, is it? Place I've always wanted to see.' Miller paused. 'Where the hell's Termoli?'

'Italy, so I believe. Somewhere on the south Adriatic coast.'

'Oh, no!' Miller turned on his side and pulled a blanket over his head. 'I *hate* spaghetti.'

CHAPTER TWO

Thursday 1400–2330

The landing on Termoli airfield, on the Adriatic coast of Southern Italy, was every bit as bumpy as the harrowing take-off from the Mandrakos airstrip had been. The Termoli fighter airbase was officially and optimistically listed as newly-constructed but in point of fact was no more than half-finished and felt that way for every yard of the excruciating touchdown and the jack-rabbit run-up to the prefabricated control tower at the eastern end of the field. When Mallory and Andrea swung down to terra firma, neither of them looked particularly happy: Miller, who came a very shaky last, and who was widely known to have an almost pathological loathing and detestation of all conceivable forms of transport, looked very ill indeed.

Miller was given time neither to seek nor receive commiseration. A camouflaged British 5th Army jeep pulled up alongside the plane, and the sergeant at the wheel, having briefly established their identity, waved them inside in silence, a silence which he stonily maintained on their drive through the shambles of the war-torn streets of Termoli. Mallory was unperturbed by the apparent unfriendliness. The driver was obviously under the strictest instructions not to talk to them, a situation which Mallory had encountered all too often in the past. There were not, Mallory reflected, very many groups of untouchables, but his, he knew, was one of them: no one, with two or three rare exceptions, was ever permitted to talk to them. The process, Mallory knew, was perfectly understandable and justifiable, but it was an attitude that did tend to become increasingly wearing with the passing of the years. It tended to make for a certain lack of contact with one's fellow men.

After twenty minutes, the jeep stopped below the broad-flagged steps of a house on the outskirts of the town. The jeep driver gestured briefly to an armed sentry on the top of the steps who responded with a similarly perfunctory greeting. Mallory took this as a sign that they had arrived at their destination and, not wishing to violate the young sergeant's vow of silence, got out without being told. The others followed and the jeep at once drove off.

The house – it looked more like a modest palace – was a rather splendid example of late Renaissance architecture, all colonnades and columns and everything in veined marble, but Mallory was more interested in what was inside the house than what it was made of on the outside. At the head of the steps their path was barred by the young corporal sentry armed with a Lee-Enfield .303. He looked like a refugee from high school.

'Names, please.'

'Captain Mallory.'

'Identity papers? Pay-books?'

'Oh, my God,' Miller moaned. 'And me feeling so sick, too.'

'We have none,' Mallory said gently. 'Take us inside, please.'

'My instructions are – '

'I know, I know,' Andrea said soothingly. He leaned across, effortlessly removed the rifle from the corporal's desperate grasp, ejected and pocketed the maga-

339

zine and returned the rifle. 'Please, now.'

Red-faced and furious, the youngster hesitated briefly, looked at the three men more carefully, turned, opened the door behind him and gestured for the three to follow him.

Before them stretched a long, marble-flagged corridor, tall leaded windows on one side, heavy oil paintings and the occasional set of double-leather doors on the other. Halfway down the passage Andrea tapped the corporal on the shoulder and handed the magazine back without a word. The corporal took it, smiling uncertainly, and inserted it into his rifle without a word. Another twenty paces and he stopped before the last pair of leather doors, knocked, heard a muffled acknowledgement and pushed open one of the doors, standing aside to let the three men pass him. Then he moved out again, closing the door behind him.

It was obviously the main drawing-room of the house – or palace – furnished in an almost medieval opulence, all dark oak, heavily brocaded silk curtains, leather upholstery, leather-bound books, what were undoubtedly a set of Old Masters on the walls and a flowing sea of dull bronze carpeting from wall to wall. Taken all in all, even a member of the old-pre-war Italian nobility wouldn't have turned up his nose at it.

The room was pleasantly redolent with the smell of burning pine, the source of which wasn't difficult to locate: one could have roasted a very large ox indeed in the vast and crackling fireplace at the far end of the room. Close by this fireplace stood three young men who bore no resemblance whatsoever to the rather ineffectual youngster who had so recently tried to prevent their entry. They were, to begin with, a good few years older, though still young men. They were heavily-built, broad-shouldered characters

340

and had about them a look of tough and hard-bitten competence. They were dressed in the uniform of that élite of combat troops, the Marine Commandos, and they looked perfectly at home in those uniforms.

But what caught and held the unwavering attention of Mallory and his two companions was neither the rather splendidly effete decadence of the room and its furnishings nor the wholly unexpected presence of the three commandos: it was the fourth figure in the room, a tall, heavily built and commanding figure who leaned negligently against a table in the centre of the room. The deeply-trenched face, the authoritative expression, the splendid grey beard and the piercing blue eyes made him a prototype for the classic British naval captain, which, as the immaculate white uniform he wore indicated, was precisely what he was. With a collective sinking of their hearts, Mallory, Andrea and Miller gazed again, and with a marked lack of enthusiasm, upon the splendidly piratical figure of Captain Jensen, RN, Chief of Allied Intelligence, Mediterranean, and the man who had so recently sent them on their suicidal mission to the island of Navarone. All three looked at one another and shook their heads in slow despair.

Captain Jensen straightened, smiled his magnificent sabre-toothed tiger's smile and strode forward to greet them, his hand outstretched.

'Mallory! Andrea! Miller!' There was a dramatic five-second pause between the words. 'I don't know what to say! I just don't know what to say! A magnificent job, a magnificent – ' He broke off and regarded them thoughtfully. 'You – um – don't seem at all surprised to see me, Captain Mallory?'

'I'm not. With respect, sir, whenever and wherever there's dirty work afoot, one looks to find – '

'Yes, yes, yes. Quite, quite. And how are you all?'

341

'Tired,' Miller said firmly. 'Terribly tired. We need a rest. At least, I do.'

Jensen said earnestly: 'And that's exactly what you're going to have, my boy. A rest. A long one. A *very* long one.'

'A *very* long one?' Miller looked at him in frank incredulity.

'You have my word.' Jensen stroked his beard in momentary diffidence. 'Just as soon, that is, as you get back from Yugoslavia.'

'Yugoslavia!' Miller stared at him.

'Tonight.'

'Tonight!'

'By parachute.'

'By *parachute*!'

Jensen said with forbearance: 'I am aware, Corporal Miller, that you have had a classical education and are, moreover, just returned from the Isles of Greece. But we'll do without the Ancient Greek Chorus bit, if you don't mind.'

Miller looked moodily at Andrea. 'Bang goes your honeymoon.'

'What was that?' Jensen asked sharply.

'Just a private joke, sir.'

Mallory said in mild protest: 'You're forgetting, sir, that none of us has ever made a parachute jump.'

'I'm forgetting nothing. There's a first time for everything. What do you gentlemen know about the war in Yugoslavia?'

'What war?' Andrea asked warily.

'Precisely.' There was satisfaction in Jensen's voice.

'I heard about it,' Miller volunteered. 'There's a bunch of what-do-you-call-'em – Partisans, isn't it – offering some kind of underground resistance to the German occupation troops.'

'It is probably as well for you,' Jensen said heavily, 'that the Partisans cannot hear you. They're not underground, they're very much over ground and at the last count there were 350,000 of them tying down twenty-eight German and Bulgarian divisions in Yugoslavia.' He paused briefly. 'More, in fact, than the combined Allied armies are tying down here in Italy.'

'Somebody should have told me,' Miller complained. He brightened. 'If there's 350,000 of them around, what would they want us for?'

Jensen said acidly: 'You must learn to curb your enthusiasm, Corporal. The fighting part of it you may leave to the Partisans – and they're fighting the cruellest, hardest, most brutal war in Europe today. A ruthless, vicious war with no quarter and no surrender on either side. Arms, munitions, food, clothes – the Partisans are desperately short of all of those. But they have those twenty-eight divisions pinned down.'

'I don't want any part of that,' Miller muttered.

Mallory said hastily: 'What do you want us to do, sir?'

'This.' Jensen removed his glacial stare from Miller. 'Nobody appreciates it yet, but the Yugoslavs are our most important Allies in Southern Europe. Their war is our war. And they're fighting a war they can never hope to win. Unless – '

Mallory nodded. 'The tools to finish the job.'

'Hardly original, but true. The tools to finish the job. We are the *only* people who are at present supplying them with rifles, machine-guns, ammunition, clothing and medical supplies. And those are not getting through.' He broke off, picking up a cane, walked almost angrily across the room to a large wall-map hanging between a couple of Old Masters and rapped the tip of the bamboo against it. 'Bosnia-Herzegovina,

343

gentlemen. West-Central Yugoslavia. We've sent in four British Military Missions in the past two months to liaise with the Yugoslavs – the Partisan Yugoslavs. The leaders of all four missions have disappeared without trace. Ninety per cent of our recent airlift supplies have fallen into German hands. They have broken all our radio codes and have established a network of agents in Southern Italy here with whom they are apparently able to communicate as and when they wish. Perplexing questions, gentlemen. Vital questions. I want the answers. Force 10 will get me the answers.'

'Force 10?' Mallory said politely.

'The code name for your operation.'

'Why that particular name?' Andrea said.

'Why not? Ever heard of *any* code name that had *any* bearing on the operation on hand? It's the whole essence of it, man.'

'It wouldn't, of course,' Mallory said woodenly, 'have anything to do with a frontal attack on something, a storming of some vital place.' He observed Jensen's total lack of reaction and went on in the same tone: 'On the Beaufort Scale, Force 10 means a storm.'

'A storm!' It is very difficult to combine an exclamation and a moan of anguish in the same word, but Miller managed it without any difficulty. 'Oh, my God, and all I want is a flat calm, and that for the rest of my life.'

'There are limits to my patience, Corporal Miller,' Jensen said. 'I may – I say *may* – have to change my mind about a recommendation I made on your behalf this morning.'

'On my behalf?' Miller said guardedly.

'For the Distinguished Conduct Medal.'

'*That* should look nice on the lid of my coffin,' Miller muttered.

344

'What was that?'

'Corporal Miller was just expressing his appreciation.' Mallory moved closer to the wall-map and studied it briefly. 'Bosnia-Herzegovina – well, it's a fair-sized area, sir.'

'Agreed. But we can pinpoint the spot – the approximate location of the disappearances – to within twenty miles.'

Mallory turned from the map and said slowly: 'There's been a lot of homework on this one. That raid this morning on Navarone. The Wellington standing by to take us here. All preparations – I infer this from what you've said – laid on for tonight. Not to mention – '

'We've been working on this for almost two months. You three were supposed to have come here some days ago. But – ah – well, you know.'

'We know.' The threatened withholding of his DCM had left Miller unmoved. 'Something else came up. Look, sir, why us? We're saboteurs, explosives experts, combat troops – this is a job for undercover espionage agents who speak Serbo-Croat or whatever.'

'You must allow me to be the best judge of that,' Jensen gave them another flash of his sabre-toothed smile. 'Besides, you're lucky.'

'Luck deserts tired men,' Andrea said. 'And we are very tired.'

'Tired or not, I can't find another team in Southern Europe to match you for resource, experience and skill.' Jensen smiled again. 'And luck. I have to be ruthless, Andrea. I don't like it, but I have to. But I take the point about your exhaustion. That's why I have decided to send a back-up team with you.'

Mallory looked at the three young soldiers standing by the hearth, then back to Jensen, who nodded.

'They're young, fresh and just raring to go. Marine

Commandos, the most highly trained combat troops we have today. Remarkable variety of skills, I assure you. Take Reynolds, here.' Jensen nodded to a very tall, dark sergeant in his late twenties, a man with a deeply-tanned aquiline face. 'He can do anything from underwater demolition to flying a plane. And he will be flying a plane tonight. And, as you can see, he'll come in handy for carrying any heavy cases you have.'

Mallory said mildly: 'I've always found that Andrea makes a pretty fair porter, sir.'

Jensen turned to Reynolds. 'They have their doubts. Show them you can be of some use.'

Reynolds hesitated, then stooped, picked up a heavy brass poker and proceeded to bend it between his hands. Obviously, it wasn't an easy poker to bend. His face turned red, the veins stood out on his forehead and the tendons in his neck, his arms quivered with the strain, but slowly, inexorably, the poker was bent into a figure 'U'. Smiling almost apologetically, Reynolds handed the poker over to Andrea. Andrea took it reluctantly. He hunched his shoulders, his knuckles gleamed white but the poker remained in its 'U' shape. Andrea looked up at Reynolds, his expression thoughtful, then quietly laid the poker down.

'See what I mean?' Jensen said. 'Tired. Or Sergeant Groves here. Hot-foot from London, via the Middle East. Ex-air navigator, with all the latest in sabotage, explosives and electrics. For booby-traps, time-bombs and concealed microphones, a human mine-detector. And Sergeant Saunders here – a top-flight radio operator.'

Miller said morosely to Mallory: 'You're a toothless old lion and you're over the hill.'

'Don't talk rubbish, Corporal!' Jensen's voice was sharp. 'Six is the ideal number. You'll be duplicated in every department, and those men are *good*. They'll be invaluable. If it's any salve to your pride, they weren't originally picked to go with you: they were picked as a reserve team in case you – um – well – '

'I see.' The lack of conviction in Miller's voice was total.

'All clear then?'

'Not quite,' Mallory said. 'Who's in charge?'

Jensen said in genuine surprise: 'You are, of course.'

'So.' Mallory spoke quietly and pleasantly. 'I understand the training emphasis today – especially in the Marine Commandos – is on initiative, self-reliance, independence in thought and action. Fine – if they happen to be caught out on their own.' He smiled, almost deprecatingly. 'Otherwise I shall expect immediate, unquestioning and total compliance with orders. My orders. Instant and total.'

'And if not?' Reynolds asked.

'A superfluous question, Sergeant. You know the wartime penalty for disobeying an officer in the field.'

'Does that apply to your friends, too?'

'No.'

Reynolds turned to Jensen. 'I don't think I like that, sir.'

Mallory sank wearily into a chair, lit a cigarette, nodded at Reynolds and said, 'Replace him.'

'What!' Jensen was incredulous.

'Replace him, I said. We haven't even left and already he's questioning my judgement. What's it going to be like in action? He's dangerous. I'd rather carry a ticking time-bomb with me.'

'Now, look here, Mallory – '

'Replace him or replace me.'

347

'And me,' Andrea said quietly.

'And me,' Miller added.

There was a brief and far from companionable silence in the room, then Reynolds approached Mallory's chair.

'Sir.'

Mallory looked at him without encouragement.

'I'm sorry,' Reynolds went on. 'I stepped out of line. I will never make the same mistake twice. I *want* to go on this trip, sir.'

Mallory glanced at Andrea and Miller. Miller's face registered only his shock at Reynolds's incredibly foolhardy enthusiasm for action. Andrea, impassive as ever, nodded almost imperceptibly. Mallory smiled and said: 'As Captain Jensen said, I'm sure you'll be a great asset.'

'Well, that's it, then.' Jensen affected not to notice the almost palpable relaxation of tension in the room. 'Sleep's the thing now. But first I'd like a few minutes – report on Navarone, you know.' He looked at the three sergeants. 'Confidential, I'm afraid.'

'Yes, sir,' Reynolds said. 'Shall we go down to the field, check flight plans, weather, parachutes and supplies?'

Jensen nodded. As the three sergeants closed the double doors behind them, Jensen crossed to a side door, opened it and said: 'Come in, General.'

The man who entered was very tall, very gaunt. He was probably about thirty-five, but looked a great deal older. The care, the exhaustion, the endless privations inseparable from too many years' ceaseless struggle for survival had heavily silvered the once-black hair and deeply etched into the swarthy, sunburnt face the lines of physical and mental suffering. The eyes were dark and glowing and intense, the hypnotic eyes of a man inspired by a fanatical dedication to some as yet

348

unrealized ideal. He was dressed in a British Army officer's uniform, bereft of insignia and badges.

Jensen said: 'Gentlemen, General Vukalovic. The general is second-in-command of the Partisan forces in Bosnia-Herzegovina. The RAF flew him out yesterday. He is here as a Partisan doctor seeking medical supplies. His true identity is known only to us. General, those are your men.'

Vukalovic looked them over severally and steadily, his face expressionless. He said: 'Those are tired men, Captain Jensen. So much depends ... too tired to do what has to be done.'

'He's right, you know,' Miller said earnestly.

'There's maybe a little mileage left in them yet,' Jensen said mildly. 'It's a long haul from Navarone. Now then – '

'Navarone?' Vukalovic interrupted. 'These – these are the men – '

'An unlikely-looking lot, I agree.'

'Perhaps I was wrong about them.'

'No, you weren't, General,' Miller said. 'We're exhausted. We're completely – '

'Do you mind?' Jensen said acidly. 'Captain Mallory, with two exceptions the General will be the only person in Bosnia who knows who you are and what you are doing. Whether the General reveals the identity of the others is entirely up to him. General Vukalovic will be accompanying you to Yugoslavia, but not in the same plane.'

'Why not?' Mallory asked.

'Because his plane will be returning. Yours won't.'

'Ah!' Mallory said. There was a brief silence while he, Andrea and Miller absorbed the significance behind Jensen's words. Abstractedly, Andrea threw some more wood on the sinking fire and looked around for a poker:

349

but the only poker was the one that Reynolds had already bent into a 'U'-shape. Andrea picked it up. Absent-mindedly, effortlessly, Andrea straightened it out, poked the fire into a blaze and laid the poker down, a performance Vukalovic watched with a very thoughtful expression his face.

Jensen went on: 'Your plane, Captain Mallory, will not be returning because your plane is expendable in the interests of authenticity.'

'Us, too?' Miller asked.

'You won't be able to accomplish very much, Corporal Miller, without actually putting your feet on the ground. Where you're going, no plane can possibly land: so you jump – and the plane crashes.'

'That sounds very authentic,' Miller muttered.

Jensen ignored him. 'The realities of total war are harsh beyond belief. Which is why I sent those three youngsters on their way – I don't want to dampen their enthusiasm.'

'Mine's water-logged,' Miller said dolefully.

'Oh, do be quiet. Now, it would be fine if, by way of a bonus, you could discover why eighty per cent of our air-drops fall into German hands, fine if you could locate and rescue our captured mission leaders. But not important. Those supplies, those agents are militarily expendable. What are not expendable are the seven thousand men under the command of General Vukalovic here, seven thousand men trapped in an area called the Zenica Cage, seven thousand starving men with almost no ammunition left, seven thousand men with no future.'

'We can help them?' Andrea asked heavily. 'Six men?'

Jensen said candidly: 'I don't know.'

'But you have a plan?'

'Not yet. Not as such. The glimmerings of an idea. No more.' Jensen rubbed his forehead wearily. 'I myself arrived from Alexandria only six hours ago.' He hesitated, then shrugged. 'By tonight, who knows? A few hours' sleep this afternoon might transform us all. But, first, the report on Navarone. It would be pointless for you three other gentlemen to wait – there are sleeping quarters down the hall. I daresay Captain Mallory can tell me all I want to know.'

Mallory waited till the door closed behind Andrea, Miller and Vukalovic and said: 'Where shall I begin my report, sir?'

'What report?'

'Navarone, of course.'

'The hell with Navarone. That's over and done with.' He picked up his cane, crossed to the wall, pulled down two more maps. 'Now, then.'

'You – you *have* a plan,' Mallory said carefully.

'Of course I have a plan,' Jensen said coldly. He rapped the map in front of him. 'Ten miles north of here. The Gustav Line. Right across Italy along the line of the Sangro and Liri rivers. Here the Germans have the most impregnable defensive positions in the history of modern warfare. Monte Cassino here – our finest Allied divisions have broken on it, some for ever. And here – the Anzio beachhead. Fifty thousand Americans fighting for their lives. For five solid months now we've been battering our heads against the Gustav Line and the Anzio perimeter. Our losses in men and machines – incalculable. Our gains – not one solitary inch.'

Mallory said diffidently: 'You mentioned something about Yugoslavia, sir.'

'I'm coming to that,' Jensen said with restraint. 'Now, our only hope of breaching the Gustav Line is

351

by weakening the German defensive forces and the only way we can do *that* is by persuading them to withdraw some of their front-line divisions. So we practise the Allenby technique.'

'I see.'

'You don't see at all. General Allenby, Palestine, 1918. He had an east-west line from the Jordan to the Mediterranean. He planned to attack from the west – so he convinced the Turks the attack was coming from the east. He did this by building up in the east a huge city of army tents occupied by only a few hundred men who came out and dashed around like beavers whenever enemy planes came over on reconnaissance. He did this by letting the same planes see large army truck convoys pouring to the east all day long – what the Turks didn't know was that the same convoys poured back to the west all night long. He even had fifteen thousand canvas dummies of horses built. Well, we're doing the same.'

'Fifteen thousand canvas horses?'

'Very, very amusing.' Jensen rapped the map again. 'Every airfield between here and Bari is jammed with dummy bombers and gliders. Outside Foggia is the biggest military encampment in Italy – occupied by two hundred men. The harbours of Bari and Taranto are crowded with assault landing craft, the whole lot made of plywood. All day long columns of trucks and tanks converge on the Adriatic coast. If you, Mallory, were in the German High Command, what would you make of this?'

'I'd suspect an airborne and sea invasion of Yugoslavia. But I wouldn't be sure.'

'The German reaction exactly,' Jensen said with some satisfaction. 'They're badly worried, worried to the extent that they have already transferred two divisions from Italy to Yugoslavia to meet the threat.'

'But they're not certain?'

'Not quite. But almost.' Jensen cleared his throat. 'You see, our four captured mission leaders were all carrying unmistakable evidence pointing to an invasion of Central Yugoslavia in early May.'

'They carried evidence –' Mallory broke off, looked at Jensen for a long and speculative moment, then went on quietly: 'And how *did* the Germans manage to capture them all?'

'We told them they were coming.'

'You did what!'

'Volunteers all, volunteers all,' Jensen said quickly. There were, apparently, some of the harsher realities of total war that even he didn't care to dwell on too long. 'And it will be your job, my boy, to turn near-conviction into absolute certainty.' Seemingly oblivious of the fact that Mallory was regarding him with a marked lack of enthusiasm, he wheeled round dramatically and stabbed his cane at a large-scale map of Central Yugoslavia.

'The valley of the Neretva,' Jensen said. 'The vital sector of the main north-south route through Yugoslavia. Whoever controls this valley controls Yugoslavia – and no one knows this better than the Germans. If the blow falls, they know it must fall here. They are fully aware that an invasion of Yugoslavia is on the cards, they are terrified of a link-up between the Allies and the Russians advancing from the east and they *know* that any such link-up must be along this valley. They already have two armoured divisions along the Neretva, two divisions that, in the event of invasion, could be wiped out in a night. From the north – here – they are trying to force their way south to the Neretva with a whole army corps – but the only way is through the Zenica Cage here. And Vukalovic and his seven thousand men block the way.'

'Vukalovic knows about this?' Mallory asked. 'About what you really have in mind, I mean?'

'Yes. And the Partisan command. They know the risks, the odds against them. They accept them.'

'Photographs?' Mallory asked.

'Here.' Jensen pulled some photographs from a desk drawer, selected one and smoothed it out on the table. 'This is the Zenica Cage. Well named: a perfect cage, a perfect trap. To the north and west, impassable mountains. To the east, the Neretva dam and the Neretva gorge. To the south, the Neretva river. To the north of the cage here, at the Zenica gap, the German 11th Army Corps is trying to break through. To the west here – they call it the West Gap – more units of the 11th trying to do the same. And to the south here, over the river and hidden in the trees, two armoured divisions under a General Zimmermann.'

'And this?' Mallory pointed to a thin black line spanning the river just north of the two armoured divisions.

'That,' Jensen said thoughtfully, 'is the bridge at Neretva.'

Close-up, the bridge at Neretva looked vastly more impressive than it had done in the large-scale photograph: it was a massively cantilevered structure in solid steel, with a black asphalt roadway laid on top. Below the bridge rushed the swiftly-flowing Neretva, greenish-white in colour and swollen with melting snow. To the south there was a narrow strip of green meadowland bordering the river and, to the south of this again, a dark and towering pine forest began. In the safe concealment of the forest's gloomy depths, General Zimmermann's two armoured divisions crouched waiting.

Parked close to the edge of the wood was the divisional command radio truck, a bulky and very long vehicle so beautifully camouflaged as to be invisible at more than twenty paces.

General Zimmermann and his ADC, Captain Warburg, were at that moment inside the truck. Their mood appeared to match the permanent twilight of the woods. Zimmermann had one of those high-fore-headed, lean and aquiline and intelligent faces which so rarely betray any emotion, but there was no lack of emotion now, no lack of anxiety and impatience as he removed his cap and ran his hand through his thinning grey hair. He said to the radio operator seated behind the big transceiver:

'No word yet? Nothing?'

'Nothing, sir.'

'You are in constant touch with Captain Neufeld's camp?'

'Every minute, sir.'

'And his operator is keeping a continuous radio watch?'

'All the time, sir. Nothing. Just nothing.'

Zimmermann turned and descended the steps, fol-lowed by Warburg. He walked, head down, until he was out of earshot of the truck, then said: 'Damn it! Damn it! God damn it all!'

'You're as sure as that, sir.' Warburg was tall, good-looking, flaxen-haired and thirty, and his face at the moment reflected a nice balance of apprehension and unhappiness. 'That they're coming?'

'It's in my bones, my boy. One way or another it's coming, coming for all of us.'

'You can't be *sure*, sir,' Warburg protested.

'True enough.' Zimmermann sighed. 'I can't be sure. But I'm sure of this. If they do come, if the 11th Army Group can't break through from the north, if we can't wipe out those damned Partisans in the Zenica Cage – '

Warburg waited for him to continue, but Zimmermann seemed lost in reverie. Apparently apropos of nothing, Warburg said: 'I'd like to see Germany again, sir. Just once more.'

'Wouldn't we all, my boy, wouldn't we all.' Zimmermann walked slowly to the edge of the wood and stopped. For a long time he gazed out over the bridge at Neretva. Then he shook his head, turned and was almost at once lost to sight in the dark depths of the forest.

The pine fire in the great fireplace in the drawing-room in Termoli was burning low. Jensen threw on some more logs, straightened, poured two drinks and handed one to Mallory.

Jensen said: 'Well?'

'That's the plan?' No hint of his incredulity, of his near-despair, showed in Mallory's impassive face. 'That's *all* of the plan?'

'Yes.'

'Your health.' Mallory paused. 'And mine.' After an even longer pause he said reflectively: 'It should be interesting to watch Dusty Miller's reactions when he hears this little lot this evening.'

As Mallory had said, Miller's reactions were interesting, even if wholly predictable. Some six hours later, clad now, like Mallory and Andrea, in British Army uniform, Miller listened in visibly growing horror as Jensen outlined what he considered should be their

356

proposed course of action in the next twenty-four hours or so. When he had finished, Jensen looked directly at Miller and said: 'Well? Feasible?'

'Feasible?' Miller was aghast. 'It's suicidal!'

'Andrea?'

'Andrea shrugged, lifted his hands palms upwards and said nothing.

Jensen nodded and said: 'I'm sorry, but I'm fresh out of options. We'd better go. The others are waiting at the airstrip.'

Andrea and Miller left the room, began to walk down the long passageway. Mallory hesitated in the doorway, momentarily blocking it, then turned to face Jensen who was watching him with a surprised lift of the eyebrows.

Mallory said in a low voice: 'Let me tell Andrea, at least.'

Jensen looked at him for a considering moment or two, shook his head briefly and brushed by into the corridor.

Twenty minutes later, without a further word being spoken, the four men arrived at the Termoli airstrip to find Vukalovic and two sergeants waiting for them: the third, Reynolds, was already at the controls of his Wellington, one of them standing at the end of the airstrip, propellers already turning. Ten minutes later both planes were airborne, Vukalovic in one, Mallory, Miller, Andrea, and the three sergeants in the other, each plane bound for its separate destination.

Jensen, alone on the tarmac, watched both planes climbing, his straining eyes following them until they disappeared into the overcast darkness of the moonless sky above. Then, just as General Zimmermann had done that afternoon, he shook his head in slow finality, turned and walked heavily away.

CHAPTER THREE

Friday 0030–0200

Sergeant Reynolds, Mallory reflected, certainly knew how to handle a plane, especially this one. Although his eyes showed him to be always watchful and alert, he was precise, competent, calm and relaxed in everything he did. No less competent was Groves: the poor light and cramped confines of his tiny plotting-table clearly didn't worry him at all and as an air navigator he was quite clearly as experienced as he was proficient. Mallory peered forward through the windscreen, saw the white-capped waters of the Adriatic rushing by less than a hundred feet beneath their fuselage, and turned to Groves.

'The flight plan calls for us to fly as low as this?'

'Yes. The Germans have radar installations on some of the outlying islands off the Yugoslav coast. We start climbing when we reach Dalmatia.'

Mallory nodded his thanks, turned to watch Reynolds again. He said, curiously: 'Captain Jensen was right about you. As a pilot. How on earth does a Marine Commando come to learn to drive one of those things?'

'I've had plenty of practice,' Reynolds said. 'Three years in the RAF, two of them as sergeant-pilot in a Wellington bomber squadron. One day in Egypt I took a Lysander up without permission. People did it all the time – but the crate I'd picked had a defective fuel gauge.'

'You were grounded?'

'With great speed.' He grinned. 'There were no objections when I applied for a service transfer. I think they felt I wasn't somehow quite right for the RAF.'

Mallory looked at Groves. 'And you?'

Groves smiled broadly. 'I was his navigator in that old crate. We were fired on the same day.'

Mallory said consideringly: 'Well, I should think that might be rather useful.'

'What's useful?' Reynolds asked.

'The fact that you're used to this feeling of disgrace. It'll enable you to act your part all the better when the time comes. If the time comes.'

Reynolds said carefully: 'I'm not quite sure – '

'Before we jump, I want you – all of you – to remove every distinguishing badge or emblem of rank on your clothes.' He gestured to Andrea and Miller at the rear of the flight-deck to indicate that they were included as well, then looked at Reynolds again. 'Sergeants' stripes, regimental flashes, medal ribbons – the lot.'

'Why the hell should I?' Reynolds, Mallory thought, had the lowest boiling-point he'd come across in quite some time. 'I *earned* those stripes, those ribbons, that flash. I don't see – '

Mallory smiled. 'Disobeying an officer on active service?'

'Don't be so damned touchy,' Reynolds said.

'Don't be so damned touchy, *sir.*'

'Don't be so damned touchy, *sir.*' Reynolds suddenly grinned. 'OK, so who's got the scissors?'

'You see,' Mallory explained, 'the last thing we want to happen is to fall into enemy hands.'

'Amen,' Miller intoned.

'But if we're to get the information we want we're

359

going to have to operate close to or even inside their lines. We might get caught. So we have our cover story.'

Groves said quietly: 'Are we permitted to know just what that cover story is, sir?'

'Of course you are,' Mallory said in exasperation. He went on earnestly: 'Don't you realize that, on a mission like this, survival depends on one thing and one thing only – complete and mutual trust? As soon as we start having secrets from each other – we're finished.'

In the deep gloom at the rear of the flight-deck, Andrea and Miller glanced at each other and exchanged their wearily cynical smiles.

As Mallory left the flight-deck for the fuselage, his right hand brushed Miller's shoulder. After about two minutes Miller yawned, stretched and made his way aft. Mallory was waiting towards the rear of the fuselage. He had two pieces of folded paper in his hand, one of which he opened and showed to Miller, snapping on a flashlight at the same time. Miller stared at it for some moments, then lifted an eyebrow.

'And what is this supposed to be?'

'It's the triggering mechanism for a 1,500-pound submersible mine. Learn it by heart.'

Miller looked at it without expression, then glanced at the other paper Mallory held.

'And what have you there?'

Mallory showed him. It was a large-scale map, the central feature of which appeared to be a winding lake with a very long eastern arm which bent abruptly at right-angles into a very short southern arm, which in turn ended abruptly at what appeared to be a dam wall. Beneath the dam, a river flowed away through a winding gorge.

Mallory said: 'What does it look like to you? Show them both to Andrea and tell him to destroy them.'

Mallory left Miller engrossed in his homework and moved forward again to the flight-deck. He bent over Groves's chart table.

'Still on course?'

'Yes, sir. We're just clearing the southern tip of the island of Hvar. You can see a few lights on the mainland ahead.' Mallory followed the pointing hand, located a few clusters of lights, then reached out a hand to steady himself as the Wellington started to climb sharply. He glanced at Reynolds.

'Climbing now, sir. There's some pretty lofty stuff ahead. We should pick up the Partisan landing lights in about half an hour.'

'Thirty-three minutes,' Groves said. 'One-twenty, near enough.'

For almost half an hour Mallory remained on a jump-seat in the flight-deck, just looking ahead. After a few minutes Andrea disappeared and did not reappear. Miller did not return. Groves navigated, Reynolds flew, Saunders listened in to his portable transceiver and nobody talked at all. At one-fifteen Mallory rose, touched Saunders on the shoulders, told him to pack up his gear and headed aft. He found Andrea and a thoroughly miserable-looking Miller with their parachute snap-catches already clipped on to the jumping wire. Andrea had the door pulled back and was throwing out tiny pieces of shredded paper which swirled away in the slipstream. Mallory shivered in the suddenly intense cold. Andrea grinned, beckoned him to the open doorway and pointed downwards. He yelled in Mallory's ear: 'There's a lot of snow down there.'

There was indeed a lot of snow down there. Mallory understood now Jensen's insistence on not landing a

361

plane in those parts. The terrain below was rugged in the extreme, consisting almost entirely of a succession of deep and winding valleys and steep-sided mountains. Maybe half of the landscape below was covered in dense forests of pine trees: all of it was covered in what appeared to be a very heavy blanket of snow. Mallory drew back into the comparative shelter of the Wellington's fuselage and glanced at his watch.

'One-sixteen.' Like Andrea, he had to shout.

'Your watch is a little fast, maybe?' Miller bawled unhappily. Mallory shook his head, Miller shook his. A bell rang and Mallory made his way to the flight-deck, passing Saunders going the other way. As Mallory entered, Reynolds looked briefly over his shoulder, then pointed directly ahead. Mallory bent over his shoulder and peered forwards and downwards. He nodded.

The three lights, in the form of an elongated V, were still some miles ahead, but quite unmistakable. Mallory turned, touched Groves on the shoulder and pointed aft. Groves rose and left. Mallory said to Reynolds: 'Where are the red and green jumping lights?'

Reynolds indicated them.

'Press the red light. How long?'

'Thirty seconds. About.'

Mallory looked ahead again. The lights were less than half as distant as they had been when first he'd looked. He said to Reynolds: 'Automatic pilot. Close the fuel switches.'

'Close the – for the petrol that's left – '

'Shut off the bloody tanks! And get aft. Five seconds.'

Reynolds did as he was told. Mallory waited, briefly made a last check of the landing lights ahead, pressed the green light button, rose and made his way swiftly aft. By the time he reached the jump door, even

Reynolds, the last of the first five, was gone. Mallory clipped on his snap-catch, braced his hands round the edge of the doorway and launched himself out into the bitter Bosnian night.

The sudden jarring impact from the parachute harness made him look quickly upwards: the concave circle of a fully open parachute was a reassuring spectacle. He glanced downwards and saw the equally reassuring spectacle of another five open parachutes, two of which were swaying quite wildly across the sky – just as was his own. There were some things, he reflected, about which he, Andrea and Miller had a great deal to learn. Controlling parachute descents was one of those things.

He looked up and to the east to see if he could locate the Wellington, but it was no longer visible. Suddenly, as he looked and listened, both engines, almost in perfect unison, cut out. Long seconds passed when the only sound was the rush of the wind in his ears, then there came an explosively metallic sound as the bomber crashed either into the ground or into some unseen mountainside ahead. There was no fire or none that he could see: just the crash, then silence. For the first time that night, the moon broke through.

Andrea landed heavily on an uneven piece of ground, rolled over twice, rose rather experimentally to his feet, discovered he was still intact, pressed the quick-release button of his parachute, then automatically, instinctively – Andrea had a built-in computer for assuring survival – swung through a complete 360° circle. But no immediate danger threatened, or none that he could see. Andrea made a more leisurely survey of their landing spot.

They had, he thought grimly, been most damnably lucky. Another hundred yards to the south and they'd have spent the rest of the night, and for all he knew, the rest of the war, clinging to the tops of the most impossibly tall pine trees he had ever seen. As it was, luck had been with them and they had landed in a narrow clearing which abutted closely on the rocky scarp of a mountainside.

Or rather, all but one. Perhaps fifty yards from where Andrea had landed, an apex of the forest elbowed its way into the clearing. The outermost tree in this apex had come between one of the parachutists and terra firma. Andrea's eyebrows lifted in quizzical astonishment, then he broke into an ambling run.

The parachutist who had come to grief was dangling from the lowermost bough of the pine. He had his hands twisted in the shrouds, his legs bent, knees and ankles close together in the classic landing position, his feet perhaps thirty inches from the ground. His eyes were screwed tightly shut. Corporal Miller seemed acutely unhappy.

Andrea came up and touched him on the shoulder, gently. Miller opened his eyes and glanced at Andrea, who pointed downwards. Miller followed his glance and lowered his legs, which were then four inches from the ground. Andrea produced a knife, sliced through the shrouds and Miller completed the remainder of his journey. He straightened his jacket, his face splendidly impassive, and lifted an enquiring elbow. Andrea, his face equally impassive, pointed down the clearing. Three of the other four parachutists had already landed safely: the fourth, Mallory, was just touching down.

Two minutes later, just as all six were coming together some little distance away from the most easterly landing flare, a shout announced the appearance of a young soldier running towards them from the edge of the forest. The parachutists' guns came up and were almost immediately lowered again: this was no occasion for guns. The soldier was trailing his by the barrel, excitedly waving his free hand in greeting. He was dressed in a faded and tattered near-uniform that had been pillaged from a variety of armies, had long flowing hair, a cast to his right eye and a straggling ginger beard. That he was welcoming them, was beyond doubt. Repeating some incomprehensible greeting over and over again, he shook hands all round and then a second time, the huge grin on his face reflecting his delight.

Within thirty seconds he'd been joined by at least a dozen others, all bearded, all dressed in the same nondescript uniforms, no two of which were alike, all in the same almost festive mood. Then, as at a signal almost, they fell silent and drew slightly apart as the man who was obviously their leader appeared from the edge of the forest. He bore little resemblance to his men. He differed in that he was completely shaven and wore a uniform, a British battledress, which appeared to be all of one piece. He differed in that he was not smiling: he had about him the air of one who was seldom if ever given to smiling. He also differed from the others in that he was a hawk-faced giant of a man, at least six feet four inches in height, carrying no fewer than four wicked-looking Bowie-type knives in his belt – an excess of armament that on another man might have looked incongruous or even comical but which on this man provoked no mirth at all. His face was dark and sombre and when he spoke it was in English, slow and stilted, but precise.

'Good evening.' He looked round questioningly. 'I am Captain Droshny.'

Mallory took a step forward. 'Captain Mallory.'

'Welcome to Yugoslavia, Captain Mallory – Partisan Yugoslavia.' Droshny nodded towards the dying flare, his face twitched in what may have been an attempt at a smile, but he made no move to shake hands. 'As you can see, we were expecting you.'

'Your lights were a great help,' Mallory acknowledged.

'Thank you.' Droshny stared away to the east, then back to Mallory, shaking his head. 'A pity about the plane.'

'All war is a pity.'

Droshny nodded. 'Come. Our headquarters is close by.'

No more was said. Droshny, leading, moved at once into the shelter of the forest. Mallory, behind him, was intrigued by the footprints, clearly visible in the now bright moonlight, left by Droshny in the deep snow. They were, thought Mallory, most peculiar. Each sole left three V-shaped marks, the heel one: the right-hand side of the leading V on the right sole had a clearly defined break in it. Unconsciously, Mallory filed away this little oddity in his mind. There was no reason why he should have done so other than that the Mallorys of this world always observe and record the unusual. It helps them to stay alive.

The slope steepened, the snow deepened and the pale moonlight filtered thinly down through the spreading, snow-laden branches of the pines. The light wind was from the east: the cold was intense. For almost ten minutes no voice was heard, then Droshny's came, softly but clearly and imperative in its staccato urgency.

'Be still.' He pointed dramatically upward. 'Be still! Listen!'

They stopped, looked upward and listened intently.

At least, Mallory and his men looked upward and listened intently, but the Yugoslavs had other things on their minds: swiftly, efficiently and simultaneously, without either spoken or gestured command being given, they rammed the muzzles of their machine-guns and rifles into the sides and backs of the six parachutists with a force and uncompromising authority that rendered any accompanying orders quite superfluous.

The six men reacted as might have been expected. Reynolds, Groves and Saunders, who were rather less accustomed to the vicissitudes of fate than their three older companions, registered a very similar combination of startled anger and open-mouthed astonishment. Mallory looked thoughtful. Miller lifted a quizzical eyebrow. Andrea, predictably, registered nothing at all: he was too busy exhibiting his usual reaction to physical violence.

His right hand, which he had instantly lifted halfway to his shoulder in an apparent token of surrender, clamped down on the barrel of the rifle of the guard to his right, forcing it away from him, while his left elbow jabbed viciously into the solar plexus of the guard to his left, who gasped in pain and staggered back a couple of paces. Andrea, with both hands now on the rifle of the other guard, wrenched it effortlessly free, lifted it high and brought the barrel down in one continuous blur of movement. The guard collapsed as if a bridge had fallen on him. The winded guard to the left, still bent and whooping in agony, was trying to line up his rifle when the butt of Andrea's rifle struck him in the face: he made a brief coughing sound and fell senseless to the forest floor.

It took all of the three seconds that this action had lasted for the Yugoslavs to release themselves from their momentary thrall of incredulity. Half-a-dozen soldiers flung themselves on Andrea, bearing him to the ground. In the furious, rolling struggle that followed, Andrea laid about him in his usual willing fashion, but when one of the Yugoslavs started pounding him on the head with the barrel of a pistol, Andrea opted for discretion and lay still. With two guns in his back and four hands on either arm Andrea was dragged to his feet: two of his captors already looked very much the worse for wear.

Droshny, his eyes bleak and bitter, came up to Andrea, unsheathed one of his knives and thrust its point against Andrea's throat with a force savage enough to break the skin and draw blood that trickled on to the gleaming blade. For a moment it seemed that Droshny would push the knife home to the hilt, then his eyes moved sideways and downwards to look at the two huddled men lying in the snow. He nodded to the nearest man.

'How are they?'

A young Yugoslav dropped to his knees, looked first at the man who had been struck by the rifle-barrel, touched his head briefly, examined the second man, then stood up. In the filtered moonlight, his face was unnaturally pale.

'Josef is dead. I think his neck is broken. And his brother – he's breathing – but his jaw seems to be –' The voice trailed away uncertainly.

Droshny transferred his gaze back to Andrea. His lips drew back, he smiled the way a wolf smiles and leaned a little harder on the knife.

'I *should* kill you now. I *will* kill you later.' He sheathed his knife, held up his clawed hands in front of Andrea's face, and shouted: 'Personally. With those hands.'

'With those hands.' Slowly, meaningly, Andrea examined the four pairs of hands pinioning his arms, then looked contemptuously at Droshny. He said: 'Your courage terrifies me.'

There was a brief and unbelieving silence. The three young sergeants stared at the tableau before them with faces reflecting various degrees of consternation and incredulity. Mallory and Miller looked on impassively. For a moment or two, Droshny looked as if he hadn't heard aright, then his face twisted in savage anger as he struck Andrea backhanded across the face. Immediately a trickle of blood appeared at the right-hand corner of Andrea's mouth but Andrea himself remained unmoving, his face without expression.

Droshny's eyes narrowed. Andrea smiled again, briefly. Droshny struck again, this time with the back of the other hand. The effect was as before, with the exception that this time the trickle of blood came from the left-hand corner of the mouth. Andrea smiled again but to look into his eyes was to look into an open grave. Droshny wheeled and walked away, then halted as he approached Mallory.

'You *are* the leader of those men, Captain Mallory?'

'I am.'

'You're a very — *silent* leader, Captain?'

'What am I to say to a man who turns his guns on his friends and allies?' Mallory looked at him dispassionately. 'I'll talk to your commanding officer, not to a madman.'

Droshny's face darkened. He stepped forward, his arm lifted to strike. Very quickly, but so smoothly and calmly that the movement seemed unhurried, and totally ignoring the two rifle-muzzles pressing into his side, Mallory lifted his Luger and pointed it at Droshny's face. The click of the Luger safety-catch being released came like a hammer-blow in the suddenly unnatural intensity of silence.

And unnatural intensity of silence there was. Except for one little movement, so slow as to be almost imperceptible, both Partisans and parachutists had frozen into a tableau that would have done credit to the frieze on an Ionic temple. The three sergeants, like most of the Partisans, registered astonished incredulity. The two men guarding Mallory looked at Droshny with questioning eyes. Droshny looked at Mallory as if he were mad. Andrea wasn't looking at anyone, while Miller wore that look of world-weary detachment which only he could achieve. But it was Miller who made that one little movement, a movement that now came to an end with his thumb resting on his Schmeisser's safety-release. After a moment or two he removed his thumb: there would come a time for Schmeissers, but this wasn't it.

Droshny lowered his hand in a curious slow-motion gesture and took two paces backwards. His face was still dark with anger, the dark eyes cruel and unforgiving, but he had himself well in hand. He said: 'Don't you know we have to take precautions? Till we are satisfied with your identity?'

'How should I know that?' Mallory nodded at Andrea. 'Next time you tell your men to take precautions with my friend here, you might warn them to stand a little farther back. He reacted the only way he knows how. And I know why.'

'You can explain later. Hand over your guns.'

'No.' Mallory returned the Luger to its holster.

'Are you mad? I can take them from you.'

'That's so,' Mallory said reasonably. 'But you'd have

370

to kill us first, wouldn't you? I don't think you'd remain a captain very long, my friend.'

Speculation replaced anger in Droshny's eyes. He gave a sharp order in Serbo-Croat and again his soldiers levelled their guns at Mallory and his five companions. But they made no attempt to remove the prisoners' guns. Droshny turned, gestured and started moving up the steeply-sloping forest floor again. Droshny wasn't, Mallory reflected, a man likely to be given to taking too many chances.

For twenty minutes they scrambled awkwardly up the slippery hillside. A voice called out from the darkness ahead and Droshny answered without breaking step. They passed by two sentries armed with machine-carbines and, within a minute, were in Droshny's HQ.

It was a moderately-sized military encampment – if a wide circle of rough-hewn adze-cut cabins could be called an encampment – set in one of those very deep hollows in the forest floor that Mallory was to find so characteristic of the Bosnian area. From the base of this hollow grew two concentric rings of pines far taller and more massive than anything to be found in western Europe, massive pines whose massive branches interlocked eighty to a hundred feet above the ground, forming a snow-shrouded canopy of such impenetrable density that there wasn't even a dusting of snow on the hard-packed earth of the camp compound: by the same token, the same canopy also effectively prevented any upward escape of light: there was no attempt at any black-out in several illuminated cabin windows and there were even some oil lamps suspended on outside hooks to illuminate the compound itself. Droshny stopped and said to Mallory:

'You come with me. The rest of you stay here.'

He led Mallory towards the door of the largest hut

371

in the compound. Andrea, unbidden, slipped off his pack and sat on it, and the others, after various degrees of hesitation, did the same. Their guards looked them over uncertainly, then withdrew to form a ragged but watchful semi-circle. Reynolds turned to Andrea, the expression on his face registering a complete absence of admiration and goodwill.

'You're crazy.' Reynolds's voice came in a low, furious whisper. 'Crazy as a loon. You could have got yourself killed. You could have got all of us killed. What are you, shell-shocked or something?'

Andrea did not reply. He lit one of his obnoxious cigars and regarded Reynolds with mild speculation or as near an approach to mildness as it was possible for him to achieve.

'Crazy isn't half the word for it.' Groves, if anything, was even more heated than Reynolds. 'Or didn't you *know* that was a Partisan you killed? Don't you *know* what that means? Don't you *know* people like that must always take precautions?'

Whether he knew or not, Andrea wasn't saying. He puffed at his cigar and transferred his peaceable gaze from Reynolds to Groves.

Miller said soothingly: 'Now, now. Don't be like that. Maybe Andrea *was* a mite hasty but –'

'God help us all,' Reynolds said fervently. He looked at his fellow-sergeants in despair. 'A thousand miles from home and help and saddled with a trigger-happy bunch of has-beens.' He turned back to Miller and mimicked: ' "Don't be like that." '

Miller assumed his wounded expression and looked away.

The room was large and bare and comfortless. The only concession to comfort was a pine fire crackling

372

in a rough hearth-place. The only furniture consisted of a cracked deal table, two chairs and a bench.

Those things Mallory noted only subconsciously. He didn't even register when he heard Droshny say: 'Captain Mallory. This is my commanding officer.' He seemed to be too busy staring at the man seated behind the table.

The man was short, stocky and in his mid-thirties. The deep lines around eyes and mouth could have been caused by weather or humour or both: just at that moment he was smiling slightly. He was dressed in the uniform of a captain in the German Army and wore an Iron Cross at his throat.

CHAPTER FOUR

Friday 0200–0330

The German captain leaned back in his chair and steepled his fingers. He had the air of a man enjoying the passing moment.

'Hauptmann Neufeld, Captain Mallory.' He looked at the places on Mallory's uniform where the missing insignia should have been. 'Or so I assume. You are surprised to see me?'

'I am *delighted* to meet you, Hauptmann Neufeld.' Mallory's astonishment had given way to the beginnings of a long, slow smile and now he sighed in deep relief. 'You just can't imagine *how* delighted.' Still smiling, he turned to Droshny, and at once the smile gave way to an expression of consternation. 'But who *are* you? Who is this man, Hauptmann Neufeld? Who in the name of God are those men out there? They must be – they must be – '

Droshny interrupted heavily: 'One of his men killed one of my men tonight.'

'What!' Neufeld, the smile now in turn vanishing from his face, stood abruptly: the backs of his legs sent his chair crashing to the floor. Mallory ignored him, looked again at Droshny.

'*Who are you?* For God's sake, tell me!'

Droshny said slowly: 'They call us Cetniks.'

'Cetniks? Cetniks? What on earth are Cetniks?'

'You will forgive me, Captain, if I smile in weary disbelief.' Neufeld was back on balance again, and his face had assumed a curiously wary impassivity, an expression in which only the eyes were alive: things, Mallory reflected, unpleasant things could happen to people misguided enough to underrate Hauptmann Neufeld. 'You? The leader of a special mission to this country and you haven't been well enough briefed to know that the Cetniks are our Yugoslav allies?'

'Allies? Ah!' Mallory's face cleared in understanding. 'Traitors? Yugoslav Quislings? Is that it?'

A subterranean rumble came from Droshny's throat and he moved towards Mallory, his right hand closing round the haft of a knife. Neufeld halted him with a sharp word of command and a brief downward-chopping motion of his hand.

'And what do you mean by a special mission?' Mallory demanded. He looked at each man in turn and smiled in wry understanding. 'Oh, we're special mission all right, but not in the way you think. At least, not in the way I think you think.'

'No?' Neufeld's eyebrow-raising technique, Mallory reflected, was almost on a par with Miller's. 'Then why do you think we were expecting you?'

'God only knows,' Mallory said frankly. 'We thought the Partisans were. That's why Droshny's man was killed, I'm afraid.'

'That's why Droshny's man – ' Neufeld regarded Mallory with his warily impassive eyes, picked up his chair and sat down thoughtfully. 'I think, perhaps, you had better explain yourself.'

As befitted a man who had adventured far and wide in the West End of London, Miller was in the habit of using a napkin when at meals, and he was using one now, tucked into the top of his tunic, as he sat on his rucksack in the compound of Neufeld's camp and fastidiously consumed some indeterminate goulash from a mess-tin. The three sergeants, seated nearby, briefly observed this spectacle with open disbelief, then resumed a low-voiced conversation. Andrea, puffing the inevitable nostril-wrinkling cigar and totally ignoring half-a-dozen watchful and understandably apprehensive guards, strolled unconcernedly about the compound, poisoning the air wherever he went. Clearly through the frozen night air came the distant sound of someone singing a low-voiced accompaniment to what appeared to be guitar music. As Andrea completed his circuit of the compound, Miller looked up and nodded in the direction of the music.

'Who's the soloist?'

Andrea shrugged. 'Radio, maybe.'

'They want to buy a new radio. My trained ear – '

'Listen.' Reynolds's interrupting whisper was tense and urgent. 'We've been talking.'

Miller performed some fancy work with his napkin and said kindly: 'Don't. Think of the grieving mothers and sweethearts you'd leave behind you.'

'What do you mean?'

'About making a break for it is what I mean,' Miller said. 'Some other time, perhaps?'

'Why not now?' Groves was belligerent. 'They're off guard – '

'Are they now.' Miller sighed. 'So young, so young. Take another look. You don't think Andrea *likes* exercise, do you?'

The three sergeants took another look, furtively, surreptitiously, then glanced interrogatively at Andrea.

'Five dark windows,' Andrea said. 'Behind them, five dark men. With five dark machine-guns.'

Reynolds nodded and looked away.

*

'Well, now.' Neufeld, Mallory noted, had a great propensity for steepling his fingers: Mallory had once known a hanging judge with exactly the same propensity. 'This *is* a most remarkably odd story you have to tell us, my dear Captain Mallory.'

'It is,' Mallory agreed. 'It would have to be, wouldn't it, to account for the remarkably odd position in which we find ourselves at this moment.'

'A point, a point.' Slowly, deliberately, Neufeld ticked off other points on his fingers. 'You have for some months, you claim, been running a penicillin and drug-running ring in the south of Italy. As an Allied liaison officer you found no difficulty in obtaining supplies from American Army and Air Force bases.'

'We found a little difficulty towards the end,' Mallory admitted.

'I'm coming to that. Those supplies, you also claim, were funnelled through to the Wehrmacht.'

'I wish you wouldn't keep using the word "claim" in that tone of voice,' Mallory said irritably. 'Check with Field-Marshal Kesselring's Chief of Military Intelligence in Padua.'

'With pleasure.' Neufeld picked up a phone, spoke briefly in German and replaced the receiver.

Mallory said in surprise: 'You have a direct line to the outside world? From *this* place?'

'I have a direct line to a hut fifty yards away where we have a very powerful radio transmitter. So. You further claim that you were caught, court-martialled and were awaiting the confirmation of your death sentence. Right?'

'If your espionage system in Italy is all we hear it is, you'll know about it tomorrow,' Mallory said drily.

'Quite, quite. You then broke free, killed your

guards and overheard agents in the briefing room being briefed on a mission to Bosnia.' He did some more finger-steepling. 'You may be telling the truth at that. What did you say their mission was?'

'I didn't say. I didn't really pay attention. It had something to do with locating missing British mission leaders and trying to break your espionage set-up. I'm not sure. We had more important things to think about.'

'I'm sure you had,' Neufeld said distastefully. 'Such as your skins. What happened to your epaulettes, Captain? The medal ribbons? The buttons?'

'You've obviously never attended a British court-martial, Hauptmann Neufeld.'

Neufeld said mildly: 'You could have ripped them off yourself.'

'And then, I suppose, emptied three-quarters of the fuel from the tanks before we stole the plane?'

'Your tanks were only a quarter full?' Mallory nodded. 'And your plane crashed without catching fire?'

'We didn't mean to crash,' Mallory said in a weary patience. 'We meant to land. But we were out of fuel – and, as we know now, at the wrong place.'

Neufeld said absently: 'Whenever the Partisans put up landing flares we try a few ourselves – and we knew that you – or someone – were coming. No petrol, eh?' Again Neufeld spoke briefly on the telephone, then turned back to Mallory. 'All very satisfactory – if true. There just remains to explain the death of Captain Droshny's man here.'

'I'm sorry about that. It was a ghastly blunder. But surely you can understand. The last thing we wanted was to land among you, to make direct contact with you. We've heard what happens to British parachutists dropping over German territory.'

Neufeld steepled his fingers again. 'There is a state of war. Proceed.'

'Our intention was to land in Partisan territory, slip across the lines and give ourselves up. When Droshny turned his guns on us we thought the Partisans were on to us, that they had been notified that we'd stolen the plane. And that could mean only one thing for us.'

'Wait outside. Captain Droshny and I will join you in a moment.'

Mallory left. Andrea, Miller and the three sergeants were sitting patiently on their rucksacks. From the distance there still came the sound of distant music. For a moment Mallory cocked his head to listen to it, then walked across to join the others. Miller patted his lips delicately with his napkin and looked up at Mallory.

'Had a cosy chat?'

'I spun him a yarn. The one we talked about in the plane.' He looked at the three sergeants. 'Any of you speak German?'

All three shook their heads.

'Fine. Forget you speak English too. If you're questioned you know nothing.'

'If I'm not questioned,' Reynolds said bitterly, 'I still don't know anything.'

'All the better,' Mallory said encouragingly. 'Then you can never tell anything, can you?'

He broke off and turned round as Neufeld and Droshny appeared in the doorway. Neufeld advanced and said: 'While we're waiting for some confirmation, a little food and wine, perhaps.' As Mallory had done, he cocked his head and listened to the singing. 'But first of all, you must meet our minstrel boy.'

'We'll settle for just the food and wine,' Andrea said.

'Your priorities are wrong. You'll see. Come.'

The dining-hall, if it could be dignified by such a name, was about forty yards away. Neufeld opened the door to reveal a crude and makeshift hut with two rickety trestle tables and four benches set on the earthen floor. At the far end of the room the inevitable pine fire burnt in the inevitable stone hearth-place. Close to the fire, at the end of the farther table, three men – obviously, from their high-collared coats and guns propped by their sides, some kind of temporarily off-duty guards – were drinking coffee and listening to the quiet singing coming from a figure seated on the ground by the fire.

The singer was dressed in a tattered anorak type jacket, an even more incredibly tattered pair of trousers and a pair of knee boots that gaped open at almost every possible seam. There was little to be seen of his face other than a mass of dark hair and a large pair of rimmed dark spectacles.

Beside him, apparently asleep with her head on his shoulder, sat a girl. She was clad in a high-collared British Army greatcoat in an advanced state of dilapidation, so long that it completely covered her tucked-in legs. The uncombed platinum hair spread over her shoulders would have done justice to any Scandinavian, but the broad cheekbones, dark eyebrows and long dark lashes lowered over very pale cheeks were unmistakably Slavonic.

Neufeld advanced across the room and stopped by the fireside. He bent over the singer and said: 'Petar, I want you to meet some friends.'

Petar lowered his guitar, looked up, then turned and touched the girl on the arm. Instantly, the girl's head lifted and her eyes, great dark sooty eyes, opened wide. She had the look, almost, of a hunted animal. She glanced around her, almost wildly, then jumped

380

quickly to her feet, dwarfed by the greatcoat which reached almost to her ankles, then reached down to help the guitarist to his feet. As he did so, he stumbled: he was obviously blind.

'This is Maria,' Neufeld said. 'Maria, this is Captain Mallory.'

'Captain Mallory.' Her voice was soft and a little husky: she spoke in almost accentless English. 'You are English, Captain Mallory?'

It was hardly, Mallory thought, the time or the place for proclaiming his New Zealand ancestry. He smiled. 'Well, sort of.'

Maria smiled in turn. 'I've always wanted to meet an Englishman.' She stepped forward towards Mallory's outstretched hand, brushed it aside and struck him, open-handed and with all her strength, across the face.

'Maria!' Neufeld stared at her. 'He's on our side.'

'An Englishman *and* a traitor!' She lifted her hand again but the swinging arm was suddenly arrested in Andrea's grip. She struggled briefly, futilely, then subsided, dark eyes glowing in an angry face. Andrea lifted his free hand and rubbed his own cheek in fond recollection.

He said admiringly: 'By heavens, she reminds me of my own Maria,' then grinned at Mallory. 'Very handy with their hands, those Yugoslavs.'

Mallory rubbed his cheek ruefully with his hand and turned to Neufeld. 'Perhaps Petar – that's his name – '

'No.' Neufeld shook his head definitely. 'Later. Let's eat now.' He led the way across to the table at the far end of the room, gestured the others to seats, sat down himself and went on: 'I'm sorry. That was my fault. I should have known better.'

Miller said delicately: 'Is she – um – all right?'

381

'A wild animal, you think?'

'She'd make a rather dangerous pet, wouldn't you say?'

'She's a graduate of the University of Belgrade. Languages. With honours, I'm told. Some time after graduation she returned to her home in the Bosnian mountains. She found her parents and two small brothers butchered. She – well, she's been like this ever since.'

Mallory shifted in his seat and looked at the girl. Her eyes, dark and unmoving and unwinking, were fixed on him and their expression was less than encouraging. Mallory turned back to Neufeld.

'Who did it? To her parents, I mean.'

'The Partisans,' Droshny said savagely. 'Damn their black souls, the Partisans. Maria's people were our people. Cetniks.'

'And the singer?' Mallory said.

'Her elder brother.' Neufeld shook his head. 'Blind from birth. Wherever she goes, she leads him by the hand. She is his eyes: she is his life.'

They sat in silence until food and wine were brought in. If an army marched on its stomach, Mallory thought, this one wasn't going to get very far: he had heard that the food situation with the Partisans was close to desperate, but, if this were a representative sample, the Cetniks and Germans appeared to be in little better case. Unenthusiastically, he spooned – it would have been impossible to use a fork – a little of the greyish stew, a stew in which little oddments of indefinable meat floated forlornly in a mushy gravy of obscure origin, glanced across at Andrea and marvelled at the gastronomic fortitude that lay behind the already almost empty plate. Miller averted his eyes from the plate before him and delicately sipped the rough red

382

wine. The three sergeants, so far, hadn't even looked at their food: they were too occupied in looking at the girl by the fireside. Neufeld saw their interest, and smiled.

'I do agree, gentlemen, that I've never seen a more beautiful girl and heaven knows what she'd look like if she had a wash. But she's not for you, gentlemen. She's not for any man. She's wed already.' He looked at the questioning faces and shook his head. 'Not to any man. To an ideal – if you can call death an ideal. The death of the Partisans.'

'Charming,' Miller murmured. There was no other comment, for there was none to make. They ate in silence broken only by the soft singing from the fireside, the voice was melodious enough, but the guitar sounded sadly out of tune. Andrea pushed away his empty plate, looked irritably at the blind musician and turned to Neufeld.

'What's that he's singing?'

'An old Bosnian love song, I've been told. Very old and very sad. In English you have it too.' He snapped his fingers. 'Yes, that's it. "The girl I left behind me".'

'Tell him to sing something else,' Andrea muttered. Neufeld looked at him, puzzled, then looked away as a German sergeant entered and bent to whisper in his ear. Neufeld nodded and the sergeant left.

'So.' Neufeld was thoughtful. 'A radio report from the patrol that found your plane. The tanks *were* empty. I hardly think we need await confirmation from Padua, do you, Captain Mallory?'

'I don't understand.'

'No matter. Tell me, have you ever heard of a General Vukalovic?'

'General which?'

'Vukalovic.'

'He's not on our side,' Miller said positively. 'Not with a name like that.'

'You must be the only people in Yugoslavia who *don't* know him. Everybody else does. Partisans, Cetniks, Germans, Bulgarians, everyone. He is one of their national heroes.'

'Pass the wine,' Andrea said.

'You'd do better to listen.' Neufeld's tone was sharp. 'Vukalovic commands almost a division of Partisan infantry who have been trapped in a loop of the Neretva river for almost three months. Like the men he leads. Vukalovic is insane. They have no shelter, none. They are short of weapons, have almost no ammunition left and are close to starvation. Their army is dressed in rags. They are finished.'

'Then why don't they escape?' Mallory asked.

'Escape is impossible. The precipices of the Neretva cut them off to the east. To the north and west are impenetrable mountains. The only conceivable way out is to the south, over the bridge at Neretva. And we have two armoured divisions waiting there.'

'No gorges?' Mallory asked. 'No passes through the mountains?'

'Two. Blocked by our best combat troops.'

'Then why don't they give up?' Mallory asked reasonably. 'Has no one told them the rules of war?'

'They're insane, I tell you,' Neufeld said. 'Quite insane.'

At that precise moment in time, Vukalovic and his Partisans were proving to some other Germans just how extraordinary their degree of insanity was.

The Western Gap was a narrow, tortuous, boulder-strewn and precipitously walled gorge that afforded the only passage through the impassable mountains that shut off the Zenica Cage to the east. For three months now German infantry units – units which had recently included an increasing number of highly-skilled Alpine troops – had been trying to force the pass: for three months they had been bloodily repulsed. But the Germans never gave up trying and on this intensely cold night of fitful moonlight and gently, intermittently falling snow, they were trying again.

The Germans carried out their attack with the coldly professional skill and economy of movement born of long and harsh experience. They advanced up the gorge in three fairly even and judiciously spaced lines: the combination of white snow suits, of the utilization of every scrap of cover and of confining their brief forward rushes to those moments when the moon was temporarily obscured made it almost impossible to see them. There was, however, no difficulty in locating them: they had obviously ammunition and to spare for machine-pistols and rifles alike and the fire-flashes from those muzzles were almost continuous. Almost as continuous, but some distance behind them, the sharp flat cracks of fixed mountain pieces pinpointed the source of the creeping artillery barrage that preceded the Germans up the boulder-strewn slope of that narrow defile.

The Yugoslav Partisans waited at the head of the gorge, entrenched behind a redoubt of boulders, hastily piled stones and splintered tree-trunks that had been shattered by German artillery fire. Although the snow was deep and the east wind full of little knives, few of the Partisans wore greatcoats. They were clad in an extraordinary variety of uniforms, uniforms that had belonged in the past to members of British, German, Italian, Bulgarian and Yugoslav armies: the one identifying feature that all had in common was a red star sewn on to the right-hand side of their forage caps. The uniforms, for the most part, were thin and tattered, offering little protection against the piercing cold, so that the men shivered almost continuously. An astonishing proportion of them appeared to be wounded: there were splinted legs, arms in slings and bandaged heads everywhere. But the most common characteristic among this rag-tag collection of defenders was their pinched and emaciated faces, faces where the deeply etched lines of starvation were matched only by the calm and absolute determination of men who have no longer anything to lose.

Near the centre of the group of defenders, two men stood in the shelter of the thick bole of one of the few pines still left standing. The silvered black hair, the deeply trenched – and now even more exhausted – face of General Vukalovic was unmistakable. But the dark eyes glowed as brightly as ever as he bent forward to accept a cigarette and light from the officer sharing his shelter, a swarthy, hook-nosed man with at least half of his black hair concealed under a blood-stained bandage. Vukalovic smiled.

'Of course I'm insane, my dear Stephan. You're insane – or you would have abandoned this position weeks ago. We're all insane. Didn't you know?'

'I know this.' Major Stephan rubbed the back of his hand across a week-old growth of beard. 'Your parachute landing, an hour ago. That was insane. Why, you – ' He broke off as a rifle fired only feet away, moved to where a thin youngster, not more than seventeen years of age, was peering down into the white gloom of the gorge over the sights of a Lee-Enfield. 'Did you get him?'

The boy twisted and looked up. A child. Vukalovic thought despairingly, no more than a child: he should still have been at school. The boy said: 'I'm not sure, sir.'

'How many shells have you left? Count them.'

'I don't have to. Seven.'

'Don't fire till you are sure.' Stephan turned back to Vukalovic. 'God above, General, you were almost blown into German hands.'

'I'd have been worse off without the parachute,' Vukalovic said mildly.

'There's so little time.' Stephan struck a clenched fist against a palm. 'So little time left. You were crazy to come back. They need you far more – ' He stopped abruptly, listened for a fraction of a second, threw himself at Vukalovic and brought them both crashing heavily to the ground as a whining mortar shell buried itself among loose rocks a few feet away, exploding on impact. Close by, a man screamed in agony. A second mortar shell landed, then a third and a fourth, all within thirty feet of one another.

'They've got the range now, damn them.' Stephan rose quickly to his feet and peered down the gorge. For long seconds he could see nothing, for a band of dark cloud had crossed the face of the moon: then the moon broke through and he could see the enemy all too clearly. Because of some almost certainly prearranged signal, they were no longer making any attempt to seek cover: they were pounding straight up the slope with all the speed they could muster, machine-carbines and rifles at the ready in their hands – and as soon as the moon broke through they squeezed the triggers of those guns. Stephan threw himself behind the shelter of a boulder.

'Now!' he shouted. 'Now!'

The first ragged Partisan fusillade lasted for only a

few seconds, then a black shadow fell over the valley. The firing ceased.

'Keep firing,' Vukalovic shouted. 'Don't stop now. They're closing in.' He loosed off a burst from his own machine-pistol and said to Stephan, 'They know what they are about, our friends down there.'

'They should.' Stephan armed a stick grenade and spun it down the hill. 'Look at all the practice we've given them.'

The moon broke through again. The leading German infantry were no more than twenty-five yards away. Both sides exchanged hand-grenades, fired at point-blank range. Some German soldiers fell, but many more came on, flinging themselves on the redoubt. Matters became temporarily confused. Here and there bitter hand-to-hand fighting developed. Men shouted at each other, cursed each other, killed each other. But the redoubt remained unbroken. Suddenly, dark heavy clouds again rolled over the moon, darkness flooded the gorge and everything slowly fell quiet. In the distance the thunder of artillery and mortar fire fell away to a muted rumble, then finally died.

'A trap?' Vukalovic said softly to Stephan. 'You think they will come again?'

'Not tonight.' Stephan was positive. 'They're brave men, but – '

'But not insane?'

'But not insane.'

Blood poured down over Stephan's face from a reopened wound in his face, but he was smiling. He rose to his feet and turned as a burly sergeant came up and delivered a sketchy salute.

'They've gone, Major. We lost seven of ours this time, and fourteen wounded.'

'Set pickets two hundred metres down,' Stephan

said. He turned to Vukalovic. 'You heard, sir? Seven dead. Fourteen hurt.'

'Leaving how many?'

'Two hundred. Perhaps two hundred and five.'

'Out of four hundred.' Vukalovic's mouth twisted. 'Dear God, out of four hundred.'

'And sixty of those are wounded.'

'At least you can get them down to the hospital now.'

'There is no hospital,' Stephan said heavily. 'I didn't have time to tell you. It was bombed this morning. Both doctors killed. All our medical supplies – poof! Like that.'

'Gone? All gone?' Vukalovic paused for a long moment. 'I'll have some sent up from HQ. The walking wounded can make their own way to HQ.'

'The wounded won't leave, sir. Not any more.'

Vukalovic nodded in understanding and went on: 'How much ammunition?'

'Two days. Three, if we're careful.'

'Sixty wounded.' Vukalovic shook his head in slow disbelief. 'No medical help whatsoever for them. Ammunition almost gone. No food. No shelter. And they won't leave. Are they insane, too?'

'Yes, sir.'

'I'm going down to the river,' Vukalovic said. 'To see Colonel Lazlo at HQ.'

'Yes, sir.' Stephan smiled faintly. 'I doubt if you'll find his mental equilibrium any better than mine.'

'I don't suppose I will,' Vukalovic said.

Stephan saluted and turned away, mopping blood from his face, walked a few short swaying steps then knelt down to comfort a badly wounded man. Vukalovic looked after him expressionlessly, shaking his head: then he, too, turned and left.

*

Mallory finished his meal and lit a cigarette. He said, 'So what's going to happen to the Partisans in the Zenica Cage, as you call it?'

'They're going to break out,' Neufeld said. 'At least, they're going to try to.'

'But you've said yourself that's impossible.'

'Nothing is too impossible for those mad Partisans to try. I wish to heaven,' Neufeld said bitterly, 'that we were fighting a normal war against normal people, like the British or Americans. Anyway, we've had information – reliable information – that an attempted break-out is imminent. Trouble is, there are those two passes – they might even try to force the bridge at Neretva – and we don't know where the break-out is coming.'

'This is very interesting.' Andrea looked sourly at the blind musician who was still giving his rendering of the same old Bosnian love-song. 'Can we get some sleep now?'

'Not tonight, I'm afraid.' Neufeld exchanged a smile with Droshny. 'You are going to find out for us where this break-out is coming.'

'We are?' Miller drained his glass and reached for the bottle. 'Infectious stuff, this insanity.'

Neufeld might not have heard him. 'Partisan HQ is about ten kilometres from here. You are going to report there as the bona-fide British mission that has lost its way. Then, when you've found out their plans, you tell them that you are going to their main HQ at Drvar, which of course, you don't. You come back here instead. What could be simpler?'

'Miller's right,' Mallory said with conviction. 'You *are* mad.'

'I'm beginning to think there's altogether too much talk of this madness.' Neufeld smiled. 'You would prefer, perhaps, that Captain Droshny here turned you over to his men. I assure you, they are most unhappy about their – ah – late comrade.'

'You can't ask us to do this!' Mallory was hard-faced in anger. 'The Partisans are bound to get a radio message about us. Sooner or later. And then – well, you know what then. You just can't ask this of us.'

'I can and I will.' Neufeld looked at Mallory and his five companions without enthusiasm. 'It so happens that I don't care for dope-peddlers and drug-runners.'

'I don't think your opinion will carry much weight in certain circles,' Mallory said.

'And that means?'

'Kesselring's Director of Military Intelligence isn't going to like this at all.'

'If you don't come back, they'll never know. If you do –' Neufeld smiled and touched the Iron Cross at his throat – 'they'll probably give me an oak leaf to this.'

'Likeable type, isn't he?' Miller said to no one in particular.

'Come then.' Neufeld rose from the table. 'Petar?'

The blind singer nodded, slung his guitar over his shoulder and rose to his feet, his sister rising with him.

'What's this, then?' Mallory asked.

'Guides.'

'*Those* two?'

'Well,' Neufeld said reasonably, 'you can't very well find your own way there, can you? Petar and his sister – well, his sister – know Bosnia better than the foxes.'

'But won't the Partisans – ' Mallory began, but Neufeld interrupted.

391

'You don't know your Bosnia. These two wander wherever they like and no one will turn them from their door. The Bosnians believe, and God knows with sufficient reason, that they are accursed and have the evil eye on them. This is a land of superstition, Captain Mallory.'

'But — but how will they know where to take us?'

'They'll know.' Neufeld nodded to Droshny, who talked rapidly to Maria in Serbo-Croat: she in turn spoke to Petar, who made some strange noises in his throat.

'That's an odd language,' Miller observed.

'He's got a speech impediment,' Neufeld said shortly. 'He was born with it. He can sing, but not talk — it's not unknown. Do you wonder people think they are cursed?' He turned to Mallory. 'Wait outside with your men.'

Mallory nodded, gestured to the others to precede him. Neufeld, he noted, was immediately engaged in a short, low-voiced discussion with Droshny, who nodded, summoned one of his Cetniks and dispatched him on some errand. Once outside, Mallory moved with Andrea slightly apart from the others and murmured something in his ear, inaudible to all but Andrea, whose nodded acquiescence was almost imperceptible.

Neufeld and Droshny emerged from the hut, followed by Maria who was leading Petar by the hand. As they approached Mallory's group, Andrea walked casually towards them, smoking the inevitable noxious cigar. He planted himself in front of a puzzled Neufeld and arrogantly blew smoke into his face.

'I don't think I care for you very much, Hauptmann Neufeld,' Andrea announced. He looked at Droshny. 'Nor for the cutlery salesman here.'

Neufeld's face immediately darkened, became tight

392

in anger. But he brought himself quickly under control and said with restraint: 'Your opinion of me is of no concern to me.' He nodded to Droshny. 'But do not cross Captain Droshny's path, my friend. He is a Bosnian and a proud one – and the best man in the Balkans with a knife.'

'The best man – ' Andrea broke off with a roar of laughter, and blew smoke into Droshny's face. 'A knife-grinder in a comic opera.'

Droshny's disbelief was total but of brief duration. He bared his teeth in a fashion that would have done justice to any Bosnian wolf, swept a wickedly-curved knife from his belt and threw himself on Andrea, the gleaming blade hooking viciously upwards, but Andrea, whose prudence was exceeded only by the extraordinary speed with which he could move his vast bulk, was no longer there when the knife arrived. But his hand was. It caught Droshny's knife wrist as it flashed upwards and almost at once the two big men crashed heavily to the ground, rolling over and over in the snow while they fought for possession of the knife.

So unexpectedly, so wholly incredible the speed with which the fight had developed from nowhere that, for a few seconds, no one moved. The three young sergeants, Neufeld and the Cetniks registered nothing but utter astonishment. Mallory, who was standing close behind the wide-eyed girl, rubbed his chin thoughtfully while Miller, delicately tapping the ash off the end of his cigarette, regarded the scene with a sort of weary interest.

Almost at the same instant, Reynolds, Groves and two Cetniks flung themselves upon the struggling pair on the ground and tried to pull them apart. Not until Saunders and Neufeld lent a hand did they succeed.

393

Droshny and Andrea were pulled to their feet, the former with contorted face and hatred in his eyes, Andrea calmly resuming the smoking of the cigar which he'd somehow picked up after they had been separated.

'You madman!' Reynolds said savagely to Andrea. 'You crazy maniac. You – you're a bloody psychopath. You'll get us all killed.'

'That wouldn't surprise me at all,' Neufeld said thoughtfully. 'Come. Let us have no more of this foolishness.'

He led the way from the compound, and as he did so they were joined by a group of half-a-dozen Cetniks, whose apparent leader was the youth with the straggling ginger beard and cast to his eye, the first of the Cetniks to greet them when they had landed.

'Who are they and what are they for?' Mallory demanded of Neufeld. 'They're not coming with us.'

'Escort,' Neufeld explained. 'For the first seven kilometres only.'

'Escorts? What would we want with escorts? We're in no danger from you, nor, according to what you say, will we be from the Yugoslav Partisans.'

'We're not worried about you,' Neufeld said drily. 'We're worried about the vehicle that is going to take you most of the way there. Vehicles are very few and very precious in this part of Bosnia – and there are many Partisan patrols about.'

Twenty minutes later, in a now moonless night and with snow falling, they reached a road, a road which was little more than a winding track running through a forested valley floor. Waiting for them there was one of the strangest four-wheeled contraptions Mallory or his companions had ever seen, an incredibly ancient and battered truck which at first sight, from the vast clouds of smoke emanating from it, appeared to be on fire. It was, in fact, a very much pre-war wood-burning truck, of a type at one time common in the Balkans. Miller regarded the smoke-shrouded truck in astonishment and turned to Neufeld.

'You call this a vehicle?'

'You call it what you like. Unless you'd rather walk.'

'Ten kilometres? I'll take my chance on asphyxiation.' Miller climbed in, followed by the others, till only Neufeld and Droshny remained outside.

Neufeld said: 'I shall expect you back before noon.'

'If we ever come back,' Mallory said. 'If a radio message has come through – '

'You can't make an omelette without breaking eggs,' Neufeld said indifferently.

With a great rattling and shaking and emission of smoke and steam, all accompanied by much red-eyed coughing from the canvas-covered rear, the truck jerked uncertainly into motion and moved off slowly along the valley floor, Neufeld and Droshny gazing after it. Neufeld shook his head. 'Such clever little men.'

'Such *very* clever little men,' Droshny agreed. 'But I want the big one, Captain.'

Neufeld clapped him on the shoulder. 'You shall have him, my friend. Well, they're out of sight. Time for you to go.'

Droshny nodded and whistled shrilly between his fingers. There came the distant whirr of an engine starter, and soon an elderly Fiat emerged from behind a clump of pines and approached along the hard-packed snow of the road, its chains clanking violently, and stopped beside the two men. Droshny climbed into the front passenger seat and the Fiat moved off in the wake of the truck.

CHAPTER FIVE

Friday 0330–0500

For the fourteen people jammed on the narrow side benches under the canvas-hooped roof, the journey could hardly be called pleasurable. There were no cushions on the seats just as there appeared to be a total absence of springs on the vehicle, and the torn and badly fitting hood admitted large quantities of icy night air and eye-smarting smoke in about equal proportions. At least, Mallory thought, it all helped considerably to keep them awake.

Andrea was sitting directly opposite him, seemingly oblivious of the thick choking atmosphere inside the truck, a fact hardly surprising considering that the penetrating power and the pungency of the smoke from the truck was of a lower order altogether than that emanating from the black cheroot clamped between Andrea's teeth. Andrea glanced idly across and caught Mallory's eye. Mallory nodded once, a millimetric motion of the head that would have gone unremarked by even the most suspicious. Andrea dropped his eyes until his gaze rested on Mallory's right hand, lying loosely of his knee. Mallory sat back and sighed, and as he did his right hand slipped until his thumb was pointing directly at the floor. Andrea puffed out another Vesuvian cloud of acrid smoke and looked away indifferently.

For some kilometres the smoke-enshrouded truck clattered and screeched its way along the valley floor, then swung off to the left on to an even narrower track, and began to climb. Less than two minutes later, with Droshny sitting impassively in the front passenger seat, the pursuing Fiat made a similar turn off.

The slope was now so steep and the spinning driving wheels losing so much traction on the frozen surface of the track that the ancient wood-burning truck was reduced to little more than walking pace. Inside the truck, Andrea and Mallory were as watchful as ever, but Miller and the three sergeants seemed to be dozing off, whether through exhaustion or incipient asphyxiation it was difficult to say. Maria and Petar, hand in hand, appeared to be asleep. The Cetniks, on the other hand, could hardly have been more wide awake, and were making it clear for the first time that the rents and holes in the canvas cover had not been caused by accident: Droshny's six men were now kneeling on the benches with the muzzles of their machine-pistols thrust through the apertures in the canvas. It was clear that the truck was now moving into Partisan territory, or, at least, what passed for no-man's-land in that wild and rugged territory.

The Cetnik farthest forward in the truck suddenly withdrew his face from a gap in the canvas and rapped the butt of his gun against the driver's cab. The truck wheezed to a grateful halt, the ginger-bearded Cetnik jumped down, checked swiftly for any signs of ambush, then gestured the others to disembark, the repeatedly urgent movements of his hand making it clear that he was less than enamoured of the idea of hanging around that place for a moment longer than necessity demanded. One by one Mallory and his companions jumped down on to the frozen snow. Reynolds guided the blind singer down to the ground, then reached up a hand to help Maria as she clambered over the tailboard.

Wordlessly, she struck his hand aside and leapt nimbly to the ground: Reynolds stared at her in hurt astonishment. The truck, Mallory observed, had stopped outside a small clearing in the forest. Backing and filling and issuing denser clouds of smoke than ever, it used this space to turn around in a remarkably short space of time and clanked its way off down the forest path at a considerably higher speed than it had made the ascent. The Cetniks gazed impassively from the back of the departing truck, made no gesture of farewell.

Maria took Petar's hand, looked coldly at Mallory, jerked her head and set off up a tiny footpath leading at right-angles from the track. Mallory shrugged and set off, followed by the three sergeants. For a moment or two, Andrea and Miller remained where they were, gazing thoughtfully at the corner round which the truck had just disappeared. Then they, too, set off, talking in low tones to each other.

The ancient wood-burning truck did not maintain its initial impetus for any lengthy period of time. Less than four hundred yards after rounding the corner which blocked it from the view of Mallory and his companions it braked to a halt. Two Cetniks, the ginger-bearded leader of the escort and another black-bearded man, jumped over the tailboard and moved at once into the protective covering of the forest. The truck rattled off once more, its belching smoke hanging heavily in the freezing night air.

A kilometre farther down the track, an almost identical scene was taking place. The Fiat slid to a halt, Droshny scrambled from the passenger's seat and vanished among the pines. The Fiat reversed quickly and moved off down the track.

398

The track up through the heavily wooded slope was very narrow, very winding: the snow was no longer hard-packed, but soft and deep and making for very hard going. The moon was quite gone now, the snow, gusted into their faces by the east wind, was becoming steadily heavier and the cold was intense. The path frequently arrived at a V-shaped branch but Maria, in the lead with her brother, never hesitated: she knew, or appeared to know, exactly where she was going. Several times she slipped in the deep snow, on the last occasion so heavily that she brought her brother down with her. When it happened yet again, Reynolds moved forward and took the girl by the arm to help her. She struck out savagely and drew her arm away. Reynolds stared at her in astonishment, then turned to Mallory.

'What the devil's the matter with – I mean, I was only trying to help – '

'Leave her alone,' Mallory said. 'You're one of them.'

'I'm one of – '

'You're wearing a British uniform. That's all the poor kid understands. Leave her be.'

Reynolds shook his head uncomprehendingly. He hitched his pack more securely on his shoulders, glanced back down the trail, made to move on, then glanced backwards again. He caught Mallory by the arm and pointed.

Andrea had already fallen thirty yards behind. Weighed down by his rucksack and Schmeisser and weight of years, he was very obviously making heavy weather of the climb and was falling steadily behind by the second. At a gesture and word from Mallory the rest of the party halted and peered back down through the driving snow, waiting for Andrea to make up on them. By this time Andrea was beginning to stumble almost drunkenly and clutched at his right side as if in pain. Reynolds looked at Groves: they both looked at Saunders: all three slowly shook their heads. Andrea came up with them and a spasm of pain flickered across his face.

'I'm sorry.' The voice was gasping and hoarse. 'I'll be all right in a moment.'

Saunders hesitated, then advanced towards Andrea. He smiled apologetically, then reached out a hand to indicate the rucksack and Schmeisser.

'Come on, Dad. Hand them over.'

For the minutest fraction of a second a flicker of menace, more imagined than seen, touched Andrea's face, then he shrugged off his rucksack and wearily handed it over. Saunders accepted it and tentatively indicated the Schmeisser.

'Thanks.' Andrea smiled wanly. 'But I'd feel lost without it.'

Uncertainly, they resumed their climb, looking back frequently to check on Andrea's progress. Their doubts were well-founded. Within thirty seconds Andrea had stopped, his eyes screwed up and bent almost double in pain. He said, gaspingly: 'I must rest . . . Go on. I'll catch up with you.'

Miller said solicitously: 'I'll stay with you.'

'I don't need anybody to stay with me,' Andrea said surlily. 'I can look after myself.'

Miller said nothing. He looked at Mallory and jerked his head in an uphill direction. Mallory nodded, once, and gestured to the girl. Reluctantly, they moved off, leaving Andrea and Miller behind. Twice, Reynolds looked back over his shoulder, his expression an odd mixture of worry and exasperation: then he shrugged his shoulders and bent his back to the hill.

Andrea, scowling blackly and still clutching his ribs, remained bent double until the last of the party had rounded the nearest uphill corner, then straightened effortlessly, tested the wind with a wetted forefinger, established that it was moving up-trail, produced a cigar, lit it and puffed in deep and obvious contentment. His recovery was quite astonishing, but it didn't appear to astonish Miller, who grinned and nodded downhill. Andrea grinned in return, made a courteous gesture of precedence.

Thirty yards down-trail, at a position which gave them an uninterrupted view of almost a hundred yards of the track below them they moved into the cover of the bole of a giant pine. For about two minutes they stood there, staring downhill and listening intently, then suddenly Andrea nodded, stooped and carefully laid his cigar in a sheltered dried patch of ground behind the bole of the pine.

They exchanged no words: there was need of none. Miller crawled round to the downhill-facing front of the pine and carefully arranged himself in a spread-eagled position in the deep snow, both arms outflung, his apparently sightless face turned up to the falling snow. Behind the pine, Andrea reversed his grip on his Schmeisser, holding it by the barrel, produced a knife from the recesses of his clothing and stuck it in his belt. Both men remained as motionless as if they had died there and frozen solid over the long and bitter Yugoslav winter.

Probably because his spreadeagled form was sunk so deeply in the soft snow as to conceal most of his body, Miller saw the two Cetniks coming quite some time before they saw him. At first they were no more than two shapeless and vaguely ghostlike forms gradually materializing from the falling snow: as they drew nearer, he identified them as the Cetnik escort leader and one of his men.

They were less than thirty yards away before they saw Miller. They stopped, stared, remained motionless for at least five seconds, looked at each other, unslung their machine-pistols and broke into a stumbling uphill run. Miller closed his eyes. He didn't require them any more, his ears gave him all the information he wanted, the closing sound of crunching footsteps in the snow, the abrupt cessation of those, the heavy breathing as a man bent over him.

Miller waited until he could actually feel the man's breath in his face, then opened his eyes. Not twelve inches from his own were the eyes of the ginger-bearded Cetnik. Miller's outflung arms curved upwards and inwards, his sinewy fingers hooked deeply into the throat of the startled man above him.

Andrea's Schmeisser had already reached the limit of its backswing as he stepped soundlessly round the bole of the pine. The black-bearded Cetnik was just beginning to move to help his friend when he caught sight of Andrea from the corner of one eye, and flung up both arms to protect himself. A pair of straws would have served him as well. Andrea grimaced at the sheer physical shock of the impact, dropped the Schmeisser, pulled out his knife and fell upon the other Cetnik still struggling desperately in Miller's stranglehold.

Miller rose to his feet and he and Andrea stared down at the two dead men. Miller looked in puzzlement at the ginger-bearded man, then suddenly stooped, caught the beard and tugged. It came away in his hand, revealing beneath it a clean-shaven face and a scar which ran from the corner of a lip to the chin.

Andrea and Miller exchanged speculative glances, but neither made comment. They dragged the dead men some little way off the path into the concealment of some undergrowth. Andrea picked up a dead branch and swept away the dragmarks in the snow and, by the base of the pine, all traces of the encounter: inside the hour, he knew, the brushmarks he had made would have vanished under a fresh covering of snow. He picked up his cigar and threw the branch deep into the woods. Without a backward glance, the two men began to walk briskly up the hill.

Had they given this backward glance, it was barely possible that they might have caught a glimpse of a face peering round the trunk of a tree further downhill. Droshny had arrived at the bend in the track just in time to see Andrea complete his brushing operations and throw the branch away: what the meaning of this might be he couldn't guess.

He waited until Andrea and Miller had disappeared from his sight, waited another two minutes for good measure and safety, then hurried up the track, the expression on his swarthy brigand's face nicely balanced between puzzlement and suspicion. He reached the pine where the two Cetniks had been ambushed, briefly quartered the area, then followed the line of brushmarks leading into the woods, the puzzlement on his face giving way first to pure suspicion, then the suspicion to complete certainty.

He parted the bushes and peered down at the two Cetniks lying half-buried in a snow-filled gully with that curiously huddled shapelessness that only the dead can achieve. After a few moments he straightened, turned and looked uphill in the direction in which Andrea and Miller had vanished: his face was not pleasant to look upon.

Andrea and Miller made good time up the hill. As they approached one of the innumerable bends in the trail they heard up ahead the sound of a softly-played

403

guitar, curiously muffled and softened in tone by the falling snow. Andrea slowed up, threw away his cigar, bent forward and clutched his ribs. Solicitously, Miller took his arm.

The main party, they saw, was less than thirty yards ahead. They, too, were making slow time: the depth of snow and the increasing slope of the track made any quicker movement impossible. Reynolds glanced back — Reynolds was spending a great deal of his time in looking over his shoulder, he appeared to be in a highly apprehensive state — caught sight of Andrea and Miller and called out to Mallory who halted the party and waited for Andrea and Miller to make up with them. Mallory looked worriedly at Andrea.

'Getting worse?'

'How far to go?' Andrea asked hoarsely.

'Must be less than a mile.'

Andrea said nothing, he just stood there breathing heavily and wearing the stricken look of a sick man contemplating the prospect of another upward mile through deep snow. Saunders, already carrying two rucksacks, approached Andrea diffidently, tentatively. He said: 'It would help, you know, if — '

'I know.' Andrea smiled painfully, unslung his Schmeisser and handed it to Saunders. 'Thanks, son.'

Petar was still softly plucking the strings of his guitar, an indescribably eerie sound in those dark and ghostly pine woods. Miller looked at him and said to Mallory: 'What's the music while we march for?'

'Petar's password, I should imagine.'

'Like Neufeld said? Nobody touches our singing Cetnik?'

'Something like that.'

They moved on up the trail. Mallory let the others pass by until he and Andrea were bringing up the rear. Mallory glanced incuriously at Andrea, his face registering no more than a mild concern for the condition of his friend. Andrea caught his glance and nodded fractionally: Mallory looked away.

Fifteen minutes later they were halted, at gunpoint, by three men, all armed with machine-pistols, who simply appeared to have materialized from nowhere, a surprise so complete that not even Andrea could have done anything about it – even if he had had his gun. Reynolds looked urgently at Mallory, who smiled and shook his head.

'It's all right. Partisans – look at the red star on their forage caps. Just outposts guarding one of the main trails.'

And so it proved. Maria talked briefly to one of the soldiers, who listened, nodded and set off up the path, gesturing to the party to follow him. The other two Partisans remained behind, both men crossing themselves as Petar again strummed gently on his guitar. Neufeld, Mallory reflected, hadn't exaggerated about the degree of awed respect and fear in which the blind singer and his sister were held.

They came to Partisan HQ inside another ten minutes, an HQ curiously similar in appearance and choice of location to Hauptmann Neufeld's camp: the same rough circle of crude huts set deep in the same *jamba* – depression – with similar massive pines towering high above. The guide spoke to Maria and she turned coldly to Mallory, the disdain on her face making it very plain how much against the grain it went for her to speak to him at all.

'We are to go to the guest hut. You are to report to the commandant. This soldier will show you.'

The guide beckoned in confirmation. Mallory followed him across the compound to a fairly large, fairly well-lit hut. The guide knocked, opened the door and waved Mallory inside, he himself following.

The commandant was a tall, lean, dark man with that aquiline, aristocratic face so common among the Bosnian mountainmen. He advanced towards Mallory with outstretched hand and smiled.

'Major Broznik, and at your service. Late, late hours, but as you see we are still up and around. Although I must say I did expect you before this.'

'I don't know what you're talking about.'

'You don't know – you *are* Captain Mallory, are you not?'

'I've never heard of him.' Mallory gazed steadily at Broznik, glanced briefly sideways at the guide, then looked back to Broznik again. Broznik frowned for a moment, then his face cleared. He spoke to the guide, who turned and left. Mallory put out his hand.

'Captain Mallory, at your service. I'm sorry about that, Major Broznik, but I insist we must talk alone.'

'You trust no one? Not even in *my* camp?'

'No one.'

'Not even your own men?'

'I don't trust them not to make mistakes. I don't trust myself not to make mistakes. I don't trust *you* not to make mistakes.'

'Please?' Broznik's voice was as cold as his eyes.

'Did you ever have two of your men disappear, one with ginger hair, the other with black, the ginger-haired man with a cast to his eye and a scar running from mouth to chin?'

Broznik came closer. 'What do you know about those men?'

'Did you? Know them, I mean?'

Broznik nodded and said slowly: 'They were lost in action. Last month.'

406

'You found their bodies?'

'No.'

'There were no bodies to be found. They had deserted – gone over to the Cetniks.'

'But they *were* Cetniks – converted to our cause.'

'They'd been reconverted. They followed us tonight. On the orders of Captain Droshny. I had them killed.'

'You – had – them – killed?'

'Think, man,' Mallory said wearily. 'If they had arrived here – which they no doubt intended to do a discreet interval after our arrival – we wouldn't have recognized them and you'd have welcomed them back as escaped prisoners. They'd have reported our every movement. Even if we had recognized them after they had arrived here and done something about it, you may have *other* Cetniks here who would have reported back to their masters that we had done away with their watchdogs. So we disposed of them very quietly, no fuss, in a very remote place, then hid them.'

'There are no Cetniks in my command, Captain Mallory.'

Mallory said drily: 'It takes a very clever farmer, Major, to see two bad apples on the top of the barrel and be quite certain that there are none lower down. No chances. None. Ever.' Mallory smiled to remove any offence from his words and went on briskly: 'Now, Major, there's some information that Hauptmann Neufeld wants.'

To say that the guest hut hardly deserved so hospitable a title would have been a very considerable understatement. As a shelter for some of the less-regarded domesticated animals it might have been barely acceptable: as an overnight accommodation for human beings it was conspicuously lacking in what our modern effete European societies regard as the minimum essentials for civilized living. Even the Spartans of ancient Greece would have considered it as too much of a good thing. One rickety trestle table, one bench, a dying fire and lots of hard-packed earthen floor. It fell short of being a home from home.

There were six people in the hut, three standing, one sitting, two stretched out on the lumpy floor. Petar, for once without his sister, sat on the floor, silent guitar clasped in his hands, gazing sightlessly into the fading embers. Andrea, stretched in apparently luxurious ease in a sleeping-bag, peacefully puffed at what, judging from the frequent suffering glances cast in his direction, appeared to be a more than normally obnoxious cigar. Miller, similarly reclining, was reading what appeared to be a slender volume of poetry. Reynolds and Groves, unable to sleep, stood idly by the solitary window, gazing out abstractedly into the dimly-lit compound: they turned as Saunders removed his radio transmitter from its casing and made for the door.

With some bitterness Saunders said: 'Sleep well.'

'Sleep well?' Reynolds raised an eyebrow. 'And where are you going?'

'Radio hut across there. Message to Termoli. Mustn't spoil your beauty sleep while I'm transmitting.'

Saunders left. Groves went and sat by the table, cradling a weary head in his hands. Reynolds remained by the window, watched Saunders cross the compound and enter a darkened hut on the far side. Soon a light appeared in the window as Saunders lit a lamp.

Reynolds's eyes moved in response to the sudden appearance of an oblong of light across the compound. The door to Major Broznik's hut had opened and Mallory stood momentarily framed there, carrying what appeared to be a sheet of paper in his hand.

Then the door closed and Mallory moved off in the direction of the radio hut.

Reynolds suddenly became very watchful, very still. Mallory had taken less than a dozen steps when a dark figure detached itself from the even darker shadow of a hut and confronted him. Quite automatically, Reynolds's hand reached for the Luger at his belt, then slowly withdrew. Whatever this confrontation signified for Mallory it certainly wasn't danger, for Maria, Reynolds knew, did not carry a gun. And unquestionably it was Maria who was now in such apparent close conversation with Mallory.

Bewildered now, Reynolds pressed his face close against the glass. For almost two minutes he stared at this astonishing spectacle of the girl who had slapped Mallory with such venom, who had lost no opportunity of displaying an animosity bordering on hatred, now talking to him not only animatedly but also clearly very amicably. So total was Reynolds's baffled incomprehension at this inexplicable turn of events that his mind moved into a trance-like state, a spell that was abruptly snapped when he saw Mallory put a reassuring arm around her shoulder and pat her in a way that might have been comforting or affectionate or both but which in any event clearly evoked no resentment on the part of the girl. This was still inexplicable: but the only interpretation that could be put upon it was an uncompromisingly sinister one. Reynolds whirled round and silently and urgently beckoned Groves to the window. Groves rose quickly, moved to the window and looked out, but by the time he had done so there was no longer any sign of Maria: Mallory was alone, walking across the compound towards the radio hut, the paper still in his hand. Groves glanced questioningly at Reynolds.

'They were together,' Reynolds whispered. 'Mallory and Maria. I saw them! They were talking!'

'What? You sure?'

'God's my witness. I *saw* them, man. He even had his arm around – Get away from this window – Maria's coming.'

Without haste, so as to arouse no comment from Andrea or Miller, they turned and walked unconcernedly towards the table and sat down. Seconds later, Maria entered and, without looking at or speaking to anyone, crossed to the fire, sat by Petar and took his hand. A minute or so later Mallory entered, and sat on a palliasse beside Andrea, who removed his cigar and glanced at him in mild enquiry. Mallory casually checked to see that he wasn't under observation, then nodded. Andrea returned to the contemplation of his cigar.

Reynolds looked uncertainly at Groves, then said to Mallory, 'Shouldn't we be setting a guard, sir?'

'A guard?' Mallory was amused. 'Whatever for? This is a Partisan camp, Sergeant. Friends, you know. And, as you've seen, they have their own excellent guard system.'

'You never know – '

'*I* know. Get some sleep.'

Reynolds went on doggedly: 'Saunders is alone over there. I don't like – '

'He's coding and sending a short message for me. A few minutes, that's all.'

'But – '

'Shut up,' Andrea said. 'You heard the captain?'

Reynolds was by now thoroughly unhappy and uneasy, an unease which showed through in his instantly antagonistic irritation.

'Shut up? Why should I shut up? I don't take orders

from you. And while we're telling each other what to do, you might put out that damned stinking cigar.'

Miller wearily lowered his book of verse.

'I quite agree about the damned cigar, young fellow. But do bear in mind that you are talking to a ranking colonel in the army.'

Miller reverted to his book. For a few moments Reynolds and Groves stared open-mouthed at each other, then Reynolds stood up and looked at Andrea.

'I'm extremely sorry, sir. I – I didn't realize – '

Andrea waved him to silence with a magnanimous hand and resumed his communion with his cigar. The minutes passed in silence. Maria, before the fire, had her head on Petar's shoulder, but otherwise had not moved: she appeared to be asleep. Miller shook his head in rapt admiration of what appeared to be one of the more esoteric manifestations of the poetic muse, closed his book reluctantly and slid down into his sleeping-bag. Andrea ground out his cigar and did the same. Mallory seemed to be already asleep. Groves lay down and Reynolds, leaning over the table, rested his forehead on his arms. For five minutes, perhaps longer, Reynolds remained like this, uneasily dozing off, then he lifted his head, sat up with a jerk, glanced at his watch, crossed to Mallory and shook him by the shoulder. Mallory stirred.

'Twenty minutes,' Reynolds said urgently. 'Twenty minutes and Saunders isn't back yet.'

'All right, so it's twenty minutes,' Mallory said patiently. 'He could take that long to make contact, far less transmit the message.'

'Yes, sir. Permission to check, sir?'

Mallory nodded wearily and closed his eyes. Reynolds picked up his Schmeisser, left the hut and closed the door softly behind him. He released the safety-catch on his gun and ran across the compound.

411

The light still burned in the radio hut. Reynolds tried to peer through the window but the frost of that bitter night had made it completely opaque. Reynolds moved around to the door. It was slightly ajar. He set his finger to the trigger and opened the door in the fashion in which all Commandos were trained to open doors – with a violent kick of his right foot.

There was no one in the radio hut, no one, that is, who could bring him to any harm. Slowly, Reynolds lowered his gun and walked in in a hesitant, almost dreamlike fashion, his face masked in shock.

Saunders was leaning tiredly over the transmitting table, his head resting on it at an unnatural angle, both arms dangling limply towards the ground. The hilt of a knife protruded between his shoulderblades: Reynolds noted, almost subconsciously, that there was no trace of blood: death had been instantaneous. The transmitter itself lay on the floor, a twisted and mangled mass of metal that was obviously smashed beyond repair. Tentatively, not knowing why he did so, he reached out and touched the dead man on the shoulder: Saunders seemed to stir, his cheek slid along the table and he toppled to one side, falling heavily across the battered remains of the transmitter. Reynolds stooped low over him. Grey parchment now, where a bronzed tan had been, sightless, faded eyes uselessly guarding a mind now flown. Reynolds swore briefly, bitterly, straightened and ran from the hut.

Everyone in the guest hut was asleep, or appeared to be. Reynolds crossed to where Mallory lay, dropped to one knee and shook him roughly by the shoulder. Mallory stirred, opened weary eyes and propped himself up on one elbow. He gave Reynolds a look of unenthusiastic enquiry.

'Among friends, you said!' Reynolds's voice was

low, vicious, almost a hissing sound. 'Safe, you said. Saunders will be all right, you said. You *knew*, you said. You bloody well knew.'

Mallory said nothing. He sat up abruptly on his palliasse, and the sleep was gone from his eyes. He said: 'Saunders?'

Reynolds said, 'I think you'd better come with me.'

In silence the two men left the hut, in silence they crossed the deserted compound and in silence they entered the radio hut. Mallory went no farther than the doorway. For what was probably no more than ten seconds but for what seemed to Reynolds to be an unconsciously long time, Mallory stared at the dead man and the smashed transmitter, his eyes bleak, his face registering no emotional reaction. Reynolds mistook the expression, or lack of it, for something else, and could suddenly no longer contain his pent-up fury.

'Well, aren't you bloody well going to do something about it instead of standing there all night?'

'Every dog's entitled to his one bite,' Mallory said mildly. 'But don't talk to me like that again. Do what, for instance?'

'Do what?' Reynolds visibly struggled for self-control. 'Find the nice gentleman who did this.'

'Finding him will be very difficult.' Mallory considered. 'Impossible, I should say. If the killer came from the camp here, then he'll have gone to earth in the camp here. If he came from outside, he'll be a mile away by this time and putting more distance between himself and us every second. Go and wake Andrea and Miller and Groves and tell them to come here. Then go and tell Major Broznik what's happened.'

'I'll tell them what's happened,' Reynolds said bitterly. 'And I'll also tell them it never *would* have

413

happened if you'd listened to me. But oh no, you wouldn't listen, would you?'

'So you were right and I was wrong. Now do as I ask you.'

Reynolds hesitated, a man obviously on the brink of outright revolt. Suspicion and defiance alternated in the angry face. Then some strange quality in the expression in Mallory's face tipped the balance for sanity and compliance and he nodded in sullen antagonism, turned and walked away.

Mallory waited until he had rounded the corner of the hut, brought out his torch and started, not very hopefully, to quarter the hard-packed snow outside the door of the radio hut. But almost at once he stopped, stooped, and brought the head of the torch close to the surface of the ground.

It was a very small portion of footprint indeed, only the front half of the sole of a right foot. The pattern showed two V-shaped marks, the leading V with a cleanly-cut break in it. Mallory, moving more quickly now, followed the direction indicated by the pointed toeprint and came across two more similar indentations, faint but unmistakable, before the frozen snow gave way to the frozen earth of the compound, ground so hard as to be incapable of registering any footprints at all. Mallory retraced his steps, carefully erasing all three prints with the toe of his boot and reached the radio hut only seconds before he was joined by Reynolds, Andrea, Miller and Groves. Major Broznik and several of his men joined them soon after.

They searched the interior of the radio hut for clues as to the killer's identity, but clues there were none. Inch by inch they searched the hard-packed snow surrounding the hut, with the same completely negative results. Reinforced, by this time, by perhaps sixty or seventy sleepy-eyed Partisan soldiers, they carried out a simultaneous search of all the buildings and of the woods surrounding the encampment: but neither the encampment nor the surrounding woods had any secrets to yield.

'We may as well call it off,' Mallory said finally. 'He's got clean away.'

'It looks that way,' Major Broznik agreed. He was deeply troubled and bitterly angry that such a thing should have happened in his encampment. 'We'd better double the guards for the rest of the night.'

'There's no need for that,' Mallory said. 'Our friend won't be back.'

'There's no need for that,' Reynolds mimicked savagely. 'There was no need for that for poor Saunders, you said. And where's Saunders now? Sleeping comfortably in his bed? Is he hell! No need – '

Andrea muttered warningly and took a step nearer Reynolds, but Mallory made a brief conciliatory movement of his right hand. He said: 'It's entirely up to you, of course, Major. I'm sorry that we have been responsible for giving you and your men so sleepless a night. See you in the morning.' He smiled wryly. 'Not that that's so far away.' He turned to go, found his way blocked by Sergeant Groves, a Groves whose normally cheerful countenance now mirrored the tight hostility of Reynolds's.

'So he's got clear away, has he? Away to hell and gone. And that's the end of it, eh?'

Mallory looked at him consideringly. 'Well, no. I wouldn't quite say that. A little time. We'll find him.'

'A little time? Maybe even before he dies of old age?' Andrea looked at Mallory. 'Twenty-four hours?'

'Less.'

Andrea nodded and he and Mallory turned and walked away towards the guest hut. Reynolds and Groves, with Miller slightly behind them, watched the two men as they went, then looked at each other, their faces still bleak and bitter.

'Aren't they a nice warm-hearted couple now? Completely broken up about old Saunders.' Groves shook his head. 'They don't care. They just don't care.'

'Oh, I wouldn't say that,' Miller said diffidently. 'It's just that they don't *seem* to care. Not at all the same thing.'

'Faces like wooden Indians,' Reynolds muttered. 'They never even said they were *sorry* that Saunders was killed.'

'Well,' Miller said patiently, 'it's a cliché, but different people react in different ways. Okay, so grief and anger is the natural reaction to this sort of thing, but if Mallory and Andrea spent their time in reacting in that fashion to all the things that have happened to *them* in their lifetimes, they'd have come apart at the seams years ago. So they don't react that way any more. They do things. Like they're going to do things to your friend's killer. Maybe you didn't get it, but you just heard a death sentence being passed.'

'How do *you* know?' Reynolds said uncertainly. He nodded in the direction of Mallory and Andrea who were just entering the guest hut. 'And how did *they* know? Without talking, I mean.'

'Telepathy.'

'What do you mean – "telepathy"?'

'It would take too long,' Miller said wearily. 'Ask me in the morning.'

CHAPTER SIX

Friday 0800–1000

Crowning the tops of the towering pines, the dense, interlocking snow-laden branches formed an almost impenetrable canopy that effectively screened Major Broznik's camp, huddled at the foot of the *jamba*, from all but the most fleeting glimpses of the sky above. Even at high noon on a summer's day, it was never more than a twilit dusk down below: on a morning such as this, an hour after dawn with snow falling gently from an overcast sky, the quality of light was such as to be hardly distinguishable from a starlit midnight. The interior of the dining hut, where Mallory and his company were at breakfast with Major Broznik, was gloomy in the extreme, the darkness emphasized rather than alleviated by the two smoking oil lamps which formed the only primitive means of illumination.

The atmosphere of gloom was significantly deepened by the behaviour and expression of those seated round the breakfast table. They ate in a moody silence, heads lowered, for the most part not looking at one another: the events of the previous night had clearly affected them all deeply but none so deeply as Reynolds and Groves in whose faces was still unmistakably reflected the shock caused by Saunders's murder. They left their food untouched.

To complete the atmosphere of quiet desperation, it was clear that the reservations held about the standard of the Partisan early-morning cuisine were of a profound and lasting nature. Served by two young *partisankas* – women members of Marshal Tito's army – it consisted of *polenta*, a highly unappetizing dish made from ground corn, and *raki*, a Yugoslav spirit of unparalleled fierceness. Miller spooned his breakfast with a marked lack of enthusiasm.

'Well,' he said to no one in particular, 'it makes a change, I'll say that.'

'It's all we have,' Broznik said apologetically. He laid down his spoon and pushed his plate away from him. 'And even that I can't eat. Not this morning. Every entrance to the *jamba* is guarded, yet there was a killer loose in my camp last night. But maybe he *didn't* come in past the guards, maybe he was already inside. Think of it – a traitor in my own camp. And if there is, I can't even find him. I can't even believe it!'

Comment was superfluous, nothing could be said that hadn't been said already, nobody as much as looked in Broznik's direction: his acute discomfort, embarrassment and anger were apparent to everyone in his tone of voice. Andrea, who had already emptied his plate with apparent relish, looked at the two untouched plates in front of Reynolds and Groves and then enquiringly at the two sergeants themselves, who shook their heads. Andrea reached out, brought their plates before him and set to with every sign of undiminished appetite. Reynolds and Groves looked at him in shocked disbelief, possibly awed by the catholicity of Andrea's taste, more probably astonished by the insensitivity of a man who could eat so heartily only a few hours after the death of one of his comrades. Miller, for his part, looked at Andrea in near horror, tried another tiny portion of his *polenta* and wrinkled his nose in delicate distaste. He laid down his spoon and looked

418

morosely at Petar who, guitar slung over his shoulder, was awkwardly feeding himself.

Miller said irritably: 'Does he *always* wear that damned guitar?'

'Our lost one,' Broznik said softly. 'That's what we call him. Our poor blind lost one. Always he carries it or has it by his side. Always. Even when he sleeps – didn't you notice last night? That guitar means as much to him as life itself. Some weeks ago, one of our men, by way of a joke, tried to take it from him: Petar, blind though he is, almost killed him.'

'He must be stone tone deaf,' Miller said wonderingly. 'It's the most god-awful guitar I ever heard.'

Broznik smiled faintly. 'Agreed. But don't you understand? He can feel it. He can touch it. It's his own. It's the only thing left to him in the world, a dark and lonely and empty world. Our poor lost one.'

'He could at least tune it,' Miller muttered.

'You are a good man, my friend. You try to take our minds off what lies ahead this day. But no man can do that.' He turned to Mallory. 'Any more than you can hope to carry out your crazy scheme of rescuing your captured agents and breaking up the German counter-espionage network here. It is insanity. Insanity!'

Mallory waved a vague hand. 'Here you are. No food. No artillery. No transport. Hardly any guns – and practically no ammunition for those guns. No medical supplies. No tanks. No planes. No hope – and you keep on fighting. That makes you sane?'

'Touché.' Broznik smiled, pushed across the bottle of *raki*, waited until Mallory had filled his glass. 'To the madmen of this world.'

'I've just been talking to Major Stephan up at the

Western Gap,' General Vukalovic said. 'He thinks we're all mad. Would you agree, Colonel Lazlo?'

The man lying prone beside Vukalovic lowered his binoculars. He was a burly, sun-tanned, thickset, middle-aged man with a magnificent black moustache that had every appearance of being waxed. After a moment's consideration, he said: 'Without a doubt, sir.'

'Even you?' Vukalovic said protestingly. 'With a Czech father?'

'He came from the High Tatra,' Lazlo explained. 'They're all mad there.'

Vukalovic smiled, settled himself more comfortably on his elbows, peered downhill through the gap between two rocks, raised his binoculars and scanned the scene to the south of him, slowly raising his glasses as he did so.

Immediately in front of where he lay was a bare, rocky hillside, dropping gently downhill for a distance of about two hundred feet. Beyond its base it merged gradually into a long flat grassy plateau, no more than two hundred yards wide at its maximum, but stretching almost as far as the eye could see on both sides, on the right-hand side stretching away to the west, on the left curving away to the east, north-east and finally north.

Beyond the edge of the plateau, the land dropped abruptly to form the bank of a wide and swiftly flowing river, a river of that peculiarly Alpine greenish-white colour, green from the melting ice-water of spring, white from where it foamed over jagged rocks and overfalls in the bed of the river. Directly to the south of where Vukalovic and Lazlo lay, the river was spanned by a green-and-white-painted and very solidly-constructed cantilevered steel bridge. Beyond the river, the grassy bank on the far side rose in a very easy slope for a distance of about a hundred yards to the very regularly defined limit of a forest of giant pines which stretched away into the southern distance. Scattered through the very outermost of the pines were a few dully metallic objects, unmistakably tanks. In the farthest distance, beyond the river and beyond the pines, towering, jagged mountains dazzled in their brilliant covering of snow and above that again, but more to the south-east, an equally white and dazzling sun shone from an incongruously blue patch in an otherwise snow-cloud-covered sky.

Vukalovic lowered his binoculars and sighed.

'No idea at all how many tanks are across in the woods there?'

'I wish to heaven I knew.' Lazlo lifted his arms in a small, helpless gesture. 'Could be ten. Could be two hundred. We've no idea. We've sent scouts, of course, but they never came back. Maybe they were swept away trying to cross the Neretva.' He looked at Vukalovic, speculation in his eyes. 'Through the Zenica Gap, through the Western Gap or across that bridge there – you don't know where the attack is coming from, do you, sir?'

Vukalovic shook his head.

'But you expect it soon?'

'Very soon.' Vukalovic struck the rocky ground with a clenched fist. 'Is there *no* way of destroying that damned bridge?'

'There have been five RAF attacks,' Lazlo said heavily. 'To date, twenty-seven planes lost – there are two hundred AA guns along the Neretva and the nearest Messerschmitt station is only ten minutes' flying time away. The German radar picks up the British bombers crossing our coast – and the Messerschmitts are here, waiting, by the time they arrive. And don't forget that the bridge is set in rock on either side.'

'A direct hit or nothing?'

'A direct hit on a target seven metres wide from three thousand metres. It is impossible. And a target so camouflaged that you can hardly see it five hundred metres away on land. Doubly impossible.'

'And impossible for us,' Vukalovic said bleakly.

'Impossible for us. We made our last attempt two nights ago.'

'You made – I told you not to.'

'You *asked* us not to. But of course I, Colonel Lazlo, knew better. They started firing star-shells when our troops were halfway across the plateau, God knows how they knew they were coming. Then the searchlights –'

'Then the shrapnel shells,' Vukalovic finished. 'And the Oerlikons. Casualties?'

'We lost half a battalion.'

'Half a battalion! And tell me, my dear Lazlo, what would have happened in the unlikely event of your men reaching the bridge?'

'They had some amatol blocks, some hand-grenades – '

'No fireworks?' Vukalovic asked in heavy sarcasm. 'That might have helped. That bridge is built of steel set in reinforced concrete, man! You were mad even to try.'

'Yes, sir.' Lazlo looked away. 'Perhaps you ought to relieve me.'

'I think I should.' Vukalovic looked closely at the exhausted face. 'In fact I would. But for one thing.'

'One thing?'

'All my other regimental commanders are as mad as you are. And if the Germans do attack – maybe even tonight?'

'We stand here. We are Yugoslavs and we have no place to go. What else can we do?'

'What else? Two thousand men with pop-guns, most of them weak and starving and lacking ammunition, against what may perhaps be two first-line German armoured divisions. And you stand there. You could always surrender, you know.'

Lazlo smiled. 'With respect, General, this is no time for facetiousness.'

Vukalovic clapped his shoulder. 'I didn't think it funny, either. I'm going up to the dam, to the north-eastern redoubt. I'll see if Colonel Janzy is as mad as you are. And Colonel?'

'Sir?'

'If the attack comes, I may give the order to retreat.'

'Retreat!'

'Not surrender. Retreat. Retreat to what, one hopes, may be victory.'

'I am sure the General knows what he is talking about.'

'The General isn't.' Oblivious to possible sniper fire from across the Neretva, Vukalovic stood up in readiness to go. 'Ever heard of a man called Captain Mallory. Keith Mallory, a New Zealander?'

'No,' Lazlo said promptly. He paused, then went on: 'Wait a minute, though. Fellow who used to climb mountains?'

'That's the one. But he has also, I'm given to understand, other accomplishments.' Vukalovic rubbed a stubbly chin. 'If all I hear about him is true, I think you could quite fairly call him a rather gifted individual.'

'And what about this gifted individual?' Lazlo asked curiously.

'Just this.' Vukalovic was suddenly very serious, even sombre. 'When all things are lost and there is no

423

hope left, there is always, somewhere in the world, one man you can turn to. There may be only that one man. More often than not there *is* only that one man. But that one man is always there.' He paused reflectively. 'Or so they say.'

'Yes, sir,' Lazlo said politely. 'But about this Keith Mallory – '

'Before you sleep tonight, pray for him. I will.'

'Yes, sir. And about us? Shall I pray for us, too?'

'That,' said Vukalovic, 'wouldn't be at all a bad idea.'

The sides of the *jamba* leading upwards from Major Broznik's camp were very steep and very slippery and the ascending cavalcade of men and ponies were making very heavy going of it. Or most of them were. The escort of dark stocky Bosnian Partisans, to whom such terrain was part and parcel of existence, appeared quite unaffected by the climb: and it in no way appeared to interfere with Andrea's rhythmic puffing of his usual vile-smelling cigar. Reynolds noticed this, a fact which fed fresh fuel to the already dark doubts and torments in his mind.

He said sourly: 'You seem to have made a remarkable recovery in the night-time, Colonel Stavros, sir.'

'Andrea.' The cigar was removed. 'I have a heart condition. It comes and goes.' The cigar was replaced.

'I'm sure it does,' Reynolds muttered. He glanced suspiciously, and for the twentieth time, over his shoulder. 'Where the hell is Mallory?'

'Where the hell is *Captain* Mallory,' Andrea chided.

'Well, where?'

'The leader of an expedition has many responsibilities,' Andrea said. 'Many things to attend to. Captain Mallory is probably attending to something at this very moment.'

'You can say that again,' Reynolds muttered.

'What was that?'

'Nothing.'

Captain Mallory was, as Andrea had so correctly guessed, attending to something at that precise moment. Back in Broznik's office, he and Broznik were bent over a map spread out on the trestle table. Broznik pointed to a spot near the northern limit of the map.

'I agree. This *is* the nearest possible landing strip for a plane. But it is very high up. At this time of year there will still be almost a metre of snow up there. There are other places, better places.'

'I don't doubt that for a moment,' Mallory said. 'Faraway fields are always greener, maybe even faraway airfields. But I haven't the time to go to them.' He stabbed his forefinger on the map. 'I want a landing-strip here and only here by night-fall. I'd be most grateful if you'd send a rider to Konjic within the hour and have my request radioed immediately to your Partisan HQ at Drvar.'

Broznik said drily: 'You are accustomed to asking for instant miracles, Captain Mallory?'

'This doesn't call for miracles. Just a thousand men. The feet of a thousand men. A small price for seven thousand lives?' He handed Broznik a slip of paper. 'Wavelength and code. Have Konjic transmit it as soon as possible.' Mallory glanced at his watch. 'They have twenty minutes on me already. I'd better hurry.'

'I suppose you'd better,' Broznik said hurriedly. He hesitated, at a momentary loss for words, then went on awkwardly: 'Captain Mallory, I – I – '

'I know. Don't worry. The Mallorys of this world never make old bones anyway. We're too stupid.'

'Aren't we all, aren't we all?' Broznik gripped Mallory's hand. 'Tonight, I make a prayer for you.'

Mallory remained silent for a moment, then nodded. 'Make it a long one.'

The Bosnian scouts, now, like the remainder of the party, mounted on ponies, led the winding way down through the gentle slope of the thickly-forested valley, followed by Andrea and Miller riding abreast, then by Petar, whose pony's bridle was in the hand of his sister. Reynolds and Groves, whether by accident or design, had fallen some little way behind and were talking in soft tones.

Groves said speculatively: 'I wonder what Mallory and the Major are talking about back there?'

Reynolds's mouth twisted in bitterness. 'It's perhaps as well we don't know.'

'You may be right at that. I just don't know.' Groves paused, went on almost pleadingly: 'Broznik is on the up-and-up. I'm sure of it. Being what he is, he *must* be.'

'That's as may be. Mallory too, eh?'

'*He* must be, too.'

'Must?' Reynolds was savage. 'God alive, man, I tell you I saw him with my own eyes.' He nodded towards Maria, some twenty yards ahead, and his face was cruel and hard. 'That girl hit him – and *how* she hit him – back in Neufeld's camp and the next thing I see is the two of them having a cosy little lovey-dovey chat outside Broznik's hut. Odd, isn't it? Soon after, Saunders was murdered. Coincidence, isn't it? I tell you, Groves, Mallory could have done it himself. The girl *could* have had time to do it before she met Mallory – except that it would have been physically impossible for her to drive a six-inch knife home to the hilt. But Mallory

426

could have done it all right. He'd time enough – and opportunity enough – when he handed that damned message into the radio hut.'

Groves said protestingly: 'Why in God's name should be do that?'

'Because Broznik had given him some urgent information. Mallory *had* to make a show of passing this information back to Italy. But maybe sending that message was the last thing he wanted. Maybe he stopped it in the only way he knew how – and smashed the transmitter to make sure no one else could send a message. Maybe that's why he stopped me from mounting a guard or going to see Saunders – to prevent me from discovering the fact that Saunders was already dead – in which case, of course, because of the time factor, suspicion would have automatically fallen on him.'

'You're imagining things.' Despite his discomfort, Groves was reluctantly impressed by Reynolds's reasoning.

'You think so? That knife in Saunders's back – did I imagine that too?'

Within half an hour, Mallory had rejoined the party. He jogged past Reynolds and Groves, who studiously ignored him, past Maria and Petar, who did the same, and took up position behind Andrea and Miller.

It was in this order, for almost an hour, that they passed through the heavily-wooded Bosnian valleys. Occasionally, they came to clearings in the pines, clearings that had once been the site of human habitation, small villages or hamlets. But now there were no humans, no habitations, for the villages had ceased to exist. The clearings were all the same, chillingly and depressingly the same. Where the hard-working but happy Bosnians had once lived in their simple but sturdy homes, there were now only the charred and blackened remains of what had once been thriving communities, the air still heavy with the acrid smell of ancient smoke, the sweet-sour stench of corruption and death, mute testimony to the no-quarter viciousness and total ruthlessness of the war between the Germans and the Partisan Yugoslavs. Occasionally, here and there, still stood a few small, stone-built houses which had not been worth the expenditure of bombs or shells or mortars or petrol: but few of the larger buildings had escaped complete destruction. Churches and schools appeared to have been the primary targets: on one occasion, as evidenced by some charred steel equipment that could have come only from an operating theatre, they passed by a small cottage hospital that had been so razed to the ground that no part of the resulting ruins was more than three feet high. Mallory wondered what would have happened to the patients occupying the hospital at the time: but he no longer wondered at the hundreds of thousands of Yugoslavs – 350,000 had been the figure quoted by Captain Jensen, but, taking women and children into account, the number must have been at least a million – who had rallied under the banner of Marshal Tito. Patriotism apart, the burning desire for liberation and revenge apart, there was no place else left for them to go. They were a people, Mallory realized, with literally nothing left, with nothing to lose but their lives which they apparently held of small account, but with everything to gain by the destruction of the enemy: were he a German soldier, Mallory reflected, he would not have felt particularly happy about the prospect of a posting to Yugoslavia. It was a war which the Wehrmacht could never win, which the soldiers of no Western

European country could ever have won, for the peoples of the high mountains are virtually indestructible.

The Bosnian scouts, Mallory observed, looked neither to left nor right as they passed through the lifeless shattered villages of their countrymen, most of whom were now almost certainly dead. They didn't *have* to look, he realized: they had their memories, and even their memories would be too much for them. If it were possible to feel pity for an enemy, then Mallory at that moment felt pity for the Germans.

By and by they emerged from the narrow winding mountain track on to a narrow, but comparatively wide road, wide enough, at least, for single-file vehicular traffic. The Bosnian scout in the lead threw up his hand and halted his pony.

'Unofficial no-man's-land, it would seem,' Mallory said. 'I think this is where they turfed us off the truck this morning.'

Mallory's guess appeared to be correct. The Partisans wheeled their horses, smiled widely, waved, shouted some unintelligible words of farewell and urged their horses back the way they had come.

With Mallory and Andrea in the lead and the two sergeants bringing up the rear, the seven remaining members of the party moved off down the track. The snow had stopped now, the clouds above had cleared away and the sunlight was filtering down between the now thinning pines. Suddenly Andrea, who had been peering to his left, reached out and touched Mallory on the arm. Mallory followed the direction of Andrea's pointing hand. Downhill, the pines petered out less than a hundred yards away and through the trees could be glimpsed some distant object, a startling green in colour. Mallory swung round in his saddle.

'Down there. I want to take a look. *Don't* move below the tree-line.'

The ponies picked their delicate sure-footed way down the steep and slippery slope. About ten yards from the tree-line and at a signal from Mallory, the riders dismounted and advanced cautiously on foot, moving from the cover of one pine to the next. The last few feet they covered on hands and knees, then finally stretched out flat in the partial concealment of the boles of the lowermost pines. Mallory brought out his binoculars, cleared the cold-clouded lenses and brought them to his eyes.

The snow-line, he saw, petered out some three or four hundred yards below them. Below that again was a mixture of fissured and eroded rock-faces and brown earth and beyond that again a belt of sparse and discouraged-looking grass. Along the lower reaches of this belt of grass ran a tarmacadam road, a road which struck Mallory as being, for that area, in remarkably good condition: the road was more or less exactly paralleled, at a distance of about a hundred yards, by a single-track and extremely narrow-gauge railway: a grass-grown and rusted line that looked as if it hadn't been used for many years. Just beyond the line the land dropped in a precipitous cliff to a narrow winding lake, the farther margin of which was marked by far more towering precipices leading up without break and with hardly any variation in angle to rugged snow-capped mountains.

From where he lay Mallory was directly overlooking a right-angled bend in the lake, a lake which was almost incredibly beautiful. In the bright clear sparkling sunlight of that spring morning it glittered and gleamed like the purest of emeralds. The smooth surface was occasionally ruffled by errant catspaws of

430

wind, catspaws which had the effect of deepening the emerald colour to an almost translucent aquamarine. The lake itself was nowhere much more than a quarter of a mile in width, but obviously miles in length: the long right-hand arm, twisting and turning between the mountains, stretched to the east almost as far as the eye could see: to the left, the short southern arm, hemmed in by increasingly vertical walls which finally appeared almost to meet overhead, ended against the concrete ramparts of a dam. But what caught and held the attention of the watchers was the incredible mirrored gleam of the far mountains in that equally incredible emerald mirror.

'Well, now,' Miller murmured, 'that *is* nice.' Andrea gave him a long expressionless look, then turned his attention to the lake again.

Groves's interest momentarily overcame his animosity.

'What lake is that, sir?'

Mallory lowered the binoculars. 'Haven't the faintest idea. Maria?' She made no answer. 'Maria! What – lake – is – that?'

'That's the Neretva dam,' she said sullenly. 'The biggest in Yugoslavia.'

'It's important, then?'

'It is important. Whoever controls that controls Central Yugoslavia.'

'And the Germans control it, I suppose?'

'They control it. *We* control it.' There was more than a hint of triumph in her smile. 'We – the Germans – have got it completely sealed off. Cliffs on both sides. To the east there – the upper end – they have a boom across a gorge only ten yards wide. And that boom is patrolled night and day. So is the dam wall itself. The only way in is by a set of steps –

431

ladders, rather – fixed to the cliff-face just below the dam.'

Mallory said drily: 'Very interesting information – for a parachute brigade. But we've other and more urgent fish to fry. Come on.' He glanced at Miller, who nodded and began to ease his way back up the slope, followed by the two sergeants, Maria and Petar. Mallory and Andrea lingered for a few moments longer.

'I wonder what it's like,' Mallory murmured.

'What's what like?' Andrea said.

'The other side of the dam.'

'And the ladder let into the cliff?'

'And the ladder let into the cliff.'

From where General Vukalovic lay, high on a cliff-top on the right-hand or western side of the Neretva gorge, he had an excellent view of the ladder let into the cliff: he had, in fact, an excellent view of the entire outer face of the dam wall and of the gorge which began at the foot of the wall and extended southwards for almost a mile before vanishing from sight round an abrupt right-hand corner.

The dam wall itself was quite narrow, not much more than thirty yards in width, but very deep, stretching down in a slightly V-formation from between overhanging cliff-faces to the greenish-white torrent of water foaming from the outlet pipes at the base. On top of the dam, at the eastern end and on a slight eminence, were the control station and two small huts, one of which, judging from the clearly visible soldiers patrolling the top of the wall, was almost certainly a guard-room. Above those buildings the walls of the gorge rose quite vertically for about thirty feet, then jutted out in a terrifying overhang.

From the control-room, a zig-zag, green-painted iron

432

ladder, secured by brackets to the rock-face, led down to the floor of the gorge. From the base of the ladder a narrow path extended down the gorge for a distance of about a hundred yards, ending abruptly at a spot where some ancient landslide had gouged a huge scar into the side of the gorge. From here a bridge spanned the river to another path on the right-hand bank.

As bridges go, it wasn't much, an obviously very elderly and rickety wooden swing bridge which looked as if its own weight would be enough to carry it into the torrent at any moment: what was even worse, it seemed, at first glance, as if its site had been deliberately picked by someone with an unhinged mind, for it lay directly below an enormous boulder some forty feet up the landslide, a boulder so clearly in a highly precarious state of balance that none but the most foolhardy would have lingered in the crossing of the bridge. In point of fact, no other site would have been possible.

From the western edge of the bridge, the narrow, boulder-strewn path followed the line of the river, passing by what looked like an extremely hazardous ford, and finally curving away from sight with the river.

General Vukalovic lowered his binoculars, turned to the man at his side and smiled.

'All quiet on the eastern front, eh, Colonel Janzy?'

'All quiet on the eastern front,' Janzy agreed. He was a small, puckish, humorous-looking character with a youthful face and incongruous white hair. He twisted round and gazed to the north. 'But not so quiet on the northern front, I'm afraid.'

The smile faded from Vukalovic's face as he turned, lifted his binoculars again and gazed to the north. Less than three miles away and clearly visible in the morning sunlight, lay the heavily wooded Zenica Gap,

for weeks a hotly contested strip of territory between
Vukalovic's northern defensive forces, under the command of Colonel Janzy, and units of the invading German
11th Army Corps. At that moment frequent puffs of
smoke could be seen, to the left a thick column of
smoke spiralled up to form a dark pall against the now
cloudless blue of the sky, while the distant rattle of
small-arms fire, punctuated by the occasional heavier
boom of artillery, was almost incessant. Vukalovic
lowered his glasses and looked thoughtfully at Janzy.

'The softening-up before the main attack?'

'What else? The final assault.'

'How many tanks?'

'It's difficult to be sure. Collating reports, my staff
estimate a hundred and fifty.'

'One hundred and fifty!'

'That's what they make it – and at least fifty
of those are Tiger tanks.'

'Let's hope to heaven your staff can't count.' Vukalovic rubbed a weary hand across his bloodshot eyes:
he'd had no sleep during the night just gone, no sleep
during the night previous to that. 'Let's go and see how
many *we* can count.'

Maria and Petar led the way now, with Reynolds and
Groves, clearly in no mood for other company, bringing
up the rear almost fifty yards behind. Mallory, Andrea
and Miller rode abreast along the narrow road. Andrea
looked at Mallory, his eyes speculative.

'Saunders's death? Any idea?'

Mallory shook his head. 'Ask me something else.'

'The message you'd given him to send. What was it?'

'A report of our safe arrival in Broznik's camp.
Nothing more.'

'A psycho,' Miller announced. 'The handy man

with the knife, I mean. Only a psycho would kill for that reason.'

'Maybe he didn't kill for that reason,' Mallory said mildly. 'Maybe he thought it was some other kind of message.'

'Some other kind of message?' Miller lifted an eyebrow in the way that only he knew how. 'Now what kind – ' He caught Andrea's eye, broke off and changed his mind about saying anything more. Both he and Andrea gazed curiously at Mallory who seemed to have fallen into a mood of intense introspection.

Whatever its reason, the period of deep preoccupation did not last for long. With the air of a man who has just arrived at a conclusion about something, Mallory lifted his head and called to Maria to stop, at the same time reining in his own pony. Together they waited until Reynolds and Groves had made up on them.

'There are a good number of options open to us,' Mallory said, 'but for better or worse this is what I have decided to do.' He smiled faintly. 'For better, I think, if for no other reason than that this is the course of action that will get us out of here fastest. I've talked to Major Broznik and found out what I wanted. He tells me – '

'Got your information for Neufeld, then, have you?' If Reynolds was attempting to mask the contempt in his voice he made a singularly poor job of it.

'The hell with Neufeld,' Mallory said without heat. 'Partisan spies have discovered where the four captured Allied agents are being held.'

'They have?' Reynolds said. 'Then why don't the Partisans do something about it?'

'For a good enough reason. The agents are held deep in German territory. In an impregnable block-house high up in the mountains.'

'And what are *we* going to do about the Allied agents held in this impregnable block-house?'

'Simple.' Mallory corrected himself. 'Well, in theory it's simple. We take them out of there and make our break tonight.'

Reynolds and Groves stared at Mallory, then at each other in frank disbelief and consternation. Andrea and Miller carefully avoided looking at each other or at anyone else.

'You're mad!' Reynolds spoke with total conviction.

'You're mad, *sir*,' Andrea said reprovingly.

Reynolds looked uncomprehendingly at Andrea, then turned back to Mallory again.

'You must be!' he insisted. 'Break? Break for where, in heaven's name?'

'For home. For Italy.'

'Italy!' It took Reynolds all of ten seconds to digest this startling piece of information, then he went on sarcastically: 'We're going to fly there, I suppose?'

'Well, it's a long swim across the Adriatic, even for a fit youngster like you. How else?'

'Flying?' Groves seemed slightly dazed.

'Flying. Not ten kilometres from here is a high – a very high mountain plateau, mostly in Partisan hands. There'll be a plane there at nine o'clock tonight.'

In the fashion of people who have failed to grasp something they have just heard, Groves repeated the statement in the form of a question. 'There'll be a plane there at nine o'clock tonight? You've just arranged this?'

'How could I? We've no radio.'

Reynolds's distrustful face splendidly complemented the scepticism in his voice. 'But *how* can you be sure – well, at nine o'clock?'

'Because, starting at six o'clock this evening, there'll

be a Wellington bomber over the airstrip every three hours for the next week if necessary.'

Mallory kneed his pony and the party moved on, Reynolds and Groves taking up their usual position well to the rear of the others. For some time Reynolds, his expression alternating between hostility and speculation, stared fixedly at Mallory's back: then he turned to Groves.

'Well, well, well. Isn't that very convenient indeed. We just *happen* to be sent to Broznik's camp. He just *happens* to know where the four agents are held. It just *happens* that an airplane will be over a certain airfield at a certain time – and it also so happens that I know for an absolute certainty that there are no airfields up in the high plateau. Still think everything clean and above-board?'

It was quite obvious from the unhappy expression on Groves's face that he thought nothing of the kind. He said: 'What in God's name are we going to do?'

'Watch our backs.'

Fifty yards ahead of them Miller cleared his throat and said delicately to Mallory: 'Reynolds seems to have lost some of his – um – earlier confidence in you, sir.'

Mallory said drily: 'It's not surprising. He thinks I stuck that knife in Saunders's back.'

This time Andrea and Miller did exchange glances, their faces registering expressions as close to pure consternation as either of those poker-faced individuals was capable of achieving.

CHAPTER SEVEN

Friday 1000–1200

Half a mile from Neufeld's camp they were met by
Captain Droshny and some half-dozen of his Cetniks.
Droshny's welcome was noticeably lacking in cordial-
ity but at least he managed, at what unknown cost, to
maintain some semblance of inoffensive neutrality.

'So you came back?'

'As you can see,' Mallory agreed.

Droshny looked at the ponies. 'And travelling in
comfort.'

'A present from our good friend Major Broznik.'
Mallory grinned. 'He thinks we're heading for Konjic
on them.'

Droshny didn't appear to care very much what Major
Broznik had thought. He jerked his head, wheeled his
horse and set off at a fast trot for Neufeld's camp.

When they had dismounted inside the compound,
Droshny immediately led Mallory into Neufeld's hut.
Neufeld's welcome, like Droshny's, was something
less than ecstatic, but at least he succeeded in impart-
ing a shade more benevolence to his neutrality. His face
held, also, just a hint of surprise, a reaction which he
explained at once.

'Candidly, Captain, I did not expect to see you
again. There were so many – ah – imponderables.
However, I am delighted to see you – you would not
have returned without the information I wanted. Now
then, Captain Mallory, to business.'

Mallory eyed Neufeld without enthusiasm. 'You're not a very business-like partner, I'm afraid.'

'I'm not?' Neufeld said politely. 'In what way?'

'Business partners don't tell lies to each other. Sure you said Vukalovic's troops are massing. So they are indeed. But not, as you said, to break out. Instead, they're massing to defend themselves against the final German attack, the assault that is to crush them once and for all, and this assault they believe to be imminent.'

'Well, now, you surely didn't expect me to give away our military secrets — which you might, I say just might, have relayed to the enemy — before you had proved yourselves,' Neufeld said reasonably. 'You're not that naïve. About this proposed attack. Who gave you the information?'

'Major Broznik.' Mallory smiled in recollection. 'He was very expansive.'

Neufeld leaned forward, his tension reflected in the sudden stillness of his face, in the way his unblinking eyes held Mallory's. 'And did they say where they expected this attack to come?'

'I only know the name. The bridge at Neretva.'

Neufeld sank back into his chair, exhaled a long soundless sigh of relief and smiled to rob his next words of any offence. 'My friend, if you weren't British, a deserter, a renegade and a dope-peddler, you'd get the Iron Cross for this. By the way,' he went on, as if by casual afterthought, 'you've been cleared from Padua. The bridge at Neretva? You're sure of this?'

Mallory said irritably: 'If you doubt my word — '

'Of course not, of course not. Just a manner of speaking.' Neufeld paused for a few moments, then said softly: 'The bridge at Neretva.' The way he spoke them, the words sounded almost like a litany.

439

Droshny said softly: 'This fits in with all we suspected.'

'Never mind what you suspected,' Mallory said rudely. 'To *my* business now, if you don't mind. We have done well, you would say? We have fulfilled your request, got the precise information you wanted?' Neufeld nodded. 'Then get us the hell out of here. Fly us deep into some German-held territory. Into Austria or Germany itself, if you like – the farther away from here the better. You know what will happen to us if we ever again fall into British or Yugoslav hands?'

'It's not hard to guess,' Neufeld said almost cheerfully. 'But you misjudge us, my friend. Your departure to a place of safety has already been arranged. A certain Chief of Military Intelligence in northern Italy would very much like to make your personal acquaintance. He has reason to believe that you can be of great help to him.'

Mallory nodded his understanding.

General Vukalovic trained his binoculars on the Zenica Gap, a narrow and heavily-wooded valley floor lying between the bases of two high and steep-shouldered mountains, mountains almost identical in both shape and height.

The German 11th Army Corps tanks among the pines were not difficult to locate, for the Germans had made no attempt either to camouflage or conceal them, measure enough, Vukalovic thought grimly, of the Germans' total confidence in themselves and in the outcome of the battle that lay ahead. He could clearly see soldiers working on some stationary vehicles: other tanks were backing and filling and manoeuvring into position as if making ready to take up battle formation for the actual attack: the deep rumbling

440

roar of the heavy engines of Tiger tanks was almost incessant.

Vukalovic lowered his glasses, jotted down a few more pencil marks on a sheet of paper already almost covered with similar pencil marks, performed a few exercises in addition, laid paper and pencil aside with a sigh and turned to Colonel Janzy, who was similarly engaged.

Vukalovic said wryly: 'My apologies to your staff, Colonel. They can count just as well as I can.'

For once, Captain Jensen's piratical swagger and flashing, confident smile were not very much in evidence: at that moment, in fact, they were totally absent. It would have been impossible for a face of Jensen's generous proportions ever to assume an actually haggard appearance, but the set, grim face displayed unmistakable signs of strain and anxiety and sleeplessness as he paced up and down the 5th Army Operations Headquarters in Termoli in Italy.

He did not pace alone. Beside him, matching him step for step, a burly grey-haired officer in the uniform of a lieutenant-general in the British Army accompanied him backwards and forwards, the expression on his face an exact replica of that on Jensen's. As they came to the farther end of the room, the General stopped and glanced interrogatively at a head-phone-wearing sergeant in front of a large RCA transceiver. The sergeant slowly shook his head. The two men resumed their pacing.

The General said abruptly: 'Time is running out. You do appreciate, Jensen, that once you launch a major offensive you can't possibly stop it?'

'I appreciate it,' Jensen said heavily. 'What are the latest reconnaissance reports, sir?'

'There is no shortage of reports, but God alone knows what to make of them all.' The General sounded bitter. 'There's intense activity all along the Gustav Line, involving – as far as we can make out – two Panzer divisions, one German infantry division, one Austrian infantry division and two Jaeger battalions – their crack Alpine troops. They're not mounting an offensive, that's for sure – in the first place, there's no possibility of their making an offensive from the areas in which they are manoeuvring and in the second place if they *were* contemplating an offensive they'd take damn good care to keep all their preparations secret.'

'All this activity, then? If they're not planning an attack.'

The General sighed. 'Informed opinion has it that they're making all preparations for a lightning pull-out. Informed opinion! All that concerns me is that those blasted divisions are still in the Gustav Line. Jensen, *what has gone wrong?*'

Jensen lifted his shoulders in a gesture of helplessness. 'It was arranged for a radio rendezvous every two hours from four a.m. – '

'There have been no contacts whatsoever.'

Jensen said nothing.

The General looked at him, almost speculatively. 'The best in Southern Europe, you said.'

'Yes, I did say that.'

The General's unspoken doubts as to the quality of the agents Jensen had selected for operation Force 10 would have been considerably heightened if he had been at that moment present with those agents in the guest hut in Hauptmann Neufeld's camp in Bosnia. They were exhibiting none of the harmony, understanding and implicit mutual trust which one would have expected to find among a team of agents rated as the best in the business. There was, instead, tension and anger in the air, an air of suspicion and mistrust so heavy as to be almost palpable. Reynolds, confronting Mallory, had his anger barely under control.

'I want to know now!' Reynolds almost shouted the words.

'Keep your voice down,' Andrea said sharply.

'I want to know now,' Reynolds repeated. This time his voice was little more than a whisper, but none the less demanding and insistent for that.

'You'll be told when the time comes.' As always, Mallory's voice was calm and neutral and devoid of heat. 'Not till then. What you don't know, you can't tell.'

Reynolds clenched his fists and advanced a step. 'Are you damn well insinuating that – '

Mallory said with restraint: 'I'm insinuating nothing. I was right, back in Termoli, Sergeant. You're no better than a ticking time-bomb.'

'Maybe.' Reynolds's fury was out of control now. 'But at least there's something honest about a bomb.'

'Repeat that remark,' Andrea said quietly.

'What?'

'Repeat it.'

'Look, Andrea – '

'Colonel Stavros, sonny.'

'Sir.'

'Repeat it and I'll guarantee you a minimum of five years for insubordination in the field.'

'Yes, sir.' Reynolds's physical effort to bring himself under control was apparent to everyone. 'But *why* should he *not* tell us his plans for this afternoon and at the same time let us all know that we'll be leaving from this Ivenici place tonight?'

'Because our plans are something the Germans can do something about,' Andrea said patiently. 'If they find out. If one of us talked under duress. But they can't do anything about Ivenici — that's in Partisan hands.'

Miller pacifically changed the subject. He said to Mallory: 'Seven thousand feet up, you say. The snow must be thigh-deep up there. How in God's name does anyone hope to clear all that lot away?'

'I don't know,' Mallory said vaguely. 'I suspect somebody will think of something.'

And seven thousand feet up on the Ivenici plateau, somebody had indeed thought of something.

The Ivenici plateau was a wilderness in white, a bleak and desolate and, for many months of the year, a bitterly cold and howling and hostile wilderness, totally inimical to human life, totally intolerant of human presence. The plateau was bounded to the west by a five-hundred-foot-high cliff-face, quite vertical in some parts, fractured and fissured in others. Scattered along its length were numerous frozen waterfalls and occasional lines of pine trees, impossibly growing on impossibly narrow ledges, their frozen branches drooped and laden with the frozen snow of six long months gone by. To the east the plateau was bounded by nothing but an abrupt and sharply defined line marking the top of another cliff-face which dropped away perpendicularly into the valleys below.

The plateau itself consisted of a smooth, absolutely level, unbroken expanse of snow, snow which at that height of 2,000 metres and in the brilliant sunshine gave off a glare and dazzling reflection which was positively hurtful to the eyes. In length, it was perhaps half a mile: in width, nowhere more than a hundred yards.

At its southern end, the plateau rose sharply to merge with the cliff-face which here tailed off and ran into the ground.

On this prominence stood two tents, both white, one small, the other a large marquee. Outside the small tent stood two men, talking. The taller and older man, wearing a heavy greatcoat and a pair of smoked glasses, was Colonel Vis, the commandant of a Sarajevo-based brigade of Partisans: the younger, slighter figure was his adjutant, a Captain Vlanovich. Both men were gazing out over the length of the plateau.

Captain Vlanovich said unhappily: 'There must be easier ways of doing this, sir.'

'You name it, Boris, my boy, and I'll do it.' Both in appearance and voice Colonel Vis gave the impression of immense calm and competence. 'Bull-dozers, I agree, would help. So would snow-ploughs. But you will agree that to drive either of them up vertical cliff-faces in order to reach here would call for considerable skill on the part of the drivers. Besides, what's an army for, if not for marching?'

'Yes, sir,' Vlanovich said, dutifully and doubtfully.

Both men gazed out over the length of the plateau to the north.

To the north, and beyond, for all around a score of encircling mountain peaks, some dark and jagged and sombre, others rounded and snow-capped and rose-coloured, soared up into the cloudless washed-out pale blue of the sky. It was an immensely impressive sight.

Even more impressive was the spectacle taking place on the plateau itself. A solid phalanx of a thousand uniformed soldiers, perhaps half in the buff grey of

445

the Yugoslav army, the rest in a motley array of other countries' uniforms, were moving, at a snail-pace, across the virgin snow.

The phalanx was fifty people wide but only twenty deep, each line of fifty linked arm-in-arm, heads and shoulders bowed forward as they laboriously trudged at a painfully slow pace through the snow. That the pace was so slow was no matter for wonder, the leading line of men were ploughing their way through waist-deep snow, and already the signs of strain and exhaustion were showing in their faces. It was killingly hard work, work which, at that altitude, doubled the pulse rate, made a man fight for every gasping breath, turned a man's legs into leaden and agonized limbs where only the pain could convince him that they were still part of him.

And not only men. After the first five lines of soldiers, there were almost as many women and girls in the remainder of the phalanx as there were men, although everyone was so muffled against the freezing cold and biting winds of those high altitudes that it was impossible almost to tell man from woman. The last two lines of the phalanx were composed entirely of *partisankas* and it was significantly ominous of the murderous labour still to come that even they were sinking knee-deep in the snow.

It was a fantastic sight, but a sight that was far from unique in wartime Yugosalavia. The airfields of the lowlands, completely dominated by the armoured divisions of the Wehrmacht, were permanently barred to the Yugoslavs and it was thus that the Partisans constructed many of their airstrips in the mountains. In snow of this depth and in areas completely inaccessible to powered mechanical aids, there was no other way open to them.

Colonel Vis looked away and turned to Captain Vlanovich.

'Well, Boris, my boy, do you think you're up here for the winter sports? Get the food and soup kitchens organized. We'll use up a whole week's rations of hot food and hot soup in this one day.'

'Yes, sir.' Vlanovich cocked his head, then removed his ear-flapped fur cap the better to listen to the newly-begun sound of distant explosions to the north. 'What on earth is that?'

Vis said musingly: 'Sound does carry far in our pure Yugoslavian mountain air, does it not?'

'Sir? Please?'

'That, my boy,' Vis said with considerable satisfaction, 'is the Messerschmitt fighter base at Novo Derventa getting the biggest plastering of its lifetime.'

'Sir?'

Vis sighed in long-suffering patience. 'I'll make a soldier of you some day. Messerschmitts, Boris, are fighters, carrying all sorts of nasty cannons and machine-guns. What, at this moment, is the finest fighter target in Yugoslavia?'

'What is – ' Vlanovich broke off and looked again at the trudging phalanx. 'Oh!'

' "Oh," indeed. The British Air Force have diverted six of their best Lancaster heavy bomber squadrons from the Italian front just to attend to our friends at Novo Derventa.' He in turn removed his cap, the better to listen. 'Hard at work, aren't they? By the time they're finished there won't be a Messerschmitt able to take off from that field for a week. If, that is to say, there are any left to take off.'

'If I might venture a remark, sir?'

'You may so venture, Captain Vlanovich.'

'There are other fighter bases.'

447

'True.' Vis pointed upwards. 'See anything?'

Vlanovich craned his neck, shielded his eyes against the brilliant sun, gazed into the empty blue sky and shook his head.

'Neither do I,' Vis agreed. 'But at seven thousand metres – and with their crews even colder than we are – squadrons of Beaufighters will be keeping relief patrol up there until dark.'

'Who – who *is* he, sir? Who can ask for all our soldiers down here, for squadrons of bombers and fighters?'

'Fellow called Captain Mallory, I believe.'

'A *captain*? Like me?'

'A captain. I doubt, Boris,' Vis went on kindly, 'whether he's quite like you. But it's not the rank that counts. It's the name. Mallory.'

'Never heard of him.'

'You will, my boy, you will.'

'But – but this man Mallory. What does he want all this *for*?'

'Ask him when you see him tonight.'

'When I – he's coming here tonight?'

'Tonight. If,' Vis added sombrely, 'he lives that long.'

Neufeld, followed by Droshny, walked briskly and confidently into his radio hut, a bleak, ramshackle lean-to furnished with a table, two chairs, a large portable transceiver and nothing else. The German corporal seated before the radio looked up enquiringly at their entrance.

'The Seventh Armoured Corps HQ at the Neretva bridge,' Neufeld ordered. He seemed in excellent spirits. 'I wish to speak to General Zimmermann personally.'

The corporal nodded acknowledgment, put through the call-sign and was answered within seconds. He listened briefly, looked up at Neufeld. 'The General is coming now, sir.'

Neufeld reached out a hand for the ear-phones, took them and nodded towards the door. The corporal rose and left the hut while Neufeld took the vacated seat and adjusted the head-phones to his satisfaction. After a few seconds he automatically straightened in his seat as a voice came crackling over the ear-phones.

'Hauptmann Neufeld here, Herr General. The Englishmen have returned. Their information is that the Partisan division in the Zenica Cage is expecting a full-scale attack from the south across the Neretva bridge.'

'Are they now?' General Zimmermann, comfortably seated in a swivel chair in the back of the radio truck parked on the tree-line due south of the Neretva bridge, made no attempt to conceal the satisfaction in his voice. The canvas hood of the truck was rolled back and he removed his peaked cap the better to enjoy the pale spring sunshine. 'Interesting, very interesting. Anything else?'

'Yes,' Neufeld's voice crackled metallically over the loudspeaker. 'They've asked to be flown to sanctuary. Deep behind our lines, even to Germany. They feel – ah – unsafe here.'

'Well, well, well. Is that how they feel.' Zimmermann paused, considered, then continued. 'You are fully informed of the situation, Hauptmann Neufeld? You are aware of the delicate balance of – um – niceties involved?'

'Yes, Herr General.'

'This calls for a moment's thought. Wait.'

Zimmermann swung idly to and fro in his swivel chair as he pondered his decision. He gazed thoughtfully but almost unseeingly to the north, across the meadows bordering the south bank of the Neretva, the river spanned by the iron bridge, then the meadows on the far side rising steeply to the rocky redoubt which served as the first line of defence for Colonel Lazlo's Partisan defenders. To the east, as he turned, he could look up the green-white rushing waters of the Neretva, the meadows on either side of it narrowing until, curving north, they disappeared suddenly at the mouth of the cliff-sided gorge from which the Neretva emerged. Another quarter turn and he was gazing into the pine forest to the south, a pine forest which at first seemed innocuous enough and empty of life – until, that was, one's eyes became accustomed to the gloom and scores of large rectangular shapes, effectively screened from both observation from the air and from the northern bank of the Neretva by camouflage canvas, camouflage nets and huge piles of dead branches. The sight of those camouflaged spearheads of his two Panzer divisions somehow helped Zimmermann to make up his mind. He picked up the microphone.

'Hauptmann Neufeld? I have decided on a course of action and you will please carry out the following instructions precisely . . .'

Droshny removed the duplicate pair of ear-phones that he had been wearing and said doubtfully to Neufeld: 'Isn't the General asking rather a lot of us?'

Neufeld shook his head reassuringly. 'General Zimmermann *always* knows what he is doing. His psychological assessment of the Captain Mallorys of this world is invariably a hundred per cent right.'

'I hope so.' Droshny was unconvinced. 'For our sakes, I hope so.'

They left the hut. Neufeld said to the radio operator: 'Captain Mallory in my office, please. And Sergeant Baer.'

450

Mallory arrived in the office to find Neufeld, Droshny and Baer already there. Neufeld was brief and businesslike.

'We've decided on a ski-plane to fly you out — they're the only planes that can land in those damned mountains. You'll have time for a few hours' sleep — we don't leave till four. Any questions?'

'Where's the landing-strip?'

'A clearing. A kilometre from here. Anything else?'

'Nothing. Just get us out of here, that's all.'

'You need have no worry on that score,' Neufeld said emphatically. 'My one ambition is to see you safely on your way. Frankly, Mallory, you're just an embarrassment to me and the sooner you're on your way the better.'

Mallory nodded and left. Neufeld turned to Baer and said: 'I have a little task for you, Sergeant Baer. Little but very important. Listen carefully.'

Mallory left Neufeld's hut, his face pensive, and walked slowly across the compound. As he approached the guest hut, Andrea emerged and passed wordlessly by, wreathed in cigar smoke and scowling. Mallory entered the hut where Petar was again playing the Yugoslavian version of 'The girl I left behind me'. It seemed to be his favourite song. Mallory glanced at Maria, Reynolds and Groves, all sitting silently by, then at Miller who was reclining in his sleeping-bag with his volume of poetry.

Mallory nodded towards the doorway. 'Something's upset our friend.'

Miller grinned and nodded in turn towards Petar. 'He's playing Andrea's tune again.'

Mallory smiled briefly and turned to Maria. 'Tell him to stop playing. We're pulling out late this afternoon and we all need all the sleep we can get.'

451

'We can sleep in the plane,' Reynolds said sullenly. 'We can sleep when we arrive at our destination – wherever that may be.'

'No, sleep now.'

'Why now?'

'Why now?' Mallory's unfocused eyes gazed into the far distance. He said in a quiet voice: 'For now is all the time there may be.'

Reynolds looked at him strangely. For the first time that day his face was empty of hostility and suspicion. There was puzzled speculation in his eyes, and wonder and the first faint beginnings of understanding.

On the Ivenici plateau, the phalanx moved on, but they moved no more like human beings. They stumbled along now in the advanced stages of exhaustion, automatons, no more, zombies resurrected from the dead, their faces twisted with pain and unimaginable fatigue, their limbs on fire and their minds benumbed. Every few seconds someone stumbled and fell and could not get up again and had to be carried to join scores of others already lying in an almost comatose condition by the side of the primitive runway, where *partisankas* did their best to revive their frozen and exhausted bodies with mugs of hot soup and liberal doses of *raki*.

Captain Vlanovich turned to Colonel Vis. His face was distressed, his voice low and deeply earnest.

'This is madness, Colonel, madness! It's – it's impossible, you can see it's impossible. We'll never – look, sir, two hundred and fifty dropped out in the first two hours. The altitude, the cold, sheer physical exhaustion. It's madness.'

'All war is madness,' Vis said calmly. 'Get on the radio. We require five hundred more men.'

CHAPTER EIGHT

Friday 1500–2115

Now it had come, Mallory knew. He looked at Andrea and Miller and Reynolds and Groves and knew that they knew it too. In their faces he could see very clearly reflected what lay at the very surface of his own mind, the explosive tension, the hair-trigger alertness straining to be translated into equally explosive action. Always it came, this moment of truth that stripped men bare and showed them for what they were. He wondered how Reynolds and Groves would be: he suspected they might acquit themselves well. It never occurred to him to wonder about Miller and Andrea, for he knew them too well: Miller, when all seemed lost, was a man above himself, while the normally easy-going, almost lethargic Andrea was transformed into an unrecognizable human being, an impossible combination of an icily calculating mind and berserker fighting machine entirely without the remotest parallel in Mallory's knowledge or experience. When Mallory spoke his voice was as calmly impersonal as ever.

'We're due to leave at four. It's now three. With any luck we'll catch them napping. Is everything clear?'

Reynolds said wonderingly, almost unbelievingly: 'You mean if anything goes wrong we're to shoot our way out?'

'You're to shoot and shoot to kill. That, Sergeant, is an order.'

'Honest to God,' Reynolds said, 'I just don't know what's going on.' The expression on his face clearly indicated that he had given up all attempts to understand what was going on.

Mallory and Andrea left the hut and walked casually across the compound towards Neufeld's hut. Mallory said: 'They're on to us, you know.'

'I know. Where are Petar and Maria?'

'Asleep, perhaps? They left the hut a couple of hours ago. We'll collect them later.'

'Later may be too late ... They are in great peril, my Keith.'

'What can a man do, Andrea? I've thought of nothing else in the past ten hours. It's a crucifying risk to have to take, but I have to take it. They are expendable, Andrea. You know what it would mean if I showed my hand now.'

'I know what it would mean,' Andrea said heavily. 'The end of everything.'

They entered Neufeld's hut without benefit of knocking. Neufeld, sitting behind his desk with Droshny by his side, looked up in irritated surprise and glanced at his watch.

He said curtly: 'Four o'clock, I said, not three.'

'Our mistake,' Mallory apologized. He closed the door. 'Please do not be foolish.'

Neufeld and Droshny were not foolish, few people would have been while staring down the muzzles of two Lugers with perforated silencers screwed to the end: they just sat there, immobile, the shock slowly draining from their faces. There was a long pause then Neufeld spoke, the words coming almost haltingly.

'I have been seriously guilty of underestimating – '

'Be quiet. Broznik's spies have discovered the whereabouts of the four captured Allied agents. We know

454

roughly where they are. You know precisely where they are. You will take us there. Now.'

'You're mad,' Neufeld said with conviction.

'We don't require you to tell us that.' Andrea walked round behind Neufeld and Droshny, removed their pistols from their holsters, ejected the shells and replaced the pistols. He then crossed to a corner of the hut, picked up two Schmeisser machine-pistols, emptied them, walked back round to the front of the table and placed the Schmeissers on its top, one in front of Neufeld, one in front of Droshny.

'There you are, gentlemen,' Andrea said affably. 'Armed to the teeth.'

Droshny said viciously: 'Suppose we decide not to come with you?'

Andrea's affability vanished. He walked unhurriedly round the table and rammed the Luger's silencer with such force against Droshny's teeth that he gasped in pain. 'Please – ' Andrea's voice was almost beseeching – *'please* don't tempt me.'

Droshny didn't tempt him. Mallory moved to the window and peered out over the compound. There were, he saw, at least a dozen Cetniks within thirty feet of Neufeld's hut, all of them armed. Across the other side of the compound he could see that the door to the stables was open indicating that Miller and the two sergeants were in position.

'You will walk across the compound to the stables,' Mallory said. 'You will talk to nobody, warn nobody, make no signals. We will follow about ten yards behind.'

'Ten yards behind. What's to prevent us making a break for it? You wouldn't dare hold a gun on us out there.'

'That's so,' Mallory agreed. 'From the moment you

455

open this door you'll be covered by three Schmeissers from the stables. If you try anything – *anything* – you'll be cut to pieces. That's why we're keeping well behind you – we don't want to be cut to pieces too.'

At a gesture from Andrea, Neufeld and Droshny slung their empty Schmeissers in angry silence. Mallory looked at them consideringly and said: 'I think you'd better do something about your expressions. They're a dead giveaway that something is wrong. If you open that door with faces like that, Miller will cut you down before you reach the bottom step. Please try to believe me.'

They believed him and by the time Mallory opened the door had managed to arrange their features into a near enough imitation of normality. They went down the steps and set off across the compound to the stables. When they had reached halfway Andrea and Mallory left Neufeld's hut and followed them. One or two glances of idle curiosity came their way, but clearly no one suspected that anything was amiss. The crossing to the stables was completely uneventful.

So also, two minutes later, was their departure from the camp. Neufeld and Droshny, as would have been proper and expected, rode together in the lead, Droshny in particular looking very warlike with his Schmeisser, pistol and the wickedly-curved knives at his waist. Behind them rode Andrea, who appeared to be having some trouble with the action of his Schmeisser, for he had it in his hands and was examining it closely: he certainly wasn't looking at either Droshny or Neufeld and the fact that the gun barrel, which Andrea had sensibly pointed towards the ground, had only to be lifted a foot and the trigger pressed to riddle the two men ahead was a preposterous idea that would not have occurred to even the most suspicious. Behind Andrea,

Mallory and Miller rode abreast: like Andrea, they appeared unconcerned, even slightly bored. Reynolds and Groves brought up the rear, almost but not quite attaining the degree of nonchalance of the other three: their still faces and restlessly darting eyes betrayed the strain they were under. But their anxiety was needless for all seven passed from the camp not only unmolested but without as much as even an enquiring glance being cast in their direction.

They rode for over two and a half hours, climbing nearly all the time, and a blood-red sun was setting among the thinning pines to the west when they came across a clearing set on, for once, a level stretch of ground. Neufeld and Droshny halted their ponies and waited until the others came up with them. Mallory reined in and gazed at the building in the middle of the clearing, a low, squat, immensely strong-looking block-house, with narrow, heavily barred windows and two chimneys, from one of which smoke was coming.

'This is the place?' Mallory asked.

'Hardly a necessary question.' Neufeld's voice was dry, but the underlying resentment and anger unmistakable. 'You think I spent all this time leading you to the wrong place?'

'I wouldn't put it past you,' Mallory said. He examined the building more closely. 'A hospitable-looking place.'

'Yugoslav Army ammunition dumps were never intended as first-class hotels.'

'I dare say not,' Mallory agreed. At a signal from him they urged their ponies forward into the clearing, and as they did so two metal strips in the facing wall of the block-house slid back to reveal a pair of embrasures with machine-pistols protruding. Exposed as they were, the seven mounted men were completely at the mercy of those menacing muzzles.

'Your men keep a good watch,' Mallory acknowledged to Neufeld. 'You wouldn't require many men to guard and hold a place like this. How many are there?'

'Six,' Neufeld said reluctantly.

'Seven and you're a dead man,' Andrea warned.

'Six.'

As they approached, the guns — almost certainly because the men behind them had identified Neufeld and Droshny — were withdrawn, the embrasures closed, the heavy metal front door opened. A sergeant appeared in the doorway and saluted respectfully, his face registering a certain surprise.

'An unexpected pleasure, Hauptmann Neufeld,' the sergeant said. 'We had no radio message informing us of your arrival.'

'It's out of action for the moment.' Neufeld waved them inside but Andrea gallantly insisted on the German officer taking precedence, reinforcing his courtesy with a threatening hitch of his Schmeisser. Neufeld entered, followed by Droshny and the other five men.

The windows were so narrow that the burning oil lamps were obviously a necessity, the illumination they afforded being almost doubled by a large log fire blazing in the hearth. Nothing could ever overcome the bleakness created by four rough-cut stone walls, but the room itself was surprisingly well furnished with a table, chairs, two armchairs and a sofa: there were even some pieces of carpet. Three doors led off from the room, one heavily barred. Including the sergeant who had welcomed them, there were three armed soldiers in the room. Mallory glanced at Neufeld who nodded, his face tight in suppressed anger.

Neufeld said to one of the guards: 'Bring out the prisoners.' The guard nodded, lifted a heavy key from the wall and headed for the barred door. The sergeant and the other guard were sliding the metal screens back across the embrasures. Andrea walked casually towards the nearest guard, then suddenly and violently shoved him against the sergeant. Both men cannoned into the guard who had just inserted the key into the door. The third man fell heavily to the ground: the other two, though staggering wildly, managed to retain a semblance of balance or at least remain on their feet. All three twisted round to stare at Andrea, anger and startled incomprehension in their faces, and all three remained very still, and wisely so. Faced with a Schmeisser machine-pistol at three paces, the wise man always remains still.

Mallory said to the sergeant: 'There are three other men. Where are they?'

There was no reply: the guard glared at him in defiance. Mallory repeated the question, this time in fluent German: the guard ignored him and looked questioningly at Neufeld, whose lips were tight-shut in a mask of stone.

'Are you mad?' Neufeld demanded of the sergeant. 'Can't you see those men are killers? Tell him.'

'The night guards. They're asleep.' The sergeant pointed to a door. 'That one.'

'Open it. Tell them to walk out. Backwards and with their hands clasped behind their necks.'

'Do exactly as you're told,' Neufeld ordered.

The sergeant did exactly what he was told and so did the three guards who had been resting in the inner room, who walked out as they had been instructed, with obviously no thought of any resistance in their minds. Mallory turned to the guard with the key who

459

had by this time picked himself up somewhat shakily from the floor, and nodded to the barred door.

'Open it.'

The guard opened it and pushed the door wide. Four British officers moved out slowly and uncertainly into the outer room. Long confinement indoors had made them very pale, but apart from this prison pallor and the fact that they were rather thin they were obviously unharmed. The man in the lead, with a major's insignia and a Sandhurst moustache – and, when he spoke, a Sandhurst accent – stopped abruptly and stared in disbelief at Mallory and his men.

'Good God above! What on earth are you chaps – '

'Please.' Mallory cut him short. 'I'm sorry, but later. Collect your coats, whatever warm gear you have, and wait outside.'

'But – but where are you taking us?'

'Home. Italy. Tonight. Please hurry!'

'Italy. You're talking – '

'Hurry!' Mallory glanced in some exasperation at his watch. 'We're late already.'

As quickly as their dazed condition would allow, the four officers collected what warm clothing they had and filed outside. Mallory turned to the sergeant again. 'You must have ponies here, a stable.'

'Round the back of the block-house,' the sergeant said promptly. He had obviously made a rapid readjustment to the new facts of life.

'Good lad,' Mallory said approvingly. He looked at Groves and Reynolds. 'We'll need two more ponies. Saddle them up, will you?'

The two sergeants left. Under the watchful guns of Mallory and Miller, Andrea searched each of the six guards in turn, found nothing, and ushered them all into the cell, turning the heavy key and hanging it up on the wall. Then, just as carefully, Andrea searched Neufeld and Droshny: Droshny's face, as Andrea carelessly flung his knives into a corner of the room, was thunderous.

Mallory looked at the two men and said: 'I'd shoot you if necessary. It's not. You won't be missed before morning.'

'They might not be missed for a good few mornings,' Miller pointed out.

'So they're over-weight anyway,' Mallory said indifferently. He smiled. 'I can't resist leaving you with a last little pleasant thought, Hauptmann Neufeld. Something to think about until someone comes and finds you.' He looked consideringly at Neufeld, who said nothing, then went on: 'About that information I gave you this morning, I mean.'

Neufeld looked at him guardedly. 'What about the information you gave me this morning?'

'Just this. It wasn't, I'm afraid, quite accurate. Vukalovic expects the attack from the *north*, through the Zenica Gap, not across the bridge at Neretva from the south. There are, we know, close on two hundred of your tanks massed in the woods just to the north of the Zenica Gap – but there won't be at two a.m. this morning when your attack is due to start. Not after I've got through to our Lancaster squadrons in Italy. Think of it, think of the target. Two hundred tanks bunched in a tiny trap a hundred and fifty yards wide and not more than three hundred yards long. The RAF will be there at 1.30. By two this morning there won't be a single tank left in commission.'

Neufeld looked at him for a long moment, his face very still, then said, slowly and softly: 'Damn you! Damn you! Damn you!'

'Damning is all you'll have for it,' Mallory said

agreeably. 'By the time you are released – hopefully assuming that you will be released – it will all be over. See you after the war.'

Andrea locked the two men in a side room and hung the key up by the one to the cell. Then they went outside, locked the outer door, hung the key on a nail by the door, mounted their ponies – Groves and Reynolds had already two additional ones saddled – and started climbing once again, Mallory, map in hand, studying in the fading light of dusk the route they had to take.

Their route took them up alongside the perimeter of a pine forest. Not more than half a mile after leaving the block-house, Andrea reined in his pony, dismounted, lifted the pony's right foreleg and examined it carefully. He looked up at the others who had also reined in their ponies.

'There's a stone wedged under the hoof,' he announced. 'Looks bad – but not too bad. I'll have to cut it out. Don't wait for me – I'll catch you up in a few minutes.'

Mallory nodded, gave the signal to move on. Andrea produced a knife, lifted the hoof and made a great play of excavating the wedged stone. After a minute or so, he glanced up and saw that the rest of the party had vanished round a corner of the pine wood. Andrea put away his knife and led the pony, which quite obviously had no limp whatsoever, into the shelter of the wood and tethered it there, then moved on foot some way down the hill towards the block-house. He sat down behind the bole of a convenient pine and removed his binoculars from their case.

He hadn't long to wait. The head and shoulders of a figure appeared in the clearing below peering out cautiously from behind the trunk of a tree. Andrea flat in the snow now and with the icy rims of the binoculars clamped hard against his eyes, had no difficulty at all in making an immediate identification: Sergeant Baer, moon-faced, rotund and about seventy pounds overweight for his unimpressive height, had an unmistakable physical presence which only the mentally incapacitated could easily forget.

Baer withdrew into the woods, then reappeared shortly afterwards leading a string of ponies, one of which carried a bulky covered object strapped to a pannier bag. Two of the following ponies had riders, both of whom had their hands tied to the pommels of their saddles. Petar and Maria, without a doubt. Behind them appeared four mounted soldiers. Sergeant Baer beckoned them to follow him across the clearing and within moments all had disappeared from sight behind the block-house. Andrea regarded the now empty clearing thoughtfully, lit a fresh cigar and made his way uphill towards his tethered pony.

Sergeant Baer dismounted, produced a key from his pocket, caught sight of the key suspended from the nail beside the door, replaced his own, took down the other, opened the door with it and passed inside. He glanced around, took down one of the keys hanging on the wall and opened a side door with it. Hauptmann Neufeld emerged, glanced at his watch and smiled.

'You have been very punctual, Sergeant Baer. You have the radio?'

'I have the radio. It's outside.'

'Good, good, good.' Neufeld looked at Droshny and smiled again. 'I think it's time for us to make our rendezvous with the Ivenici plateau.'

Sergeant Baer said respectfully: 'How can you be

463

so sure that it is the Ivenici plateau, Hauptmann Neufeld?'

'How can I be so sure? Simple, my dear Baer. Because Maria – you have her with you?'

'But of course, Hauptmann Neufeld.'

'Because Maria told me. The Ivenici plateau it is.'

Night had fallen on the Ivenici plateau, but still the phalanx of exhausted soldiers was trudging out the landing-strip for the plane. The work was not by this time so cruelly and physically exacting, for the snow was now almost trampled and beaten hard and flat: but, even allowing for the rejuvenation given by the influx of another five hundred fresh soldiers, the overall level of utter weariness was such that the phalanx was in no better condition than its original members who had trudged out the first outline of the airstrip in the virgin snow.

The phalanx, too, had changed its shape. Instead of being fifty wide by twenty deep it was now twenty wide by fifty deep: having achieved a safe clearance for the wings of the aircraft, they were now trudging out what was to be as close as possible an iron-hard surface for the landing wheels.

A three-quarters moon, intensely white and luminous, rode low in the sky, with scattered bands of cloud coming drifting down slowly from the north. As the successive bands moved across the face of the moon, the black shadows swept lazily across the surface of the plateau: the phalanx, at one moment bathed in silvery moonlight, was at the next almost lost to sight in the darkness. It was a fantastic scene with a remarkably faery-like quality of eeriness and foreboding about it. In fact it was, as Colonel Vis had just unromantically mentioned to Captain Vlanovich, like something out

464

of Dante's *Inferno*, only a hundred degrees colder. At least a hundred degrees, Vis had amended: he wasn't sure how hot it was in hell.

It was this scene which, at twenty minutes to nine in the evening, confronted Mallory and his men when they topped the brow of a hill and reined in their ponies just short of the edge of the precipice which abutted on the western edge of the Ivenici plateau. For at least two minutes they sat there on their ponies, not moving, not speaking, mesmerized by the other-world quality of a thousand men with bowed heads and bowed shoulders, shuffling exhaustedly across the level floor of the plain beneath, mesmerized because they all knew they were gazing at a unique spectacle which none of them had ever seen before and would never see again. Mallory finally broke free from the trance-like condition, looked at Miller and Andrea, and slowly shook his head in an expression of profound wonder conveying his disbelief, his refusal to accept the reality of what his own eyes told him was real and actual beyond dispute. Miller and Andrea returned his look with almost identical negative motions of their own heads. Mallory wheeled his pony to the right and led the way along the cliff-face to the point where the cliff ran into the rising ground below.

Ten minutes later they were being greeted by Colonel Vis.

'I did not expect to see you, Captain Mallory.' Vis pumped his hand enthusiastically. 'Before God, I did not expect to see you. You – and your men – must have a remarkable capacity for survival.'

'Say that in a few hours,' Mallory said drily, 'and I would be very happy indeed to hear it.'

'But it's all over now. We expect the plane – ' Vis glanced at his watch – 'in exactly eight minutes. We have a bearing surface for it and there should be no difficulty in landing and taking off provided it doesn't hang around too long. You have done all that you came to do and achieved it magnificently. Luck has been on your side.'

'Say that in a few hours,' Mallory repeated.

'I'm sorry.' Vis could not conceal his puzzlement. 'You expect something to happen to the plane?'

'I don't expect anything to happen to the plane. But what's gone, what's past, is – was, rather – only the prologue.'

'The – the prologue?'

'Let me explain.'

Neufeld, Droshny and Sergeant Baer left their ponies tethered inside the woodline and walked up the slight eminence before them, Sergeant Baer making heavy weather of their uphill struggle through the snow because of the weight of the large portable transceiver strapped to his back. Near the summit they dropped to their hands and knees and crawled forward till they were within a few feet of the edge of the cliff overlooking the Ivenici plateau. Neufeld unslung his binoculars and then replaced them: the moon had just moved from behind a dark barred cloud highlighting every aspect of the scene below: the intensely sharp contrast afforded by black shadow and snow so deeply and gleamingly white as to be almost phosphorescent made the use of binoculars superfluous.

Clearly visible and to the right were Vis's command tents and, near by, some hastily erected soup kitchens. Outside the smallest of the tents could be seen a group of perhaps a dozen people, obviously, even at that distance, engaged in close conversation. Directly beneath where they lay, the three men could see the phalanx

466

turning round at one end of the runway and beginning to trudge back slowly, so terribly slowly, so terribly tiredly, along the wide path already tramped out. As Mallory and his men had been, Neufeld, Droshny and Baer were momentarily caught and held by the weird and other-worldly dark grandeur of the spectacle below. Only by a conscious act of will could Neufeld bring himself to look away and return to the world of normality and reality.

'How very kind,' he murmured, 'of our Yugoslav friends to go to such lengths on our behalf.' He turned to Baer and indicated the transceiver. 'Get through to the General, will you?'

Baer unslung his transceiver, settled it firmly in the snow, extended the telescopic aerial, pre-set the frequency and cranked the handle. He made contact almost at once, talked briefly then handed the microphone and head-piece to Neufeld, who fitted on the phones and gazed down, still half mesmerized, at the thousand men and women moving antlike across the plain below. The head-phones cracked suddenly in his ears and the spell was broken

'Herr General?'

'Ah. Hauptmann Neufeld.' In the ear-phones the General's voice was faint but very clear, completely free from distortion or static. 'Now then. About my psychological assessment of the English mind?'

'You have mistaken your profession, Herr General. Everything has happened exactly as you forecast. You will be interested to know, sir, that the Royal Air Force is launching a saturation bombing attack on the Zenica Gap at precisely 1.30 a.m. this morning.'

'Well, well, well,' Zimmermann said thoughtfully. 'That is interesting. But hardly surprising.'

'No, sir.' Neufeld looked up as Droshny touched

467

him on the shoulder and pointed to the north. 'One moment, sir.'

Neufeld removed the ear-phones and cocked his head in the direction of Droshny's pointing arm. He lifted his binoculars but there was nothing to be seen. But unquestionably there was something to be heard – the distant clamour of aircraft engines, closing. Neufeld readjusted the ear-phones.

'We have to give the English full marks for punctuality, sir. The plane is coming in now.'

'Excellent, excellent. Keep me informed.'

Neufeld eased off one ear-phone and gazed to the north. Still nothing to be seen, the moon was now temporarily behind a cloud, but the sound of the aircraft engines was unmistakably closer. Suddenly, somewhere down on the plateau, came three sharp blasts on a whistle. Immediately, the marching phalanx broke up, men and women stumbling off the runway into the deep snow on the eastern side of the plateau, leaving behind them, obviously by pre-arrangement, about eighty men who spaced themselves out on either side of the runway.

'They're organized, I'll say that for them,' Neufeld said admiringly.

Droshny smiled his wolf's smile. 'All the better for us, eh?'

'Everybody seems to be doing their best to help us tonight,' Neufeld agreed.

Overhead, the dark and obscuring band of cloud drifted away to the south and the white light of the moon raced across the plateau. Neufeld could immediately see the plane, less than half a mile away, its camouflaged shape sharply etched in the brilliant moonlight as it sank down towards the end of the runway. Another sharp blast of the whistle and at once the men lining both sides of the runway switched on hand lamps – a superfluity, really, in those almost bright as day perfect landing conditions, but essential had the moon been hidden behind cloud.

'Touching down now,' Neufeld said into the microphone. 'It's a Wellington bomber.'

'Let's hope it makes a safe landing,' Zimmermann said.

'Let's hope so indeed, sir.'

The Wellington made a safe landing, a perfect landing considering the extremely difficult conditions. It slowed down quickly, then steadied its speed as it headed towards the end of the runway.

Neufeld said into the microphone: 'Safely down, Herr General, and rolling to rest.'

'Why doesn't it stop?' Droshny wondered.

'You can't accelerate a plane over snow as you can over a concrete runway,' Neufeld said. 'They'll require every yard of the runway for the take-off.'

Quite obviously, the pilot of the Wellington was of the same opinion. He was about fifty yards from the end of the runway when two groups of people broke from the hundreds lining the edge of the runway, one group heading for the already opened door in the side of the bomber, the other heading for the tail of the plane. Both groups reached the plane just as it rolled to a stop at the very end of the runway, a dozen men at once flinging themselves upon the tail unit and beginning to turn the Wellington through 180°.

Droshny was impressed. 'By heavens, they're not wasting much time, are they?'

'They can't afford to. If the plane stays there any time at all it'll start sinking in the snow.' Neufeld lifted his binoculars and spoke into the microphone.

'They're boarding now, Herr General. One, two, three
. . . seven, eight, nine. Nine it is.' Neufeld sighed in
relief and at the relief of tension. 'My warmest congratulations, Herr General. Nine it is, indeed.'

The plane was already facing the way it had come.
The pilot stood on the brakes, revved the engines up to
a crescendo, then twenty seconds after it had come to a
halt the Wellington was on its way again, accelerating
down the runway. The pilot took no chances, he
waited till the very far end of the airstrip before
lifting the Wellington off, but when he did it rose
cleanly and easily and climbed steadily into the night
sky.

'Airborne, Herr General,' Neufeld reported. 'Everything perfectly according to plan.' He covered the
microphone, looking after the disappearing plane, then
smiled at Droshny. 'I think we should wish them *bon
voyage*, don't you?'

Mallory, one of the hundreds lining the perimeter
of the airstrip, lowered his binoculars. 'And a very
pleasant journey to them all.'

Colonel Vis shook his head sadly. 'All this work
just to send five of my men on a holiday to Italy.'

'I dare say they needed a break,' Mallory said.

'The hell with them. How about us?' Reynolds
demanded. In spite of the words, his face showed no
anger, just a dazed and total bafflement. 'We should
have been aboard that damned plane.'

'Ah. Well. I changed my mind.'

'Like hell you changed your mind,' Reynolds said
bitterly.

Inside the fuselage of the Wellington, the moustached
major surveyed his three fellow-escapees and the five

470

Partisan soldiers, shook his head in disbelief and turned to the captain by his side.

'A rum do, what?'

'Very rum, indeed, sir,' said the captain. He looked curiously at the papers the major held in his hand. 'What have you there?'

'A map and papers that I'm to give to some bearded naval type when we land back in Italy. Odd fellow, that Mallory, what?'

'Very odd indeed, sir,' the captain agreed.

Mallory and his men, together with Vis and Vlanovich, had detached themselves from the crowd and were now standing outside Vis's command tent.

Mallory said to Vis: 'You have arranged for the ropes? We must leave at once.'

'What's all the desperate hurry, sir?' Groves asked. Like Reynolds, much of his resentment seemed to have gone to be replaced by a helpless bewilderment. 'All of a sudden, like, I mean?'

'Petar and Maria,' Mallory said grimly. 'They're the hurry.'

'What about Petar and Maria?' Reynolds asked suspiciously. 'Where do they come into this?'

'They're being held captive in the ammunition block-house. And when Neufeld and Droshny get back there – '

'Get back there,' Groves said dazedly. 'What do you mean, get back there? We – we left them locked up. And how in God's name do you know that Petar and Maria are being held in the block-house? How can they be? I mean, they weren't there when we left there – and that wasn't so long ago.'

'When Andrea's pony had a stone in its hoof on the way up here from the block-house, it didn't have

471

a stone in its hoof. Andrea was keeping watch.'

'You see,' Miller explained, 'Andrea doesn't trust anyone.'

'He saw Sergeant Baer taking Petar and Maria there,' Mallory went on. 'Bound. Baer released Neufeld and Droshny and you can bet your last cent our precious pair were up on the cliffside there checking that we really did fly out.'

'You don't tell us very much, do you, sir?' Reynolds said bitterly.

'I'll tell you this much,' Mallory said with certainty. 'If we don't get there soon, Maria and Petar are for the high jump. Neufeld and Droshny don't *know* yet, but by this time they must be pretty convinced that it was Maria who told me where those four agents were being kept. They've always known who we really were – Maria told them. Now they know who Maria is. Just before Droshny killed Saunders – '

'Droshny?' Reynolds's expression was that of a man who has almost given up all attempt to understand. 'Maria?'

'I made a miscalculation.' Mallory sounded tired. 'We all make miscalculations, but this was a bad one.' He smiled, but the smile didn't touch his eyes. 'You will recall that you had a few harsh words to say about Andrea here when he picked that fight with Droshny outside the dining hut in Neufeld's camp?'

'Sure I remember. It was one of the craziest – '

'You can apologize to Andrea at a later and more convenient time,' Mallory interrupted. 'Andrea provoked Droshny because I asked him to. I knew that Neufeld and Droshny were up to no good in the dining hut after we had left and I wanted a moment to ask Maria what they had been discussing. She told me that they intended to send a couple of Cetniks after

472

us into Broznik's camp – suitably disguised, of course – to report on us. They were two of the men acting as our escort in that wood-burning truck. Andrea and Miller killed them.'

'Now you tell us,' Groves said almost mechanically. 'Andrea and Miller killed them.'

'What I didn't know was that Droshny was also following us. He saw Maria and myself together.' He looked at Reynolds. 'Just as you did. I didn't know at the time that he'd seen us, but I've known for some hours now. Maria has been as good as under sentence of death since this morning. But there was nothing I could do about it. Not until now. If I'd shown my hand, we'd have been finished.'

Reynolds shook his head. 'But you've just said that Maria betrayed us – '

'Maria,' Mallory said, 'is a top-flight British espionage agent. English father, Yugoslav mother. She was in this country even before the Germans came. As a student in Belgrade. She joined the Partisans, who trained her as a radio operator, then arranged for her defection to the Cetniks. The Cetniks had captured a radio operator from one of the first British missions. They – the Germans, rather – trained her to imitate this operator's hand – every radio operator has his own unmistakable style – until their styles were quite indistinguishable. And her English, of course, was perfect. So then she was in direct contact with Allied Intelligence in both North Africa and Italy. The Germans thought they had us completely fooled: it was, in fact, the other way round.'

Miller said complainingly: 'You didn't tell me any of this, either.'

'I've so much on my mind. Anyway, she was notified direct of the arrival of the last four agents to be parachuted in. She, of course, told the Germans. And all those agents carried information reinforcing the German belief that a second front – a full-scale invasion – of Yugoslavia was immiment.'

Reynolds said slowly: 'They knew we were coming too?'

'Of course. They knew everything about us all along, what we really were. What they didn't know, of course, is that we knew they knew and though what they knew of us was true it was only part of the truth.'

Reynolds digested this. He said, hesitating: 'Sir?'

'Yes?'

'I could have been wrong about you, sir.'

'It happens,' Mallory agreed. 'From time to time, it happens. You were wrong, Sergeant, of course you were, but you were wrong from the very best motives. The fault is mine. Mine alone. But my hands were tied.' Mallory touched him on the shoulder. 'One of these days you might get round to forgiving me.'

'Petar?' Groves asked. 'He's not her brother?'

'Petar is Petar. No more. A front.'

'There's still an awful lot – ' Reynolds began, but Mallory interrupted him.

'It'll have to wait. Colonel Vis, a map, please.' Captain Vlanovich brought one from the tent and Mallory shone a torch on it. 'Look. Here. The Neretva dam and the Zenica Cage. I told Neufeld that Broznik had told me that the Partisans believe that the attack is coming across the Neretva bridge from the south. But, as I've just said, Neufeld knew – he knew even before we had arrived – who and what we *really* were. So he was convinced I was lying. He was convinced that I was convinced that the attack was coming through the Zenica Gap to the north here. Good reason for believing

474

that, mind you: there are two hundred German tanks up there.'

Vis stared at him. 'Two hundred!'

'One hundred and ninety of them are made of plywood. So the only way Neufeld – and, no doubt, the German High Command – could ensure that this useful information got through to Italy was to allow us to stage this rescue bid. Which, of course, they very gladly did, assisting us in every possible way even to the extent of gladly collaborating with us in permitting themselves to be captured. They *knew*, of course, that we had no option left but to capture them and force them to lead us to the block-house – an arrangement they had ensured by previously seizing and hiding away the only other person who could have helped us in this – Maria. And, of course, knowing this in advance, they had arranged for Sergeant Baer to come and free them.'

'I see.' It was plain to everyone that Colonel Vis did not see at all. 'You mentioned an RAF saturation attack on the Zenica Gap. This, of course, will now be switched to the bridge?'

'No. You wouldn't have us break our word to the Wehrmacht, would you? As promised, the attack comes on the Zenica Gap. As a diversion. To convince them, in case they have any last doubts left in their minds, that we have been fooled. Besides, you know as well as I do that that bridge is immune to high-level air attack. It will have to be destroyed in some other way.'

'In what way?'

'We'll think of something. The night is young. Two last things, Colonel Vis. There'll be another Wellington in at midnight and a second at three a.m. Let them both go. The next in, at six a.m., hold it against our arrival. Well, our possible arrival. With any luck we'll be flying out before dawn.'

'With any luck,' Vis said sombrely.

'And radio General Vukalovic, will you? Tell him what I've told you, the exact situation. And tell him to begin intensive small-arms fire at one o'clock in the morning.'

'What are they supposed to fire at?'

'They can fire at the moon for all I care.' Mallory swung aboard his pony. 'Come on, let's be off.'

'The moon,' General Vukalovic agreed, 'is a fair-sized target, though rather a long way off. However, if that's what our friend wants, that's what he shall have.' Vukalovic paused for a moment, looked at Colonel Janzy who was sitting beside him on a fallen log in the woods to the south of the Zenica Gap, then spoke again into the radio mouth-piece.

'Anyway, many thanks, Colonel Vis. So the Neretva bridge it is. And you think it will be unhealthy for us to remain in the immediate vicinity of this area after 1 a.m. Don't worry, we won't be here.' Vukalovic removed the head-phones and turned to Janzy. 'We pull out, quietly, at midnight. We leave a few men to make a lot of noise.'

'The ones who are going to fire at the moon?'

'The ones who are going to fire at the moon. Radio Colonel Lazlo at Neretva, will you? Tell him we'll be with him before the attack. Then radio Major Stephan. Tell him to leave just a holding force, pull out of the Western Gap and make his way to Colonel Lazlo's HQ.' Vukalovic paused for a thoughtful moment. 'We should be in for a few very interesting hours, don't you think?'

'Is there any chance in the world for this man Mallory?' Janzy's tone carried with it its own answer.

'Well, look at it this way,' Vukalovic said reasonably. 'Of course there's a chance. There has to be a chance. It is, after all, my dear Janzy, a question of options – and there are no other options left open to us.'

Janzy made no reply but nodded several times in slow succession as if Vukalovic had just said something profound.

CHAPTER NINE

Friday 2115–Saturday 0040

The pony-back ride downhill through the thickly wooded forests from the Ivenici plateau to the block-house took Mallory and his men barely a quarter of the time it had taken them to make the ascent. In the deep snow the going underfoot was treacherous to a degree, collision with the bole of a pine was always an imminent possibility and none of the five riders made any pretence towards being an experienced horseman, with the inevitable result that slips, stumbles and heavy falls were as frequent as they were painful. Not one of them escaped the indignity of involuntarily leaving his saddle and being thrown headlong into the deep snow, but it was the providential cushioning effect of that snow that was the saving of them, that and, more often, the sure-footed agility of their mountain ponies: whatever the reason or combination of reasons, bruises and winded falls there were in plenty, but broken bones, miraculously, there were none.

The block-house came in sight. Mallory raised a warning hand, slowing them down until they were about two hundred yards distant from their objective, where he reined in, dismounted and led his pony into a thick cluster of pines, followed by the others. Mallory tethered his horse and indicated to the others to do the same.

Miller said complainingly: 'I'm sick of this damned

pony but I'm sicker still of walking through deep snow. Why don't we just ride on down there?'

'Because they'll have ponies tethered down there. They'll start whinnying if they hear or see or smell other ponies approaching.'

'They might start whinnying anyway.'

'And there'll be guards on watch,' Andrea pointed out. 'I don't think, Corporal Miller, that we could make a very stealthy and unobtrusive approach on pony-back.'

'Guards. Guarding against what? As far as Neufeld and company are concerned, we're halfway over the Adriatic at this time.'

'Andrea's right,' Mallory said. 'Whatever else you may think about Neufeld, he's a first-class officer who takes no chances. There'll be guards.' He glanced up to the night sky where a narrow bar of cloud was just approaching the face of the moon. 'See that?'

'I see it,' Miller said miserably.

'Thirty seconds, I'd say. We make a run for the far gable end of the block-house – there are no embrasures there. And for God's sake, once we get there, keep dead quiet. If they hear anything, if they as much as suspect that we're outside, they'll bar the doors and use Petar and Maria as hostages. Then we'll just have to leave them.'

'You'd do that, sir?' Reynolds asked.

'I'd do that. I'd rather cut a hand off, but I'd do that. I've no choice, Sergeant.'

'Yes, sir. I understand.'

The dark bar of cloud passed over the moon. The five men broke from the concealment of the pines and pounded downhill through the deep clogging snow, heading for the farther gable-wall of the block-house. Thirty yards away, at a signal from Mallory, they

479

slowed down lest the sound of their crunching, running footsteps be heard by any watchers who might be keeping guard by the embrasures and completed the remaining distance by walking as quickly and quietly as possible in single file, each man using the footprints left by the man in front of him.

They reached the blank gable-end undetected, with the moon still behind the cloud. Mallory did not pause to congratulate either himself or any of the others. He at once dropped to his hands and knees and crawled round the corner of the block-house, pressing close in to the stone wall.

Four feet from the corner came the first of the embrasures. Mallory did not bother to lower himself any deeper into the snow – the embrasures were so deeply recessed in the massive stone walls that it would have been quite impossible for any watcher to see anything at a lesser distance than six feet from the embrasure. He concentrated, instead, on achieving as minimal a degree of sound as was possible, and did so with success, for he safely passed the embrasure without any alarm being raised. The other four were equally successful even though the moon broke from behind the cloud as the last of them, Groves, was directly under the embrasure. But he, too, remained undetected.

Mallory reached the door. He gestured to Miller, Reynolds and Groves to remain prone where they were: he and Andrea rose silently to their feet and pressed their ears close against the door.

Immediately they heard Droshny's voice, thick with menace, heavy with hatred.

'A traitress! That's what she is. A traitress to our cause. Kill her now!'

'Why did you do it, Maria?' Neufeld's voice, in contrast to Droshny's, was measured, calm, almost gentle.

'Why did she do it?' Droshny snarled. 'Money. That's why she did it. What else?'

'Why?' Neufeld was quietly persistent. 'Did Captain Mallory threaten to kill your brother?'

'Worse than that.' They had to strain to catch Maria's low voice. 'He threatened to kill me. Who would have looked after my blind brother then?'

'We waste time,' Droshny said impatiently. 'Let me take them both outside.'

'No.' Neufeld's voice, still calm, admitted of no argument. 'A blind boy? A terrified girl? What are you, man?'

'A Cetnik!'

'And I'm an officer of the Wehrmacht.'

Andrea whispered in Mallory's ear: 'Any minute now and someone's going to notice our foot-tracks in the snow.'

Mallory nodded, stood aside and made a small gesturing motion of his hand. Mallory was under no illusion as to their respective capabilities when it came to bursting open doors leading into rooms filled with armed men. Andrea was the best in the business – and proceeded to prove it in his usual violent and lethal fashion.

A twist of the door handle, a violent kick with the sole of the right foot and Andrea stood framed in the doorway. The wildly swinging door had still not reached the full limit of travel on its hinges when the room echoed to the flat staccato chatter of Andrea's Schmeisser: Mallory, peering over Andrea's shoulder through the swirling cordite smoke, saw two German soldiers, lethally cursed with over-fast reactions, slumping wearily to the floor. His own machine-pistol levelled, Mallory followed Andrea into the room.

481

There was no longer any call for Schmeissers. None of the other soldiers in the room was carrying any weapon at all while Neufeld and Droshny, their faces frozen into expressions of total incredulity, were clearly, even if only momentarily, incapable of any movement at all, far less being capable of the idea of offering any suicidal resistance.

Mallory said to Neufeld: 'You've just bought yourself your life.' He turned to Maria, nodded towards the door, waited until she had led her brother outside, then looked again at Neufeld and Droshny and said curtly: 'Your guns.'

Neufeld managed to speak, although his lips moved in a strangely mechanical fashion. 'What in the name of God – '

Mallory was in no mind for small talk. He lifted his Schmeisser. 'Your guns.'

Neufeld and Droshny, like men in a dream, removed their pistols and dropped them to the floor.

'The keys.' Droshny and Neufeld looked at him in almost uncomprehending silence. 'The keys,' Mallory repeated. 'Now. Or the keys won't be necessary.'

For several seconds the room was completely silent, then Neufeld stirred, turned to Droshny and nodded. Droshny scowled – as well as any man can scowl when his face is still overspread with an expression of baffled astonishment and homicidal fury – reached into his pocket and produced the keys. Miller took them, unlocked and opened wide the cell door wordlessly and with a motion of his machine-pistol invited Neufeld, Droshny, Baer and the other soldiers to enter, waited until they had done so, swung shut the door, locked it and pocketed the key. The room echoed again as Andrea squeezed the trigger of his machine-pistol and destroyed the radio beyond any hope of repair. Five seconds later they were all outside, Mallory, the last man to leave, locking the door and sending the key spinning to fall yards away, buried from sight in the deep snow.

Suddenly he caught sight of the number of ponies tethered outside the block-house. Seven. Exactly the right number. He ran across to the embrasure outside the cell window and shouted: 'Our ponies are tethered two hundred yards uphill just inside the pines. Don't forget.' Then he ran quickly back and ordered the other six to mount. Reynolds looked at him in astonishment.

'You think of this, sir? At such a time?'

'I'd think of this at any time.' Mallory turned to Petar, who had just awkwardly mounted his horse, then turned to Maria. 'Tell him to take off his glasses.'

Maria looked at him in surprise, nodded in apparent understanding and spoke to her brother, who looked at her uncomprehendingly, then ducked his head obediently, removed his dark glasses and thrust them deep inside his tunic. Reynolds looked on in astonishment, then turned to Mallory.

'I don't understand, sir.'

Mallory wheeled his pony and said curtly: 'It's not necessary that you do.'

'I'm sorry, sir.'

Mallory turned his pony again and said, almost wearily: 'It's already eleven o'clock, boy, and almost already too late for what we have to do.'

'Sir.' Reynolds was deeply if obscurely pleased that Mallory should call him boy. 'I don't really want to know, sir.'

'You've asked. We'll have to go as quickly as our ponies can take us. A blind man can't see obstructions, can't balance himself according to the level of the terrain, can't anticipate in advance how he should brace himself for an unexpectedly sharp drop, can't lean in the saddle for a corner his pony knows is coming. A blind man, in short, is a hundred times more liable to fall off in a downhill gallop than we are. It's enough that a blind man should be blind for life. It's too much that we should expose him to the risk of a heavy fall with his glasses on, expose him to the risk of not only being blind but of having his eyes gouged out and being in agony for life.'

'I hadn't thought – I mean – I'm sorry, sir.'

'Stop apologizing, boy. It's really my turn, you know – to apologize to you. Keep an eye on him, will you?'

Colonel Lazlo, binoculars to his eyes, gazed down over the moonlit rocky slope below him towards the bridge at Neretva. On the southern bank of the river, in the meadows between the south bank and the beginning of the pine forest beyond, and, as far as Lazlo could ascertain, in the fringes of the pine forest itself, there was a disconcertingly ominous lack of movement, of any sign of life at all. Lazlo was pondering the disturbingly sinister significance of this unnatural peacefulness when a hand touched his shoulder. He twisted, looked up and recognized the figure of Major Stephan, commander of the Western Gap.

'Welcome, welcome. The General has advised me of your arrival. Your battalion with you?'

'What's left of it.' Stephan smiled without really smiling. 'Every man who could walk. And all those who couldn't.'

'God send we don't need them all tonight. The General has spoken to you of this man Mallory?' Major Stephan nodded, and Lazlo went on: 'If he fails? If the Germans cross the Neretva tonight –'

'So?' Stephan shrugged. 'We were all due to die tonight anyway.'

'A well-taken point,' Lazlo said approvingly. He lifted his binoculars and returned to his contemplation of the bridge at Neretva.

So far, and almost incredibly, neither Mallory nor any of the six galloping behind him had parted company with their ponies. Not even Petar. True, the incline of the slope was not nearly as steep as it had been from the Ivenici plateau down to the block-house, but Reynolds suspected it was because Mallory had imperceptibly succeeded in slowing down the pace of their earlier headlong gallop. Perhaps, Reynolds thought vaguely, it was because Mallory was sub-consciously trying to protect the blind singer, who was riding almost abreast with him, guitar firmly strapped over his shoulder, reins abandoned and both hands clasped desperately to the pommel of his saddle. Unbidden, almost, Reynolds's thoughts strayed back to that scene inside the block-house. Moments later, he was urging his pony forwards until he had drawn alongside Mallory.

'Sir?'

'What is it?' Mallory sounded irritable.

'A word, sir. It's urgent. Really it is.'

Mallory threw up a hand and brought the company to a halt. He said curtly: 'Be quick.'

'Neufeld and Droshny, sir.' Reynolds paused in a moment's brief uncertainty, then continued. 'Do you reckon they know where you're going?'

'What's that to do with anything?'

'Please.'

'Yes, they do. Unless they're complete morons. And they're not.'

485

'It's a pity, sir,' Reynolds said reflectively, 'that you hadn't shot them after all.'

'Get to the point,' Mallory said impatiently.

'Yes, sir. You reckoned Sergeant Baer released them earlier on?'

'Of course.' Mallory was exercising all his restraint. 'Andrea saw them arrive. I've explained all this. They – Neufeld and Droshny – had to go up to the Ivenici plateau to check that we'd really gone.'

'I understand that, sir. So you knew that Baer was following us. How did he get into the block-house?'

Mallory's restraint vanished. He said in exasperation: 'Because I left both keys hanging outside.'

'Yes, sir. You were expecting him. But Sergeant Baer didn't know you were expecting him – and even if he did he wouldn't be expecting to find keys so conveniently to hand.'

'Good God in heaven! Duplicates!' In bitter chagrin, Mallory smacked the fist of one hand into the palm of the other. 'Imbecile! Imbecile! Of *course* he would have his own keys.'

'And Droshny,' Miller said thoughtfully, 'may know a short cut.'

'That's not all of it.' Mallory was completely back on balance again, outwardly composed, the relaxed calmness of the face the complete antithesis of his racing mind. 'Worse still, he may make straight for his camp radio and warn Zimmermann to pull his armoured divisions back from the Neretva. You've earned your passage tonight, Reynolds. Thanks, boy. How far to Neufeld's camp, do you think, Andrea?'

'A mile.' The words came over Andrea's shoulder, for Andrea, as always in situations which he knew called for the exercise of his highly specialized talents, was already on his way.

486

Five minutes later they were crouched at the edge of the forest less than twenty yards from the perimeter of Neufeld's camp. Quite a number of the huts had illuminated windows, music could be heard coming from the dining hut and several Cetnik soldiers were moving about in the compound.

Reynolds whispered to Mallory: 'How do we go about it, sir?'

'We don't do anything at all. We just leave it to Andrea.'

Groves spoke, his voice low. 'One man? Andrea? We leave it to one man?'

Mallory sighed. 'Tell them, Corporal Miller.'

'I'd rather not. Well, if I have to. The fact is,' Miller went on kindly, 'Andrea is rather good at this sort of thing.'

'So are we,' Reynolds said. 'We're commandos. We've been trained for this sort of thing.'

'And very highly trained, no doubt,' said Miller approvingly 'Another half-dozen years' experience and half a dozen of you might be just about able to cope with him. Although I doubt it very much. Before the night is out, you'll learn — and I don't mean to be insulting, Sergeants — that you are little lambs to Andrea's wolf.' Miller paused and went on sombrely: 'Like whoever happens to be inside that radio hut at this moment.'

'Like whoever happens —' Groves twisted round and looked behind him. 'Andrea? He's gone. I didn't see him go.'

'No one ever does,' Miller said. 'And those poor devils won't ever see him come.' He looked at Mallory. 'Time's a-wasting.'

Mallory glanced at the luminous hands of his watch. 'Eleven-thirty. Time *is* a-wasting.'

487

For almost a minute there was a silence broken only by the restless movements of the ponies tethered deep in the woods behind them, then Groves gave a muffled exclamation as Andrea materialized beside him. Mallory looked up and said: 'How many?'

Andrea held up two fingers and moved silently into the woods towards his pony. The others rose and followed him, Groves and Reynolds exchanging glances which indicated more clearly than any words could possibly have done that they could have been even more wrong about Andrea than they had ever been about Mallory.

At precisely the moment that Mallory and his companions were remounting their ponies in the woods fringing Neufeld's camp, a Wellington bomber came sinking down towards a well-lit airfield – the same airfield from which Mallory and his men had taken off less than twenty-four hours previously. Termoli, Italy. It made a perfect touchdown and as it taxied along the runway an army radio truck curved in on an interception course, turning to parallel the last hundred yards of the Wellington's run down. In the left-hand front seat and in the right-hand back seat of the truck sat two immediately recognizable figures: in the front, the piratical splendidly bearded figure of Captain Jensen, in the back the British lieutenant-general with whom Jensen had recently spent so much time in pacing the Termoli Operations Room.

Plane and truck came to a halt at the same moment. Jensen, displaying a surprising agility for one of his very considerable bulk, hopped nimbly to the ground and strode briskly across the tarmac and arrived at the Wellington just as its door opened and the first of the passengers, the moustached major, swung to the ground.

Jensen nodded to the papers clutched in the major's hand and said without preamble: 'Those for me?' The major blinked uncertainly, then nodded stiffly in return, clearly irked by this abrupt welcome for a man just returned from durance vile. Jensen took the papers without a further word, went back to his seat in the jeep, brought out a flashlight and studied the papers briefly. He twisted in his seat and said to the radio operator seated beside the General: 'Flight plan as stated. Target as indicated. Now.' The radio operator began to crank the handle.

Some fifty miles to the south-east, in the Foggia area, the buildings and runways of the RAF heavy bomber base echoed and reverberated to the thunder of scores of aircraft engines: at the dispersal area at the west end of the main runway several squadrons of Lancaster heavy bombers were lined up ready for take-off, obviously awaiting the signal to go. The signal was not long in coming.

Halfway down the airfield, but well to one side of the main runway, was parked a jeep identical to the one in which Jensen was sitting in Termoli. In the back seat a radio operator was crouched over a radio, earphones to his head. He listened intently, then looked up and said matter-of-factly: 'Instructions as stated. Now. Now. Now.'

'Instructions as stated,' a captain in the front seat repeated. 'Now. Now. Now.' He reached for a wooden box, produced three Very pistols, aimed directly across the runway and fired each in turn. The brilliantly arcing flares burst into incandescent life, green, red and green again, before curving slowly back to earth. The thunder at the far end of the airfield mounted to a rumbling crescendo and the first of the Lancasters began to move. Within a few minutes the last of them had taken off and was lifting into the darkly hostile night skies of the Adriatic.

'I did say, I believe,' Jensen remarked conversationally and comfortably to the General in the back seat, 'that they are the best in the business. Our friends from Foggia are on their way.'

'The best in the business. Maybe. I don't know. What I do know is that those damned German and Austrian divisions are still in position in the Gustav Line. Zero hour for the assault on the Gustav Line is – ' he glanced at his watch – 'in exactly thirty hours.'

'Time enough,' Jensen said confidently.

'I wish I shared this blissful confidence.'

Jensen smiled cheerfully at him as the jeep moved off, then faced forward in his seat again. As he did, the smile vanished completely from his face and his fingers beat a drum tattoo on the seat beside him.

The moon had broken through again as Neufeld, Droshny and their men came galloping into camp and reined in ponies so covered with steam from their heaving flanks and distressed breathing as to have a weirdly insubstantial appearance in the pale moonlight. Neufeld swung from his pony and turned to Sergeant Baer.

'How many ponies left in the stables?'

'Twenty. About that.'

'Quickly. And as many men as there are ponies. Saddle up.'

Neufeld gestured to Droshny and together they ran towards the radio hut. The door, ominously enough on that icy night, was standing wide open. They were still ten feet short of the door when Neufeld shouted: 'The

490

Neretva bridge at once. Tell General Zimmermann – '

He halted abruptly in the doorway, Droshny by his shoulder. For the second time that evening the faces of both men reflected their stunned disbelief, their total uncomprehending shock.

Only one small lamp burned in the radio hut, but that one small lamp was enough. Two men lay on the floor in grotesquely huddled positions, the one lying partially across the other: both were quite unmistakably dead. Beside them, with its face-plate ripped off and interior smashed, lay the mangled remains of what had once been a transmitter. Neufeld gazed at the scene for some time before shaking his head violently as if to break the shocked spell and turned to Droshny.

'The big one,' he said quietly. 'The big one did this.'

'The big one,' Droshny agreed. He was almost smiling. 'You will remember what you promised, Hauptmann Neufeld? The big one. He's for me.'

'You shall have him. Come They can be only minutes ahead.' Both men turned and ran back to the compound where Sergeant Baer and a group of soldiers were already saddling up the ponies.

'Machine-pistols only,' Neufeld shouted. 'No rifles. It will be close-quarter work tonight. And Sergeant Baer?'

'Hauptmann Neufeld?'

'Inform the men that we will not be taking pris-oners.'

As those of Neufeld and his men had been, the ponies of Mallory and his six companions were almost invisible in the dense clouds of steam rising from their sweat-soaked bodies: their lurching gait, which could not now even be called a trot, was token enough of the obvious fact that they had reached the limits of exhaustion. Mallory glanced at Andrea, who nodded and said: 'I agree. We'd make faster time on foot now.'

'I must be getting old,' Mallory said, and for a moment he sounded that way. 'I'm not thinking very well tonight, am I?'

'I do not understand.'

'Ponies. Neufeld and his men will have fresh ponies from the stables. We should have killed them – or at least driven them away.'

'Age is not the same thing as lack of sleep. It never occurred to me, either. A man cannot think of everything, my Keith.' Andrea reined in his pony and was about to swing down when something on the slope below caught his attention. He pointed ahead.

A minute later they drew up alongside a very narrow-gauge railway line, of a type common in Central Yugoslavia. At this level the snow had petered out and the track, they could see, was overgrown and rusty, but for all that, apparently in fair enough mechanical condition: undoubtedly, it was the same track that had caught their eye when they had paused to examine the green waters of the Neretva dam on the way back from Major Broznik's camp that morning. But what simultaneously caught and held the attention of both Mallory and Miller was not the track itself, but a little siding leading on to the track – and a diminutive, wood-burning locomotive that stood on the siding. The locomotive was practically a solid block of rust and looked as if it hadn't moved from its present position since the beginning of the war: in all probability, it hadn't.

Mallory produced a large-scale map from his tunic and flashed a torch on it. He said: 'No doubt of it, this is the track we saw this morning. It goes down along the Neretva for at least five miles before bearing off to the south.' He paused and went on thoughtfully: 'I wonder if we could get that thing moving.'

'What?' Miller looked at him in horror. 'It'll fall to pieces if you touch it – it's only the rust that's holding the damn thing together. And that gradient there!' He peered in dismay down the slope. 'What do you think our terminal velocity is going to be when we hit one of those monster pine trees a few miles down the track?'

'The ponies are finished,' Mallory said mildly, 'and you know how much you love walking.'

Miller looked at the locomotive with loathing. 'There must be some other way.'

'Shh!' Andrea cocked his head. 'They're coming. I can hear them coming.'

'Get the chocks away from those front wheels,' Miller shouted. He ran forward and after several violent and well-directed kicks which clearly took into no account the future state of his toes, succeeded in freeing the triangular block which was attached to the front of the locomotive by a chain: Reynolds, no less energetically, did the same for the other chock.

All of them, even Maria and Petar helping, flung all their weight against the rear of the locomotive. The locomotive remained where it was. They tried again, despairingly: the wheels refused to budge even a fraction of an inch. Groves said, with an odd mixture of urgency and diffidence: 'Sir, on a gradient like this, it would have been left with its brakes on.'

'Oh my God!' Mallory said in chagrin. 'Andrea. Quickly. Release the brake lever.'

Andrea swung himself on to the footplate. He said complainingly: 'There are a dozen damned levers up here.'

'Well, open the dozen damned levers, then.' Mallory

glanced anxiously back up the track. Maybe Andrea had heard something, maybe not: there was certainly no one in sight yet. But he knew that Neufeld and Droshny, who must have been released from the block-house only minutes after they had left there themselves and who knew those woods and paths better than they did, must be very close indeed by this time.

There was a considerable amount of metallic screeching and swearing coming from the cab and after perhaps half a minute Andrea said: 'That's the lot.'

'Shove,' Mallory ordered.

They shoved, heels jammed in the sleepers and backs to the locomotive, and this time the locomotive moved off so easily, albeit with a tortured squealing of rusted wheels, that most of those pushing were caught wholly by surprise and fell on their backs on the track. Moments later they were on their feet and running after the locomotive which was already perceptibly beginning to increase speed. Andrea reached down from the cab, swung Maria and Petar aboard in turn, then lent a helping hand to the others. The last, Groves, was reaching for the footplate when he suddenly braked, swung round, ran back to the ponies, unhitched the climbing ropes, flung them over his shoulder and chased after the locomotive again. Mallory reached down and helped him on to the footplate.

'It's not my day,' Mallory said sadly. 'Evening rather. First, I forget about Baer's duplicate keys. Then about the ponies. Then about the brakes. Now the ropes. I wonder what I'll forget about next?'

'Perhaps about Neufeld and Droshny.' Reynolds's voice was carefully without expression.

'What about Neufeld and Droshny?'

Reynolds pointed back up the railway track with the barrel of his Schmeisser. 'Permission to fire, sir.'

Mallory swung round. Neufeld, Droshny and an indeterminate number of other pony-mounted soldiers had just appeared around a bend in the track and were hardly more than a hundred yards away.

'Permission to fire,' Mallory agreed. 'The rest of you get down.' He unslung and brought up his own Schmeisser just as Reynolds squeezed the trigger of his. For perhaps five seconds the closed metallic confines of the tiny cabin reverberated deafeningly to the crash of the two machine-pistols, then, at a nudge from Mallory, the two men stopped firing. There was no target left to fire at. Neufeld and his men had loosed off a few preliminary shots but immediately realized that the wildly swaying saddles of their ponies made an impossibly unsteady firing position as compared to the cab of the locomotive and had pulled their ponies off into the woods on either side of the track. But not all of them had pulled off in time: two men lay motionless and face down in the snow while their ponies still galloped down the track in the wake of the locomotive.

Miller rose, glanced wordlessly at the scene behind, then tapped Mallory on the arm. 'A small point occurs to me, sir. How do we stop this thing.' He gazed apprehensively through the cab window. 'Must be doing sixty already.'

'Well, we're doing at least twenty,' Mallory said agreeably. 'But fast enough to out-distance those ponies. Ask Andrea. He released the brake.'

'He released a dozen levers,' Miller corrected. 'Any one could have been the brake.'

'Well, you're not going to sit around doing nothing, are you?' Mallory asked reasonably. 'Find out how to stop the damn thing.'

495

Miller looked at him coldly and set about trying to find out how to stop the damn thing. Mallory turned as Reynolds touched him on the arm. 'Well?'

Reynolds had an arm round Maria to steady her on the now swaying platform. He whispered: 'They're going to get us, sir. They're going to get us for sure. Why don't we stop and leave those two, sir? Give them a chance to escape into the woods?'

'Thanks for the thought. But don't be mad. With us they have a chance – a small one to be sure, but a chance. Stay behind and they'll be butchered.'

The locomotive was no longer doing the twenty miles per hour Mallory had mentioned and if it hadn't approached the figure that Miller had so fearfully mentioned it was certainly going quickly enough to make it rattle and sway to what appeared to be the very limits of its stability. By this time the last of the trees to the right of the track had petered out, the darkened waters of the Neretva dam were clearly visible to the west and the railway track was now running very close indeed to the edge of what appeared to be a dangerously steep precipice. Mallory looked back into the cab. With the exception of Andrea, everyone now wore expressions of considerable apprehension on their faces. Mallory said: 'Found out how to stop this damn thing yet?'

'Easy.' Andrea indicated a lever. 'This handle here.'

'Okay, brakeman. I want to have a look.'

To the evident relief of most of the passengers in the cab, Andrea leaned back on the brake-lever. There was an eldritch screeching that set teeth on edge, clouds of sparks flew up past the sides of the cab as some wheels or other locked solid in the lines, then the locomotive eased slowly to a halt, both the intensity of sound from the squealing brakes and the number of sparks diminishing as it did so. Andrea, duty done, leaned out of the side of the cab with all the bored aplomb of the crack loco engineer: one had the feeling that all he really wanted in life that moment was a piece of oily waste and a whistle-cord to pull.

Mallory and Miller climbed down and ran to the edge of the cliff, less than twenty yards away. At least Mallory did. Miller made a much more cautious approach, inching forward the last few feet on hands and knees. He hitched one cautious eye over the edge of the precipice, screwed both eyes shut, looked away and just as cautiously inched his way back from the edge of the cliff: Miller claimed that he couldn't even stand on the bottom step of a ladder without succumbing to the overwhelming compulsion to throw himself into the abyss.

Mallory gazed down thoughtfully into the depths. They were, he saw, directly over the top of the dam wall, which, in the strangely shadowed half-light cast by the moon, seemed almost impossibly far below in the dizzying depths. The broad top of the dam wall was brightly lit by floodlights and patrolled by at least half a dozen German soldiers, jack-booted and helmeted. Beyond the dam, on the lower side, the ladder Maria had spoken of was invisible, but the frail-looking swing bridge, still menaced by the massive bulk of the boulder on the scree on the left bank, and farther down, the white water indicating what might or might not have been a possible – or passable – ford were plainly in sight. Mallory, momentarily abstracted in thought, gazed at the scene below for several moments, recalled that the pursuit must be again coming uncomfortably close and hurriedly made his way back to the locomotive. He said to Andrea: 'About a mile and a half, I should think. No more.' He turned to Maria. 'You know there's a ford – or what seems to be a ford – some way below the dam. Is there a way down?'

'For a mountain goat.'

'Don't insult him,' Miller said reprovingly.

'I don't understand.'

'Ignore him,' Mallory said. 'Just tell us when we get there.'

Some five or six miles below the Neretva dam General Zimmermann paced up and down the fringe of the pine forest bordering the meadow to the south of the bridge at Neretva. Beside him paced a colonel, one of his divisional commanders. To the south of them could just dimly be discerned the shapes of hundreds of men and scores of tanks and other vehicles, vehicles with all their protective camouflage now removed, each tank and vehicle surrounded by its coterie of attendants making last-minute and probably wholly unnecessary adjustments. The time for hiding was over. The waiting was coming to an end. Zimmermann glanced at his watch.

'Twelve-thirty. The first infantry battalions start moving across in fifteen minutes, and spread out along the north bank. The tanks at two o'clock.'

'Yes, sir.' The details had been arranged many hours ago, but somehow one always found it necessary to repeat the instructions and the acknowledgements. The colonel gazed to the north. 'I sometimes wonder if there's *anybody* at all across there.'

'It's not the north I'm worrying about,' Zimmermann said sombrely. 'It's the west.'

'The Allies? You – you think their air armadas will come soon? It's still in your bones, Herr General?'

'Still in my bones. It's coming soon. For me, for

498

you, for all of us.' He shivered, then forced a smile. 'Some ill-mannered lout has just walked over my grave.'

CHAPTER TEN

Saturday 0040–0120

'We're coming up to it now,' Maria said. Blonde hair streaming in the passing wind, she peered out again through the cab window of the clanking, swaying locomotive, withdrew her head and turned to Mallory. 'About three hundred metres.'

Mallory glanced at Andrea. 'You heard, brakeman?'

'I heard.' Andrea leaned hard on the brake lever. The result was as before, a banshee shrieking of locked wheels on the rusty lines and a pyrotechnical display of sparks. The locomotive came to a juddering halt as Andrea looked out his cab window and observed a V-shaped gap in the edge of the cliff directly opposite where they had come to a stop. 'Within the yard, I should say?'

'Within the yard,' Mallory agreed. 'If you're unemployed after the war, there should always be a place for you in a shunter's yard.' He swung down to the side of the track, lent a helping hand to Maria and Petar, waited until Miller, Reynolds and Groves had jumped down, then said impatiently to Andrea: 'Well, hurry up, then.'

'Coming,' Andrea said peaceably. He pushed the handbrake all the way off, jumped down, and gave the locomotive a shove: the ancient vehicle at once moved off, gathering speed as it went. 'You never know,' Andrea said wistfully. 'It might hit somebody somewhere.'

They ran towards the cut in the edge of the cliff, a cut which obviously represented the beginning of some prehistoric landslide down to the bed of the Neretva, a maelstrom of white water far below, the boiling rapids resulting from scores of huge boulders which had slipped from this landslide in that distant aeon. By some exercise of the imagination, that scar in the side of the cliff-face might just perhaps have been called a gully, but it was in fact an almost perpendicular drop of scree and shale and small boulders, all of it treacherous and unstable to a frightening degree, the whole dangerous sweep broken only by a small ledge of jutting rock about halfway down. Miller took one brief glance at this terrifying prospect, stepped hurriedly back from the edge of the cliff and looked at Mallory in a silently dismayed incredulity.

'I'm afraid so,' Mallory said.

'But this is terrible. Even when I climbed the south cliff in Navarone — '

'You didn't climb the south cliff in Navarone,' Mallory said unkindly. 'Andrea and I pulled you up at the end of a rope.'

'Did you? I forget. But this — this is a climber's nightmare.'

'So we don't have to climb it. Just lower ourselves down. You'll be all right — as long as you don't start rolling.'

'I'll be all right as long as I don't start rolling,' Miller repeated mechanically. He watched Mallory join two ropes together and pass them around the bole of a stunted pine. 'How about Petar and Maria?'

'Petar doesn't have to see to make this descent. All he has to do is to lower himself on this rope — and Petar is as strong as a horse. Somebody will be down there before him to guide his feet on to

501

the ledge. Andrea will look after the young lady here. Now hurry. Neufeld and his men will be up with us any minute here – and if they catch up on this cliff-face, well that's that. Andrea, off you go with Maria.'

Immediately, Andrea and the girl swung over the edge of the gully and began to lower themselves swiftly down the rope. Groves watched them, hesitated, then moved towards Mallory.

'I'll go last, sir, and take the rope with me.'

Miller took his arm and led him some feet away. He said, kindly: 'Generous, son, generous, but it's just not on. Not as long as Dusty Miller's life depends on it. In a situation like this, I must explain, all our lives depend upon the anchorman. The Captain, I am informed, is the best anchorman in the world.'

'He's what?'

'It's one of the non-coincidences why he was chosen to lead this mission. Bosnia is known to have rocks and cliffs and mountains all over it. Mallory was climbing the Himalayas, laddie, before you were climbing out of your cot. Even you are not too young to have heard of him.'

'*Keith* Mallory? The New Zealander?'

'Indeed. Used to chase sheep around, I gather. Come on, your turn.'

The first five made it safely. Even the last but one, Miller, made the descent to the ledge without incident, principally by employing his favourite mountain-climbing technique of keeping his eyes closed all the time. Then Mallory came last, coiling the rope with him as he came, moving quickly and surely and hardly ever seeming to look where he put his feet but at the same time not as much as disturbing the slightest pebble or piece of shale. Groves observed the descent with a look of almost awed disbelief in his eyes.

Mallory peered over the edge of the ledge. Because of a slight bend in the gorge above, there was a sharp cut-off in the moonlight just below where they stood so that 'while the phosphorescent whiteness of the rapids was in clear moonlight, the lower part of the slope beneath their feet was in deep shadow. Even as he watched, the moon was obscured by a shadow, and all the dimly-seen detail in the slope below vanished. Mallory knew that they could never afford to wait until the moon reappeared, for Neufeld and his men could well have arrived by then. Mallory belayed a rope round an outcrop of rock and said to Andrea and Maria: 'This one's really dangerous. Watch for loose boulders.'

Andrea and Maria took well over a minute to make this invisible descent, a double tug on the rope announcing their safe arrival at the bottom. On the way down they had started several small avalanches, but Mallory had no fears that the next man down would trigger off a fall of rock that would injure or even kill Andrea and Maria; Andrea had lived too long and too dangerously to die in so useless and so foolish a fashion – and he would undoubtedly warn the next man down of the same danger. For the tenth time Mallory glanced up towards the top of the slope they had just descended but if Neufeld, Droshny and his men had just arrived they were keeping very quiet about it and being most circumspect indeed: it was not a difficult conclusion to arrive at that, after the events of the past few hours, circumspection would be the last thing in their minds.

The moon broke through again as Mallory finally made his descent. He cursed the exposure it might offer if any of the enemy suddenly appeared on the clifftop, even although he knew that Andrea would be guarding against precisely that danger; on the other

503

hand it afforded him the opportunity of descending at twice the speed he could have made in the earlier darkness. The watchers below watched tensely as Mallory, without any benefit of rope, made his perilous descent: but he never even looked like making one mistake. He descended safely to the boulder-strewn shore and gazed out over the rapids.

He said to no one in particular: 'You know what's going to happen if they arrive at the top and find us halfway across here and the moon shining down on us?' The ensuing silence left no doubt but they all knew what was going to happen. 'Now is all the time. Reynolds, you think you can make it?' Reynolds nodded. 'Then leave your gun.'

Mallory knotted a bowline round Reynolds's waist, taking the strain, if one were to arise, with Andrea and Groves. Reynolds launched himself bodily into the rapids, heading for the first of the rounded boulders which offered so treacherous a hold in that seething foam. Twice he was knocked off his feet, twice he regained them, reached the rock, but immediately beyond it was washed away off balance and swept down-river. The men on the bank hauled him ashore again, coughing and spluttering and fighting mad. Without a word to or look at anybody Reynolds again hurled himself into the rapids, and this time so determined was the fury of his assault that he succeeded in reaching the far bank without once being knocked off his feet.

He dragged himself on to the stony beach, lay there for some moments recovering from his exhaustion, then rose, crossed to a stunted pine at the base of the cliff rising on the other side, undid the rope round his waist and belayed it securely round the bole of the tree. Mallory, on his side, took two turns round a large rock and gestured to Andrea and the girl.

Mallory glanced upwards again to the top of the gully. There were still no signs of the enemy. Even so, Mallory felt that they could afford to wait no longer, that they had already pushed their luck too far. Andrea and Maria were barely halfway across when he told Groves to give Petar a hand across the rapids. He hoped to God the rope would hold, but hold it did for Andrea and Maria made it safely to the far bank. No sooner had they grounded than Mallory sent Miller on his way, carrying a pile of automatic arms over his left shoulder.

Groves and Petar also made the crossing without incident. Mallory himself had to wait until Miller reached the far bank, for he knew the chances of his being carried away were high and if he were, then Miller too would be precipitated into the water and their guns rendered useless.

Mallory waited until he saw Andrea give Miller a hand into the shallow water on the far bank and waited no longer. He unwound the rope from the rock he had been using as a belay, fastened a bowline round his own waist and plunged into the water. He was swept away at exactly the same point where Reynolds had been on his first attempt and was finally dragged ashore by his friends on the far bank with a fair amount of the waters of the Neretva in his stomach but otherwise unharmed.

'Any injuries, any cracked bones or skulls?' Mallory asked. He himself felt as if he had been over Niagara in a barrel. 'No? Fine.' He looked at Miller. 'You stay here with me. Andrea, take the others up round the first corner there and wait for us.'

'Me?' Andrea objected mildly. He nodded towards the gully. 'We've got friends that might be coming down there at any moment.'

Mallory took him some little way aside. 'We also

505

have friends,' he said quietly, 'who might just possibly be coming down-river from the dam garrison.' He nodded at the two sergeants, Petar and Maria. 'What would happen to them if they ran into an Alpenkorps patrol, do you think?'

'I'll wait for you round the corner.'

Andrea and the four others made their slow way up-river, slipping and stumbling over the wetly slimy rocks and boulders. Mallory and Miller withdrew into the protection and concealment of two large boulders and stared upwards.

Several minutes passed. The moon still shone and the top of the gully was still innocent of any sign of the enemy. Miller said uneasily: 'What do you think has gone wrong? They're taking a damned long time about turning up.'

'No, I think that it's just that they are taking a damned long time in turning back.'

'Turning back?'

'They don't *know* where we've gone.' Mallory pulled out his map, examined it with a carefully hooded pencil-torch. 'About three-quarters of a mile down the railway track, there's a sharp turn to the left. In all probability the locomotive would have left the track there. Last time Neufeld and Droshny saw us we were aboard that locomotive and the logical thing for them to have done would have been to follow the track till they came to where we had abandoned the locomotive, expecting to find us somewhere in the vicinity. When they found the crashed engine, they would know at once what would have happened – but that would have given them another mile and a half to ride – and half of that uphill on tired ponies.'

'That must be it. I wish to God,' Miller went on grumblingly, 'that they'd hurry up.'

'What is this?' Mallory queried. 'Dusty Miller yearning for action?'

'No, I'm not,' Miller said definitely. He glanced at his watch. 'But time is getting very short.'

'Time,' Mallory agreed soberly, 'is getting terribly short.'

And then they came. Miller, glancing upward, saw a faint metallic glint in the moonlight as a head peered cautiously over the edge of the gully. He touched Mallory on the arm.

'I see him,' Mallory murmured. Together both men reached inside their tunics, pulled out their Lugers and removed their waterproof coverings. The helmeted head gradually resolved itself into a figure standing fully silhouetted in the moonlight against the sharply etched skyline. He began what was obviously meant to be a cautious descent, then suddenly flung up both arms and fell backwards and outwards. If he cried out, from where Mallory and Miller were the cry could not have been heard above the rushing of the waters. He struck the ledge halfway down, bounced off and outwards for a quite incredible distance, then landed spread-eagled on the stony river bank below, pulling down a small avalanche behind him.

Miller was grimly philosophical. 'Well, you said it was dangerous.'

Another figure appeared over the lip of the precipice to make the second attempt at a descent, and was followed in short order by several more men. Then, for the space of a few minutes, the moon went behind a cloud, while Mallory and Miller stared across the river until their eyes ached, anxiously and vainly trying to pierce the impenetrable darkness that shrouded the slope on the far side.

The leading climber, when the moon did break

through, was just below the ledge, cautiously negotiating the lower slope. Mallory took careful aim with his Luger, the climber stiffened convulsively, toppled backwards and fell to his death. The following figure, clearly oblivious of the fate of his companion, began the descent of the lower slope. Both Mallory and Miller sighted their Lugers but just then the moon was suddenly obscured again and they had to lower their guns. When the moon again reappeared, four men had already reached the safety of the opposite bank, two of whom, linked together by a rope, were just beginning to venture the crossing of the ford.

Mallory and Miller waited until they had safely completed two thirds of the crossing of the ford. They formed a close and easy target and at that range it was impossible that Mallory and Miller should miss, nor did they. There was a momentary reddening of the white waters of the rapids, as much imagined as seen, then, still lashed together they were swept away down the gorge. So furiously were their bodies tumbled over and over by the rushing waters, so often did cartwheeling arms and legs break surface, that they might well have given the appearance of men who, though without hope, were still desperately struggling for their lives. In any event, the two men left standing on the far bank clearly did not regard the accident as being significant of anything amiss in any sinister way. They stood and watched the vanishing bodies of their companions in perplexity, still unaware of what was happening. A matter of two or three seconds later and they would never have been aware of anything else but once more a wisp of errant dark cloud covered the moon and they still had a little time, a very little time, to live. Mallory and Miller lowered their guns.

Mallory glanced at his watch and said irritably:

508

'Why the hell don't they start firing? It's five past one.'

'Why don't who start firing?' Miller said cautiously.

'You heard. You were there. I asked Vis to ask Vukalovic to give us sound cover at one. Up by the Zenica Gap there, less than a mile away. Well, we can't wait any longer. It'll take —' He broke off and listened to the sudden outburst of rifle fire, startlingly loud even at that comparatively close distance, and smiled. 'Well, what's five minutes here or there. Come on. I have the feeling that Andrea must be getting a little anxious about us.'

Andrea was. He emerged silently from the shadows as they rounded the first bend in the river. He said reproachfully: 'Where have you two been? You had me worried stiff.'

'I'll explain in an hour's time — if we're all still around in an hour's time,' Mallory amended grimly. 'Our friends the bandits are two minutes behind. I think they'll be coming in force — although they've lost four already — six including the two Reynolds got from the locomotive. You stop at the next bend up-river and hold them off. You'll have to do it by yourself. Think you can manage?'

'This is no time for joking,' Andrea said with dignity. 'And then?'

'Groves and Reynolds and Petar and his sister come with us up-river, Reynolds and Groves as nearly as possible to the dam, Petar and Maria wherever they can find some suitable shelter, possibly in the vicinity of the swing bridge — as long as they're well clear of that damned great boulder perched above it.'

'Swing bridge, sir?' Reynolds asked. 'A boulder?'

'I saw it when we got off the locomotive to reconnoitre.'

509

'*You* saw it. Andrea didn't.'

'I mentioned it to him,' Mallory went on impatiently. He ignored the disbelief in the sergeant's face and turned to Andrea. 'Dusty and I can't wait any longer. Use your Schmeisser to stop them.' He pointed north-westwards towards the Zenica Gap, where the rattle of musketry was now almost continuous. 'With all that racket going on, they'll never know the difference.'

Andrea nodded, settled himself comfortably behind a pair of large boulders and slid the barrel of his Schmeisser into the V between them. The remainder of the party moved upstream, scrambling awkwardly around and over the slippery boulders and rocks that covered the right-hand bank of the Neretva, until they came to a rudimentary path that had been cleared among the stones. This they followed for perhaps a hundred yards, till they came to a slight bend in the gorge. By mutual consent and without any order being given, all six stopped and gazed upwards.

The towering breath-taking ramparts of the Neretva dam wall had suddenly come into full view. Above the dam on either side precipitous walls of rock soared up into the night sky, at first quite vertical then both leaning out in an immense overhang which seemed to make them almost touch at the top, although this, Mallory knew from the observation he had made from above, was an optical illusion. On top of the dam wall itself the guardhouses and radio huts were clearly visible, as were the pigmy shapes of several patrolling German soldiers. From the top of the eastern side of the dam, where the huts were situated, an iron ladder – Mallory knew it was painted green, but in the half-shadow cast by the dam wall it looked black – fastened by iron supports to the bare rock face, zig-zagged downwards to the foot of the gorge, close by

510

where foaming white jets of water boiled from the outlet pipes at the base of the dam wall. Mallory tried to estimate how many steps there would be in that ladder. Two hundred, perhaps two hundred and fifty, and once you started to climb or descend you just had to keep on going, for nowhere was there any platform or backrest to afford even the means for a temporary respite. Nor did the ladder at any point afford the slightest scrap of cover from watchers on the bridge. As an assault route, Mallory mused, it was scarcely the one he would have chosen: he could not conceive of a more hazardous one.

About halfway between where they stood and the foot of the ladder on the other side, a swing bridge spanned the boiling waters of the gorge. There was little about its ancient, rickety and warped appearance to inspire any confidence: and what little confidence there might have been could hardly have survived the presence of an enormous boulder, directly above the eastern edge of the bridge, which seemed in imminent danger of breaking loose from its obviously insecure footing in the deep scar in the cliff-side.

Reynolds assimilated all of the scene before him, then turned to Mallory. He said quietly: 'We've been very patient, sir.'

'You've been very patient, Sergeant – and I'm grateful. You know, of course, that there is a Yugoslav division trapped in the Zenica Cage – that's just behind the mountains to our left, here. You know, too, that the Germans are going to launch two armoured divisions across the Neretva bridge at two a.m. this morning and that if once they do get across – and normally there would be nothing to stop them – the Yugoslavs, armed with their pop-guns and with hardly any ammunition left, would be cut to pieces. You know the only way

511

to stop them is to destroy the Neretva bridge? You know that this counter-espionage and rescue mission was only a cover for the real thing?'

Reynolds said bitterly: 'I know that – now.' He pointed down the gorge. 'And I also know that the bridge lies that way.'

'And so it does. I also know that even if we could approach it – which would be quite impossible – we couldn't blow that bridge up with a truckload of explosives; steel bridges anchored in reinforced concrete take a great deal of destroying.' He turned and looked at the dam. 'So we do it another way. See that dam wall there – there's thirty million tons of water behind it – enough to carry away the Sydney bridge, far less the one over the Neretva.'

Groves said in a low voice: 'You're crazy,' and then, as an afterthought, 'sir.'

'Don't we know it? But we're going to blow up that dam all the same. Dusty and I.'

'But – but all the explosives we have are a few hand-grenades,' Reynolds said, almost desperately. 'And in that dam wall there must be ten- to twenty-feet thicknesses of reinforced concrete. Blow it up? How?'

Mallory shook his head. 'Sorry.'

'Why, you close-mouthed –'

'Be quiet! Dammit, man, will you never, never learn. Even up to the very last minute you could be caught and made to tell – and then what would happen to Vukalovic's division trapped in the Zenica Cage? What you don't know, you can't tell.'

'But you know.' Reynolds's voice was thick with resentment. 'You and Dusty and Andrea – Colonel Stavros – you know. Groves and I knew all along that you knew, and you could be made to talk.'

Mallory said with considerable restraint: 'Get Andrea

512

to talk? Perhaps you might – if you threatened to take away his cigars. Sure, Dusty and I could talk – but *someone* had to know.'

Groves said in the tone of a man reluctantly accepting the inevitable: 'How do you get behind that dam wall – you can't blow it up from the front, can you?'

'Not with the means at present available to us,' Mallory agreed. 'We get behind it. We climb up there.' Mallory pointed to the precipitous gorge wall on the other side.

'We climb up there, eh?' Miller said conversationally. He looked stunned.

'Up the ladder. But not all the way. Three-quarters of the way up the ladder we leave it and climb vertically up the cliff-face till we're about forty feet above the top of the dam wall, just where the cliff begins to overhang there. From there, there's a ledge – well, more of a crack, really – '

'A crack!' Miller said hoarsely. He was horror-stricken.

'A crack. It stretches about a hundred and fifty feet clear across the top of the dam wall at an ascending angle of maybe twenty degrees. We go that way.'

Reynolds looked at Mallory in an almost dazed incredulity. 'It's madness!'

'Madness!' Miller echoed.

'I wouldn't do it from choice,' Mallory admitted. 'Nevertheless, it's the only way in.'

'But you're bound to be seen,' Reynolds protested.

'Not bound to be.' Mallory dug into his rucksack and produced from it a black rubber frogman's suit, while Miller reluctantly did the same from his. As both men started to pull their suits on, Mallory continued: 'We'll be like black flies against a black wall.'

'He hopes,' Miller muttered.

513

'Then with any luck we expect them to be looking the other way when the RAF start in with the fireworks. And if we do seem in any danger of discovery – well, that's where you and Groves come in. Captain Jensen was right – as things have turned out, we couldn't have done this without you.'

'Compliments?' Groves said to Reynolds. 'Compliments from the Captain? I've a feeling there's something nasty on the way.'

'There is,' Mallory admitted. He had his suit and hood in position now and was fixing into his belt some pitons and a hammer he had extracted from his rucksack. 'If we're in trouble, you two create a diversion.'

'What kind of diversion?' Reynolds asked suspiciously.

'From somewhere near the foot of the dam you start firing up at the guards atop the dam wall.'

'But – but we'll be completely exposed.' Groves gazed across at the rocky scree which composed the left bank at the base of the dam and at the foot of the ladder. 'There's not an ounce of cover. What kind of chance will we have?'

Mallory secured his rucksack and hitched a long coil of rope over his shoulder. 'A very poor one, I'm afraid.' He looked at his luminous watch. 'But then, for the next forty-five minutes you and Groves are expendable. Dusty and I are not.'

'Just like that?' Reynolds said flatly. 'Expendable.'

'Just like that.'

'Want to change places?' Miller said hopefully. There was no reply for Mallory was already on his way. Miller, with a last apprehensive look at the towering rampart of rock above, gave a last hitch to his rucksack and followed. Reynolds made to move off, but Groves caught him by the arm and signed to Maria to go ahead with Petar. He said to her: 'We'll wait a bit and bring up the rear. Just to be sure.'

'What is it?' Reynolds said in a low voice.

'This. Our Captain Mallory admitted that he has already made four mistakes tonight. I think he's making a fifth now.'

'I'm not with you.'

'He's putting all our eggs in one basket and he's overlooked certain things. For instance, asking the two of us to stand by at the base of the dam wall. If we have to start a diversion, one burst of machine-gun fire from the top of the dam wall will get us both in seconds. One man can create as successful a diversion as two — and where's the point in the two of us getting killed? Besides, with one of us left alive, there's always the chance that something can be done to protect Maria and her brother. I'll go to the foot of the dam while you — '

'Why should you be the one to go? Why not — '

'Wait, I haven't finished yet. I also think Mallory's very optimistic if he thinks that Andrea can hold off that lot coming up the gorge. There must be at least twenty of them and they're not out for an evening's fun and games. They're out to kill us. So what happens if they do overwhelm Andrea and come up to the swing bridge and find Maria and Petar there while we are busy being sitting targets at the base of the dam wall? They'll knock them both off before you can bat an eyelid.'

'Or maybe not knock them off,' Reynolds muttered. 'What if Neufeld were to be killed before they reached the swing bridge? What if Droshny were the man in charge — Maria and Petar might take some time in dying.'

'So you'll stay near the bridge and keep our backs covered? With Maria and Petar in shelter somewhere near?'

'You're right, I'm sure you're right. But I don't like it,' Reynolds said uneasily. 'He gave us his orders and he's not a man who likes having his orders disobeyed.'

'He'll never know – even if he ever comes back, which I very much doubt, he'll never know. *And* he's started to make mistakes.'

'Not this kind of mistake.' Reynolds was still more than vaguely uneasy.

'Am I right or not?' Groves demanded.

'I don't think it's going to matter a great deal at the end of the day,' Reynolds said wearily. 'Okay, let's do it your way.'

The two sergeants hurried off after Maria and Petar.

Andrea listened to the scraping of heavy boots on stones, the very occasional metallic chink of a gun striking against a rock, and waited, stretched out flat on his stomach, the barrel of his Schmeisser rock-steady in the cleft between the boulders. The sounds heralding the stealthy approach up the river bank were not more than forty yards away when Andrea raised himself slightly, squinted down the barrel and squeezed the trigger.

The reply was immediate. At once three or four guns, all of them, Andrea realized, machine-pistols, opened up. Andrea stopped firing, ignoring the bullets whistling above his head and ricocheting from the boulders on either side of him, carefully lined up on one of the flashes issuing from a machine-pistol and fired a one-second burst. The man behind the machine-pistol straightened convulsively, his upflung right arm sending his gun spinning, then slowly toppled sideways in the Neretva and was carried away in the whitely swirling waters. Andrea fired again and a second man twisted round and fell heavily among the rocks. There came a suddenly barked order and the firing down-river ceased.

There were eight men in the down-river group and now one of them detached himself from the shelter of a boulder and crawled towards the second man who had been hit: as he moved, Droshny's face revealed his usual wolfish grin, but it was clear that he was feeling very far from smiling. He bent over the huddled figure in the stones, and turned him on his back: it was Neufeld, with blood streaming down from a gash in the side of the head. Droshny straightened, his face vicious in anger, and turned round as one of his Cetniks touched his arm.

'Is he dead?'

'Not quite. Concussed and badly. He'll be unconscious for hours, maybe days. I don't know, only a doctor can tell.' Droshny beckoned to two other men. 'You three – get him across the ford and up to safety. Two stay with him, the other come back. And for God's sake tell the others to hurry up and get here.'

His face still contorted with anger and for the moment oblivious of all danger, Droshny leapt to his feet and fired a long continuous burst upstream, a burst which apparently left Andrea completely unmoved, for he remained motionless where he was, resting peacefully with his back to his protective boulder, watching with mild interest but apparent unconcern as ricochets and splintered fragments of rock flew off in all directions.

The sound of the firing carried clearly to the ears of the guards patrolling the top of the dam. Such was

517

the bedlam of small-arms fire all around and such were the tricks played on the ears by the baffling variety of echoes that reverberated up and down the gorge and over the surface of the dam itself, that it was quite impossible precisely to locate the source of the recent bursts of machine-pistol fire: what was significant, however, was that it *had* been machine-gun fire and up to that moment the sounds of musketry had consisted exclusively of rifle fire. And it *had* seemed to emanate from the south, from the gorge below the dam. One of the guards on the dam went worriedly to the captain in charge, spoke briefly, then walked quickly across to one of the small huts on the raised concrete platform at the eastern end of the dam wall. The hut, which had no front, only a rolled-up canvas protection, held a large radio transceiver manned by a corporal.

'Captain's orders,' the sergeant said. 'Get through to the bridge at Neretva. Pass a message to General Zimmermann that we – the captain, that is – is worried. Tell him that there's a great deal of small-arms fire all around us and that some of it seems to be coming from down-river.'

The sergeant waited impatiently while the operator put the call through and even more impatiently as the earphones crackled two minutes later and the operator started writing down the message. He took the completed message from the operator and handed it to the captain, who read it out aloud.

'General Zimmermann says, "There is no cause at all for anxiety, the noise is being made by our Yugoslav friends up by the Zenica Gap who are whistling in the dark because they are momentarily expecting an all-out assault by units of the 11th Army Corps. And it will be a great deal noisier later on when the

RAF starts dropping bombs in all the wrong places. But they won't be dropping them near you, so don't worry." ' The captain lowered the paper. 'That's good enough for me. If the General says we are not to worry, then that's good enough for me. You know the General's reputation, sergeant?'

'I know his reputation, sir.' Some distance away and from some unidentifiable direction, came several more bursts of machine-pistol fire. The sergeant stirred unhappily.

'You are still troubled by something?' the captain asked.

'Yes, sir. I know the general's reputation, of course, and trust him implicitly.' He paused then went on worriedly: 'I could have sworn that that last burst of machine-pistol fire came from down the gorge there.'

'You're becoming just an old woman, sergeant,' the captain said kindly, 'and you must report to our divisional surgeon soon. Your ears need examining.'

The sergeant, in fact, was not becoming an old woman and his hearing was in considerably better shape than that of the officer who had reproached him. The current burst of machine-pistol firing was, as he'd thought, coming from the gorge, where Droshny and his men, now doubled in numbers, were moving forward, singly or in pairs, but never more than two at a time, in a series of sharp but very short rushes, firing as they went. Their firing, necessarily wildly inaccurate as they stumbled and slipped on the treacherous going underfoot, elicited no response from Andrea, possibly because he felt himself in no great danger, probably because he was conserving his ammunition. The latter supposition seemed the more likely as Andrea had slung his Schmeisser and was now examining with

519

interest a stick-grenade which he had just withdrawn from his belt.

Farther up-river, Sergeant Reynolds, standing at the eastern edge of the rickety wooden bridge which spanned the narrowest part of the gorge where the turbulent, racing, foaming waters beneath would have offered no hope of life at all to any person so unfortunate as to fall in there, looked unhappily down the gorge towards the source of the machine-pistol firing and wondered for the tenth time whether he should take a chance, re-cross the bridge and go to Andrea's aid: even in the light of his vastly revised estimate of Andrea, it seemed impossible, as Groves had said, that one man could for long hold off twenty others bent on vengeance. On the other hand, he had promised Groves to remain there to look after Petar and Maria. There came another burst of firing from down-river. Reynolds made his mind up. He would offer his gun to Maria to afford herself and Petar what protection it might, and leave them for as little time as might be necessary to give Andrea what help he required.

He turned to speak to her, but Maria and Petar were no longer there. Reynolds looked wildly around, his first reaction was that they had both fallen into the rapids, a reaction that he at once dismissed as ridiculous. Instinctively he gazed up the bank towards the base of the dam, and even although the moon was then obscured by a large bank of cloud, he saw them at once, making their way towards the foot of the iron ladder, where Groves was standing. For a brief moment he puzzled why they should have moved upstream without permission, then remembered that neither he nor Groves had, in fact, remembered to give them instructions to remain by the bridge. Not to worry, he thought, Groves will soon send them back down to the bridge again and when they arrived he would tell them of his decision to return to Andrea's aid. He felt vaguely relieved at the prospect, not because he entertained fears of what might possibly happen to him when he rejoined Andrea and faced up to Droshny and his men but because it postponed, if even only briefly, the necessity of implementing a decision which could be only marginally justifiable in the first place.

Groves, who had been gazing up the seemingly endless series of zig-zags of that green iron ladder so precariously, it seemed, attached to that vertical cliff-face, swung round at the soft grate of approaching footsteps on the shale and stared at Maria and Petar, walking, as always, hand in hand. He said angrily: 'What in God's name are you people doing here? You've no right to be here – can't you see, the guards have only to look down and you'll be killed? Go on. Go back and rejoin Sergeant Reynolds at the bridge. Now!'

Maria said softly: 'You are kind to worry, Sergeant Groves. But we don't want to go. We want to stay here.'

'And what in hell's name good can you do by staying here?' Groves asked roughly. He paused, then went on, almost kindly: 'I know who you are now, Maria. I know what you've done, how good you are at your own job. But this is not your job. Please.'

'No.' She shook her head. 'And I *can* fire a gun.'

'You haven't got one to fire. And Petar here, what right have you to speak for him. Does he know where he is?'

Maria spoke rapidly to her brother in incomprehensible Serbo-Croat: he responded by making his customary odd sounds in his throat. When he had finished, Maria turned to Groves.

'He says he knows he is going to die tonight. He has what you people call the second sight and

521

he says there is no future beyond tonight. He says he is tired of running. He says he will wait here till the time comes.'

'Of all the stubborn, thick-headed – '

'Please, Sergeant Groves.' The voice, though still low, was touched by a new note of asperity. 'His mind is made up, and you can never change it.'

Groves nodded in acceptance. He said: 'Perhaps I can change yours.'

'I do not understand.'

'Petar cannot help us anyway, no blind man could. But you can. If you would.'

'Tell me.'

'Andrea is holding off a mixed force of at least twenty Cetniks and German troops.' Groves smiled wryly. 'I have recent reason to believe that Andrea probably has no equal anywhere as a guerilla fighter, but one man cannot hold off twenty for ever. When he goes, then there is only Reynolds left to guard the bridge – and if he goes, then Droshny and his men will be through in time to warn the guards, almost certainly in time to save the dam, certainly in time to send a radio message through to General Zimmermann to pull his tanks back on to high ground. I think, Maria, that Reynolds may require your help. Certainly, you can be of no help here – but if you stand by Andrea you *could* make all the difference between success and failure. And you did say you can fire a gun.'

'And as *you* pointed out, I haven't got a gun.'

'That was then. You have now.' Grove unslung his Schmeisser and handed it to her along with some spare ammunition.

'But – ' Maria accepted gun and ammunition reluctantly. 'But now *you* haven't a gun.'

'Oh yes I have.' Groves produced his silenced Luger

522

from his tunic. 'This is all I want tonight. *I* can't afford to make any noise tonight, not so close to the dam as this.'

'But I *can't* leave my brother.'

'Oh, I think you can. In fact, you're going to. No one on earth can help your brother any more. Not now. Please hurry.'

'Very well.' She moved off a few reluctant paces, stopped, turned and said: 'I suppose you think you're very clever, Sergeant Groves?'

'I don't know what you're talking about,' Groves said woodenly. She looked at him steadily for a few moments, then turned and made her way down-river. Groves smiled to himself in the near-darkness.

The smile vanished in the instant of time that it took for the gorge to be suddenly flooded with bright moonlight as a black, sharply-edged cloud moved away from the face of the moon. Groves called softly, urgently to Maria: 'Face down on the rocks and keep still,' saw her at once do what he ordered, then looked up the green ladder, his face registering the strain and anxiety in his mind.

About three-quarters of the way up the ladder, Mallory and Miller, bathed in the brilliant moonlight, clung to the top of one of the angled sections as immobile as if they had been carved from the rock itself. Their unmoving eyes, set in equally unmoving faces, were obviously fixed on – or transfixed by – the same point in space.

That point was a scant fifty feet away, above and to their left, where two obviously jumpy guards were leaning anxiously over the parapet at the top of the dam: they were gazing into the middle distance, down the gorge, towards the location of what seemed to be the sound of firing. They had only to move their eyes

downwards and discovery for Groves and Maria was certain: they had only to shift their gaze to the left and discovery for Mallory and Miller would have been equally certain. And death for all inevitable.

CHAPTER ELEVEN

Saturday 0120–0135

Like Mallory and Miller, Groves, too, had caught sight
of the two German sentries leaning out over the parapet at the top of the dam and staring anxiously down
the gorge. As a situation for conveying a feeling of
complete nakedness, exposure and vulnerability, it
would, Groves felt, take a lot of beating. And if he
felt like that, how must Mallory and Miller, clinging
to the ladder and less than a stone's throw from the
guards, be feeling? Both men, Groves knew, carried
silenced Lugers, but their Lugers were inside their
tunics and their tunics encased in their zipped-up
frogmen's suits, making them quite inaccessible. At
least, making them quite inaccessible without, clinging as they were to the ladder, performing a variety of
contortionist movements to get at them – and it was
certain that the least untoward movement would have
been immediately spotted by the two guards. How it
was that they hadn't already been seen, even without
movement, was incomprehensible to Groves: in that
bright moonlight, which cast as much light on the
dam and in the gorge as one would have expected on
any reasonably dull afternoon, any normal peripheral
vision should have picked them all up immediately.
And it was unlikely that any front-line troops of the
Wehrmacht had less than standard peripheral vision.
Groves could only conclude that the intentness of the
guards' gaze did not necessarily mean that they were

looking intently: it could have been that all their being was at that moment concentrated on their hearing, straining to locate the source of the desultory machine-pistol fire down the gorge. With infinite caution Groves eased his Luger from his tunic and lined it up. At that distance, even allowing for the high muzzle-velocity of the gun, he reckoned his chances of getting either of the guards to be so remote as to be hardly worth considering: but at least, as a gesture, it was better than nothing.

Groves was right on two counts. The two sentries on the parapet, far from being reassured by General Zimmermann's encouraging reassurance, were in fact concentrating all their being on listening to the down-river bursts of machine-pistol fire, which were becoming all the more noticeable, not only because they seemed – as they were – to be coming closer, but also because the ammunition of the Partisan defenders of the Zenica Gap was running low and their fire was becoming more sporadic. Groves had been right, too, about the fact that neither Mallory nor Miller had made any attempt to get at their Lugers. For the first few seconds, Mallory, like Groves, had felt sure that any such move would be bound to attract immediate attention, but, almost at once and long before the idea had occurred to Groves, Mallory had realized that the men were in such a trance-like state of listening that a hand could almost have passed before their faces without their being aware of it. And now, Mallory was certain, there would be no need to do anything at all because, from his elevation, he could see something that was quite invisible to Groves from his position at the foot of the dam: another dark band of cloud was almost about to pass across the face of the moon.

Within seconds, a black shadow flitting across the

526

waters of the Neretva dam turned the colour from dark green to the deepest indigo, moved rapidly across the top of the dam wall, blotted out the ladder and the two men clinging to it, then engulfed the gorge in darkness. Groves sighed in soundless relief and lowered his Luger. Maria rose and made her way down-river towards the bridge. Petar moved his unseeing gaze around in the sightless manner of the blind. And, up above, Mallory and Miller at once began to climb again.

Mallory now abandoned the ladder at the top of one of its zigs and struck vertically up the cliff-face. The rockface, providentially, was not completely smooth, but such hand- and footholds as it afforded were few and small and awkwardly situated, making for a climb that was as arduous as it was technically difficult: normally, had he been using the hammer and pitons that were stuck in his belt, Mallory would have regarded it as a climb of no more than moderate difficulty: but the use of pitons was quite out of the question. Mallory was directly opposite the top of the dam wall and no more than 35 feet from the nearest guard: one tiny chink of hammer on metal could not fail to register on the hearing of the most inattentive listener: and, as Mallory had just observed, inattentive listening was the last accusation that could have been levelled against the sentries on the dam. So Mallory had to content himself with the use of his natural talents and the vast experience gathered over many years of rock-climbing and continue the climb as he was doing, sweating profusely inside the hermetic rubber suit, while Miller, now some forty feet below, peered upwards with such tense anxiety on his face that he was momentarily oblivious of his own precarious perch on top of one of the slanted ladders, a predicament which would normally have sent him into a case of mild hysterics.

Andrea, too, was at that moment peering at something about fifty feet away, but it would have required a hyperactive imagination to detect any signs of anxiety in that dark and rugged face. Andrea, as the guards on the dam had so recently been doing, was listening rather than looking. From his point of view all he could see was a dark and shapeless jumble of wetly glistening boulders with the Neretva rushing whitely alongside. There was no sign of life down there, but that only meant that Droshny, Neufeld and his men, having learnt their lessons the hard way – for Andrea could not know at this time that Neufeld had been wounded – were inching their way forward on elbows and knees, not once moving out from one safe cover until they had located another.

A minute passed, then Andrea heard the inevitable: a barely discernible 'click', as two pieces of stone knocked together. It came, Andrea estimated, from about thirty feet away. He nodded as if in satisfaction, armed the grenade, waited two seconds, then gently lobbed it downstream, dropping flat behind his protective boulder as he did so. There was the typically flat crack of a grenade explosion, accompanied by a briefly white flash of light in which two soldiers could be seen being flung bodily sideways.

The sound of the explosion came clearly to Mallory's ear. He remained still, allowing only his head to turn slowly till he was looking down on top of the dam wall, now almost twenty feet beneath him. The same two guards who had been previously listening so intently stopped their patrol a second time, gazed down the gorge again, looked at each other uneasily, shrugged uncertainly, then resumed their patrol. Mallory resumed his climb.

He was making better time now. The former negligible finger and toe holds had given way, occasionally, to small fissures in the rock into which he was able to insert the odd piton to give him a great deal more leverage than would have otherwise been possible. When next he stopped climbing and looked upwards he was no more than six feet below the longitudinal crack he had been looking for – and, as he had said to Miller earlier, it *was* no more than a crack. Mallory made to begin again, then paused, his head cocked towards the sky.

Just barely audible at first above the roaring of the waters of the Neretva and the sporadic small-arms fire from the direction of the Zenica Gap, but swelling in power with the passing of every second, could be heard a low and distant thunder, a sound unmistakable to all who had ever heard it during the war, a sound that heralded the approach of squadrons, of a fleet of heavy bombers. Mallory listened to the rapidly approaching clamour of scores of aero engines and smiled to himself.

Many men smiled to themselves that night when they heard the approach from the west of those squadrons of Lancasters. Miller, still perched on his ladder and still exercising all his available will-power not to look down, managed to smile to himself, as did Groves at the foot of the ladder and Reynolds by the bridge. On the right bank of the Neretva, Andrea smiled to himself, reckoned that the roar of those fast-approaching engines would make an excellent cover for any untoward sound and picked another grenade from his belt. Outside a soup tent high up in the biting cold of the Ivenici plateau, Colonel Vis and Captain Vlanovich smiled their delight at each other and solemnly shook hands. Behind the southern redoubts of the Zenica

Cage, General Vukalovic and his three senior officers, Colonel Janzy, Colonel Lazlo and Major Stephan, for once removed the glasses through which they had been so long peering at the Neretva bridge and the menacing woods beyond and smiled their incredulous relief at one another. And, most strangely of all, already seated in his command truck just inside the woods to the south of the Neretva bridge, General Zimmermann smiled perhaps the most broadly of all.

Mallory resumed his climb, moving even more quickly now, reached the longitudinal crack, worked his way up above it, pressed a piton into a convenient crack in the rock, withdrew his hammer from his belt and prepared to wait. Even now, he was not much more than forty feet above the dam wall, and the piton that Mallory now wanted to anchor would require not one blow but a dozen of them, and powerful ones at that: the idea that, even above the approaching thunder of the Lancasters' engines, the metallic hammering would go unremarked was preposterous. The sound of the heavy aero engines was now deepening by the moment.

Mallory glanced down directly beneath him. Miller was gazing upward, tapping his wristwatch as best a man can when he has both arms wrapped round the same rung of a ladder, and making urgent gestures. Mallory, in turn, shook his head and made a downward restraining motion with his free hand. Miller shook his head in resignation.

The Lancasters were on top of them now. The leader arrowed in diagonally across the dam, lifted slightly as it came to the high mountains on the other side and then the earth shook and ripples of dark waters shivered their erratic way across the surface of the Neretva dam before the first explosion reached their ears, as the first stick of 1,000-pound bombs crashed squarely into the Zenica Gap. From then on the sounds of the explosions of the bombs raining down on the Gap were so close together as to be almost continuous: what little time-lapse there was between some of the explosions was bridged by the constantly rumbling echoes that rumbled through the mountains and valleys of central Bosnia.

Mallory had no longer any need to worry about sound any more, he doubted he could even have heard himself speak, for most of those bombs were landing in a concentrated area less than a mile from where he clung to the side of the cliff, their explosions making an almost constant white glare that showed clearly above the mountains to the west. He hammered home his piton, belayed a rope around it, and dropped the rope to Miller, who immediately seized it and began to climb: he looked, Mallory thought, uncommonly like one of the early Christian martyrs. Miller was no mountaineer, but, no mistake, he knew how to climb a rope: in a remarkably short time he was up beside Mallory, feet firmly wedged into the longitudinal crack, both hands gripping tightly to the piton.

'Think you can hang on that piton?' Mallory asked. He almost had to shout to make himself heard above the still undiminished thunder of the falling bombs.

'Just try to prise me away.'

'I won't,' Mallory grinned.

He coiled up the rope which Miller had used for his ascent, hitched it over his shoulder and started to move quickly along the longitudinal crack. 'I'll take this across the top of the dam, belay it to another piton. Then you can join me. Right?'

Miller looked down into the depths and shuddered. 'If you think I'm going to stay here, you must be mad.'

531

Mallory grinned again and moved away.

To the south of the Neretva bridge, General Zimmermann, with an aide by his side, was still listening to
the sounds of the aerial assault on the Zenica Gap. He
glanced at his watch.

'Now,' he said. 'First-line assault troops into position.'

At once heavily armed infantry, bent almost double
to keep themselves below parapet level, began to move
quickly across the Neretva bridge: once on the other
side, they spread out east and west along the northern
bank of the river, concealed from the Partisans by the
ridge of high ground abutting on the river bank. Or they
thought they were concealed: in point of fact a Partisan
scout, equipped with night-glasses and field telephone,
lay prone in a suicidally positioned slit-trench less than
a hundred yards from the bridge itself, sending back a
constant series of reports to Vukalovic.

Zimmermann glanced up at the sky and said to his
aide: 'Hold them. The moon's coming through again.'
Again he looked at his watch. 'Start the tank engines
in twenty minutes.'

'They've stopped coming across the bridge, then?'
Vukalovic said.

'Yes, sir.' It was the voice of his advance scout. 'I
think it's because the moon is about to break through
in a minute or two.'

'I think so too,' Vukalovic said. He added grimly:
'And I suggest you start working your way back before
it does break through or it will be the last chance you'll
ever have.'

Andrea, too, was regarding the night sky with interest. His gradual retreat had now taken him into a

particularly unsatisfactory defensive position, practically bereft of all cover: a very unhealthy situation to be caught in, he reflected, when the moon came out from behind the clouds. He paused for a thoughtful moment, then armed another grenade and lobbed it in the direction of a cluster of dimly seen boulders about fifty feet away. He did not wait to see what effect it had, he was already scrambling his way up-river before the grenade exploded. The one certain effect it did have was to galvanize Droshny and his men into immediate and furious retaliation, at least half a dozen machine-pistols loosing off almost simultaneous bursts at the position Andrea had so recently and prudently vacated. One bullet plucked at the sleeve of his tunic, but that was as near as anything came. He reached another cluster of boulders without incident and took up a fresh defensive position behind them: when the moon did break through it would be Droshny and his men who would be faced with the unpalatable prospect of crossing that open stretch of ground.

Reynolds, crouched by the swing bridge with Maria now by his side, heard the flat crack of the exploding grenade and guessed that Andrea was now no more than a hundred yards downstream on the far bank. And like so many people at that precise instant, Reynolds, too, was gazing up at what could be seen of the sky through the narrow north-west gap between the precipitous walls of the gorge.

Reynolds had intended going to Andrea's aid as soon as Groves had sent Petar and Maria back to him, but three factors had inhibited them from taking immediate action. In the first place, Groves had been unsuccessful in sending back Petar: secondly, the frequent bursts of machine-pistol firing down the gorge, coming steadily closer, were indication enough that Andrea was making a very orderly retreat and was still in fine fighting fettle: and thirdly, even if Droshny and his men did get Andrea, Reynolds knew that by taking up position behind the boulder directly above the bridge, he could deny Droshny and his men the crossing of the bridge for an indefinite period.

But the sight of the large expanse of starlit sky coming up behind the dark clouds over the moon made Reynolds forget the tactically sound and cold-blooded reasons for remaining where he was. It was not in Reynolds's nature to regard any other man as an expendable pawn and he suspected strongly that when he was presented with a sufficiently long period of moonlight Droshny would use it to make the final rush that would overwhelm Andrea. He touched Maria on the shoulder.

'Even the Colonel Stavroses of this world need a hand at times. Stay here. We shouldn't be long.' He turned and ran across the swaying swing bridge.

Damn it, Mallory thought bitterly, damn it, damn it and damn it all. Why couldn't there have been heavy dark cloud covering the entire sky? Why couldn't it have been raining? Or snowing? Why hadn't they chosen a moonless night for this operation? But he was, he knew, only kicking against the pricks. No one had had any choice, for tonight was the only time there was. But still, that damnable moon.

Mallory looked to the north, where the northern wind, driving banded cloud across the moon, was leaving behind it a large expanse of starlit sky. Soon the entire dam and gorge would be bathed in moonlight for a considerable period: Mallory thought wryly that he could have wished himself to be in a happier position for that period.

By this time, he had traversed about half the length of the longitudinal crack. He glanced to his left and reckoned he had still between thirty and forty feet to go before he was well clear of the dam wall and above the waters of the dam itself. He glanced to his right and saw, not to his surprise, that Miller was still where he had left him, clinging to the piton with both hands as if it were his dearest friend on earth, which at that moment it probably was. He glanced downwards: he was directly above the dam wall now, some fifty feet above it, forty feet above the roof of the guardhouse. He looked at the sky again: a minute, no more, and the moon would be clear. What was it that he had said to Reynolds that afternoon? Yes, that was it. For now is all the time there may be. He was beginning to wish he hadn't said that. He was a New Zealander, but only a second-generation New Zealander: all his forebears were Scots and everyone knew how the Scots indulged in those heathenish practices of second sight and peering into the future. Mallory briefly indulged in the mental equivalent of a shoulder shrug and continued on his traverse.

At the foot of the iron ladder, Groves, to whom Mallory was now no more than a half-seen, half-imagined dark shape against a black cliff-face, realized that Mallory was soon going to move out of his line of sight altogether, and when that happened he would be in no position to give Mallory any covering fire at all. He touched Petar on the shoulder and with the pressure of his hand indicated that he should sit down at the foot of the ladder. Petar looked at him sightlessly, uncomprehendingly, then suddenly appeared to gather what was expected of him, for he nodded obediently

535

and sat down. Groves thrust his silenced Luger deep inside his tunic and began to climb.

A mile to the west, the Lancasters were still pounding the Zenica Gap. Bomb after bomb crashed down with surprising accuracy into that tiny target area, blasting down trees, throwing great eruptions of earth and stones into the air, starting all over the area scores of small fires which had already incinerated nearly all the German plywood tanks. Seven miles to the south, Zimmermann still listened with interest and still with satisfaction to the continuing bombardment to the north. He turned to the aide seated beside him in the command car.

'You will have to admit that we must give the Royal Air Force full marks for industry, if for nothing else. I hope our troops are well clear of the area?'

'There's not a German soldier within two miles of the Zenica Gap, Herr General.'

'Excellent, excellent.' Zimmermann appeared to have forgotten about his earlier forebodings. 'Well, fifteen minutes. The moon will soon be through, so we'll hold our infantry. The next wave of troops can go across with the tanks.'

Reynolds, making his way down the right bank of the Neretva towards the sound of firing, now very close indeed, suddenly became very still indeed. Most men react the same way when they feel the barrel of a gun grinding into the side of their necks. Very cautiously, so as not to excite any nervous trigger-fingers, Reynolds turned both eyes and head slightly to the right and realized with a profound sense of relief that this was one instance where he need have no concern about jittery nerves.

'You had your orders,' Andrea said mildly. 'What are you doing here?'

'I – I thought you might need some help.' Reynolds rubbed the side of his neck. 'Mind you, I could have been wrong.'

'Come on. It's time we got back and crossed the bridge.' For good measure and in very quick succession, Andrea spun another couple of grenades down-river, then made off quickly up the river bank, closely followed by Reynolds.

The moon broke through. For the second time that night, Mallory became absolutely still, his toes jammed into the longitudinal crack, his hands round the piton which he had thirty seconds earlier driven into the rock and to which he had secured the rope. Less than ten feet from him Miller, who with the aid of the rope had already safely made the first part of the traverse, froze into similar immobility. Both men stared down on to the top of the dam wall.

There were six guards visible, two at the farther or western end, two at the middle and the remaining two almost directly below Mallory and Miller. How many more there might have been inside the guardhouse neither Mallory nor Miller had any means of knowing. All they could know for certain was that their exposed vulnerability was complete, their position desperate.

Three-quarters of the way up the iron ladder, Groves, too, became very still. From where he was, he could see Mallory, Miller and the two guards very clearly indeed. He knew with a sudden conviction that this time there would be no escape, they could never be so lucky again. Mallory, Miller, Petar or himself – who would be the first to be spotted? On balance, he thought he himself was the most likely candidate. Slowly, he wrapped his left arm round the ladder, pushed his right hand inside his tunic, withdrew his Luger and laid the barrel along his left forearm.

The two guards on the eastern end of the dam wall were restless, apprehensive, full of nameless fears. As before, they both leaned out over the parapet and stared down the valley. They can't help but see me, Groves thought, they're *bound* to see me, good God, I'm almost directly in their line of sight. Discovery must be immediate.

It was, but not for Groves. Some strange instinct made one of the guards glance upwards and to his left and his mouth fell open at the astonishing spectacle of two men in rubber suits clinging like limpets to the sheer face of the cliff. It took him several interminable seconds before he could recover himself sufficiently to reach out blindly and grab his companion by the arm. His companion followed the other guard's line of sight, then his jaw, too, dropped in an almost comical fashion. Then, at precisely the same moment, both men broke free from their thrall-like spell and swung their guns, one a Schmeisser, the other a pistol, upwards to line up on the two men pinned helplessly to the cliff-face.

Groves steadied his Luger against both his left arm and the side of the ladder, sighted unhurriedly along the barrel and squeezed the trigger. The guard with the Schmeisser dropped the weapon, swayed briefly on his feet and started to fall outwards. Almost three seconds passed before the other guard, startled and momentarily quite uncomprehending, reached out to grab his companion, but he was far too late, he never even succeeded in touching him. The dead man, moving in an almost grotesquely slow-motion fashion, toppled wearily over the edge of the parapet and tumbled head over heels into the depths of the gorge beneath.

The guard with the pistol leaned far out over the parapet, staring in horror after his falling comrade. It was quite obvious that he was momentarily at a total loss to understand what had happened, for he had heard no sound of a shot. But realization came within the second as a piece of concrete chipped away inches from his left elbow and a spent bullet ricocheted its whistling way into the night sky. The guard's eyes lifted and widened in shock, but this time the shock had no inhibiting effect on the speed of his reactions. More in blind hope than in any real expectation of success, he loosed off two quick snap-shots and bared his teeth in satisfaction as he heard Groves cry out and saw the right hand, the forefinger still holding the Luger by the trigger guard, reach up to clutch the shattered left shoulder.

Groves's face was dazed and twisted with pain, the eyes already clouded by the agony of the wound, but those responsible for making Groves a commando sergeant had not picked him out with a pin and Groves was not quite finished yet. He brought his Luger down again. There was something terribly wrong with his vision now, he dimly realized, he thought he had a vague impression that the guard on the parapet was leaning far out, pistol held in both hands to make sure of his killing shot, but he couldn't be sure. Twice Groves squeezed the trigger of his Luger and then he closed his eyes, for the pain was gone and he suddenly felt very sleepy.

The guard by the parapet pitched forward. He reached out desperately to grab the coaming of the parapet, but to pull himself back to safety he had to swing his legs up to retain his balance and he found he could no longer control his legs, which slid helplessly over the edge of the parapet. His body followed his legs almost of its own volition, for the last vestiges of strength remain for only a few seconds with a man through whose lungs two Luger bullets have just passed. For a moment of time his clawed hands hooked despairingly on to the edge of the parapet and then his fingers opened.

Groves seemed unconscious now, his head lolling on his chest, the left-hand sleeve and left-hand side of his uniform already saturated with blood from the terrible wound in his shoulder. Were it not for the fact that his right arm was jammed between a rung of the ladder and the cliff-face behind it, he must certainly have fallen. Slowly, the fingers of his right hand opened and the Luger fell from his hand.

Seated at the foot of the ladder, Petar started as the Luger struck the shale less than a foot from where he was sitting. He looked up instinctively, then rose, made sure that the inevitable guitar was firmly secured across his back, reached out for the ladder and started climbing.

Mallory and Miller stared down, watching the blind singer climb up towards the wounded and obviously unconscious Groves. After a few moments, as if by telepathic signal, Mallory glanced across at Miller who caught his eyes almost at once. Miller's face was strained, almost haggard. He freed one hand momentarily from the rope and made an almost desperate gesture in the direction of the wounded sergeant. Mallory shook his head.

Miller said hoarsely: 'Expendable, huh?'

'Expendable.'

Both men looked down again. Petar was now not more than ten feet below Groves, and Groves, though Mallory and Miller could not see this, had his eyes closed and his right arm was beginning to slip through the gap between the rung and the rock. Gradually, his right arm began to slip more quickly, until his elbow was free, and then his arm came free altogether and slowly, so very slowly, he began to topple outwards from the wall. But Petar got to him first, standing on the step beneath Groves and reaching out an arm to encircle him and press him back against the ladder. Petar had him and for the moment Petar could hold him. But that was all he could do.

The moon passed behind a cloud.

Miller covered the last ten feet separating him from Mallory. He looked at Mallory and said: 'They're both going to go, you know that?'

'I know that.' Mallory sounded even more tired than he looked. 'Come on. Another thirty feet and we should be in position.' Mallory, leaving Miller where he was, continued his traverse along the crack. He was moving very quickly now, taking risks that no sane cragsman would ever have contemplated, but he had no option now, for time was running out. Within a minute he had reached a spot where he judged that he had gone far enough, hammered home a piton and securely belayed the rope to it.

He signalled to Miller to come and join him. Miller began the last stage of the traverse, and as he was on his way across, Mallory unhitched another rope from his shoulders, a sixty-foot length of climbers' rope, knotted at fifteen-inch intervals. One end of this he fastened to the same piton as held the rope that Miller was using for making his traverse: the other end he let fall down the cliff-side. Miller came up and Mallory touched him on the shoulder and pointed downwards.

The dark waters of the Neretva dam were directly beneath them.

CHAPTER TWELVE

Saturday 0135–0200

Andrea and Reynolds lay crouched among the boulders at the western end of the elderly swing bridge over the gorge. Andrea looked across the length of the bridge, his gaze travelling up the steep gully behind it till it came to rest on the huge boulder perched precariously at the angle where the steep slope met the vertical cliff-face behind it. Andrea rubbed a bristly chin, nodded thoughtfully and turned to Reynolds.

'You cross first. I'll give you covering fire. You do the same for me when you get to the other side. Don't stop, don't look round. Now.'

Reynolds made for the bridge in a crouching run, his footsteps seeming to him abnormally loud as he reached the rotting planking of the bridge itself. The palms of his hands gliding lightly over the hand ropes on either side he continued without check or diminution of speed, obeying Andrea's instructions not to risk a quick backward glance, and feeling a very strange sensation between his shoulderblades. To his mild astonishment he reached the far bank without a shot being fired, headed for the concealment and shelter offered by a large boulder a little way up the bank, was startled momentarily to see Maria hiding behind the same boulder, then whirled round and unslung his Schmeisser.

On the far bank there was no sign of Andrea. For a brief moment Reynolds experienced a quick stab of

542

anger, thinking Andrea had used this ruse merely to get rid of him, then smiled to himself as he heard two flat explosive sounds some little way down the river on the far bank. Andrea, Reynolds remembered, had still had two grenades left and Andrea was not the man to let such handy things rust from disuse. Besides, Reynolds realized, it would provide Andrea with extra valuable seconds to make good his escape, which indeed it did for Andrea appeared on the far bank almost immediately and, like Reynolds, effected the crossing of the bridge entirely without incident. Reynolds called softly and Andrea joined them in the shelter of the boulder.

Reynolds said in a low voice: 'What next?'

'First things first.' Andrea produced a cigar from a waterproof box, a match from another waterproof box, struck the match in his huge cupped hands and puffed in immense satisfaction. When he removed the cigar, Reynolds noticed that he held it with the glowing end safely concealed in the curved palm of his hand. 'What's next? I tell you what's next. Company coming to join us across the bridge, and coming very soon, too. They've taken crazy risks to try to get me – and paid for them – which shows they are pretty desperate. Crazy men don't hang about for long. You and Maria here move fifty or sixty yards nearer the dam and take cover there – and keep your guns on the far side of the bridge.'

'You staying here?' Reynolds asked.

Andrea blew out a noxious cloud of cigar smoke. 'For the moment, yes.'

'Then I'm staying, too.'

'If you want to get killed, it's all right by me,' Andrea said mildly. 'But this beautiful young lady here wouldn't look that way any more with the top of her head blown off.'

Reynolds was startled by the crudeness of the words. He said angrily: 'What the devil do you mean?'

'I mean this.' Andrea's voice was no longer mild. 'This boulder gives you perfect concealment from the bridge. But Droshny and his men can move another thirty or forty yards farther up the bank on their side. What concealment will you have then?'

'I never thought of that,' Reynolds said.

'There'll come a day when you say that once too often,' Andrea said sombrely, 'and then it will be too late to think of anything again.'

A minute later they were in position. Reynolds was hidden behind a huge boulder which afforded perfect concealment both from the far side of the bridge and from the bank on the far side up to the point where it petered out: it did not offer concealment from the dam. Reynolds looked to his left where Maria was crouched farther in behind the rock. She smiled at him, and Reynolds knew he had never seen a braver girl, for the hands that held the Schmeisser were trembling. He moved out a little and peered down-river, but there appeared to be no signs of life whatsoever at the western edge of the bridge. The only signs of life at all, indeed, were to be seen behind the huge boulder up in the gully, where Andrea, completely screened from anyone at or near the far side of the bridge, was industriously loosening the foundations of rubble and earth round the base of the boulder.

Appearances, as always, were deceptive. Reynolds had judged there to be no life at the western end of the bridge but there was, in fact, life and quite a lot of it, although admittedly there was no action. Concealed in the massive boulders about twenty feet back from the bridge, Droshny, a Cetnik sergeant and perhaps a dozen German soldiers and Cetniks lay in deep concealment among the rocks.

Droshny had binoculars to his eyes. He examined the ground in the neighbourhood of the far side of the swing bridge, then traversed to his left up beyond the boulder where Reynolds and Maria lay hidden until he reached the dam wall. He lifted the glasses, following the dimly-seen zig-zag outline of the iron ladder, checked, adjusted the focus as finely as possible, then stared again. There could be no doubt: there were two men clinging to the ladder, about three-quarters of the way up towards the top of the dam.

'Good God in heaven!' Droshny lowered the binoculars, the gaunt craggy features registering an almost incredulous horror, and turned to the Cetnik sergeant by his side. 'Do you know what they mean to do?'

'The dam!' The thought had not occurred to the sergeant until that instant but the stricken expression on Droshny's face made the realization as immediate as it was inevitable. 'They're going to blow up the dam!' It did not occur to either man to wonder how Mallory could possibly blow up the dam: as other men had done before them, both Droshny and the sergeant were beginning to discover in Mallory and his *modus operandi* an extraordinary quality of inevitability that transformed remote possibilities into very likely probabilities.

'General Zimmermann!' Droshny's gravelly voice had become positively hoarse. 'He must be warned! If that dam bursts while his tanks and troops are crossing – '

'Warn him? Warn him? How in God's name can we warn him?'

'There's a radio up on the dam.'

The sergeant stared at him. He said: 'It might as well be on the moon. There'll be a rearguard, they're bound to have left a rearguard. Some of us are going to get killed crossing that bridge, Captain.'

'You think so?' Droshny glanced up sombrely at the dam. 'And just what do you think is going to happen to us all down here if *that* goes?'

Slowly, soundlessly and almost invisibly, Mallory and Miller swam northwards through the dark waters of the Neretva dam, away from the direction of the dam wall. Suddenly Miller, who was slightly in the lead, gave a low exclamation and stopped swimming.

'What's up?' Mallory asked.

'This is up.' With an effort Miller lifted a section of what appeared to be a heavy wire cable just clear of the water. 'Nobody mentioned this little lot.'

'Nobody did,' Mallory agreed. He reached under the water. 'And there's a steel mesh below.'

'An anti-torpedo net?'

'Just that.'

'Why?' Miller gestured to the north where, at a distance of less than two hundred yards, the dam made an abrupt right-angled turn between the towering cliff-faces. 'It's impossible for any torpedo bomber – any bomber – to get a run-in on the dam wall.'

'Someone should have told the Germans. They take no chances – and it makes things a damned sight more difficult for us.' He peered at his watch. 'We'd better start hurrying. We're late.'

They eased themselves over the wire and started swimming again, more quickly this time. Several minutes later, just after they had rounded the corner of the dam and lost sight of the dam wall, Mallory touched Miller on the shoulder. Both men trod water, turned and looked back in the direction from which they had come. To the south, not much more than two miles away, the night sky had suddenly blossomed into an incandescent and multi-coloured beauty as scores of parachute flares, red and green and white and orange, drifted slowly down towards the Neretva river.

'Very pretty, indeed,' Miller conceded. 'And what's all this in aid of?'

'It's in aid of us. Two reasons. First of all, it will take any person who looks at that – and *everyone* will look at it – at least ten minutes to recover his night-sight, which means that any odd goings-on in this part of the dam are all that less likely to be observed: and if everyone is going to be busy looking that way, then they can't be busy looking this way at the same time.'

'Very logical,' Miller approved. 'Our Captain Jensen doesn't miss out on very much, does he?'

'He has, as the saying goes, all his marbles about him.' Mallory turned again and gazed to the east, his head cocked the better to listen. He said: 'You have to hand it to them. Dead on target, dead on schedule. I hear him coming now.'

The Lancaster, no more than five hundred feet above the surface of the dam, came in from the east, its engine throttled back almost to stalling speed. It was still two hundred yards short of where Mallory and Miller were treading water when suddenly huge black silk parachutes bloomed beneath it: almost simultaneously, engine-power was increased to maximum revolutions and the big bomber went into a steeply banking climbing turn to avoid smashing into the mountains on the far side of the dam.

Miller gazed at the slowly descending black parachutes, turned, and looked at the brilliantly burning flares to the south. 'The skies,' he announced, 'are full of things tonight.'

547

He and Mallory began to swim in the direction of the falling parachutes.

Petar was near to exhaustion. For long minutes now he had been holding Groves's dead weight pinned against the iron ladder and his aching arms were beginning to quiver with the strain. His teeth were clenched hard, his face, down which rivulets of sweat poured, was twisted with the effort and the agony of it all. Plainly, Petar could not hold out much longer.

It was by the light of those flares that Reynolds, still crouched with Maria in hiding behind the big boulder, first saw the predicament of Petar and Groves. He turned to glance at Maria: one look at the stricken face was enough to tell Reynolds that she had seen it, too.

Reynolds said hoarsely: 'Stay here. I must go and help them.'

'No!' She caught his arm, clearly exerting all her will to keep herself under control: her eyes, as they had been when Reynolds had first seen her, had the look of a hunted animal about them. 'Please, Sergeant, no. You must stay here.'

Reynolds said desperately: 'Your brother – '

'There are more important things – '

'Not for you there aren't.' Reynolds made to rise, but she clung to his arm with surprising strength, so that he couldn't release himself without hurting her. He said, almost gently: 'Come on, lass, let me go.'

'No! If Droshny and his men get across – ' She broke off as the last of the flares finally fizzled to extinction, casting the entire gorge into what was, by momentary contrast, an almost total darkness. Maria went on simply: 'You'll have to stay now, won't you?'

'I'll have to stay now.' Reynolds moved out from

the shelter of the boulder and put his night-glasses to his eyes. The swing bridge, and as far as he could tell, the far bank seemed innocent of any sign of life. He traversed up the gully and could just make out the form of Andrea, his excavations finished, resting peacefully behind the big boulder. Again with a feeling of deep unease, Reynolds trained his glasses on the bridge. He suddenly became very still. He removed the glasses, wiped the lenses very carefully, rubbed his eyes and lifted the glasses again.

His night-sight, momentarily destroyed by the flares, was now almost back to normal and there could be no doubt or any imagination about what he was seeing — seven or eight men, Droshny in the lead, flat on their stomachs, were inching their way on elbows, hands and knees across the wooden slats of the swing bridge.

Reynolds lowered the glasses, stood upright, armed a grenade and threw it as far as he could towards the bridge. It exploded just as it landed, at least forty yards short of the bridge. That it achieved nothing but a flat explosive bang and the harmless scattering of some shale was of no account, for it had never been intended to reach the bridge: it had been intended as a signal for Andrea, and Andrea wasted no time.

He placed the soles of both feet against the boulder, braced his back against the cliff-face and heaved. The boulder moved the merest fraction of an inch. Andrea momentarily relaxed, allowing the boulder to roll back, then repeated the process: this time the forward motion of the boulder was quite perceptible. Andrea relaxed again, then pushed for the third time.

Down below on the bridge, Droshny and his men, uncertain as to the exact significance of the exploding grenade, had frozen into complete immobility. Only their eyes moved, darting almost desperately from side to side to locate the source of a danger that lay so heavily in the air as to be almost palpable.

The boulder was distinctly rocking now. With every additional heave it received from Andrea, it was rocking an additional inch farther forward, an additional inch farther backwards. Andrea had slipped farther and farther down until now he was almost horizontal on his back. He was gasping for breath and sweat was streaming down his face. The boulder rolled back almost as if it were going to fall upon him and crush him. Andrea took a deep breath, then convulsively straightened back and legs in one last titanic heave. For a moment the boulder teetered on the point of imbalance, reached the point of no return and fell away.

Droshny could most certainly have heard nothing and, in that near darkness, it was certain as could be that he had seen nothing. It could only have been an instinctive awareness of impending death that made him glance upwards in sudden conviction that this was where the danger lay. The huge boulder, just rolling gently when Droshny's horror-stricken eyes first caught sight of it, almost at once began to bound in ever-increasing leaps, hurtling down the slope directly towards them, trailing a small avalanche behind it. Droshny screamed a warning. He and his men scrambled desperately to their feet, an instinctive reaction that was no more than a useless and token gesture in the face of death, because, for most of them, it was already far too late and they had no place to go.

With one last great leap the hurtling boulder smashed straight into the centre of the bridge, shattering the flimsy woodwork and slicing the bridge in half. Two men who had been directly in the path of the boulder died instantaneously: five others were catapulted into the torrent below and swept away to almost equally immediate death. The two broken sections of the bridge, still secured to either bank by the suspension ropes, hung down into the rushing waters, their lowermost parts banging furiously against the boulder-strewn banks.

There must have been at least a dozen parachutes attached to the three dark cylindrical objects that now lay floating, though more than half submerged, in the equally dark waters of the Neretva dam. Mallory and Miller sliced those away with their knives, then joined the three cylinders in line astern, using short wire strops that had been provided for that precise purpose. Mallory examined the leading cylinder and gently eased back a lever set in the top. There was a subdued roar as compressed air violently aerated the water astern of the leading cylinder and sent it surging forward, tugging the other two cylinders behind it. Mallory closed the lever and nodded to the other two cylinders.

'These levers on the right-hand side control the flooding valves. Open that one till you just have negative buoyancy and no more. I'll do the same on this one.'

Miller cautiously turned a valve and nodded at the leading cylinder. 'What's that for?'

'Do you fancy towing a ton and a half of amatol as far as the dam wall? Propulsion unit of some kind. Looks like a sawn-off section of a twenty-one-inch torpedo tube to me. Compressed air, maybe at a pressure of five thousand pounds a square inch, passing through reduction gear. Should do the job all right.'

'Just so long as Miller doesn't have to do it.' Miller closed the valve on the cylinder. 'About that?'

'About that.' All three cylinders were now just barely submerged. Again Mallory eased back the compressed air lever on the leading cylinder. There was a throaty burble of sound, a sudden flurry of bubbles streaming out astern and then all three cylinders were under way, heading down towards the angled neck of the dam, both men clinging to and guiding the leading cylinder.

When the swing bridge had disintegrated under the impact of the boulder, seven men had died: but two still lived.

Droshny and his sergeant, furiously buffeted and badly bruised by the torrent of water, clung desperately to the broken end of the bridge. At first, they could do no more than hold on, but gradually, and after a most exhausting struggle, they managed to haul themselves clear of the rapids and hang there, arms and legs hooked round broken sections of what remained of the bridge, fighting for breath. Droshny made a signal to some unseen person or persons across the rapids, then pointed upwards in the direction from which the boulder had come.

Crouched among the boulders on the far side of the river, three Cetniks – the fortunate three who had not yet moved on to the bridge when the boulder had fallen – saw the signal and understood. About seventy feet above where Droshny – completely concealed from sight on that side by the high bank of the river – was still clinging grimly to what was left of the bridge, Andrea, now bereft of cover, had begun to make a precarious descent from his previous hiding-place. On the other side of the river, one of the three Cetniks took aim and fired.

Fortunately for Andrea, firing uphill in semi-darkness is a tricky business at the best of times. Bullets smashed into the cliff-face inches from Andrea's left shoulder, the whining ricochets leaving him almost miraculously unscathed. There would be a correction factor for the next burst, Andrea knew: he flung himself to one side, lost his balance and what little precarious purchase he had and slid and tumbled helplessly down the boulder-strewn slope. Bullets, many bullets, struck close by him on his way down, for the three Cetniks on the right bank, convinced now that Andrea was the only person left for them to deal with, had risen, advanced to the edge of the river and were concentrating all their fire on Andrea.

Again fortunately for Andrea, this period of concentration lasted for only a matter of a few seconds. Reynolds and Maria emerged from cover and ran down the bank, stopping momentarily to fire at the Cetniks across the river, who at once forgot all about Andrea to meet this new and unexpected threat. Just as they did so, Andrea, in the midst of a small avalanche, still fighting furiously but hopelessly to arrest his fall, struck the bank of the river with appalling force, struck the side of his head against a large stone and collapsed, his head and shoulders hanging out over the wild torrent below.

Reynolds flung himself flat on the shale of the river bank, forced himself to ignore the bullets striking to left and right of him and whining above him and took a slow and careful aim. He fired a long burst, a very long one, until the magazine of his Schmeisser was empty. All three Cetniks crumpled and died.

Reynolds rose. He was vaguely surprised to notice that his hands were shaking. He looked at Andrea, lying unconscious and dangerously near the side of the bank, took a couple of paces in his direction, then checked and turned as he heard a low moan behind him. Reynolds broke into a run.

Maria was half-sitting, half-lying on the stony bank. Both hands cradled her leg just above the right knee and the blood was welling between her fingers. Her face, normally pale enough, was ashen and drawn with shock and pain. Reynolds cursed bitterly but soundlessly, produced his knife and began to cut away the cloth around the wound. Gently, he pulled away the material covering the wound and smiled reassuringly at the girl: her lower lip was caught tightly between her teeth and she watched him steadily with eyes dimmed by pain and tears.

It was a nasty enough looking flesh wound, but, Reynolds knew, not dangerous. He reached for his medical pack, gave her a reassuring smile and then forgot all about his medical pack. The expression in Maria's eyes had given way to one of shock and fear and she was no longer looking at him.

Reynolds twisted round. Droshny had just hauled himself over the edge of the river bank, had risen to his feet and was now heading purposefully towards Andrea's prostrate body, with the obvious intention of heaving the unconscious man into the gorge.

Reynolds picked up his Schmeisser and pulled the trigger. There was an empty click — he'd forgotten the magazine had been emptied. He glanced around almost wildly in an attempt to locate Maria's gun, but there was no sign of it. He could wait no longer. Droshny was only a matter of feet from where Andrea lay. Reynolds picked up his knife and rushed along the bank. Droshny saw him coming and he saw too that Reynolds was armed with only a knife. He smiled as a wolf would smile, took one of his wickedly-curved knives from his belt and waited.

The two men approached closely and circled warily. Reynolds had never wielded a knife in anger in his life and so had no illusions at all as to his chances: hadn't Neufeld said that Droshny was the best man in the Balkans with a knife? He certainly looked it, Reynolds thought. His mouth felt very dry.

Thirty yards away Maria, dizzy and weak with pain and dragging her wounded leg, crawled towards the spot where she thought her gun had fallen when she had been hit. After what seemed a very long time, but what was probably no more than ten seconds, she found it half-hidden among rocks. Nauseated and faint from the pain of her wounded leg, she forced herself to sit up and brought the gun to her shoulder. Then she lowered it again.

In her present condition, she realized vaguely, it would have been impossible for her to hit Droshny without almost certainly hitting Reynolds at the same time: in fact, she might well have killed Reynolds while missing Droshny entirely. For both men were now locked chest to chest, each man's knife-hand – the right – clamped in the grip of the other's left.

The girl's dark eyes, which had so recently reflected pain and shock and fear, now held only one expression – despair. Like Reynolds, Maria knew of Droshny's reputation – but, unlike Reynolds, she had seen Droshny kill with that knife and knew too well how lethal a combination that man and that knife were. A wolf and a lamb, she thought, a wolf and a lamb. After he kills Reynolds – her mind was dulled now, her thoughts almost incoherent – after he kills Reynolds I shall kill him. But first, Reynolds would have to die, for there could be no help for him. And then the despair left the dark eyes to be replaced by an almost unthinkable hope for she knew with an intuitive certainty that with Andrea by one's side hope need never be abandoned.

Not that Andrea was as yet by anyone's side. He had forced himself up to his hands and knees and was gazing down uncomprehendingly at the rushing white waters below, shaking his leonine head from side to side in an attempt to clear it. And then, still shaking his head, he levered himself painfully to his feet and he wasn't shaking his head any more. In spite of her pain, Maria smiled.

Slowly, inexorably, the Cetnik giant twisted Reynolds's knife-hand away from himself while at the same time bringing the lancet point of his own knife nearer to Reynolds's throat. Reynolds's sweat-sheened face deflected his desperation, his total awareness of impending defeat and death. He cried out with pain as Droshny twisted his right wrist almost to breaking-point, forcing him to open his fingers and drop his knife. Droshny kneed him viciously at the same time, freeing his left hand to give Reynolds a violent shove that sent him staggering to crash on his back against the stones and lie there winded and gasping in agony.

Droshny smiled his smile of wolfish satisfaction. Even although he must have known that the need for haste was paramount he yet had to take time off to carry out the execution in a properly leisurely fashion, to savour to the full every moment of it, to prolong the exquisite joy he always felt at moments like these. Reluctantly, almost, he changed to a throwing grip on his knife and slowly raised it high. The smile was broader than ever, a smile that vanished in an instant of time as he felt a knife being plucked from his own belt. He whirled round. Andrea's face was a mask of stone.

Droshny smiled again. 'The gods have been kind

to me.' His voice was low, almost reverent, his tone a caressing whisper. 'I have dreamed of this. It is better that you should die this way. This will teach you, my friend – '

Droshny, hoping to catch Andrea unprepared, broke off in mid-sentence and lunged forward with cat-like speed. The smile vanished again as he looked in almost comical disbelief at his right wrist locked in the vice-like grip of Andrea's left hand.

Within seconds, the tableau was as it had been in the beginning of the earlier struggle, both knife-wrists locked in the opponents' left hands. The two men appeared to be absolutely immobile, Andrea with his face totally impassive, Droshny with his white teeth bared, but no longer in a smile. It was, instead, a vicious snarl compounded of hate and fury and baffled anger – for this time Droshny, to his evident consternation and disbelief, could make no impression whatsoever on his opponent. The impression, this time, was being made on him.

Maria, the pain in her leg in temporary abeyance, and a slowly recovering Reynolds stared in fascination as Andrea's left hand, in almost millimetric slow-motion, gradually twisted Droshny's right wrist so that the blade moved slowly away and the Cetnik's fingers began, almost imperceptibly at first, to open. Droshny, his face darkening in colour and the veins standing out on forehead and neck, summoned every last reserve of strength to his right hand: Andrea, rightly sensing that all of Droshny's power and will and concentration were centred exclusively upon breaking his crushing grip, suddenly tore his own right hand free and brought his knife scything round and under and upwards with tremendous power: the knife went in under the breastbone, burying itself to the hilt. For a moment or two the giant stood there, lips drawn far back over bared teeth smiling mindlessly in the rictus of death, then, as Andrea stepped away, leaving the knife still embedded, Droshny toppled slowly over the edge of the ravine. The Cetnik sergeant, still clinging to the shattered remains of the bridge, stared in uncomprehending horror as Droshny, the hilt of the knife easily distinguishable, fell head-first into the boiling rapids and was immediately lost to sight.

Reynolds rose painfully and shakily to his feet and smiled at Andrea. He said: 'Maybe I've been wrong about you all along. Thank you, Colonel Stavros.'

Andrea shrugged. 'Just returning a favour, my boy. Maybe I've been wrong about you, too.' He glanced at his watch. 'Two o'clock! *Two* o'clock! Where are the others?'

'God, I'd almost forgotten. Maria there is hurt. Groves and Petar are on the ladder. I'm not sure, but I think Groves is in a pretty bad way.'

'They may need help. Get to them quickly. I'll look after the girl.'

At the southern end of the Neretva bridge, General Zimmermann stood in his command car and watched the sweep-second hand of his watch come up to the top.

'Two o'clock,' Zimmerman said, his tone almost conversational. He brought his right hand down in a cutting gesture. A whistle shrilled and at once tank engines roared and treads clattered as the spearhead of Zimmermann's first armoured division began to cross the bridge at Neretva.

CHAPTER THIRTEEN

Saturday 0200–0215

'Maurer and Schmidt! Maurer and Schmidt!' The captain in charge of the guard on top of the Neretva dam wall came running from the guard-house, looked around almost wildly and grabbed his sergeant by the arm. 'For God's sake, where are Maurer and Schmidt? No one seen them? No one? Get the searchlight.'

Petar, still holding the unconscious Groves pinned against the ladder, heard the sound of the words but did not understand them. Petar, with both arms round Groves, now had his forearms locked at an almost impossible angle between the stanchions and the rock-face behind. In this position, as long as his wrists or forearms didn't break, he could hold Groves almost indefinitely. But Petar's grey and sweat-covered face, the racked and twisted face, was mute testimony enough to the almost unendurable agony he was suffering.

Mallory and Miller also heard the urgently shouted commands, but, like Petar, were unable to understand what it was that was being shouted. It would be something, Mallory thought vaguely, that would bode no good for them, then put the thought from his mind: he had other and more urgently immediate matters to occupy his attention. They had reached the barrier of the torpedo net and he had the supporting cable in one hand, a knife in the other when Miller exclaimed and caught his arm.

'For God's sake, no!' The urgency in Miller's voice

559

had Mallory looking at him in astonishment. 'Jesus, what do I use for brains. That's not a wire.'

'It's not – '

'It's an insulated power cable. Can't you see?'

Mallory peered closely. 'Now I can.'

'Two thousand volts, I'll bet.' Miller still sounded shaken. 'Electric chair power. We'd have been frizzled alive. *And* it would have triggered off an alarm bell.'

'Over the top with them,' Mallory said.

Struggling and pushing, heaving and pulling, for there was only a foot of clear water between the wire and the surface of the water, they managed to ease the compressed air cylinder over and had just succeeded in lifting the nose of the first of the amatol cylinders on to the wire when, less than a hundred yards away, a six-inch searchlight came to life on the top of the dam wall, its beam momentarily horizontal, then dipping sharply to begin a traverse of the water close in to the side of the dam wall.

'That's all we bloody well need,' Mallory said bitterly. He pushed the nose of the amatol block back off the wire, but the wire strop securing it to the compressed air cylinder held it in such a position that it remained with its nose nine inches clear of the water. 'Leave it. Get under. Hang on to the net.'

Both men sank under the water as the sergeant atop the dam wall continued his traverse with the searchlight. The beam passed over the nose of the first of the amatol cylinders, but a black-painted cylinder in dark waters makes a poor subject for identification and the sergeant failed to see it. The light moved on, finished its traverse of the water alongside the dam, then went out.

Mallory and Miller surfaced cautiously and looked swiftly around. For the moment, there was no other

560

sign of immediate danger. Mallory studied the luminous hands of his watch. He said: 'Hurry! For God's sake, hurry! We're almost three minutes behind schedule.'

They hurried. Desperate now, they had the two amatol cylinders over the wire inside twenty seconds, opened the compressed air valve on the leading cylinder and were alongside the massive wall of the dam inside another twenty. At that moment, the clouds parted and the moon broke through again, silvering the dark waters of the dam. Mallory and Miller were now in a helplessly exposed position but there was nothing they could do about it and they knew it. Their time had run out and they had no option other than to secure and arm the amatol cylinders as quickly as ever possible. Whether they were discovered or not could still be all-important: but there was nothing they could do to prevent that discovery.

Miller said softly: 'Forty feet apart and forty feet down, the experts say. We'll be too late.'

'No. Not yet too late. The idea is to let the tanks across first then destroy the bridge before the petrol bowsers and the main infantry battalions cross.'

Atop the dam wall, the sergeant with the searchlight returned from the western end of the dam and reported to the captain.

'Nothing, sir. No sign of anyone.'

'Very good.' The captain nodded towards the gorge. 'Try that side. You might find something there.'

So the sergeant tried the other side and he did find something there, and almost immediately. Ten seconds after he had begun his traverse with the searchlight he picked up the figures of the unconscious Groves and the exhausted Petar and, only feet below them and climbing steadily, Sergeant Reynolds. All three were hopelessly trapped, quite powerless to do anything to defend themselves: Reynolds had no longer even his gun.

On the dam wall, a Wehrmacht soldier, levelling his machine-pistol along the beam of the searchlight, glanced up in astonishment as the captain struck down the barrel of his gun.

'Fool!' The captain sounded savage. 'I want them alive. You two, fetch ropes, get them up here for questioning. We *must* find out what they have been up to.'

His words carried clearly to the two men in the water for, just then, the last of the bombing ceased and the sound of the small-arms fire died away. The contrast was almost too much to be borne, the suddenly hushed silence strangely ominous, deathly, almost, in its sinister foreboding.

'You heard?' Miller whispered.

'I heard.' More cloud, Mallory could see, thinner cloud but still cloud, was about to pass across the face of the moon. 'Fix these float suckers to the wall. I'll do the other charge.' He turned and swam slowly away, towing the second amatol cylinder behind him.

When the beam of the searchlight had reached down from the top of the dam wall Andrea had been prepared for instant discovery, but the prior discovery of Groves, Reynolds and Petar had saved Maria and himself, for the Germans seemed to think that they had caught all there were to be caught and, instead of traversing the rest of the gorge with the searchlights, had concentrated, instead, on bringing up to the top of the wall the three men they had found trapped on the ladder. One man, obviously unconscious – that would be Groves, Andrea thought – was hauled up at the end of a rope: the other two, with one man lending assistance

562

to the other, had completed the journey up the ladder by themselves. All this Andrea had seen while he was bandaging Maria's injured leg, but he had said nothing of it to her.

Andrea secured the bandage and smiled at her. 'Better?'

'Better.' She tried to smile her thanks but the smile wouldn't come.

'Fine. Time we were gone.' Andrea consulted his watch. 'If we stay here any longer I have the feeling that we're going to get very, very wet.'

He straightened to his feet and it was this sudden movement that saved his life. The knife that had been intended for his back passed cleanly through his upper left arm. For a moment, almost as if uncomprehending, Andrea stared down at the tip of the narrow blade emerging from his arm then, apparently oblivious of the agony it must have cost him, turned slowly round, the movement wrenching the hilt of the knife from the hand of the man who held it.

The Cetnik sergeant, the only other man to have survived with Droshny the destruction of the swing bridge, stared at Andrea as if he were petrified, possibly because he couldn't understand how a man could suffer such a wound in silence and, in silence, still be able to tear the knife from his grasp. Andrea had now no weapon left him nor did he require one. In what seemed an almost grotesque slow motion, Andrea lifted his right hand: but there was nothing slow-motion about the dreadful edge-handed chopping blow which caught the Cetnik sergeant on the base of the neck. The man was probably dead before he struck the ground.

Reynolds and Petar sat with their backs to the guard-hut at the eastern end of the dam. Beside them lay the still unconscious Groves, his breathing now stertorous, his face ashen and of a peculiar waxed texture. From overhead, fixed to the roof of the guard-house, a bright light shone down on them, while nearby was a watchful guard with his carbine trained on them. The Wehrmacht captain of the guard stood above them, an almost awestruck expression on his face.

He said incredulously but in immaculate English: 'You hoped to blow up a dam this size with a few sticks of dynamite? You must be mad!'

'No one told us the dam was as big as this,' Reynolds said sullenly.

'No one told you – God in heaven, talk of mad dogs and Englishmen! And where is this dynamite?'

'The wooden bridge broke.' Reynolds's shoulders were slumped in abject defeat. 'We lost all the dynamite – and all our other friends.'

'I wouldn't have believed it, I just wouldn't have believed it.' The captain shook his head and turned away, then checked as Reynolds called him. 'What is it?'

'My friend here.' Reynolds indicated Groves. 'He is very ill, you can see that. He needs medical attention.'

'Later.' The captain turned to the soldier in the open transceiver cabin. 'What news from the south?'

'They have just started to cross the Neretva bridge, sir.'

The words carried clearly to Mallory, at that moment some distance apart from Miller. He had just finished securing his float to the wall and was on the point of rejoining Miller when he caught a flash of light out of the corner of his eye. Mallory remained still and glanced upward and to his right.

There was a guard on the dam wall above, leaning over the parapet as he moved along, flashing a torch

564

downwards. Discovery, Mallory at once realized, was certain. One or both of the supporting floats were bound to be seen. Unhurriedly, and steadying himself against his float, Mallory unzipped the top of his rubber suit, reached under his tunic, brought out his Luger, unwrapped it from its waterproof cover and eased off the safety-catch.

The pool of light from the torch passed over the water, close in to the side of the dam wall. Suddenly, the beam of the torch remained still. Clearly to be seen in the centre of the light was a small, torpedo-shaped object fastened to the dam wall by suckers and, just beside it, a rubber-suited man with a gun in his hand. And the gun – it had, the sentry automatically noticed, a silencer screwed to the end of the barrel – was pointed directly at him. The sentry opened his mouth to shout a warning but the warning never came for a red flower bloomed in the centre of his forehead, and he leaned forward tiredly, the upper half of his body over the edge of the parapet, his arms dangling downwards. The torch slipped from his lifeless hand and tumbled down into the water.

The impact of the torch on the water made a flat, almost cracking sound. In the now deep silence it was bound to be heard by those above, Mallory thought. He waited tensely, the Luger ready in his hand, but after twenty seconds had passed and nothing happened Mallory decided he could wait no longer. He glanced at Miller, who had clearly heard the sound, for he was staring at Mallory, and at the gun in Mallory's hand with a puzzled frown on his face. Mallory pointed up towards the dead guard hanging over the parapet. Miller's face cleared and he nodded his understanding. The moon went behind a cloud.

*

Andrea, the sleeve of his left arm soaked in blood, more than half carried the hobbling Maria across the shale and through the rocks: she could hardly put her right foot beneath her. Arrived at the foot of the ladder, both of them stared upwards at the forbidding climb, at the seemingly endless zig-zags of the iron ladder reaching up into the night. With a crippled girl and his own damaged arm, Andrea thought, the prospects were poor indeed. And God only knew when the wall of the dam was due to go up. He looked at his watch. If everything was on schedule, it was due to go now: Andrea hoped to God that Mallory, with his passion for punctuality, had for once fallen behind schedule. The girl looked at him and understood.

'Leave me,' she said. 'Please leave me.'

'Out of the question,' Andrea said firmly. 'Maria would never forgive me.'

'Maria?'

'Not you.' Andrea lifted her on to his back and wound her arms round his neck. 'My wife. I think I'm going to be terrified of her.' He reached out for the ladder and started to climb.

The better to see how the final preparations for the attack were developing, General Zimmermann had ordered his command car out on to the Neretva bridge itself and now had it parked exactly in the middle, pulled close in to the right-hand side. Within feet of him clanked and clattered and roared a seemingly end-less column of tanks and self-propelled guns and trucks laden with assault troops: as soon as they reached the northern end of the bridge, tanks and guns and trucks fanned out east and west along the banks of the river, to take temporary cover behind the steep escarpment ahead before launching the final concerted attack.

From time to time, Zimmermann raised his binoculars and scanned the skies to the west. A dozen times he imagined he heard the distant thunder of approaching air armadas, a dozen times he deceived himself. Time and again he told himself he was a fool, a prey to useless and fearful imaginings wholly unbecoming to a general in the Wehrmacht: but still this deep feeling of intense unease persisted, still he kept examining the skies to the west. It never once occurred to him, for there was no reason why it should, that he was looking in the wrong direction.

Less than half a mile to the north, General Vukalovic lowered his binoculars and túrned to Colonel Janzy.

'That's it, then.' Vukalovic sounded weary and inexpressibly sad. 'They're across – or almost all across. Five more minutes. Then we counter-attack.'

'Then we counter-attack,' Janzy said tonelessly. 'We'll lose a thousand men in fifteen minutes.'

'We asked for the impossible,' Vukalovic said. 'We pay for our mistakes.'

Mallory, a long trailing lanyard in his hand, rejoined Miller. He said: 'Fixed?'

'Fixed.' Miller had a lanyard in his own hand. 'We pull those leads to the hydrostatic chemical fuses and take off?'

'Three minutes. You know what happens to us if we're still in this water after three minutes?'

'Don't even talk about it,' Miller begged. He suddenly cocked his head and glanced quickly at Mallory. Mallory, too, had heard it, the sound of running footsteps up above. He nodded at Miller. Both men sank beneath the surface of the water.

The captain of the guard, because of inclination, a certain rotundity of figure and very proper ideas as to

567

how an officer of the Wehrmacht should conduct himself, was not normally given to running. He had, in fact, been walking, quickly and nervously, along the top of the dam wall when he caught sight of one of his guards leaning over the parapet in what he could only consider an unsoldierly and slovenly fashion. It then occurred to him that a man leaning over a parapet would normally use his hands and arms to brace himself and he could not see the guard's hands and arms. He remembered the missing Maurer and Schmidt and broke into a run.

The guard did not seem to hear him coming. The captain caught him roughly by the shoulder, then stood back aghast as the dead man slid back off the parapet and collapsed at his feet, face upwards: the place where his forehead had been was not a pretty sight. Seized by a momentary paralysis, the captain stared for long seconds at the dead man, then, by a conscious effort of will, drew out both his torch and pistol, snapped on the beam of the one and released the safety catch of the other and risked a very quick glance over the dam parapet.

There was nothing to be seen. Rather, there was nobody to be seen, no sign of the enemy who must have killed his guard within the past minute or two. But there *was* something to be seen, additional evidence, as if he ever needed such evidence, that the enemy had been there: a torpedo-shaped object – no, *two* torpedo-shaped objects – clamped to the wall of the dam just at water level. Uncomprehendingly at first, the captain stared at those, then the significance of their presence there struck him with the violence, almost, of a physical blow. He straightened and started running towards the eastern end of the dam, shouting 'Radio! Radio!' at the top of his voice.

Mallory and Miller surfaced. The shouts – they were

almost screams – of the running captain to the guard
– carried clear over the now silent waters of the dam.
Mallory swore.

'Damn and damn and damn again!' His voice was
almost vicious in his chagrin and frustration. 'He can
give Zimmermann seven, maybe eight minutes' warning. Time to pull the bulk of his tanks on to the high
ground.'

'So now?'

'So now we pull those lanyards and get the hell
out of here.'

The captain, racing along the wall, was now less
than thirty yards from the radio and where Petar and
Reynolds sat with their backs to the guard-house.

'General Zimmermann!' he shouted. 'Get through. Tell
him to pull his tanks to the high ground. Those damned
English have mined the dam!'

'Ah, well.' Petar's voice was almost a sigh. 'All
good things come to an end.'

Reynolds stared at him, his face masked in astonishment. Automatically, involuntarily, his hand reached
out to take the dark glasses Petar was passing him,
automatically his eyes followed Petar's hand moving
away again and then, in a state of almost hypnotic
trance, he watched the thumb of that hand press a catch
in the side of the guitar. The back of the instrument
fell open to reveal inside the trigger, magazine and
gleamingly-oiled mechanism of a sub-machine gun.

Petar's forefinger closed over the trigger. The sub-
machine gun, its first shell shattering the end of the
guitar, stuttered and leapt in Petar's hands. The dark
eyes were narrowed, watchful and cool. And Petar had
his priorities right.

The soldier guarding the three prisoners doubled over
and died, almost cut in half by the first blast of shells.

569

Two seconds later the corporal guard by the radio hut, while still desperately trying to unsling his Schmeisser, went the same way. The captain of the guard, still running, fired his pistol repeatedly at Petar, but Petar still had his priorities right. He ignored the captain, ignored a bullet which struck his right shoulder, and emptied the remainder of the magazine into the radio transceiver, then toppled sideways to the ground, the smashed guitar falling from his nerveless hands, blood pouring from his shoulder and a wound on his head.

The captain replaced his still smoking revolver in his pocket and stared down at the unconscious Petar. There was no anger in the captain's face now, just a peculiar sadness, the dull acceptance of ultimate defeat. His eyes moved and caught Reynolds's: in a moment of rare understanding both men shook their heads in a strange and mutual wonder.

Mallory and Miller, climbing the knotted rope, were almost opposite the top of the dam wall when the last echoes of the firing drifted away across the waters of the dam. Mallory glanced down at Miller, who shrugged as best a man can shrug when hanging on to a rope and shook his head wordlessly. Both men resumed their climb, moving even more quickly than before.

Andrea, too, had heard the shots, but had no idea what their significance might be. At that moment, he did not particularly care. His left upper arm felt as if it were burning in a fierce bright flame, his sweat-covered face reflected his pain and near-exhaustion. He was not yet, he knew, halfway up the ladder. He paused briefly, aware that the girl's grip around his neck was slipping, eased her carefully in towards the ladder, wrapped his left arm round her waist and continued his painfully slow and dogged climb. He wasn't seeing very much now and he thought vaguely that it must be because of the loss of blood. Oddly enough, his left arm was beginning to become numb and the pain was centring more and more on his right shoulder which all the time took the strain of their combined weights.

'Leave me!' Maria said again. 'For God's sake, leave me. You can save yourself.'

Andrea gave her a smile or what he thought was a smile and said kindly: 'You don't know what you're saying. Besides, Maria would murder me.'

'Leave me! Leave me!' She struggled and exclaimed in pain as Andrea tightened his grip. 'You're hurting me.'

'Then stop struggling,' Andrea said equably. He continued his pain-racked, slow-motion climb.

Mallory and Miller reached the longitudinal crack running across the top of the dam wall and edged swiftly along crack and rope until they were directly above the arc lights on the eaves of the guard house some fifty feet below: the brilliant illumination from those lights made it very clear indeed just what had happened. The unconscious Groves and Petar, the two dead German guards, the smashed radio transceiver and, above all, the sub-machine gun still lying in the shattered casing of the guitar told a tale that could not be misread. Mallory moved another ten feet along the crack and peered down again: Andrea, with the girl doing her best to help by pulling on the rungs of the ladder, was now almost two-thirds of the way up, but making dreadfully slow progress of it: they'll never make it in time, Mallory thought, it is impossible that they will ever make it in time. It comes to us all, he thought tiredly, some day it's bound to come to us all: but that it should come to the indestructible Andrea pushed fatalistic acceptance beyond its limits. Such a thing was inconceivable: and the inconceivable was about to happen now.

Mallory rejoined Miller. Quickly he unhitched a rope – the knotted rope he and Miller had used to descend to the Neretva dam – secured it to the rope running above the longitudinal crack and lowered it until it touched softly on the roof of the guard-house. He took the Luger in his hand and was about to start sliding down when the dam blew up.

The twin explosions occurred within two seconds of each other: the detonation of 3,000 pounds of high explosive should normally have produced a titanic outburst of sound, but because of the depth at which they took place, the explosions were curiously muffled, felt, almost, rather than heard. Two great columns of water soared up high above the top of the dam wall, but for what seemed an eternity of time but certainly was not more than four or five seconds, nothing appeared to happen. Then, very, very slowly, reluctantly, almost, the entire central section of the dam wall, at least eighty feet in width and right down to its base, toppled outwards into the gorge: the entire section seemed to be all still in one piece.

Andrea stopped climbing. He had heard no sound, but he felt the shuddering vibration of the ladder and he knew what had happened, what was coming. He wrapped both arms around Maria and the stanchions, pressed her close to the ladder and looked over her head. Two vertical cracks made their slow appearance on the outside of the dam wall, then the entire wall fell slowly towards them, almost as if it were hinged on its base, and then was abruptly lost to sight as countless millions of gallons of greenish-dark water came boiling through the shattered dam wall. The sound of the crash of a thousand tons of masonry falling into the gorge below should have been heard miles away: but Andrea could hear nothing above the roaring of the escaping waters. He had time only to notice that the dam wall had vanished and now there was only this mighty green torrent, curiously smooth and calm in its initial stages, then pouring down to strike the gorge beneath in a seething white maelstrom of foam before the awesome torrent was upon them. In a second of time Andrea released one hand, turned the girl's terrified face and buried it against his chest for he knew that if she should impossibly live, then that battering-ram of water, carrying with it sands and pebbles and God only knew what else, would tear the delicate skin from her face and leave her forever scarred. He ducked his own head against the fury of the coming onslaught and locked his hands together behind the ladder.

The impact of the waters drove the breath from his gasping body. Buried in this great falling crushing wall of green, Andrea fought for his life and that of the girl. The strain upon him, battered and already bruising badly from the hammer-blows of this hurtling cascade of water which seemed so venomously bent upon his instant destruction, was, even without the cruel handicap of his badly injured arm, quite fantastic. His arms, it felt, were momentarily about to be torn from their sockets, it would have been the easiest thing in the world to unclasp his hands and let kindly oblivion take the place of the agony that seemed to be tearing limbs and muscles asunder. But Andrea did not let go and Andrea did not break. Other things broke. Several of the ladder supports were torn away from the wall and it seemed that both ladder and climbers must be

573

inevitably swept away. The ladder twisted, buckled and leaned far out from the wall so that Andrea was now as much lying beneath the ladder as hanging on to it: but still Andrea did not let go, still some remaining supports held. Then very gradually, after what seemed to the dazed Andrea an interminable period of time, the dam level dropped, the force of the water weakened, not much but just perceptibly, and Andrea started to climb again. Half a dozen times, as he changed hands on the rungs, his grip loosened and he was almost torn away: half a dozen times his teeth bared in the agony of effort, the great hands clamped tight and he impossibly retained his grip. After almost a minute of this titanic struggle he finally won clear of the worst of the water and could breathe again. He looked at the girl in his arms. The blonde hair was plastered over her ashen cheeks, the incongruously dark eyelashes closed. The ravine seemed almost full to the top of its precipitously-sided walls with this whitely boiling torrent of water sweeping everything before it, its roar, as it thundered down the gorge with a speed faster than that of an express train, a continuous series of explosions, an insane and banshee shrieking of sound.

Almost thirty seconds elapsed from the time of the blowing up of the dam until Mallory could bring himself to move again. He did not know why he should have been held in thrall for so long. He told himself, rationalizing, that it was because of the hypnotic spectacle of the dramatic fall in the level of the dam coupled with the sight of that great gorge filled almost to the top with those whitely seething waters: but, without admitting it to himself, he knew it was more than that, he knew he could not accept the realization that Andrea and Maria had been swept to their

574

deaths, for Mallory did not know that at that instant Andrea, completely spent and no longer knowing what he was doing, was vainly trying to negotiate the last few steps of the ladder to the top of the dam. Mallory seized the rope and slid down recklessly, ignoring or not feeling the burning of the skin on the palms of his hands, his mind irrationally filled with murder – irrationally, because it was he who had triggered the explosion that had taken Andrea to his death.

And then, as his feet touched the roof of the guard-house, he saw the ghost – the ghosts, rather – as the heads of Andrea and a clearly unconscious Maria appeared at the top of the ladder. Andrea, Mallory noticed, did not seem to be able to go any further. He had a hand on the top rung, and was making con-vulsive, jerking movements, but making no progress at all. Andrea, Mallory knew, was finished.

Mallory was not the only one who had seen Andrea and the girl. The captain of the guard and one of his men were staring in stupefaction over the awesome scene of destruction, but a second guard had whirled round, caught sight of Andrea's head and brought up his machine-pistol. Mallory, still clinging to the rope, had no time to bring his Luger to bear and release the safety catch and Andrea should have assuredly died then: but Reynolds had already catapulted himself forward in a desperate dive and brought down the gun in the precise instant that the guard opened fire. Reynolds died instantaneously. The guard died two seconds later. Mallory lined up the still smoking barrel of his Luger on the captain and the guard.

'Drop those guns,' he said.

They dropped their guns. Mallory and Miller swung down from the guard-house roof, and while Miller cov-ered the Germans with his guns, Mallory ran quickly across to the ladder, reached down a hand and helped the unconscious girl and the swaying Andrea to safety. He looked at Andrea's exhausted, blood-flecked face, at the flayed skin on his hands, at the left sleeve saturated in blood and said severely: 'And where the hell have you been?'

'Where have I been?' Andrea asked vaguely. 'I don't know.' He stood rocking on his feet, barely conscious, rubbed a hand across his eyes and tried to smile. 'I think I must have stopped to admire the view.'

General Zimmermann was still in his command car and his car was still parked in the right centre of the bridge at Neretva. Zimmermann had again his binoculars to his eyes, but for the first time he was gazing neither to the west nor to the north. He was gazing instead to the east, up-river towards the mouth of the Neretva gorge. After a little time he turned to his aide, his face at first uneasy, then the uneasiness giving way to apprehension, then the apprehension to something very like fear.

'You hear it?' he asked.

'I hear it, Herr General.'

'And feel it?'

'And I feel it.'

'What in the name of God almighty can it be?' Zimmermann demanded. He listened as a great and steadily increasing roar filled all the air around them. 'That's not thunder. It's far too loud for thunder. And too continuous. And that wind – that wind coming out of the gorge there.' He could now hardly hear himself speak above the almost deafening roar of sound coming from the east. 'It's the dam! The dam at Neretva! They've blown the dam! Get out of here!' he screamed to the driver. 'For God's sake get out of here!'

The command car jerked and moved forward, but it was too late for General Zimmermann, just as it was too late for his massed echelons of tanks and thousands of assault troops concealed on the banks of the Neretva by the low escarpment to the north of them and waiting to launch the devastating attack that was to annihilate the seven thousand fanatically stubborn defenders of the Zenica Gap. A mighty wall of white water, eighty feet high, carrying with it the irresistible pressure of millions of tons of water and sweeping before it a gigantic battering ram of boulders and trees, burst out of the mouth of the gorge.

Mercifully for most of the men in Zimmermann's armoured corps, the realization of impending death and death itself were only moments apart. The Neretva bridge, and all the vehicles on it, including Zimmermann's command car, were swept away to instant destruction. The giant torrent overspread both banks of the river to a depth of almost twenty feet, sweeping before its all-consuming path tanks, guns, armoured vehicles, thousands of troops and all that stood in its way: when the great flood finally subsided, there was not one blade of grass left growing along the banks of the Neretva. Perhaps a hundred or two of combat troops on both sides of the river succeeded in climbing in terror to higher ground and the most temporary of safety for they too would not have long to live, but for ninety-five per cent of Zimmermann's two armoured divisions destruction was as appallingly sudden as it was terrifyingly complete. In sixty seconds, no more, it was all over. The German armoured corps was totally destroyed. But still that mighty wall of water continued to boil forth from the mouth of the gorge.

'I pray God that I shall never see the like again.' General

Vukalovic lowered his glasses and turned to Colonel Janzy, his face registering neither jubilation nor satisfaction, only an awestruck wonder mingled with deep compassion. 'Men should not die like that, even our enemies should not die like that.' He was silent for a few moments, then stirred. 'I think a hundred or two of their infantry escaped to safety on this side, Colonel. You will take care of them?'

'I'll take care of them,' Janzy said sombrely. 'This is a night for prisoners, not killing, for there won't be any fight. It's as well, General. For the first time in my life I'm not looking forward to a fight.'

'I'll leave you then.' Vukalovic clapped Janzy's shoulder and smiled, a very tired smile. 'I have an appointment. At the Neretva dam – or what's left of it.'

'With a certain Captain Mallory?'

'With Captain Mallory. We leave for Italy tonight. You know, Colonel, we could have been wrong about that man.'

'I never doubted him,' Janzy said firmly.

Vukalovic smiled and turned away.

Captain Neufeld, his head swathed in a blood-stained bandage and supported by two of his men, stood shakily at the top of the gully leading down to the ford in the Neretva and stared down, his face masked in shocked horror and an almost total disbelief, at the whitely boiling maelstrom, its seething surface no more than twenty feet below where he stood, of what had once been the Neretva gorge. He shook his head very, very slowly in unspeakable weariness and final acceptance of defeat, then turned to the soldier on his left, a youngster who looked as stupefied as he, Neufeld, felt.

'Take the two best ponies,' Neufeld said. 'Ride

to the nearest Wehrmacht command post north of the Zenica Gap. Tell them that General Zimmermann's armoured divisions have been wiped out – we don't *know*, but they must have been. Tell them the valley of Neretva is a valley of death and that there is no one left to defend it. Tell them the Allies can send in their airborne divisions tomorrow and that there won't be a single shot fired. Tell them to notify Berlin immediately. You understand, Lindemann?'

'I understand, sir.' From the expression on Lindemann's face, Neufeld thought that Lindemann had understood very little of what he had said to him: but Neufeld felt infinitely tired and he did not feel like repeating his instructions. Lindemann mounted a pony, snatched the reins of another and spurred his pony up alongside the railway track.

Neufeld said, almost to himself: 'There's not all that hurry, boy.'

'Herr Hauptmann?' The other soldier was looking at him strangely.

'It's too late now,' Neufeld said.

Mallory gazed down the still foaming gorge, turned and gazed at the Neretva dam whose level had already dropped by at least fifty feet, then turned to look at the men and the girl behind him. He felt weary beyond all words.

Andrea, battered and bruised and bleeding, his left arm now roughly bandaged, was demonstrating once again his quite remarkable powers of recuperation: to look at him it would have been impossible to guess that, only ten minutes ago, he had been swaying on the edge of total collapse. He held Maria cradled in his arms: she was coming to, but very, very slowly. Miller finished dressing the head wound of a now sitting Petar who, though wounded in shoulder and head, seemed more than likely to survive, crossed to Groves and stooped over him. After a moment or two he straightened and stared down at the young sergeant.

'Dead?' Mallory asked.

'Dead.'

'Dead.' Andrea smiled, a smile full of sorrow. 'Dead – and you and I are alive. Because this young lad is dead.'

'He was expendable,' Miller said.

'And young Reynolds.' Andrea was inexpressibly tired. 'He was expendable too. What was it you said to him this afternoon, my Keith – for now is all the time there may be? And that was all the time there was. For young Reynolds. He saved my life tonight – twice. He saved Maria's. He saved Petar's. But he wasn't clever enough to save his own. *We* are the clever ones, the old ones, the wise ones, the knowing ones. And the old ones are alive and the young ones are dead. And so it always is. We mocked them, laughed at them, distrusted them, marvelled at their youth and stupidity and ignorance.' In a curiously tender gesture he smoothed Maria's wet blonde hair back from her face and she smiled at him. 'And in the end they were better men than we were . . .'

'Maybe they were at that,' Mallory said. He looked at Petar sadly and shook his head in wonder. 'And to think that all three of them are dead, Reynolds dead, Groves dead, Saunders dead, and not one of them ever knew that you were the head of British espionage in the Balkans.'

'Ignorant to the end.' Miller drew the back of his sleeve angrily across his eyes. 'Some people never learn. Some people just never learn.'

EPILOGUE

Once again Captain Jensen and the British lieutenant-general were back in the Operations Room in
Termoli, but now they were no longer pacing up
and down. The days of pacing were over. True, they
still looked very tired, their faces probably fractionally more deeply lined than they had been a few days
previously: but the faces were no longer haggard, the
eyes no longer clouded with anxiety, and, had they
been walking instead of sitting deep in comfortable
armchairs, it was just conceivable that they might
have had a new spring in their steps. Both men had
glasses in their hands, large glasses.

Jensen sipped his whisky and said, smiling: 'I
thought a general's place was at the head of his
troops?'

'Not in these days, Captain,' the General said firmly.
'In 1944 the wise general leads from behind his troops
— about twenty miles behind. Besides, the armoured
divisions are going so quickly I couldn't possibly hope
to catch up with them.'

'They're moving as fast as that?'

'Not quite as fast as the German and Austrian divisions that pulled out of the Gustav Line last night and
are now racing for the Yugoslav border. But they're
coming along pretty well.' The General permitted himself a large gulp of his drink and a smile of considerable
satisfaction. 'Deception complete, break-through complete. On the whole, your men have done a pretty fair
job.'

581

Both men turned in their chairs as a respectful rat-a-tat of knuckles preceded the opening of the heavy leather doors. Mallory entered, followed by Vukalovic, Andrea and Miller. All four were unshaven, all of them looked as if they hadn't slept for a week. Andrea carried his arm in a sling.

Jensen rose, drained his glass, set it on a table, looked at Mallory dispassionately and said: 'Cut it a bit bloody fine, didn't you?'

Mallory, Andrea and Miller exchanged expressionless looks. There was a fairly long silence, then Mallory said: 'Some things take longer than others.'

Petar and Maria were lying side by side, hands clasped, in two regulation army beds in the Termoli military hospital when Jensen entered, followed by Mallory, Miller and Andrea.

'Excellent reports about both of you, I'm glad to hear,' Jensen said briskly. 'Just brought some – ah – friends to say goodbye.'

'What sort of hospital is this, then?' Miller said severely. 'How about the high army moral tone, hey? Don't they have separate quarters for men and women?'

'They've been married for almost two years,' Mallory said mildly. 'Did I forget to tell you?'

'Of course you didn't forget,' Miller said disgustedly. 'It just slipped your mind.'

'Speaking of marriage – ' Andrea cleared his throat and tried another tack. 'Captain Jensen may recall that back in Navarone – '

'Yes, yes.' Jensen held up a hand. 'Quite so. Quite. Quite. But I thought perhaps – well, the fact of the matter is – well, it so happens that another little job, just a tiny little job really, has just come

582

up and I thought that seeing you were here anyway . . .'

Andrea stared at Jensen. His face was horror-stricken.

Storm Force from Navarone

Sam Llewellyn

The action-filled sequel to Alistair MacLean's *Force 10 from Navarone*

Alistair MacLean's gritty heroes from Navarone are not dead, and definitely not forgotten. Mallory, Miller and Andrea, the surviving commandoes of *Force 10 from Navarone* are sent on operation Storm Force – a perilous mission through the Pyrenees to disable the greatest threat to the success of the D-Day landings – the 'Werwolf' U-boats.

The Storm Force have less than six days to locate the submarines and destroy them. With communications insecure, the Force must operate outside normal channels, cut off from any back-up. Their Basque guides declare it mission impossible.

But of course they have never worked with Mallory.

Full of action, intrigue and betrayal, *Storm Force from Navarone* is a truly worthy modern successor to the original novels.

Now available in hardback

ISBN 0 00 225296 1

HMS Ulysses
Alistair MacLean

'A brilliant, overwhelming piece of descriptive writing'
Observer

This is one of the great war novels of our century and one of the finest achievements of Alistair MacLean's best-selling career. It is the story of Convoy FR77 to Murmansk – a voyage that pushes men to the limits of human endurance, crippled by enemy atack and the bitter cold of the Arctic.

'A story of exceptional courage which grips the imagination'
Daily Telegraph

'It deserves an honourable place among twentieth-century war books'
Daily Mail

'*HMS Ulysses* is in the same class as *The Cruel Sea*'
Evening Standard

ISBN 0 00 613512 9

Ice Station Zebra
Alistair MacLean

'Tense, terrifying . . . moves at a breathless pace'
Daily Express

The atomic submarine *Dolphin* has impossible orders: to sail beneath the ice-floes of the Arctic Ocean to locate and rescue the men of weather-station Zebra, gutted by fire and drifting with the ice-pack somewhere north of the Arctic Circle.

But the orders do not say what the *Dolphin* will find if she succeeds – that the fire at Ice Station Zebra was sabotage, and that one of the survivors is a killer . . .

'A thoroughly professional cliff-hanger'   *Sunday Telegraph*

ISBN 0 00 616141 3

Where Eagles Dare
Alistair MacLean

'A real humdinger. The best MacLean yet.'   *Daily Mirror*

'There is a splendid audacity about *Where Eagles Dare* in which a handful of British agents invade an "impenetrable" Gestapo command post . . . MacLean offers a real dazzler of a thriller, with vivid action, fine set pieces of suspense, and a virtuoso display of startling plot twists.'
New York Times

'Alistair MacLean has done it again: produced another king-sized thriller of tremendous pace and excitement. The tension is almost unbearable at times, but you can't stop turning the pages in a feverish desire to know what happens next.'   *Liverpool Echo*

ISBN 0 00 615804 8